The Dream Walker

The Dream Walker

The Forgotten Legacies Series Book Four

K.J. Simmill

Published 2020 by Shadow City – A Next Chapter Imprint
Cover art by Cover Mint

Titles by K.J. Simmill

Fiction:

The Forgotten Legacies Series:

Darrienia
The Severaine
Remedy
The Dreamwalker

Other Titles:

The Grimoire - coming 2021

Non-Fiction:

Herbal Lore

In loving memory of my nan, Alma Cox (1924-2018).
A supportive, inspiring, and loving woman. The world is a little darker without you here.

Contents

Chapter 1

The Earth Maiden

It had been so long, too long, since last he had traversed this realm. Even in this ethereal form the world made way for his presence. Shadows wrapped around him, casting haunting images on scarcely lit walls. The sounds of the wind chasing fallen leaves through the streets warped into haunting whispers. The murmurs stilled as parents ran into the room of their screaming child, offering false reassurances that there were no such thing as monsters; that the long fingers they had seen stretching across towards their bed were nothing more than the moon's light playing tricks through the heavy branches of the surrounding trees. Yet they too would startle when the wind began anew, sending the tree branches to claw at the windows as if to gain entry.

Íkelos watched from darkened paths and shadowed nooks as those on patrol would raise their collars, shuddering against the chill of his eyes upon them. These were people wise enough to still fear the dark, and all things that walked within. They raised their lanterns to drive back the shadows, not comforted by flawed explanations of inexplicable phenomenon. Those of instinct, of true courage, knew there were things no man could explain away with logic. Monsters were real.

While his name had long been forgotten by those of this plane, it would soon be on each of their lips. It would be spoken with a fear and reverence owed to one who was known as the Father of Nightmares. For too long he had been nothing more than a prisoner who sent his Epiales across the boundaries and into Darrienia to haunt the dreams of those he could ensnare. Soon he would have everything he needed and those who would stand against him were still oblivious to the threat. By the time they realised, it would already be too late. Boundaries were no longer a concern and the world would atone for how far it had strayed.

The Mystics should have ensured his destruction when they had the chance. Their act of cruelty in preserving him would return to haunt them. He would achieve the task for which he was born and so much more. They had given him time, and time had given him the means to achieve his ambitions.

He flitted through the shadows, seeking the bait needed to ensure his prey had no choice but to don the mantle she was born for. The dawn of his return was imminent and with it would come the birth of a new era. For so long he had guided the path from the shadows, influenced dreams and the flow of history.

Now was the moment to release the shadows of his exile and once more feel the touch of light, and with him he would bring a darkness so old even the gods once feared it.

* * *

Xantara sighed in nervous frustration as she pulled and tugged at her unyielding hair. The darkening circles beneath her brown eyes told tales of her restless nights. She glared critically at the exhausted looking reflection, startling slightly as her handmaid snatched the brush from her grasp with a pained sigh.

Closing her eyes, she leaned back into the motherly touch as Guinevere separated her hair with skilled hands. She wove and threaded several brown strands into a beautiful half-braid, adorned with silvery-white flowers and hand-dyed golden thread that cascaded down the length of her hair.

"Come now, child, you mustn't keep him waiting," Guinevere warned, adding an extra dusting of gold powder around the young woman's eyes, hoping to mask the dark rings. "This way, come. Dawn is almost upon us and you're not even dressed."

Stifling a yawn, Xantara allowed herself to be escorted across the room where a bodice woven of vines and leaves awaited. With short, quick adjustments it was secured into place to hug her slender figure tightly. She was led in a daze through various sections of the room; each brief pause added layers onto her garments until only a spray of leaves remained. Stepping to their centre she raised her arms allowing Guinevere to secure the arrangement at her waist, where the weave ensured the delicate composition cascaded like an elegant ball gown. "You are still sleeping poorly?" she ventured, trying to bring the young woman's focus back from wherever her mind had strayed. Her effort was rewarded with a slight nod.

It had only been four days since the unnatural sleep had claimed the health of the current Maiden. Even now, Leona lay comatose, unreachable by magic or stimuli. Such an aliment had caused panic. Kerõs was renowned for its healers, and yet even they could not discover the cause for the unusual slumber. It was during this time of disarray Xantara had agreed to take on the role of leader prematurely, if their guardian accepted her.

Kerõs' residents were blessed by the Earth Spirit, and it was through him they received their healing artes. The village's ruler, a woman of exceptional talent and grace chosen by the people, held the title of Maiden. The rites and rituals she performed acted like a beacon for his energy, allowing him to bless them with his gifts and boons without having to be in their presence. Until Xantara's birth, no one could remember a time when their guardian had chosen a person to lead them. They recognised its significance from ancient fables, and knew she would be granted insight and blessings unknown to any who bore the mantle before her.

Whilst she was almost twenty-one, there were those who still considered her too young to accept the responsibilities. However, Kerõs could not be without an active Maiden for long or the enchantments bestowing the guardian's blessings upon them would fade, and so too would his own strength.

For days prior to Leona's illness, Xantara had been suffering nightmares. At first, she thought they had been signs, a warning she should have understood in order to prevent the Maiden's illness. However, when the nightmares continued she could discern no meaning. Day and night she felt as if someone, or something, was watching her. She swore she had felt their breath upon her as she slept, but as she startled awake her stalker would be nowhere to be seen. More than once she had cried out, believing the wind through the curtains had been the shifting of a figure. With each passing day the feelings of foreboding had grown. She saw movement in the flickering of every shadow and dared not sleep in case the figure returned.

"Quickly now, the sun is rising." Guinevere's voice pulled her from her concerns, kindling fresh nervous flutters in the pit of her stomach. Today she would take her place as the priestess of this town, and formally accept the mantle of Earth Maiden from the sacred creature who protected their village.

The morning air seemed unseasonably warm upon her cool flesh as she began her slow walk through the town towards the forest. Everything was still. Barely audible against the tense silence, she could hear the birds singing quietly in a soft harmonious chorus along with the frogs and crickets. People peered from their shuttered windows, hoping to glimpse their priestess, but no one would dare stray outside. Even being close to her could taint her, or cause disquiet to her mind. Only the selected handmaiden could be in her attendance since the purification first began, and even she could not taint the ground with her presence as Xantara made her slow procession.

With each step her apprehension built. She tried to recall all she had been told about their guardian. He was now the last embodiment of earthen elemental magic. As time had passed, his brethren, and those of the other Great Spirits, had all reduced in numbers until but one for each element remained living. He had accepted his isolation, knowing that to appear freely before others would see his demise and the imbalance of nature. He had founded this village, a place where he could bestow his boons upon choice few while he waited for his Maiden to be born. She was his spiritual companion, but as centuries passed her presence had never appeared. It was said he had feared her essence was lost, until the day Xantara had been born. This was the first time he had appeared before a gathering, and it was a tale still spoken about today.

Before undertaking this role, Xantara had needed to spend two days from dawn to dusk in prayer and purification, disturbed by no one whilst he observed from the light. Just as creatures of darkness hid in shadows, creatures of purity were concealed by the light. Once he had been certain he could accept her, he answered her request. At long last he would take that which was his and share with her a gift known only to his one true Maiden.

Xantara meandered, her pace slowing as her nerves rose. The grass felt like silk beneath her bare feet and her skin prickled with fear as her gaze fell upon the large circle of flowers within a small sheltered clearing. She was familiar with everything inside their forest's boundary, and yet, these flowers were unknown to her. They were an unusual midnight blue in colour and appeared to have been spun from light and silk. The air was heavy with their intoxicating scent, a fragrance which caused her heart to pound and her head to grow light. As she approached the boundary the green leaves weaving her dress began to alter, turning to autumnal shades. Whispering a quick blessing, she took a deep breath before stepping within the circle as her vision had instructed. She knelt in its centre, trying to calm herself as her dress continued to change and the leaves shed to reveal her freckled flesh.

When she heard the whinny of the beast, she felt as if she were both awake and within a dream. Her eyes opened, revealing a world that was both spiritual and corporeal. A white mist rose from the ground outside the flowers, twisting and distorting as if brushed by an invisible presence. Slowly it began to thicken, centring around a single location, seeming almost solid as a figure emerged. Still in motion, the creature continued to circle the boundary of flowers until its form became solid and she beheld, for the first time, his true splendour.

His hooves were the first part to be freed from the mist. Never had she seen an animal with a golden hoof wall, nor one whose skin was so pure white it seemed almost aglow. Each time one of his hooves met with the earth, flowers bloomed at his feet. Her eyes traced up his powerful, muscular legs, her breath quickening in fear and awe as her own brown eyes met with the creature's. His silver mane seemed to be spun from fine weaves of silken thread, parting only where the magnificent horn of gold and ivory twisted from his forehead.

Her stomach tightened and, for a moment as her head spun and she gasped for breath, she wondered if she would faint. She had been told by the current priestess of the wonder and beauty of this majestic creature, but words alone had not been enough to prepare her. She knelt, transfixed, unable to breathe as he moved to look down upon her. It was only then she realised he was still within his spirit form, and fine wisps of his silky mane faded into a light mist similar to that he had emerged from.

The figure became enshrouded in mist once more as his hoof passed over the blue flower border to enter the circle. As it touched the grass Xantara gasped as the haze cleared to reveal the figure of a man. His hair was the same long, spun silk that had made up the guardian's mane. Looking upon him she felt her body tremble.

He walked with the same grace and, just as it had before, beneath his human feet life bloomed. His eyes met hers and once again she felt the heat rise to her cheeks. Her neckline, now visible through the shedding leaves of her garment, mirrored the flushed colour of her embarrassment. She understood what would follow, what being his true Maiden entailed. Taking a breath, she prepared herself for his touch.

* * *

Zoella sat on the bed plaiting her daughter's rich, auburn hair while the six-year-old squirmed and protested. She voiced her most adamant objections, insisting she was a grown-up and far too old to need an afternoon nap. Screwing her face tightly into a pout, she almost succeeded in suppressing the building yawn. Zo looked at her daughter in the mirror, which hung on the adjacent wall, with a gentle smile lifting the corner of her lips. She could see so much of her husband in Alana. However, her striking blue eyes, currently welled with tears barely being held back by her thick, dark lashes, were a trait from her side of the family. Scooping her up tenderly Zo lay her daughter down, wrapping the soft burgundy covers around her.

"But—"

"But nothing." Zo tried to disguise the smile, knowing there were few within Crystenia who could resist such a look. She fought harder to suppress it as she felt Seiken's presence lingering in the doorway. "Even Rowmeow, the elder of all Oneirois, takes several naps throughout the day, and he is the oldest and wisest of us all," she asserted, playfully tapping her daughter's nose.

"Really?" she quizzed, pretending to hide her face to disguise the fact she was rubbing her eyes.

"Really," Zo declared firmly. Alana frowned, pursing her lips as she seemed to think on this for a moment before allowing her drooping eyelids to close. Feeling the soothing sensation of Seiken's hand upon the small of her back, Zo turned, smiling warmly before they left the room, neither daring to speak a word until far beyond the child's earshot.

"I was wondering how you felt about a visit to Misora this afternoon," Seiken reached out taking his wife's hand in his, "and perhaps a picnic?" He glanced fervently around, ensuring there was no one in the vicinity to hear his words. His lips turned up into a mischievous smile.

"Don't you have to attend—"

"I briefly excused myself. It's not my fault that my wife looks hungry. What kind of husband could I claim to be if I allowed my family to starve?" He offered her a charming smile, interlacing his fingers with hers before leading her down the corridor and into the magnificent gardens. He swiftly escorted her down the winding pathways, leaving her barely enough time to appreciate their splendour. Seiken was notorious for these spontaneous outings. Any moment now, Zo half expected one of the council members to step out before them. They knew by now whenever their prince sneaked away to tuck his daughter into bed, he somehow always seemed to lose his way back.

Seiken spun, wrapping his arms around Zo's waist as he pulled her into the shelter of the nearby willows. He placed his lips to hers, silencing any protests that could have alerted the passersby he had sighted to their presence. He savoured her taste upon his lips long after the dark shadow of the Oneiroi had faded from sight. Only then did he release her, grinning childishly.

"You're going to get into trouble," she whispered, reaching out to brush a strand of his auburn hair from his brown eyes.

"I've barely seen you in weeks. I'm painfully aware how all-consuming the formation of this new ministry is. Surely they can't begrudge me a few stolen moments with my wife."

"And you know I understand how important it is. With everything that happened, first with Night, and then the unnatural energies crossing into our realm, we need to make sure our lands *and* its dreamers are safe. If that means for a short time I can't see you as much, then it's a price I will pay. Besides, we still don't know what happened to those missing Outcasts."

"Aidan and Jude?" Zoella nodded as Seiken's brow furrowed with concern.

"You know we need to find out, I—"

"You still feel responsible?"

"I asked Aidan to watch over Elly. Whatever happened, happened because he was with her. Surely you don't think it's a coincidence she was expelled from Darrienia, and only minutes later both Aidan and Jude's cluster felt their energy vanish."

"He volunteered for the task, from what you told me." Seiken's face grew serious for a moment, weighted with the pressure of his newest responsibilities. He shook his head, dislodging the intrusive thoughts. Grabbing her hand, he pulled her from the cover of the trees and towards the gate where the two Cynocephali, Fenyang and Abasi, stood eternal vigil. Zo called out a greeting to them as they rushed past and towards the portal which led below to the surface of Darrienia.

The tall cliffs sheltered a small untouched cove from the winds that chased across the ocean. This was but one of their hidden retreats, a place whose resting and unmanipulated form was the one they now beheld. Zo could see Seiken had warded against dreamers, something which implied he had been planning their visit a little longer than their impulsive sprint had suggested. A large beige blanket lay spread across the sand with a woven picnic basket upon its centre. Seeing all he had done for her, Zo kissed him gently.

"This is beautiful," she whispered. Seiken guided her towards the shore where small pebbles tickled the sand trying to break free from the pull of the gentle waves. "Thank you."

"No, thank *you.* Eight years ago today we offered you a chance to return home, to your life and friends." Zo's vision turned towards the platinum ring upon her finger as he spoke. "I have never known such fear as that I felt thinking you would leave," he admitted, taking her hand in his.

"That was never an option. My heart would have stilled had I betrayed it. It wants only you, now, forever, and always."

Zo had not once regretted the decision to stay, and could imagine nothing that would make her do so. Not long after, Seiken finally mustered the courage to ask for her hand in marriage. She had accepted without delay, and later became one of only two Oneirois to conceive a child. Seiken had been the first to be born in Darrienia, and now their daughter, Alana, was the second.

Zo felt the warmth spreading through her as her eyes locked on Seiken's. Even now she found it difficult to believe that, of all people, he had chosen her. He had said they were destined to be together, and the fact she survived the rite of claiming with her own will intact was a testament to that truth. Seiken had been reluctant to claim her. It was an archaic rite employed only by ancient gods. It had been a means to identify their devotees, and once claimed by soul manipulation—or psychíkinesis as it was commonly known—a person's will was often no longer their own. Their every desire became solely about making the one who claimed them happy.

Seiken lay back on the blanket, raising his arm so Zo could lie beside him and rest her head upon his chest. She loved lying with him like this, simply the two of them together as she listened to the soothing sound of his powerful heartbeat. She knew she could stay in his embrace forever. She felt her eyes growing heavy, and soon the rhythmic beat of his heart lulled her to sleep and she did something no other Oneiroi could, she dreamt.

The steady tattoo of his heart reached into her dreams, becoming the drums of war. She turned full circle, but a blanket of darkness shrouded her vision.

She was not alone. Another presence was here with her, watching. Movement flashed through obstructed sight, and agonising screams filled the blackened canvas, streaking the air and staining the dark clouds with crimson fury as an unseen assailant tore its way through the shadows.

'*See what your actions have wrought,*' whispered a voice. She felt the breath of something upon her neck, its pressure increasing until the breath became a wind and the dark clouds lifted to reveal a scene of carnage. Men, women, and children had been reduced to an amalgamation of twisted, unidentifiable limbs, strewn across a blood-stained field, and yet somehow she still heard their tormented screams. She startled, once more finding comfort in the familiar sound of her lover's heart but, despite the security of his embrace, she could find no warmth.

Chapter 2

Xantara's Plight

Fey, like his father, and his forefathers, had been raised as a guide. Their family had long-standing ties in the Travellers' Plexus, but few people called on such services. A guide was often a local to an area and well-versed in the lay of the land. He knew where the rarest herbs grew, how to track and trap, and where the most dangerous beasts roamed. Given his aptitude for the wild, he was often mistaken for a ranger. But as a guide it was his duty to extend his services to any who asked.

Today he had the pleasure of escorting two ladies from Steelforge, one of his neighbouring villages, to Castlefort found in the westernmost area of Therascia. Normally, those of standing would request an escort from the Hunters' Plexus, but their prices were much steeper given the specialised training their members had to undergo. To become a guide, one simply had to have knowledge. Fortunately, as those in the area knew, Fey himself had received an invitation to partake in the trials of the Hunters' Plexus, but he had opted to remain true to his family's calling. It was days like these, however, he questioned his decision.

One of the two ladies in his company was extremely challenging. At every possible opportunity she deliberately attempted to undermine him. Now they were finally on their way she found other means to infuriate him, such as complaining about their rapid pace, while simultaneously moaning that they would be late.

Being a guide was a job he loved, most days. He would often find himself with the honour of escorting herbalists and apothecaries to sheltered and difficult locations, and help them gather their much needed supplies. By seeing the omens left by nature's spirits, and what their signs implied, he himself could pass warnings of plague and illness onto others. Other days, he would find himself in the service of a hunter who needed aid in tracking a bounty in his territory. And then there were days like these. He often reflected during such journeys that, if not for people like these, his hair would still be lustrous and dark, instead of streaked with grey. He swore, as he listened to the ceaseless barrage of complaints, he could feel another strand of hair being stripped of its once vibrant shade.

On the occasions he caught glimpses of himself, and witnessed the latest damage to his moderate vanity, he would not smile fondly, as someone who had raised a family might. He would *not* remember his charges kindly as he beheld the deepening frown-lines upon his furrowed brow, caused by those who thought themselves of some important standing or significant influence. Fey was too young to be turning white, and as he looked upon each strand the voice of each complaint would return, *'the pace is too slow,' 'the horse is too bumpy,' 'the wind is messing my hair,'*. The two he now rode with were no different. They had the same complaints he had heard countless times before, but with the addition of '*my clothes will be creased.*'

Fey had insisted, no less than twice, that they changed into more appropriate attire for riding. But the older of the two women—the one who seemed to have taken a deep breath at his arrival and spouted nothing but an endless stream of complaints and criticisms—had insisted they ride in their finest silks so they may arrive in the glory expected.

He had explained that the final part of the journey was through marshland, but his warning had met only with the woman's flustered looking husband heaving her hefty frame onto the carefully positioned sidesaddle. He, at least, had the decency to look somewhat apologetic, although Fey could see his poorly guarded relief at the promise of a few days of respite from the cantankerous woman he had married.

If not for the fee, he would have refused his services there and then. However, as much as he loathed to admit it, these were the tasks that paid in coin. Healers paid in treatments and remedies, hunters paid him in meat and hide, blacksmiths in services. The exchange of service for service was more common than it was believed. Often, when Fey found he was in need of something, he would have to trade and barter with his service tokens, and often found himself far from satisfied with the deal. These undertakings were essential and, in order to obtain some of his rarer supplies, he was forced to deal with traders who would only accept coin, precious metals, or jewels as payment.

"And it looks like it is going to rain!" The older woman was still complaining. Years of practice had ensured Fey could, for the most part, drown out the incessant noise. He focused his attention on their surroundings. Due to a migration in bandit activities along the main trade route, and the anticipation of wagons filled with supplies, Fey had guided their horses through the woodland. They were in the heart of bandit territory, and such scoundrels did not take kindly to trespassers. Today, however, this route was the lesser of two evils. Travelling the roads they were certain to be attacked. The two women were draped in fine silks and jewels, some of which he knew to have been borrowed from other members of the community in order to portray an image of wealth. The main routes would have meant certain death. This path, however, was merely dangerous.

"Look," Fey warned sternly as he pulled on the reins of his horse, causing the two steeds behind him to stop. This was the reason he always used his own horses. His own beasts had no question as to who was in charge. "If you don't quieten down you'll have more to worry about than the state of your hair and the sores on your backside. I told you before we entered, the bandits here won't be any gentler because your clothes are pretty. I think you'll find it's just the opposite. So, unless you want to find yourself beaten, and making a living on your back, then I suggest you be quiet!" The look slowly transforming the woman's face went from indignant to outraged, almost in the blink of an eye. Her portly face grew red, visible even through the thick layers of makeup she had applied to hide her age-lines. She opened her mouth to protest, but the sharp gesture from Fey saw her mouth, instead, snapping shut. He turned back towards the path, spurring the horses onward as, in his peripheral vision, he saw the woman shaking her head in disbelief and patting down her windswept hair.

Fey had not exaggerated. If anything he had underplayed the danger. The bandits in this area were well-known Slavers and Fleshmongers. Their trade varied from selling their wares to high-standing households, to providing expendable resources to the overseers in the mines. The slaves they trained would become anything their new master would ask of them, servant or whore. The Fleshmongers traded with shady brothels, those whose patrons were often disease-ridden, rough-handed men and women. There were more reputable dens of iniquities, but they ensured a genuine debt and crosschecked the history of the ones being sold something which, given the bandits' methods of acquisitions, could not always be supplied.

It was said if a whore could earn enough they could buy their freedom—at a price of three times their purchase fee—their master would release them from the binding spell. Few survived long enough to earn this right. Before many had even saved half, their master had already prepared a replacement for when the unthinkable befell them. Finding fresh meat was never an issue.

Fey slowed his horse slightly, watching for movement in the undergrowth as he reached down removing his throwing knives from his saddlebags. Normally he was more prepared, armed and ready, but the woman's incessant droning had distracted him. Patches of darkened shadows wove through the camouflage of the forest. They thought their positioning towards the group's rear would conceal them for longer, but Fey's peripheral vision was better than most. Slowing his horse further he positioned himself between the two women.

Their trackers were few, but he had no doubt they would eliminate him given the chance. They would not, however, risk damaging the spoils. Fey glanced from left to right, looking for any indication the two women had realised what was about to happen. The younger one still sat submissively, her eyes closed as her mother droned on. The silence had lasted but a few minutes before she had once more found her voice.

By Fey's best estimation, there were currently four figures in pursuit. Given their alternating positions, it seemed two had been tasked to dispatch him allowing the remaining ones to claim the women. He exhaled sharply, he had warned them the noise would attract unsavoury characters. The track before them began to darken as the trees reached out onto the bridleway causing a visible narrowing, presenting the opportune position for an ambush. Bracing himself, Fey gave the reins a sharp tug bringing his animals to a halt. The undergrowth rustled as two of the assailants sprung forwards, their rapid steps faltering as they overshot their mark. Fey studied the men as they recovered quickly, his eyes narrowing impatiently as they took the reins of the ladies' horses in their dirt-encrusted hands.

"I was promised safe passage," he announced, his tone harsh and unamused as he positioned himself to sit taller upon his saddle.

"These are two mighty fine wenches y've got 'ere, lad." Another figure emerged from the forest, a little too far away for Fey to distinguish any identifying marks.

"Whores can appear however you dress them. Does Raz know you're disrupting his agreements?"

"What y' mean?"

"You're his clan, or at least your men wear his sigil. These were his"—Fey gestured towards the women—"inspect them if you must. They're branded and will-bound, but don't sully the merchandise." The men in possession of the reins looked towards their leader questioningly. Fey attempted to project confidence, but was all too aware that the look of terror on the women's faces was betraying his ruse. Besides, given the slow approach of those still concealed in the forest he could tell his words had no effect. He tucked his fingers into his sleeves, grasping the knife handles before quickly releasing them.

The reins slid from the men's hands before their bodies crumpled to the forest floor, adding further sprays of red to the crimson blanket of autumn leaves. Maintaining eye contact with the leader Fey slowly dismounted, closing the distance between them slightly, enough to be able to watch the shadows behind him where the concealed figures still lay in wait. "Step aside." Fey released another knife. Hearing it strike wood he released a second. This time he was rewarded with the dull thump of the blade penetrating flesh, and the crumbling thud of another body. Fey's fingers slid the final knife from its holder in his sleeve. One knife, two adversaries. "Don't think I'll hesitate because she's a woman," Fey warned, inclining his head towards the remaining figure, who still stalked through the camouflage of the forest. The leader raised his hand and the shadow's movement stilled.

"That's a good eye, for a guide."

"And you've got some nerve, for a stalker." A piercing cry echoed from above as several dark shadows cast from circling birds penetrated the canopies and open track. The bandit cast his gaze warily skyward, at first marvelling how carrion birds arrived to pick the bones of the dead on par with the speed he could strip a corpse of its valuables. His face grew serious as he saw the outlines of the circling creatures.

"Harpies!" The birds let out a wispy wail as they began their rapid descent, diving towards them. Fey secured the reins of the horses, ready to protect the women, and lead them deeper into the shelter of the forest, but the attack was solely focused on the bandit and his hidden companion. The harpy eagles dove, their enormous bear-like talons extended. One of the creatures swooped close to Fey, flapping its wings to hover until he extended his arm. He strained against the sudden weight of the young creature, watching in awe as the bandits fled into the forest trailed by the predators.

Fey looked to the eagle questioningly. This species had been dubbed harpies due to their almost human shaped face bringing to mind the beautiful monsters of fables, but as Fey looked upon it he saw but a few features which could be thought of as such. The bird ruffled its slate-black feathers, moving its grey head to study him as intently as he studied it. A silent understanding seemed to pass between them. Then, in a flurry of movement, its strong grip uncurled from his arm, and it took to the sky allowing him a brief glimpse of its white underbelly before it vanished from sight.

"Must we delay further?" The woman huffed, resuming her confident posture as she patted her hair down, tucking stray strands into the large honeycomb. Fey stared after the bird for a moment, almost in disbelief of what had just occurred. Then, accepting it as simply what had been, without a word mounted his horse and resumed leading the way. "Is it far?" she demanded, but Fey retained his silence, biting back a venomous reply.

The journey across the sodden waste of the marshland had so far taken a few hours. They had been carefully skirting along the edges of the lakes and peat bogs, when Fey once more caught sight of the circling birds in the distance. Slowly, he adjusted his course to lead them closer. Even at a glance he knew the actions were not those of carrion birds. When the harpy eagle's massive frame had first grasped his arm he hadn't known the purpose of their intervention, but he knew their unexpected aid had not been for his own benefit. The woman behind him was still complaining—now about the mud and water being kicked up by the horses' movements onto their fine clothes—and he once more drowned out her irritating voice, focusing instead on the dark clouds. Here, on this open plain, the wind swept so violently across the land even the horses were forced to stagger against its ceaseless barrage, and yet it seemed where the birds patrolled sunlight broke the clouds, touching the land as to provide a beacon.

A familiar cry sounded from above. Turning his gaze skyward, Fey recognised the markings of the harpy eagle. It began to circle them, and whilst the wind continued to batter the land, the area surrounding them grew still. At their approach to the illuminated area, the circling birds broke formation to scatter across the sky. Darkness closed in from above as the clouds encroached across the area of blue and began to release the first fat, heavy drops of the promised rain.

Fey studied the surroundings, as his vision was drawn to a slumped figure upon the ground he brought the mounts to a stop. "Now what?" The woman demanded bitterly as Fey slid from his horse, quickly approaching the motionless form.

"Excuse me, miss?" he questioned softly, already knowing the woman would not respond. She had been oblivious to their approach, it was doubtful words alone could rouse her. As he reached out to touch her, his eyes recognised the symbolism of her attire. She wore a silken high-collared dress. Her shoulders were bare but for a finely spun scarf which was currently wrapped around her like a shawl that billowed wildly in the returning wind. Its delicate mesh seemed almost invisible, woven with a thread so fine it appeared to be made from mist and clouds. The area in which she lay was firm, surrounded by a strange blue flower. It was a symbol Fey rarely saw, one that suggested the land had been touched by a Great Spirit.

The harpy eagle called out from beyond the flower circle. At its prompt Fey nodded and watched as it took flight to join its brethren. Reaching down, he checked her carefully for injuries. Even through her elbow-length gloves he could feel her flesh was cold, the only warmth remaining seemed to be that from the sun which had shielded her. Glancing around, he lifted the woman into his arms, carefully making his way back towards his horse.

"Do put that back," the woman ordered as Fey lifted the limp figure to straddle his steed. He whispered softly in its ear as he positioned the woman securely. "You don't know where it has been, it could have a disease."

"Surely you would wish someone to aid you, if it were you here." The younger woman finally spoke, the tenderness of her voice surprised Fey almost as much as the tone of shame barely concealed within.

"Don't be silly, child, I wouldn't be found dead out here." Ignoring the woman Fey mounted, carefully positioning himself behind the woman. She was a dainty figure, her long ash-blonde hair, which once would have fallen in beautiful curls to rest just below her shoulders, was matted and tangled. Pulling his cloak from his saddlebag, Fey wrapped it around her before leaning her back to rest against him so her frigid body could absorb some of his own heat.

He did not know this woman, but her attire, and the reactions of the birds and clouds to her presence, meant she could only be Sylph's chosen. Within his arms lay the Air Maiden, and given how shallow her breathing was he feared she may never wake.

* * *

Alana giggled as she ducked under the outstretched arms of the pursuing Eorthád, weaving around another to skid across the sand. Her vision desperately panned from left to right as she sought a place to hide. She could hear the cries of the other captured children warning her to keep moving, lest she be caught and forced to remain in the wolves' den until one of the other lambs could free them. It was a favoured game of the children, as yet they had not come to realise it was a teaching exercise in strategy, quick thinking, and stealth. Tonight the wolves—comprised of six Eortháds, one from each area of expertise—were showing no quarter, or at least it seemed that way to the children.

Alana squealed in surprise as a figure sprung from a nearby rock pool, wrapping his wet arms around her as he hauled her dramatically towards the den. He placed her down gently beside the bamboo and woven grass structure, shaking his hair playfully to send droplets of water spraying over the children. They squealed and giggled, hiding behind the shelter until he walked away in search of his next victim.

Seiken sat with his hand interlaced with Zo's, his gaze fixed upon her as she watched the spectacle from their place near one of the small fires that littered the beach. Happiness traced the edge of her smile.

The Eortháds were always thrilled when they would visit, more so when they brought their newest addition to the family along. Alana still giggled when they addressed her as Mistress, and it had taken Zo some time to become accustomed to her new name as well. Here she was known as Thea. The name, bestowed upon her when she became an Oneiroi, had been the one by which Seiken had always addressed her.

"I can't believe how much she's grown." Daniel stepped over one of the large wooden benches as he approached, smoothing his brown hair before joining them at the fireside. He had been in the middle of training when news of their arrival had reached him and, despite the importance of their visitors, he had been forbidden from leaving his duties prematurely.

He had already surpassed their expectations for this phase of his awakening into the role of Wita. His connection to the Underworld allowed him to call upon the wisdom of those departed, but this was difficult and exhausting to maintain. Nemean—the Grand Master and eldest of the wyrms—instead of solely allowing Daniel to focus on retaining the link in a calm environment, had now introduced physical burdens to the exercise, forcing him to practice maintaining the tether during times of distraction. If he could achieve this, he would be able to draw on not only the wisdom and power of the deceased, but their perception as well, allowing him to see beyond the scope of a normal warrior.

Daniel had never considered himself to be gifted in combat, nor had he expected the role of Wita to ask him to become versed in such things. The passing years had seen them all grow and change in ways none of them could have predicted. "I see so much of you both in her," he added gesturing towards the youngsters while nodding his head in greeting towards Seiken.

"Is that a polite way of saying she's trouble?" Zo teased.

"I don't think trouble is a strong enough word," Seiken interjected as he rose to his feet. Daniel's gesture had brought his attention to the fine billows of smoke from the place his daughter had last stood. He gave a humoured sigh, his pace increasing as the flickering embers of a fire became more noticeable. Seiken skilfully lifted a pail from the hands of an approaching Eorthád, who more than had the situation under control. With an exaggerated swing he covered the squealing children from head to toe in the sea water while Adel, Thegnalar of Drá»^{3}cræft, schooled one of the younger children showing promise in the arcane on how to create a barrier around the fire to extinguish it.

"Sorry, Daddy." Alana scuffed her feet, her sight focusing upon them briefly before glancing timidly towards him with her big, blue, deer-like eyes. She knew it made his heart melt. It was a look she quickly learnt worked on almost everyone. "I tried to stop it."

"How?" he questioned, trying to keep his voice firm. He narrowed his eyes, hoping to disguise the smile that threatened to appear.

"Well," she sang, rocking backwards and forwards on her heels. "It said it was hungry, so I fed it some leaves. *Everybody* knows a full tummy makes you sleepy." She flashed him a brilliant smile as she presented her logic.

"You, young lady, need to study more. And don't you believe everything you hear."

"So, I don't need to study more?" she questioned innocently.

"Sorry about that." Seiken looked apologetically to Alessia, who had joined them to see what all the commotion was about. Alana ran to her, lifting her arms up. As if by second nature the Master and Commander of the Eorthåds scooped the child into her arms, positioning her to sit on her hip. Alana pushed back some of Alessia's black hair, being careful to avoid the silver wyrm winged circlet she always wore as a symbol of her rank, before snuggling closer to her.

"Concern yourself not, many of our young are coming into magic, Lord Seiken. Mistress Alana is no different."

"But still..." Seiken trailed off, his vision turning to focus on his wife. He couldn't be sure, but there was something about the manner in which she sat, and Daniel's concerned expression, that suggested something important was being discussed. He felt a frown furrow his brow as he wondered what fresh mischief his wife was causing while he had dispelled the trouble caused by their daughter.

"Daddy, it's rude to stare." Alana's scolding returned his focus. He gave a slight shrug. Surely there was nothing more to their discussion than Daniel, once again, trying to fill in the gaps in his knowledge. And yet, a strange sensation washed over him as he watched them. "Daddy!"

"Yes, sorry. Shall we join Mummy and Uncle Daniel? I think you've had quite enough excitement for one day." Seiken and Alessia made their way over to the small fire, where they made themselves comfortable. Alana ran straight for her mother, fidgeting until Zo had no choice but to reposition herself so her daughter could lie with her head on her lap. "I guess she's run out of trouble and needs to recharge," Seiken teased.

"It's been an eventful day," Zo whispered, tenderly stroking Alana's hair as her eyes began to close. When she spoke again, she maintained the same soft tone. "So, you were telling me about the Daimon," Zo prompted. Daniel barely hid his surprise at the sudden change in conversation. He *had* been telling her about his encounter with Kitaia Ethelyn, but then, as soon as Seiken was otherwise distracted, she had interrupted to tell him of something of such magnitude that her sudden return to the topic at hand was unexpected.

Daniel had so many questions about what she had just revealed. He glanced towards Seiken, understanding that perhaps she was once more interfering in forbidden things. She had been warned countless times about involving herself in the mortal realm, and that was only for the times her indiscretions had been discovered. Perhaps this secret was better kept between the two of them, for now. How she expected him to forget it was another matter. He could not leave it unaddressed, but perhaps that had been her intention.

"Yes, as I was saying, she was the one who had Remedy attached to her. I never imagined they would look so much like us. Every book I've ever seen depicted them as monsters, yet aside from the additional bones she did not differ from you or I. I've been meaning to visit their land, but Alessia thinks I should wait until I've mastered the voices from these lands first."

"Of course, Seiken explained what it meant to be selected as Wita. I can't believe you've advanced so far already. Do you hear them now?" Zo questioned eagerly, her eyes sparkling with intrigue and pride. Seiken had told her in great detail the path that awaited her closest friend. Being the Eorthóds' Wita meant he possessed a talent surpassing those of a sage. Daniel could commune with the spirits of the ancestors. He would see things beyond the scope of man, and be given insight most could only imagine.

"I'm still learning. I can't always control when I hear them, or focus enough to retain a link to ask for specifics, but I am improving."

"You are doing amazingly. Grand Master is impressed by your progress. You have come so far in such a short time. We have never known one to have the aptitude you do and view ourselves fortunate our paths crossed when they did. You were already a sage, even if you were unaware of it the spirits were not. It would have been difficult to understand the transition if not for our presence. I must give my thanks to you for guiding him to us, Lady Thea." Alessia noticed the subtle shifting of Zo's position as she tried to make herself comfortable under the weight of the sleeping child. "My home is available, she is welcome to rest there."

"Thank you, Commander, but we really must be returning." Seiken approached Zo, lifting his daughter into his arms with a well-practised skill. He adjusted her slightly, holding her close, without waking her.

"Of course, it's nightfall already," Daniel observed, much to his surprise. It seemed his friends had only arrived mere moments ago, and already they were having to leave. "We're keeping you from your duties."

"Not really, we are expecting a quiet night this evening. There's very little preordained."

"Preordained, you mean you know when someone will suffer terrors?"

"It's complicated, but many of the negative areas present omens before a dreamer arrives, otherwise we would be unprepared to protect them. However, there are many we cannot anticipate, and of course there's the Epiales interference and corruption. Tonight we have the easy task of the expected, whilst others walk the land." It surprised Daniel when it was Seiken who answered. He had always circumvented the details wherever possible, often leaving his answers vague and open to interpretation.

"I still don't understand how it works," Daniel complained. He hated not comprehending it fully, but there was no one who could offer him information on that world except for the Oneirois themselves. Any of their race who passed away had either taken the blind-step to become mortal—and as such lost all insight into that world—or had been corrupted and joined the ranks of the Epiales. There was no insight to be gained from either.

"It's relatively simple when you stop thinking about it in your own terms. Our entire existence is forged from energy waves, and within a dreamscape they adapt to become a visual representation of what the dreamer sees. When an area of negativity begins to form we know those entering there will be subjected to terrors, as you call them. We have the added benefit of the fact our kind do not require sleep, and thus are keeping constant vigil should something untoward occur." Seiken glanced to Zo, so far they had kept the fact she still dreamt a closely guarded secret. It was unfathomable for one of their own kind. Until it became apparent it was occurring with her they had thought it impossible.

Seiken noticed Daniel glance towards his daughter questioningly. "Alana herself is unusual. Our kind don't possess the ability to procreate and yet, like myself, she was born to our world. Since we exist in a world of REM we can't dream, but we do enter a sleep-like state we call NREM which allows us to absorb the theta waves we use to sustain ourselves. It helps the younger of our kind to learn and process information, but the same can also be achieved by eating. Our sustenance is nothing more than condensed energy," he revealed. Daniel exchanged a curious look with Zo, who simply nodded, her eyes crinkling in amusement at Daniel's curious expression.

"You're the Eorthåds' Wita, as such you already know who my husband is to them. Concealing information from you serves no purpose now," Zo offered, explaining Seiken's sudden openness. "On that note, whilst it is restful to be here the benefits are far less than those of our own world, and this young lady needs all the rest she can get."

"It has been an honour to see you again." Alessia dropped to one knee to bow before them.

"You too." Zo smiled awkwardly. Alessia's people bowed before her and Seiken whenever they visited. It was a show of respect they insisted on as Seiken was the reincarnation of the Wyrm god. He was an ancient being, born near the time the universe first began to hold life. His divine form had been slain and reborn into Darrienia, but the Eorthåds and wyrms remained his to command; as such they offered him and his family this tribute. Zo understood the importance this ritual held for the Eorthåds and whilst it made her uncomfortable to have those she thought of as friends kneel before her, she had been warned asking them not to would be disrespectful. Even knowing this she doubted it was something she would ever become accustomed to.

* * *

Xantara let the refreshing water of the small natural pool wash over her, soothing her aching body and cleansing the earth and sweat from her flesh. The gown she had approached the Spirit in had returned to the earth, and in its place he had presented her with clothes of his own design.

Emerging from the waters refreshed and rejuvenated, she slid the silver cloth of the sleeveless, high-necked bodysuit over her head, amazed at the silken feel of its texture. The Spirit had informed her that this top had been spun from his own mane, and whilst delicate in appearance it possessed a strength and durability that the finest warrior would envy. She fastened it carefully between her legs before pulling up the dark brown, hide trousers. As she fastened them, she couldn't help but wonder how she could be so covered, and yet feel so exposed at the same time. The fabric clung to her like a second skin, made tighter by the belts around either thigh which held hunting blades, and yet as she moved it felt almost as if she wore nothing at all.

Finally she pulled on the boots, fashioned from the same hide as the trousers and edged with golden stitching. They felt rigid as she pulled on the laces to fasten them over her shins but, like everything else, once in place, they felt comfortable. As a final gift he had presented a long coat, mottled with the colours of earth that altered subtly to provide the most beneficial camouflage.

The Spirit had informed her that this attire would identify her as his chosen Maiden, and that just as her clothes were an embodiment of all the earth had to offer, she would recognise the chosen Maidens of any other Spirits by a similar aura. He had warned her that from this day forth she should only wear garments fashioned by himself. They appeared delicate, but the Maidens chosen by the Spirits were their mortal warriors and this was the armour he had bestowed upon her.

It was only as Xantara returned to her home and gazed upon her reflection she realised how different she looked to the current Maiden. Her freckles, since joining with the Spirit had become more pronounced, altering to appear the subtle red and brown shades associated with autumnal leaves, and her brown hair shone in multi-toned shades of earthen brown. The current Maiden, the one whom she would now replace, was fair, and wore a flowing gown woven by the tailors in a fashion they thought would appeal to their guardian. Looking deeper into the mirror she noticed the brown shades of her eyes had now intensified, showing intense golden freckles.

Despite everything she had just experienced, the power surging through her veins from their encounter, her body trembled. It was time to take up the mantle preordained by her birth. She had been called to become the Maiden prematurely and had to prove herself worthy. Now more than ever she feared failure. After a decisive stare at her reflection in the surface of the looking glass she once more stepped out onto the streets.

Unlike moments ago, when she had returned, the streets were no longer deserted. On seeing Xantara the town had become animated, awaiting eagerly the re-emergence of their Spirit's chosen Maiden.

"My lady." A figure awaited her at the door. "It is my understanding that there are no Fangers awakened, perhaps you would permit me the honour until your protector makes himself known to us?" Xantara looked upon her childhood friend in astonishment, her freckles seemed to grow more pronounced as her skin flushed. For as long as she remembered he had trained to be their village's protector. He was their most competent hunter and their greatest scout.

"William," she whispered, her voice almost failing. A murmur of excitement delayed her answer as her attention was drawn towards the small man pushing his way through the gathering crowd towards her.

"My lady, what of Leona?" he asked when she acknowledged his presence. Before giving her answer she extended her hand to William, beckoning him to rise.

"Have her taken to the temple's prayer room. You, and you"—she gestured towards two of the larger men within the crowd—"help move her. Deliver this to the apothecary, I need it prepared without delay." She handed a scrap of parchment to a nearby villager who scurried away, her face beaming with happiness at being called upon. With purposeful strides Xantara made her way towards the temple, with William falling into step beside her. "You have always been my guardian," she whispered. "Once this is official I shall name you such." He gave a slight bow. "But that stops this instant."

"My lady?" he questioned with a mischievous smirk.

"You are still ten years my senior. I have not changed since yesterday, and yet now you distance yourself from me with titles. You're my friend, my brother in all but blood."

"Xan, I—"

"I know. You mean only respect, but do you not think my heart already knows. Since I was born and named so many have been guarded around me. You, however, dragged me into trouble." William laughed at her words.

"I swear, the first time I put a knife in your hand your father almost slaughtered me."

"You didn't go easy on me because I was born with this privilege, although sometimes I wished you had. If anything, you were harder on me because of it. I shed many tears because of you."

"And I don't regret causing you a single one," he admitted in earnest. "I couldn't stand how people spoilt you. How did they expect you to learn when they were afraid to challenge you? I swear they were more afraid of you at six than they were of any wild beast. If not for me you'd have never seen the forest outside the town."

"Yes... although I've never forgiven you for abandoning me out there."

"The whole town was looking for you." He laughed. "Besides, you were never in any real danger. I was never far, but it taught them a valuable lesson.

You may have been their future, but you still needed to learn the skills to fend for yourself."

"They punished you though," she whispered, looking to the scarring across his arms. When she had been found they had decided that William needed to be disciplined. Given his natural skill he had become arrogant and at sixteen had thought himself invincible. They pitted him, unarmed, against one of their trained wolves. It had taught him a valuable lesson, and even now he bore the claw and tooth marks as a reminder. He had never endangered her again, but he would change nothing. His actions had made them realise the importance of Xantara being able to defend herself, hunt, and track.

"I think I did rather well," he chuckled light heartedly, seeing her gaze towards his old scars.

"Raff used you like his own personal gnawing bit."

"I learnt, and became stronger because of it. Now, my lady, your temple awaits." Xantara raised her hand as he moved to follow her inside. She alone could prepare the area for what must be done. There could be no distractions. The symbols she had to reproduce from memory were complex.

As she entered the sanctuary her thoughts returned to her time resting beside the Great Spirit upon the flattened grass. He had listened as she had explained what ailed the current Maiden, and had offered her the solution. But a warning had also been imparted. Within the lands of Darrienia lay many dangers and, in order to retrieve the part of Leona which had become ensnared, Xantara would first have to face whatever force had detained her.

Chapter 3

Ádlíc

Fey drew the horses to a stop outside the large gates of the confined city of Castlefort. This world had but two castles of such grandeur, Albeth Castle, also known as Oureas' Rest, and the one he stood before now. Rumour had it that Castlefort had once been known by another name, but it was one that seemed to have been long forgotten.

Both castles had their own allure and shared but a few similarities. They both stood when they should have fallen, and were strongholds, nearly impossible to infiltrate. For two constructions believed to have been built in the time of the ancients, they were immensely different in architecture.

Albeth Castle was an enormous building, spanning the width of many cities. It was protected by a moat and drawbridge, and the castle itself was fused with mountains. Its rear overlooked one of the largest inland bodies of water known, which granted sailing vessels access into a secured port. Castlefort, however, was a city surrounded by an enormous fortified wall. Within, small houses littered the streets, and barely visible from outside was the royal castle, known as Castle Iris. This structure had earned its name due to the iris-shaped, purple flower wind-vane which stood prominent against the castle's roof. The outer petals rotated, while the inner ones remained stationary. Its breeze-driven motion was said to bestow blessings upon the surrounding land. Rumours suggested that this vane was a symbol of a blood-pact made by the royal house, and as long as one of royal blood was within the walls its boons would be granted.

Over a decade ago, when the king had been assassinated, the iris had closed and drought and famine had taken the land. The Chancellor had acted as Regent, guiding his people through the crisis, and yet whispers of underhanded deeds, and suspicion about his role in the king's death, had kept him from earning support. Even when the great flower opened once more, it brought no recognition of his actions, only suspicious tongues that spun tales of a prisoner escorted into the castle under night's cloak.

Without trust in its leader Castlefort had become divided, and no plans to name a successor to the throne had been made. There was an uneasy order across the land, and Fey noted the increased numbers of guards patrolling the battlements above, keeping close vigil on everything both within the walls and beyond.

Seeing Fey's approach, a guard from the battlements gave an order. At once the deafening grinding of metal echoed through the air as the enormous chains began to pull up the larger of the two impressive portcullises that protected the city's doors. Castlefort had two entrances, a small shielded door for travellers on foot, and the larger trade entrance for horses and wagons. Due to its location across marshland, and its rear border of steep cliffs, it was rare for people to approach on foot. Despite it being an infrequent occurrence, a well-maintained, wrought iron knocker could just be seen within arm's reach through the smaller door's portcullis. Both gateways progressed into a transitional area within the thick wall, where vehicles and people were searched thoroughly, and their business and intentions recorded.

There were stables inside the city but, quite often, those arriving on horseback were asked to leave their animals outside and enter through the smaller gate, with assurances that a stable hand would attend to their animals. This ensured the main gates were not opened and closed more than necessary. Fey's arrival, by luck rather than intention, had coincided with the evening traders. While the first large gate was still being raised a large wagon pulled to a slow halt beside them. Fey had been aware of its approach, but the driver had not sought to pass them, possibly in a show of respect for his finely dressed company. He forced back a slight smile as images of the mud-soaked figures played on his mind.

Inside, Fey and the two ladies waited in silence as the trader's carriage was surveyed, and the inventory checked along with the appropriate trading documents. While one small group attended to that task a familiar guard approached, chuckling as he saw the relief on Fey's face at finally arriving. He studied the invitations with care and scrutiny. The huffing and sighing of the older woman made him consider turning them away and saying he believed they were forgeries, and subjecting Fey to further torture, but the ill health of the woman astride his friend's saddle gave him second thoughts.

"Sam." Fey nodded his head greeting the guard.

"Still rescuing damsels?" His smile faltered as he caught a glimpse of a woman's boots from beneath the blanket. They were a very distinguishable white and pale green knee-length leather. "By the Gods' breath Fey, that's Lady Mayrah. Please tell me this wasn't your doing."

"No, Sam, I found her in the marsh. There was no sign of a struggle, I thought it best to bring her straight here."

"Scavenger food. I told him he should have left her. Those filthy creatures were everywhere, who knows what disease they passed on." The elder woman once more found her voice, earning herself a scowl from her own daughter. "A lady you say, by title alone I tell you. What kind of nobility would walk the marshes, wearing that no less? Oh well, dear, it looks like there's a little less competition for you."

"Mother!" Her daughter's cheeks flushed with embarrassment as she glanced towards the awaiting crowds, who were all now looking on with interest at the unfolding events.

"Fey, take her to Val. I'll see to your nag, and I'll stable your horses too." Sam grinned. "The suitor ball is it? If you'll dismount and follow me please, I'll show you to the appointed changing areas. I assume you ladies will wish to dress appropriately." He gave Fey a knowing wink having seen all too clearly that they had ridden in their best attire, and could only imagine the headache this outspoken woman had inflicted upon his friend.

Fey dismounted, before sliding the woman carefully into his arms and exiting towards the main street.

He was no stranger to this great city. Despite how often he attempted to avoid such fares his tasks always seemed to bring him here. There was always some manner of social event. Today's gathering was once more centred on finding a partner for the son of one of the more recognised nobles. For months his mother had organised banquets and galas trying to pair him with the perfect bride or groom.

Time after time he would sit and watch the spectacle in mild amusement, seeing only the arrogant sons and daughters of pompous fools who thought low cut tops and heaving bosoms, or oiled, glistening muscles would draw his eye long enough for him to overlook the fact that the depths of their personality could turn a fertile land barren. He would watch in polite boredom, humouring his mother's wishes. He turned his affection to no one, and still every father thought their own vacuous child would be the exception.

Unfortunately, for Fey, suitors often arrived in advance. As a respected guide he was less expensive than commissioning someone from the Hunters' Plexus, and thus his services during such events were often in great demand.

The remaining guards stepped aside, leaving Fey to his task. He walked the symmetrical streets. This entire town, almost down to its last cobblestone, gave the impression of uniformity. It was only the positioning of the water sources and farmlands that deterred this illusion. A uniform space separated each house, the bricks were a matching shade of reddish-brown, and the doors were planed to a smooth and uniform finish.

Each house, however, had its own individual touches. The trade houses hung iron signs announcing their services, tailors, clothiers, alchemists, produce stores, Fleshmongers, even armouries. The trade within the city was diverse, but there were rules. No two shops could sell the same speciality items. Although, there was always some overlap, and it was particularly noticeable in potions and alchemy, but the laws were strictly adhered to. Of course, what occurred beyond sight was another matter entirely.

Finally, Fey reached the small property belonging to the healer. Surrounding her home was a modest area of land contained within a low fence. Here she grew herbs and medicinal items. Fey had often told her some sections would be better served for growing food, but she would hear none of it. Stepping over the small fence, to save struggling with the gate, he approached the door, surprised when it opened before he had even had a chance to ring the small bell which was bolted onto the wall by the door. He remembered fitting it for her. It was less than ideal, in times of strong winds the weighted chime would bluster causing it to ring itself. Val often corrected his observation, saying it was the spirits of the land making their presence known to those around.

Whilst not an innate healer, Val had a talent which saw people flock to her in times of need. Even the nobles—much to the frustration of the court's physician—would seek her services. She had once welcomed many through her door as friends, but hateful rumours started by jealous competition saw those she once counted as companions turned away. Fey thought this was the greatest injustice of all. Val gave everything she had to those who called upon her, more so since the death of her husband and son, and was repaid only with loneliness until something was sought from her.

Healers were uncommon, it was thought that they were able to harness the part of magic associated with life. Unlike other users of the arcane who could use healing artes, such as a sorceress and the long extinct Hectarians, healers trained hard to develop the skill. It was by no means instinctive and required firm dedication and a strong aptitude. With enough practise they could assess ailments and even heal small wounds. But unlike those attuned to magic, they could do little more.

Seeing the young woman cradled in his arms she hurried them inside, quickly placing a fresh sheet over a long table specifically crafted for this purpose.

"Lay her there, my boy. We'll postpone the pleasantries until later. Go through, I've made scones, and the preserve should be just about cool now. We'll talk later." As Fey gently lowered the figure in his arms, Val shuffled across the large room returning with a soft pillow which she placed under the woman's head. As Val began her scrutiny, he moved carefully, silencing the rattling of the bead curtains as he passed through them into the rear rooms.

Being welcomed into Val's home was something Fey had grown accustomed to over the years, and yet the unusual layout of the interior never failed to amaze him. He had been given cause to enter many of the businesses and dwellings here, and hers was the only one to differ. They were small houses, built from brick and wood, and each had a uniform square layout with an identical number of rooms. He had seen make-shift partitions for larger families, but never had he seen another house with such a large, singular reception room.

Val often recounted the tale of her husband returning home after trying to prove to the younger Shantymen he could not only out-pace them in work, but in drinking as well. Apparently his misadventure had resulted in a minor injury for him, and the near demolishing of the interior wall. Even as she told the tale she would let slip just some of the berating words he received about the thickness of his skull. It had taken some specialist intervention, but the wall was torn down, allowing her to relax in the living area while keeping vigil on resting patients.

"She's the second one this week." Val appeared through the bead curtains to see Fey standing at the kitchen counter, using a small knife to spread the strawberry preserve across one of the scones. He placed it onto a tray with a cup of tea before laying it on the table at her habitual place. "I'm afraid there's nothing I can do for her. She has contracted Ádlíc, a corruption or sickness of her spirit. We have a house down the way that is caring for the other one. It's something they have to come out of on their own, we just try to keep them nourished." She paused for a moment, her brow furrowing.

"I've not heard of such a thing."

"It's rare. The last case reported was so long ago it's but a reference in history. We had a senior member of the Physicians' Plexus attend after my first report, that's the only reason we know it by name. I have studied both of the people afflicted, it appears as if part of their essence has been corrupted. We can't even begin to comprehend its cause. We are hoping that, just as the body would, the spirit will heal. The only thing I can ascertain is both victims could channel magical energies, and that link is now sealed because of the corruption."

"Is it contagious, Val, are you safe?" Fey pushed a hand through his hair in distress. He had brought this woman to her, if the disease could be transmitted when Val touched her she would have been infected.

"We're not sure how it passes, but I examined the first and I remain unharmed. You worry too much."

"Val, is something—"

"I saw that, you put that away!" Val insisted, as Fey slipped three gold coins onto her table, thinking he had concealed them beneath the tray.

"No arguments. This will cover her care, and your expenses. Something tells me this is going to get a lot worse before it gets better. You'll be no use to anyone hungry. You can't afford to get sick, you need to take better care of yourself." He could see her fragile frame had shed more pounds since his last visit. Her face was gaunt, her eyes sunken. Val would attend to people without rest, but the one person she always forgot was in need of care was herself.

"Fine, but I warn you, I'll be filling my cupboards, and the next time you come there'll be a steak and kidney pie with your name on it, and I'll watch you eat the whole darn thing," she lectured realising that while she had been looking at the young woman Fey had taken an inventory of her kitchen, probably realising the only thing she had was the scones and preserve she had offered him. "Did no one ever teach you it's not polite to go poking around in people's cupboards when their backs are turned tending to the sick?"

"Did no one ever teach you that you need to eat?" he retorted, pulling out the chair at the table and gesturing for her to sit.

* * *

Xantara opened her eyes and knew herself to be within a lucid dream. She stood slowly, trying to become accustomed to the strangeness of her surroundings. Her body felt both light and heavy. It protested against her attempts to move and then seemed to execute her requests in quick succession. It was several moments before her mind and dream-form aligned to work simultaneously, and the world around her came into focus.

This was like no dreamscape she had witnessed before, but she knew dreams came in many forms. Dark ivy hung from the trees and the wind whispered, rattling the leaves to give the impression of sinister laughter. The deeper she advanced into the forest the darker the trees became. She swore each groan and creak was a cry of pain and torment from the dying giants. The thought sent ice-cold tremors chasing across her flesh and she hugged her arms around herself for warmth.

The drooping undergrowth reached down its decaying tendrils, filling the air with a rancid odour. Despite its coarse appearance, the grass at her feet felt soft and luscious. Looking down, she saw in this world—just as it had in the Earth Spirit's presence—life returned to the undergrowth at her touch, causing the putrid and rotting ground to revive, leaving soft blankets of flourishing grasses and flowers in her wake. The beauty lasted for but a moment until death ravaged it once more.

She focused on locating Leona. Her new master had instructed her on how to navigate her way into Leona's dreamscape. It was apparent something within was preventing her from waking, but Xantara had been instructed on the many things she could do to rouse her. In the distance, as if answering her request for guidance, the canopies of trees began to part, allowing sunlight to stream through.

Kneeling in the clearing Xantara could see the figure of a woman. Her tear-streaked face raised to look at her in horror. She called out, the animation of her movements showing the force behind the words, but no sound reached her.

"Xantara." A deep voice penetrated the silence. It possessed a sinister delight in the way it spoke her name. Shadows began to take form behind Leona, her figure rose rigidly until she stood upon tiptoes, fighting for breath as an unseen hand choked her. "You're so full of his power, I can almost taste it."

"Release her." Her own voice trembled as much as her body as the shadows writhed and pulsed, their swirling mass never quite taking solid form.

"It was the only way to bring you to me. An invitation if you will. I know you've felt me on the tip of your dreams, watching you from the shadows. Your awareness stilled my approach but this time you came to me. I have no use for this impostor. It's you my soul craves." At once the pressure surrounding Leona released, sending her rigid body tumbling to the floor.

"Run," Leona gasped, choking out the words while clutching at her throat. "He has no use for me. Run!" The urgency forced her feet to move, pushing herself through the undergrowth. The grass that once bloomed at Xantara's touch turned to thorns, impaling her flesh and hindering her escape as it grasped and tore, shredding her skin. Leona's terrified cries of warning echoed just moments before a burning pain radiated through Xantara's back. Her insides lurched as the shadow's hand penetrated to tear something from deep within her core. She fought to breathe, her body growing weaker until she felt herself falling. A single shimmer of light danced within Xantara's fading vision, a glowing orb clutched within the hands of the writhing shadow. The illumination began to fade, devoured by darkness as its forming chest accepted the gift, and as it extinguished, so too did her awareness fade.

* * *

Daniel marched with a determined stride through the forest. All warding and magic aimed at disorientating him failed to cause even the slightest hesitation. He saw through them to the path he must walk. The voices of the ancestors, more specifically those who knew Kerõs, guided him desperately, as if they too could sense the unease. Alessia remained in step beside him, like himself she wore their everyday clothing. Her black hide trousers and brown leather laced top looked casual, yet in a blink her armour could appear on top of it, released from the crystal pendent she wore around her neck to transform her into the formidable warrior he knew. She refrained from asking him *again* about his reason for wishing to visit here. It had become apparent it was a question he refused to answer. She had caught him trying to leave undetected using the irfeláfa, which was the Eorthåds' equivalent of portal travel, but without having to pass through Collateral.

He had managed to convince her it was a task of the utmost importance, yet refused to disclose anything further. He had thought on what Zo had told him for days and had been suppressing the urge to act. Now he could deny this desire no longer. His spirit was in turmoil, and the ancestors advised the only way to quieten it was to follow his instincts.

It wasn't that he didn't trust Alessia with the details; he trusted her with his life and soul. However, he realised Zo had taken a great risk in revealing what she had. Many times she had been warned not to interfere with the preordained matters of Gaea's Star, and yet continued to keep vigil over its people whenever possible. If he were to reveal to Alessia the cause of his concern she would feel duty bound to inform Seiken. Zo's words had been vague, her warning cryptic, as if intended to shield its true meaning from any who could overhear. That such measures seemed necessary spoke volumes of the danger she perceived.

For the last mile Daniel had been aware of someone tracking them, concealing themselves within the shadows, but it was only as they reached the final enchantment the figure revealed himself.

"You've navigated our wards with ease, your focus never faltered. What brings one such as yourself to Kerõs?" the figure questioned, emerging behind them. His hands rested comfortably at his sides, ready to draw the weapons he carried if the need presented itself.

"I am Daniel Eliot, Wita of the Eorthåds. Beside me stands Alessia, Master and Commander. I come regarding a matter of great importance. I must speak with your lady, Xantara."

"I am William, soon to be named Fanger of our Maiden. Such an audience is impossible at this time," William explained formally, instantly put at ease in their presence. He gestured forward, guiding them through the final stretch of the woods and into the small town. "She has been in healing for the past two days."

"For two days, without food or water? Please, I mean no disrespect, but this is a matter of urgency." Daniel realised from the look in William's eyes insistence alone would not convince him, no matter the desperation infused into his request. “I had a vision that she is in great danger. If I cannot speak with her can you at least confirm she is unharmed?” William beckoned for a priestess belonging to the temple to approach, their quiet exchange unheard against the rising murmurs of the gathering crowd. Strangers within their boundaries always set them ill at ease. Daniel watched as the slender figure hurried towards the distant structure, cracking the door slightly before daring to step inside. Seconds felt like minutes as an uneasy silence fell over the town. The priestess emerged from the door, her stricken face considerably paler than when she entered. No words were needed, her expression had revealed the truth of Daniel’s concerns.

William advanced, the crowd parting to grant him passage. Daniel followed on his heels. Pausing at the threshold they waited to be granted permission to enter the sacred grounds. Before words of entry were uttered, the sound of boots and nails upon the wooden floor, chorused by strangled cries, saw all ceremony discarded. Alessia hurried within, instantly placing herself at the side of Leona’s flailing figure, stroking her sweat-soaked hair and whispering softly. She became still for but a moment, her eyes opening and her body reacting on instinct as she thrust Alessia away, screaming and retreating until attendants rushed to her aid, sheltering and calming her within their embrace.

The silence became as piercing as Leona’s screams had been as the Eorthád examined the figure of the one who had yet to stir. Daniel felt his stomach tighten as her eyes met his and she gently shook her head. He studied Xantara from afar, keeping a respectful distance, but approaching enough to see the rise and fall of her chest, but if she could not be roused—given the influence the Eortháds held within Darrienia—the warning he had received rang true. He felt himself cringe as Alessia rose, her expression knotted with concern as she marched towards him with intention, before pulling him away.

“How did you do that?” Daniel questioned, inclining his head towards the blond-haired woman, before Alessia had the opportunity to speak.

“She was trapped within Darrienia. I woke her.” There was a harshness to her tone which made him flinch.

“You can do that? Force—”

“You are rambling. You are attempting to distract me. What is going on here? She is not dreaming”—Alana gestured towards the other figure—“and *you* do not have visions.”

"What do you mean not dreaming? All this symbology is to invoke just that," Daniel observed, forcing himself to focus on the chalk symbols in a ploy to avoid Alessia's penetrating stare.

"Her essence is corrupted, your people had a name for it..."

"Ádlíc," Daniel muttered. "Is there anything that can be done?"

"No. There is no means to assist her. It was once rumoured it could be contracted through healing magic, it is better if no one attempts such a thing." Alessia raised her voice so that those present could hear her suggestion. "It was believed unfounded, but since healing will not assist in repair caution is best advised."

"Alessia..." She looked up to him sharply, her expression softening as she saw his concern.

"I am unharmed, but I cannot risk remaining here longer, not when we live with beings who are essentially magical in nature." Alessia turned her focus to the woman she had awoken. "Honoured elder, keep her warm and sustained. But do nothing else. Do not permit your master to approach, although I imagine he knows of the dangers already." Alessia looked to the brighter rays of light as they receded and knew he had understood her warning. She pulled Daniel from the temple, marching him towards the town's border. "How did you know Ádlíc would take her?" she demanded.

"I didn't. I was told she was in danger."

"What exactly were you told, and by whom?"

Chapter 4

The Birth of a Prophet

Zo sat watching the dancing flame as it flicked upon the small table as she sat curled in Seiken's embrace upon the large, cushioned seats. A leather-bound tome was held loosely open in her grasp as her attention wandered. To any recognising the symbols, it would be clear she was studying Oneiroikinesis. She had been an Oneiroi for many years, but Seiken had been convinced that her transition had unlocked a new affinity within her. Since she lacked any talents beyond the basic manipulation, she was beginning to doubt his words. The more Zo read about the amazing feats possible by those who could manipulate dreams, the more understanding was gained into their diversity.

Zo was in no way envious, after all, her own magic had adapted during the transition, altering to tether itself to Darrienia instead of Gaea's star. Seiken advised the alteration had changed her artes from Hectarian to simple energy manipulation. Most Oneirois, to one extent or another, could influence the surrounding energies. Her ability to do so simply came from an alternative source. He assured her there was a great gift sealed within her, to which her response was to remind him she had already shown the greatest magic of all, the ability to bear a child in a world where life was created by ritual, not conception. There was no argument that Alana was both a surprise, and a blessing.

"Sorry?" Seiken questioned, startling Zo from her focus. She drew her gaze from the flame to look deep into his rich brown eyes.

"Was I reading aloud?" she asked in confusion, almost able to hear the echo of her own voice, but the words were lost to her.

"It depends, are you reading about dreamless sleep?"

"No, I've just reached the—what's wrong?"

"Thea, you said Xantara was lost to the dreamless sleep. I'm not familiar with such a tale." As a child he had heard many fables, and he still recalled the smile on his mother's lips as the soothing sound of her voice had relayed them to him, but this was a story he was unfamiliar with. Then again, their world was always evolving and creating new adventures.

"I must have been daydreaming." Zo shrugged, returning her attention back towards the book. Several moments passed before Seiken felt her startle once more, this time as the crystal around her neck summoned her attention. She groaned slightly as she pulled herself from his embrace, seeing him lower his own tome.

"Zo, I'm really sorry. I had to tell her," Daniel blurted out before Alessia snatched the gossip crystal from him.

"Did you know about the Ádlíc?" she demanded, forsaking all formalities in her haste and urgency. As she looked at Alessia's image, her perspective shifted to project the scene into her mind. They were stood within the borders of a forest. Daniel stood behind the Master and Commander looking apologetic, while Alessia seemed almost alarmed.

"The Ádlíc?" Zo glanced towards Seiken, wondering if her question had been directed towards him.

"The Earth Maiden, Xantara, has been afflicted. Lady Thea, did you know it was Ádlíc before you sent him there?" Seeing the look of genuine confusion on Zo's face Daniel stepped closer to Alessia, a puzzled expression knitting his brows together.

"Zo, the other night at the fire you said to me, and I quote, 'In Kerõs, Xantara will be lost as the elder sleeps.' I was about to ask you more but you warned if she fell two more would follow." Zo stared at him blankly, flinching as she heard Seiken growl a powerful curse beneath his breath. She turned to look towards him in bewilderment, aware of Alessia's expression altering to one of deep concern. His eyes were tightly closed as he took a slow deep breath, releasing it with care before he brought himself to look upon his wife.

"How long have you been giving prophecy, Thea?" His voice was guarded of emotion to the point its absence caused her alarm.

"I-I haven't, I don't know—"

"A sage and a prophet," he muttered raising a hand to his forehead. There was a moment of silence before he lowered it and spoke again. "Commander, have the Wita escorted to Crystenia as soon as possible."

"Yes, my lord," Alessia turned to Daniel, who appeared as confused as Zo. As their connection terminated, Zo's gaze sought Seiken in hope of an explanation. As their eyes met, she felt herself retreat slightly under the pressure of the powerful emotions he was attempting to suppress.

"There's a reason we have no sages amongst the Oneirois. An awakening prophet can only give their first prophecy to a sage, who must then confirm it as valid to give the power its foundation." Seiken walked to the door as Zo felt the tears begin to burn in her eyes. She did not understand what she had done to cause him so much anger that he couldn't even bear to look at her. "Congratulations, you've been granted the gift of visions." He left their rooms without looking back. The door pulled firmly closed behind him, warning her not to follow.

* * *

Seiken marched down the hallway, the ground at his feet quivering under the force of his anger. He had to leave, the destructive power was welling within him. He needed to find release before discussing what this meant with his wife. Creatures and beings all altered their direction rather than be in the presence of their heir, or risk crossing his path as the very foundation of their world shuddered and wilted around him.

Behind him, the charred and damaged ground began to repair, knitting the severed energies together until all evidence of his fury had been concealed. Seiken's pace never slowed. There was no friendly greeting called out to the Cynocephali, and no acknowledgement of the devastation he left in his wake. It was all he could do to hold back the rage and anguish he felt bursting within him. He needed solitude.

As his feet touched the surface of Darrienia, he took a deep breath, but the fury would not quell. Extending his arms a shimmering barrier surrounded the area and he let out a piercing scream, a sound of anger and grief made from the vocal chords of one who was man, beast, and god. Its tones penetrated the shielding, causing countless dreamers in Gaea's Star to inexplicably startle awake. He panted, drawing in another deep breath, knowing he must dispel this venom before he could face another living soul.

* * *

Rowmeow heard the violent distortion of the land below Crystenia. As the first created of their kind he was attuned to their world in ways unfathomable to any other being. He raced through the gardens, his feline ears pressed back against his head as he dashed rapidly towards the portal to transport himself to the source of the destructive energies. Pausing, with his paw hovering uncertainly in the air, he beheld the devastation that lay within the barrier. The land tried to knit and reform in order to repair the deep craters within. Yet its efforts to heal met with another barrage of destruction. The energy inside was slowly being destroyed leaving large scars, scars which became a void of nothingness and chaos.

The small black and white cat sat outside the barrier, watching the carnage that poured from their heir. Seiken was a unique creature, he did not possess a single soul; he was joined to another, a being of timeless power. He protected and shielded this ancient part of himself, the part the Eorthǻds worshipped. More often than not he was able to control its primal urges.

Only once before had he lost control, and that had related to the claiming ritual. It had been a desire he had suppressed from the moment he had realised Zoella had been his soul-mate. She had insisted he embraced it should he wish to call her his wife. It had been a wise decision, had she not been prepared to risk the danger then their mating would have destroyed her own essence almost completely. This, however, was a different reaction, and Rowmeow could not fathom what could stir such pain and anguish. The cat closed his eyes to confirm both Zoella and Alana were safe and well, and then simply watched, waiting for their prince to tire.

When the barest slither of life remained within Seiken's isolating ward, he sank to his knees upon the small butte, exhausted. Rowmeow fractured the barrier with a swipe of his paw, allowing energy to rush inside to mend the ravaged land. Using subtle manipulation, he created a walkway to allow his approach, before releasing the energies to allow them to focus on repairing the more extensive damage. Seiken's bowed head snapped up, turning to look at the approaching figure. His eyes burned with tired fury.

"Prophecies," he growled, clenching his fists so tightly that his nails drew blood. He felt the power rising again, but this time he succeeded in restraining it.

"Alana? Worry not, we don't have a sage here, we—"

"Thea. She gave the Wita a prophecy when last we visited," he fumed through gritted teeth.

"As long as he doesn't—"

"I found out because Alessia wanted to know how much she had known, *after* they had confirmed the danger to be real." He dropped his gaze towards the ground where the grass slowly began to grow upon the freshly formed land. "Why, Row? We have a child. What cruel fate would give her this curse?" Rowmeow approached, nuzzling his head against Seiken's arm.

"Seiken, I'm sorry."

"We have a child," he repeated softly, wiping his damp cheeks. "We were happy."

"I'm sorry. She doesn't deserve this, none of you do. But staying here solves nothing." He nudged Seiken again, encouraging him to his feet. "Have you told her?"

"No, how can I?" he whispered, following Rowmeow with a defeated slump as he led him back towards the portal. They had barely reached the garden when Seiken felt the pull of the summons. He gave an exhausted, resigned sigh.

"You sent for the Wita?" Rowmeow questioned, feeling Seiken grant permission to the Cynocephali to permit his guest entry.

"What else could I have done?" he asked dejectedly. Rowmeow looked to him with what could only be interpreted as regret before he excused himself, allowing Seiken to greet Daniel alone. Seiken gave a heavy sigh, his limbs now burning from the earlier exertion.

"Lord Seiken." Daniel offered a polite greeting as he moved to stand beside his friend. Concern crossed his brow as he noticed Seiken's haggard appearance.

"Wita," he acknowledged respectfully. "Did the Commander not accompany you?" he questioned after a short moment of silence.

"No." Daniel thought back to their return to Kalia. Alessia had seemed strangely troubled and had barely spoken since her conversation with Zo. When Daniel had said he was prepared to leave she had been with the Thegnalar, deep in what appeared to be a solemn conversation. Glancing up to him, almost apologetically, she had requested he attended alone. On reaching the irfeláfa Daniel had looked back with a feeling of strange foreboding.

But, when he sought insight from the ancients as to its cause, all voices were silent. "Is... is Zo in trouble?" he questioned.

"Daniel, Thea has awakened the power of prophecy. She is the first to receive such insight in Darrienia for many of your cycles."

"That's fantastic!" Daniel's enthusiasm died the instant he saw Seiken's expression harden. "Isn't it?"

"No." He paused for a moment, before bringing himself to look at Daniel once more. "The last prophet struck their own name from the Pillar of Life many cycles ago, as had those who awakened before them. They sought to extinguish this bane and spare others the suffering."

"They took their own lives?" he questioned uncertainly. "Zo, is she..."

"She's well, for now. She doesn't know about any of this. She can't." Seiken released his clenched fist, attempting to breathe some tension from his body.

"Then why bring me here?"

"In order to ensure there were no prophets in Darrienia we also had to ensure we possessed no sages. That way, even if the trait awakened it could not be realised. A new prophet can only give their first prophecies to a sage. For the ability to take root the sage must then validate it by visual confirmation of its passing."

"What Zo said, about Xantara, that was a prophecy?"

"Yes, and your journey to Kerõs validated it, allowing the curse to manifest. So now, as much as it pains me to do so, I must ask for you to go to her and document any insight revealed." Seiken turned his gaze towards the amber skies with a heavy sigh, blinking back the tears he knew he could not afford to shed.

"Why? Surely if a prophecy can only be taken by a sage keeping her away from me would be the answer." Daniel focused upon the castle before them, trying to allow Seiken's raw emotions the privacy they warranted. He was clearly struggling to keep himself composed, anger and despair radiated from him.

"It would, had you not validated the first. Now the gift has awakened we must release her dependency on a sage. To do so, she must present you with two more."

"And if she doesn't?"

"The pain of suppressing them will become unbearable."

"She'll die?" Daniel shuddered as he heard Seiken cough out a bitter chuckle.

"Die? Her name is not upon the Pillar, her existence, like my own, is no longer finite." Seiken saw the realisation in Daniel's horror-filled eyes. "And now you understand."

* * *

Within Crystenia were many nooks and crannies, secret rooms, warded areas, and studies. Such things had been necessary to ensure Seiken's presence as a child had remained unnoticed, until such a time came that he could step into another Oneiroi's role. The room in which Daniel now sat was a grand study. It was an area normally reserved for the meetings of the newly forming ministry. A large heptagonal table stood central within the vast space. Its positioning below the glowing crystal chandelier, which hung from the tall roof, ensured ample lighting to any wishing to peruse the many tomes that lined the seemingly endless bookshelves.

Despite the vast quantity of literature, it was not a library. As Daniel sat, he admired the deep chestnut glow of the wooden table before allowing his gaze to stray to the spines of the books, which appeared to be texts belonging to specific people. This realisation allowed him to recall how Oneiroi literature also served to record anything they encountered. A book, in their hands, could display the knowledge they had accumulated. Time was infinite, and facts, laws, and myths forever changed. To document such history would be near impossible, and as such this method had been conceived in order to allow all events, which the Oneirois bore witness to, to be recalled. The tomes within the bookshelf he currently observed seemed to belong mainly to Rowmeow.

With a stretch Daniel rose to his feet, ambling towards the bookshelf. His fingers traced the smooth wooden surface before selecting one of the many volumes. Removing it he peered inside discovering, as he had suspected, the pages held no wisdom for him. With a disheartened sigh he slid the leather-bound tome back into place. As he returned to the table his gaze inadvertently met Zo's, and he looked away, lowering his vision to the blank parchment before him as he sat. His sight burned into the blotting ink left upon the page from when he had first taken the quill in hand, and brought him to question if such attention to detail was necessary in a world where all he beheld was merely energy.

"Daniel?" Zo prompted. Several minutes ago, when she had been escorted to this room, she had been overjoyed to see her friend. But the awkwardness of his greeting, and his subsequent descent into silence had unnerved her. He refused to look at her and, whilst she had asked him before, she found it once more necessary to ask the reason for his presence.

"Zo, I..." He puffed out a deep breath, his mind diverting to the question if something such as breathing was required here. After all, when he crossed to this realm he too became pure energy, and only when he returned to the mortal realm would his corporeal form be solidified once more.

"Look, I don't know what I've done, but first Seiken, now you. If you don't mind, unless I am a prisoner, I have better things I can be doing than, well, whatever this is." Zo stood, marching towards the door, pulling on it firmly she realised it was stuck. She rattled the handle, straining and shoving against it, but it refused to grant her leave. "What is this?" she demanded, gesturing towards her sealed escape. "*Am* I a prisoner? Do I at least get to know what I'm meant to have done?"

"Zo, I'm here to record prophecy," he answered softly, his attention never lifting from the parchment. He watched as another drop of ink slid from the end of the quill, the nearly silent impact against the parchment seemed so loud. He traced the extending outline of the blot, not trusting himself to look upon her.

"Then do so. I don't see why I have to be here too."

"I'm here to record your words, not ones already spoken." He heard Zo give a frustrated sigh as she returned to the table, dragging the chair across the wooden floor before unceremoniously dropping herself onto it with yet another exasperated sigh.

"I tried to tell Seiken, and now I'll tell you. I do not have visions. How much clearer can I be about this?" she snapped, her patience wearing thin. "It's nearly time for Alana's nap. Please, can we just forget this nonsense?"

"Zo, you warned me about Xantara. How could you have known if you didn't see it?" Daniel touched the quill to the paper, spreading the ink blots and joining them with intricate lines.

"I was tired. I was probably daydreaming."

"Oneirois don't dream." Zo sat taller, opening her mouth ready to impart wisdom upon her misinformed friend, but before she could speak another voice silenced her. His gentle tones almost apologetic at intruding.

"Any progress?" Seiken sealed the door behind him, ensuring it would not open until he was prepared. Placing a tray—holding a small candelabrum and a bowl of fruit—upon the table his gaze flitted over the blank parchment. Zo smiled by instinct as his vision turned to her, but it was a greeting he returned emptily.

"Have I done something wrong?" Zo questioned, rising to step between Seiken and break the focused stare he directed towards the Wita. She shivered against the sudden chill, her breath escaping her chattering teeth in plumes as she turned to lock vision with Daniel in demand of an answer. "Will someone ple—" her breath caught, instead of seeing her friends her gaze became transfixed upon the candles. She felt the heat radiating from the fire as her flesh cooled. The golden orange embers crackled softly, drawing her towards them. She squeezed her eyes closed, yet still the flame remained in sight. The world around her burned, devouring all until everything became the same hue as the fire. Attempting to ground herself she forced her gaze to stray beyond the flame, finally turning her back to it in the hope of beholding Seiken. But he no longer stood behind her. She turned again, seeing only the pure white whips of distant clouds far beneath her feet as the frigid air enveloped her.

Light exploded all around her, the radiant beams rushing towards the ground below as they were forced from the unfamiliar landmass that hovered above. She heard a voice, the pain of hearing the ancient words caused her to clamp her hands tightly against her ears. It was loud, deafening, and powerful. Above her she saw the island tremble as another ray of light erupted from its jagged base.

"Talaria will fall," she whispered, repeating the words of the voice and understanding what she saw.

Zo gasped for breath, a new scene coming into focus. Blood-stained hands held her tightly as she fought against the stifling grip while drawing ragged breaths. It was a moment before she realised the warm touch upon her frigid flesh belonged to Seiken, and the blood upon his hands was hers. She felt the dampness on her face from her eyes and ears. Her sight sought his face, he looked concerned, afraid. His mouth moved, but she could hear nothing. Daniel skidded across the table to land beside her, a damp cloth already in his hand. He dabbed her face before relinquishing the duty to her husband, excusing himself a few paces to collect the inkwell which had sent the blue fluid spilling across the desk's surface, soaking into wood and parchment alike.

Seiken stroked her hair and, noticing her eyes were now open, attempted to offer a smile. He glanced towards Daniel and nodded. The etching of his quill across the paper was the first sound she heard.

"Talaria will fall," Daniel whispered, echoing the words Zo herself had spoken just moments ago. Her view of him was obstructed by the table, but she heard the unmistakable quiver in his voice. Seiken pulled her close, holding her to his chest in a strong embrace. She closed her eyes, relishing the warmth and energy his embrace sent flooding back into her.

"I'm sorry, Thea," Seiken whispered. He had hoped to be wrong that, somehow, she had witnessed events as she dreamt and thought to repeat what she had seen to Daniel. In his heart he had known the truth and felt the rage of this revelation, this curse, and yet he had still been foolish enough to find hope.

Chapter 5

Tainted

Talaria was not even a myth, it was a forgotten legend spanning back to the early cycles of the world. It was home to a race known as the Moirai, beings which invoked feelings of love and serenity in all they encountered. The energies that resulted from these powerful feelings fuelled and strengthened their magic. It was the manner in which they stored this power that saw their image remained embedded through time as bringers of peace and love.

Moirai, like Daimons, did not channel magic through themselves to manipulate the forces, instead they stored and utilised it. Daimons stored their magic internally and worked to suppress it. The Moirai, however, gathered the energies through the unique bone appendages upon their back, converting it into a visible form where it took the appearance of white plumes, which in turn created brilliant wings. The energies harnessed saw all Moirai possessed wings of white, although the shades often varied from brilliantly pure to dirty-greys. It was thought, the purer the white the stronger the magic.

Talaria itself had been long lost to those of Gaea's star. Fearing for the safety of their race the Moirai had raised their lands into the heavens, and when their magic began to fade they tethered it to the world below by several imperceivable anchors. As time moved forward the powers sustaining these anchors began to falter, but a solution was placed within their grasp. By capturing and fracturing the essence of one of the seven Great Spirits they were once more able to harness the energies they craved from the land below, thus ensuring their own longevity. In addition, they utilised the Spirit Elemental's powers to bind the land and protect them from sight and detection. Once this had been achieved, they slowly ensured all who could connect with the power of this Great Spirit met with misfortune before being able to pass the skills along to another Elementalist. It had taken several cycles to ensure the Spirit's cries for aid would remain unheard, but they had achieved it.

The main landmass was comprised of a large, crystalline tower, its structure more impressive than any of the thousand foot high sentry islands which stood guard around it, tethered by ice and crystal walkways. This central edifice was known as The Tower of the Prophets. It was an immense structure surrounded by several smaller duplicates in which the more prestigious noble houses resided. Those of power, such as the Seraphim, lived within the outer-spires of the great tower, but the central spire—which had once towered into the clouds when their home had been upon Gaea—was rumoured to be a paradise reserved solely for prophets and sages. Only those with access knew the warped truth.

The interiors were a honeycomb of chambers and corridors that burrowed through the solid structures to present magnificent and grand spaces. Each corridor stood a uniform twenty metres across. The only variation in design was the carvings upon the smooth surfaces which identified the passage by art and symbols. The several corridors which led inward towards the chamber of the Seraphim were engraved with daunting figures, and powerful wardings and protections.

The normally still corridors hummed with life as Moirai gathered in crowds outside the sealed walls of the chamber. Their panicked tones each holding the same concern, questioning if the whispers regarding the latest prophecy were true. Never before had rumours reached their ears at such urgency, but never before had the fate of their race hung on the truth of these words.

Moments prior to this gathering one of the Virtues had careened from The Tower of the Prophets, his pallor almost matching the pure white shade of his luscious wings. Something of this magnitude had not occurred for time immemorial. Somewhere, a powerful diviner had been born, one whose words could destroy the predictions of any who had come before them. This one person possessed a power unseen for generations, and their first real prediction had been of Talaria's downfall.

The Seraphim council listened with horror. Through time they had acted as secret butchers, steering the course of the world's future to the one they deemed suitable. They had hunted people, purged bloodlines, razed towns, all in the name of creating the best possible world. This person, whoever it was, could destroy all they had achieved.

"Talaria will fall," the Virtue gasped, repeating the prophecy once more. "What should we do, what can we do? It is a bound prophecy. There's no hope of a divergence, no means to prevent it." The voice was panicked, bordering on hysterical.

"Who made this prediction?" The oldest of the Seraphim stood and lifted one of the many blood-crystal tears from the Virtue's hand. He studied the prophecy contained within. "This is a second-hand repetition. Who gave the original?" he demanded, placing the droplet on the round table for all to see. The Virtue scattered the remaining along with it. Each prophet had declared the same thing in unison.

"That's what I've been trying to tell you, we don't know."

The Moirai had gone to great lengths to ensure the prophets, both earth-bound and Moirai, were under their control. Prophecy often came with the curse of the Maniae and they had constructed an elaborate ruse to draw all those gifted to one location, herding them like cattle with the promise of protection from the torment. When the gathering was complete, they had taken them all, bringing them into Talaria, while monitoring those with limited sight such as Seers and Soothsayers allowing them to remain on Gaea's Star.

It was true the Daimon kingdom of Kólasi had rejoined the mortal plane, but the Moirai had no cause to be concerned about their prophets, for a different force guided them. They heard whispers from the earth mother, who granted some insight into events her future-self could see, however, as they had once touched upon all realms their gifts had developed to see into the futures of all the multi-verse. The power witnessed here was not one the Daimons could harness.

* * *

Daniel watched as Seiken cradled Zo's limp body in his arms. He followed the path of the drying blood, bringing his attention to the small movements of her mouth. Daniel strained to hear the words, leaning closer until her voice found strength.

"Phobetor," she coughed before pain enveloped her, sending her body into sharp spasms. She gulped for air, thrashing and writhing until powerful words streamed from her. "Phobetor, The Dream Walker, will claim the Maidens and seek the power of those who would oppose him." Zo took a choking gasp of air. Her arms briefly flailed as she tried to free herself from an imaginary grip. Grounding herself, she looked to Seiken in dismay, but her eyes were empty. "She shouldn't have spoken his name aloud." The voice which left her was her own, yet with undertones of another. As her control was returned she filled with panic as her consciousness slipped away.

"What did she mean?" Daniel questioned, quickly scribing her words, his focus flitting between his task and his friends.

"I don't know, but it is best we speak of this to no one. Repeat nothing of what she has entrusted to you. I will seek Rowmeow's council on the matter." Seiken glanced towards the candles upon the table, willing the flame from existence as he lowered Zo to the floor before rising. "Thank you for your assistance. We should have no cause to call on you again for this matter," he stated rather formally but, despite this front, Daniel heard the agony etched into the prince's voice.

"Will the visions become easier?" Daniel questioned, fearing he already knew the answer. There was a noticeable difference each time she had spoken. At the fire in Kalia she had shown no signs of distress; this time had seemed torturous.

"No. At this time she is granted the luxury of lapsing into unconsciousness, but such is not a state befitting a prophet. They must retain a connection to the plane where predictions are granted, and to do that, to give full verse, they must suffer." He lifted her into his arms, summoning an orb of light to guide his path as he exited the study.

"Is there nothing we can do, no means to inhibit this?" Daniel asked, following closely on Seiken's heels.

"You're the Wita, you tell me," Seiken challenged harshly, failing to bite back his emotions.

"Both times she has been near a flame...so we limit her exposure to the stimulus." Seiken nodded, confirming he had already considered this. "But..."

"But there's no means to prevent it. Our people, before the trait was extinguished, sought many methods to alleviate the burden. Our resources are endless, and we found no solution, save one." There was a long and solemn silence as they walked the deserted halls. Seiken wondered if the hour had really grown so late, or if rumours of his wife's ability had already spread and his subjects simply retreated from his sight.

"She spoke of the Maidens, do you know of them?" His question earned him a scowl.

"I thought I was clear when I instructed you to repeat nothing of what was spoken," he growled. "But no, to answer your question, I know nothing of them. I had believed them unborn until you spoke of Xantara." Seiken knew much of the old ways. He possessed a kindred relationship with beings from other planes. He knew the Spirits would, on rare occasions, take a Maiden as their own, an essence reborn time again as their warrior and servant. However, he also knew none had been born for a time beyond measure. To learn of one being claimed had been surprising, when their very existence appeared to have been extinguished.

* * *

Seiken parted ways with Daniel near Rowmeow's private quarters and bid him farewell. After stepping inside he scanned the surroundings quickly. The room was in almost complete darkness, with a small candle lighting an area near a large assortment of pillows and blankets. He willed the flame from existence, mentally casting his small glowing orb of light towards the centre of the room. He couldn't risk returning to their own dwellings. This was the quietest area he could find, and Rowmeow would be elsewhere attending to matters of importance.

Slowly he placed his wife down upon the assortment of soft, and multi-textured materials, startling when a small figure dashed from the folds with sounds of frustration.

"What in the name of—Seiken?" the black and white cat hissed, calming slightly to see who had disturbed him in such a careless manner.

"Sorry, Row. I thought you'd be elsewhere."

"So this is what you get up to when my back is turned?" The cat climbed upon the mound, sniffing the sleeping figure before rubbing his head against her cool arm. "I take it the time with the Wita served its purpose."

"I'm sorry, Row, I couldn't take her back to our room like this, not with Alana..."

"I understand. How are you faring?" Seiken covered his wife, stroking her face tenderly before moving to sit at the table, cradling his head in his hands.

"I feel useless. I almost dread to ask, but how many did the others give before they...." He pushed his hands through his hair with a sigh.

"No less than five, no more than ten." Rowmeow jumped upon the table's surface to brush himself against Seiken's arm comfortingly. "What insight have you gained? For things to happen as they have we must believe there is a cause, a purpose."

"She spoke a name she shouldn't have. She was terrified, so much so I dare not speak it aloud in fear it may invoke some terrible evil."

"Wise indeed. I will ask her when she wakes. Better to have her speak it again than it pass through another's lips." Names had power, none more so than those belonging to great beings, and to use true names without caution could prove disastrous. That Zoella feared she should not have spoken it told Rowmeow two very important things, first, that speaking the name gave it power, and second, that when she awoke her mere presence could sow danger.

"No need. I have the Wita's recording." Seiken produced the parchment from his pocket, placing it upon the table with great restraint.

"He didn't forge the crystals?" Crystal tears were the optimum way to record prophecy in its purest form. When the predictions were spoken it fell to a sage to harvest the blood shed and forge it into a solid state by archaic rituals. Doing so was the sole means to record an enduring and truly accurate transcript of what had been spoken.

"I thought it would be too much to ask of him. It pains him almost as much as it does myself." Rowmeow edged forwards as the parchment unfurled before him. His eyes flickered across the scrawl. His body tensed, visibly recoiling as he read the second prophecy she had spoken. An involuntary hiss escaped him, and that hiss carried with it a name.

"Íkelos." Rowmeow's fur stood on end. "He should be bound to the forest. You say she uttered this name aloud?" Seiken confirmed with a nod. "She spoke his true name? He is not an Oneiroi, but given his mother that specific rule of our world will apply."

"What does that mean for her?" Seiken questioned. In the mortal plane, to speak a being's true name gave the speaker the power to manipulate it, but here, in Darrienia, the reverse was true. It was intended as a safeguard, a means for the Oneirois to be both protected and protectors, but Nyx had also ensured the same safety for her other children.

"We must confine her. I'm sorry, but until I can complete a rite of severing she will put us all in danger." Rowmeow paused, scratching behind his ear thoughtfully. "Check the forest, ensure he is still bound to The Betwixt."

Seiken lifted a looking glass from one of Rowmeow's display cases—all of which housed functional tools—and passed his hand above its surface. He visualised the Forest of the Epiales upon its surface, focusing on the land mass it was confined to, then concentrated on the magic which sealed gateways between the worlds and prevented Íkelos from emerging. He looked to Rowmeow in dismay. "Your expression speaks volumes, dare I enquire how long?"

"The decay shows he has been walking Darrienia for two years," Seiken revealed in distress. Rowmeow's concern was founded. By speaking such an ancient name aloud his wife had unwittingly pledged herself to his service as a vessel to be controlled in any way this entity saw fit. His gaze lingered on Zoella as a curse slipped, unguarded, through his lips. She had been forced, through prophecy, to speak his name, and being so inexperienced had lacked the knowledge to protect herself from such manipulation.

"And the mortal world?" Rowmeow prompted, seeing he was losing Seiken's focus to the intense fire of anger burning in his eyes.

"Open, but not yet breached," he relayed in a deep growl.

"You understand that we have no choice. We have to move her to a tower. We must isolate her."

"You're asking me to banish her to The Sealed Ruins? Row, she's my wife, Alana's mother." Seiken shuddered as he remembered the only time he had gazed upon this place. It was a dark and dreary landmass with no connection to either Darrienia or the Oneirois' cities. Things banished to this dark region were starved of the energies needed to live, to the point where the only means of survival was to sleep. It was a prison reserved for the greatest dangers. Captured Epiales and threats to the realm all slumbered within, their life preserved by the barest slither of energy.

"And in her current state she could very well spread this plague. We cannot risk everything. I know she is your soul-mate, you claimed her, and perhaps that is the sole reason speaking his name did not render her an immediate puppet, but do not be deceived, his strings are in place. Until I can sever them we must protect everyone. We must protect Alana. It's what she would want."

"Damn you, Row, don't bring Al—"

"He's right," Zo whispered weakly.

"Thea, you're awake?" Seiken's voice was filled with concern. "How much did you hear?"

"Enough to know I can't remain here. When do we leave?" She struggled, fighting against her body's weakened protest as she attempted to pull herself into a sitting position, but failed.

"Immediately. But I will have you escorted. We cannot risk touching you with magic. I must ask you to sleep, it will be easier for you that way."

"Thea, we'll find a means to make this right. I promise." Zo raised her hand as Seiken approached, but pulled back, not knowing if she dared to touch him. He took her hand forcefully in his, pressing it to his lips. "We are already joined as one, you need not fear."

"Surely if we are one I have cause to fear more?" she whispered, her voice almost failing her.

"You are mine. I claimed you. Had it been the other way then your concerns would be founded." He brushed a stray piece of her hair behind her ears as he lifted her into his arms. "I will take her myself."

"You'll forgive me this measure, but I will see that Cenehard escorts you," Rowmeow asserted. He knew Seiken's love for his wife was without bounds, without compromise. It would take but a sweet, honeyed word, whispered from her lips, and he would risk them all.

* * *

Never had he expected anyone to invoke him. When the words had tumbled carelessly from her lips he had been unable to hide the trace of a smile that had momentarily curled his lips upwards. For so long there had been none with her potential born of Darrienia, and those who he could have once manipulated were wise in the rules of their worlds. They had been protected, but she was a lamb to slaughter under his prowess. Hunting the Maidens—who he had painstakingly safeguarded against assassination—was not without its challenges. With her at his disposal his task had become far more simple.

Within the world of Darrienia, any speaking the true name of an Oneiroi would find themselves under its control. After all, it had long been recognised that the only beings with cause to look for such a thing would be those seeking to exploit them. It was with this in mind that the rules had been reversed for this realm, especially given their duties to seize and dispel conjurings, summons, and monsters who had strayed too far from their purpose. Íkelos had been born of Nyx, and his mother had protected all her children with a similar safeguard. No one had referred to him as Phobetor since he had been tricked into taking form on the mortal plane. Upon his birth he came to be known as Íkelos. But a being such as he developed many aliases as time moved ever onward, within Darrienia they favoured Melas-Oneiros, for he had been the one to bring darkness and nightmares to their land.

Íkelos had been deceived by his allies—gods now long forgotten by both time and legend—into pursuing his bride, unaware he was giving up his divinity to become a puppet who could never return to his former position. They had convinced him that in order to retrieve the power she had retained, that he too must be born to the mortal lands. They ensured he would remain focused, permitting him full recollection of his godly identity while instilling a drive which ensured everything he did would be to further this goal. She had been a goddess of great strength, and her gifts needed to be returned to the realm of the divine.

Their deception, however, had not ended there. There were those who believed her father's decree was nothing more than a means to claim his daughter's power as his own, and thus they secretly crafted a soul to defend her from those who would cause her harm. This essence would be eternally tethered to her own, both dying and being reborn in almost perfect synchronicity. This Fanger, this hero, had been the one responsible for Íkelos' banishment. But what they thought would destroy him was twisted to his own devices, becoming the Forest of the Epiales, a place no living creature would dare to tread.

He corrupted what had once been a thoroughfare for those passing through The Stepping Realm, into a dark kingdom twisted to his own design. As this land submitted to him Mankind came to know its first night terrors. They had sealed him, but the minions he created by using the shredded essences of those imprisoned before him, were free to plague Darrienia, bringing him fresh souls and new energy. Occasionally, he could even relay a message to a lucid dreamer through one of his creatures, but long had he sought to corrupt a prophet, and now that he had there was nothing he could not achieve.

Zoella's essence was unique in more ways than he could possibly imagine, and a fraction of her diversity was by his own design. Unbeknown to her, she was his niece, a daughter of his little brother, Night, but she was now so much more than that. Her rebirth as an Oneiroi had left certain vulnerabilities, such as the unusual fact she still sought to dream. This race lacked this capability since their world was comprised from the energy generated by this force. When she had been mortal she had been within his clutches, and he had left a mark upon her soul, one which ensured in death she would become a spirit destined to fade from existence, leaving Night with no choice but to intervene, and by doing so he had delivered the very future Íkelos had planned.

Everything Íkelos had done since Night's rebirth as a god had been to see her born, and his involvement had been deeper than any could imagine. To bring himself to this moment he had started countless wars. Wars that created factions amongst the Elves leading to the fated meeting between those who would come to be Zoella's parents.

Seiken had once commented that she possessed two true names, such a blessing had been Íkelos' gift to her, one which ensured when the future he forged came to pass, she would possess the potential he needed.

He could feel her watching him now. She was dreaming, but she did not walk Darrienia as he did at this moment. She merely observed events, powerless to intervene. Some of the things she beheld had already come to pass, some would be, others occurred as she bore witness, and some he orchestrated just for her, and because she saw them they would come into being. A prophet was a powerful thing indeed.

* * *

Zo was dreaming, a realisation that came with the familiar feeling of entrapment. Her mind showed her images, but she could neither move nor speak as the events unfolded before her. She wanted to call out, to warn the strawberry-blond haired man he was in danger. He lived within his dream as a picture of unease, wracked with coughs even within his slumber. It was not an overly interesting dream; the figure was in a small rowing boat upon a lake. He pulled on the oars firmly, causing small waves and ripples in the wind-kissed surface of the lake.

He gave a sniff, wiping his nose on his sleeve quickly before setting down the oars and lying back. Zo mentally cried for him to look at the water, to notice the trail of darkness his boat had left as it had glided across the surface. But her pleas went unheard. The dark waters gathered, forming a silhouette beneath the water's surface, and still the figure lay in his boat, absentmindedly watching the blue sky overhead, occasionally raising his right hand to shield his eyes from the sun's glare. From her seemingly limitless perspective as she observed, Zoella could see his sight had turned from the blue sky to the deep scarring across his right palm, and at once she recognised the injury.

There were four people with similar markings. The scarring he bore could only have been made by the sceptre used to open the path to the Spiritwest. Whilst she had never known his name, in his dreamscape she knew him to be Marc Asvin.

The light surrounding him seemed to darken. As if expecting to see a cloud he tore his sight from the scar, sitting in confusion as he saw the cloudless sky. His boat jerked as the figure beneath collided with the wooden frame. Gripping the sides, Marc scanned the water's tranquil surface, unaware of the form which seemed to always be just beyond his line of sight. The figure passed the boat again, its collision this time sending ripples of negative colours spanning out to consume everything within the dreamscape. Within his chest, Zoella could see a bright bulb of energy pulsing. Fearing what could happen she called out again with her soundless voice.

The figure broke through the water's surface, its brilliant white shade a contrast to its once darkened appearance. Black rivulets of water ran from the elevating form, racing to meet the darkened pool below. Zoella cried out again, pleading, begging him to flee, and still the silence prevented her warning from reaching his ears. As if hearing her desperation Marc seemed to tense, his vision slowly panning from left to right as if sensing something was amiss. He turned slowly, his body jerked sending him falling into the seat well. Looming over him, the figure lunged forward, his wisp-like appendage reaching through the arms raised in protection, to plummet deep into his chest.

Agonising cries pierced the silence. A harmonious chorus of Marc's voice mingled with Zo's own terror as she saw the energy within him alter and warp. The violation stemmed from the very core of his being, spreading to consume him. She felt his anguish, his terror, and the wrongness of all that occurred. Then, as Marc's limp body was discarded over the side of the boat, and colour returned to the world, she felt nothing from the dreamer.

As if sensing her presence, the apparition turned its eyes towards her as the dreamscape, and all within it, began to dissipate into nothingness.

Zo gasped as dizziness encompassed her and she was released from the dream. It was not like waking when she had been mortal; instead of a gentle rousing there was the wrenching pull of her awareness being snatched violently back into her body. She briefly glimpsed herself within Seiken's arms. They were walking a meadow with two armed guards either side. Blood streamed from her eyes and ears as her body thrashed in an attempt to break free of Seiken's protective and restraining grasp. The collision of her two parts being forced into unity caused a sharp intake of breath to accompany her awakening.

"The fourth Maiden will be lost this night," Zo gasped, hearing the warning which had accompanied her return. She looked desperately towards Seiken, feeling his embrace around her trembling body tighten. "They alone are not enough, he too must claim those who would stand against him. The forgers of his realm. Seiken, he's after the—" She felt a strange sensation wash over her, realising too late that Cenehard had pierced her flesh, forcing her to sleep.

"It'll just help you rest. It's for our own safety, and yours," Cenehard assured, placing the creature back within his flesh. Oneirois came in many forms, from insects and flowers to impressive beasts, but Cenehard was one of the more unusual. He was created to be a guardian, his flesh appeared like the bark of a petrified tree and his several limbs emerged from his trunk-like torso as if they were branches. In rest he could easily be mistaken for a tree. In movement he was something to behold. Limbs would adjust and twigs would realign to create fingers or appendages as needed. When with humanoids, he attempted to duplicate their appearance as much as was possible. Large branches formed legs and numerous arms, most he kept wrapped around himself to give the impression of but two. Near the top of his trunk a face, of sorts, would emerge, and he would attempt to make this wooden carving mirror the expressions and movements of the beings he was with.

Through his magic he could temporarily give life to any small creature native to Darrienia's land, but he was limited to those he had encountered and touched. He could then forge its image inside his trunk, and pull the carving from his body to give it solidity and sentience. His creations were always the colour of his own flesh, and most lived for but a short span of time before they returned to their carved form. He was known as an Empsychó, a being who could add a spirit to another object for a brief time. There were few of them in existence, and their forms greatly varied.

When he was not in demand, Cenehard would entertain the occasional child dreamer, who would watch in awe as his limbs became animated with wildlife dashing through his branches in displays of daring acrobatics. He was thought to be a gentle soul, but he was also not one to endanger others needlessly. His actions towards Zo may have seemed harsh to their small group, but they had been necessary.

Chapter 6

Revelations

Peter Stert pushed his hand through his mop of limp, mouse-brown hair. He almost never left the remote cabin he called home, not unless it was absolutely unavoidable. To help keep his interactions with anyone to a minimum, there were people who would deliver any wares he required. Such things were a necessity.

During his training with Amelia he had gained some control over the visions. It had been needed in order to allow the Mystics the strength required to force Paion's monstrous tower beyond their own realm and deep into The Betwixt. He still needed to hone his control, but was reluctant to further his training until he had mastered the exercises she had given him.

He walked through the busy courtyard of Albeth Castle, a place bestowed the moniker of Oureas' Rest due to its unique combination of man's architecture and nature's glory. His arms were wrapped protectively against his chest in an attempt to make himself as small as possible. He concentrated on keeping his aura close to avoid crossing energies with another living person. Peter had been dubbed the Seer of Misfortune. His mother had been a powerful Soothsayer, and he the product of brutality and rape. Those in his home town said the methods of conception had tainted his gift and, hoping to silence it, had branded the rune Gebo across Peter's third eye, permanently scarring him symmetrically from forehead to cheek as they drew hot pokers down his flesh to brand him with the x-shaped symbol. Their cruelty had not silenced the gift, but it caused people to shun the scarred figure.

He walked briskly, yet with great unrest, as he navigated his way across the courtyard towards the central towers which were home to the royal house.

Entry was prohibited by the large gated archways segregating all possible points of entry to those outside. To be granted admission, let alone an audience, bordered on impossible.

Albeth Castle was divided into areas known as wards, and its agricultural area alone spanned many miles. The size of the structure in its entirety was beyond any comprehension, and the mountains, with their high and sheer cliffs which extended outward to fuse to the outer drum towers, only added to the impression of its magnificent scope.

Reaching the arch, he wiped the beading sweat from his face, taking a moment to catch his breath before beckoning one of the guards. The archway was large enough for six carriages to pass through simultaneously. It was a secure area, with several sections for the close inspection of transport and those of the standing required to be permitted entry. Tasked to stand vigil were part of the King's Guard, and the area had been made to ensure their comfort during the long postings. Several large benches had been placed at various sections, and covered with soft fabrics. Few were granted passage through to the Royal Ward, and thus they operated in a squad of eight.

"Excuse me, I must speak with Helen Farmbrook. Tell her it's Peter Stert. It's urgent." The figure at one of the tables stood, raising his hand. He quickly shuffled the stack of papers before him, his vision tracing the contents. The guard's posture stiffened as he saw the name upon Lady Helen's personal visitor list, and he gave a confirming gesture. But the guards made no attempt to open the thick iron gates.

"It's Wolfraine now, but I'm afraid she's not accepting visitors. She's been taken ill."

"Please, even if she's samded, if you tell her of my visit she will see me," Peter pleaded.

"It would do no good. The healers called it Ádlíc, she's unresponsive," the guard revealed formally, his tone laced with a hint of regret.

"I'm too late? Has anyone else seeking her passed through, Stacy maybe?" Peter asked desperately, shifting uncomfortably. He shuddered, feeling the grasp on his energy weaken. He stepped back quickly, trying to slow his breathing and regain control of his aura before being forced to bear witness to things he would rather not see.

"Stacy Psáltis?" Peter confirmed his question with a nod, desperately searching the surrounding area in hope of a familiar face. He could feel his restraint crumbling. Helen had been lost, but the warning still needed to be heard. "Not for some time." Peter's shoulders slumped at the feared reply. If possible, he somehow looked more dejected than he had just moments ago. He grasped his hair in tight fists before dragging his hands down his face. He needed to pass this message on before it was too late. Peter braced himself against the coarse stone wall, taking several deep breaths as he fought off his fatigue.

"I think I know how to find her," he realised. "Please, can you direct me to the Plexus?"

* * *

Rob kept his face stern as he slid yet another silver coin across the counter towards the balding barkeep, his eyes never leaving the severe face of the man he was negotiating with. Without breaking the stare the man placed his finger on the coin, sliding it from the counter and into his apron pocket with a sleight of hand that betrayed how often he engaged in the exchange of information for coin.

"Hmm, yes, it's coming back to me now. 'Twas about a sennight ago, there was someone matching that description, was looking for a Seer or Soothsayer. I tell him we ain't seen their like here for some time now. So off he went." The faintest hint of a smile tickled the barkeep's lips.

"Did he happen to say where he was heading?" Rob asked, knowing all too well the deliberate tells of the figure before him withholding further information. The barkeep started to wipe the counter, bringing back a shine to its otherwise dull surface with each absentminded stroke.

"I reckon he did, but the details are a little hazy." Rob fished another coin from his pocket. In a rare act of showmanship the barkeep swiped his cloth over it, before shaking it dramatically, disclosing the coin had, in fact, vanished. Rob forced a smile, knowing if he didn't the information was likely to double in price.

It was times like these he missed Bray. He could have retrieved the information without spending a single coin, in fact, they would likely have enjoyed an endless stream of complimentary beverages. "Those coins of yours must be enchanted with potent magic, my friend. I hear the voice as clear as a bell, 'twas my own, I suggested he try Therascia." Rob slid two more coins over the counter.

"Potent magic indeed. I trust if you hear any more on him these will help you remember to have the Plexus notify me?"

"As I said," the barkeep grinned, "potent magic."

Rob walked away, attempting to conceal his disappointment. It had been almost a year since Paion had escaped, and yet still he was no closer to locating him. He and Bray had sworn a solemn oath. They would hunt him down, ensuring he was never granted another opportunity to weave his vicious plans to purge the world, ready for his people's return.

After everything he had done, all the manipulation and torture, he could not remain loose. The fact he now sought a Seer suggested he had another scheme in mind. He had used Kitaia Ethelyn before, forcing her visions to build a future where his victory had been assured. He had not anticipated the intervention of one who lived outside the sight of vision and prophecy, but even then the line between victory and destruction had been paper thin. If he was now seeking another person who could gaze forward, to what will be, then it was an ill-tiding indeed. Rob sighed, deciding to return to Collateral to see if any of his alternative contacts had discovered anything new. Despite the confidence of his source's words, he wasn't certain he was even following the correct person anymore, and could only hope Bray was having more success in Misora.

As he entered the Plexus, Barnett, the Plexus master grasped his spectacles from the counter's surface. Placing them upon his hooked nose with a smile, he raised his head in a friendly acknowledgement.

"Aeolos, I've got something for you. But it seems I must remind you the importance of asking people to use your Plexus name when requesting your services. You never know whose hands these pass through." The Plexus, for security of its members, operated solely on assigned aliases. It kept a level on anonymity, essential for people undertaking the more prolific tasks.

"I don't recall giving anyone my—may I?" Rob gestured to the parchment Barnett now held in his hand.

"You're lucky it came to me as a query, else it would likely have been rejected. You need to be more—that bad?" he questioned seeing Rob's hardened expression.

"You could say that. Thanks, Barnett, I owe you for this." Rob raised the parchment in a gesture of gratitude, before turning to dash from the Plexus. He had a transport carriage take him to the outer borders of Collateral, where he made haste towards Boa street. His pace never slowed until he stood hammering at the door of a small cottage on the outskirts of Drevera. The delicate aroma of fresh herbs, that had been hung to dry on the twine stretching outside the windows, carried on the gentle breeze, bringing a measure of calmness to his agitated mind. Within this modest hut was a warmth he had never felt elsewhere. It was a home to anyone who crossed its threshold, but it was also home to one of the most powerful and influential beings this world had known. She worked from the shadows, guiding people towards the path fate had set before them. Most of the time, even they were unaware of her intervention.

"What's the meaning of this, laying siege to an old lady's house in the dead of night!" Amelia snapped as she pulled the door open forcefully. Rob glanced upward, realising the sun had long since set and the stars shone brightly through the cloudless sky. "You'll wake the dead. Now, wipe yer boots if yer coming in." Amelia seemed to look a little younger than the last time they had met. Her hair was still the same stark white, but given the hour it was no longer secured in its regal fashion, instead a single plait secured it in place. It was her face, Rob realised. Since the Mystics had awoken, the wrinkles betraying her age had all but vanished. "Don't just stand there catching flies with yer gaping mouth."

"Sorry," he mumbled. The low light of the fire crackled, casting darkened shadows from the sparse furniture within the small modest dwelling. His gaze set upon the table, it was the focus of the room and with good reason. He himself had sat around it debating the very future, and had no doubt others had done the same. The slow creaking of the rear door shifted his focus as he lingered on the doorstep. Seeing who emerged, his thoughts returned to the present and his reason for being here. "Psáltis, get dressed, grab your cloak, we're leaving."

"It's the middle of the night," Stacy snapped smoothing down her brown hair. "Can't it wait until morning?"

"You tell me, Stert posted a request from Oureas' Rest." Amelia and Stacy exchanged concerned glances. They hadn't seen Peter since the Mystics parted ways following the raising of Kólasi. Stacy had chosen to stay with Amelia and hone her talents. Marc, Helen, and Peter had been given exercises and tasks better practised away from this small and xenophobic island.

"Why wouldn't he come straight to me?" Amelia questioned in concern, motioning that Stacy should do as bid, and quickly.

"Maybe the thought of a boat or Collateral was too much for him," Stacy called from the bedroom, emerging a few moments later wearing her hide trousers and top.

"Whatever the reason, he insisted it was urgent."

"For him to go there, it would have to be. Come on then, what are you waiting for?" Stacy questioned with a sharp tug on the belt strap of her backpack.

* * *

Seiken placed Zo down as the escorts began to manipulate the complex energies which prevented access to The Sealed Ruins. He stroked her face softly, noticing the fresh flow of blood matting her hair. He pulled her close, gently kissing her forehead while cradling her as they sat upon the soft and luscious grass. He waited for the pain to pass, knowing even Cenehard's venom would not keep her in slumber long.

She opened her eyes to look up directly into his, her breathing came in sharp and rapid succession as her body trembled within his embrace.

"Tell me?" Seiken prompted, his voice soft, harbouring the regret he felt about the actions they were taking to detain her.

"She said he's targeting the Mystics as well, that some have already fallen to him. I need you to tell Daniel." She reached out, grasping his lapel tightly in her trembling fingers.

"What do you mean, she said?"

"The voice, the one that causes the pain. She also said those of Talaria would seek to silence the forger of forks." Her eyes searched his desperately for any sign he was taking to heart her warnings.

"That's what you saw?"

"No, I saw him claim a man called Marc, and then a woman baring the same scarring on her hand. Like him she seemed familiar, like our paths have crossed, but I-I can't place where. I think I remembered before, but," Zo shook her head, closing her eyes against the pounding sensation the movement caused. "I must speak with Daniel, please." She stilled his hand as it stroked her face, clasping it as she looked pleadingly into his eyes. He could not keep the tether between them, and looked away to focus on the task being performed just several feet away.

Rowmeow had prepared Seiken for this, the desperation she would show before being sealed. He had been right to insist someone had accompanied him. Even now, he wanted nothing more to believe her, to let her pass along her warnings, and believe her words were something more than just manipulation.

"I'm sorry, Thea, for his own safety, and that of the Eorthåds, I can't allow it. But this voice, you said she?" Seiken clenched his jaw, instantly regretting the feeling of hope that had risen within him. It was a deception, one aimed at ensuring she remained free to do as Íkelos bid. He needed to remember no matter what she said, or how dire the situation, he could not trust her words, even those which came with the markers of prophecy. Not when a simple word could be altered, or a meaning distorted.

"While I'm dreaming I've been aware of another presence, but it's only since what happened with Daniel I can hear her. There's so much power in her voice." She placed her hand to her ears finding the sticky warmth of blood. She rubbed it between her fingers. "Please, believe me," she begged, tears flooding her eyes. "Something terrible—"

"Lord Seiken, it's time." The guard announced stepping aside. As he did so a small crack fractured the ground, allowing illumination to spill upwards from within. Through the fissure a sparse landscape anointed with large grey towers expanded beyond the horizon. The view was but a slither of the vast expanse, and looking upon it caused dread and fear to knot her stomach. The world inside the fracture was a stark contrast to the plains they stood upon. Where her world was flooded with life and colour, this strange and disjointed landscape seemed lacking in both.

"That's where I'll be held?" Zo questioned, trying to keep the tremble of fear from her voice. Even from her current location she could feel the desolation and despair from within. A haunting sadness roamed that land, a land that thrived solely on the minute energies allowed to pass through. But there was something else there too, she could feel it, something alive that stood sentry over the prisoners, and thrived on their captivity. She wondered if they could sense it too.

"It may seem cliche, but your fairytale ideas all have foundations in one reality or another. When the door to your tower is sealed, you'll be forced into slumber. You'll feel no pain," he reassured, helping her to her feet and supporting her weight as fear took the strength from her legs. It was just a few moments before she found the courage to advance. Duty triumphing over fear, she knew she should show no weakness. Her every instinct told her to flee, and that Seiken may even allow her to. With a shiver she slid her hand into his, gripping it tightly. His touch brought heat to her icy flesh. "You need not be afraid. While you rest, I'll be with Rowmeow, helping him to prepare the severing. We will return as soon as we are able. To you, it will feel like mere moments," he comforted as he led her through the fissure.

Darrienia, as a land, was filled with vibrant colours, shades more intense than those of the waking world. Here, however, was a complete contrast. The colours were dull, the sky, the land, the towers, everything was so lacklustre that it took great effort to perceive the colours as anything other than shades of grey.

"If he succeeds in claiming the Mystics..." Zo paused looking fearfully upon the first tower's door. Cenehard stood awaiting their approach by the gaping opening into what she feared would become her tomb. "If he does this, he can emerge in their world, and there is no living being with the power required to banish him. Please, I must speak with—" Zo collapsed as Cenehard quickly secured the energy tether from inside the tower to her aura. He could see how difficult it was for their prince to take this action, how impossible it felt for him to ignore her warnings and pleas. It was better he acted quickly, than prolong the torture for either of them.

Seiken caught her. For a moment, as he lay her upon the floor of the cold stone building, he thought of lying beside her, joining her in slumber until they could be reunited once more. But he knew she would not forgive him such an indulgence, especially when Alana would need him to be strong. Forcing himself to leave, he had promised himself he would not look back, but he had. He had seen the vibrant shades of life being subdued within her as her own energy receded leaving her to look as lost and haunted as the grey world around them. With his trembling hand resting upon the outside of the tower, he summoned the energy through the portal in order to forge a thick panelled iron and wood door. With a heavy heart, he placed his forehead briefly upon it, closing his eyes as he felt the scope of the distance between them and whispered a promise to return.

"My lord, it would be unwise to linger." Cenehard's thick branches encouraged Seiken forward, towards the portal where the second guard stood vigil, ensuring the barrier did not close while those seeking to return were still within.

Their journey back to Crystenia was made in silence. The weight of their heir's emotions was almost crushing. They loved her too, Thea had a way of bringing light into a room. She was a beautiful soul, and Seiken was not the only one who would miss her presence. Telling him such would offer no comfort, and so all bore the burden of their actions in silence, wondering if, in his moments of hope, he had yet to realise that even should Íkelos' will be severed her gift of prophecy would still remain. It was likely the very tower which housed her now, would one day become her permanent home.

After passing the immense gateway to Seiken's homeland, the emptiness filled him. His allies peeled away, bringing awareness to his solitude as he sombrely retired to his rooms. His thoughts lingered on his wife, the deep ache her absence caused within his soul. He thought of nothing else, not even their daughter. She consumed his every thought. He had sworn to protect her, to keep her from harm, and now she lay amongst the worst sinners of their land, those who could not be afforded life for the dangers they could bring. She did not belong there, and yet he had delivered her into this prison himself, abandoning her fate to others while he could do nothing but mourn her absence.

Seiken sat on the bed, allowing himself to fall backward to stare at the canopy above. His blurred gaze burnt through it unseeingly, and the room darkened with the passing of hours. He lay and stared, his mind empty, his heart aching, and felt neither hot nor cold, tired or energised. He simply was, and he could bring himself to be nothing more than still.

"Cenehard has informed me of events. Although, I think given the situation, it was a report better to have come from yourself." Rowmeow's voice seemed overly stern as he leapt up onto the bed. He head-butted Seiken's elbow forcing him to move for the first time in hours.

"Why? My telling you would not alter the situation." Now he had stirred, Seiken became aware of the weight of his limbs, and the aches caused by not having moved for so long.

"Actually, it would have. You would not have had to wait so long to hear the news. Your wife is not a prophet." Seiken sat upright on hearing the feline's words. His intense stare searching Rowmeow's eyes to ensure he'd heard him correctly. For a moment he dared to hope, but images of her blood-streaked face, and the torture of the visions returned to haunt him.

"How can you say that?"

"Prophets do not hear a voice within their visions. They are left to interpret windows into the future. They are not presented in the manner she described."

"Surely it was a ploy by Íkelos to have us rethink our action," Seiken ventured, but the glimmer in Rowmeow's eyes showed him to believe her words to be truth. "Well, if she's not a prophet, then… what is she?"

* * *

The horses' hooves hammered the untrodden path, two beasts, running as one as their riders pushed them harder, faster. Glancing over to the finely dressed noble Fey could see the sweat glistening on his forehead. Yet unlike most dressed in such finery, he had followed Fey's every lead without hesitation. If it wasn't for knowing those who travelled in the circles of knighthood, he would have considered this well-mannered man more knight than noble.

When first the gentleman had petitioned his attention, it was all Fey could do to withhold a groan. He had cast a glance upwards, towards the timeworn rafters, offering a silent prayer that this man sought the barkeep, who had just moments ago stepped aside after depositing a chilled beverage before him.

Introducing himself as Arlen, he had made a most unusual request. He sought a Seer, but first had a small errand in need of attending. He seemed confident Fey could assist him on both counts, and the coin deposited before him made refusal nearly impossible.

On more than one occasion Fey had assisted many Diviners and Seers with the obtaining of a specific herb said to possess futuresight. Using it provided a temporary boon, strengthening their inherent abilities. Their uses were many, and the demand was always high. He remained the only guide who had successfully taken his clients to this rare flower.

The challenge, when dealing with plants that could predict the future, was if they foresaw danger or misuse they moved on. They would shed their seeds, dispersing them upon the winds to ensure those who were unworthy could not happen upon them. Fey's family had been able to follow the path of these plants across the land, thus, whenever a Seer found themselves in great need they were gifted wisdom of this plant, and told from whom to seek aid.

He had watched as Arlen harvested just one of these rare flowers, surprised when he had not thought to question why Fey himself was careful not to touch their growing land. The only time his foot would be placed upon the soils was if someone attempted to harvest more than they were in need of. His contact with the land saw them shed, moving on before they faced exploitation. While most would seek to only procure the quantity required, temptation was a cruel device. He knew many, when faced with such a rare and profitable bounty, would be unable to resist the call to return, just as he knew that greeting their arrival would be no markers of the flower's existence.

When they had reached the first Seer, Fey had lingered outside the modest ramshackle hut, savouring the sound of spirit bells hung within the nearby trees. The gentle chimes echoed a blessing to those nearby, whilst driving away darker intentions. Arlen had spoken little about his needs, and Fey wondered what could cause such separation of coin for a task which would be so quick to complete. Even the most complex readings took little time, but he was surprised when, no sooner had he made himself comfortable against the gnarled wood, Arlen exited, the flower still in hand, and requesting he be led to an alternative Seer.

Thus far they had travelled for several days, and not one of the Diviners had met his needs. On every occasion Fey would make an introduction, Arlen would gaze upon the figure with a critical eye, shake his head, and then request their search continue. Their path had systematically tested all those possessing such talents, and whilst the words exchanged between them were few, Fey knew none seemed to possess the power he was seeking. He understood now why such a vast amount of coin had been offered for such a task. Arlen was not just seeking a Seer, he was seeking someone particular, but all attempts to tease more information from his lips met with but a single response. Whilst the task was of vital importance, Arlen would not know whom he sought until his gaze fell upon them.

Chapter 7

A Human amongst Moirai

Rob knocked firmly on the door to Peter's room for what was easily the third time. Each strike sounding more impatient than the last. When he crouched to begin his assessment of the locking mechanisms, Stacy continued to knock. The speed increasing with the urgency she felt rising within her.

The innkeeper had advised them that the gentleman had paid in advance, left explicit instructions not to be disturbed, and had not left his room at all since his arrival. Stacy glared down at Rob as the lock clicked, allowing him to turn the handle and enter.

"Would you prefer we attempted to convince the innkeeper to go against a paid client's wishes?" he hissed seeing the look of disapproval.

"I suppose it's a good job he didn't bolt it," she grumbled stepping in front of Rob to enter. She pushed through the door, cringing slightly as it impacted with the small table near the wall.

"I've a tool for that too," Rob grinned, patting one of the many pouches on his belt. He stepped inside, a strange chill causing the hairs on the back of his neck to rise as he looked upon the sight before him.

The room was modest, consisting of nothing more than a bed, a small table, and a single chair. This was a fairly common layout for the cheapest accommodations in Castlefort. They had many rooms, but the grandeur and privacy afforded depended on the cost. A room such as this would incur the smallest fee, or be granted in exchange for a bailiff token which were earned for labours completed within Castlefort. The room had a cold, confined feel, and seemed to lack any real ventilation. Edging carefully between the small table and the base of the bed, Stacy made her way towards Peter. He lay in slumber, peacefully unaware of their intrusion.

"Do you want to, or shall I?" Rob questioned gesturing towards him. He imagined being woken by the touch of another person was less than ideal for someone with Peter's unusual talent.

"Given how your life is just begging for despair and disaster, I think I'll do the honours," Stacy chided, reaching out to touch him. She shook him gently and stepped back, expecting him to startle awake, but instead he lay there motionless.

"And I guess your life is simply too dull," Rob retorted. Stacy glared at him in contempt, stepping forward she tried again, laying her hand upon him for longer. Pulling her water-skin from her bag she poured the contents over him, her face a mask of concern as she glanced towards Rob, seeking his aid.

Guiding her aside he approached. Leaning over him he searched for any indications of puncture wounds to explain such a deep and unrelenting slumber. There was nothing. Furthering his examination, Rob touched him, lifting his hands to check the more subtle places for administration. Stacy was not wrong about the danger he frequently found himself in, if anything could wake someone, surely it would be the horror Rob imagined his own future, even death, would hold. When there was still no sign of movement, Rob fished a small container from his belt. Carefully removing the lid of the ornate tin, he sprinkled a fine application of the shimmering dust beneath Peter's nose, watching in satisfaction as the fine particles were inhaled, but his expression soon turned to concern as his compound had no effect.

"Psáltis, you best fetch the physician."

* * *

Teanna sat within The Library of the Oracles, red crystal teardrops were scattered across the opaque table before her. With trembling hands she took another within her grasp, connecting to the energy that had been used to forge it. She felt herself being drawn into the blood-red world to behold the words forged by the prophet's understanding of what they had seen.

The prophet—in this instance a young human male—stood beside her. The impression of his image long since lost. She watched the movements of his mouth form the words he had spoken. Whilst unheard to the viewer, they became letters in the air surrounding them, ones that she could read.

"The darkness will be sacrificed, and the untamed beast shall free its bindings, but the light will give her power so that the leash can be returned to Gaea." Teanna spoke these words aloud, pushing her silver-shaded hair behind her ears. It was not the colour of age, but almost the same shade as the fur of silver wolves and foxes. She fingered the fine fracture upon the crystal before finding the one it paired with. It was a newer prediction, thus, as she was drawn once more into the silent world, she could see the prophet's features as clearly as if they shared the room with her. Again the words formed around her. "The light will be sacrificed, and the untamed beast shall free its bindings. The Mystics will give of their power to return the leash to Gaea."

"Teanna!" The young woman startled as she heard the harsh tones accompanying the sound of her name. "How many times must I tell you not to view the crystals? We keep such things in the archives for a reason, why waste your time with ones that failed? Use the chronicles." The chronicles correlated all of the information in the archives and compiled a list of future arcs which could be viewed by any without the need to search for individual prophecies, or match them by hand to any which may be related. Each possible future emitted its own energy, and the chronicles paired paths and time-lines with ease.

"I'm sorry, Master Bibliothecary," she whispered, addressing Clarke, the ancient librarian, by his full title. "I was curious—"

"And what do those fables you waste your time with say about such traits and a rather ill-fated feline, hmm?" He cast a quick glance towards one of the storage areas, his posture visibly relaxing when he saw it remained undisturbed.

"Sorry. But I heard them speaking about the forks that should not have been, I wanted to see."

"Ah, the pull of the inexplicable. Come now, you should be studying, not wasting your time on prophecy."

"Yes, Master, only... I heard they plan to silence the person responsible." She raised an eyebrow inquisitively, the playful look upon her features making her appear far younger than her twenty-five years.

"And gossip breeds?" he prompted sternly, with the slightest hint of a smile reflected in his eyes as he folded his arms to give her his best disapproving look.

"Ignorance and hatred." She tried to look ashamed, but he could see from her expression she had more to say.

"Teanna, gossip is a plague, better you purge it from your system here and now than infect others." He gestured for her to continue.

"I hear they're attempting to silence the fork-maker, but not before they try to exploit her gift to stop this land from falling. Is it true?"

"Ah yes, this mysterious force of malaise. Thus far she has damaged the power of the Mystics, ensured two weapons of destruction were unearthed instead of one and, as if those actions alone were not enough, this allowed Íkelos to gain access to The Stepping Realm. This figure is sowing peril with each choice they make, what would you have us do?" Teanna's brow furrowed as she considered the options.

"I'm uncertain, but I know this..." She grinned at the thought of revealing something even the Master Bibliothecary was unaware of. "They believe she is native to Darrienia. They say she died and was resurrected as one of their race. There are plans in motion to retrieve her."

"And now you have purged that nonsense, do you feel like replacing that tedious gossip with some useful facts?" He dropped a large tome on the table before her. "Chapters one through twenty, if you please."

"Yes, Master Bibliothecary," she sighed, opening the metal binding to reveal the ball of energy within. She placed her hands around the orb and groaned at the chosen subject matter.

"And if you manage to complete the task before dusk, I shall request someone to show you the practical application, if it pleases you." His eyes sparkled as he saw her smile, but there was something slightly haunted to her normally bright gesture. He lifted the chair, pulling it out carefully so not to draw it across the highly polished floor, and sat beside her, suddenly realising the reason she had sought such isolation in a place no one but himself had cause to venture. He placed his hand upon the tome, stilling the energies and disrupting her concentration. "The pairing was this morning, was it not?" He placed his wrinkled hand upon her own giving it a reassuring squeeze.

"Yes," she whispered, disguising the hurt from her voice.

"You are a fine young woman, Teanna. That you remain unmatched is a crime unto itself."

"I'm used to it now. Why would anyone seek to be mated with a dirty human? Even my hair is the colour of impure magic. To have me beside any would be to lower their status considerably." She knew all too well the Moirai judged by shades of white. Those who were deemed more powerful possessed a magic which was displayed as feathers of brilliant white. They were noble, highly sought to be partnered. Those with duller shades were weaker, and never allowed to rise above certain stations. Their responsibilities depended upon the colour of their magic. If a pure paired with a dull their status dropped, for none of brilliant magic wished to be associated, even indirectly, with those of lesser standing. For a Moirai to marry her they would have to possess no concern for titles. She was not only human, but her hair was the shade of the weak magic, even grey was thought superior to silver, because silver was thought to be forged by black impurities, rather than weakness. She never questioned this, not when her own hair grew the occasional strand of black, which she would quickly pluck before any could see.

"Why even save me, why bring me here to live like this, trapped in this existence seeing happiness only through the eyes of others? My friends, those I studied with, all have families of their own, but I cannot get anyone, male or female, to even look upon me with anything but friendship." Teanna supposed she should be grateful for that. Given the elitism of the Moirai it seemed strange that she was never without a friend or company, only without a partner. Being seen with her was acceptable, sought even. She had dined with the noblest of families, was invited to their gatherings, and yet despite her acceptance into even the highest echelons, she remained without love.

"Oh my darling girl, you are so much more than they could ever realise. Let us leave the study for this day. Go, find yourself in the Rumination Room, be at one with all you are." Teanna looked to Clarke in surprise, his aged face wrinkled into a sad smile. This man had been one of many who had been like a father to her. Despite all, she now had more family than she could ever ask for, and somehow she still felt so desperately alone.

"I will do as you ask." She nodded rising to her feet. She had sought her solitude here for a reason aside from curiosity. After remaining unpaired after her twenty-first birthday it seemed the Virtues had gathered and assigned her a task. Aside from her current role, she was to spend an hour each day in meditation within *that* room. Irrelevant whether day or night it was always empty. She would climb the small tower to its peak and enter the small crystal chamber which looked up to the vast and endless sky, and there she would lie.

She was instructed to find herself within these walls. If her true self was fractured and suffering then she could claim success. Every time she lay within the small enclosure she felt pain, a feeling of being lost and broken.

As she let her mind wander she also felt affection and warmth flowing into her. Her every sense became awash with confusion. To feel such affliction and anguish aligned with comfort and need was unbalancing in itself. Her presence there seemed to be sweet torture, both painful and comforting. Often she would close her eyes, imagining herself within the presence of another, one who longed desperately to take her within their arms, but was somehow forbidden from the contact it so desired.

* * *

Unlike those normally bound within the sealed ruins, Zoella's sleep was anything but restful. She—unlike the others confined here—could dream, as such, visions came to her through sleep. As the haunting images danced within her mind, the deafening voice roused her. Clutching her chest, she gasped for breath as beads of sweat trickled down her face. The air within these walls seemed thin, but she knew it was an illusion caused by the lack of energy available to this area. But her dreams had recharged her somewhat and, whilst doubting she possessed the strength to stand, she knew what must be done.

Her trembling hands raised to the small crystal that still hung around her neck. She needed to warn Daniel. Removing the cord she clutched it tightly, focusing her waning energy on reaching him.

"Zo?" She could hear the strain in Daniel's voice as he addressed her. "By The Gods, you look awful... is that a dungeon? Zo, what's happening, where are you?" Feeling his alarm she shook her head, trying to find the energy to speak.

"Later." Feeling the fatigue returning she drew her dry tongue against her parched lips. "Warn Amelia, he's got the four Maidens, now he hunts Mystics."

"The Mystics, who is? Zo, you're not making any sense. Where are you?"

"I can't," she panted. "I've been compromised."

"You tell me where you are right now. Where's Seiken?"

"He had no choice... I can't be near..."

She heard Daniel calling her name desperately as their connection faded and the darkness enveloping her gave way to another dream. The land below twisted into shimmering colours, crafting a new dreamscape before her gaze. As she looked down she saw a familiar figure, but the warmth spreading through her chest at seeing her was soon replaced by the icy tendrils of dread.

Zo's voiceless form cried out, but even should she hear the warning it was already too late. Íkelos had found his next quarry. Ensnared within the dream Zoella heard something portrayed but a few times in Amelia's voice, fear.

"You... but that's, you should not possess the power to call *me* to dream. How did you bring me here?" Amelia looked startled, her vision scanning the dreamscape desperately.

"It seems you do remember me after all. I suppose I should be flattered. I must say, time has not been kind to you. You have grown careless. Of all those I have stalked, I did not expect claiming you to be this easy. Then again, with the tool I have at my disposal your fate was inevitable.

"What I did to your world before will seem like paradise compared to the fear I will wrought, the chaos I must bring. I wish you could bear witness, but we both know that cannot be," he mocked, his shadowed hand already placed upon her chest. The shifting of colours occurred once more. Zoella knew what would follow, and grief consumed her as she witnessed him claim the power from the woman she considered her grandmother. The shadowy figure cast his gaze skyward towards Zo and whispered a single phrase. "Speak so it shall be."

Zo awoke with a start, hearing her own voice echoing within her mind, almost unable to recall the words she had spoken. Fear flooded through her as she recalled the look of terror upon Amelia's face. She sucked in deep breaths, noticing the air seemed saturated with energy where before it had been sparse. She knew this image had yet to be, but had no idea how long had passed since her conversation with Daniel. She only hoped the warning issued would reach Amelia in time. Rubbing her hand across her face she noticed only clear tears had fallen, unlike the times she had heard the secondary, more powerful voice address her.

* * *

The physician trotted behind Stacy, his arms still ladened with the scrolls and parchments he had been transporting before she had intercepted him. Her recognition had been instant. When last she had stayed within these walls he had been the understudy, the apprentice, of the Royal Physician. The old man had used him to gather herbs and prepare them for use. It had seemed to Galen that he had not wanted an assistant, merely an errand boy so he may better spend his time assessing the viability of strong alcohol for use in tinctures, or such was the reason he presented for his frequent intoxication. Galen spent his own time in study, his knowledge increasing exponentially as his master spent more time in contemplation than attending to his tasks.

Even with time's passage, it appeared to Stacy he was still the same mild-mannered errand boy, yet his demeanour now reflected the additional responsibilities he bore. She knew he was too gracious to expose his master. Unbeknown to Galen, the royals and nobles were aware of the alteration in roles and, when need required it, often waited until the old physician was suitably incapacitated before seeking aid and potions.

"So, it has been some time. Where have your adventures taken you?" he enquired awkwardly, as she strode through the castle leading him towards the place Peter lay.

"About," she answered curtly. "What aren't you telling me?" She stopped sharply, turning upon her heel to look at him as her eyes narrowed.

"It is best I leave such news until after I have seen to your friend, but you are correct, I have news for you. I sent a pigeon, but I feared it had not made harbour when you did not reply."

"You sent me a pigeon?" she questioned, concern now edging her voice. He gave a firm nod, stepping around her to continue his path before stopping outside a door as a shudder escaped him.

"Is this the room?" Galen asked, knowing without question it would be. He had felt this strange sensation before, and entered without awaiting her confirmation. His quickened entry saw him collide with the table before quickly adjusting his path to the bedside, where another man stood vigil over the sleeping figure. "This is... Peter Stert if memory serves," he observed. He briefly remembered the man from the time he had spent living within the castle walls years ago. Galen placed a small clear crystal upon the figure's chest, a device of his own design and forging. It drew a fraction of the figure's energy into it, its clear shades first turning opaque before altering to a smoky shade of grey. He shook his head, retrieving the item. "It is as I feared, Ádlíc. This makes him the seventh victim."

"Ádlíc?" Rob queried, his eyes trained upon the curious crystal the physician had now secured back into its place inside the unusual bracelet upon his wrist. Witnessing what he had, it made Rob wonder what the other gems adorning it were capable of, and how much the physician knew about the rare talent he seemed to possess.

"His spirit has been damaged, fractured. Whilst not contagious, as such, healers have been warned not to cross energies with those afflicted. There is a concern it may carry through magic. Looking at those affected it seems unlikely, but it is true they are all of unusual blessings. You should be careful, Stacy, of the four of you who resided here, you are the sole one not yet taken."

"You mean Helen?" Stacy felt her chest tighten as Galen nodded in response.

"And I hear Marc is being attended to in Castlefort. His illness, given his predisposition for such things, was expected but he was the first male to fall. Until then, we thought only women were susceptible. The distance rules out touch transmission, so we're at a loss."

"Peter crosses paths with no one, he rarely leaves. What exactly is this thing and how is it being transferred?" Stacy demanded, but her answer came in the form of an apologetic shrug.

"Has anyone without magic been affected?" Rob questioned.

"No, from what I have heard all are touched in one way or another." Galen narrowed his eyes, his brow furrowed in concentration.

"What is it?"

"Well, before Helen was taken ill she came to me asking for a compound to prevent sleep. She looked exhausted, but her pleas were desperate. She was terrified of falling asleep. I made the potion but before I could deliver it the master returned, saying he had done the poor thing a service. I didn't connect events until I saw the sleeping draught within her grasp. I let her sleep, what else could I do when escorted into a lady's room? But not twelve hours later her husband sought me out, unable to wake her."

"So we have incidents in both Therascia and Albeth," Rob muttered, scratching his chin in quiet contemplation.

"I was wondering if it was a Daimon-born disease myself, something they carry that we are not yet immune to," Galen volunteered as if reading Rob's thoughts. "My sources date this illness back to before we discovered their continent though, and there are humans who live amongst them already, none of whom have been afflicted."

"We have a friendship of sorts, we can enquire with Kitaia Ethelyn and see if she knows of a means to counter—"

"What is it?" Stacy asked sharply as Rob's speech halted abruptly.

"Would you call her a prophet?" Rob posed.

"Sorry?"

"Ethelyn, would she be called a prophet?"

"I guess so, I don't see what—"

"Of course, why didn't I consider it before? He's not looking for just any prophet, he wants the one he knows works." Rob cast a quick glance around the room as the realisation struck him.

"What are you talking about?"

"Paion. My last source said a man matching his description was asking about prophets. Psáltis, you need to warn Amelia about this sickness, she may have some insight. I need to warn Ethelyn, she could be in danger. There is no way, while I draw breath, that he will *ever* get his hands on her again."

Chapter 8

Will Speaker

Daniel pounded on Amelia's door after trying the handle for what was easily the third time. No matter what the hour he had visited before, never had he found the door to be locked. His hands once more became tangled in the wild sprays of herbs growing around the cottage as he desperately foraged for a key, hoping he had somehow overlooked it on his first search. All the time unease gnawed within him. Loose splinters pierced his flesh as he searched the knotted wooden structure for hidden nooks, but to no avail. His heart hammered inside his chest with the desperation of his next knock, and still the summons remained unanswered.

Remembering the time he had spent in this matriarch's company, he tried to lever the window open. Despite there being no manner of bolts, it remained fast, unmoving against his relentless attempts. It was only as a voice invaded his thoughts, warning that it was something far more powerful than a lock which had sealed this home from invasion, that he abandoned his efforts with a despairing sigh.

His attempts to gain entry had done nothing but disguise the small vibrations of the gossip crystal as it had tried to summon his attention. When a futile glance for aid strayed toward the distant town he groaned, slumping dejectedly to rest with his back against the door while devising another method to gain entry.

Those of the town would spare him no aid, if they even acknowledged his presence. The people of Drevera were by far the most xenophobic people he had encountered. No outsider would find themselves welcome here. Even in the times of great festivals the presence of foreigners was merely tolerated. Allowing his head to fall back against the door he heaved a sigh, startling as the door gave way, swinging inward. A figure stood looking down upon his sitting figure, her eyes reddened.

"I was too late," Stacy whispered as Daniel rose to his feet. He reached out, touching her arm gently. "Wita?" she questioned in surprise, her tear-filled eyes finally clearing enough to recognise the figure before her. Their paths had crossed before, over a year ago when the world had been threatened by the combined power of Remedy and Sunrise. She had silently marvelled at his insight and courage, but now questioned what had brought him to this door.

"Amelia?" Daniel questioned softly, already knowing the answer even before she had shaken her head.

"Just like the others. She's been taken by Ádlíc." Daniel shuddered hearing this word as images of Earth Maiden flashed through his mind and he recalled Zo's warning.

"Ádlíc, it's not a sickness it's a symptom," he stated in understanding.

"What do you mean?"

"I came because I was warned someone had taken the four Elemental Maidens, and now sought the Mystics. If she's afflicted by this Ádlíc then it's not a disease, it's something being forcibly done. I only wish I knew why." He paused, hoping to hear a whisper providing him with the answers.

"Warned, by who?" Stacy stepped aside, allowing Daniel to enter the modest dwelling. Amelia's home had always possessed a comforting warmth, but now it seemed cold and empty.

"A prophet, I guess. Who else has been afflicted?" He peered through the bedroom door, to see the elderly woman's sleeping figure. She lay fully dressed, sprawled horizontally across the bed as if barely reaching it before being taken by sleep. A cover had been draped over her, no doubt by Stacy when she had first discovered her.

"Have you contacted Eiji?" Stacy questioned.

"No, his crystal is with Acha. I'm waiting for him to return from his errands, why?"

"Then it is possible just the two of us remain untouched." Stacy turned away from the bedroom, unable to look any longer. "I wasn't quick enough."

"What brought you here?"

"Before falling ill Helen had been attended to by the castle physician, he said she feared to sleep. I thought this fear was somehow related to the fact the people are trapped in slumber. If anyone knew what this threat could be it would have been Amelia."

"Don't you hold the memories of your previous incarnations?" Daniel asked with concern.

"We should, but for some reason the memories of our past actions have not returned to us." Stacy glanced towards the door. "We should have her moved to Albeth, we can't leave her here." Daniel nodded, studying Stacy critically. If Zo's prediction was coming to pass then the woman before him was also in danger. He knew himself the difficulty of evading sleep, it was a near impossible feat. They needed to get a warning to Eiji, but he feared what leaving Stacy alone would subject her to. Fearful for the safety of his friend, he attempted to contact Acha only to become more distressed when he received no response.

* * *

The sudden and surprising discovery of Kólasi had caused confusion amongst many well-travelled explorers. It was true that the waters surrounding this island were indeed treacherous to sail, but the thought of being completely unaware of such an impressive landmass defied belief.

The enormous island was a sight to behold, and many vessels approached as close as they dared just to look upon the enormous city of Eremalche. Be it day or night this was a wonder to behold. In the day there stood a great city, divided into small districts upon an enormous plateau with five large, frost-blue vistas extending from its central structure. As night fell, these platforms would rise and close, sealing the city within. These unusual walls appeared almost fluid and delicate, like petals, as they wrapped protectively around the city which had taken its name from the flower it mimicked. These protective petals were forged from magic and fibres resistant to even the most powerful attacks, and rumours of this city implied it had withstood many.

Its people were something of a mystery, pale-skinned and dark-haired, they were few in number and belonged to a race known as the Daimons, beings who lived in harmony with nature and its spirits. It was said they could manipulate the world around them to a degree that those outside their race had difficulty understanding and thus accepted the acts as a form of magic. Over the last year, several of their naturopaths and shamans had agreed to work alongside the Physicians' Plexus, and the result had been the development of new, but simple techniques which had already saved many lives. The Plexus, once diverting towards the path of new sciences in healing, was slowly being returned to natural methods and rites. Although this return was not welcomed by all, particularly those of The Order.

In older times, when Hectarian magic had been bountiful and healers many in number, those practising such arts would give thanks to the Elemental Spirits, and invoke the magic of these beings into their workings to grant them additional power. Over time, The Order had used its influence to see this practice diminish, and even managed to turn the hand of healers away from herbs and nature towards chemistry and divine artefacts.

The Order was responsible for the temples of the world, and ensuring that The Gods remained the focal point of all worship. They found profit in such things and as such had risen to a state of power that could overthrow the monarchy itself. The Daimons' methods had reversed decades of manipulation, and seeking to bring their own agenda back to the forefront, they now wondered if it was time to bring back the rites of sacrifice and prayer for healing.

Fey had little cause to venture from his homeland of Therascia, so was unaware that the map in Collateral had only recently been updated to include the portals to the island of Kólasi. Not that it mattered, given Arlen's unfamiliarity with the Travellers' City, Fey opted to secure a vessel to cross the ocean.

Kólasi had only recently invited trade, and with such a hazardous approach had seen the need to construct clear markers to guide vessels into their port. These markers were a wonder unto themselves. They sprung from the ocean, and appeared to be stone pillars which birthed countless layers of soft-glowing petals woven by magic. The soft hues of their gentle chasing lights guided sailors to port, as well as soothed the mind of those who gazed upon the mesmerising display.

Kólasi's exports had been more reserved than anticipated following their addition to the Traders' Plexus register, and whilst some travellers would venture to the island to gaze upon its mystery, many chose to visit for another reason. Tales of the fiefdom's Regent had spread far and wide, comparing his form to that of a monster pulled straight from myths and fables. Many hunters had journeyed here in the hope to cross swords and test their mettle in friendly combat with such a powerful being.

"Are there any more Diviners you know of?" questioned Arlen as they once more boarded the vessel. The man's spirit had visibly dropped since he had laid eyes upon the queen of their land, Kitaia Ethelyn. Her husband had stood beside her, his jaw set firmly as his piercing eyes watched Arlen for any minor indiscretion. Given all Arlen had been privileged to, he could understand why one of his kind would not be welcomed within their land. Paion, once a noble of Talaria, had been responsible for the unimaginable suffering which had nearly resulted in Kitaia's death. Even after a year of healing she had not yet regained the ability to walk. That she had permitted him an audience at all spoke volumes with regard to her character. Her husband, however, had been less than accommodating. Arlen had feared the repercussions of even the slightest provocation.

"None that I know of. Have you visited there before?" Fey questioned. He had felt unnerved by the fact they had been escorted into and out of the city. Even now the ones who had accompanied them here stood guard near the ship's boarding ramp, as if to ensure they remained aboard. It was impossible not to observe that such precaution had not been taken with any of their other visitors. Fortunately, the ship they boarded was returning to Therascia, he doubted their hosts would have cared which vessel took them away, they were just eager for them to leave their shores.

"The Sfaíra, their queen, has reason to be mindful of my presence. Although I intend no ill will, their caution is understandable. I am fortunate they allowed me to approach. Are there truly no more Soothsayers, not even a Diviner?"

"None that I know of, but I really only know my own territory. Neither here, Albeth, or the islands fall into such jurisdiction. Perhaps if you told me why it was important."

"The prophet I seek is not a Seer in the traditional sense. They do not just see visions, they hear words. In my homeland we called them Paravátis, violators of the future, but here I suppose Willsayer would be apt. To understand the danger, you must first understand that a vision, by itself, is fallible. It is open to many interpretations, as images can be changed or beheld in different ways depending on the Seer. When a prophet translates the vision to words it becomes their understanding of what they witnessed. On the other hand, if someone was told what their vision implied it can only have that singular outcome. Those who hear a voice are in fact being imprinted with the will of another to force the outcome of a vision. When this person speaks the words aloud they validate the prediction and, by doing so, ensure it comes to pass. A prediction by a Willsayer overcomes any visions or prophecies, that's why we call them violators, because they force the future to change to reflect the wishes of the one for whom they speak."

"You said the will of another, do you mean divinity?"

"If it were only that simple. Anyone with the power to manipulate another into seeing a vision could force them to direct the path of the future. Do not misunderstand, it is a difficult task. To create a vision in itself is near impossible. I myself believed the knowledge had been all but lost. Due to the danger, the divinity, as you call them, opted to place an impediment on those who could behold visions. It ensured that a prophet could only give their first prediction to a sage who, in turn, had to confirm it came to be, before the power could truly awaken. My homeland have kept vigil on the known sages for longer than you would imagine, tracing their heritage through blood, and we know none of them have taken a new prophet under their wing, thus this Willsayer must be someone in which the gift has already been awakened."

"Or a new sage, perhaps?" Fey mused. "The Eorthāds once more grace our skies, but their land remains unseen. Did your ancestors possess the ability to track those sealed?"

"A new sage," Arlen mused. "The Eorthāds had none, but maybe there could be one not born by ancestry. With crises such as those you have witnessed here these past decades, perhaps such a thing is possible," Arlen acknowledged thoughtfully. "Thus, it would also not be beyond belief that they unwittingly crossed paths with an unawakened prophet. While we ensure prophets can't be corrupted by the will of another, a new sage would be unaware of the measures to be taken. They could allow the prophet to become tainted without even realising it."

"What will happen when you find this Willsayer?"

"I am an Appraiser. It is my duty to assess whose will is being channelled, and whether its purpose is one of benevolence or malice. Given what has come to pass I fear the force is not one of good. I have been assigned the arduous task of silencing them should that be the case."

"And if it is pure?"

"Then we listen in fear."

* * *

Daniel pushed the horse to gallop faster, aware that Stacy, who led the way on her own chestnut mare, fought desperately against the onslaught of fatigue. They had travelled directly to Collateral and, on seeing that the store belonging to their friends had been closed, had immediately departed. Daniel had sent Stacy to procure the mounts while he obtained some horrifically familiar supplies from a local grocer. Even now the scent of the coffee beans turned his stomach as the odour was carried towards him on the wind as they rode.

He understood her plight more than she would imagine. There had been a time when he had resorted to many means to ensure dreams could not find him. It had been due to one such episode that his path had crossed with Amelia's. If not for the elderly woman attending to him, he would not still be amongst the living. At that time he had thought life itself a curse, and would have welcomed the peace. She had nursed him, scolded him, and purged the opiates and poisons from his system, all while attempting to hide his suffering from his friends. It had been a dark time, his lowest point, and his dreams had served only to worsen his fragile mind.

After that incident he had needed to obtain other means to prevent sleep, ones which would evade the notice of his constant supervision. It was then he had discovered this solution, recommended by a rather weary looking Keeper of Records in Albeth Castle. They lacked the potency of his more dangerous vices, but they had served their purpose better than willpower alone. Even now, the bitter scent caused his throat to turn dry and his stomach to lurch but, given all that Stacy had revealed, it was better she did not succumb to sleep.

"How are you faring?" Daniel called above the sound of the roaring wind as his horse drew alongside hers. "Are we close?" It seemed a strange thing for him to be asking, given that Eiji was one of his closest friends. Daniel had visited Eiji's home on but a few occasions, and they were times he struggled to recall with any clarity. When they realised the store had been closed, Stacy suggested they try his home deep within the forest on Therascia.

Even after their less than amicable parting, Eiji had ensured the Mystics all possessed the information needed to locate him should a matter of urgency arise. Daniel was certain, if he concentrated, he could draw the path from his distorted memories and locate his friend without encountering many difficulties, but having her act as his guide was another method of keeping her alert and ensuring she remained awake.

"How do you think?" she snarled, grinding her teeth. "It's not too much further." She kicked her horse, spurring it to run faster, clinging to the hope he was safe. The thought of being alone with this burden was as all-consuming as the blanket of autumn leaves lining the tracks before them.

* * *

Rob always received a hero's welcome when he visited Eremalche. It was one of the reasons he avoided doing so. The other sat before him now, studying him intently with her smoky-grey eyes. She looked upon him in frustration as his gaze lingered upon the chair she still remained confined to after all this time. It was unlike those of his own lands. Vines and metals mingled with energy to form a mailable structure which created braces and supports to the locations her broken body needed it most. Every time Rob looked upon her he felt the waves of guilt and shame. If not for his actions she would not be confined there.

"If not for your actions I would not be anywhere." Taya intruded upon the thoughts of guilt and self-berating she was all too familiar with.

"You've made progress?" Rob asked hopefully, to which Taya dipped her head slightly in a nod. "I've still heard nothing on the whereabouts of my sister but, I assure you, when she is found she will be delivered to you to face whatever punishment you deem fit," Rob advised. Yuri seemed to stiffen beside her slightly. Twisting, he bent to scoop up a small figure who was exploring the area behind him.

"You visit us rarely. How will your goddaughter come to learn of her uncle if he is forever absent?" Yuri questioned stiffly, approaching to place the squirming child into Rob's arms. He held her uncomfortably for a moment, before relaxing slightly. The young girl was the mirror image of her mother, her black hair now growing to crown her head beautifully. Catrina quickly voiced her protest at her adventure being cut short, wriggling within his arms, desperate to return to her explorations.

"She has your spirit for adventure it seems," Taya jested as Rob crouched to place the child down, watching her hasty departure on hands and knees. A small smile turned the edge of his lips before his eyes lifted to meet with

Taya's. Seeing his expression she gave a slight sigh, beckoning for him to approach. "Why do I sense this is not an informal visit, what troubles you?"

"You know myself and Bray have been trying to locate Paion. So far we have had little luck. Bray returned to Misora to use their means, and I've been tracking rumour." Rob paused, noticing Yuri gesture towards the guards, indicating that they should allow them some privacy, possibly due to the fear he saw barely suppressed upon his wife's face. She detested showing weakness, and yet she had felt nothing but since her return. "I fear he may be seeking your talents once more. The last insight I received had him searching for a prophet. I am concerned he plans to exploit you again."

Taya released a breath she had been unaware of holding, her posture visibly relaxing.

"It wasn't him. Just a number of hours ago a Moirai braved our land and sought an audience. It is true he seeks a prophet, but it was not I he sought." A large Herculean form swung the audience chamber's doors open, his hard stare carefully observing those within the room. "Lord Geburah," Taya acknowledged as the figure lingered. "We have much to discuss, shall we?" She gestured towards the tactical room, suggesting they continue their conversation within, knowing Geburah would also wish to hear what she had to say. The enormous figure placed his hand to his chest, offering a respectful bow, before scooping Catrina up into his arms. The young child giggled, reaching towards the brightly coloured plumes of his once Moiraic wings.

Rob felt himself tense as the figure strode past. The blue, green, and purple shades of the fire-like feathers caused great disquiet to his already troubled soul. He knew the magic, which sparked and died to create the plumes of maddening colours, was a gift bestowed by the Lampads, beings whose light could drive a man to insanity. He was also aware that being in the presence of the Daimons softened the effect Geburah's feathers had on those looking upon him.

When Yuri pulled the large doors closed behind them Taya spoke, first informing Geburah of the Moirai's visit and the figure he sought, before explaining the true intention behind his appearance upon their world.

"What is an Appraiser exactly?" Rob questioned, his brow furrowed. Handling one rogue Moirai had been difficult enough, but if another had been sent to them with the blessing of this race there was no knowing what devastation he could bring. Paion had nearly destroyed them all in an attempt to purge all life and open a path for the return of the Moirai. The fact that they now openly walked amongst them was concerning indeed.

"The Moirai have long taken your prophets into their care, helping to protect them from the madness of futuresight. His role is basically to ascertain if those he looks upon are powerful and, if they are, offer to take them to a location they will be safe," Taya explained, casting a glance towards Catrina. When the combined powers of Sunrise and Remedy were about to be unleashed, Taya had sworn to do anything Paion asked of her in exchange for keeping her daughter safe, should she survive the power's release. Taya had been desperate, weakened, and nothing she could have done would have prevented what was to come. There had been only one life that could have been saved, and she had offered everything to attempt to do just that.

"But you are one of the most powerful Seers I have crossed paths with," Rob stated earnestly.

"Yes and no. I am the Sfaíra of the Daimons. My sight comes from elsewhere, from the connections we have with nature. The spirits open windows through which we can observe many futures, both of our world, and ones that run parallel to us. We see what can be, but we have no concept of which or whose future we behold.

"Paion found a means to exploit my connection to witness the outcome of his many attempts throughout the different futures. By doing so he could amend his own plans to ensure they did not meet failure. He did not need to know if it was his future, he only needed to witness the mistakes and ensure they would not occur. Does that make sense?" Rob nodded whilst still looking confused. "Think of it like this, we were banished to the Betwixt, a place The Stepping Realm crosses to unite worlds and realms. In this place we thrived and evolved, we could see the future of anything touched by the pathways. In some ways, while isolated, we were also connected to all. Humans, all those here on this world, even the Moirai, have evolved solely in contact with and dependent on this land, and thus their prophets only witness the future of that they are bound to."

"Okay, but what does that have to do with the Appraiser?"

"He's looking for someone who has awakened a powerful and dangerous gift. The problem he has stems from the fact his knowledge is incomplete. He has exhausted the known Seers. He will soon come to realise he must seek a newly awakened sage, and there is only one who will have escaped their notice, because he remains unseen by fate."

"Daniel Eliot," Rob whispered in understanding.

"When last our paths crossed he was already a sage, and was receptive to the voices of the ancestors. I have no doubt this is who this Moirai seeks, and he alone will know from whom he has taken a prophecy." Taya shifted uncomfortably, wincing against her body's protest to movement. She felt Yuri's hand squeeze her shoulder gently, and glanced up to smile at him as he moved to stand beside her.

"This person they seek, are they a danger to us or the Moirai?"

"With just three words this prophet condemned their race. They predicted Talaria, the home of the Moirai, will fall."

"Then surely there is nothing they can do?"

"Quite the contrary, this person is a Willsayer. Their prophecies are fulfilled when they are spoken aloud. It was an ancient lore that invokes powerful binding magic. It is very dangerous, and not just to the Moirai. Little is known about it, but it was once considered that everything they said while in a trance would come to pass. We witnessed a Willsayer only once before we were sealed, but there's more I must tell you."

"More? What could be worse than a person who could kill with a word?" Rob snatched a goblet from the table and drank deeply, but it did little to alleviate the dryness in his throat.

"There's something else, something greater at risk. When this prophet speaks all connected to any form of futuresight hear their words. What they said affects someone you know directly."

"Tell me,"

"They warned of a being who walks through dreams and seeks to claim the power of the Elemental Maidens, and the Mystics. On hearing this I asked Eadward of the Kyklos to make contact with Darrienia via meditation, to see if they could offer any insight." Taya paused, seeming almost hesitant to continue.

"And, what did he discover?"

"Nothing, he did not awaken. His body shows signs of his essence being present, but fractured. He is neither lucid nor dreaming, and his magic is somehow displaced. We dare not make another attempt, and our healers are at a loss."

"Ádlíc," Rob whispered recognising the symptoms. "Wait, you mean to say you attempted to heal him?"

"We did," Yuri acknowledged. "Unsuccessfully."

"And there were no ill-affects?"

"The shamans are in good health, why?" Geburah rose to his feet, his Herculean form seeming to tower above them all as he waited to hear what Rob had to say.

"There was a theory it might be passed through magic, I guess it was wrong. It just proves how little we know of the ailment," Rob revealed, he lifted the drink again before replacing it without partaking.

"You've seen it before?"

"Two Mystics, that I know of, have contracted it, but I have only witnessed one. I must return to Stacy. It appears whatever is happening occurs within Darrienia. I must warn her not to sleep." He rose to his feet, making his way towards the door before Taya called out to him.

"Trust me, no matter what you believe, seeking Daniel Eliot must be a priority. If this Willsayer is broken by the Moirai they may be able to manipulate them. With enough power they could be forced to speak anyone's desires aloud. Anyone's," she stressed.

"I know how to find him, but I'll need help. If what you say is true then I fear for this prophet." Rob shuddered, knowing but a little of the torture Taya had been forced to endure in order for Paion to exploit her.

"Whoever this prophet may be, they are well-hidden. Be careful you do not lead someone to their door."

Chapter 9

Warnings in Blood

Zoella swiped her arm across her eyes, leaving smears of blood streaking her already tinted flesh. She sat on the floor gasping for breath. Rivulets of sweat ran from her, both soothing her burning skin and sending shivers through her fever wracked body. It was several moments before she could grasp the leather chord from the place it had fallen when her consciousness had left her, and another few long minutes before she collected enough strength to attempt contacting Daniel.

They had said this location would keep her imprisoned in sleep, that the energy here would be only enough to sustain her life, and yet she continued to dream. Every time she awoke it was almost as if some energy was drawn back with her, allowing her moments of clear lucidity. There were times of delirium too, phases marked by the scrawling of bloody symbols which now adorned the floors and walls. Each one held their own message, although she could no longer discern what important warnings had been scribed.

She felt a wave of energy from the crystal replenish her fleeting reserves as Daniel's image appeared upon its surface, before being projected into her mind. The slight delay in this transfer was a clear indication of her sheer exhaustion.

"Daniel." She swallowed as she forced the words from her parched lips. "Have you found the Mystics?" She could see the worry on his brow and could only imagine the image he beheld in order to invoke such a reaction. He seemed to bite back a question before giving a slight nod.

"All but for Eiji. Stacy is taking me there now. Zo wh—"

"I know what he wants," she whispered, her weakened voice almost failing her. She blinked slowly, swaying as her balance faltered even from her seated position "It was denied to him once before, and is something you've held, but it's not in that form now." Zo tried to force the words, her tongue feeling numb as if something attempted to prevent her from speaking the words. "He's seeking—" Zo's words were cut short by a gut wrenching cry. Daniel could almost feel her pain, but he heard a single whisper escape her before their connection severed, and he swore she said 'the light'.

* * *

Daniel whistled for the mounts to stop, leaping from his own with a dexterity he could not have imagined possessing years ago. He surveyed their surroundings, his hand still tightly clasping the crystal. Stacy's head raised from its bowed position, sending a brief wave of relief to swell within him.

"Whaddya doing?" she muttered incoherently as Daniel released his own horse before mounting behind her. He took the reins from her slack grasp.

"We need to move faster," Daniel enforced, a little too loudly for her sensitive ears. He spurred the horse into motion, his mind racing. He noticed her supply of coffee beans had been depleted, even the scent no longer lingered. There was no choice but to force her to remain awake. Now more than ever he was confident the danger came through dreams.

Trees flashed by as the horse skilfully navigated the terrain. Daniel was certain it knew the path without the need for any instruction. He felt as if they were being guided, and only hoped he was not leading them off track. Stacy's need for sleep had become all-consuming, forcing him to resort to causing her physical pain when her body started to slump, but even this reflex was dulling. "Talk to me," he commanded in a tone which betrayed his own authority.

"What?" she muttered, attempting to sit a little straighter.

"Talk to me. Tell me something, anything." He knew he was losing her focus, she could barely force words through her exhaustion. By the time they reached the base of the tree harbouring Eiji's home, he already knew his efforts to keep her awake had failed.

Eiji's home was something not often seen. It was constructed high in the branches of an ancient tree known as the Akegata tree. Its dark and ancient trunk was easily the width of a small home, and the mottled, gnarled texture of this ancient giant seemed to imply it had taken other trees into itself as it grew. The lower area contained no branches, and was lined by enormous roots which created the impression of dark tunnels burrowing into the land below. With all that Daniel knew of this rare species, he knew better than to explore the truth of the mythos.

High above, concealed by the natural bend of branches and the heavy foliage, was Eiji's home. It appeared as if the tree had grown to embrace it, and in a manner of speaking this was true. Eiji's master, Nikki, had been the guardian of this forest and this towering beast was also deemed its protector. The tree, known as Kago, had accepted Eiji's master, parting his branches so that he may live upon him and further enhance the protection he bestowed upon the forest.

The home of an Elementalist was a blessed thing indeed. It was forged by their hands and the materials would absorb portions of their magical energy, thus becoming enchanted. Often such dwellings were passed from master to student and, for each generation who resided there, the enchantment gained power. By nature most Elementalists were forced into a life of solitude. The power of the energies within their aura acted as a deadly poison to any who spent an extended time in their vicinity. For this reason most sought isolation, but Eiji was an exception to this age old rule for but a single reason, and she now stood upon the small platform outside his treetop home, having watched their approach with a smile. As he drew near she dropped the ladder to allow him entry.

"Daniel," Acha greeted brightly, her oaken brown hair whipped wildly around her as the wind rustled through the trees.

"Where's Eiji?" Daniel's urgency caused a frown upon her face he could not see due to the sheer height.

"He's just getting dressed. It's still night to some of us you know."

"We woke you?" For the first time Daniel realised the dawn sun had yet to make an appearance on the horizon. Far above, through the thinning canopies of autumn leaves, he could still see the stars.

"I felt your approach, something is troubling you. Come, I'll warm some water." Acha studied the second figure who lay slumped forward against the horse's thick neck. "She's not just sleeping, is she?" Acha asked, her tone filled with concern.

"Come down, I'll explain what I can. It's best if Eiji remains away." Daniel pushed his hands through his hair. "Ic forþence," he muttered. His accidental slip into the language spoken by the Eorthåds saw Acha's descent quicken. This language had effortlessly become his native dialect, ingrained to be second nature by the fact all he conversed with spoke it. Even conversations with Zoella would be carried out in this dialect since the Oneirois didn't speak a language as such. Oneirois possessing a humanoid form simply spoke, and the sound waves were adapted to be understood by those they addressed. Such was necessary with a race as diverse as they, but only the humanoid Oneirois could ensure their words were understood by those not dreaming. Daniel, outside of Kalia, only reverted to this dialect in times of heightened emotions.

* * *

Íkelos surveyed the landscape of Darrienia, watching the orbs of light in the sky. They were markers only he could see, a suggestion of magical entities who were dreaming. This was the method by which he had pursued the Maidens, even the Mystics gave off brilliant heliographs. Those currently sleeping were weak, they could not further his ambition, and yet there was still one he sought, another power he needed to claim before he could make the final step onto the mortal plane. The time was nearing, and yet this individual somehow continued to evade detection.

He knew this figure well. Once before, many years ago, he had approached him through Darrienia's interpretation of The Courts of Twilight, and gained his trust. He implored this figure to seek solitude, and ensured that he would be cooperative when the time came for their paths to cross once more.

This man, this Mystic, should have been the easiest to obtain. Whilst he would know of his approach, he had also confirmed that when he asked it of him that he would go with him willingly. But not once over the years had he seen the beacon of his power. Not once. He knew his target lived, but he could not locate him. Something was protecting him, shielding him from sight. If that were truly the case then Íkelos knew of only one means to ensure he revealed himself, after all, he had a powerful tool at his disposal as well.

* * *

Cenehard escorted Seiken towards The Sealed Ruins while Rowmeow sat within one of his branched appendages. Their pace was almost a sprint, and the small feline had been having great difficulties in keeping pace with beings whose strides far outmatched his own. Or at least that was how he had secured passage on Cenehard. The truth was, he simply enjoyed lounging in the branches, and Cenehard didn't seem to mind the extra weight, although more than once Rowmeow had caught himself moments before giving in to his nature and attempting to sharpen his claws upon the Empsychó's wooden flesh.

For security reasons there were but a few beings who could open the portal to this area. They were called Guardians of the Gateways, and their rank had been presented to them by Rowmeow himself. It was a high honour. In addition to guarding the portals, they acted as heralds to announce the corruption within dreamscapes, and most had the ability to observe great distances. Cenehard often released a great bird named Merle to watch from above and warn of disruptive energies. While most of his creatures could live for but a few minutes before returning to their carved form he—like all Empsychós—had one extension they could animate for prolonged periods. In Cenehard's case this was Merle, who was a carving of a great and rare falcon, a creature who had been conjured from the imagination of a dreamer and had come to shelter within his branches.

Seiken paced impatiently as Cenehard began the ritual to open the tower with Rowmeow almost matching him step for step.

"Are you certain you can sever his influence?" Seiken questioned, almost not daring to reveal the hope within his voice. When Rowmeow had revealed that her gift must have been Will Speaking, and not prophecy, a measure of relief had coursed through him. But even if Rowmeow could undo the invocation of her speaking Íkelos' true name, there was still the matter of whose desires she originally spoke.

"I can, but it will not be pleasant." Rowmeow sat with his front paws placed upon his tail as it curled around him. It was only upon seeing this Seiken noticed how cold the lack of energy had made this sinister landscape. Rowmeow's ears pricked the instant the door dissolved from the tower. His whiskers twitched as he sprung to his feet, back arched and fur raised. "Moirai magic," Rowmeow hissed, feeling the all too familiar sensation and scent. Seiken stepped around him, already fearing what he would find within.

"How is this possible?" Seiken pushed his hands through his hair, turning a full circle to behold the empty prison. Blood smeared the floor and walls, creating symbols Seiken had not seen for a very long time. The scant light from the grey-hued sky caused something within the near-darkness to shimmer, calling his attention, beckoning him deeper inside. Crouching, Seiken retrieved the small crystal from the cold, stone floor, wrapping its leather binding around his fingers as he cursed silently at having forgotten it was in her possession. Fearfully, he pushed a small amount of energy into the fragment, surprised at the toll it took upon him.

"We're in a place of near-negative energy. It's unlikely she could have found the strength to make it function," Rowmeow asserted as he brushed against Seiken's legs, transferring a fraction of his own stored energy to him.

"This is Hectarian script. I can't decipher it, not without access to Hecate's gift." Seiken continued to study the symbols, begging his mind to recall the intricacies of this ancient dialect. It was to no avail. When Hectarian magic had been sacrificed, so too had the ability to read its symbology.

"You think it's important?"

"Why else would she write it? She shouldn't have been able to have visions here." Seiken paced, feeling the weight of his limbs increasing with each step.

"If we would have realised the true nature of her gift sooner, we would have realised she could enter dreamstate and never would have placed her here. We facilitated this." Rowmeow swiped a paw through the air meaningfully.

"Daniel?" Seiken saw his image appear on the crystal's surface.

"What happened, where's Zo?" he glanced around, surveying the area behind Seiken. The images would be faded due to the lack of energy, but Seiken knew he was not surprised at the surroundings which confirmed his fears. She had managed to reach out to him.

"Thea, she... we don't know. We need your help."

"What can I do?" The offer came without pause or delay.

"How quickly can you reach us?"

"I'm with Eiji at the moment. We need to transfer Stacy back to Albeth. Zo said someone was hunting the Mystics. Eiji is the only one who remains untouched by Ádlíc," Daniel revealed, glancing upwards towards the treetop.

"You have spoken to her?"

"Yes, twice. First she warned of the Mystics, then..." Daniel paused, frowning, "that she knew what he sought, that I've held it in another form," he recalled.

"Daniel, have Eiji and Acha attend to Stacy. This must take priority. I'm sending Rowmeow and Cenehard to meet you." He glanced towards the gaping doorway where the small feline seemed to nod his understanding before departing. "They'll bring you to me." Something in his voice seemed almost hesitant. "You will not like what I have to show you." Seiken terminated their connection, taking a moment to once again cast his gaze across the tower before lowering his head in shame. His stomach tightened with guilt as memories of abandoning his wife here returned to haunt him. He sank towards the floor, eyes closed, unable to look any longer upon the fate he had inflicted upon the woman he loved.

Seiken waited impatiently, even he struggled to breathe within this location. Cenehard had sealed the portal behind himself and Rowmeow, and whilst he was not tethered to a tower he still felt its tiring effects. He sat within the dark, cylindrical room, head in hands, diverting his thoughts of self-loathing towards questioning why she had thought to revert to a script she was surely aware few but herself could read.

Feeling the rush of energy as the portal opened, Seiken stood, unaware he had been lost to slumber. Hurried footsteps echoed through the silent terrain, but only Daniel approached. Rowmeow and Cenehard remained at a distance, allowing them their privacy.

Daniel hesitated in the doorway, his brow furrowed as he looked upon the stone tower streaked with blood.

"You kept her here!" he growled entering to behold the dark prison. When he had questioned if she was in a dungeon he was, in part, jesting. He never thought her to have been a prisoner.

"We had no choice." Seiken's voice begged him to understand, and knew at least a part of him did, but that part was overridden by the love for his closest friend.

"No choice? Spirits, Seiken, she's your wife, and you imprisoned her like this?" Daniel's arms extended in an exaggerated gesture of their surroundings.

"The name she spoke belonged to an old power. By doing so she relinquished her will to him. We placed her here because we believed it was the one place he, and the prophecies, wouldn't be able to reach her."

"And how'd that work out, hmm?" Daniel's jaw clenched as he bit back a more scathing comment. He could see how much the decision wore upon Seiken, he had witnessed first-hand the depth of his love. This remembrance only served to fuel his anger, again bringing him to question how *this* could have been the only option.

"It was temporary. We returned as soon as we had prepared everything to sever his hold on her, but this was all that remained." Seiken gestured towards the symbols.

"This is why you need me. What makes you think I can read it?" Daniel glanced around the cold stone of the tower walls, he only hint of colour beyond the grey-scale tones as that of her blood, and it shone almost like a beacon in the dreary surroundings.

"You're probably the only one who can. At the time of her death, and even after her rebirth as one of us, Thea had been psychically linked to you, as such an imprint of the language would remain with you, and if not, you can ask someone who would know. You are the Wita after all."

"This is automatic writing," Daniel observed, touching one of the symbols. He rubbed his thumb over his finger, realising dsepite its shimmer, the blood had dried.

"Can you read it?"

"Some, but parts are nonsensical. It says a lot to her state of mind." Daniel paced, mentally trying to separate the messages which had been written, some contained several symbols overlapping each other. He approached a darker stain. "This is from when she first contacted me, warning me about the Mystics..." Mentally he scrubbed that message from his sight leaving only the newer symbols. "This is what she said before she vanished—"

"Vanished, you saw her abduction?" Seiken asked in disbelief, his hand gripped Daniel's shoulder, forcing him to turn.

"Not as such. The first time she contacted me we lost contact, I believe she had another vision, or maybe lost consciousness. Who knows with this place? When we spoke again the same thing occurred. I didn't notice it at the time, but standing here now, replaying our conversation in my mind, just a moment before it happened I swear there was a burning light."

"What did she say?"

"Not much, but I'm certain she said he was seeking the light." Daniel's eyebrows drew together in concentration. A single symbol burned as if lit by embers in his mind. The more he looked, the more he saw its repetition. It stood alone, within phrases, or shielded beneath layers of additional writing. It was written as both a warning and a revelation. "Lavender!" He clicked his fingers in realisation and once more began to pace. "But he can't be after the Light of Lavender, it was extinguished in opening the path to the Spiritwest."

Daniel mumbled to himself. "By the Gods, she meant the princess! The figure from the Light of Lavender's origin story, the Elvin Thane shared it with us. But that would mean... Seiken, you said this figure was old, how old exactly?"

"Our people refer to him as Melas-Oneiros, the black dream. Your history may once have known him as Íkelos. It was his forest you visited to rescue Zo and Acha all those years ago. He is old, ancient, why do you ask?"

"That's whose name she invoked?" Daniel exhaled with a sharp breath, closing his eyes in fear his expression would reveal more than he could currently voice.

"What do you know?"

"Can we do this somewhere else?"

"I must agree with the Wita," Rowmeow intruded. "I have news to share as well. I finally know whose will Thea speaks and I am certain, now more than ever, the Moirai are responsible for her abduction, but they don't realise her importance."

"What do you mean?" Daniel questioned stepping from the tower to join the feline and Cenehard.

"You understand me now? Well now, it seems you have advanced much since last our paths crossed," Rowmeow observed. The last time he and Daniel had cause to meet the human had heard his instructions as nothing more than a series of meows and howls, with Seiken acting to translate. Daniel's posture straightened, he hadn't even realised he'd been conversing with the cat directly. "As for my implications, Seiken, you said they sought to silence the forger of forks. In their eyes, Thea would be just that."

As they exited the Sealed Towers, the world around them transitioned from desolate to the luscious, thriving planes of Darrienia, and a collective pause stilled each of their steps. Lifting his head towards the light, Seiken relished the warmth on his flesh as sights and sounds assailed his senses, and the scent of death and oppression was swept away on the gentle breeze which carried with it delicate fragrances of fresh water and blooming flowers. A moment of adjustment, when stepping between such areas, was always required and, having being starved of essential energy for so long, his body overflowed with both vitality and impatience.

"Because she shouldn't have died," Daniel declared matter-of-factly. Seiken looked to him questioningly. "Despite how things appeared, I don't believe it had been Night's intention for Zo to die, at least not in the manner she had. When Zo released the seal on the final Grimoire her remaining essence should have been consumed, leaving Marise to pay the life-debt for the spells invocation. Unfortunately, because I refused to let her go, Zo's tether to me sustained her long enough to ensure she satisfied both costs."

"Night planned to invoke Trítra Thysías to restore her?" Seiken questioned.

"Yes, why else choose a location so flooded with Grand Planetary Magic if not to utilise the greatest aspect of that power. Zo would have sacrificed herself for the greater good, and as such would have been restored."

"That is but one of the paths she has altered," Rowmeow interjected. "The fact she died created a delay in the retrieval of the Spiritwest, and the ancient prophecy had placed the key to access this power in *her* hands. As she died, instead the Mystics were forced into sacrificing a portion of their powers. Even more damning, being Hectarian, she could have removed Remedy from the Daimon, but instead Sunrise was unbound and part of Talaria was pulled to Gaea's star. She has created alternative pathways in what were bound prophecies, and each were events the Moirai would not have permitted to come to pass," he explained.

"Row, whose will is she speaking?" Seiken questioned, his expression hardening.

"Darrienia's." On hearing this Seiken's hurried steps came to an abrupt stop.

"Our Goddess?"

"It appears that by preventing a prophet's birth we also sealed the only means she could commune with us. Thea opened this gateway again, and it seems there are corrections in need of being addressed."

"What kind of corrections?" Daniel asked.

"I'm uncertain. All I know is that since the seals that bound the Severaine were released her presence has been felt again. I believe when your race last sealed the Severaine they somehow imprisoned her as well."

"The fixed locations, you think they acted as a cage of sorts?" Daniel remembered their adventure here well. They had been deceived into destroying the tethers between their two worlds which forced areas of Darrienia to remain unchanged, and by doing so they were responsible for the Severaine's release.

"I believe it was just that. My other concern is that I am unclear on whether or not it is by her will that Íkelos can roam our land."

"Wait a second, you said the Moirai were going to silence the forger of forks, but if she's Darrienia's chosen vassal, then..." Daniel paused, pinching the bridge of his nose, attempting to absorb everything that had just been implied.

"Darrienia has only ever forced her will in times of great peril. If she is using Thea as a medium to change the future it is because there is no other option," Rowmeow confirmed. "Wita, what do you know of this Lavender you spoke of?"

"Only what Thane Algar imparted, that she was a princess sought by a power-hungry sorcerer, and in death she created the Light of Lavender to dispel the darkness he had conjured." Daniel heard the cry of many voices as he revealed what he knew. "But it seems there's much more to that story, but there's so many different versions."

"Can you not ask the imprint of the princess herself?" Seiken knew the complexities of reincarnation, but there was something Daniel had not yet come to realise for himself. When a person passed through the Gate of Shades they left an imprint of who they had been there. This ensured when they drank of Lithe in preparation for rebirth, be it years or centuries from their death, their wisdom and knowledge was never truly lost. This remembrance would await their next passing to be reunited with the essence it had belonged to, and this continuous process allowed the soul to evolve through the experience of many lives. Through ritual and trance some people were able to call on this imprint and remember parts of their life from before, but the Wita could touch this energy with ease, and this was the source of the voices he heard.

"She's not present, does that mean she has been reborn?"

"No, Wita, that means she was never simply mortal." Rowmeow's tail swished, his eyes narrowing. "There is someone we could ask, but I don't think you'll like it."

"Since when has that made any difference to what must be done?" Seiken asserted. "But how will knowledge even help us?"

"Zo thought this warning important, perhaps understanding it could give us an advantage when we attempt to retrieve her."

"What do you mean?"

"Do you think the Moirai are going to simply allow us to enter their land and take her? We will need to prove she is needed, and that somehow the forks she has made are for the betterment of the future. To do this, we must first understand the past." Rowmeow scratched behind his ear before quickly grooming his paw. He knew neither would like what he was suggesting.

"And who exactly do you plan on asking?" Seiken posed, his eyes narrowing in suspicion at Rowmeow's sudden interest in cleanliness.

"Lain."

Chapter 10

Awakening of the Old

Elly cried out, her screams unheard through the silence of the chamber. Raising her fists she pounded at the glass above her, drawing laboured breaths. Her hands came into focus as they struck against her prison. All movement ceased as she witnessed the black material which covered her flesh completely. Her mouth grew dry as her focus shifted through the glass to see the endless spiral of tomes. She knew this room. It was filled to capacity with ancient and forgotten literature, shelves upon shelves, books upon books, to the point she thought perhaps the tower itself had been constructed from them.

"No, no, no, no, no." Her voice broke more with each repeated word as she resumed pounding on the surface, attempting to force the glass lid from the metal casket. This was not where she should be. This was impossible. "What did you do?" she cried, her strength failing as tremors consumed her body. She felt the warmth of tears upon her cheeks, the warmth of her flesh, the beating of her heart, and the small shocks generated by the strange clothes which had served to ensure her muscles had never atrophied.

The glass case opened slowly, her body grew light as she felt herself lifted into someone's arms. But the light outside the case was different. It hurt too much to keep her eyes open, and each sound was deafening. Even this person's gentle touch brought pain. She felt the pressure ease as she was placed upon something soft, draped in warm silken sheets.

"But her hair, it's—"

"Thank you, Elisha, that will be all." Night's voice echoed through her head. He was speaking in a tone barely recognisable as a whisper, yet to her, to the senses unused for centuries, it all seemed too loud. Her chamber had been designed to filter the light and mute sound. She had wanted this day for so long, and now would give anything to find herself within the golem. Her mind raced, unable to comprehend all that had transpired. Confusion washed over her as strange sensations, long forgotten, resurfaced with the warmth of tears as they spilt involuntarily from her burning eyes. "Welcome back." She felt his hand pass over her eyes, dulling the pain. "You can open them now." She did so warily, finding herself looking directly into Night's blue eyes as he crouched before her. "I must say, this is most unexpected. How are you feeling?"

"What happened?" she rasped.

"I am afraid I have no definite answer. What has occurred was thought to be impossible, the strength needed to wake you in this form is beyond any I can comprehend," Night answered. "I can tell you that the tether to your golem decayed long before you awoke. In earnest, I feared you lost."

"The Daimons," Elly whispered, straightening herself.

"The Daimons did this?" Night questioned uncertainly.

"No, Melas has breached The Stepping Realm to their world. Kólasi cannot rise."

"I'm afraid your warning comes a year too late."

"What?" Elly gasped. "How is that possible, Aidan just woke me." Elly felt heat rush through her body. He had achieved something no other Oneiroi had, he had woken her. The image of him touching the obelisk flashed through her mind. He had used what she had told him to push her here, to her flesh.

"Lain, you were expelled from Darrienia quite some time ago. Given that you had suppressed your tethers we feared the worst, more so when the anchor to your golem decayed. We thought you lost, like the Oneiroi you travelled with. Given events, I can only imagine you were expelled to this form, but it has taken until now for your mind to realign."

"I'm mortal?" Elly questioned, raising her hand into her line of sight.

"Well, that remains to be seen. But part of your curse has indeed been broken."

"Which part? How can you be certain?" Night reached back, grasping one of the many mirrors from within this room. He raised it, allowing her to see her reflection. She stared in astonishment at the mousy-brown shade of her hair, she looked now as she had in Darrienia. "Your eyes remain altered, even I cannot be certain what all of this suggests."

"We have to warn them. If Kólasi has risen that means he can access the human plane through The Stepping Realm, just as he can Darrienia."

"Lain, this is one matter in which I must not intervene," Night asserted, pulling the mirror from her grasp.

"Your promises are meaningless if there are no mortals to protect."

"It is not that which binds me in this matter. Íkelos, or Melas, whichever name he goes by now, before being known as such was a god, and he was birthed by Nyx."

"He is your brother?" Elly looked to him, she had long known he had siblings, but never had he admitted to such, not even to her.

"For me to intervene now, when Nyx forbade the offer of aid, would create strife between the Gods themselves. Do as you must, but know that I cannot be the one to guide you."

"But..." Elly raised a hand to her head as a wave of dizziness consumed her, her stomach tightened as heat once more chased across her flesh.

"You're fevered, your awakening has caused great shock to a body that has lain in wait for so long. You must rest, we can discuss things further when your health improves."

Elly opened her eyes, staring at the familiar ceiling. Mere weeks had passed and still she dreamt of her awakening in this fragile form with such vividness. Each time she awoke it was as if she had been newly roused from her prolonged sleep. At the end of the last cycle, when Kronos still possessed the Throne of Eternity, she had unknowingly assisted Zeus in overthrowing his father. The result had been a curse bestowed upon her by the angered god. She had been sealed in a timeless slumber, aware of all, yet unable to interact, that was, until Night had liberated her.

Night, newly born as a god following an audacious covenant with Hades, had recreated the ancient Arte of golemancy in order to construct a vessel her consciousness could be tethered to, allowing her to walk and live within the world she had once been sealed from. For countless centuries she had existed in this form, journeying with the time's greatest heroes and sharing their epic adventures. She had lived and died in every way imaginable. On the golem's death her essence would become confined to The Stepping Realm, stranded between worlds, until such a time the damage to her golem was repaired and she could return to the mortal plane. She had been unable to dream without invoking the rune of boundaries to permit her to pierce the gateway into another realm. Following her latest death she had done just that, and retreated into Darrienia to mourn the loss of Marise.

When her golem had been repaired, she had simply suppressed the tethers between her and the other world. She had never expected that an Oneiroi would not only possess the power needed to wake her, but the strength to force her back into mortal form, but it seemed doing so had been at the cost of his own life.

Elly sat slowly, staring at herself in the mirror on the large dressing table. She raised a hand to her hair, still unable to become accustomed to the shade that was both old and new.

Recently, Night had attempted to encourage her to leave her rooms and explore the towers, or even the world outside, and yet, Elly could not bring herself to leave her chambers. She felt something she had never felt before, vulnerable. She had died times beyond count, never actively seeking death, and the experiences of such ill-fate reminded her she was now flesh and blood. There had been no progress in determining which parts of Kronos' curse remained. She knew she could still access the volumes of information within the library through her watcher, Elisha, although it would not be as convenient as before. Recently, however, it had come to light that there were certain records, those not within the library, she could now recall. By thought alone it seemed Elly could see divine history, the exploits of gods, old and new, as if she herself had bore witness to the events.

* * *

Zo's body was wracked with tremors as she collapsed to the floor. She was vaguely aware of the dull light radiating from the vast array of symbols drawn upon the floor surrounding her. The iridescent shades seemed to pulse with each rapid beat of her heart. Memories flashed before her eyes as she recalled having seen such workings before. Many years ago, Elly had used something very similar to obtain the hair of an Oneiroi. With each laboured breath the true extent of the situation became apparent, her energies had been forced into a physical manifestation. She was no longer within Darrienia but upon the planes of the mortal world.

"Quickly, bind her," commanded an authoritarian female voice.

Zoella pushed herself to her knees, each movement seeming unusually strenuous. Slowly moving her head, she became aware of the cautiously approaching figures. Their guarded steps ensured they avoided the vast array of symbols which, now she studied them more closely, appeared not to be drawn but somehow encased just beneath the surface of the room's walls, and spanned from ceiling to floor. The approaching figures' individual features were lost in the uniformity of their appearance, and any attempt to focus on them saw her vision drawn towards the large feathered wings of brilliant white that trailed behind them.

A chill chased across her flesh as the weight of something being secured around her neck startled her trembling body. The awareness of a rapid flurry of movement from behind had come too late for her to react, too late for her to realise the two figures before her had not been alone in their advance. Thrusting herself away from the firm grasp of the assailant, she retreated, crying out silently. Rising to her feet she grappled with the collar, tearing at the restraint until it released its grasp upon her, and with it removed her voice returned. Blood streaked with tears ran rivulets down her cheeks, her words giving warnings as she backed away from the one who had reclaimed the artifact that had somehow silenced her words.

"The final Mystic will fall as that which protects him leaves," she warned. "With the last fallen he will step into the mortal realm." Zo felt the solid impact of something against her back, realising now she stood at the edge of a marked circle. The symbols had created a barrier through which she could not step. She evaded the approaching figure, falling as their slight scuffle saw her thrown to the floor. He sat upon her back, once more securing the device into place.

"Pass me the bindings, hurry." Zoella screamed silently as she felt him insert the pin within the collar before binding her wrists to a long tether attached to the back of the collar. "A precaution I'm certain you understand. No voice no forks, no energy no magic." It was only as the figure spoke Zoella realised she could no longer feel the flow of her energy. The tether binding her arms to the collar had fused to her flesh, preventing the flow of magic through her. She cried out in silent desperation.

"My lady, it appears she is more than just the forger of forks."

"Your observations are very astute. It appears we have no choice but to call him back. We cannot force her to create a fork when she may speak the will we are attempting to silence." Zo watched the figures fearfully. "If we can harness this power though, imagine what we could accomplish. Call back the Appraiser. In the meantime, I'll see if there isn't a method we can devise to force her cooperation." The female paced for a moment. "Hmm, if we were to induce the correct state of lucidity it would be possible." She crouched down to look into Zo's fear stricken eyes. "It will be some time until the Appraiser returns, in the meantime, I have plans for you, suffice to say it will be anything but pleasant. Who do you think you are to predict our lands will fall? If they let you live, I'll show you what it means to be a *real* prophet, just you wait and see."

* * *

"Lain." Night announced his presence with a knock on the door to her chambers before granting himself entry into the large sitting area. She had lived with him for countless centuries, having her own dwellings in alternative areas as well, but this was one of the two places she truly called home. Yet, even this familiar setting did little to bring her comfort. He crossed the room towards the sleeping area, knocking once more before permitting himself entry.

Elly sat at the foot of her bed, a hardened expression upon her delicate features as she stared at the reflection of herself within the mirror. On the times he had visited her, Night had often found her in such contemplation. He wondered how long it would take for her to accept what had come to pass and embrace life once more. The haunted expression, so unfamiliar to see upon her, made him believe that without action she would remain here indefinitely. "Lain, I have a task for you." She looked towards him as if noticing his presence for the first time.

"I do not believe myself to be adequately adjusted to"—she gestured a hand over herself—"this."

"No matter, I require you to deliver something for me."

"What is it you are asking me to do?"

"You are surely aware it approaches Alana's birthday. I find myself otherwise indisposed and ask that you would deliver a gift in my stead. I would not wish my only grandchild to think she had been forgotten."

"You are passing up an opportunity to see your granddaughter?" Elly's eyes narrowed suspiciously. From what she had been told, for many years he had been undertaking the monumental task of rebuilding trust with the Oneirois, and more specifically with his daughter Zoella. He was still not warmly received within Darrienia but, once Alana had been born, Zoella had ensured that he was given every opportunity to bond with his granddaughter.

"As I said, I have urgent matters here that require my undivided attention. Even the divine have responsibilities. I have already secured the necessary passage and will visit her as soon as I am able, but I would hate for my sweet Alana to be disappointed."

"I doubt I will be welcomed."

"It is taken care of, you're expected." Night presented a small box to Elly, hesitantly she reached forward, diverting her hand to rest upon her chest where Seiken had once delivered a deadly blow. "You will be perfectly safe," Night assured as he offered the box once again. This time she grasped it firmly.

"I am uncertain that I am prepared for my path to cross with Zoella and her husband, but it seems you are offering me little choice." Night's posture stiffened a little in response to Elly's words. "What are you keeping from me?"

"Nothing, I wish my gift to be delivered to Alana, that is all. I assume you are aware of the pathway?"

"Am I to assume you wish me to leave immediately?" Elly questioned, looking down at her nightgown. She could sense Night's impatience, a trait she rarely saw in him.

"Perhaps you could dress first?" Night gestured towards the large wardrobe before leaving her in peace, allowing her the privacy needed. Approaching the large wooden doors she released a slight sigh, her trembling fingers reached out to seize the cool metal handles before giving the doors a tentative pull. Stepping backward, Elly beheld the array of clothes in her possession. She had everything a person could need, from formal gowns to battle attire. Longevity could be tedious, and her desire for obscurity often saw the need to follow the fickle fashions of nobles and warriors alike. Reaching out, she stroked one of the gowns affectionately as it rekindled fond memories, but all too soon her expression soured. She had lived long enough to be blessed in love, but so too did she outlive those whom she had cared for.

Tucked away in the far reaches was an outfit which had once brought her much comfort. With a decisive nod, she pulled on her black leggings and old highwayman boots, before fastening a black front-lacing corset over a high-necked top. Pulling her knee-length coat around her shoulders she carefully adjusted the folded cuffs. To complete the roguish appearance, she buckled the two belts to secure the coat closed around her waist.

She pulled the old tricorn hat from inside the wardrobe. Her fingers tracing the hidden blade within its folds as she looked back at the ghost in the mirror. Memories of fighting rings and a quest for knowledge surfaced. She had been mortal back then, but had known no fear. Perhaps this was exactly what she needed to remember who she was. With a spark of determination she snatched the box from the bed. Night would not allow her to fester here and lose such a large part of who she was. Adventure was in her spirit, and perhaps this small step was the encouragement she needed. Besides, she was going to Crystenia, surely no harm would befall her there.

She looked at herself once more, biting her lower lip. If she was truly attempting to rekindle who she had been, then there was one more thing she needed to do. Removing the small knife from her hat she grabbed her long hair. After centuries of sleep it had grown too long. With a quick and decisive stroke she severed part of the braid at her elbow, and released it from the tie. As she adjusted her plait-curled locks in the mirror, a smile turned her lips. She still barely recognised herself, so perhaps those she must encounter would not realise her identity either. She retrieved her six dice from her bedside table, and carefully secured them in the two secret pockets within her sleeves. With a final glance towards the mirror she departed, her heart pounding in her chest as the door to her rooms closed behind her.

* * *

Arlen encouraged his horse faster, calling to attract Fey's attention as they neared their destination. Slowing his mount, Fey drew to a halt before sliding gracefully from the saddle.

"I must know, if they found this prophet was the will good or evil?" Fey had been mulling over this question since Arlen had first received the communication and requested an escort to this seemingly deserted area for his retrieval.

"They lack the skills to determine such things. Appraisers are few, and the situation appears to be complex." Arlen drew his sword from his scabbard in a smooth motion, his actions instantly alerting Fey to the sheltered isolation he had guided them to. "Well, I must thank you for your service, but this concludes our contract." Fey tensed as he approached. "Your payment, along with a, what do you call it, gratuity." Arlen tossed him a small pouch. "I'm afraid

I need one more thing from you." Arlen placed his hand on Fey's shoulder, instantly he felt his knees weaken as Arlen seemed to draw strength from him. "This world is not the place it once was." He shook his head, extending his blade towards the sky.

Embers of fire burned from deep within the metal, brandishing symbols upon its surface as Fey began to tremble beneath his touch. With a rapid flurry of movement, Arlen sliced his blade across the air, cutting through the landscape and opening a tear in the very fabric of reality. With the removal of his hand, Fey crumbled to the ground just moments before Arlen stepped through the tear to emerge within Talaria. The frigid air assailed him instantly causing his warm breath misted before his gaze.

A small escort awaited his arrival impatiently, relieving him of his weapon and the concealed armour that he had donned for his excursion. Once more in his homeland, he allowed the energies surrounding him to dispel, revealing his radiant wings.

He had received a confused message, distorted by the distance the energies had been required to travel to relay the information. The only thing he knew for certain was they had found the one he had been seeking. The figure to his left wrapped a full-length, fur-lined parka around Arlen's shivering body while the rest of the entourage attended to other measures to help him acclimatise to the cold climate they called home. By the time they reached their destination, all but a single person had broken away from the escort, and he was the one who carried the Appraiser's Caribou skin clothes.

Once inside, his retainer dressed him in the appropriate trappings for his station. Arlen took a brief moment to appreciate the warmth of his attire, and its softness upon his flesh, before continuing on his path.

"We saw fit to bind her to the Labradorite chamber."

"Wise, a Paravátis receives their messages through REM. Hopefully, this will counter the need to sleep," he acknowledged with an authoritarian tone.

"We used quartz restraints and attuned them to keep her in levels of heightened consciousness, but, there is a slight problem..." His retainer hastened, before opening the door. Arlen beheld the symbols drawn upon the ground, his eyes fervently scanning them before his vision came to rest upon the convulsing figure.

"She's an Oneiroi," Arlen observed in horror watching the figure thrash about in violent fits and silent screams. Bruises already marred her flesh, which appeared paler due to the darkening circles and dried blood around her exhausted looking eyes.

"We didn't know what else we could do." Arlen thought for a moment, remembering one of the unique creatures his world had bred.

"Fetch Echo, that should address the concerns without killing the girl." Arlen lowered his hand, aware he was scratching his ear uncomfortably.

"But, I shouldn't leave you."

"I am here to fulfil my purpose. I suggest you attend to yours," he growled impatiently. With a slight shudder he approached the brown-haired woman. He sat upon her back, holding her still to allow himself the motion needed to work the pegs free from her restrains. The instant the collar was free he heard her tormented cries, cries which turned to gasping breaths as he removed the shackles, leaving only the tether, preventing the use of her magic, still fused to her flesh.

He continued to straddle her, attempting to prevent any more injuries as her convulsions slowly calmed. Studying his surroundings, he shook his head in slight disapproval. The selection of this room, when paired with the bonds restraining her, had created an almost perfect, anti-energy alignment for the woman struggling beneath him. They utilised such methods on their own prophets to keep them at a continual level of heightened pain to ensure they could receive their divinations with ease. The difference was, if she received a prophecy she couldn't voice it. He wondered if whoever placed her here had deliberately bound her in this manner. There was much animosity held towards the forger of forks, especially since it seemed she was also responsible for their approaching fall. "Despite how this may appear, we mean you no harm." He kept his tone soothing as he lifted his weight from her. She sat quickly, pushing herself to the edge of the invisible barrier before finding her voice.

"You say that, but you intend to silence me, and I'm not foolish enough to think that binding of yours is what you had in mind." She rubbed her neck, where her skin had burnt angrily in response to her contact with the collar. Restraints like these had not been made with beings such as her in mind.

"I'm sorry young lady, but you don't realise just how dangerous you are."

"No, I think it is you who doesn't realise." Zo stood, feeling the thrill of energy surge through her. The area they had bound her in had contradictory effects, the Labradorite chamber seemed to charge and empower her, granting her strength and awareness, but the surrounding symbols, and the tether still fused to her back, prevented her from harnessing the magic she knew she could call upon. "I warn you now, this will not go unpunished. I am a mother, a wife, and there is nothing that will stop my husband tearing down your door to find me."

"You've already sealed our fate, our 'door' seems meaningless when you've condemned our entire city."

"I'm in Talaria?" Her voice softened for a moment, and she realised she was pacing, almost unable to remain still. The need to utilise the energy flooding through her sent her mind and body into chaos. "What is it you want from me?" she questioned, realising that the effects from the room were not the blessing she had first perceived when the binding had been released. She blew into her hands, realising how cold the air surrounding her was.

"You've put me in a difficult situation. You made the forks in bound prophecy, but it seems you're also the Paravátis I've been searching for. Troubling indeed. Firstly, I must determine for whom you speak." Zo felt herself grow rigid as he cupped his hands mere inches from her face yet, despite the pressure and electricity that seemed to chase across her flesh, their skin never touched. She attempted to raise her hands to distance herself from the oppressive energy. Heat burned within her, bringing a flush of colour to her cheeks as she realised her limbs remained unresponsive. "You, young lady, have a habit of changing things that should have been, changing that which was destined and bringing chaos and uncertainty." His eyes narrowed as he studied her. "This is worse than I imagined."

"Lord Appraiser, I've secured Echo." A silver-haired woman stepped into the room with a small box clutched within her grasp.

"That's—" Zo felt her sight grow dark, and then, as if in a dream, she was watching herself from above.

"Teanna, out!"

"But Errol was detained by the Virtues, they sent me in his stead," she explained placing the box containing some small, opaque crystal pods upon the floor before retreating. Arlen still held Zoella, but he knew it was too late, she had seen her, the human who walked amongst the Moirai. He turned his vision to the woman paralysed within his grasp, her eyes were closed, her eyelids fluttering with the movement of REM. Quickly he grasped one of the chrysalises from the box, placing it within her ear where it splintered, allowing the small creature sleeping within to emerge.

"I'm sorry." His hand clamped across her mouth as he spoke, seeing her tear-filled eyes were now open "You've left me with no choice." He placed another pod in her other ear, repeating the process, his grip on her mouth remaining firm. "Echo is the name we've given to the creature I've just inserted. It affixes itself to the inside of your ears to create Delayed Auditory Feedback. It evolved from a primal species who worked symbiotically with small predators. They would first infect their intended prey, ensuring that when attacked it could not alert its pack to the danger.

"Even now, as I am talking, your brain is being tricked into thinking it's your voice it hears. Now Echo is in place you will hear any words, or any sound, as if they came from your own voice, when combined with the natural inhibitors it secretes it will cause what we call vocal submission. To ensure it remains effective, the lava emits a constant hum, effectively silencing you until it's removed." Arlen nodded to himself knowing his speech was adequately timed to ensure this submission would have taken effect. He released Zoella physically, pausing for but a moment before releasing the paralysis his Appraiser skill had induced. "I'm sorry, but you can't speak a will if you can't speak, and Darrienia's wishes are not all you are voicing." Arlen glanced back towards the door, knowing all too well Teanna had been seen. There was little question now as to the action they must take. This woman could not be permitted to speak, not at the risk of losing Teanna, the woman who, if not for their actions, would have been named the Spirit Maiden.

* * *

Elly walked hesitantly through the castle of Crystenia. She had been more than a little surprised that the Cynocephali standing guard had permitted her entrance. A large bird, whose form had no real substance and was merely suggested by a flurry of leaves and feathers, squawked a greeting of sorts before escorting her to Alana.

The child had been thrilled to receive a gift from her grandfather, but was a little confused as her birthday was still not for a number of months. Elly had tried to explain it away as a surprise, but had a sneaking suspicion there was more to her presence here than the delivery of a bracelet woven from what appeared to be leather and hair. Elly was certain she had detected the colours of both Night's and Seiken's hair within the weave. It was well-made, but not the kind of gift he normally presented.

"Lain!" Elly recognised the voice by the powerful elemental rhythm it possessed, it was all she could manage not to flinch. "I did not believe it would be so, yet here you stand. What purpose brought you here?" Rowmeow had just moments ago requested Seiken to fetch him some pomberries from the garden, a timing which seemed to have ensured their paths would cross.

"I was asked to deliver a gift. I—" Elly felt her right foot slide backward. With her hand raised to her chest, she glanced over her shoulder in preparation to flee. This man had already killed her once. Now, she was in his own domain, and vulnerable.

"The past is just that, but it's convenient you're here. There's something we would ask of you." Seiken gestured towards the opening behind him. She beheld it skeptically, still considering the option of retreat, but she had never been a coward, and refused to show this man any more weakness than she already had. Studying him intently, she noticed the slight droop of his shoulders, and an emptiness within his gaze that somehow failed to mask the deep fury smouldering within. Something was concerning him, something of importance. Elly stood a little taller with the sudden revelation of why she had been sent here.

"Íkelos?" Elly asked, a knowing smile turned the corner of her lips. Night had spoken of his brother, of how he could not intervene. "That is why he had me deliver the gift," she muttered, holding herself now with the posture of confidence she once displayed without effort.

"Pardon?"

"Forgive me, I was thinking aloud. It appears I am at your disposal." She extended her hand, gesturing towards the door so that he may lead the way. She was more confident, not a fool.

"As you said, it is related to Íkelos." A small cat appeared at the opening and sat with a satisfied look upon his face before grooming himself briefly.

"Did you know she'd be here?" Seiken asked.

"I attempted to inform Night of our predicament." Rowmeow gave a small snort. "He would not even listen and was quite adamant he could not be of aid."

"And so he is not, I was tasked to deliver a gift. However, since I am here, shall we?" She inclined her head towards the opening. Seiken responded with a gentlemanly gesture, encouraging her inside.

On entering, the wall seemed to melt behind them, creating the impression of a vast space and infinite horizons. Even for Elly—who had witnessed more wonder and mystery than any one person could hope to glimpse—entering into such an expanse caused surges of vertigo to envelop her.

"You're different," Seiken observed, subtly cupping his hand on her elbow to steady her.

"I am unaccustomed to mortality." She knew hiding such things from him would serve no purpose. The manner in which his eyes critically assessed her revealed he had already felt something from her he had never noticed before, the energy of a dreamer.

"You're human?"

"I am... something. What, has not quite been determined. But when Aidan woke me it was in the flesh." Her eyelids lowered towards the floor for a second as she thought of the annoyingly persistent figure who had shared her last journey.

"You were with Aidan, do you know his fate?" Elly lifted her gaze to meet his.

"Your wife did not inform you? She charged him with watching over me while I distanced myself from the world." Seiken nodded, suggesting he knew this much at least. "Aidan was sacrificed by Íkelos' general to open a pathway through The Stepping Realm and into Darrienia." Elly shuddered, recalling the horrific creature. She had been its intended prey, and would no longer be drawing breath if not for Aidan's sacrifice. "When Kólasi rose Íkelos gained access to the mortal plane as well. Although from what I have seen he has not yet breached the gateway." Elly felt the tightness in her chest as her thoughts lingered on the Oneiroi.

Rowmeow brushed past her legs, moving to sit in the centre of the dead-space before a room slowly emerged from the shadows. Soon flickering candles lined a grey wall, bookcases and mirrors grew from vines in the floor while dust particles, now visible in the candlelight, swirled and became solid, creating a table at which they could sit. Many of the rooms in Crystenia would reforge themselves to meet the desired purpose of the occupant but, to Elly, watching this creation from nothing was spectacular.

"Please, be seated, Daniel will join us shortly. Given the circumstances, we have agreed to overlook past transgressions. In short, we need your help."

"As you have said, but you still have yet to tell me what exactly it is you believe I can be of aid with."

"We need to understand all there is to know regarding the Light of Lavender, its origins to be precise." Daniel appeared to step through the wall to enter the room. He glanced around, noticing how it differed to the last time he had sat in this identical space. He strode purposefully forwards, his stride stilling as the mousy-haired figure—dressed in an attire reminiscent of a highwayman—turned to face him. If not for hearing her voice, he may have not recognised the woman before him as the traitor who had ensured Zoella's death. He saw her stiffen as their eyes met, causing a brief disruption in the confident posture she now displayed.

"My, my, Daniel Eliot, look at what you have become. I never would have imagined it possible." She turned to address Seiken. "With him at your disposal, what possible aid could I hope to be?"

"Lain, we only have knowledge of the lore. Myth, history, and fables become tangled. We need to know the truth, we need to glimpse that which you alone have touched," Rowmeow revealed.

"The knowledge of the Gods?" Elly asked rhetorically. The surface of the round table, which was now the centre-point of the room, began to sink creating a concave dish which soon shimmered with a silvery liquid. Elly knew it was not water within, but liquefied ether itself.

"If you and Daniel could take your positions at opposite sides, we can begin."

The Table of Scrying was a treasure of the Oneirois, handed to them through the dreams of an ill-fated alchemist. When filled with ether it could draw on the knowledge of those who touched it and discern the answer to a question, displaying the truth for all to see. It had once been a tool of justice, used to settle disputes.

The accused and the accuser would each place a hand within the liquid. Their presence would stir the fluids creating animated figures and events, awash with colour and conjured by truth. It had been the product of error—as most genius creations often were—and a magnificent invention which spurred much hatred. There was no question to truth, and those who would normally be acquitted of murder proved their own guilt.

The artefact had been destroyed in the mortal world when disgruntled ruffians—thought to have been heftily rewarded by more affluent members of society—had raided the alchemist's home, but in death the secret was passed to the psychopomps who stored its wisdom in The Cave of Possession, to later be bestowed upon someone they deemed worthy. As something protected by Darrienia, the tools within were available to be used by the Oneirois, to assist the psychopomps in finding a suitable possessor. This time, however, they had requested it for their own use, swearing to return the concept once its purpose had been fulfilled. Since they were in the realm of dreams, the actual table itself did not sit before them, simply the idea of it.

With determined strides Daniel approached, his hand barely rippling the surface of the fluid as he placed it within. His gaze lingered upon Elly, as if sensing her reluctance to draw closer. Swirling tendrils, seeming to be formed from liquid, gas, and solids, danced tumultuously within the depression. Seeing his gaze upon her, Elly slid her fingers within. No sooner had it welcomed her touch, when light wisps formed from the gas, rising to create figures and structures upon the once smooth surface. With bated breath and great curiosity, they watched the images unfold as those touching the fluids spoke the narrative in unison.

Chapter 11

The truth of Lavender

A beautiful goddess had once sat within the heavens, her tears falling upon the bountiful land below. The glistening drops caused small flowers to sprout and thrive, and any who approached these purple flowers were overcome by feelings of serenity and calmness that the goddess, Levánta Lavender, herself had lacked. She had discovered her father had betrayed her. He had known of her alignment to the great Elemental Spirit, and how she was one with this sacred creature in an eternal kinship of loyalty and respect. But he had other plans. She was a powerful goddess, and great power and influence would result from pairing her with the right mate. He had kept her union with the Spirit a secret, and pledged her hand in marriage to the one he had deemed most suitable, a god and the enforcer of his divine laws.

The arrangement had been finalised, and her father would hear no more on the matter. Three days before the eve of their binding she visited the mortal realm. She embraced the freedom in the form of a bird, feeling the escape of the wind beneath her wings, flying without reprieve until she came to rest upon a perch overlooking a meadow, awash with the flowers created by her tears. Within the purple hue sat an Elvin woman, her hands clasped in prayer. Levánta knew her wish by heart, she had heard this voice call to her many times, begging for a divine blessing that was beyond her power to bestow.

The Elvin queen had been a victim of a powerful and spiteful curse, rendering her forever barren. The greatest magical users in the land had tried to lift this enchantment, but all had failed. It was said to have been placed upon her as a child, by one whose loyalty lay with the land-dwelling enforcers of the gods, for they had warned that if this woman should bear a child, it would bring about darkness and despair. There were other oracles, however, who said this child would be a saviour, a bringer of light, and the queen's own dreams spoke of this truth. Yet no power, not even that of true love, could break this spell.

Levánta followed the queen for three days, judging her to be pure of heart. On the eve of her wedding, she watched as the woman slept within the arms of her husband. On silent wings she entered the bedchamber and, blessing the union of the two, embraced a form of pure spiritual magic to become the seed of the child they had so desperately yearned for, unaware that her actions would have repercussions on all those bound to the Great Spirits.

Levánta was born months later, her past forgotten, for any divine being born into this plane loses their ability to recall the life before. They become mortal in all but one respect, their essence would never pass through the underworld and their energies are fated to be reborn in an endless cycle of reincarnation. The child was born with the same beautiful silver hair as the goddess herself and, in honour of this gift, the queen had named her Lavender, as a tribute to the one she believed had answered her prayers.

Lavender was much loved by her people and was unaware of the danger she had unleashed. When Levánta's father had learnt of her actions, he sent her betrothed, a son of the goddess Nyx, to pursue her. Only a god born mortal could hope to apprehend her and reclaim the divine power she had removed from their domain. Retrieving her essence was never the priority of her father. He saw in her mortal birth an opportunity to obtain an even greater power for himself. He convinced her betrothed to follow the path of his bride and be born in mortal form, but the gods aided in his development ensuring, unlike Lavender, he would remember his task and former identity. They made the retrieval of this power the focal point of his existence. When he was born he was named Íkelos, and his parents had no thought to fear the babe in their arms. Had they possessed any arcane skills, however, they would have seen the dark powers he possessed.

This deception had not been well received by those who had befriended the goddess and, secretly, with the aid of the Spirit Elemental she had been protected. Together her allies crafted a new essence, a Fanger. This being would be born in unison with the goddess. The Spirit Elemental would claim her mortal incarnation and share with her his power, and also grant her Fanger the means needed to protect her. This Fanger would act as a guardian, but its birth as a single entity would be noted and so, the Spirit Elemental used fragments of himself to forge more, bestowing them into the service of the other six Elemental Spirits. He knew, given the need for balance, that Lavender's actions would have condemned the other Spirits' counterparts into entering the mortal birth cycle, and so, he bound to each one a Fanger to watch over and protect their newly vulnerable selves.

The Fangers would be drawn to the Maidens whenever they were in danger. It was the only means by which he could now protect them until they became of the maturity required to accept their role. There had, however, been a greater cost to these actions. There was one Maiden who could not be saved, a being of such immense power she was not bound to a single Spirit but to all of them. She had been known as the Mitéra, and she alone kept the peace between the realms of man, god, and spirit.

The princess grew into a beautiful young lady, and the kingdom knew nought but happiness and prosperity until the day her path crossed with Íkelos. For years this young man had walked the land, stripping and stealing the magic from any he could as a means to grant himself more power while seeking his missing bride, but she was always shielded from detection by something stronger than himself.

Íkelos had sought the Elves in order to further advance himself. He had heard of the princess' beauty and thought he may take her as a bride, allowing him to access the hidden troves of treasures and powers guarded by their kind, items that were rumoured to possess such force that even in the hands of man the gods would have cause to fear. He had caught but a glimpse of her as she was placed inside a carriage and escorted away, but from the moment their eyes had briefly met, he knew she was meant for him.

Having spent countless years traversing the lands, Íkelos had gained a fearful reputation. His rage and frustrations had condemned cities to plagues, famines, and death. In his wake, those of great power had been struck down by an unusual malady to which there was no cure. The healers named this spirit sickness Ádlíc, and scribed warnings to any who would find themselves in this monster's path.

When news of his approach reached the Elves, the Elemental Spirit had intervened and had immediately sent Lavender away into hiding. He entrusted a human, whose identity was obscured through a thick-hooded cloak, to ensure she remained concealed from all, even her parents. The Spirit had warned that if Íkelos became her husband, willingly or by force, the power he would wield could enslave the world itself.

The human with Lavender, unbeknown to her or any other, was the Fanger forged to be her protector. She had not yet reached the age where the Spirit Elemental could claim and empower her, but at least he knew this human would protect her until his last breath. The Elves' actions had been praised by those of other races, and they offered their support, understanding what was at stake should their daughter fall into the hands of one so corrupted by the desire for power. They understood, until the strain became too much to bear.

Íkelos had seen this united front, and knew the only way to destroy it was through fear and hysteria. He blanketed the sky with darkness, forcing day into artificial night, and vowed that unless she was presented to him, he would allow all life to stagnate and die. At first the people held strong, certain their prayers would reach the ears of the gods. But as their crops failed and hunger burned, they questioned why *their* family should suffer, why *their* children should go hungry, all for the sake of a spoilt princess who refused to accept a marriage of convenience. They had sacrificed enough, and decided it was her turn to submit.

Their fear turned to malice, and they demanded the Elves revealed the location of the princess. But no matter how many they slaughtered, how many villages they burned, or people they tortured, her location remained undisclosed for one simple reason; there was but a single person who knew where to find her. But no one believed this to be the truth, and the fires across the land poured black smoke into the sky, further thickening the all-consuming darkness.

Lavender was painfully aware of the suffering her absence caused, and it was more than she could bear. Countless times she had tried to flee the sanctuary and surrender herself, if only to see an end to the suffering. However, the barrier that shielded her from detection also prevented her escape. Often she pleaded with Cadel to guide her from that place, and each time, he would speak the words which had implored him to guide his childhood friend to safety.

He would tell her that while her surrender would clear the sky, the darkest shadow of all would be cast upon the world. Íkelos sought power and the adoration and unquestioning servitude of others. He believed he was worthy of worship, of claiming the Throne of Eternity for his own, and creating a world where even The Gods would bow before him. She was the means to see his ambition realised, because she possessed more power than she knew, and by being joined with him, before he stripped all magic from her, he would also gain access to powers that should never be disturbed.

Lavender, for the first time, turned her prayers to the gods. She begged for their aid in saving those beyond her seal more times than could be counted. Her pleas went unheard through the thick, cushioned sky, and she was unaware that this was perhaps a blessing in itself, for if her divine father were to recognise the light from her soul he would guide Íkelos to her sanctuary.

Cadel visited her frequently, presenting her with the meagre scraps of food he had scavenged. With sorrow he had delivered the news of her father's death. Just weeks after, he informed her that her mother had attempted to take her own life. Íkelos, unaware only the first husband of royalty would be granted access to the sealed powers, had plotted and executed the King's murder, forcing her mother to become his bride in hope to claim the power needed before disposing of her. He had doomed himself to failure as, with the loss of her husband, the queen became more resolute not to retrieve that which Íkelos desired.

Íkelos adapted. If he could not exploit the queen, then he could sire a child who would possess her blood, and use it to gain entry. The queen suffered under his touch, but her curse became a blessing, ensuring he could father no heir.

As Lavender wept in Cadel's arms for all the lives lost, and all those who suffered because of her, he noticed the small purple flowers in bloom, each seeming to sprout where her tears fell. He uttered not a word, but he had understood the implications, and pulled her closer, vowing he would keep her safe, no matter the cost.

The path to reach Lavender's sanctuary was a treacherous one, filled with such danger and peril that many-a-hero would retreat, rather than brave the sinister track. Each time Cadel visited, the trial seemed to become more hostile. The longer the darkness held dominance, the more terrors that thrived in such environments emerged. He became a man quickly, learning to trap and hunt these nightmare creatures, but each time a new challenge awaited. Monsters thrived in darkness, becoming larger, more deadly predators in a time so short it defied belief. Long ago he had refused to slay the young, but now the farrows he had once spared had reached maturity, and like all creatures they were not spared hunger's madness.

When he finally reached the sanctuary, he could no longer retain consciousness, but Lavender had known of his arrival. She had rushed to greet him, only to witness the gored wounds staining the ground with his life's blood. With his life in jeopardy she did the only thing she could; she laid her hands upon him and called her Elvin magic to heal his wounds. Cadel's injuries were not the only thing to be replenished by the touch of her magic, the ground beneath him flourished as if creating a soft blanket for him to lie upon.

She knew then what she must do. Stealing the charm—which allowed Cadel to breach the barrier of protection—she stole away, using her knowledge to locate a portal to the land of the Daimons. There she called to them and used the powers within the amulet to enter their realm. They met her as she emerged, and removed her royal crest, returning after some time with a small item wrapped in cloth. The Daimons knew all too well of the humans' plight, but they were bound to Kólasi for all but the single moon at the year's end, and there were those who still resented their kind for their part in their lands being sealed. The princess retrieved a single item with their blessing, and a small gift of fruit and vegetables to sustain her for the task they knew she was about to undertake.

When Lavender returned, Cadel had still not awoken, and so, after returning the charm she placed the food beside him for when he awoke, and set about her task. Carefully she unwrapped the bundle to reveal a small seed, a gift from one of the first deities. Planting it, she placed her hands upon the soil and gave it life. Elvin magic, however, needed balance. Each time she used her skills it stripped time from her life, balancing the energies of life and death. The cost of an Elf using magic was always tallied against their longevity.

Lavender knew the history of this tree and the cost of her actions. The tree needed to not only grow, but flower, something this rare breed had never done. They would shed but four seeds upon their death, having never budded or flowered, but she knew she must succeed. For the sake of all she would unleash the ancient sun god's gift.

She refused to surrender to exhaustion and watched in awe as the tree towered above. Her hands trembled as each laboured breath warned of her approaching end. The world around her descended into gradual darkness until the tree, and the small bud of hope forming upon its bough, were all she could see. As she died, she offered the tree the very essence of the magic bound to her soul, hoping the flower would bloom.

Lavender never saw the petals part as it opened to reveal a beautiful crystal stigma, nor felt the light's soft caress upon her flesh. The light within was radiant, unbeknown to anyone it contained the core of her divine power, and shone with such force that it was later said the clouds themselves were burnt away as the light enveloped the world, restoring life to the decaying vegetation.

Cadel was roused by the dazzling light to find his wounds were healed. He lay within an area luscious with life, yet the joy of all he beheld turned sour as his gaze came to rest upon the aged and withered figure lying at the base of the magnificent tree. Cadel fashioned a weapon from its branches, and vowed to destroy Íkelos, the one who had caused this to come to pass, and for a time he left the crystal stigma—which he had dubbed the Light of Lavender—and the sanctuary to do just that.

When he returned, while victorious, he was close to death, and once more beheld the greed of man. Hunters, merchants, thieves, and noblemen, all attempted to breach the barrier to claim the stigma for their own. When the hour was late, and their attempts had ceased for another day, Cadel stole inside, retrieving the light and entrusting it to the Elvin queen. With Íkelos banished, and Lavender's magic in safe hands, his mission was deemed as complete and he was allowed to reenter the reincarnation cycle. While Lavender no longer possessed her divine gift, she would always remain the Spirit Maiden, and as such, his fate would be tied to hers.

Cycles past, and this divine power went undiscovered. Lavender's Light was forgotten as time moved on, until the moment came for the Spiritwest to be revealed. As four of the Mystics took the sceptre in their hands to unlock the ancient path, the container for Lavender's divine power shattered, allowing this essence of magic to return to the soul to whom it belonged.

* * *

The wisps of ether released their forms, sinking slowly to return to their resting state upon the surface of the Table of Scrying. Daniel and Elly, who had spoken the narrative in unison, fell silent, released from the compulsion to speak the tale. Elly withdrew her hand from the liquid, watching as the fluid upon her flesh became fine threads weaving across her fingers to return to the now still pool.

"What do we know of Lavender's reincarnation? That's what we saw wasn't it, the power returning to her mortal form?" Daniel questioned, his fingers still idly playing within the fluid. He concentrated for a moment, reshaping the ether to the three dimension shape that had briefly been visible before the story ended. As with the reenactment itself, no features were visible. It was just a representation of a humanoid shape, not even their sex was discernible. He removed his hand, allowing the ether to once more rest.

"Nothing, but we can assume that she is whom Íkelos now seeks. If the tale is accurate, then the compulsion given to him by the long-fallen deities will still burn," Seiken mused.

"I was not the only person in this room party to deception," Elly snapped accusingly, hearing the clear doubt in Seiken's tone. "If you care to question my accuracy—"

"That is not what I was suggesting." Seiken raised his hand placatingly. "There's no time for this, we need answers."

"Were the ones dowsed not sufficient, what other questions do you have?" Elly crossed her arms, fixing her piercing gaze upon him. There was something else, something he was deliberately withholding. Her suspicions were confirmed as she witnessed him momentarily glance towards the cat, who sat perched on the outer-rim of the table.

"Well, what became of Íkelos, how did he end up being trapped in the Betwixt and sealed from the Stepping Realm?" he posed. The table had only revealed the answers regarding Lavender, but in doing so had presented more questions about their adversary.

"The Fanger crafted a legendary weapon from the tree which was referred to as The Hand of Deliverance." Elly noticed Seiken raise a disbelieving eyebrow. "Do not presume to blame me for their lack of imagination. Under the Mystic's guidance this weapon was used to sever Íkelos' essence from his body and push him into the Perpetual Forest, where it was thought he would become a prisoner. Instead, he twisted this domain to his own will."

"How do you know this? If that were true would it not have been shown there?" Seiken gestured towards the ether.

"Simple." Elly smiled, she rotated her wrists to reveal the six dice now held within her grasp. "You asked only of the tale of Lavender. I have this knowledge because I am a collector of weaponry." Daniel scrutinised the small cubes in her hand, noticing now they were not as simple as they first appeared. He recalled the few occasions he had seen her cast them, each time a weapon had appeared within her grasp within moments. A voice whispered to him through the silence, causing his mouth to hang agape as understanding and confusion washed over him, and he realised exactly what she held. "Daniel Eliot, speechless? I never imagined it could be so. Perhaps I should have reconsidered showing you such things."

Daniel remained awestruck as he tried to understand the information and the mechanics of what she had just revealed. He stared at the dice, unable to speak, and that in itself brought a genuine smile to her lips. "It would appear I have broken your Wita," she mused, replacing her dice, removing them from his sight. "There is one more thing I know which the ether failed to reveal. Each incarnation of Lavender contained a trace of the power she once held, as such the Spirit Element used to ensure she slept within a dreamer's web, lest the Epiales find her in her slumber and take her essence to Íkelos. I imagine her presence in the Forest of the Epiales would have been sufficient to meet his needs."

"You said used to?" Daniel blinked hard, trying to dispel the dizzying information he had received by gazing upon Elly's weapons. To think such a creation could exist was staggering, within those six innocent cubes was every imaginable potential.

"Indeed. Many cycles ago the lands belonging to the Moirai were in danger of falling. Their lands were so far removed from the world below that there was a drought of the emotions they harnessed for magic. At first they attempted to rectify this by abducting humans, but it was not enough. They discovered, probably through some twisted pathway conjured by Íkelos, that if they were to capture the Spirit Elemental they could shatter its form and bind it, allowing them to utilise its powers to anchor themselves to the land, and draw on the energies they were lacking."

"So that would mean once the Spirit was captured Lavender was unprotected?"

"I believe that was Íkelos' intention. As he had been offered her hand in marriage, he would have been unaware of her connection to the Spirit Elemental, he would only be aware that this being was somehow shielding her mortal incarnation. But it was his own actions which ultimately protected her.

In order to force the Great Spirit into submission the Moirai identified her as his maiden and she was used as collateral, to ensure no comeuppance for their actions. This should inform you of one very important thing, the figure you seek is either with them, or somehow under their protection."

"Seiken, that means Zo is—"

"And what of this Fanger?" Seiken interrupted Daniel. The harsh tone in which he did so causing suspicion to rise as Elly studied each of them intently.

"The Fangers were born of the Spirit Elemental, so when he was captured their awakening halted. They likely still walk the world, but have no tether to draw them to their duty," Elly explained.

"You said a dreamer's web?" Rowmeow batted the fluid within the table, causing its surface to grow flat as the ether was dispelled by his desire. He shook his paw, wisps of the fluid leaving it hastily. "If I remember correctly your kind used to call it a dream catcher, a charm woven of wood, leather, and sinew. The web followed the dreamer. Unknown to them they stood within the centre, and the sinew surrounding them would cause any Epiales, or terrors, to become ensnared and unable to approach. We, however, could see the web, and ride the feathers across to the dreamer if the need arose."

"Do you have any here, perhaps we could give one to Eiji?" Daniel questioned urgently, knowing it was only a matter of time before his friend also fell into Íkelos' clutches.

"They represent dreams, as we are perceived as such they can only be crafted on Gaea's star, but I can give instruction." Daniel thought for a moment and shook his head at Seiken's offer, the voices had already informed him how they could be made.

"Why would Eiji require protection, what have you neglected to tell me?" Elly glanced around, once more noting Zoella's continued absence. "Seiken, where is your wife?"

"Lain, we cannot thank you enough for your help, but unless you know a way to reach Talaria then there's no need for you to become further involved."

"You are seeking a passage to the Moirai?" Her eyes narrowed in suspicion before turning her attention to Daniel. A smile traced the corners of her lips. "From your expression would I be correct in my assumption that your need for this information not only relates to Íkelos, but to his wife?" She inclined her head towards Seiken, never tearing her eyes from Daniel. He could never hide the truth from her, she could read him as easily as if he spoke aloud.

"Of course, why else would you be concerned by the thought Zoella and the Light are in the same proximity?" Elly's vision turned sharply to meet Seiken's horrified stare. "Could it be Íkelos has found a means to corrupt your wife?" Her question met with silence, and a brief glance exchanged between Seiken and Daniel. "Your wife is going to lead him to the Light." Elly gave a harsh sounding chuckle. "Like a moth to a flame, it seems she draws danger to her."

Elly took a deep breath, her foot tapping for a moment as she weighed her options before heaving a sigh. "As it would happen, I do know how you can access the distant lands. I am sure you can recall yourself I have great insight when it comes to archaic methods of traversing realms. After all, Seiken, was it not by such an administration we first came to meet?" Seiken nodded, briefly recalling the time he had been pulled from his home to stand before her in the mortal world. "However, before I show you my hand, *you* must deal answers. There are still some pieces missing from my deduction."

Chapter 12

The Forks

Elly had listened with interest as they recapped everything they knew. Íkelos, as she had suspected, was preparing to step into the mortal realm and, following a carelessly uttered prophecy and subsequent corruption of her gift, he was using Zoella to ensure his desires came to pass. In retaliation to one of her prophecies, the Moirai appeared to have abducted her from Darrienia, but they were aware they had delivered a more dangerous threat to their doors.

Of all the powers he needed to claim to free himself completely, only Eiji remained unaffected by the malady that had afflicted the others, and their theory was that the tree he called home was shielding him from detection.

"Then, I would be accurate in assuming you need to rescue Zoella as quickly as possible. It is likely they will induce a prophetic state and manipulate the fact she can speak wills to force their own divinations and, by doing so, spare themselves from the fate she inflicted upon them. It should prove a simple task, they have the power needed to force such a binding and expel Íkelos' hold on her. However, it is likely once they have spared themselves they will seek to silence her, lest she contradict their plans," Elly deduced coldly, expressing the theory they had all been too concerned to voice.

"You said you know of a way to reach Talaria," Seiken pressed.

"And I do." Elly approached Daniel, leaning in as if she were about to whisper her secrets into his ear. Instead, her fingers unhooked his weapon, seizing it in her grasp. It resisted her touch as she flicked the sections of the folded staff together. "You are the Eortháds Wita, and yet still you do not know what you possess." She marvelled at the simplicity of the design and the ancient symbols carved upon the wooden surface. It seemed incomplete to her gaze, but it would serve this purpose.

Zoella had made this weapon for him as a means to defend himself against Marise. The staff itself had a heart of magical energy, allowing it to split into its different sections to be used in a manner of ways, while remaining joined by a tether of energy. She had made it to protect him, and no other weapon in history could have done so. Daniel had possessed no skill for combat but, with this staff in hand, theories and renditions of techniques he had only seen or read about came to life within his grasp, as if it drew upon his knowledge to force a physical prowess he had never known.

Elly winced as the weapon released a surge of energy, followed by a second, more forceful warning against her unwanted touch. She returned it to Daniel quickly, having no desire to see the ramifications of prolonged exposure to this weapon, not in this body. In her golem, however, she would have been tempted to see the true power it possessed.

"What do I have?" he questioned. He had sought the aid of the ancestors in an attempt to decipher the carvings and understand their meanings, but every time he looked upon it the voices fell into silence.

"How shall I put this?" Elly clicked her tongue in thought before continuing. "When calling upon a lord, you never simply enter their home, you are announced. *That* is your Herald." Daniel looked at the staff with confusion.

"So how does it—"

"You really do not change. Always questioning. It is little wonder you were born for your title." Elly chuckled lightly, remembering how much his constant questions had infuriated her when their paths had first crossed. "To continue the analogy, you cannot enter through a wall, you must first find the doorway. I have already mentioned this, but Talaria is tethered to the land, you need to find a convergence and charge the incantation." Elly looked towards Seiken. "I trust I have proven myself?" She knew Seiken too knew of this staff's latent abilities. He was testing her, ensuring she could be trusted.

"Would you accompany us?" Seiken requested.

"I cannot. Although Zoella may not have realised it at the time, that staff was also forged to protect him from people such as myself." She turned her palm towards Seiken to reveal the angry red welt caused by the weapon she had grasped. "You are still in contact with Miss Night I presume. Talaria is a complex location, you may find her skills in demand." Elly turned to walk away, flinching slightly as she felt Seiken's hand upon her shoulder.

"Lain, thank you."

"Tell your wife my debt to her is settled once more."

* * *

Acha knew it had not pleased Eiji when he had been told he could not accompany them, especially when he heard everything that was occurring. More than anything he wanted to be of assistance to his friends, but it seemed his involvement would incur a greater danger. Eventually he had relented, agreeing to remain within his home, which appeared to keep his presence concealed from Íkelos. Acha knew he was a man of his word, but her stomach still knotted at the thought of leaving him alone.

Acha and Eiji had a relationship of the likes rarely seen. As an Elementalist the aura of wild energy surrounding him had condemned him to a life of solitude, lest he cause injury or death to those remaining in his presence for prolonged periods. She, however, was immune to such things. Her mere existence in this time was nothing more than an oversight made by a powerful being attempting to reclaim his lost divinity. Her father, Night, had once been mortal. He had been torn from Nyx as Zeus had tried to force the primordial deity into mortality, for refusing to align with him in the divine war known as Titanomachy. But one can never destroy that which bore existence itself, and Night had been the result of his effort, an aspect of the goddess born in a mortal form.

Knowing Zeus would attempt to destroy him, Night subtly concealed himself within the mortal world, taking a wife, and conceiving a child, all so he could approach Hades and make a deal to reclaim his divinity. Hades and Night had intended to substitute Acha's essence with that of Metis, in order to trick Zeus into conceiving a second child with this soul. Acha's soul had been displaced but instead of being thrust into the underworld, it had diverted into an ancient shamanic talisman which had been lost and forgotten, buried in the soil, and there it remained until fate found her a body to claim.

The form offered to her had been on the brink of death. As she was set upon by attackers, Acha soon discovered her touch absorbed the life from others, utilising the energy to ensure her own body could remain functioning. For a long time she had believed contact was required, but in times of great need she had inadvertently drawn on the life-energy of the things around her. She had learnt control and balance, but when an act of heroics had seen her and Eiji's flesh meet, she realised the power of his aura more than satisfied the cost of her touch. Being with him sustained her, and in return, her presence ensured the more harmful aspects of his power were neutralised, allowing him to live the life he chose, rather than an existence of solitude.

Her ability to draw on the life of another was not the reason Daniel needed her to accompany him. There was another aspect to her unusual gift. With concentration she could push aside the consciousness of a person she touched, allowing her to possess their form and divulge all the wisdom and knowledge of this being. Over the years, she had learnt much and now, something as simple as a handshake could unearth a person's darkest secrets. She knew Daniel foresaw the need for her skills, and given the task they were about to undertake, Eiji agreed it was better she accompanied them.

Zoella was Acha's half-sister. Whilst Acha had been fathered by Night in his mortal form, Zoella's mother, Kezia, centuries later, had married the god but, as was often the case when a god took a mortal bride, it ended in tragedy.

Acha returned from her reverie in time to see Daniel and Seiken arrive on the borders of what had once been Napier village. When last Daniel had stood here, he had been mounting an assault on a tower drawn down from the lands of the Moirai. The Mystics had forced the monument through to be sealed within The Betwixt, their actions almost condemning all life itself. For the first time, in its long-standing history of disaster, no one had tried to rebuild the ruined village. When the tower had collided with the earth it had caused massive devastation, reducing the small town to dust. Now, all that remained was the still-scorched land bearing countless fissures, and miles of broken shards left scattered and partially buried across the once majestic landscape. Where once the elements had fought for dominance, disaster now reigned.

The small group descended the steep crater, walking upon the scorched, compacted earth until Seiken motioned for them to stop.

"Do you think we're likely to receive a warm welcome?" Acha questioned, tugging at the neck of the fur-lined coat Daniel had supplied her with when they met. Even with the slight chill in the air, it was too warm for this season. "What is the plan exactly?"

"We're going to negotiate for her release."

"And what's preventing them from imprisoning us with her?" Acha posed.

"You." Daniel offered a faint smile as he raised the staff towards the sky. Acha and Seiken placed a hand upon his shoulder as he focused on pushing the energy within it to activate the invocation.

* * *

Zoella lay curled upon the floor. She had tried in vain to remove the strange tether they had affixed to her back. Whilst she was no longer bound, the combined effects of her prison, the dizziness caused by the creatures within her ears, and the suppressing energies of the tether, had exhausted her. She slapped the floor in weakened frustration, wishing she could break the vocal submission.

There was a warning which needed to be heard, something which could still be prevented if only she could force the words. Despite her resolve, despite the importance, her every attempt met with failure, plunging her into a more desperate and weakened state than before. Her arm slapped the floor again as silent, bloody tears mingled with those of her own grief, and ran in rivulets from her eyes as she mentally pleaded for someone to understand the desperation.

"Relax, it will soon be over." Zo startled as Arlen spoke, his voice sending her inner gyroscope spinning as waves of nausea encompassed her. Clutching the floor, as if to steady herself, her blurred vision noticed the addition of newer symbols joining those within the near transparent crystal of the prison. She knew he had been amending the script, and with each alteration her ability to resist and will to fight diminished. Her body grew heavier, yet she still tried to gain his attention with another attempt at drawing his gaze. If he could only see her expression she was certain he would understand the gravity of what she knew. Her breath momentarily stilled as she forced her burdened limb to move. "I understand your discomfort. Our actions are in no way related to yours. We will separate you from Darrienia. If you wish for your goddess to remain unharmed, then I suggest you cooperate. You may not save yourself, but at least your goddess will remain uninjured." He fell silent, for the briefest moment she allowed herself a glimmer of hope, he had looked upon her surely he had seen the importance of the newest message, but when the silence was once more replaced by the sound of his movement all hope, like her remaining energy, was extinguished.

* * *

As the world warped around Daniel, Seiken, and Acha the temperature plummeted. Even their cloaks did little to protect them from the frigid climate. At once each breath became more difficult for Daniel, whilst both Acha and Seiken seemed mostly unaffected by the thinning of the air. When the vertigo from the step through the portal subsided, they found themselves surrounded. Guards laden in fur parkas pointed unusual glass-like weaponry towards them. Spears, swords, and curious instruments were held poised and ready to strike.

Daniel placed his arm on Seiken's elbow, both to steady himself against the nausea, and to prevent his friends from acting impulsively. Daniel had climbed to great heights upon the back of a wyrm, but here he could scarcely draw a satisfying breath.

"Identify yourselves!" A figure demanded, his eyes traversing the surface of the staff Daniel was using to support his weight. He studied them each critically, noticing only this one figure was affected by their altitude.

"You will take me to my property this instant," Seiken growled. He knew little of the Moirai, but they like all other creatures dreamt, and their desire within the dream was to have the brightest plumes, similar to those of the figure before him. By this alone Seiken knew the figure to be a man of standing. "I am heir to Crystenia, God of the Wyrms, Prince of Dreams, and *you* have stolen something claimed as my own. Return it this instant or I will bring a war of the likes you could *never* imagine. I will raze your home and haunt your dreams, and should any survive when I drag you from your perch, then I will make Anámesa seem like a paradise." The figures raised their weapons in response to his threats, to which Seiken growled his next words. "Do *not* test me."

"You claim we have your consort?" The figure stepped forward, his own weapon, unlike that of his guards, was not yet drawn. His hand merely rested upon it.

"You would not dare presume to abduct it from our lands without knowing its heritage. Do not play ignorant, you will take me to it this instant."

"What we have taken was cast away inside a dungeon."

"What I do with my playthings is none of your concern," he growled.

"And how do we know you are who you claim to be?" the figure challenged, his glare fixed firmly upon Seiken.

"Who else would travel beside the Wita, who else would know how to enter your domain? But if it is my power you wish to test..." Fractures in the invisible barrier between them rippled "Darrienia said you would fall, but I did not anticipate it being by my hand." Seiken raised his arms, the anger in his eyes adding power to the stifling aura of his presence.

"Lower your weapons," the guard commanded hastily, feeling the lands tremble beneath his feet.

"You *will* escort me immediately."

"At once, my lord," The figure conceded. Daniel, having watched the exchange, narrowed his eyes suspiciously.

"Your dream webs only protect you against the Epiales. You would do well to remember this," Daniel threatened. He saw the corner of Seiken's mouth turn in a slight approving smile and was relieved to know the weakness of his voice had in no way diminished the threat.

"Summon Appraiser Arlen, it seems we must enter a covenant."

* * *

Acha had watched with interest as heated words and veiled hostilities exchanged between the blond-haired man and Seiken, but the matter of dispute was simple. The Moirai had stolen the claimed property of a god, and imprisoned it for their own exploitation. Acha had never heard Seiken refer to Zoella in such a manner before, and each time he did his posture seemed to tense a little more.

"Why does he keep referring to her as property?" Acha whispered to Daniel.

"Because, in ancient laws, that is precisely what she became when he claimed her. When the divine used to claim humans they became vassals to the will of that god. They lost all thought and reason and lived solely to serve the one who claimed them. They became objects to be used and traded as deemed fit. Eventually the practise was surceased between god and mortal, but one law has remained since the birth of time. You *never* steal the property of a god. The claiming rite is archaic, the fact Seiken even pursued it speaks of his age and the intensity of his feelings towards Zo.

"But there is more than one reason he needed to claim her. You have heard the timeless tales of children born from a union between god and mortal.

There is a reason such a joining results in the rise of a hero. A child of part-god origin will always be in service to their parent until claimed by another. More often than not, they became vessels to channel their divine parent's will and were forced to undertake tasks to see their parent receive recognition and prestige. Did you never wonder why great armies of the past have often had a demigod as their figurehead? The whole army would shed blood in the name of said god, granting this divinity the same power as if those killed had pledged their life as a sacrifice to them."

"So to prevent her from being a tool for Night to exploit, she had to become Seiken's property instead?" Acha reasoned, relieved to see she had understood when Daniel nodded.

"Yes, but Zo was not mortal, and the fact she retained sentience speaks to the truth of their match. I have no doubt he views her as at least his equal, but the Moirai learning this could place us all in danger. The one advantage he has at this moment is that they have no way of knowing claiming was abolished, and so they don't know the true value of what they have."

Daniel startled as Seiken slammed his hands upon the table as Appraiser Arlen's protests became more animated. Extending his finger, as if to punctuate whatever point he was making, Seiken allowed the weave of magic to gather around the gesture. Seizing the energy he cast it aside, causing numerous symbols to come aglow in the air surrounding them. Upon seeing this, Arlen's posture visibly slumped as he looked upon them in dismay before finally giving a slow, begrudging nod.

"What was that?" Acha whispered, feeling the weight of all which just transpired.

"I think they've just reached an agreement."

* * *

Zo was uncertain at what point she had succumbed to sleep. She had known it was inevitable, her body was exhausted and far beyond the reaches of Darrienia. When she felt his touch upon her face, she thought she had entered a dream. His cool flesh soothed her fevered skin and, whilst she couldn't understand what he was saying, he glared above her angrily, as if his vision bore into another figure.

It was a few more moments before Zo could hear the hushed tones of conversation over the pressure-filled ringing in her ears. It took several moments for her to realise her paralysis was no longer caused by her prison, but by the thick, fur-line blankets draped over her. Tentatively she wriggled her fingers, wondering if she had the strength to free herself from their oppressive weight. As Seiken's concerned gaze examined her, she gave a weakened nod, reassuring him. It was only then she realised she was no longer within the walls of the crystal prison. Carefully, he tucked his arm behind her, raising her slightly before dipping his finger within a small bowl of water and tracing it across her dry lips.

"Have they hurt you?" Zo opened her mouth to speak, but no words would come. "Release the submission."

"But, she has a will. If we do that and—"

"It was not a request," he growled. Zo glanced around the room, confusion knitting her brow as she saw Daniel, Appraiser Arlen, and finally Acha. Zo's gaze snapped back to Arlen, rage shattering the final hold Echo had possessed over her.

"You idiot," she hissed, much to his surprise. "Do you know what you've done?"

"That's the will, the prophecy you wished to reveal?" Arlen stammered in confusion. He had never heard of an insult being carried along in such a manner.

"No. This is your fault. Gods, why wouldn't you listen, you could have stopped it."

"Stopped what... what is your prophecy, how can you reject speaking it?"

"I can't reject what has already happened. But you could have stopped it." Zo's body grew tense as the familiar pain radiated through her, trying to force her to speak the words she fought against. She gritted her teeth, resisting. "Daniel, get her out of here." She glanced towards Acha, noticing the look of bewilderment on the Appraiser's face.

"Fascinating, I never thought it could be suppressed."

"Thea, you're speaking the will of Darrienia, she only speaks in times of great importance. We must hear what she has to say."

"She's not the only voice I hear." Zo shuddered. Daniel had taken Acha's arm, but she resisted. The look on her sister's face had already betrayed the message she bore, she feared she did not need to hear it to know what it meant. Zo closed her eyes, there was little point denying it any longer.

"The final Mystic, if left unprotected, will fall to the dreamless sleep." Zo gave a weighted sigh. "I'm sorry Acha, if they'd have listened... she warned this would happen, they could have stopped it." Acha let out a slight breath.

"He'll be okay, he has the tree," she whispered in denial.

"Acha, you're the one who was shielding him. I've seen Íkelos hunt, he can see their magic in Darrienia, it acts like a beacon. He couldn't find Eiji because..." Zo lowered her gaze, "because you were there. Your gift absorbs the power from his aura, it is what lets him live so long with people. It is also what made him invisible to our uncle."

"Your uncle?" Arlen questioned in surprise.

"Apparently so, like our father he is a child of Nyx." She turned back to Acha, who stood with her hands cupped over her mouth, fighting back the tears. "I'm so sorry, Acha. If you hadn't come..." She felt Seiken's hand give her shoulder a reassuring squeeze.

"We need to get you home," Seiken whispered softly.

"There's something I must know first." Zo turned her enraged vision to Arlen, speaking in a slow, emotionless manner. "You said my forks caused problems. I need answers. You said I made the wrong choices at each turn, but perhaps there is a reason that you fail to see."

"First, tell me, how did you refuse the prophecy?"

"I didn't want to say it. When you said my words acted as validation I decided not to, not that it would make any difference now."

"You can decide that?"

"To some degree. It is similar to the times I attempted to suppress Marise, and while it is true she would eventually emerge, I could often delay her appearance. The same appears to hold true here. Now, about my forks," she prompted, finding the strength to push the remaining covers back.

"What do you know?" Arlen questioned, knowing there was more to this than simple curiosity.

"The other prophecy I received, it said, through her forks lies the only hope. We must talk now, while he is busy. He cannot see through my eyes while he is otherwise occupied."

"What do you want to know?" Appraiser Arlen leaned in to confirm her words to be the truth, despite the fact she had already relayed the most dangerous piece of information she could. "Well, I will start at the beginning, feel free to interrupt if I've not answered something. We first became aware of you at the time of your prophesied death. Your essence should have faded into nothingness leaving Marise's essence to satisfy the life-debt required to fully release the Grimoire. You should have faded and she should have died. To reward your noble sacrifice the powers of Grand Planetary Magic would have restored you to life. However, somehow you tethered yourself to the mortal coil, and thus it was you who Hades collected."

"What repercussions did we see from that?" Zo prompted quickly. She didn't know how long she had to seek the truth before she became a risk once more.

"Unbeknown to you, an exiled Moirai known as Geburah had tethered himself to your essence. Your final act of becoming a sacrifice freed him from his prison in The Betwixt. The Severaine's release was always inevitable, but since you were no longer mortal you didn't uncover the information about the Spiritwest and, instead of you opening the way, the sceptre was activated by the Mystics, and it stripped a portion of their power. Thus, your death resulted in the weakening of this world's most influential powers."

"And?"

"We believed the future had the potential to correct itself when we heard tales that the Oneirois had found the means to offer you mortality once more. They intended to utilise the energy created by the return of the Spiritwest to permit you to take the Blind-step and become mortal, but you chose to remain an Oneiroi." Zo looked up to Seiken giving a slight smile. There had really been no choice in the matter. She hadn't chosen to, she had needed to.

"What issues arose from this?" Seiken questioned, squeezing Zo's hand.

"The Daimon!" Daniel exclaimed with a click of his finger followed by some excited gesturing. "You would have still been Hectarian, you could have removed Remedy."

"Indeed. You were the last person capable of wielding such magic, by refusing mortality Remedy remained affixed to the Daimon and, as a result, Sunrise was discovered. A tower was pulled from Talaria, Kólasi was forced to rise as the Mystics attempted to seal the threat, and all life was nearly forfeit."

"But that didn't happen, so what became of these weapons?" Zo prompted.

"I destroyed them," Acha intervened, subtly wiping a rogue tear from her cheek.

"So, just to make sure I'm understanding this. You abducted her because her choices caused the Mystics power to weaken, the release of Geburah, the raising of Kólasi, and two powerful weapons to be destroyed?" Arlen nodded as Daniel listed the points on his fingers. "You really are fools. Don't you see what she's done? Geburah was sealed because when he attempted to wield the Goddess Tear against the Mystics it was incomplete. The power of the Tear should have been an equal match to theirs, and thus in its entirety, when infused with his own magic, would have subdued them. Íkelos now holds the power of the four Maidens, and the Mystics. However, and here is the important part, the Goddess Tear holds a power equivalent to the Mystics at the time of their creation, not in their current condition. If this hadn't happened, there would be no force that could stand against him."

"There *is* no force that can stand against him," Arlen objected.

"You're wrong." Daniel rose from his seated position, his voice holding a tinge of excitement. "Given the Mystics' condition, even with the power of the Maidens, Íkelos' strength would only be parallel to that of the Mystics had they not sacrificed some of their power. The Goddess Tear *could* be powerful enough to stop him. It may be enough."

"Or at the very least equal to what he possesses," Seiken interjected, nodding appreciatively towards Daniel, who had processed the information at a speed only possible to him.

"I have it on good authority that Geburah still possesses his fraction of the Tear. Acha, do you still have the pendant Amelia gave you to navigate the forest when we visited the Elves?"

"I know where it is, if that's what you mean." In response to her answer Daniel gave a nod.

"This may well be true, but, we cannot just let her leave. She—"

"You *will* uphold your agreement, or do you forget she is still my property?" Seiken warned. Zo felt the heat rise to her face.

"She has yet to deliver what you promised," Arlen reminded him. With a slight nod of his head Seiken lowered his head, placing his lips at Zo's ear and softly whispered a disturbing tale. When he pulled away she looked horrified.

"You need not fall," she announced having understood all of what Seiken had said, and what was now expected from her. "If you release the Spirit Elemental, it will allow Talaria to descend safely." She looked to Arlen in disgust. "How could your people fracture a Spirit and use it in such a way? But knowing this brings me to another point I must address, the young lady, Teanna, cannot remain here. He knows where to find her."

"And what would you have us do?"

"Since you will be making preparations to release the Elemental Spirit, you don't need her as collateral any more. She does, however, need protecting," Daniel asserted.

"I never said we would—"

"And yet not to, would be to fall," Daniel interjected.

"I have an idea as to how we can keep her safe." Zo raised her hand, silencing Arlen.

"You can't speak of such things in my presence."

"Very well, I will consent to your release on one condition, we sever his influence. What use would it be to protect Teanna if you can condemn her with a sentence?" Zo looked towards Seiken, who nodded his head.

"I accept your terms," he agreed on her behalf.

Chapter 13

Íkelos Walks

Íkelos had waited for this moment since he had first found himself imprisoned within the Forest of the Epiales, known to those of Gaea's Star as the Perpetual Forest. For countless aeons he had manipulated events to ensure his escape. The seals, linking his prison to Darrienia and the mortal realm, had been breached by careful planning, and now, after finally procuring the power belonging to the last of the Mystics he had all he required to free himself of the bark prison and return.

Since Kólasi had risen he had gained access to the world of mortals. He had been able to traverse Darrienia and through it enter their plane, but only to walk between the shadows, manipulating their forms to cause fear and terror. He grew stronger from nightmares, his Epiales grew in power, and soon, when he regained a physical form, he could finally give life to the Skiá. Darrienia could keep its dreamers, it could keep its fairytale magic, and whimsical spirit of hope. He would bring nightmares to the waking, he would claim his bride, and restore the ancient order.

It was only when he had ensured the Spirit Elemental's imprisonment he come to learn of the true cost of Lavender's birth into the mortal world. Her choice had corrupted the only balance of power which had truly worked, and he would use her gift to once more restore order.

Having greater concerns than those of worship and renown, the primordial gods had once used the Great Spirits and their Maidens to govern the world, but when Lavender's actions had destroyed the essence of the Mitéra the delicate balance floundered and failed.

Íkelos had sworn a silent vow to correct this wrong, and force the return of the Mitéra the only way he knew how. He would drive the world to ruin and remake it from the corrupted soil, and restore the intended form from the time when the primordial gods had first breathed life and dust across the emptiness of space.

For cycles, spurred by the ruling Gods' greed for power and recognition, an order had been created; their task, to eliminate any mortal or being who could challenge the rule of the Gods, and thanks to Paion's intervention The Order had grown from a small congregation to a formidable force. For almost the entity of this cycle, and countless cycles before, The Order had succeeded in orchestrating the death of the Maidens before they could be granted their power. Wars had been waged, villages burned and pillaged, all for a single purpose, to prevent the union of Maiden and Spirit. They had succeeded more times than he could recall, but this time, however, things had been different.

The Moirai had always been corrupt, steering the future to the path which best served their ideals. That future was one where their relics continued to be distributed by The Order, and the love they craved continued to be harvested. Like the Gods, they had lost sight of what they should be, and instead sought only to satisfy their own needs. The Moirai would whisper the name of the mother bearing the child with a Maiden's essence, the name itself plucked from the tears of the prophets, and The Order, believing they served the Gods, saw their target would not be born.

This time, however, Íkelos had used his own influences to corrupt the messages. Parents and children *had* been killed, but they had been the wrong parents and children. For the first time, in a long time, four of the Spirits had claimed their Maidens, and yet until this very moment Teanna had remained invisible to him.

She was the only one whose birth he could never foresee, but now she was almost within his reach. Her role was so much more than that of the other Maidens, as the catalyst to these events there was a special rite he needed to perform. He could not just claim part of her magic, to undo the damage she had caused he would need to devour its every trace. He would fulfil his ancient calling, whilst restoring things to the way they should have been.

Íkelos strode through his forest, his pace never faltering as the leaves whispered despite the stillness of the air. He walked beneath the darkened canopies, to a boundary none but he could perceive, and entered an area of nothingness. No land or grass extended within this small space, and yet a majestic tree stood within, its twisting roots extended throughout the blackness to create walkways and paths in an expanse which was composed of nothingness and the tree. He walked with purpose, picking his path around the gnarled and woody roots until he stood before the base of the tree. Reaching out, he placed his hand upon its surface. Air rushed through and past him as his perspective reversed, he looked beyond the bark upon the path he had just moments ago traversed.

He had been sealed for time immemorial, but only an aspect of him had remained trapped within the prison. He had claimed this domain as his own, corrupting it to serve him. Sometimes he forgot he was still a prisoner, his form a mere shade brought into existence outside his cell. No more. With the power of the Maidens, and that of the six Mystics, this prison could hold him no longer.

Splintering cracks fractured the unnatural silence as the bark of the tree curled and opened, allowing his unified essence to emerge. Now he was complete he needed only to cross the boundary, but to do so he would need a physical body.

Íkelos strode back towards his domain. The trees' energies pooled and gathered, altering the powers he had claimed in order to create a new vessel for his spirit. He raised a foot from the earth, seeing sinew and muscle knit around bone. Segments of roots separated from the trees, coiling around his forming body, becoming blood vessels. Earth rose, coating him in flesh. Leaves and berries fell from the trees, staining his skin, tracing upon it the outline of the muscles and tendons beneath. Metals rose from the ground, thinning and weaving themselves into fine yarns, mirroring each muscular bulge of flesh and twisting into place to create armour.

The joins shone a radiant blue as they were knitted together and sculpted by magic. The metal rippled and twisted to take on the appearance of that which had been drawn by the sap upon his flesh. Everything within his domain added power to the protection he would wear. Each footfall increased his strength until he finally stood at the boundary of the forest. He was a reflection of the very image conjured by those who had once called him the Father of Nightmares. He looked like a man, grotesquely skinned, with the impression of creatures and people trapped within him. The armour appeared to move, with each step he took faces pushed against the hardened metal muscles, as things seemed to scurry below and, within this realm at least, he could hear the screams of those within his domain as his armour fed upon their energy.

Upon the ground lay a mask, the snarling face looked up at him with a twisted grin. He raised it to his face before accepting the final boon, a wooden amulet carved from the energies and power of the forest itself. With the exception of that he now possessed, no magic could be used within his presence. The amulet duplicated the forest's lore. Just as any who entered the forest found themselves unable to wield their arcane skills, no one could hope to use them against him. Everything gifted unto him by the forest ensured he remained a part of it, feeding on its energies and its connections with all things living and sealed within.

He strode across the small plane, to the place the Mystic known as Eiji had once opened a portal into the land of Collateral. The boy had been inexperienced; he had left the gateway open and, now there was no seal preventing him from emerging, Íkelos stepped through into the mortal world, into the perfect place to begin his conquest, a place that touched all others in the mortal kingdom.

Chapter 14

In the Flesh

Seiken's concerned vision traced across the engraved runic symbols throughout the room they had entered. He felt the pressure of Zo's grip intensify on his bicep as she looked upon the strange device within the room's centre. A crystal lattice, formed by an amalgamation of every imaginable colour and crystal, loomed overhead, beneath which stood a marble altar.

"Are you certain this will work?" Seiken questioned dubiously. He knew exactly what they would attempt, and was uncertain they could actually achieve what had been promised. He recognised many of the invocations that seemed to shine from within the crystal's surface, this chamber had been constructed for the sole purpose of removing an influence. That they possessed such a place readily, gave him cause to question the frequency of its use.

"We ourselves have never had cause to test it," Arlen announced, as if in tune to Seiken's thoughts. "It was performed on rare occasions by our ancestors. As the most recognised and proficient Appraiser of our land, it will be myself who undertakes this feat. I can see the energy belonging to your goddess, and that of Íkelos. I witness how they merge and join within her and am certain I can remove his influence," Arlen assured. If he were lacking in confidence, he showed no visible expression of such fears.

"And what of Darrienia?"

"I will leave her untouched. It seems she has the need to intervene. Besides, even I lack the power to remove such a bond."

"That is not what you implied before," Zo challenged, remembering his earlier threat.

"I was distorting the truth to a degree. We planned to destroy your essence, but we knew you would be more cooperative if you thought your resistance would hurt your goddess." On hearing this, Seiken clenched his jaw, biting back his anger. "Now, to the task at hand, if you would be so kind." Arlen motioned towards the altar as Zo looked to Seiken for reassurance.

"Thea," his voice faltered slightly, "do you understand how this severing will be achieved?" She shook her head. "Before you begin, please explain what is to be expected. Since it will take some time I will speak with Acha and Daniel. There is little reason for them to remain here any longer. I trust you will not deny our departure?"

"So long as this procedure succeeds, I give you my word you can depart without resistance. Shall I await your return, or do you trust your consort will be in good hands?"

"Await my return," Seiken instructed firmly, leaving the room and returning to the place Daniel and Acha were waiting.

"Well?" Daniel rose to his feet, immediately releasing his focus on the book as Seiken entered. Teanna lifted it from the table and folded the heavy binding closed. She had been surprised this man had been able to use their tomes with such minimal tuition, yet he had absorbed their techniques almost without effort.

"The Appraiser is confident it will work." Seiken moved to sit beside them. Resting his legs, even for just a moment, was a welcome reprieve.

"You mean it's not over yet?" Acha questioned softly.

"No. It's a long process, and I will remain here with her until she is able to travel. I came to you for another reason. Teanna cannot stay here." Seiken looked towards the silver-haired woman with regret, noticing the red flush upon her face from the tears he had not seen her shed. She turned away from him, collecting the other tomes which had been placed upon the table.

"I know, Master Bibliothecary Clarke already informed me such. I don't understand the reasons, but he said the moment your consort saw me I was at risk," she said softly. Clarke had revealed much more than that, part of her was relieved at finally knowing the truth. She understood now why she was never paired, why people were happy to befriend her, but immediately shied away from any romantic intentions. She also understood why the Rumination Room had always been empty. It had been a space designed for her.

"What would you have us do?" Daniel asked, reluctantly passing the remaining tome to Teanna.

"I need her to stay with you." Seiken looked to Acha meaningfully. "Your presence prevented Íkelos from locating Eiji. We must trust it will do the same for Teanna."

"I'll keep her safe," Acha confirmed, offering Teanna a reassuring smile. The woman returned the gesture before excusing herself to replace the tomes to their designated places. "Did you have something specific in mind?"

"Find somewhere safe, or keep moving. Use your judgement. It's better if I don't know the details."

"And what would you ask of me?" Daniel questioned sensing there was more to this conversation.

"When Íkelos enters the mortal realm, he will use every means at his disposal to locate her. We know he is not above wars and manipulations, but I have more pressing concerns. He is the Father of Nightmares and his presence in the waking world means with enough power at his disposal he could rebirth the Skiá."

"The Skiá?" Daniel questioned, he listened for the wisdom but no answer came.

"You will find no reference to them," Seiken confirmed, seeing the distant look in Daniel's eyes as answers evaded him. "Before this universe was born there was still life, that of the gods, but there were also the scavengers of energy known as Skiá. They fed on the energies of Chaos and Nyx, who had been banished to this void region. The Skiá were creatures able to devour the core of magic and even the essence of a god. Nyx, being of darkness herself, knew a weakness of these beings, and so began the story of creation.

"Nyx danced through the heavens, her movements giving birth to light and stars, but in their creation came a greater awareness of darkness, thus Erebus, the primordial deity of darkness, was brought into being and so too was, Aether, the first god of air and light. As the tide of battle shifted to favour the gods, a prison was needed, one capable of restraining their foes, and thus Tartarus was created.

"It was during this time Gaea's presence appeared upon one of the stars crafted by Nyx. Soon after Selene and Hecate's creation followed and, through alliances, the magic you know came into being. From that time forth deities were born from unions, each seizing power over the universe while the primal deities fought to drive back or seal the Skiá. Such is the reason we do not find the primordial gods amongst the ranks of Olympus, they are waging wars and defending their creations from things those living don't know to fear."

"So the Skiá are an ancient enemy?" Daniel questioned.

"One of many. They were but the gaolers to the void in which Chaos and Nyx had been banished. Their purpose was to consume the essence of anything placed within." Seiken looked to Daniel, recognising the spiralling thoughts that filled his mind. "So you've already realised this alone means a far greater threat lies beyond our sight. The Skiá are gaolers, grunts to other forces, and even I cannot tell you who governs them."

"How does this relate to what you need from me?" Daniel questioned, fighting back his desire to learn more with the necessity of focusing on current events.

"Nyx used light to injure the Skiá, but they never truly died, and Tartarus could only restrain them for a finite period before their presence sapped its strength. Eventually, as the primordial gods grew in power, another landmass was created in which to contain them, a place that existed on the verge of all realms allowing its energy to shift so the Skiá could not adapt. Upon this land grew prisons, designed to ensnare a living being and feed upon their energy and essence until it ceased to be. The primordial gods had mirrored the method by which the Skiá had tried to erase them, turning their own techniques against them by using a physical place to mirror the effect."

"You don't mean—"

"The Forest of the Epiales," Seiken confirmed.

"Wait, I thought the Perpetual Forest was initially a thoroughfare. A place where beings from one realm could visit those of another, how could that be, if it were a prison?"

"A thing can serve more than a single purpose. The Forest of the Epiales was created upon Gaea's Star, but it was also a part of everything. Its location existed in a physical convergence of all, simply because it was where Nyx first began her creation dance. Places such as those have power. When the Mystics fractured the realms to seal Kólasi, it was inadvertently one of the landmasses lost to The Betwixt. Its physical presence was removed from your world, but its impression and the means to gain access to it still remained. But we digress, the danger is simple, Íkelos twisted this prison into his own domain, and the Epiales were born from the essence of the Skiá."

"Wait, you don't mean..." Daniel gasped.

"All within the forests are servants to its master's will."

"So if he brings the Skiá here..."

"We need a way to engage them," Seiken confirmed. "We know they're weak to light, that was why before he was sealed Íkelos had blanketed the sky. Back then he was naive, assuming he could control their power, fortunately he was stopped before he could attempt to bring them forth. If he had tried to twist them to his will he would have failed, but now as master of their prison he can create a special opening, one to draw and revive the ancient essence, and as it will be born from the forest, it will be his to control until his purpose has been completed. He will cover the sky and call his army, an army whose power will grow, an army who will be looking for—" Seiken's eyes met with Teanna's as he heard her gasp. He realised that no one had taken the time to fully explain the situation to her.

"Then, wouldn't I be safer here? We're above his magic, even if he seals light from the land below, surely he can't reach me."

"But, Teanna, Talaria will fall, or descend. You won't remain sheltered for long. He knows you're here. It is better we take it upon ourselves to protect you from him."

"But... would it not be for the best if I were to simply surrender myself, what difference could my power make?"

"And therein lies the question. We don't know why Íkelos needs you, but if he's willing to go to such lengths, you can assume it will bring more evil than would befall the world if we defend you." Seiken stood, pacing. He had no understanding of why she was so important, or why Íkelos would go to such vast measures in order to acquire her.

"And the story begins anew," Daniel muttered. He looked to Seiken, filled with understanding. "I'll do what I can. We need a way to combat these things, to save as many people as we can, until we can devise a means to stop him. I'll see what I can discover."

"First, I need you to inform the Master and Commander of the situation. Once you have done so we will meet you in Kólasi."

"Why Kólasi?"

"We need to get the Goddess' tear, but to do so I will require both yourself and Thea to accompany me."

* * *

Rob regretted having ever considered that finding Daniel Eliot would be a simple task. He had returned to the store, where their paths had crossed before, in search of Eiji and Acha, certain they would consent to him using their gossip crystal so he might speak with their friend. However, to his frustration, the emporium was closed. The maroon tent was bare and secured, and the cascade windows—where Acha would normally attend to customers—were bolted closed, and held a note written in beautiful handwriting expressing that they would reopen during the second week of Dekatreís. Since the thirteenth month was nearing its end, this message did little more than send an uneasy feeling coursing through his veins.

Manoeuvring through the sealed partition of the awning, he approached the door. After a firm knock he rattled the handle, remembering how on one of his visits he had carefully picked the locks to gain entry to use the very crystal he now sought. The cool metal of the handle began to warm in his grasp as he contemplated his next move. He had hoped the sign within the window had been a mere oversight, but the lack of light beneath the small cracks of the door suggested the house was, as he feared, empty.

As he stood, a chill crept over him. Eiji was a Mystic, their absence here could only have one possible meaning. While tending to Peter, Galen had advised that those suffering from Ádlíc were being attended to within the walls of the two great castles. If Eiji had been afflicted, it would take very little effort for him to determine where he now resided, especially since certain portals of Collateral emerged within close proximity, and he would surely find Acha, and their crystal, beside him.

His grasp slipped from the handle as a new realisation struck him. As yet, he had received no contact from Stacy, despite her promise that she would send word via a Herald when she reached Amelia's home. The silence of the street seemed to close in around him whilst his own thoughts were riddled with disquiet. He banged on the door once more, louder, with more force, knowing it was futile, yet still hoping, praying, that someone would answer and his own instincts were wrong.

Shoving his hands into his jerkin's pockets he walked away, heading towards the main Plexus. If Stacy had tried to contact him it was possible the message had been delayed. Before journeying to either castle he would visit the Main Plexus. If nothing else, he could liaise with the Physicians' Branch to obtain the current affliction rate and see if there had been any progress on a cure. Galen had informed them Peter was the seventh victim, if the figures had increased it was likely either Stacy or Eiji, or perhaps even both, would be amongst the fallen. His pace quickened, his long strides turning into a sprint as he dashed through the great city.

* * *

Zo lay back upon the altar, a cold shiver escaped her as Arlen touched the marble platform, allowing a viscous fluid to emerge and flow across her body, sealing her upon the surface completely. Her eyes were filled with terror as she stared at the crystal lattice above.

Arlen had explained the procedure, how painful it would be to endure, and how it was unlikely she would lose consciousness.

Energy from the lattice would be channelled to simultaneously pierce multiple places along her twelve primary meridians. This was done in such a precise fashion the energy flowing through her body would freeze, allowing Arlen to identify, locate, and remove the weave of influence sown by Íkelos.

When Seiken returned, she was already in position. He reached out, touching her face gently. The Moirai's method of removing an influence were kinder and quicker to recover from than that Rowmeow would have needed to employ.

With Seiken's consent to begin, the lattice came aglow and her body appeared to tense as the energy penetrated her. Had she been able to, he knew she would have screamed. But she was paralysed, by both the altar and the energy above.

Arlen moved with speed as the lattice pulsed with energy. Painfully long seconds passed before it dulled and he took a step backwards, lifting his hands away. Seiken heard Zo draw in a gasping breath, but no sooner had her need been fulfilled, the glow began anew, the paralysis returned, and Arlen continued.

It was a slow, arduous task. Seiken watched as the barbs from one of Arlen's feathers extended to pierce her flesh. The white tethers burrowed into her to seize and remove the unwanted energy. The feather would change colour in his grasp, turning from white to black, and Arlen would place it with the others within a crystal container. Normally the feather would vanish shortly after being used, and the energy would be returned to the one who had used it. For tasks such as this, however, the impurities first had to be cleansed, lest the corrupted energy be transferred to the one who had performed the task.

Seiken noticed that whilst Arlen removed but a single feather each time, his wings visibly thinned, proof that he was consuming more magic to complete this task than a single feather could supply.

When at last the final feather was discarded, Arlen sank weakly to his knees, gasping for breath. Several moments of weighted silence passed until he looked up to Seiken and nodded.

"Thank you," Seiken acknowledged as the lattice rose. The fluid restraining Zo receded, allowing him to lift her limp and exhausted figure tenderly into his arms. "We shall take our leave, she will not recover well in this world."

Arlen watched as Seiken departed. Like himself, the Paravátis had been exhausted. He could see the skeletal structure of his almost-bare wings, their stark and jagged appearance akin to a tree in the final throes of autumnal shedding. Their bareness served as a humbling reminder of the intensity of the task he performed. Bringing his trembling hands to rest upon his knees he closed his eyes, his focus rewarding him with the warmth and weight of magic as ether flowed through him, replenishing his reserves. Opening his eyes he saw the white-energy down begin to thicken, and relished the feeling of his vigour returning.

Once he was rested, he rose to his feet, shivering against the chill of his sweat-soaked clothing, before turning his focus towards the crystal bowl, still overflowing with the blackened feathers. He began to cleanse the ether, pausing for a moment. A trick of the light briefly convinced him one of the now fading feathers had not been quite as dark as the others. He blinked, seeing the afterglow from the crystal lattice still dulling the colours of the room. Feeling the gritty sting of his eyes he looked upon the empty bowl, even now areas of it seemed lighter than the rest as the afterglow of the energies moved with his vision. Rubbing his eyes, he decided it was better to return to his chambers and rest before reporting the course of events.

* * *

The sound of Íkelos' frustrated growl echoed through his armour as he emerged from the portal. He had never visited Collateral, but he knew this mountain ledge, overlooking the fog-shrouded lands below, was not part of the Travellers' City. Through Daley's windows of scrying he had seen much of the world, however, during that time he had been seeking something specific, as such, the visions he beheld had flitted from one great power to another, as he drew upon the Daimon's gift to search for the very powers he had needed to return. Even since the gateways had been opened for him, until now he had not trod the soils of the mortal land, merely played within the shadows opened to him by the nightmares delivered by his Epiales.

Removing his helm he placed it under his arm, taking his first slow, deep breath of the fresh air. The smell of baking bread and roasting meat teased the air, altering him to the possibility of a town shrouded deep within the blanketed land below. He inhaled again, tasting the air, his olfactory senses had always been extraordinary, they had to be in order to detect and track the delicate odours of magic.

"Hail down there!" Called a chipper voice from the cliffs above, beckoning his attention. He raised his head slowly, shielding his eyes instinctively from the sun's glare. "You appear to be in a spot of bother. Luckily for you I'm passing." A thick rope descended from above, blowing wildly in the strong current of the rising winds.

"So it seems," Íkelos answered curtly, replacing his helm. An altruist was the last thing he needed, they had a tendency to talk about their good deeds, and whilst it was unlikely anyone would recognise the threat, he could not risk people knowing he had emerged.

"Secure yourself, I'll pull you up." Íkelos looked up to the slender figure, wondering how such a slight form could possibly hope to bear his great weight for the climb ahead. "I've a draught horse, really, are you going to quibble over the details?" the figure questioned. Íkelos grasped the offered rope, scaling the cliff with ease.

"Where, by all the stars, am I?" The figure moved as if to grasp Íkelos' arm and lead him towards the track, but as soon as his hand touched the chilled contours of the armour, it retracted quickly.

"That armour is... well, is it an heirloom? I couldn't fathom why else—" the figure choked, gasping for breath as Íkelos squeezed his hand around his neck. "What, are, you?" With an impatient snarl, Íkelos tightened his grasp, crushing the remaining life from the figure before tossing the limp corpse aside. His return had not gone as planned, but no matter, such an inconvenience merely delayed his progress and could easily be rectified.

Surveying his surroundings he looked for the promised draught horse, but observed no evidence of such a beast's passing. With disregard, Íkelos pushed the figure's motionless body over the cliff edge with his foot. Casting a glance towards the beaten track he shook his head. This may not be as straightforward as he had imagined. It seemed that despite his realm being connected to Collateral, he himself had been denied entry. It would delay him, but what did a manner of days matter when he had waited for a time beyond measure for the coming of this day?

Chapter 15

Debts

Bray groaned as consciousness returned. His ice-cold hands gently rubbed his swollen neck. The injury he had sustained would have killed a human, fortunately, he had been well fed when the ruffian set upon him. He was just grateful his attacker had caused no permanent damage. His body was quick to heal, but he was not immortal. That had not been the kind of gratitude he had expected when offering his assistance to the stranger. Then again, his own intentions had been anything but pure.

He had been journeying to this specific location in order to gain access to Collateral, when the powerful scent had caught his attention. It had stirred a curiosity within him he had not known since his path had first crossed with Taya's. There was a magic in his blood he did not recognise, and foolishly he had sought to learn more, incorrectly assuming he could do both a good deed and earn a rather unique meal from his heroics. Bray rolled his neck trying to quell the burning pain. With a slight shrug he glanced around, at least the portal was now accessible, it wasn't as if he could have simply descended and vanished while another person kept vigil on his movements. Collateral was a guarded location, and revealing its portals was something not to be taken lightly.

Bray had spent the last six months within Misora, utilising their knowledge in the hope of gaining some insight into the whereabouts of Paion. Updating Rob on his progress—or lack thereof—was long overdue, and besides, another pressing task had beckoned him here with haste.

After Paion had escaped, Bray had confided to Rob his intention to pursue the Moirai. He knew beings as focused and committed as Paion would never still their ambitions, they would look for new methods to achieve the same result. The latest revelation, of the person Rob was following seeking a prophet, had sat uneasily with him, forcing the recollection of how he had exploited Taya's gift to ensure his success. This expelled Moirai was too dangerous to be left to his own devices. Bray had witnessed firsthand his maliciousness.

"The cur," Bray cursed, patting down his pockets, releasing a relieved sigh as his fingers wrapped around the scroll in his possession. His brow furrowed, his hand once more caressing the bruising on his flesh. He had never felt such raw power before, the moment he had grasped his arm he had felt the dark tendrils of the figure's energy at play. Fear had gnawed at him, as if a primal part had recognised something of who, or what, that figure was. Recalling the strange armour Bray shuddered, before taking the step into Collateral and trying to push the encounter from his mind.

* * *

Zo leaned into Seiken as he wrapped his arm around her. His attempt to shield her fatigue and unsteadiness from sight ensured to any observing they would appear as two lover's walking together. Her pace was slow, her vision appearing to absorb every detail of the magnificent structure before them. She had heard much about the Daimon city known as Eremalche, but had never believed she would have cause to stand upon Kólasi's soil.

Before departing from Talaria, Seiken had arranged for a message to be relayed to the Kyklos, informing them to expect their arrival. He was certain such an announcement had caused unrest. Knowledge of the Oneirois' existence was limited, and of those who knew their dreams had guardians, few realised they could take physical form upon the mortal plane.

Taking a shaky breath, Zo leaned closer into Seiken, her bleary vision underplaying the brilliance of the magnificent, magical energy encompassing the impressive city.

"I wish I could have asked you to return home, but your presence is key to our negotiations, and we can't delay." Seiken paused for but a moment to allow her a slight reprieve.

"You worry too much," Zo whispered, her body shivering. Daniel, seeing their arrival, hurried towards them, his approach halting as he beheld the weakened condition of his friend. Removing his backpack he removed a fur-lined cloak from within, before continuing his advance to drape it around her shoulders.

"How are you holding up?" he questioned, feeling the intensity of her tremors as his hand stroked her arm.

"I've felt worse, but I'd be lying if I said I wasn't eager to return home."

"Did it work?"

"I hope so," Zo answered as Seiken nodded his head. "I don't think I could endure that again."

"You'll feel better after some rest," Daniel reassured, relief washing over him. They continued at a slow pace, towards the magnificent city. Night had fallen, and the walls had closed around the city, protecting it from danger. Seiken gestured towards the sky, hoping the beauty of the ribboned lights above would distract her enough to encourage her to continue. He knew she didn't wish to appear weak before them, and he fought the urge to take her within his arms to carry her.

"What are they?" Zo asked in awe, watching the magnificent lights snake across the sky in a vast array of colours.

"It's known as the Dance of the Spirits." Daniel smiled, a mischievous glint reflecting in his own eyes. Now he had set foot upon this land he could hear the voices of their dead. Not those belonging to the Daimons, but of the partners they had taken from other species. He heard tales of how the Daimons, like gods, did not pass through the Gate of Shades, their essence became of the earth, cleansing and recharging its energies and becoming part of the land and sky until it could be reborn. "It is magic and spirits, combining in an ethereal dance. The Daimons were created to stand as a being between the gods and the first humans and forge an understanding. They were the mediators of all disputes because they were created with a gift exceeding empathy, allowing them to fully embrace the perspective of another, seeing, hearing, even feeling as they did. These lights were a beacon of hope, a force uniting earth and sky. They've not been seen on our world since the Daimons were first imprisoned."

"Can you commune with their impressions?" Seiken asked in surprise.

"No, but they have taken partners from many species, those are the ones who speak with me now." He looked as if he wanted to say more, but fell silent as a figure approached them. Her dark brown hair had been elegantly braided to accommodate the gemstone-adorned, crown-like headdress that identified her as a member of the Kyklos. Delight reflected in her eyes as she offered them a welcoming smile.

"Lord Seiken, I am Meredith of the Kyklos. Have you eaten?" Seiken felt Daniel grasp his arm gently before Seiken could speak. The gesture amused him, as did the thought that the Wita was concerned he did not possess the required insight into politics and etiquette to understand the respect intended in the greeting.

"Thank you, Lady Meredith, we would be honoured to join you at your table," Seiken advised, feeling Daniel's grip soften. "Might I introduce my wife, Lady Thea, and the Wita of the Eorthåds, Daniel Eliot." Seiken turned and winked at Daniel, a gesture only he could see, and smiled as the Wita relaxed with a slight look of embarrassment briefly crossing his face.

"Spirits, I never imagined we would receive such honoured guests." Meredith turned and bowed to Daniel. "I must thank you for all you did for our Sfaíra. If not for your intervention our future would have been very different."

"I was not alone, everyone involved was pivotal. How is she faring? When last I saw Taya we were transporting her from Kalia, her situation was grave."

"She hopes to speak with you herself before you depart. She regrets she cannot be here personally to greet you. I have been tasked to escort you to the Regent in her stead." Daniel nodded his understanding. Over the last year he had often wondered how the Daimon had fared. "If you will follow me." The figure turned with grace extending her hand forward in a flowing motion as she led the way. "Eremalche was designed countless of your cycles ago, it was to be a stronghold city to protect us from the war. Although the walls surround us now, you will witness they take on a near-transparent hue, allowing us to see the spirits of our people who are awaiting their rebirth." Meredith had felt the tension amongst the group, and decided rather than an uncomfortable silence she would put them at ease with a tale of their city. "Our five outer districts are connected by portals, but given your origins I imagine nothing you witness here will be beyond your comprehension, but if you have questions, please ask." She paused as they reached a structure forged from stone and wood. When Meredith placed her hand upon it a shimmer expanded, tracing the internal framework before converging at the gateway's centre, causing an iridescent glow to ripple the air before them.

"Lady Meredith, my wife and I are unable to use Gaea-based portals."

"Do not concern yourself, our connection to the ethereal saw its architects allow transference of spirit and flesh. You will find no issues here. You have already noticed I am not actually present beside you." Meredith smiled as she saw Daniel study her again, he glanced to Seiken, reading a new meaning into the wink he had received. "The Sfaíra requested I attended in ethereal form to greet you, in case you harboured any such concerns."

"She need not have worried, we would have taken you at your word," Zo assured, Meridith looked to her with a concerned frown at hearing the weakness in her voice.

"Some transgressions of the Order left deep scars. For ten years she was lost to us and made to believe her identity was a lie. Sometimes she still doubts herself, and if she doubts she assumes others will also, hence my apparition." Meredith paused for a moment, as if considering whether to say more. After a short period of silence she gestured toward to portal before stepping through.

"It seems you underplayed your role when you told us of your heroics." Zo smiled, looking to Daniel.

"Really, Zo, I didn't do much. Shall we?" Daniel stepped through, allowing Seiken to remain by her side providing the support she needed.

"You know you'll never hear the full rendition don't you?" Seiken whispered. "He's too modest to seek glory, and not arrogant enough to be a braggart."

* * *

Geburah sat within the tactical room, watching as the cuisiniers placed a cloth upon his table, covering the engraving of the ancient map. He groaned inwardly.

"I thought I was having an audience, not a dinner party," he grumbled, rubbing his stomach. Cold meats and cheeses ladened the table, interspaced with dishes of vegetables and fruits, most of which had been dressed and prepared in a way unique to their people. He swore with each new dish the overburdened table groaned as much as his own stomach, which protested at the thought of another banquet. Since Kólasi had opened its ports to visitors he had sampled more varieties of food than he had imagined existed.

The Traders' Plexus, excited by the prospect of new trade, had been sending packages of their many wares for him to sample. The thought of sharing another meal with someone sent his stomach into a frenzy. It wasn't only the

Plexus, each time someone would arrive for an audience their escort would greet them, asking if they had eaten, not wanting to appear impolite they always accepted the offer of hospitality. His room grew more like a banquet hall with each passing day.

He had suggested their guests be taken to dine *before* meeting with him, but Taya had insisted that he broke bread with his visitors when she could not do so herself. He tried to dissuade her, saying his appearance would likely ruin their appetite, but she merely chuckled, dismissing his concerns. While Taya was slender, with the dark hair and fair skin common amongst the Daimon, he was a monster. His Herculean form towered above most who would stand before him and, if they overlooked his leathery, ash-coloured skin, their eyes would become fixated upon his wings. Occasionally, if they were unable to avert their gaze, he'd hear the cringe-worthy pitch of shrill, maniacal laughter caused by the unsettling effects of the Lampads' light reflected by his plumes. This often came as a welcome reprieve, as it gave him cause to briefly excuse himself.

Geburah, before the Daimons had been sealed, had once been a Moirai. He had once bore the same pristine shaded wings as they did, but that was before they had stripped his magic and sentenced him to eternal suffering in Anámesa. Over time, the Lampads had befriended him, their kindness causing a new magic to replace that torn from him. His feathers returned, but they were no longer white but the same hues of blue, purple, and green which burned within the Lampads' torches. It was a light said to be able to drive any mortal to insanity. The plumes burnt and died, shimmering like the burning embers of a fire. While Daimons felt mere discomfort in his presence, humans, however, suffered more visibly, and were often grateful to focus their attention upon the plates before them.

Geburah rose, stretching and twisting in an attempt to prepare himself. He wondered what possible business the Oneirois could have with him. Had they extended the request for an audience a year ago he could have, perhaps, understood. Daley had not been the only creature trapped within the forest when Geburah had attempted his rescue. The gateway he had witnessed open had been to Darrienia, but the events themselves still made little sense. To this day, all he knew for certain was that the place Daley had been held had fed on magic. Perhaps the Oneirois also sought insight.

"Show them in." Geburah nodded towards Meredith as she appeared in the doorway leading from the audience chamber. He turned towards the door, outstretching his arms in a welcoming manner as the small group entered, he plastered his well-practised smile on his face, attempting to look friendly and casual. His smile froze, and his arms hovered uncomfortably without instruction as his gaze fell upon Zo. For but a fraction of a second his entire body tensed and froze in a reaction of genuine surprise.

"It's you!" he boomed. He knew this woman, she had been his salvation. Before he was aware of his actions he had closed the distance between them to take the young lady in his crushing embrace, briefly lifting her from the floor. "Thank you." He released the fragile figure, studying her intently, and understanding more of the reason Kitaia had asked him to attend to this matter in her stead. He was certain she had known of their connection. "But how? You died." Zo's face was filled with confusion as she looked at him with unfamiliarity. "Forgive me, where are my manners. Please be seated, help yourself to refreshments. I am Geburah, Regent to the Daimons." He gestured towards the table, regaining his composure.

"You're Geburah?" Zo asked, a delicate smile tracing her lips. "So you're the one freed by my death. It's a pleasure to meet you." She wasn't sure what else to say. The figure before her had once called to her on the wind, and almost charmed her magic into prematurely committing the very sacrifice that had freed him. She recalled that Elly had referred to him as a demon of destruction, yet being in his presence did not trigger any sense of foreboding. Realising she was staring, she straightened her posture, and continued to talk. "This is my husband, Seiken, and next to him is Daniel Eliot, Wita to the Eorthåds." Daniel flinched as Geburah's giant hand wrapped around his own, clasping it with a clearly practised, gentle strength.

"It seems we owe you a great debt as well. Tell me, what brings you to our land. Whatever you would ask of us, consider it done." Geburah clapped his hands summoning one of the cuisiniers. "Bring us the finest bottle of elderberry and cherry mead. Such honoured guests deserve nothing less."

"At once, my lord."

"Please, it's not necessary—" Daniel began, growing quiet as Geburah raised his massive hand.

"Nonsense. If not for Zoella I would still be bound to my prison, and if not for you our lands would not have their Sfaíra. It is only appropriate you receive a small show of my gratitude. Please sit, and tell me how we can be of aid."

"Lord Geburah," Seiken began, thanking the returning cuisinier as he placed a goblet of pale red fluid before him. "We have just returned from Talaria."

"You're the one who's been making the bound prophecies fork?" Geburah deduced. It was the only logical explanation as to why she was alive.

"It seems I did more than just free you. My actions resulted in numerous consequences, one of which is what brings us to you." Zo leaned forwards on the table, trying to keep herself composed. Her body still trembled from pain and exhaustion. It was only as she raised the goblet to her mouth, Geburah realised what he had overlooked.

"You're an Oneiroi."

"Yes, I am the Willsayer of Darrienia, but another being had been using me to bring about their desires. It is because of them we find ourselves here."

"It must be important, I can see how much you need to return to your land. Please, eat. Whilst it's not of your world, it does contains spiritual energy. It may replenish you, if only a little." Zo placed her hand on Seiken's arm, suggesting he should continue while she accepted their host's gracious offer of food.

"Lord Geburah, you are correct, we have come here to seek a favour. The Melas-Oneiros, Íkelos as he may be known to you, found a means to reopen the gateways from the Forest of the Epiales into both Darrienia and the mortal realm. We understand how he breached our domain, he sacrificed the life of two Oneirois, one at either side of the gateway, but we have no insight as for how he reached the mortal plane. He has since gathered the power of the Mystics and the Elemental Maidens. He may already be upon this world, and we can only theorise he intends to return the Skiá and seize the divine power of Lavender."

"This Forest you speak of, does it feed on magic?" Seiken nodded. "Then I fear I may know how he breached this world, and the blame is mine. I may have inadvertently paved his return by opening the doorway to Kólasi."

"And when Kólasi rose and merged with the mortal plane the paths were unlocked," Daniel finished in realisation.

"If it happened when I believe it to have, we had no knowledge," Geburah expressed with a shake his head, "but you spoke of a sacrifice, we too lost one of our own to the forest, and another life was... lost here. If he possesses the power you believe, then what hope can you find with me?" Geburah paused for but a second, but before they could answer he realised what had brought them here. "You've come for the Goddess' Tear, you plan to confront him."

"It is the only tool with a power equal to that of the Mystics. It's our only chance of stopping him. The power he claimed, because of Thea's actions, is less than the sum of the crystal. With it in hand we might be able to banish him."

"Thea?" Geburah questioned, nodding his understanding as Seiken inclined his head towards Zo. "I will grant you its possession by all means, but be warned, it is incomplete. If you attempt to use it in its current condition you will find the power wanting, and be sealed instead. In its current condition it will be of little aid," he warned.

"We are in possession of the missing fragment. We're hoping its power will be enough to overcome him," Zo explained.

"Zo, you've mentioned this before, but how are you going to find out without facing him?" Daniel asked.

"Simple, we'll ask Rowmeow, and failing that there may be another option."

* * *

Acha knew she could not return to Eiji's home. It was one of the few places she felt safe and protected, as such, it would be the first location anyone would think to look for her. Íkelos had witnessed Teanna through Zoella's eyes, but it remained unclear whether her insight was also at his disposal. If it was, then he would already know who had been charged with Teanna's protection. Even without being privileged to the information, Acha's skills made her the only person capable of this feat, as such, she had to ensure nothing she did would be predictable.

She knew Eiji would be safe, but despite Daniel's assurances that he would be taken to Castlefort, it was impossible not to be concerned for his safety. She would like to have gazed upon him one final time, and witness what her absence had cost. It had been two days since they had departed from Talaria, and still the need to see him weighed heavily.

Teanna had not noticed her distraction, the woman was assailed by the newness of everything, marvelling at the endless landscapes as the ground at her feet swept on to touch the sky in the distant horizon. Acha had noticed her wonder, but also the sadness she carried. Having witnessed a tearful goodbye between Teanna and the librarian Clarke, she could only imagine the depths of this woman's pain. She had left everything familiar behind and been thrust upon a new land that was so different to the one she had known.

Often, Acha saw Teanna's fingers trace the contours of the small dream catcher charm Clarke had pinned to each of them before their departure. He had assured her it would keep her safe. His gaze had flickered to Acha, it seemed he too knew her role. Whilst never spoken aloud, it was a silent understanding. Should the need arise, she would sacrifice herself in order to protect the Maiden.

"What was it like living with the Moirai?" Acha questioned, breaking the strained silence. They had been pushed together, two strangers, and the air of discomfort was palatable. The least she could do was attempt to make the transition easier. She could see Teanna's uncertainty, but it was often clouded by her awe of the new environment. At first, Acha had given her time to adjust to the novelty of everything she saw, but now it was time to offer comfort and friendship.

"I'm not sure, I have nothing else to compare it against," Teanna advised. "We were forbidden from any interaction with the Gaea dwellers, although I suppose some of us, I mean some Moirai, would make such journeys, after all, they retrieved and safeguarded the prophets."

"What do you mean, safeguarded the prophets?"

"When a proficient Gaea-based Seer awakens their gift they are haunted by the Maniae. The Moirai retrieve them and grant them safe harbour in the Tower of the Prophets. They know a life of bliss and are free to offer their visions to the sages who watch over them." Teanna had been told frequently of the wondrous life a prophet would lead. They were highly respected and treated with dignity and honour. They sacrificed their freedom but wanted for nothing. There were even rumours of beautiful enclosed gardens. Often she had hoped to awaken such a gift, she felt at home with the Moirai, but there were times, especially during the pairing, that she wondered what it would be like to meet another of her own species.

"What's the tower like?"

"I am uncertain. No prophet has ever left, and the sages are forbidden from discussing details of the life within, in fear of stirring envy."

"So what was your role?"

"I was an apprentice." Teanna wasn't sure how to describe her purpose. Unlike the Moirai, she had never been assigned a station or a singular role.

"To what?"

"Everything I suppose. When a Moirai finishes their studies they are assigned duties based on their aptitude and colouring, but I alone was provided with no task. Often my elders would send me to the Rumination Room to reflect on my purpose. After much insistence on my part they finally allowed me to attend to other duties. At first I assisted the Master Bibliothecary with the cleansing of our texts. Clarke would assign me small tasks, and then give me a book to study. Once I had finished, he would intern me to the master of that topic who would show me the practical applications of what I had studied. I thought it was their way of appraising how I would fare at their tasks without their magic, but as soon as I turned twenty-one practical experience became scarce and the Virtues decided my time was better spent in the Rumination Room, sharing the energy I had with the force of the land."

"What is the Rumination Room?" Acha questioned with intrigue.

"It's difficult to explain. Lying within the small chamber was the closest to both euphoria and wretchedness I have ever experienced. I felt complete and whole yet fractured and broken. It was bittersweet. Knowing what I do now, it is understandable."

"What were you told?" Acha enquired, knowing the tome given to her by Clarke at the time of their departure would possess more answers. Tears welled in Teanna's eyes and a heavy silence surrounded them. "I'm sorry, I shouldn't have—"

"I always knew I was different," she whispered, her voice gaining resolve as she spoke. "A human allowed to walk amongst the Moirai. But I never imagined they viewed me as nothing more than a source of power. At least I understand why I was never paired. You asked what they told me? It appears they required my presence to keep their lands elevated. As long as I was present the Elemental Spirit would continue to aid them. They spilt my mother's blood just hours after I was born, and yet I was raised with tales of how they broke their laws to save me as a child.

"I was naïve. Because he sought to protect my soul, the Spirit Elemental was fractured, his power sealed between tethers to feed their magic. The Rumination Room was the sole location where the Spirit was as close to whole as his prison would allow. They sent me there so he may take comfort in my presence.

"Knowing what I do now, I'm glad your sister spoke forks, I'm glad she's condemned them to descending. At least with their fall his eternal torture will end. I thought they were kind, and yet it seems I was only embraced each rebirt to ensure I fulfilled my task. How did I not see it?" she despaired.

"What else did Clarke reveal?"

"If nothing else I know he, at least, thought fondly of me. The Virtues wished to seal me away. During other incarnations, whilst they ensured I had all I needed, they sealed me within a prison adjoining the Rumination Room. Clarke had been a young man when my last body died, apparently he befriended me through the crystal walls and swore the same fate would not await me this birth.

"He convinced the Virtues that my happiness transferred extra power to the Elemental, and in turn they would grow in strength and provide the land with more magic. Strangely, whenever something ill would befall me as a child the lands trembled, but I don't believe it was the Spirit's doing. It holds no power there as Talaria consumes it all."

"So what do you think was the cause?"

"Before I left, Clarke told me there was a faction in the Moirai who were loyal to the Elemental, and they had watched over me. I think they were responsible."

"If they were loyal to it, why not just free it from its burden?"

"Loyalty and longevity don't always mesh. Besides, only the Virtues possess the means to unbind the prisons." Teanna turned her vision towards the vast sky above them, wondering if Talaria was above them, out of sight.

"So, now you are no longer on Talaria, what is keeping them safe?"

"A promise. They're going to slowly reduce the restraints binding the Spirit, in return, it'll lower their lands safely." Clarke had told her of this arrangement, but the details had been vague. The Moirai had raised her, but now she was aware of the truth her loyalty towards them had shifted.

"I sense a but." Acha gestured towards the fork in the track, indicating which way they would continue.

"Its fragments will be forced to link with other creatures, and it will not become whole until all parts are reunited."

"So they are binding its power between hosts, similar to how the Hoi Hepta Sophoi used the Grimoires to subdue Night."

"That was their inspiration. But I believe it has some more convenient complexities." While Clarke had spoken in earnest, he had said this method of release was both a precaution, and for the Spirit's own good. Teanna believed only one was true and, given all she had come to learn, was certain the Elemental could be whole without any danger to itself. The Moirai had been its captors for longer than she could imagine, and to think it would harbour no desire for revenge would be foolish. Teanna paused, her gaze once more spanning across the distant horizon. They had walked for a long time without rest, through the rise and fall of the sun. She paused for a moment, her gaze becoming transfixed on the shift in the sky's colours, the hypnotic shades were vibrant, mesmerising, and each sunset seemed so different from this perspective.

"Are you tired?" Teanna startled at the question, and realised she had been lost to the magnificent display for some time, her mind devoid of all thoughts as she stared, not really seeing anything before her. The air was so invigorating she had, until this moment, forgotten her body's own limits. As if Acha's words had prompted a response, she gave a yawn. Now she had stopped, she felt exhausted.

"Now that you mention it, my legs are starting to ache."

"There's a journeyman's shelter near here. We can rest there, you must be hungry."

* * *

Elly hesitated as she left Darrienia. Night had informed her he could not intervene, and yet she would assume her journey there had been anything but innocent. She knew him, perhaps better than anyone else in existence, and for this sole reason had decided returning to take shelter in his home would not be for the best, not after her recent actions. Should any force be watching, her return could almost be construed as an admission of interference. She wondered if this too was part of his plan. If not for his intervention she would have taken shelter within the walls of her rooms far longer. She no longer knew her place in this world, and if there was one thing she found frustrating, it was not knowing something.

She reflected on the recent revelations, and what the next logical course of action would be. Seiken would seek to rescue his wife, but there would be consequences. The Moirai rarely interfered visibly in the lives of humans, and never in the lives of the Oneirois. Zoella had clearly caused some manner of strife for them to risk such an action.

"This all relates to Íkelos," Elly mused aloud. "But, if I were a god, now free to walk the mortal plane, what would I do?" Elly snapped her fingers. "Of course, I would finish my mission. He was intending to open the gateway for the Skiá, so—"

"You know, they say people who talk to themselves have a fool for an audience, but I would hazard a guess their paths never crossed with yours, my lady." It was only as the figure spoke Elly realised she had been pacing the length of the outdoor seating area of her favourite Collateral bistro. The heavenly aroma of freshly baked pastries and breads assailed her senses as her awareness expanded around her. The small outdoor seating area was almost deserted, but for a few people at the furthest tables sheltered within the growing shadow of the afternoon sun. Most chose to sit indoors as the autumnal months added a chill to the sun's heat.

"And they say those who eavesdrop on private conversations are often short lived." Elly turned sharply to behold the figure who had risen from his place at the table.

"Then I have no cause for concern, I have been anything but that." The brown-haired man flashed a charming smile. "And yet I sense you may be my elder. It would appear it is not only the scent of your desperation that was intriguing," he observed, motioning towards the extra seat at his small table. "Perhaps I can interest you in a beverage of sorts."

"Perhaps I can interest you in a lesson in manners," she snapped.

"Then maybe there are a few things we could teach each other?" Elly felt herself inexplicably shudder as he placed his hand upon her arm, alarmed that she had been unaware of him closing the distance between them. "Desist. My mind is not as fickle as you would like to believe," she warned, frowning as she saw him smile again.

"And yet you're sitting. Indulge me, please."

"With which vice?" Elly attempted to keep her voice level as she realised she was now seated in the very chair he had gestured to.

"Company."

"Who were you to meet?" Elly motioned towards the extra glass, shifting uncomfortably until the figure withdrew to the opposite side of the small table.

"Someone who can assist me with my current dilemma." He removed a parchment from his jacket placing it next to the empty glass. As Elly looked upon it she found herself unable to tear her sight from the broken seal. It was one she recognised.

"That is not a Plexus seal," she observed, reaching out to take the scroll within her hand before the figure could remove it from reach.

"And you are not its sender, yet I feel our paths were destined to cross. Allow me to introduce myself, I am Grayson Bray, and you are?" He filled the empty glass with the cloudy juice from the pitcher in the centre of the table, pushing it towards her.

"Alisha," she whispered recognising the handwriting. She traced her fingers across the elegant curls of the lettering on the outer part of the scroll.

"Alisha? A beautiful name for a—"

"How did you get this?"

"It was delivered by hand. Not an easy task, believe me." He lifted it from her grasp, placing it within his inside pocket before she could open it to read its contents.

"Who are you exactly?"

"I believed I've already made introductions, I am Grayson Bray."

"Yes, but what are your skills, what is your trade?" Elly queried. There was only one reason she could consider that Alisha would arrange such an encounter. Night did indeed have plans for her, and this could be his way of leading her in the correct direction.

"Since I know you to have encountered many already, I shall not attempt to deceive you. I am a monster, dangerous beyond what you can imagine." He placed his hand upon hers, causing a ripple of fine hairs to chase across her flesh. He leaned forward across the table, inhaling deeply. "Maybe we could get to know one another better, somewhere a little less crowded, perhaps?" Elly, leaned in towards him, touching her cheek to his as she felt the draw of his suggestion.

"No, thank you," she whispered softly before pulling away with a smile.

"Minx," Bray chuckled, leaning backwards in his chair, his fingers linked behind his head. "I could give you answers, Alisha. I can see the depth of your questions. I could satisfy your every curiosity and know you like no other."

"And yet you do not even know my name." Elly stood sharply, turning to leave. If this was indeed a means to set her upon the right path, it was a poor one. She was certain she could discover answers for herself without this man's help. Working alone was something she was accustomed to, and she had no qualms in doing so again. Besides, despite being in possession of the scroll, he had no idea who she was and so, she reasoned, perhaps her assumption had been wrong.

"Mistress Lain Exerevnitis." Bray rose from his chair gliding around the table as her name rolled from his tongue. "I never forget the face of a beautiful woman, no matter the years that have passed. Time has certainly been kind to us both." Elly turned back to face him, studying him intently. "Alas, you break my heart, I thought your pretence was mere enticement, but it seems you truly do not remember me. The nights we shared, did they mean so little?" Elly's frown deepened as she probed her memories. "Let me assist you in your remembrance. Firelight danced upon the walls of Hephaestus' forge as winter winds sang their mournful serenade through the volcanic caves."

"You opposed me," Elly recalled harshly, at last remembering the handsome face of the stranger before her. Centuries ago, he had almost prevented her from securing the ore needed to ensure Prometheus could be freed. Not just any weapon could have killed the eagle that had tortured him relentlessly. She had taken it upon herself to mine the ore used by the Gods themselves and use Hephaestus' own forge to craft arrow heads. Despite what the legends came to tell, not all the great heroes had travelled alone. She had stood by many of them, those remembered and forgotten. Sometimes she walked only within the shadows, but often she had been beside them.

"I was inexperienced. I thought if I pleased the Gods they would ease my burden in ways those of Misora could not. So many heroes came to attempt what you had, but you were the only one to resist my advances." He placed two of his fingers to his mouth, licking them as he drew them down his lower lip in what Elly thought was intended to be a provocative gesture.

"Your thrall does not work on a golem," Elly recalled. At first she had not understood why this humanoid not only blocked her path, but made advances towards her. It was only when he had touched her, and the look of confusion crossed his playful features, she had understood part of his nature. He was part of the Aphrodisia Clan—beings who preyed on traits associated with Aphrodite such as love, lust, and passion— which had made him the perfect sentry for any living intruder.

"But you're not a golem anymore, are you?" Elly felt her breath catch as the gravelly voice serenaded her ears. "You're flesh and blood," he whispered teasingly.

"Are we still on opposing sides?"

"We both know our reunion was no coincidence." He moved closer, brushing a stray hair from her face, allowing his fingers to trace the contours of her jawline. "I won't stand in your path, but I have been asked to discover your secret." Elly felt the resistance upon her flesh as he reached her neck. She flinched, confusion washing over her as his skin became one with her own and he drew the blood through her flesh and into his own. He closed his eyes, savouring the experience before he pulled away, releasing her from his grasp. "Well, even in the flesh you are divine. You're more of an enigma than I would dare to presume." He blinked, concerned about the shift in the shades of his vision. Her blood was powerful, more than she could imagine. There was a moment of prolonged silence. Only when Bray's shoulders relaxed and his eyes reopened, returning to their normal shade, did Elly speak.

"What did you deduce?" She looked annoyed, her arms crossed before her, her head held a little higher as she glared at him impatiently.

"That I will assist you with your deliberations. I believe together we can devise a method that would repel the Skiá."

"That is not what I was asking." Elly unrolled the parchment she had slipped from his inside pocket during his moment of distraction. Her eyes widened with surprise as she read its contents. "What is this?"

"A request for information."

"I can see that. What makes you think you can be of any help to me?" The letter was brief, requesting he locate her and use his methods to extract any information possible regarding her current nature. As she had suspected, it was signed by Alisha, with a footnote regarding payment for services rendered.

"You see this mark here," Bray moved closer, his breath tickling her neck as he gestured towards the parchment.

"It is an ink blot," Elly stated blandly, stepping away, yet her vision studied it carefully.

"And yet to me it is a plea for aid." He placed his hand upon his heart, a crooked smile teased his lips.

"You are improvising. Do not deny it."

"Who's to say what it means to you." He shrugged his shoulders. "I have lived through an age of ice, studied with Misorian masters, do you not think I may have learnt of things even you do not yet know, especially now your link to Alisha has been severed by flesh?" Elly's posture straightened as she realised his words were true.

"You mentioned creating a weapon against the Skiá. It is true I was contemplating my next action, but you deciphered all that from a blob of spilt ink?"

"No, I divined it from hearing your one-sided conversation."

"And why would I agree to this?"

"We both are searching for the same thing. Besides, I know what you are."—Elly opened her mouth to speak, but was silenced abruptly as Bray raised his hand—"What you *really* are, now part of your curse has been lifted. Surely you are aware a curse taints the blood as well as the essence. I am the only one who can answer the questions you have, and I am bored, so I propose a trade. A friend of mine will soon find himself amidst a hopeless war with no means to defend himself. Help me design a weapon to keep the Skiá at bay, it is what you intended to do anyway, and once it is in his possession, I will answer the questions no one else can."

Chapter 16

Cost of Blood

Íkelos had spent a great deal of time travelling. His armoured boots cast deep impressions across the land in earth and stone, scarring the ground with a warning tale of his passing. Within the sound of his never-faltering footfall, audible only to himself, came the rhythmic beating of a tribal drum, urging him onward. Unaccustomed to a corporeal form, it had taken him many miles to realise this driving tattoo was in fact the beating of his own heart. His gaze remained transfixed upon the distant horizon, to the location he sought. The Mountains of Light had always been shrouded in myths and fables, earning their name from the unidentifiable phenomenon which caused the land and plant-life of that location to emit a soft glow. Throughout the various cycles their light had often been mistaken as a gift from divinity, but these ice-capped peaks held more secrets than a mere mortal could ever hope to understand.

It had been his own hand, when he himself had still been amidst the gods, which had planted the seeds of these towering giants. He had not known of the impending betrayal when he was tasked with pursuing his runaway bride, but had known better than to embrace mortality blindly. A mortal vessel could harness but a fraction of the power belonging to the divine, unless other powers were factored into the equation. His own gifts were the most feared, his touch could render the gods no greater than the mortals whose praise they sought. For this reason he had been assigned the role of an enforcer because his talent lay in the ability to remove magic from another, and turn it towards his own devices for a limited time. Only a fool would assume a human could wield such force against a god. His fealty had been the only means of persuasion Lavender's father had needed to ensure complete obedience and loyalty, and by their pairing he had no doubt hoped they would bear a child with the same gifts, a child he could bend unquestioningly to his will.

His power had not come easily, but was the result of much sacrifice, labour, and training. Before being transferred to the mortal who would birth him, he had bound a Great Spirit between himself and a shrine, located where The Mountains of Light now rose. Through the link between his essence and this obelisk he could draw upon powerful magic and entities by syphoning the energy from this being to fuel his own abilities. Great strength could be found in the darkness, and it was this magical link which had seen him reborn in the Forest of the Epiales as the Father of Nightmares, because he was one with darkness, and all the terrors that lay within.

To ensure the entity remained bound, the shrine was fortified by a solar invocation. As long as the seal held true, light would be emitted from the monolith. Over countless cycles the world had grown around this power, forging mountains and complex networks of caverns and caves; and as the world grew, so too had the power of the seal. The shrine became a mountain; the mountain became a range. Rocks and crystals formed by the pressure of the magic all radiated with the power from the seal on the dark Spirit.

Fablers of this world had no doubt woven their myths and theories as to why these mountains shone, but Íkelos knew no one could ever envision or comprehend their true splendour. The shrine had attracted worshippers who would come and behold the divine monument. It would use the energies of those in its proximity to sustain it, slowly syphoning life and magic from those nearby and, like fools, the mortals forged great cities at this location, believing this light somehow connected them to the divine.

The mountain housed another secret, one he could feel from the moment his sabaton first crunched upon the loose stone of the bridal track. Another being had sought to use the magic within this location, something other than his own entity was sealed within, watching, never sleeping. It would cause him no harm. It could neither help nor hinder what he had planned and, since its resting place was near to the snow-laden peaks, he had no cause to give it any further attention.

He was unaware of what this cycle had named the city crafted upon the large plateau, near the range's centre, and thought of it as a name it would no doubt have come to bear, if only in an idle tongue, The City of Light. If any mortal or god, knew of his return it would most likely be the last place they would think to search. There were few who would realise that a place of perpetual light was the only place capable of giving rise to an army of shadows. Here, and here alone, was where the Skiá would be reborn, but first there was the matter of the town. In order to raise the Skiá the seal binding the darkness must be fractured, but only enough to allow the energy to seep across the land and open the gateway to his realm, and for that to be achieved there was a price to pay, and blood was the currency.

* * *

The Journeyman's shelter was a small, modest structure. The warped wood showed telltale signs of age, and time had blanketed it in a thick tapestry of moss and vines. Makeshift repairs had plugged the many holes worn in the roof from the persistent battering of the elements. How it still stood was a law unto itself. The shelter was located in a small glade surrounded and concealed by overgrown thickets of bramble. If not for being marked on her map, Acha would have been unaware that it existed.

The shelter was dark and dank, with a heavy odour of rotting leaves and damp. Picking up the cobweb ladened brush, Teanna began sweeping the rotting debris from the uneven floor, while Acha lit the small fire pit in the room's centre. The wood creaked and protested as Acha fought to open the central roof plate, sending new debris tumbling inside where it became quickly consumed by the fire. The flickering glow of firelight illuminated the darkened, rotting support beams which had been precariously patched with mould-ridden cloth and splints.

"We'll leave as soon as we're rested," Acha announced, eyeing the interior dubiously now it was illuminated by the fire's glow. Seeing the condition was worse than she had imagined, she was relieved that the struggle with the roof plate had not brought the entire structure down upon them. "It seems no one has been here for some time."

"You said this was a Journeyman's shelter?" Teanna enquired.

"Yes. The Travellers' Plexus erected rest points in remote areas. They're usually maintained by those using them, but I'd say this one has been all but forgotten." Acha looked at her map, they were perhaps a day's walk from the fishing village of Seine Weir, from there they could begin their journey to the island of Therascia. Whilst not as popular as the main ports, the small town still fared well ferrying people to Kalà port, which saved travellers days of riding.

"Your world is so large," marvelled Teanna looking over Acha's shoulder at the worn parchment. "No wonder you need topographical depictions."

"We call it a map," Acha smiled warmly. Teanna reminded her a little of herself when she had awoken in this strange time, but she had the bonus of her dying host's knowledge to ensure she knew things of importance.

"I see, and what are these squiggles?"

"They're our letters. They tell us the names of the areas, who owns the territory and, in some cases, predator warnings." Acha grimaced as she looked at the state of the metal pot which lay discarded next to the fire pit. She had been hoping to serve something warm, but it appeared stale bread, roots, and berries would have to suffice. "Can't you read?" Acha questioned. She cringed, realising how rude the question must have seemed. The topic gave her pause, she had assumed Teanna possessed such skills, after all, Clarke had entrusted Acha with one of their tomes. Recalling this, she removed it from her bag.

"Yes, but our letters are much different to—is that from our land?" Teanna asked, her eyes focusing on the heavily bound tome.

"Clarke asked I pass it on to you." Teanna plucked it from Acha's hand, parting the thick cover to allow the energy within to form. Taking a seat by the fireside, she cupped her hands around the orb of energy, allowing her mind to drift and the contents to be revealed. She was aware of Acha saying something in the background, and even responding, but her answer had been nothing more than autonomous.

The firm touch of Acha's hand upon her shoulder startled her, returning her focus to her surroundings, and the delicious aroma of roasting meat which now assailed her senses. Her brow furrowed as she noticed only the dying embers of the fire pit before her.

"Supper's ready, I hope you don't mind rabbit." Acha gestured towards the door. As Teanna had sat reading, Acha had heard each protest of the shelter as even the slightest breeze caused its structure to tremble, and had decided it would be safer for them to make camp outside than to risk their presence toppling the decrepit shelter.

"Sorry, I should have offered aid. I understand now why Clarke gave you this tome. There is so much information about your world, but also, hidden within was a prophecy." Inhaling appreciatively, Teanna followed Acha's lead and began to help herself to the spit-roasted meat.

"What is it regarding, the prophecy" Acha prompted, sitting back while Teanna sated her hunger.

"It's about me. It was written in rhyming verse so I assume it to be quite an aged one. Let's see," Teanna licked her fingers before once more taking the tome in her hands.

"*The one whose light has been returned must live the lesson she has learnt.*
As skies grow dark and past repeats, a victory claimed as one retreats.
The sacrifice will seem so bold, awaken a power unforetold,
but not for long they'll mourn what's lost, as each advance bears heavy cost.
The life of light's in mortal danger, as they stand before the stranger.
But victory is not unexpected, if they can do what is requested,
yet still if all falls into place,
the outcome's by the will of grace,"

Teanna recited, before slowly closing the book and resting it upon her lap. " I don't quite grasp its meaning," she confessed as a gust of wind sent a spray of ruby embers dancing from the fire as the night's sky began to darken with the threat of an unexpected storm.

"If you're okay to continue, we will seek passage to Lamperós, it may serve us better to rest on the ship, rather than here."

"Why Lamperós?"

"It's the only place I can imagine us being safe."

* * *

There were few places which could boast possessing as many breathtaking vistas as Semiazá Port, especially during sunrise or sunset. Even now, the sky in the east began to darken, and stars emerged, shimmering in the heavens to guide any upon the ocean. From their location, Elly and Bray could witness it all. The encroaching darkness and the final fires of sunset that set the ocean aflame, spilling its dying breath upon the seemingly calm surfaces of the waters. Distance concealed danger well. Elly knew storms raged mere miles from the port, relentless, unending, violent storms, set into motion by a person who, even now, never failed to surprise her.

Waves could be heard below as they caressed the cliff face adjacent to the compacted earth track they walked. They were still many hours from reaching the city, but intended to cover as much distance as possible before making camp. Elly herself had sat in this very location many times, watching the rise and fall of the sun as it played with the lighthouse's nature. As the sky darkened the last ray's of light reached across from the west to highlight this beacon, as if passing its duty to this monument. As the darkness came the lighthouse cast its warm glow out to sea, guiding travellers on their voyage until dawn when, as if relinquishing its duty, it would become nothing more than a shadow as the sun burnt fiercely behind it. Pausing, Elly took a moment to appreciate the view, recalling fond memories of the people she had once shared it with. Bray's stern voice soon interrupted her reverie as he began to set up their camp.

"I don't understand why, if you're on such good terms with the Founders of the Research Plexus, you won't just ask for their help." Bray folded his arms across his chest, his penetrative gaze demanding an answer.

"They will not recognise me in this form," Elly assured flatly. "Besides, it is not their aid we require. Through them I came to learn of two very talented artisans, a blacksmith and an inventor, both of which have chosen to reside here."

"I recognised your beauty the moment my vision traced your contours, why should they be any different?"

"Just trust me, given how their longevity is achieved it would be better for me not to cross their threshold without a new introduction." Elly knew many of their secrets, too many in fact. She had once owed them a debt. Without their assistance, some of the rarer materials that had been required to give her life within a golem would have been impossible to obtain. It was a debt she had repaid many times over. For her to approach them now, like this, would be to invite danger. As a golem she was of no interest, but in this form, this weaker vessel, she had no doubt they would try to discern just how much of her curse remained. The manner in which they would achieve such, however, would be no better than if Night had never rescued her. Alliances and camaraderie were of little consequence where longevity and power were concerned.

"Could it be? Are you afraid of them?" Bray had caught the subtle alteration in her posture as her hands rubbed the chill from her arms.

"There are few who can claim to be my seniors and, of them, none are human. The Founders were human at one time, they can even mimic the beings they once were, but one does not live as they do and remain unaltered. It would be unwise for any, especially myself, to seek their aid without protection."

"Yet they bestowed Dynamism upon the world, trained people to use it, and—"

"They did not," Elly interrupted firmly. "Whilst it is true they developed the techniques, they grew bored and left the execution to their disciples long ago. Given the urgency caused by the Severaine's rampage they were forced to take point once more and take it to completion, but they were *not* the ones to distribute it. They do not deal with those outside their fold unless needs dictate they must."

"So why not approach their disciples?"

"Because, despite what some may believe, they do not possess the imagination required for what we seek. Disciples of the Research Plexus are appointed after proving they can follow direction without question. They are not without their own will, just without the desire to use it. There were only two exceptions, and they were granted entry because they possessed a talent no others did."

"Then why not just ask Solon and Mika if they have any idea how to execute whatever it is you clearly have in mind?" Bray posed. He, like many others, knew their names and reputation well. "They were once active researchers, they uncovered plans and items beyond our imagination, perhaps they found something that—"

"Because they were promoted to the rank of Founder, and no one leaves the Founders alive, especially those who were once granted extended longevity under their wing." Elly wished this wasn't the case, but there were secrets in need of guarding. Solon and Mika had not been like the other disciples, they were not worker bees bent to the will and desires of the Founders. They had not been conditioned to ask only acceptable questions. They had kept their imagination, their drive and passion. They would have been exactly what she needed, visionaries. Elly huffed a sharp sigh, they had little choice but to approach those the Research Plexus aligned with for tasks which required a measure of outside assistance. They would be the best in their fields, and could maybe offer some inspiration.

* * *

Rowmeow snorted, pulling his nose away from the large crystal which Seiken had placed before him. After turning around he stretched his front paws as far as he could, sinking his claws into the table before pulling his body forward until his hind legs had also been stretched. He snorted again, looking back at the Goddess' Tear before focusing his attention towards Seiken, who sat between Zo and Daniel waiting expectantly.

"It's too close to call. The powers within would be almost equal to the sum he has collected if the information we have is accurate. It's impossible to determine which would be victorious. I can say this, had the Mystics been at full strength then this would have been useless, regardless of any power you could gather."

"So we could win?" Seiken questioned hopefully.

"You could lose."

"What if I were to wield it?" Zo questioned. "You said I showed incredible strength in summoning Tisiphone to Gaea's star."

"Thea!" Seiken snapped. "You know that isn't how this works. The energy required would need to match his trait for trait. There is little that could give us the power needed."

"That brings me to my other concern," Rowmeow grumbled. "His forest would have been paramount in creating his vessel, and I am certain you remember a very specific attribute of his domain."

"It prevents the use of magic," Daniel muttered, thinking about one of its many aliases, The Forest of Silence.

"Correct. Now, we can make a number assumptions based on this. The forest would create his vessel, but it would need to ensure he could use magic himself. Thus, when his body formed, the forest would make allowances for the exact patterns of magic he would manipulate."

"And the Maidens' magic is unique," Seiken groaned, leaning back in his chair. He couldn't help but feel every advance they made was accompanied by two backwards steps.

"The power wielded by a Maiden is completely different to that of the Elementalist as they receive magic through alternate methods, giving it a signature that only one bonded with the Spirits could produce." Rowmeow paused, clawing at the table in frustration.

"How is their magic different then? Maybe if I can understand..."

"There are certain rites a Maiden must complete, and by doing so she gives part of herself to the Spirit, and it in turn gives part of itself to her and through the union their essences become linked. A Maiden doesn't wield elemental magic, they become part of its source," Rowmeow explained.

"Thea, you said there was another option?" Seiken prompted, nudging Zo, who appeared lost in thought. She turned her focus to them, nodding.

"Darrienia said if the power didn't tally you must hold a gathering. We must petition the Spirits for their aid."

"But they each already have a Maiden, I doubt they would risk death to stand beside us," Daniel mused, a frown creasing his features. "Nor will they appear on Gaea's star whilst their Maidens are in their current state."

"I've not been given all the details," Zo admitted, "but Darrienia says it's essential, and that we must speak with them in our world. They alone possess the same magical signature to that of their Maidens. Perhaps they know of something, be it a tool or blessing, we've not considered. It's our only option." Darrienia had spoken of this gathering, warning that all magic has its price, and their aid would be no different. Zo shuddered at the thought, these words had weighed heavily on her mind since she had first heard them.

* * *

High within the snow-capped peaks, nestled upon a large plateau surrounded by waterfalls and lakes, stood the renowned City of Light. The mountains continued to tower above, reaching their jagged limbs high into the ever-present clouds and offering protection against the elements for those dwelling within the magnificent city. Most considered this range volcanic, but Íkelos knew the truth. There was more to this location than any would dare to imagine.

The seasonal mists rose from the low vegetation and luscious forests which surrounded the city. The haze would chase down from the sporadic growths which could be found huddled upon otherwise rocky cliffs and shale slopes. The rolling mists and reflective waters gave an almost eerie shine to Lamperós, the haze and shrouded transparency made the great city seem almost spectral. Fir trees, blue spruce, and pine shielded the city with their natural windbreak, while the veins within the shaded leaves emitted the same muted glow as the mountains from the many years of drinking in the power's source.

It was a magnificent city, and the reason for it being considered divine was abundantly clear. It looked to be a paradise. The waters flowing from above surrounded the city, and cut paths to create rivers through the tightly-knit streets. Where the great plateau came to an end, cascades of roaring water from the rivers crashed down into a natural reservoir miles below. Lower ridges and ledges caused some of the waters to gather and pool, creating multi-tiered structures which, on clear days, were so majestic it was difficult to fathom this location was not within the kingdom of the gods.

The slow rhythmic clatter of the waterwheels found throughout the city could just be heard over the white noise of the foaming rapids. Lamperós utilised both water and the light emitted from the mountains for energy and warmth. Unlike most towns and cities, following the Severaine's release there was no cause for the Research Plexus to arrange for them to have access to Dynamism. They already existed in harmony with the land, and thus had no need to appease the wrath of the Severaine.

Unlike the spacious jagged terrain of the peaks, the uneven rooftops of the houses stood crushed together. From his vantage point, Íkelos beheld the rise and fall of the tightly-packed, modest dwellings. Their construction revealed a clear attempt at erecting as many homes as possible, in a space already far too crowded to accommodate them. The town's central feature was a place of worship, its many spires reaching higher than anything in its vicinity. The pale glow from its brickwork emitted the same soft light as the natural world around it. Veins of energy traced through the town, converging at this central point, ensuring the temple became a beacon, brighter and more magnificent than anything in its shadow. By design, it was the first structure to draw anyone's attention as they entered the city.

It was just past dusk, and the glow from the mountains slowly became more prominent with each passing moment. The wildlife had fallen silent, even the nocturnal predators felt the alteration in energy that this time of night produced. The transition from day to night was powerful, and perhaps upon the wind they could even sense his intention. Unlike the residents of the town the creatures had no cause to fear. This was their natural habitat, they were a part of the delicate harmony between all things. They lived by their own order, but the humans did not, their balance had long turned askew. The land would find its equilibrium from the workings he would undertake, and the humans alone would be the one to pay the dues.

Íkelos breathed into his armoured hands, the chill of the mountain invigorated him, making him feel more alive than he had for a long time. He walked the ledges and inclines, climbing and descending as needed until he felt the pull of the shrine. It's energy felt just as he recalled, and whilst the path to it had altered, it would guide him to its core. Veins of minerals and ore illuminated the caves and caverns, growing more brilliant and intense the closer he came to his objective. The cavern, which had been constructed around the obelisk, was magnificent. The power of the being sealed within had shaped this formation, building a tribute to its resting place. Illuminated stalactites hung from above, while a fresh water spring sent ripples of light dancing across the cavern as it rose to gather in its small pool. Beneath the clear liquid's surface, gemstones and minerals reflected a spectrum of colours. Cupping his hand, Íkelos drank deeply from the invigorating spring, relishing the crisp taste and the empowerment of the crystals and energies residing within. Refreshed, he once more turned his focus to the obelisk. Steadying his resolve he sat before it, placing a single hand upon the stone as he began his rite of old.

* * *

Rob flashed a charming smile at the swooning nurse as she escorted him down the corridor with an extra swing in her homely hips. Honeyed words and innocent flirtation had melted the healer's tough exterior, to the point she had agreed to allow him a supervised moment with his brother. Her expression soured as she looked upon Eiji, before once more casting her vision over Rob.

"My father remarried late in life," he brushed a stray strand of hair from her eyes, "he is all the family I have left. What harm can befall of my sitting with him just a moment, perhaps, hearing my voice will be enough to shatter whatever ail has snared him." He knew he had succeeded when he raised his gaze to hers, sorrow filling his eyes, before allowing his vision to stray over to where Eiji lay.

"I wouldn't place your hope on such..." She faltered, seeing the desperation in his eyes. "Be quick, we were told to keep the patients in isolation." He reached forward, taking her hand in his, tracing his thumb across the back of her hand.

"Thank you, I will just whisper in his ear, surely he will wake."

"I will observe from outside."

Rob entered the room, his steps deliberately hesitant as he approached the bedside. This would have been far easier had Acha been present. There was still one hope, however. He glanced back to the nurse, who gave him an encouraging nod. Kneeling, he placed his hand upon Eiji's chest, his own heart quickening as he felt the unmistakable contours of the crystal beneath the covers. Shifting his position, he used his other hand to slacken the cord, drawing the item into his possession as he leaned close.

"Forgive me, I'll see it returned when I am able," he whispered, twisting the cord around his fingers before depositing it smoothly in his pocket as he stood. Turning from the bedside, he wiped an absent tear from his eye, his vision lowered in defeat. The healer, seeing his distress, embraced him, offering assurances that they were doing all they could.

On returning to the streets, he removed the crystal from his pocket and allowed his gaze to become focused upon it, repeating the same process as he had when last he had stolen it for his own personal use. He focused on Daniel, concentrating, waiting, but nothing occurred. He tried to discern what was different. Last time, he had incapacitated both Acha and Eiji to lift the item from their possession, and it had worked without hindrance. It could be that ancient relics such as this would require proximity to the one with whom it had linked, that being the case, as Eiji was no longer complete, and Acha's whereabouts were unknown, the crystal had become useless in his hands.

He studied the item once more. While he could not use it to contact Daniel, perhaps it could lead him to Acha. Glancing around he surveyed his surroundings, while he didn't know a Lithomancer, personally, he knew just how to find one. His life as a treasure hunter had seen him cross paths with many people worthy of note, those who possessed skills, wisdom, or knowledge he had lacked. One such person was Fey, a guide with an instinct for discovery that was on par with his own when he used to journey into The Depths of Acheron. Finding this man was integral to his success.

Chapter 17

The Corruption on Lamperós

Acha held back Teanna's hair as she hung over the side of the large vessel, heaving. The ocean reflected the darkness of the sky above. On the distant horizon was the same sight they had witnessed for nights, the unmistakable glow emanating from The Mountains of Light. Unfortunately, they did not advance towards the land, its existence was only apparent at night as this beacon seemed to mock their current predicament.

Another night had fallen, and still the eerie stillness of the winds persisted. For days they had been becalmed. The air was deadly still, and unrest had long spread amongst crew and passengers, especially since they had veered so far from their charted course when ill-weather had threatened the safety of the vessel.

The stores were well stocked, and water was in abundance, but this did little to quieten the bickering. Some blamed the navigator for steering from their charted route when reports of waterspouts in the distance had been relayed. Many now said they should have taken their chances rather than becoming stranded in this manner. Even if someone was searching for them, it was doubtful they would look so far from their designated route. More likely they would assume their ship had been set upon by pirates and consider them lost.

Most passenger freights were equipped to deal with such a sudden loss of winds, but this ship was an exception since its normal task was transferring non-perishable cargo between the islands, and thus it had no need for such expensive adaptations. They only made this journey because the passenger ship scheduled had been damaged and was undergoing repairs.

Somewhere above them, a small bell toned as a gentle tickle of wind crossed the deck for the first time in days. This soft chime rang again, piercing the air. The ship came alive with noise and the rapid movement of the crew as they climbed ratlines and riggings in hope to take advantage of the rising wind.

While people on deck were lost in the excitement of the moment, Teanna's grip tightened on Acha's arm as she looked up towards the glow on the horizon. For nights she had witnessed the soft, comforting illumination, and not once had she seen this.

Before their eyes the pale light grew dark, blending into the shadows until the sky itself seemed darker where the light once touched.

"Is that normal?" Teanna questioned, her eyes fixed upon the horizon. Acha shook her head. She knew there were many wonders of their world which reacted to the passing seasons. The approach of the Festival of Hades was thought to trigger many phenomena, but never had she witnessed something such as this. The Mountains of Light had turned dark, and the wind carried upon it a warning of threat. This was not a natural occurrence, something was forcing this shift, and its intentions were anything but pure.

"We need to get the vessel turned around. No good can come of this omen." Acha continued to stare at the mountains for a moment, before her gloved hand grasped Teanna, leading her towards anyone who may listen. After so long becalmed, the crew were pleased to be on their way, and no matter how loud she spoke, they were too busy trying to catch the wind to hear her words.

* * *

A small voice cried out as Seiken, Zo, and Daniel approached the exit to Crystenia where Abasi and Fenyang stood vigil. The presence of these sentries reinforced Crystenia's natural defences. In times past there had been gods who had sought to exploit the connection this land had on the mortal subconscious, and so, at the time of their creation, these two magnificent Cynocephali had been imbued with the power to kill a god, and they had done so times beyond count.

Alana sped across the gardens, weaving in and out of flowers and animals, evading the path of those strolling the land with a combination of poise, grace, and sheer luck. She stumbled, righting herself and leaping just in time to avoid a small toad-like creature. Snow clung to her fiery hair as a sharp turn saw her dashing beneath a winter storm hovering beneath the branches of an apple tree. A thunderous chuckle echoed from its core as the young girl shook the ice crystals from herself, calling back a rapid apology.

"No, no, no!" she called out, skidding to a halt before her parents, and stamping her foot. "I'm coming too!" She crossed her arms, frowning as she held her father's unyielding gaze with an intense stare of her own. "How could you go without me? You never take me anywhere," she whined.

"Oh no you're not young lady." Seiken answered after exchanging a concerned glance with Zo.

"But you're going to do something fun, I can tell!" She stamped her little foot again, blowing the hair from her face with an exaggerated sigh.

"And you have chores. Besides," Seiken crouched, placing his hand on his daughter's shoulder, "if you go, who's going to watch the garden. Those seedlings you planted will sprout soon, and look how busy the area is. If you come with us, who's going to charm them from the ground and help them grow?"

"But—"

"Now, I'm sure I remember a certain little girl promising that if we let her plant them she'd watch over and protect them. They're so little, what if Megálo doesn't see them, doesn't he take a walk about now?" Seiken stood tall, looking for the large figure who regularly could be found patrolling the garden. As if on cue, the castle doors opened, revealing his enormous form.

"No, no, Mister Dinosaur, look out!" Alana squealed, darting off towards the small flowerbed. Seiken chuckled, watching as she fled. He turned towards Zo. "Thank you, Thea," he whispered, taking her hand in his. He leaned in towards her, his hand cupping her face as he kissed her tenderly.

"Ahem, well, we should really be off. We don't know what to expect, do you have everything?" Daniel questioned hastily, reminding them of his presence.

* * *

Fey was just serving a humble meal to Val when a loud knock echoed through her home. His recollection of how he and Arlen had parted ways was still a little hazy. He had awoken on the back of a carriage, being tended to by one of the small travelling tribes who roamed the lands. Apparently their dogs had found him and, thinking him to be deceased, the small group had stopped intending to perform burial rites.

It had been a few days after they found him when he had finally awoken. The tribe's healer had been confused as to the cause of his condition, their investigation suggested his energy had been stripped from him, leaving him teetering on the verge of a coma. When finally he had recovered, he remained with them for three days, until he was strong enough to make the journey to Castlefort and seek advice from Val.

He was still fatigued when he had crossed the healer's threshold, but after some sweet tea, he soon took the opportunity of his short stay to ensure she was eating properly. Like him, Val now had far more colour to her face than when he had first arrived, and her light hearted scolding about the unacceptable reversal of roles proved she was feeling more like her old self again. He had known she would be overworking herself, especially with all the victims of this new aliment.

The castle physician had initially cared little for these strangers, leaving only Val and a meagre number of volunteers to watch over them. However, when a well-known Elementalist had been admitted the conditions for the patients had dramatically improved. They had offered use of some hospital rooms, and even assigned a few physician's aides to assist them. They had cared little for Lady Mayrah, but when the whispers of the Elementalist being Eiji, one of the heroes who had helped not only to restrain the Severaine, but also force the heavenly tower to a place it could cause no harm, they knew if they failed to offer hospitality the people would turn against the chancellor.

The help provided was still minimal, but Val was now being permitted time to rest while others watched over her charges. Her constant care and supervision of the afflicted had taken a great toll on her. Fey was almost thankful for whatever befell him, it had returned him to her in time for him to help ease the burden, if only by ensuring she rested and ate.

"You sit and eat," he scolded as she moved as if to stand. "I'll get that. Whatever it is can surely wait until you've some warm stew in your belly." Fey raised his hand as she continued to rise from the small table. "Sit." He left through the bead curtain, casting a scolding look back in her direction as he made certain she wasn't attempting to follow him. Seeing this she lowered herself back into the chair.

Fey opened the door cautiously to reveal the figure of a middle-aged man. His sandy-brown hair was tousled from what he assumed to have been a long journey. Recognising the man Fey smiled, he had sold this figure much information regarding the lay of Therascia over the years.

"Fey, it's good to see you again." Rob extended his hand in a friendly greeting. Over the years their paths had crossed infrequently, but there was an accord between the two which never diminished. It was only recently Fey had come to learn that Rob, and the renowned hunter Aeolos, were one and the same. It had been a surprising revelation, especially since most hunters wore their sigil with pride, craving the extra attention and respect that brandishing their badge incurred.

"Rob," Fey acknowledged. "Are you here to see Val?"

"No, my business is with you. The representative from the Travellers' Plexus said I'd find you here."

"I didn't expect them to be keeping tabs on me," Fey huffed. "Anyway, what can I do for you?"

"Show the lad in, my boy, it's blowing a bitter wind out there," Val called through from the kitchen table. As if to emphasise her point the outside bell caught in the wind ringing wildly. "Can I offer you some stew? This one thinks I plan to starve, he's made far too much. I'd stand and greet you properly, but the weight of his stare is keeping me fixed in place," she teased.

"No, thank you." Rob called back, stepping in and closing the door behind him. Val's observation about the shift in weather had been correct, the end of the year was almost upon them and the northern winds seemed to already be promising a cold winter. Rob followed Fey inside, ducking under the twine currently running across the length of the room where various herbs had been tied to dry. "I was hoping you could direct me to a Lithomancer, I figured if anyone had crossed paths with one it'd be you." Fey's brow furrowed in concentration. It was an uncommon profession, but Rob was correct in coming to him, he did indeed know where one could be found. Getting his help, however, would be another matter entirely.

"There was one, I took them through some old mining tunnels a few years ago. They lived in Eldnyng if memory serves."

"I'll start there then, thanks." Rob produced a few coins from his pouch, the usual price of doing business. Fey accepted them gratefully, slipping them onto one of Val's shelves for her to discover later. Fey turned, his fingers still resting upon the shelf for a moment in indecision. The fact Rob had no time for idle chatter suggested there was more to this than needing someone to divine his future through crystals.

"Wait," he called out as Rob reached out to grasp the metal latch securing the door. "He's a little on the... let's say eccentric side. A little while ago he was found wandering the plains, mumbling about strange lights and glowing dust. The Physicians' Plexus said he was suffering from the effects of an unfamiliar hallucinogenic. He's not been quite the same since."

"What do you suggest?"

"If you don't mind the company I have something I can trade for his help." Fey plucked his bag from the small cupboard beneath the shelf, casting a concerned look in Val's direction. Despite the compulsion he felt to travel with Rob, he was reluctant to leave.

"What's that?" Fey knew Rob had seen his concern, but if the rumours of this man's conditions were correct, keeping the business straightforward would be the most preferential method, especially since he already knew Fey.

"I've got a debenture for services rendered."

"You still don't make any coin do you?" Rob teased with a knowing chuckle.

"Who needs coin when I have tokens for anything I could want?" Fey patted his pocket. "Besides, I *will* be making coin. I'm not doing this for free you know." Fey grinned, patting Rob on the shoulder, knowing he had already weighed the options and agreed to his company. No confirmation was needed, he could feel the acceptance. If there was one thing Fey did well, something essential to being a guide, it was reading the world around him, and that included people. He could see whatever task Rob had was important, and finding this person was just the beginning. From the moment he had entered Fey had felt the pull of his energy, the need to accompany him. He had thought to fight it, to ensure Val was fully recovered from her exhaustion, but it was a feeling he knew he could not ignore. It was an instinct he had learnt to trust over the years.

"I guess I walked right into that one. Will you take a token?"

"You're a funny man, Robert Raymond, a funny man." Fey smiled as he slapped Rob's shoulder. "Let me just see if Val needs anything before we—"

"I'm tired, not incapable. Off you boys go, and give the old man my best," Val called through from the kitchen.

"Old man," Fey grinned. "He's only a year older than her. Anyway, we should make tracks if you want to reach there before nightfall."

* * *

The young boy scuffed his feet across the floor bashfully. In his grasp he held a rather pitiful looking lilac flower. It had taken him days to find the place this rare bloom grew. If his mother knew the danger he had placed himself in to retrieve it, he would be severely reprimanded. Fortunately, she was too busy to notice he had been absent from both his classes and his bed.

The sun set early in the mountains, eclipsed by the towering giants long before it finally sank beneath the horizon. Wanting to time this perfectly he hesitated by the small modest home belonging to Daisy. He often dreamt of her golden locks and stunning blue eyes, but she had never even cast her glance in his direction. That was about to change.

Three days ago he had overheard her telling her friends of her love for this rare flower. Her mother had died when she was young, and the only clear memory she had of her was a pressed flower, and a memory of its smell. Over the years the preserved flower had lost its scent, and with it the memory of her mother had also started to dwindle. Dainan wanted to return the smile to her eyes that he had watched slowly begin to fade.

He patted his unruly black hair down, picking small pieces of foliage from the untamable mess. Glimpsing himself in a window he quickly attempted to rub away the grime marking his skin. His muscles burned, and he wanted nothing more than to quench his thirst, but first, he had to wait. This flower, like other indigenous plants, would come alive. Despite being plucked it would glow with the divine blessings of the land. He wanted her to see it in its most brilliant form, in a state of beauty that would still pale in comparison to her. He could have collected several, but given their rarity he chose just one, the most beautiful one he could find. Unfortunately, the return journey had been more difficult than he expected. Its stem had bent and withered, and the wind had torn several of the petals, but despite its damage, it was still a thing of beauty.

In the Mountains of Light, smaller things were the first to noticeably come aglow, and so when the subtle radiance traced the petals he raised his hands and knocked. Her father scared him, but he knew he often worked late into the evenings, and he prayed this night was no different. The sound of a large bolt being released caused his heart to flutter, his breathing quickened with each millimetre the door cracked open.

"Oh, it's you," she huffed in disappointment, opening the door wide. "Botany class, right?" she questioned harshly glancing behind him. "What do you want?"

"I-I erm..." he stuttered, before lifting the small flower. He heard her gasp, taking it from his hands tenderly before flinching at the harsh mocking voice which pierced the air to ruin the moment.

"Well, well. Look what we got 'ere lads. Dainan's puttin' the moves on me girl." A small group of three older boys emerged from the shadows, as if they had been waiting there, waiting for this precise moment to humiliate him.

"No, I—" He looked to Daisy desperately.

"Leave him alone," she ordered, "and I'm not your girl."

"What's with the freaky flower, freak?" The older boy shoved Dainan, sending him tumbling to the ground. "Beat it." Swiping his arms across his eyes Dainan tried to stand, only to be shoved back down by one of the other boys. Anger coursed through him as a foot connected heavily with his ribs. One day these bullies would regret this. No matter what he had, they always went out of their way to take it, food, money, even friends. He felt the anger swelling as the bully continued to mock him. "Thought these things were meant to glow white, not black."

"No don't!" Daisy begged as he snatched the flower from her grasp.

"Little freak can't even pick a flower right. Look at it, all dark. Forget it, forget 'im. If it's flowers you want, I'll pick you plenty." He dropped it to the floor, twisting his boot upon it until it was nothing more than pulp. Dainan took the moment of distraction to get to his feet. He turned and ran, knowing these bullies would not be content with simply embarrassing him.

They always took their violence too far, but not so far as to receive a discipline. He had suffered many a broken bone by their hand, injuries that could both be seen and those that were invisible, but it was always pushed aside by those of the temple as boys being boys. He felt himself flinch as he heard the bullies' mocking calls, "But first, we'll 'ave to teach 'im a lesson boys. No one puts moves on me girl." The figure turned sharply, straining as his feet remained planted firmly in place. "What the—" Looking towards the ground he could see the black energy from the crushed petals coiling around his legs, holding him in place. He tried to release his boots and slide himself free, but the umbra was spreading. “Don’t just stand there, ’elp me!” he ordered. His two accomplices grasped his arms, pulling against the invisible force.

“Ah, get-it-off-get-it-off!” another yelled as the dark tendrils gripped him.

Daisy glanced around, her eyes meeting briefly with Dainan’s who watched in awestruck horror as the light surrounding the village all shifted to the darker shade.

“Dainan, please!” he heard Daisy’s desperate plea call after him, the panic in her voice an obvious suggestion she thought he was the cause. Perhaps she was right, the rage continued to envelop him, consuming him like the spreading darkness devoured the city. He had to run, to escape. Fear tightened his chest as he heard the screams of friends and neighbours alike.

He fled, never looking back, only half-heartedly willing away the darkness his rage seemed to have conjured. There had been times he had wished ill on all those of this city, those who sat back or turned a blind eye as the bullies beat him until he could no longer stand, or those who walked the other way while rocks were thrown through his windows and unsavoury messages about his mother were scrawled across their home. He had wanted this, and while he was petrified of being caught in his own anger, part of him was glad they were finally getting what they deserved.

His feet stayed one step ahead of the spreading energy. He pumped his legs harder, creating a larger gap between him and the encroaching force, trying to exhale his rage so that things would return to normal. He had wanted this, but as the screams of pain drowned out the roaring of water and the clattering of waterwheels he wished, with more sincerity, he could reseal whatever dark energies his fury had given rise to.

“Whoa, Slow down there!” He was running so quickly he hadn’t seen the group of returning hunters, he tried to dodge around them, but one grabbed him lifting him up by the scruff of his collar. “What’s the meaning of this?”

“We gotta run,” he panted desperately. The hunters glanced behind him, the crest of the darkness was upon them before they could even move.

“What is this?”

“It was me,” Dainan wailed as he saw the tendrils snare the feet of the hunters, winding their way up their legs, closer to him. “I didn’t know I had a gift, I didn’t mean to bring this,” he sobbed in genuine despair. Regretting even the briefest moments he had considered this justice.

"No lad, this is no mortal magic." The figure adjusted his grasp, wrapping his large hand around Dainan's bicep, dangling him in the air to keep him above the spreading threat. Dainan felt a strange sense of power coursing through him as the hunter pressed an unusual card into his palm. He tried to transfer it to the other hand, but found he could no longer open his fingers. "Run, boy. Run and don't look back. Seek Chrissie Kigenso, tell her the seal has been breached," the hunter ordered, hurling the boy forwards. "Run, the magic might only shield you for a matter of minutes." The hunter watched as the young boy sped away. He closed his eyes, preparing himself for what was to come.

When the cleric, Chrissie, had been sent by the temple to offer her assistance following a hunting injury, she had warned his family that she felt a powerful seal beneath these lands, one which caused the energy of her cards great disquiet. She had left one in his possession, saying that if ever the seal was damaged, it would draw the messenger to her so the danger could be known. Chrissie had been a young lady, but a few years into her adolescence, and yet she moved from town to town, wherever the wind, or the temple, called her. She fulfilled the tasks expected of a cleric with a confident hand and, whilst he had not taken her story seriously, he had kept the card safe, if for no other reason than the difficulty she had parting with it.

He was an old man now, with no family to pass her tale on to. Crossing paths with Dainan must have been fate. He could only pray the young boy would reach safety and find a way to warn others of the coming danger. Chrissie had said the cards were like her family, and eventually they would always return to her, the old hunter prayed she was right.

He bit back an agonising cry as he felt his life energy being torn from him by the dark light. Whatever was coming was hungry, and ancient.

* * *

Semiazá Port was one of the world's largest trading ports, second only to the vast expanse that was Albeth Castle. The enormous seafront area was divided into three tiers, of which the lowest was the docking areas and seafront markets. The town had survived many hardships following the devastation wrought upon it by the Severaine. Tsunamis had destroyed the lower parts of the grand city, twisting it into a tangled mass of debris. That the area survived at all was thanks only to the protection of an Elementalist, and her unique talents.

Over the years following the Severaine's attack the city had been rebuilt. New foundations had been laid, and they once again prospered. It stood now as a beacon of hope. Méros-Génos had worked alongside humans to create the sturdy looking structures which had replaced the twisted ruins left in the disaster's wake, and using their combined skills they had even crafted an area now referred to as the Floating Market. An area of longboats tethered to each other and the land to create an interchangeable walkway of goods where the stock didn't even require unloading. The year following the Severaine had brought humans and Méros-Génos together like never before. They had slaved shoulder to shoulder under the single purpose of restoration, and in some places, such as here, they had formed irrevocable bonds of respect between the two species.

Whilst Méros-Génos were often thought of as lesser beings—due to their animal-like qualities—the need for cooperation had seen each species finding common ground and accepting the other. The Severaine's release had turned the tides in discrimination, for some at least. Whilst there were still humans who saw their kind as scum and labourers, and some Méros-Génos who viewed humans in the same light, many places that had once turned away those different to themselves now openly welcomed each other. Albeit there was still an air of discomfort and suspicion, but progress had been made, and Semiazá Port was one of the lasting examples, despite some small towns and villages quickly reverting to their prejudices once their lifestyles had been restored.

Elly, like Bray, had witnessed the growth of the land and expansion of Man. This port was one of the more memorable places for Elly, once it had been nothing more than a quaint fishing village, with fishermen casting their nets and sailing the waters on unsteady and rickety boats, while giving thanks and paying tribute to the Hydra who they believed had sent great hauls towards their shore. Now it had grown into an enormous city, gone was the innocent gratitude, replaced with a firm belief that the Hydra was nothing more than a myth conjured by failing magic.

"People can be really dumb sometimes," Elly whispered with a knowing smile.

"That's the way of humans. Beliefs are sacrificed for knowledge, even if that knowledge is fallible," Bray responded as if attuned to her thoughts. The look he received was one of puzzlement, and he had wondered whether to let the air of mystery sit, or reveal she had been voicing aloud what she thought had been an internal monologue. He opted to offer some small insight, but not into what Elly had hoped. "The monsters of this world will attend to themselves. Their instincts will shelter them from the Skiá. We are equipped to walk beside such things, after all, we were born of their blood, or so it was told."

"I thought monsters were fathered by Typhon and Echidna."

"Who were birthed by blood of the Skiá. Echidna was created as their blood merged with Phorcys' kingdom, and Typhon was born through the coupling of Gaea and Tartarus, but within the bottomless expanse that was Tartarus the Skiá also dwelt and manipulated the child their union would conceive, allowing them to create an army that could march beside them, or reap havoc in their absence." Bray flashed a smile in her direction. "Did I not tell you there were things we could learn from one another?" He traced his finger suggestively up her arm towards her shoulder.

"If regrowing fingers is in your arsenal then, please, by all means do continue." She glared at him, his fingers stilling as if in thought for a moment. Slowly he retracted his hand, but before he could give whatever reply she saw tempting his lips, she spoke again. "Do you mean to imply the Skiá will not harm you?"

"They can't devour us. Monsters rarely feast on their own kin. As for harming us, it's betwixt and between."

"So I cannot use you as a shield?"

"Perhaps I could be your aegis, if certain conditions were met. How do you feel about being a mother?" A sharp slap rung though the air, turning the heads of a few passersby. Bray failed to hide the look of amusement. He licked his lips playfully before lengthening his strides to catch up to her. "I'll take that as a polite refusal then, shall I?"

"Very polite. Now let us find Tony and see what we can devise. If I cannot rely on you for protection, then I at least need a weapon that can satisfy me."

"Oh, I *could* satisfy you. Just remember my offer, there may be a time when it's preferential to death. You fear it now, don't you?" Elly's already hasty strides quickened further, once more leaving him behind. His voice in her ear as she reached the steps to the next tier made her startle. "You were deathless, and now you are nothing but uncertain. Be careful, Mistress Lain, hesitation could get you killed."

"Says the person who has the answers I seek." Her hand grasped the handrail, her grip tightening on the peeling paintwork.

"Perhaps it's an answer you are not yet ready to hear."

"And *perhaps* I should be the one to judge." Elly turned to him, hands on hips, ready to demand answers, but as her gaze fell upon him she faltered, finding she had involuntarily taken a backwards step down the stairs. Gone was his childlike amusement and playful expression. In its place she saw a mask of concern and quiet rage. His eyes altered in shade as his vision became secured upon the distant horizon. He reached out, steading himself on the rail, his knuckles turning white. For a few seconds he seemed to struggle to breathe, his hand placed upon his chest as his gaze locked upon a distant point across the land before he squeezed his unblinking eyes closed.

"It's starting," he whispered when the call released him. The cry he heard had not been of the Skiá, but of another force all monsters had once been joined to. It was the call of darkness, a plea, and as quickly as it had erupted to silently pierce the air and souls of all who took shelter within it, it had been stilled. Bray's eyes remained closed, it seems something had stirred a Great Spirit from its slumber. It was vengeful, murderous, yet still restrained. Its battle-cry had not been enough to rally its unseen children, merely long enough to remind them of its presence. He wondered if ever this being should be freed, if he, or any other, could resist its call.

* * *

Fey led Rob across the plains. His horse moved at speed, tearing tufts of grass from the soil as he spurred it onward. Rob, as expected, kept a good pace, and the pair rode almost neck and neck. Something was wrong. Fey felt a strange foreboding building in the pit of his stomach. The wind whipped at his face chilling the cold sweat that began to form. He encouraged the horse to move faster.

The magnificent Mountains of Light came into view to his left, previously hidden by the hilly terrain they had traversed before reaching the prairie. Eldnyng was south from the mountains, across a large expanse of plains and forest, granting it a magnificent view of the distant range. The sun hovered on the horizon, dazzling in its fiery brilliance as they charged towards it. Shadows stretched behind them, long and thin as if they could not keep pace with the two riders.

Rob's horse let out a loud snort, its movement halting at such speed it took all his effort to remain upon the saddle. Fey stopped, hearing the horse's distress and encouraging his own back to his companion. Instantly he felt the muscles of his own steed tense before it gave a long squeal, backing away as if aware of some threat they had yet to perceive. Fey scanned the immediate surroundings, expecting to see a predator lurking in the long grasses, but there was nothing, no visible threat, no other creatures. He watched in awe as a kettle of falcons took flight, their dark forms joining with several other flocks as they launched into the air in retreat from the distant trees.

"Great Apple of Discord!" Rob gasped watching as the northern mountains blackened, and the flocks of shrieking birds grew ever closer as they fled the unnatural occurrence. "That's not some closely guarded islander secret is it?" he questioned, his vision transfixed upon the eerie glow, its darkness becoming more prevalent as the sun began to sink beyond the horizon. For a moment he wondered how something so intensely dark, could still appear illuminated. The tumultuous light seemed to burn, becoming something more tangible than the soft tones the mountains had once been renowned for.

"Great Spirits!" Fey gasped, tearing his attention from the unusual behaviour of the birds towards the mountains as he attempted to steady his horse. "Run!" He tried to spur his mount into action, yet it refused to budge. "We've got to make cover before nightfall. I don't know what that is, but I've never seen its like." The light seemed to become increasingly more substantial, swirling together above the mountains to form a heavy darkening cloud. Fey leaned forwards, whispering into his horse's ears. It nickered softly, and ran, Rob's horse followed. "We need to reach Eldnyng, and quickly."

* * *

When Seiken, Zo, and Daniel arrived at the glade, Alessia was already waiting for them in the small clearing with the required tools in hand. As she saw their approach she dropped briefly to one knee in a show of respect, her circlet catching the sun as Seiken motioned for her to stand. Rowmeow had expended great effort to ensure the area would suit their needs, securing the section of land from dreamers and any further influence.

The Oneirois had long ago taken an oath of non-interference when it came to matters of Gaea's Star. They had no need to commune with the Spirits, thus no reason to craft the tools and keep areas sacred for such meetings to occur. Since Zoella had first crossed paths with Darrienia's prince, the oath had become somewhat malleable. Interference had occurred, and as such they were responsible for the ramifications of these actions, consequences which were still being understood and had led to this very moment.

Given all that had occurred with their Maidens, it was doubtful the Spirits would answer a plea on a plane where harm could befall them. Here they could remain in ethereal form, invincible against any harm, and yet converse with those who called upon them. This was the only option, their only chance. The land and energy had been purified to be hospitable. For the first time, a cry for aid would be made from Darrienia's planes on behalf of those of Gaea's Star, a plea they hoped would not go unheard.

The glade was picturesque in its beauty, a unison of the elements, combined to ensure life and nature thrived. Sunlight streamed from above, illuminating energy particles as they drifted serenely in the gentle breeze that carried the scents and sounds of a distant stream. The grass was silken beneath their feet, the rich soils below were fertile and hospitable to anything that would seek to grow. The energy of life surrounded them, and Rowmeow had masterfully woven it with the energy of the elements.

Seiken gave a brief greeting to Alessia as he lifted the small cloth package from her, nodding in approval as he looked over the contents. He examined their surroundings in brief contemplation before nodding once more.

"Will these be sufficient, Lord Seiken?" Alessia quickly studied Zoella, noticing the way her hand rested on Daniel for support. She said nothing, clearly she was ailing, but she attempted to mask her weakness by using subtle support from others. To draw attention to this, even by a respectful enquiry, would be wrong. Zoella saw her looking, and offered a grateful nod with a weakened smile.

"Yes, thank you. They will call the Elemental Spirits to us, those who are unbound at least."

"Unbound?" Alessia questioned, tossing her black hair over her shoulder as she refocused her vision towards Seiken.

"The laws of the universe states there must always be one Great Spirit for each element. Since Light and Darkness are lost, presumably sealed somehow, and the Element of Spirit remains bound to Talaria, this ritual will only summon those capable of answering the call."

"What do you require of us, my lord?" she enquired softly, moving to stand beside Daniel, her hand briefly passing over his arm as she ensured he was well.

"We must call to each Spirit in unison, but a tool can only be held by one person. That is the other reason I requested your presence." He produced a budded flower from the cloth and placed it in Alessia's grasp before taking Daniel's arm, leading him to a more suitable location. He studied the remaining items before handing him the candle. To Zo he gave a simple chalice, and for himself he took the silver bell. "It is essential you remain silent. I will act as the mediator because I'm the only one who can invite them here," Seiken explained.

Without waiting for their acknowledgement he began to speak. The words leaving him were no language they knew, and even with the magic of Darrienia they were unable to understand his invocation. For the most part the sounds which left him were unlike words at all. It was difficult to focus upon anything but this strange music. It was Seiken's voice, and yet it was the voice of so much more. The sounds and rhythm invoked feelings and kindled visions filled with the raw power of nature, a storm, an earthquake, fires, floods, and through him all the magnificence of nature could be heard.

When at last he fell silent, the air felt charged with unfamiliar energies, and whilst Daniel knew nothing of what had been said, he knew the figure standing before him had not requested an audience as Seiken, Prince of Crystenia. He had called to them with his older self, the part of his essence belonging to the God of Wyrms.

The electricity from the air slowly began to ebb and fade as the power of his call diminished, and still they stood in silence, frozen by both the plea's power and anticipation. Seiken turned to look towards his friends, a look of concern etched upon his tired features. It was only then he noticed the candle within Daniel's hand sparking before flickering to life. At once the bell within his hand chimed, the chalice overflowed, and the budding flower bloomed. His concern turned to relief. He knew the Spirits were present, even if they refused to reveal themselves.

"*Why do you invoke us?*" the four entities spoke as one, their words a feeling of intention rather than an audible sound. Seiken knew they were being cautious because of the fate that had befallen their chosen ones. To reveal themselves here would be to fully cross into this realm, and perhaps even risk exposure to the entity which had entrapped their Maidens.

"Our goddess, Darrienia, requested it of us. We hope you will lend us your aid and allow us to channel your power through the Goddess' Tear in order to bind the one who took your Maidens," Seiken explained, glancing towards his wife.

"*Only a chosen female can channel our energy in the manner you seek, and each of us already are bound to our counterpart.*" The power of the voices diminished, as if one no longer spoke with them.

"Is there any other way?" Seiken felt the shudder course through him as the powers rose in conflict, their argument audible through the clashing of energies.

"No—"
"Yes." The message was relayed as an overwhelming feeling of both optimism and desire. "I want her."
"Too many cycles have passed. We are but four, the risks will—"
"The risks will be welcomed to restore order, surely. If we do this our brothers and sisters will be restored."
"If we do this we will be weakened until the rite is completed, and if the rites fail, what then?"
"Then we are bound, but look at her, look at her essence, she's the one, imagine our imprint on one such as her, can you not see what I envision?"
"I've not seen such patterns in a being for a long time, do you think she could be suitable?"
"If she could succeed order would be restored. The elementals could be revived, even the lesser spirits could be returned. Is it not worth the risk?"
"But we are but four, the seven Great Spirits should vote on matters this important."
"They cannot, and if we agree our decision would hold the majority. Look at her, really look."

There was a moment of oppressive silence. The energy of the world around them bore down on them with crushing force to the point each stood paralysed against the sheer magnitude of energy.

"She is passionate, the fire of her essence is unmistakable," a voice finally spoke in something other than impression and implication alone. Whilst its form remained invisible the air was charged with the concealed presence of the Fire Elemental. "I vote in favour of naming her."

"She is filled with awe and wonder. I too would accept her," came the airy voice of the Elemental Spirit of Wind.

"Her impact both past and future would be immeasurable. I consent to bestowing my boon upon her."

"Then it is settled. We will agree to aid you, but there will be conditions."

"What are they?" Seiken asked as the energy holding them receded.

"We, the remaining four, wish to name a Mitéra. We will fuse our powers to her essence allowing her to channel our energies, she will stand beside you and wield the tear. But be warned, doing so comes with great risk, and acceptance is not to be taken lightly. Once she has harnessed the powers we offer, she will be called upon to complete the rite of the Mitéra. If she fails, the mortal world will suffer. Our presence keeps things in balance, but by doing this we will be bound, elemental magic will be greatly diminished, and our spirits will be imprisoned."

"When would the rite need to be completed?" Seiken questioned, glancing between Zo and Alessia, wondering which of the two women had been chosen. What they spoke of was a great honour, and even his older-self was unaware of what such a thing would entail for the one chosen.

"The world will call to her, show signs that our remaining influence has faded. When this occurs she must begin her journey. It may be months, even years before our absence is noted, but the signs will be there and she will know how to read them. But this contract should not be entered into lightly, the path will be difficult and shape the very future of the mortal world."

"I thought the Mitéra had to be of a specific essence, one lost," Seiken pondered, remembering how The Table of Scrying had revealed that the essence of the Mitéra had been lost by the binding of Spirits to the newly mortal Maidens.

"We have used mortals before. The conditions of her birth have created one as close as could be achieved, an almost exact imprint of the original. Do you consent?" The energy surrounding them intensified again, filled with a nervous anticipation.

"Who have you chosen?" Seiken asked, fearing he already knew the answer. He looked to his wife with regret, if they were to ask for her, he knew he could not consent. She was his. He could not, would not, share her. Seiken held his breath, fearing they would ask the impossible, fearing he would be forced to consent. He glanced to Alessia, being born of a shifted dragon and elf had made her as unique as his wife. They seemed to delay in answer, each second felt like hours as nervous sweat formed upon his clammy brow. His Master and Commander, or his wife, he would lose one, and both were without equal.

"Alana." The four spoke in unison just moments before a small squeal echoed from above. Startled at hearing her own name the young girl lost her footing on the tree branch. She scrabbled desperately to regain her grip, still hoping somehow she had not betrayed her presence. She dropped to the ground, tumbling forwards ungracefully through the nearby shrubs. Looking up to her parents she patted down her hair, picking small pieces of foliage from it as she attempted her most innocent smile. Her smile faltered as she saw the concern on their faces.

"I'm sorry, I wanted to see," she whispered, her eyes pooling with tears from the intense looks she was recipient to. Zo dashed forwards, wrapping her daughter protectively in her arms.

"No, she's just a baby. I know how you share your powers."

"If it were but that simple, but the powers we offer unto the Mitéra are not received by such means. The Mitéra must become more, her essence an amalgamation of human and spirit, and therein lies the danger. There is a reason our Maidens must be of a certain age, a mortal body finds the containment of our power difficult. Despite the alternative means of receiving our gift, the fact she is a child is the reason what we suggest carries so much risk. But of all the beings who are, she is the only one who possesses the potential to be when we seek."

"We will find another way." Alessia stated firmly, her hand resting on Zo's shoulder as she sat on the floor, cradling her daughter protectively. Daniel looked between them, questioning why their decision was meeting with such resistance. Alessia leaned in, whispering an answer he would never find through the ancestors.

"The risk lies in the fact we cannot transfer our gift, it must become part of her. She must undergo training in our realm, and our essence will be fused to her own. Had she been an adult there would be no danger, she would simply pay homage at the shrines and receive our boons. Her essence would have been developed enough to accept the alterations, but given her immaturity in order to fuse our powers with her, we must also take something."

"Training, for how long?"

"What we discuss will take years, but time in our world flows differently than that on the mortal plane, and we can alter it at a whim to serve our needs."

"But—" Zo whispered, hugging Alana tightly.

"Thea, it's not our decision to make. Our answer will make no difference here." Seiken's voice was little more than a whisper as he addressed his wife. "If her essence is indeed viable, only Alana can accept or refuse their proposition." Alessia stepped aside, allowing Seiken to approach his wife.

"I know you're right...but," Zo gave a soft sigh, swiping the tears from her eyes before her daughter saw them. "Alana, Daddy's right. As much as I want to protect you, this is something only you can decide." Speaking those words caused her chest to tighten, and despite what her heart was telling her, she released Alana from her protective embrace.

"What is?" Alana questioned wriggling away.

"The Spirits have offered to give you a powerful magic, one that can save the lives of many people. But they will want something in return."

"Like my toys and books? I'd share them anyway, if they want them I'd give them for free if they're important."

"Not your toys, dear one," Seiken whispered crouching down to run his hand through his daughter's hair. "Something even more important."

"What?"

"I don't know. Why don't you talk with them, we'll allow you some privacy. But, Alana, choose what *you* want, do not make a decision for any other reason than it being something that feels right to you. Whatever you decide we are proud of you." Seiken stood, kissing his daughter on the top of her head.

"We will wait just inside the forest," whispered Zo, fearing to add any power to her voice in case her daughter heard the sadness within. "Forget everything and just follow your heart." Zo kissed her daughter before rising to her feet and disappearing into the cover of the trees. She felt Daniel's hand upon her shoulder at the same moment Seiken slid his hand into hers.

"I am certain there's another way. This price they speak of, what could they ask from a child?"

"To forge her into a Maiden of the seven they could ask for almost anything. Each of them will have seen something they like in her essence, and each will know exactly what they will take in order to fuse their essences to her own, and the fact it was present is what spurred their decision," Seiken responded, squeezing Zo's hand gently. "This was never going to be our choice. Even had she not followed us, if it is meant to be they would have found her eventually."

"You knew this could happen?" Zo accused, fixing her gaze on the gnarled wooden bark of the tree before her.

"No, but given the circumstances of her birth her essence will be very unique." Daniel looked to Seiken questioningly. "Thea's father is part of a primordial deity, and Thea a Hectarian shade reborn as an Oneiroi who, like myself, exists here yet doesn't appear on the Pillar of Life. Thea herself is unique, but when paired with my own heritage it makes sense our child would be something new." He squeezed Zo's hand again. "If this is her destiny we have no right to stand between her and it."

"I know, but I know you feel this too." She placed one hand on Seiken's heart and the other on her own. He dropped his gaze towards the ground, knowing no answer was needed.

Chapter 18

The Skiá

Tony was easy to locate. It was dawn when they arrived so he was busying himself collecting pails of saltwater. As a blacksmith he used many different methods of quenching a hot blade, from saltwater gathered from the nearby ocean for rapid cooling, to oil or air cooling for the blades requiring a far longer period. He was an expert in his craft. Anything that encountered his hammer and anvil became all that it could be. It was for this reason Elly had thought to seek him out. He had crafted and restored various commissions for her over the years, and possessed an unrivalled skill.

"Hail, Tony." Elly raised her hand in greeting, wondering if the old blacksmith would still recognise her. It had been some years since their paths had last crossed. He seemed to enjoy her visits, mainly because of the ancient weaponry she tended to bring. In her golem she had rarely carried a weapon, but those she owned were maintained to high standards.

"Well, well, if it isn't my favourite collector. Finally decided to shed your curse did we?" the blacksmith's voice boomed as he secured a drum barrel filled with water to his back. He adjusted the straps on his broad shoulders and began to walk, knowing they would follow. "What can I be doing for you this time? Recreating antique blades, or does one of my old 'uns needs a little tempering?"

"I assure you I keep my weapons well."

"Perhaps you'll be so kind as to let me be the judge of that. You should see how well the patrols keep *their* blades. Honestly, don't they realise it's not just a hunk of metal? A single chip could be their death, and yet they let them rust in their scabbard." He cast a glance over Elly, surveying her from heel to hat. "Speaking of scabbards, you're mostly unarmed." He heaved the large barrel from his shoulder, placing it outside the forge. The metal shutters had been secured together, their slightly rust-tarnished surface causing Elly to give pause. Tony was known for his meticulous nature, it seemed strange he'd let his workshop fall into such disarray. Tony produced a silver key to the wrought iron chain, tossing it to her. She released the stiff lock, accepting Bray's help in rolling back the heavy shutters.

"I am always armed." She suppressed a shudder as she stepped into the forge. There was a strange energy to the air, one she did not recognise. It was only after a few moments she realised what was amiss. The forge had grown cold.

"My mistake. I was referring to visible weaponry. Well, come, let me see. It appears as if time has treated it as cruelly as it has myself, and while I tinker we can discuss your request." Tony paused for a moment, his gaze lingering on her hat, she raised her hand, her fingers tracing the brim for a moment before removing it. "Where you find some of these things I'll never know." He shook his head, marvelling at her hidden armaments. He had seen this woman on a number of occasions, and her commissions had always been unusual.

"I would be honoured if you would take a look. These, I confess, have suffered centuries of neglect. In truth I never thought I would have cause to need them again. As for my reason to seek your services," Elly glanced towards Bray as he lingered outside, almost as if standing sentry. Seeing her regard him suspiciously he stepped inside. "The request is not at my bequest, but I feel you are the sole person I can trust in this matter." She traced her finger across the dust laden table before removing the blade concealed in her tricorn.

The small dagger turned idly in her fingers as she placed her hat, along with her other tools and hidden weapons, upon the table. Cobwebs had infiltrated the corners of the forge, and the weapons, armour, and tools displayed with pride upon the wall had grown dull. Not at all like the pristinely maintained objects Elly recalled on her previous visits. Her thumb and forefinger closed around the blade before offering it to Tony, wondering if his grasp would reveal something she had failed to notice. He grasped it tightly, his hands not displaying the signs of ageing she expected given the lack of care for the upkeep of his workshop.

"Ah yes, your companion." Tony broke her critical assessment, turning the weapon over in his hands as he spoke. "I don't believe our paths have crossed."

Tony glanced up from his strategic examination of the blade to regard Bray with just as an intense stare as he had fixed upon the metal. "I trust you to be treating the Lady of Knightsbridge with the respect due?"

"Lady of Knightsbridge?" Bray asked, turning his gaze towards Elly in surprise. Elly dropped her head slightly, breathing out a nearly inaudible sigh.

"Blackwood was my father. With his death his deeds and titles passed to me. However, due to my prolonged absence the lands were redistributed by the crown. My nobility is not something we are here to discuss."

"Indeed it isn't," Bray chuckled to himself. "What we seek, Blacksmith Tony, is a means to forge a weapon capable of holding light."

"A flaming sword?" Tony once more lowered the weapon he was examining to glance between them. "I've heard of such a thing, impossible by all counts. Either the metal gets too hot or the oil sacks catch alight. Short of a magical enchantment you're looking at something that's more deadly to the wielder than the one at its tip."

"Do you think you could attempt it?" Bray queried. If a flaming sword was the only way to safeguard his friend, then it would have to do. Even if it meant wielding it himself.

"I could, I have. But like those before me I failed to perfect it. Why the desperation?" he queried hearing the slight tones hidden within Elly's companion's voice.

"It's essential." Bray grasped the crook of Elly's arm leading her aside. "There is another option. We can ask Solon and Mika if they know of anything that would be of any aid. I know of something, but my efforts at finding its location have been unsuccessful, perhaps they—"

"Ah yes, if only they were not deceased." Elly turned her eyes skyward, once more catching something in Bray's posture. "Are they not?"

"If we were not in times of such desperation I would be inclined to lie, but given the circumstances..." Elly stepped away from him approaching Tony.

"How long until we can depart?" She inclined her head towards the table, knowing he had assessed the requirements already.

"Given their age these have fared exceptionally well. I can temper the one from your tricorn, but it will take time. Some of the older repairs were done without due care and have turned brittle, but worry not, I can restore it to its glory for you. The other tools are well-maintained."

"Can I entrust it to your care?"

"Please do, I will see it fit for your return." Elly nodded her gratitude, placing payment on a small stool near the exit and departing. She felt the warmth of the air outside wash over her, another reminder of the uncharacteristic chill to the air of Tony's workshop. Frowning, she tried to recall any other time when his forge had not been lit, even at this early hour. The forge and workshop were located on the outskirts of this tier, where smoke and odour would not disturb those living in the town, the more she thought about it, the more she recalled the forge never cooling, even if only ablaze by embers. Tony had always taken great pride in his forge and workshop, it seemed strange to find it in a condition which implied it had remained unused for some time.

* * *

Zo had been unaware of entering a dream, unaware of the pain that normally accompanied the transition. Everything was silent. There was no voice, no words, merely a warning.

An obelisk of obsidian became highlighted from within a sheltered network of caves and caverns, far beneath what she perceived to be an enormous range of mountains. A figure shrouded in dark energies had his hand upon the black and white marbled stone. Its peak seemed to draw something from above. Shades of brilliant energy spiralled through the earth to feed the stone, widening a fissure barely perceivable beneath the armoured hand.

The energy swirled within the pillar, absorbed, converted, and syphoned by the lone figure, a figure she knew to be Íkelos. For a moment she heard something, a silent cry before a tear seemed to form just mere feet from where this figure stood. This fracture existed, and yet simultaneously it did not. Outside of a dream image it would be impossible to describe, and with that realisation, in one single, horrific moment, Zoella understood why. It could not be described outside a dream, because it reached through their plane into a place of nightmares.

Tendrils of jagged energy extended from the tear, like roots they anchored themselves into the world around it as it fed upon the power Íkelos offered from the shrine. The energy strained and groaned in sounds present and yet imperceivable as if some great force was trying to pull itself from within. Dark smoke leaked from the tear, rolling from the fissure to blanket the ground. It tensed and relaxed in spasms before expelling more of the blackened vapour into existence. For the briefest moment, she swore Íkelos looked towards the place she watched from, and smiled.

"Thea!" Zo felt herself wrapped tightly in a comforting embrace. Her vision blurred in and out of focus upon a face she knew by heart. Her body trembled violently, and she became aware of her own strangled sobs.

"The Skiá are coming," she whispered, her voice trembling with fear. She buried her head into Seiken's chest as bloody tears streaked her face, soaking into his shirt.

"Skiá?" Alessia questioned, seeing the look of horror now masking the face of the Wita.

"If Nyctophobia had a face, it would be theirs," Daniel whispered, remembering all Seiken had told him of these creatures. The world outside Darrienia had been protected by the primordial gods' own actions. There were things the Skiá needed to survive, shadows and darkness, and with their sun and moon they were granted neither in great abundance. "If he's bringing these creatures to the mortal plane, then does that mean he's created a... a... hospitable environment?"

"If not yet, then soon," Seiken confirmed, stroking Zo's hair as he attempted to offer her some small comfort.

"We need a way to fight these things, before that happens," Daniel urged. "I have an idea, but I need time. Do you need us? Whatever Alana's answer our presence will not alter it." This abrupt announcement caused Alessia to glare in his direction, warning him of his disrespect.

"Go," Zo consented, lifting her head from Seiken's chest. "We will focus on stopping Íkelos, you do whatever you can about the Skiá."

* * *

Acha's muscles tensed as the prickly sensation of foreboding washed over her. The air seemed to grow more charged the further into the docks they trekked. Despite her desperate pleas, the ship's navigator insisted with the wind's current temperament their only choice was to make port, regardless of how unsettling the scene before them was. Unrest and hushed alarm had washed over the harbour, sailors and traders alike refusing to set sail until the ill-tidings had passed, certain the alteration in the mountains somehow had influenced the winds and caused many vessels to become stranded. Everyone had witnessed the calamity and devastation brought by the Severaine, and with such ominous omens, the vow to remain docked until the cause of this recent phenomenon was uncovered only added to the quietly rising panic on everyone's lips.

Old folk muttered between themselves about ancient tales of sealed tombs and divine judgement. But not one of them had a story to offer about what could turn the once soft tones of the mountains dark. They argued about the reasons, their theories spanning anything from judgement to a shift in energies. The one thing they all agreed upon was that the shift in the light was an ill-tiding.

"We will not get off this island anytime soon," Acha whispered, pulling the travelling cloak's hood up over Teanna's hair. The silver shade was attracting some attention, despite it being nothing more than unusual. Given the tone's rarity Acha knew better than to attract unwanted attention, especially when talks of curses and sorcerers were paramount.

"What do you suggest?" Teanna whispered, sidestepping abruptly as a large man barged past without regard. Acha linked her arm through Teanna's, hoping they would not be separated by the quickly gathering crowd and rising panic the strange sight was causing. "We would do well to leave this port as quickly as possible."

"Perhaps somewhere remote would be best. Given that he saw you through Zo's eyes, we must assume there will be others who can see for him. The less we are around people the better." Ducking into a shelter created by the canvas lining of two nearby fish stores, Acha pulled out her map, struggling to unfold it as the winds blew in from the ocean with rising force. She fought with it for several moments, folding it over on itself until it was a more manageable size. Grasping Teanna's hand, and placing it upon her shoulder, she led the way. At the port's borders Acha stopped, showing Teanna the map. If they were separated for any reason, it was essential she found a place she could be safe. "Some time ago there was a town here called Morris' Mire. It was all but destroyed, but there were some places left partially standing that could grant us shelter. Given its remote location it will afford us some safety."

"Is that what you call a marsh?" Teanna asked, noticing the strange shadings and symbols on the map.

"Yes, it's mainly bog land, but if we can reach the town there's shelter. If not, we can always take advantage of willow groves. If we can make it to the marsh we should be safer, the mists will conceal us."

"Surely brume would be a double-edged sword?" Teanna offered, considering how it could be used for tactical ambush by rogues and curs.

"Normally yes, but my skills are different to most people's. I take energy from the land to live, which will conceal our presence. I would also be aware if something was present that didn't belong."

"This is why you guard me?" Teanna whispered with realisation. "You hide us from danger and know when it is near."

"That, and while you're with me no scryer could locate you. If I'd known that before then..." Acha raised her head to the heavens, blinking back a tear. She never would have left Eiji had she realised she was the sole reason Íkelos had not managed to locate him. Now, he lay alone, sealed in whatever dreamless prison the removal of his Mystic essence had trapped him in.

"Your beloved?" Teanna questioned. She had overheard some of the conversations regarding the fallen Mystic.

"By all the Gods," Acha whispered as her gaze focused on a blanket of clouds overhead. It had built so rapidly she could barely believe it was present. "Forget the Mire. We need shelter, fast."

"Why, what's wrong?" Teanna looked to the storm cloud, recalling how she had watched in fascination from Talaria as such things had formed below.

"We have to make a fire, darkness is coming."

"Darkness, what do you mean?"

"Those clouds, they're coming from the mountains." Acha fought with the map, scanning the area for somewhere sheltered and defensible. "Quickly, stay with me."

* * *

Fey and Rob watched in horror as darkness consumed the town below. The cries of terrified residents froze their advance. Rob, as if sensing Fey's desire to investigate, grasped his arm, pulling him away as the blanket of darkness permeated the surroundings like a thick mist. He knew there was something unnatural, something sinister within. What they saw was more than a shadow cast from above. It was dark, and possessed substance as it travelled the ground like a shroud for something living, a camouflage of darkness birthed from shadows in which it could hide and hunt.

"There's nothing to be done. We've got to warn someone." Rob pulled Fey harder, sensing his resistance.

"We've got no mounts, do you expect to outrun that?" The cloud expanded overhead, but as yet the dense mist remained firmly in place. Rob suspected this would only be true until whatever hid within had taken all the enjoyment it could from the town. Then it would search for new prey. He did not intend for it to be them.

"What other plan is there, stay here and die?" Rob pulled him again as a cold sweat trickled down his back. Whatever was in the town, it was becoming more proficient. One scream became a chorus of two and three, until a cacophony of blood-curdling cries filled the air. "It's feeding, but it won't stray beyond the cloud's shadow," Rob observed, noticing the parts of town below where the blackened mist had yet to touch were those still touched by the natural light of the moon as it broke through the wispy cover to the east. He was glad for the approach of the Festival of Hades. The moon was nearing full, and its large orb shone with radiance and power, glinting off the small quartz-laced pebbles that marked borders and pathways. For brief moments they glittered like a divine protection, until consumed by the clouds. He saw the flurry of movements below as people attempted to flee, only to be dragged into the shadow-mist as the darkness from above touched them.

"Shouldn't we do something?"

"If we go down there we die, and no one learns of the danger. There's a portal to Collateral about two miles from here. Twenty minutes, tops."

"Twenty? Are you getting slow in your age?" Fey joked nervously, his vision still fixed on the spreading cloud and those who tried to retreat its deadly touch.

"If we don't get moving, you won't be reaching old age. Move." He pulled Fey sharply, aware of the gaining momentum of the cloud above. Twenty minutes should see them to the portal, if whatever lived within the shadow-mist didn't catch them first. A harsh wind gave the broiling cloud acceleration, its eclipsing shadow upon their heels as they ran. Movement writhed behind them, Rob could almost swear he saw immaterial forms hopping from shadow to shadow, braving the darkness outside the dissipating shadow-mist for just a moment.

The shadows left the shelter of the mist in rapid streaks, barely perceivable to the naked eye. They sought new prey as they surfed the edges of the spreading darkness cast from above. The flicker of a fire ahead acted as a beacon, causing them to push their legs to move faster as he searched his bag, knowing he still had some flash powder somewhere. Fey kept pace with ease, acutely aware of how precarious their situation was. If they could reach the fire, he knew it would offer them some measure of safety, but it could also become a prison. It was clear these things feared the light, and this was a phobia they could manipulate. The light cast by a fire was unpredictable, and he knew its presence would buy them minutes at most. His vision locked just beyond the glow, the same sensation of being guided urging him onward and recharging his fatigued limbs.

Pulling a small cloth wrapped pouch from the bag Rob flung it towards the flame, relieved when it caused the embers of the fire to crackle before erupting with a piercing flash startling the two figures, almost causing them to retreat. There was no time to explain. The portal to Collateral was not far but, if they were going to make it, they would have to work together to form a barrier of light that would give the creatures cause to reconsider approaching them.

Light would repel them, of this he was certain. He closed his eyes, sending silent thanks to the Kyklos as they confirmed his own observations, offering what solutions they could. Still, after all this time, they seemed to reach out to him when he was in danger. He leapt across the outer circle of fire, only now noticing that they sat within such a barrier protected by its defences while a secondary fire burnt within its centre. Rob wondered what insight they could have which saw them take such an unusual precaution, but that question was low on his list of priorities. Dropping to his knees inside their makeshift sanctuary, he rummaged inside his bag as he took advantage of this brief and hurried search to catch his breath.

"Have you anything else that will burn? We need to build this up, quickly!" he commanded, "You"—he tossed a bundle of cloth to one of the women—"tear this into strips."

"Rob?" The figure next to the one he had thrown the cloth towards questioned before another blinding flash of light exploded from the bundle he had tossed into the centre of their camp.

"Acha, what are you doing out here?" Rob questioned as Fey handed her a leather skin, interrupting the reunion.

"She tears it, you soak it, carefully." Acha nodded at Rob's companion's instruction. "This is who you were looking for?"

"Yes. Why in Hades would you make camp with that closing in?" Rob demanded, gesturing towards the encroaching clouds before returning to his work. He sat on the floor, scooping small amounts of the powder from a pouch into gel capsules of varying sizes and shapes.

"I injured my ankle, we couldn't go any further," the unfamiliar woman explained, before sinking her teeth into the cloth to break the edge allowing it to tear. "Acha was binding it, but it came so quickly, we knew we'd never make the"—the figure glanced to Acha—"gateway." Fey tossed some of their limited wood stack onto the outer ring of the fire, taking the thicker pieces for himself. He took the oil soaked cloths from Acha, wrapping them around one end of the larger sticks, while adding the occasional gel capsule from Rob's rapidly growing pile.

"The Kyklos told me they are ancient beings known as Skiá, and light injures them. This should be sufficient to deter them. If we can make enough, we should be able to reach the portal."

"She's not going anywhere on that," Fey observed, noticing the thickness of the bandages which supported the swollen area. He studied the two figures carefully as he bound the other side of the stick, creating a dual sided torch. "Here." He passed it to Acha, who had now depleted their oil resources.

"Rob, what are those things?"

"I don't know any more. Only that they travel in the cloud's shadow, and it seems as if a collection of them in proximity form some kind of shroud. They're getting braver, separating to hunt. The light hurts them, thus it's our best chance of reaching Collateral." He saw Acha glance towards the other woman hesitantly.

"What are our chances if we remain here?"

"You've not got enough wood or cloth," he observed, noticing a large portion of the tinder was made from clothes, and the pile of wood gathered was quickly depleting. "The cloud isn't thinning, it's growing. If you stay you'll die." Rob glanced towards the Mountains of Light where the cloud was at its thickest.

"I'll carry her, but she must wield the torch," Fey offered, realising he had misunderstood Acha's concerns as her expression darkened further.

"Teanna," the figure offered. "If I'm going to be wrapping my legs around you, you should at least know my name." Her attempt to lighten the situation brought the slightest smile to Fey's face, mainly because, even in the firelight, he could see how her words had made her blush.

"Fey, Rob." He gestured to himself then his ally, realising how well they had worked as a team. "Now, let's get you to Collateral. Do you have access since the new protocols?"

"Acha's a trader, so Teanna can pass through with her," Rob advised as Fey hoisted the young woman onto his back. He lit both ends of the torch. "For the sake of us all, keep the shadows at bay." Teanna wasn't sure if this was a prayer or an order, but she took it in her trembling hand, increasing the pressure with her other arm as she hooked it across Fey's chest.

"I'll take flank," Acha volunteered.

"We both will. If Fey leads, we can cover the sides and rear together." Rob lifted a small pouch off his belt, nicking a hole into it and allowing the black powder within to start a trail behind him. "If it looks bad, worse, touch your flame to this. It may be enough to buy us a few moments."

"Do you still carry flash bombs?" Acha questioned as they began their rapid hike. He looked to her in surprise, knowing he had not used them in her presence, aside from the powder he had tossed into their fire. They were a rare commodity, and one he never announced he carried. "It may have been some time ago, but I touched you, remember?"

"No, I used the last of the powder for these." Rob gestured towards his torch as it gave a timely flash of piercing light as the flames melted one of the gel capsules he and Fey had placed at random intervals within the cloth.

"How much time do we have?" she asked, fearing the answer.

"At this pace, not enough." Acha looked to the torch in her hand, biting her lower lip while trying to force back the fear caused by the darkness of the cloud above having already consumed them. A horrific screech echoed from around her as another flash of light exploded. Trails of darkness seemed to break away from the shadows, hissing and squealing. "We just have to hope this holds them at bay, or at least gives them second thoughts about approaching."

* * *

Alana stood before the Great Spirits, even now they remained shrouded, not allowing their forms to materialise within this world. They had apologised to her for this, but they knew the one who had taken their Maidens also possessed a presence within this world. Revealing themselves, even here, when there was a being with such power on the prowl, could result in their own demise.

She had sat within a circle of blue flowers, and had listened with a patience and understanding not normally expected of a child her age. They had explained all that it meant for her to don the mantle of the Mitéra. Her acceptance of the role would mean a great sacrifice, and of all those touched by the price, she would be the one who would suffer the greatest consequences. Each of the four Spirits would need to take something of who she was in order to fuse with her. This fragment would be returned to her when her essence had reached the maturity needed to complete the rites at their shrines. In addition, she would be required to offer something of importance to each Spirit she trained with in this manner but, by lending her their aid before she was ready, they would sacrifice their freedom.

The moment she called fully upon their power her they would become bound, imprisoned until she completed the tasks expected from her. With their energies sealed, the four Maidens they were tied to would not wake from their affliction; instead the power from their essence would be diverted to her, allowing her to retain some minor gifts until the balance could be restored. As each Spirit was liberated, the essence of the Maiden would be returned and the associated elemental magic would once more awaken. Alana's shoulders bore a weight unfair to ask of any child. If she wielded the power she had to complete the rites, however, if she were to fail the forces keeping the world in balance would falter, and death and suffering would follow.

"You said you would mark me?" Alana asked, her terrified voice merely a whisper.

"Yes, the people of the mortal plane refer to what we would do as a tikéta. A marking of the skin, but ours would be crafted by magic. Any looking upon it would know of your position, and it will repel the Skiá."

"Will it hurt?"

"Yes. We will each need to imbue a fraction of your essence with a pact, altering it. We can complete the foundation any time, but only when you have completed our training will you be able to wear the symbol of our bond."

"Okay," she whispered. Silence was her only response, and she realised they hadn't understood she was giving consent. "To protect the world my family care for, I accept the honour of being your Mitéra." Alana spoke with the conviction of an adult.

"Young lady, what we are about to do will hurt more than any pain you have felt. Even the strongest of warriors have cried out for much less than this. Be brave, it will pass."

Alana felt heat rush through her body, pleasant at first, warming against the nervous chill which had enveloped her causing her thin frame to tremble. She inhaled deeply, feeling the increase in pain, trying not to cry out as agony burned through her very essence. No sound escaped her lips, although she screamed for all she was worth the sound remained trapped, unlike the tears which streamed down her face as she stood rigid, imprisoned in a silent scream. At first images flooded through her mind, instructions of what was expected of her, but soon the pain blinded her to further distractions.

When the tension released her fragile body crumpled to the floor, releasing her frozen breath in deep heaving sobs. Her cries were so all-consuming she didn't hear the hushed surprise as the Great Spirits looked upon her to see her essence now mirrored that of the former Mitéra perfectly. It seemed impossible, her energy had been destroyed, and yet this young girl had somehow now come to be the very reflection of the lost soul.

Each of the Spirits reached out in their ethereal form, offering what little comfort they could before withdrawing from Darrienia. When Alana's sobbing finally subsided she was aware of being cradled in her mother's embrace, her cool hands calming the burning pain across her back and collar bone.

When her daughter had calmed, Zoella carefully lifted the back of Alana's top and could not suppress the gasp that escaped her. Reaching out, her trembling fingers touched the markings on her daughter's flesh. Markings so beautiful, so real, had she not already felt otherwise she would have thought Alana was wearing jewellery.

A grey silver corded chain ran across the back of her neck almost between her collar bones in a V-shape, as if weighted down by the decorations it held. At the centre was a delicate bead with a beautiful feather attached fanning to the left. There was a slight drop before an intricate dream catcher, appearing to be woven of leather, sinew, and beads filled the space between her shoulder blades. There was another feather, and what looked to be energy ribbons woven with the occasional bead before a slight drop and a second, then third dream catcher, each shrinking in size. The design finished at the lower part of her back with three intricate feathers. This was the most beautiful and terrifying tikéta Zoella had seen. It marked her daughter as belonging in body and essence to the Spirits.

"It finishes on her shoulders," Zoella whispered, tracing her fingers across the severed lines.

"Of course, this only represents her past. The dream catchers are in part a symbolic representation of us, and her origins. They will also serve to keep her safe, despite being only essence made." Seiken bent down, placing a tender kiss on Alana's head as he slid his hand over Zo's giving it a comforting squeeze.

"So what do we do now?"

"Now, you have to take me to them." Alana pulled away from Zo, pulling her top down. "I can only learn what I need to in their own homes, so we have to go there. I hate studying, but I promise I'll be good, so don't be sad okay?" Alana threw herself into her mother's arms, hugging her tightly.

"I'm not sad," Zo whispered, trying to ensure her voice did not betray the lie. "We're just... really proud of you." She tightened her grip on her daughter as Seiken crouched to join the embrace. "What else did they tell you?"

"I can't tell you, Mummy. Not all of it, but the tikekia"—Alana scrunched her face in a frown, thinking back to the word used, knowing what she said hadn't sounded right—"ticky...tic—"

"Tikéta?" Seiken offered seeing her becoming increasingly more frustrated as the word continued to elude her.

"Yes, that, it will keep the skiers away." She gave a firm nod, causing her red locks to fall over her shoulders. "But we don't have much time."

"I can open a gateway to Gaea's Star, but once we're there we're not going to be able to cross back, we'll have to travel the lands." Seiken advised, meeting Zo's gaze above Alana's head.

"Why?" Alana asked.

"Because once we leave here, you'll only be able to return in your dreams." Seiken brushed his daughter's hair behind her ears.

"You mean I'm banished?" she questioned, her eyes moistening with tears.

"No, princess, never. But, when you agreed to become the Mitéra, you had to give up being an Oneiroi," he explained softly. "So, where are we going?" Alana closed her eyes, recalling the images.

"Daddy, the Water Elemental said I should seek him first, because otherwise my challenges would mean little." Zo and Seiken exchanged a knowing glance.

"Then, my princess, that is where we shall go."

* * *

As much as it had pained him to abandon his friends in their time of need, Daniel knew there were more important tasks in need of his attention. If what Zoella had said about the Skiá's emergence was true, there was no time to loiter. Alana was like her parents, he knew she would unquestioningly accept the role placed before her. The least he could do was to ensure that, while they focused on her, he did what he could to ensure the safety of the rest of the people.

Seiken and Elly's stories had revealed one thing, light was something they were weak to. So when he and Alessia returned to Kalia, and the Eorthāds informed him of a spreading darkness from the Mountains of Light, he knew this to be an ill omen. He had been thinking on this problem for some time, and was almost certain he had formulated a solution, but he could not do it alone.

"Where are we going?" Alessia questioned as Daniel rushed towards the nesting area of the wyrms.

"Alessia, this will be a war like we have never experienced in the history of our peoples. It's not something we can fight alone. It's not something I think you can even be involved in," Daniel explained, unconsciously returning to Alessia's native tongue.

"What do you mean, this is our du—"

"It's just a feeling. Something tells me that the presence of wyrms or those bonded to one, could turn the tide of this war against us." Daniel couldn't voice the sensation, but whenever he imagined the wyrms and Eorthāds riding into battle, a dark despair knotted his gut, flooding him with such foreboding he had no choice but to push the images aside.

"Then what are you doing in the nesting area?"

"I'm seeking Nemean's council. I must reach the mercenaries, but before that I need to visit Semiazá port," he explained, his pace becoming a jog as he entered the enormous hollow mountain.

"And what do you hope to find there?"

"A blacksmith." Daniel glanced around, not even stopping, as he often would, to marvel at the world that thrived within. Grassy meadows flowed for miles, and rainbows were majestically formed by the magnificent waterfall that fell inexplicably from the open peak, crashing down to the wide river below. Wyrms lay within the grass, their enormous wings extended to feed upon the sunlight filtering through from above. All this went noticed, but unseen as his vision fixed ahead, to the place he knew Nemean waited.

"We have blacksmiths that would attend your every whim," Alessia countered desperately.

"Yes, but my instincts tell me I need a specific blacksmith. The Skiá cannot be hurt by conventional means, and from what I've deduced there is but one thing that can hurt a shadow."

"Light. But surely our masters of Arcane—oh, you seek a béacenfýr." As she saw Daniel frown she realised she'd used a word he was unfamiliar with. She remained silent, waiting for the look of recognition. He had an intuitive understanding of their dialect from the moment they first met, perhaps because he was always destined to be their Wita, but there were still times that meanings briefly escaped him.

"Yes, that's one reason," he acknowledged after a short pause. "But there is another. We may not be able to make weapons from light, but we can make weapons capable of supporting it, for instance, a flaming blade. But any who fight won't have the luxury of applying oil to their blades at any frequency, so we need a means to keep our weapons as harmful as possible for as long as possible. Besides, I have another task for the Eorthåds, if you consent."

"You know we are at your disposal, but what makes this particular blacksmith so special?"

"My reasoning is two-fold. He is skilled, and we've only ever met one Elementalist capable of wielding the Light element, and I have a feeling he'll know where to find her."

"Chrissie?" Alessia questioned with a slight bite in her tone. Even now she recalled their clashing of opinions only worsened as innocent misunderstandings added fuel to an already volatile fire. They had overcome their differences, but still Alessia had her reservations about the unusual Elementalist.

"Yes, I believe"—Daniel pushed his hand through his hair as he was bombarded by a new voice—"þá egesan." Alessia stopped in mid-step, without context she was unsure of his meaning. Seeing him begin to tremble she knew it to be both the expression of dread and observation of horror. "They can travel between shadows," he spluttered as the young voice shared with him the horror he had witnessed before his father had shown him mercy, releasing him from life before the monstrosities could claim him. "With so many dead, why is it I only hear one voice?" He grasped Alessia's arm in panic. "From what I've just been told there should be hundreds. Why do I only hear one?"

Chapter 19

The Challenges

Bray smiled as he stood atop the crest of a hill, his hands upon his hips with his chest thrust out as he surveyed the rise and fall of the land, while Elly paced impatiently. He was reluctant to lead her to the safe haven he had found for Solon and Mika. Only he knew where they sheltered, and as long as that held true they would be safe. The Research Plexus' tendrils spread far and wide, and they were not the kind to let those once privileged to their secrets see a natural end. Since Elly herself had admitted her own connection to them, revealing they lived, while everyone believed them to be dead, was more than he should have done.

"What are you doing? We have no time for posturing, besides there is only myself who can see you, and I doubt this is for my benefit." Elly turned her back to him, had she known where they were going she would have continued alone, but she found herself in something of a conundrum. Whilst she had experienced every moment of the journey here, the scenery, the carriage ride, the hiking, she had no idea where she now stood. The landscape was familiar, yet alien at the same time. She was unaccustomed to such things. If there was one thing she always knew, it was her location. She rarely needed sun or stars to discern where she was. She had journeyed these lands countless times and knew them by heart. They were still on Albeth, of that she was certain, and yet she couldn't remember how she came to be here, whether they had ridden south or east. She frowned as she thought over the unusual realisation that she was lost.

"When was the last time you slept?" Bray enquired, turning his piercing gaze upon her. For a moment her breath caught as his intense green eyes met with hers. She saw the sparkle of amusement light his features as a playful smile traced his tempting lips. The wind whipped around them, carrying with it his earthy aroma. She shook her head, scowling.

"I have no need—" Elly paused, suddenly understanding why it was they had stopped. She rubbed her eyes, aware of her diminished sight and the heaviness of her limbs. She had been slowing him down, and he had been unusually quiet. Small gestures played on her mind. For the last mile or so, he had deliberately positioned himself upwind of her, leading the way, yet adhering to a pace she could manage. His gaze had never strayed to her, and the distance between them had never closed.

"I can build a shelter that I know will keep you safe. Sleep," he insisted.

"We have no time."

"No. What we do not have time for, Lady of Knightsbridge, is this. You know all too well the difficulties that come with sleep deprivation. Stop trying to keep up and acknowledge your weaknesses."

"I am not weak!" Elly snapped. Bray's words had struck a nerve. She was flesh and blood now, her endurance was but a fraction of what it once was, and it had not helped that she had spent her time since waking in the flesh hiding away. He took a stride towards her, one she had sought to meet defiantly in the opposite direction, and yet she found herself once more focused on his lips. She shook her head, questioning what was wrong with her, why all she could suddenly think about was how ruggedly handsome he looked as his forehead creased in annoyance.

"How else would you describe a failure to acknowledge your own limitations? I will not be placed in jeopardy because you're too proud to rest. You know better than this, I expected more from you."

"There is no time," she insisted.

"In your current state I could force the suggestion, your will has diminished."

"I am—"

"*Sit*," Bray commanded, to her surprise Elly felt herself obey, her pulse quickened in response to his domination. He placed his hand upon her cheek, leaning in until his lips were almost upon hers. Elly felt her breath hitch, heat rising to her cheeks as her eyes closed in response to the comfort of his tender touch. "Will you still question me?" he whispered seductively, his breath upon her ear causing the fine hairs over her body to rise before he pulled away. "Rest, I will ensure your safety. Is it so hard to trust me?"

"Your nature alone suggests the need for caution," Elly chided, mentally berating herself.

"And yet for hours I have been able to influence you. You have been weak. Easy prey for someone like myself, and believe me, the thought has crossed my mind on more than one occasion. But instead, ever the gentleman, I stand here now warning you, and ask you to rest, rather than take advantage of what you are so openly offering." Elly's focus snapped to attention as she realised the truth of his words. She was tired, and as a result his proximity was causing her own body and desires to betray her.

"You are certain it will be safe?" Elly questioned, realising that while he had been speaking he had retrieved a bundle of long, bound posts from somewhere nearby. "Where—"

"Enchanted cache," Bray advised. It had taken him a while to pinpoint, but he had led them here for a single reason. The equipment within would keep them safe, and he needed her to rest, for his own sake as much as hers. He saw her look of confusion. "Don't tell me a lady of your learning is unaware of them?" Elly didn't answer, she simply watched him in silence, mesmerised by the fluid movements of his body as he went about his task. She tried to look away, but found it impossible. Moistening her lips, aware of the inappropriate thoughts racing through her mind, she watched him hungrily. He unbound the posts at one end, spreading them out to create a makeshift shelter before draping the supplied woven mats in place. It was far from perfect, but it would suffice.

There were many such caches across the world. They ranged from larger ones, such as this one which supplied the items needed to make a shelter, to smaller ones with things such as leather skins or rudimentary tools. There was a rule to using them, before they would open an agreement to return the items before leaving had to be made. The legend was that enchanters and sorcerers had made these caches near the beginning of the cycle intending to aid any who survived. Items were stored in natural crevices and disguised by illusion to anyone, except for either those in dire need, or someone who already knew where to look. Bray was the latter, during his time in Misora he had memorised numerous locations, and knew there were many more he had yet to unearth.

Once he had finished some minor adjustments he motioned for Elly to enter, and placed a bowl of tinder upon the roof in the space where the poles converged. Bray touched the tinder, seeming to strike a flint across the bowl until a small fire ignited, quickly spreading to the surrounding wood until the structure stood bathed in flames.

"What are you—"

"Get some sleep." His commanding voice seemed unusually strained.

"I am *not* going in there," Elly asserted, gesturing towards the burning shelter.

"I swore I would keep you safe while you slept. Why not extend a branch of trust?" He turned his back towards her, his gaze fixed upon the horizon.

"Because the branch you are referencing is now on fire."

"Is it?" He turned, his hand extending to cup Elly's face as he touched her mind, and for a moment she saw the shelter as it had been seconds before, upon its peak was not a bowl of tinder, but a large uncut rock containing large fragments of Fire Agate.

"Enchanted cache," she whispered, her own hand now resting upon the place his had briefly touched. Realising what she was doing she crawled inside, silently condemning such thoughts. Bray sat near the entrance, his back towards her.

"In this case the word enchanted holds true on two counts. This cache has saved many lives. There was once a town not too far from here, more moons ago than I would care to remember." Bray gazed off into the distance, he had always been scolded for sneaking from the safety of Misora, especially given that he had a tendency to interfere with things. "The enchantress who made this structure bewitched her own humble home, so that those seeking her ill-will believed someone had already put a flame to her, while those seeking aid could see her place of dwelling as it was.

"The area surrounding her home became known as Everburn. It was thought that her magic was so powerful that when she burned alive within, the flames could never be extinguished. When more people saw flames than not, she knew it was time to move on. The rumours were that the town was already searching for a new wise woman, so she created a cache, in the hope that anyone facing the same dangers would use it as she had." Bray glanced over his shoulder, smiling as he saw Elly had already drifted into slumber.

As he gazed upon her sleeping form his hunger stirred. She could not become this weak again, he wasn't certain he could prevent himself from doing what his nature asked of him. He moistened his lips, daring not to look back inside the shelter. It had been too long since he had last eaten, and hunger was a dangerous trait for something like him. On more than one occasion as they walked he had felt his frenzy trying to surface as she reacted to being in his presence. He had made a vow to watch over her, and he would keep it.

The presence of the enchantment would be enough to keep her safe should the darkness reach them before he had the answers they sought. He only wished they could take the Fire Agate with them, the enchantment upon it would protect them. Alas, he knew he must honour the agreement of the cache, or pay the price in blood.

Bray allowed his eyes to close, granting himself a brief respite. Whilst he did not require as much sleep as humans, it was always better to be alert, especially since it seemed his next meal may not be for some time.

The loud shrieking of a large bird woke him. The creature descended, landing gracefully to deposit a small rolled parchment before taking to the skies once more. Breaking the seal he read it carefully, closing his eyes to visualise the lay of the land.

With this in hand it was time to begin their quest. He wondered how long it would be before Elly realised he had not really required her aid. He had been asked to provide answers, but there had been more to that letter than she had seen, as he had told her, it had been a request for help.

The note he had just received from Solon and Mika had contained exactly the information he had wanted. When they were in Semiazá Port he had sent a message, via a seagull, while Elly had been engaged in conversation with the blacksmith. One of the many benefits of his talents was his ability to connect with animals, in the past he had used it as a fun means of exploiting the rich and making coin. Those days seemed far behind him now.

He had left Solon and Mika with a carrier bird trained to find him, in case of emergencies. This safeguard ensured he could obtain any information he needed, without exposing their location.

"It would have been more beneficial if they had the plans already," Elly muttered, causing Bray to turn in alarm. She was kneeling behind him, reading the small note still grasped within his hand.

"How long have you been awake?" He had not even noticed her stirring, let alone moving so close. By this alone he knew her to be fully rested.

"It seems I do not require quite as much sleep as I thought." She gave a half smile. "Do you know where we are going, or shall I lead the way?" Elly glanced down at the note once more as Bray set it alight with his tinder box and stood to dismantle the shelter. She thought back on the note, specifically its words about a golden peak. There were many places it could be, but only one that came close to the description in the note. "Keep the stones," Elly insisted, grasping his hand as he lifted them from their place.

"Caches don't operate in that manner. I must return what I removed."

"I assume the price is attached to you?"

"It wasn't me who took refuge within its protection, my lady." Bray pulled his arm free, replacing the stone into a long narrow coffer before disassembling the rest of the structure and rebinding it. Once it was all back in place, he pulled a large marble lid over it. Elly glimpsed numerous engravings before it appeared to sink back into the earth. Bending down she touched the place it had once been, amazed to discover it felt like ordinary grass. "You honestly can't perceive it, can you?"

"Perceive what?"

"The aura." He approached until he was able to look deep into her violet eyes. He stood for longer than she was comfortable with, simply staring at her, "Of course, I should have realised it sooner," he mused stepping back.

"Realised what?"

"It will be concealed from people like you." He gave a shrug as he walked away.

"What is that supposed to mean?"

"It means the contents are not for you. Or at least they weren't, not in the time where heroes walked and legends were born. You have the eyes of a god, and most heroes quested against one deity or another. They are enchanted so a mortal afflicted or touched by a god cannot bear witness to the hidden support."

"Fine, it matters not. Let us get this over with. It has become very clear you have no intention of sharing what you know about me. The sooner we conclude our business and I have my answers, the better," she snapped.

"Don't think I haven't noticed how you look at me," Bray teased. "I find it is always preferential to keep a few mysteries in a new relationship, otherwise, what motivation would there be for helping me? Especially since you are now of the belief you know where we're going."

"You assume that this insight is worth my tolerating you?"

"I know it is. You're not the kind of lady who enjoys being left in the dark, for too long anyway." Bray gave a suggestive wink. "Besides, I know for a fact you find me dashing and charming."

"Oh?" Elly questioned, her right eyebrow spiking. "I assure you, the only time I will find you charming is when you are dashing away from me, forever."

"And yet, whenever our eyes meet your heart quickens." He grinned again as Elly placed a hand to her chest, her cheeks betraying her embarrassment.

"If it does, I assure you it is only from frustration," she growled, knowing her words to be a lie. She couldn't explain it, but being close to him did something to her and, in ways she had sworn never to experience again, made her feel human. Whenever he was near she felt her pulse quicken, her breathing catch. She thought she had been concealing her unwanted yearnings well.

"Do you think I can't taste the very thing my presence can induce?" Bray glanced over his shoulder with a knowing look.

"It is your doing!" Elly snapped in realisation.

"Not intentionally. What can I say, I just have a way with living things." He paused, taking her hands in his. "But if you ever feel like embracing that desire..." She pulled her hand from his sharply.

"I will do no such thing."

"Then it would be wise not to allow yourself to become so vulnerable in my presence again. Like yourself, I have times when my will wavers, do you understand?" Bray warned.

* * *

Standing upon the cobbled roads of Semiazá port brought back numerous memories for Daniel, both pleasant and foreboding. When last he stood in this exact spot he had seen a tsunami grow to epic proportions, threatening to destroy the port city. He had watched in fear and horror as it approached, only for it to be quelled by an Elementalist's power. Chrissie's power to be precise. This city had secrets, and he knew many of them, including his first-hand knowledge of the hydra who nested near the horizon, protecting its domain. He had seen it with his own eyes, in fact, she had saved their lives to repay an outstanding debt to Zoella, who had once protected her domain from trespassers with a self-sustaining illusion.

It was at this port where his path had first crossed with Tony. They had been sent here in search of the means to explore beneath the ocean to retrieve a fragment of the key needed to seal the Severaine. Tony had possessed the answer but, for his assistance, Daniel had to treat the rare illness his wife suffered from.

Their paths had crossed again during the reconstruction efforts, and Daniel had barely recognised the man. With his wife in good health he seemed to have doubled in size, standing taller and broader than before, and the fire in his soul had become a furnace burning through his eyes. The man he had first met had been a mere shade of the one he bore witness to on his return.

"So you believe this blacksmith will know where to find Chrissie?" Alessia questioned in Daniel's native dialect. She had found they were often better received when not communicating in her own language amongst strangers. Her steps quickened as a glance behind them, then forward across the ocean, confirmed her fears. The dark clouds on the distant horizon grew ever closer, expanding and swelling in a turbulent and broiling manner as they sealed the sun from the land below. "We have little time."

"We must secure this town first. Alessia, I'll find Tony, you do whatever it takes to make the lighthouse keeper fix its light upon the city. It may not be a solution, but a barrier of light should provide some defence against an army of shadows." Daniel gestured towards the beacon on the west side of the port. Unlike many such ship-guiding monuments, the one at this port had been constructed on the land's peninsular, rather than out at sea. Its stone and metal structure was well maintained against the elements and, with the repairs following the Severaine's unrest, it stood stronger than ever.

"As you wish, Wita." Alessia gave a single nod placing her hand to her chest, not quite upon the brilliant stone she wore that, when activated, extended her armour. All Nemean's warriors possessed one, even himself, and its magic fascinated him still. Daniel saw something behind the look she gave him, a recognition, seeing his curious expression she spoke again. "You have grown into the role beyond what we had hoped. A Wita is not just a sage, but a leader, that is why, as Master and Commander, I only take orders from you and Nemean."

"You said we were equals," Daniel frowned.

"At that time we were. I shall secure the béacenfýr." She took off in a sprint, the sound of her boots upon the floor barely discernible despite her haste. Watching her depart Daniel too made his way to his destination.

"Daniel Eliot, as I live and breathe." The figure cleared his throat as he struck the cherry red metal upon his anvil a few more times before dropping it into a vat of fluid. The metal hissed angrily, throwing steam into the air.

"You cast a daunting impression these days." Daniel smiled. "I'm glad to see you in good spirits. How's your wife?"

"Just fine. We had many fine years thanks to you." Tony looked out from his forge and sighed. "So what brings you to my door, the crease of your brow tells me this isn't a social call. Don't tell me, you're here to fix the weather," he jested, gesturing jovially towards the approaching ominous clouds. He let out a hearty laugh before his eyes came to rest on Daniel's serious expression. "By my hammer and anvil, don't tell me you're here to fix the weather?" he repeated, this time his voice devoid of humour. "By Zeus, that's it isn't it?"

"In part," Daniel admitted.

"Then you'd better flip the post and join me inside." Tony motioned towards the sign outside his smithy that announced he was open for business. Daniel let out a strained chuckle as he read the reverse side advising those seeking his services that they were closed.

"If only it were that simple." Daniel nodded towards the sign which now read, 'Closed, all warring is officially postponed,'.

Daniel made his way across to the distant table, where numerous parchments were unrolled to reveal the faded and smudged designs of time-worn plans and blueprints. His vision wandered to the unusual hat placed upon the recently disturbed, dust-ridden surface. Seeing this, Tony, after wiping his hands down his clothes, scooped it in his large hands, depositing it on the twisted, wooden coat stand near the shuttered workshop where he hung his coat. "Do you have company?" Daniel questioned, he knew exactly where he had seen that tricorn before, and wondered what business she could possibly have here.

"No, it's a special request from the Lady of Knightsbridge. Nothing to concern yourself with, we're quite alone."

Daniel knew he could take Tony at his word and so explained everything he knew of the current situation, from the return of Íkelos, to needing a weapon capable of injuring or repelling the Skiá.

"So, I was hoping you could forge a blade—"

"Capable of holding fire," Tony droned with a knowing sigh. "You're not the first to request such a thing of me." Tony produced a blade from one of the cooling vats. "It doesn't matter how I quench it, nor how I alter the design, this weapon is more dangerous to the wielder than the one at its tip." He flipped the blade over in his calloused hand, grunting. By itself it was a fine blade, but not fit for the purpose intended.

"What do you mean?"

"In order to ensure the blade continues to produce a flame there has to be a source to keep it burning, a delivery mechanism. The problem is, fire travels, and," Tony picked up some twisted shards of metal by way of an explanation. "The closest I've got has been using powders, and creating rivulets, but the metal gets too hot under the constant heat. Not only does the heat travel to the hilt, but it damages the weapon's integrity. Even if I could arrange for it to burn for prolonged periods, a single blow would render it useless." Tony gestured towards the countless plans. "I've tried old methods, and new, nothing works."

"There are many myths of flaming swords," Daniel mused quietly.

"Aye, those tempered by the Gods and passed to the hands of a mortal to lead their charge, but I know collectors, those who possess things you would not even imagine, and such a blade is not amongst them." He glanced towards Elly's hat meaningfully. "They must have been reclaimed by the Gods, or destroyed. Not a single example remains, believe me if it did I would know."

"The gateway to Olympus still exists. I wonder how difficult infiltrating their kingdom and excavating ore from Hephaestus' mine would be? Surely if he forged the weapons capable of wielding fire, we could turn the ore from his mines to our use." Daniel's eyes passed over the numerous twisted and splinted shards of weapons that had previously escaped his notice.

"A siege against the Gods, darn near impossible. What adventures you must have had to talk of such things so flippantly." Tony gave a rumbling chuckle. "But you wouldn't find the metal there. His mine used to be on mortal land,

Drevera, but there's no use heading there. It was completely depleted when the weapons were crafted for Titanomachy and that stored was used to forge items to ensure continued rule after Zeus claimed the throne.

"Not an ounce of ore remains. I'm a smithy, trust me, I know these things. I was once granted special permission to search the mines there, and you know what the Dreverians are like for their hospitality. There's nothing, not even a filing. Anything there that was once divine has long turned mundane." Tony's scarred hand scratched his chin thoughtfully for a moment. "But you know, there's a legend in my family. My ancestors once made a claim to be his mortal descendants, our name is famous, that's why I just go by Tony these days."

"What's the legend?" Daniel asked, raising his gaze to meet the intensity of Tony's penetrating stare.

"It was rumoured that Hephaestus was something of a perfectionist when it came to his creations. Only the purest of metal would suffice. He drew the ore from his mine, and from Olympus cast anything impure into Acheron. He did not want gods or mortals to possess it, and yet it was not good enough for his craft, and so he disposed of it in the only manner he knew how, but like I say, it's a myth. Why would he discard something he wanted away from the hands of a god into the kingdom of Hades?"

Daniel leaned forward resting his elbows on the table to cradle his head, hearing the tale had caused the voices within him to stir. Whispers upon whispers crashed around him until he focused on a single voice, a single thread of knowledge taken from a man who had once partnered with a Daimon.

"The Depths of Acheron," Daniel whispered thoughtfully, raising his head to look upon Tony.

"Yeah, like I say, it doesn't make a lot of sense." Tony's broad shoulders raised in an over-exaggerated shrug.

"No, it makes perfect sense, at least to someone who knows there is more than one Acheron."

"I don't follow." Tony hooked another stool from under the table with his foot before lowering his weight upon it. Taking the pitcher of water used to hold the blueprints in place, he poured Daniel a glass, inviting him to share his train of thought.

"There's Acheron, the river that runs through the Underworld, the one the dead cross, and then there are the Depths of Acheron, only it's not a river, it's a tear in realms that holds lost lands, the place through which The Stepping Realm traverses."

"I'm afraid you've lost me there." There was a strange sparkle in Tony's eyes, and for a moment Daniel wondered if this old smithy knew more than he let on. He suppressed a shiver. Surprised by the sudden chill, his focus turned to the forge. It burned with heat, and yet the air seemed almost frigid.

"There's just one problem," Daniel mused as he took a quick gulp of the water before him.

"Just one?"

"If I could procure this metal, a metal resistant to fire and heat, how could it be tempered?"

"Now that is something you can entrust to me. If you can find it, I can smelt it," Tony boasted, hooking his thumbs around the neck of his fire-resistant apron. "Can you not see, I have a fire in my blood that runs hotter than any forge." Tony's eyes sparkled with enthusiasm at the thought. "In fact, I'm willing to bet I'm one of only three who can, and the only one who'd be willing to help you, that's for sure."

"Then I guess I'm going to the Depths of Acheron," Daniel announced, rising to his feet with determination.

* * *

Darkness gave way to light as Rob, Fey, and Acha stumbled through the portal. Fey still gripped Teanna tightly upon his back. Sweat poured from his face as Teanna, her eyes wide with terror, continued to wave the torch frantically, leaving trails of embers and light. Seeing a bright flash a small group began to gather as if expecting some manner of street festivities to begin. But one look at the exhausted troupe saw them exchange cautious whispers, keeping a safe distance between them before dispersing as quickly as they appeared.

"What now?" Fey questioned, shifting Teanna's weight to allow him to reach up and still her waving arm.

"The Council. We need to get this city flooded with light, and soon." Rob glanced around to get his bearings, he stepped behind Acha, deferring to her judgement. He knew Collateral well, he knew some of the portals, but as a trader she could lead them with ease to the place they sought, a place few had cause to visit.

"But it already grows dark," Teanna observed. "Surely anyone of importance will have retired to their home." In Talaria, when the sun sank beyond the horizon it was time to sleep, they wasted little energy in attempting to dispel nature's natural cycle of light and darkness.

"And what you see is only an illusion," Acha revealed. Few knew of this deception. She had first come to learn of it from Daniel. The entire city was not within the boundaries of their own world thus, in order to suggest otherwise, it drew on the collective consciousness of those within the borders to adapt the city, lights, atmosphere, and even the air, to the dominant species. The land outside, even the sky above, was nought but an illusion to maintain this deception. Collateral was a safe haven, constructed by the Gods to keep their devout safe from the Severaine during the cycles after this force had been first sealed and then unleashed.

The Severaine was a mighty foe, an ally to Gaea, and a protector of its mother. It once ran rampant across the world, destroying any who performed irreparable harm to the land. The Gods, envious of Gaea's control of this force, whispered in the ear of early man and convinced them it should be sealed so they may develop beyond what this force allowed; but in truth, they had wanted to ensure Gaea did not control this devastating entity. For cycles untold Man sealed the Severaine, and when the possessor of The Throne of Eternity was unseated it would break its constraints and destroy all traces of that god's civilisation.

Across the cycles Man had always succeeded in sealing it. The final phase of its binding unleashed an ice age upon the world which took the lives of many survivors, but those who endured used the height of their time's knowledge to force the immense power back into submission. The new possessor of The Throne created life anew, and over time the means to control the Severaine was forgotten by many.

This time, however, things had been different. Zeus had not been overthrown, and yet Night had found the means to unleash this force, and those who should have resealed it had been foiled. Without being able to utilise the methods used by those who previously bound it, it seemed there was no hope to stop this power.

This cycle's advancement had been insufficient for them to devise a new method of restraint, and their magic had been bargained and traded away, weakened by pointless dealings with the Hoi Hepta Sophoi to see Night's powers temporarily sealed. They had no technology, and no magic. They had no hope. But there had been another choice.

Gaea had once possessed an ancient artefact, known as the Spiritwest, to keep the Severaine in balance. When the ancient gods had forced Gaea to seal the Severaine, they had also ensured this ancient tool was hidden away. The heroes, Daniel, Acha, and Eiji, with the help of Seiken, Zo, Chrissie, and Alessia, discovered a means to find this tool and return it to the goddess. Whilst the Severaine remained free, it was tamed, and man took heed of the warnings it gave, altering their methods to ensure they lived in balance, rather than consuming the world around them.

Acha had been part of the group now sung of in ditties and ballads, and she was privileged to information beyond that other people would receive. She and Eiji had decided to take over Eryx Venrent's store in Collateral, and in turn accepted all the responsibilities that came with doing so. But given their status as heroes, they were also granted one thing that would come in useful at this moment, unquestioned access to Collateral's Council.

"Do you honestly expect them to just take your word?" Teanna asked as they entered the magnificent hall. It was a simple building, humble against some of the others which had towered around it, and yet somehow it felt more powerful. The grey marble wall seemed to thrum with energy, causing the fine hairs on the small groups' arms to stand on end.

"People never do. Trust me, I have attended to their like more times than I care to recall. They will challenge, question, stall, delay, and complain, always complain. It will only be when the threat is at their gates they will realise their error. Only then will they act and it will already be too late," Fey predicated, already having recovered his breath as their hurried footfalls echoed through the corridor.

Acha gave a polite smile, drawing to a halt before the barrier which separated them from the Council. There was nothing to indicate anyone waited on the other side. Those of the Council also lived and worked within Collateral, and their anonymity was protected unless they chose to relinquish it. Acha knew the name and face of one of the Council members, but not the others. She glanced towards one of the guards, he nodded as if to suggest she should present her case.

Acha had little cause to visit this location, and avoided doing so whenever possible. Like many places in Collateral this area housed its own boon, here magic and curses were suppressed, becoming inactive to any who entered. Given Acha's nature, allowances had been made to ensure she could seek an audience when required, but the Council chambers quickly became oppressive. Already she felt a slight tremor within her limbs as her actions became more sluggish. It was due to her curse she could occupy her body, and being here any length of time saw the magic sustaining her begin to fail. Lifting an unsteady hand she placed it to the opaque barrier before them, her gaze fixed unseeing through it. Her weakness only served to remind her of how much energy she had expended during their hasty retreat.

"Light the city. The Skiá are coming," she panted, her legs weakening. She had deliberately suppressed her absorption of energy as they had fled. It had been a necessary precaution. Given the unknown nature of the Skiá it was impossible to predict how their energies would have affected her, their force was unlike anything she had encountered before. Her gifts were recognised here, and before being granted citizenship she had to consent to only drawing energy from agreed locations within the city. They didn't, however, take her at her word, she had been subjected to an enchantment which ensured the laws were obeyed. She allowed herself to sit before the barrier, trying to save her remaining energy until she could return home.

"They won't do it," Fey assured in hushed whispers. "We need to be finding somewhere—"

A loud clap resonated from behind the barrier. The sound was sudden, and the first real indication that someone was listening.

"Come on then, you heard our lady, get this city lit. Initiate city-wide lock down, seal the barriers." Acha allowed a small smile to lift the corners of her mouth, she knew that voice, he had trained her to use her gift in combat.

"Wait, what? You're going to do it?" Fey questioned, his vision snapping to the barrier in disbelief.

"One does not take the word of our heroine lightly," he advised. "Besides, better we act in caution now than regret delay later. We can reverse security measures far easier than we can repel an invasion. The barrier before them turned a red hue before disappearing to reveal the empty chamber behind. Despite what was believed, the council never actually sat within the building, their shielding barrier was a means to communicate with them simultaneously at their undisclosed locations.

"Wait, did he say lock down?" Rob questioned.

"This city was a haven, if they perceive a threat the council can seal the portals. Their first rule is save who they can. They won't risk anyone new entering the city and bringing the threat inside the walls. Collateral was designed to be able to completely isolate itself from our world. Nothing can enter or leave until the threat has passed," Acha explained.

"You say that as if it isn't part of it," Teanna observed.

"It isn't," Acha revealed.

"So that's why they could survive the power of the Severaine. So if it's not of our world, then where exactly are we?" Fey pondered, glancing to Rob who looked less surprised by this revelation than he would have expected.

"Truthfully, I doubt you would believe me." The look she received from him challenged her to answer. "Besides," she continued, "I'm bound to secrecy."

"What now?" Fey questioned, adjusting Teanna's weight upon his back.

"First you find a medic to bind her ankle properly, then regroup at my home. One way or another we're sealed here. Collateral just became the safest place we could be."

"Then why didn't you bring me here first?" Teanna asked sceptically.

"Because we had feared he may already be here. This would have been the most logical place from which to mount an assault. Think of the tactical advantages to a place that leads to anywhere. It's where I would have gone. Even stepping through the portal was a risk, but given the options there was little choice," Acha admitted. She, Daniel, and Seiken had spoke in great depths about the dangers of bringing Teanna here. It was one of the many reasons they had opted to avoid using Collateral to travel. The possibility of a lock down such as the one just initiated had been the other.

"You don't believe him to be here then?" Teanna posed, her gaze scanning each stranger's face as they emerged from the building. Even to her it seemed a silly thing to do, she had no idea what he looked like, but it brought her comfort.

"He who?" Rob questioned, his voice seemingly unheard.

"No, had he been, the cloud would have most likely spread from the portals, and we would not have entered a city of light."

"What do you mean?" Teanna pressed.

"As I said, Collateral adapts to become home to the most prevalent population. The Skiá would outnumber the humans, if for no other reason than they would all be dead. Had he been here, we would have entered a very different environment."

"And you didn't think to mention this beforehand?" Rob posed.

"Either way it would have done little good. All things considered I believed it better we thought ourselves to be running towards safety rather than death."

"So, we just wait this out?" Rob questioned doubtfully. He saw Acha cast a glance towards Teanna before she answered.

"I'm not sure that will be possible, but we can use this time to rest at least."

* * *

Being on the mortal plane was more exhausting than he had anticipated. Íkelos had chosen the time of his return with great care. The breach between this realm, and his would need to be maintained until the Skiá he drew through had fully adapted to the level where they no longer needed the energy tether to their former vessel imprisoned within his forest.

It was a complicated process. Íkelos had used the imprisoned essences of the Skiá to create the Epiales, altering and changing them on an intrinsic level. Drawing them through to this world required more power than he had expected, and the merging of several Epiales to revert their essence back to the true likeness of the Skiá had been exhausting. He could sustain but a few, but he knew their numbers would soon grow. He needed only keep the connection to his realm until their strength was at such a level they could discard the threads that tied them to his forest and be born anew in this world.

It was a tedious task, sitting far below the ground drawing and channelling energy. A distraction would be welcome, but all he could do for the moment was sit, and think. He began his introspection, regretting he had lost his influence over his niece. It was as he reflected on this he felt the slight response in his attempt to reach her. A weakened thread called to him. Even with an Appraiser of such standing, it appeared Talaria's severing had failed. Whilst they had indeed purged his influence, they had failed to remove all the corruption he had sown. The small tendril of his energy responded to his thoughts, and with it came the ideal means of distraction.

His niece had fulfilled the role he had required from her. She had spoken his will, allowed him to gain the magics he required to step into this world, and even facilitated his arrival. At this moment he had no need of her, but such power was always tempting. He could ensure his victory by simply having her speak it aloud. The possibility was thrilling. Yes, the Skiá were harvesting the essences, and once the world was cleansed he could rebuild it in its purest form, the way the first gods always intended it to be, but with her at his side there was so much potential.

The Severaine was free, magical balance had been restored, but the Spirits were weak, they needed a force to revive them, a force to restore order, and he would create it. Will speaking had its limitations, of this he was all too aware, otherwise he would have had his niece speak his desires. In order to force the path he had to have the means available. Saying a soul would be recreated was impossible without the raw materials to do so, but she could ensure that his efforts in gathering and harvesting succeeded. He would have to spare her, to grow and spread the slither of corruption concealed within her meridians. Once she was his again, he would devise a means to draw her to him. Thanks to the Moirai taking her prisoner, he now knew of many bindings that could hold an Oneiroi on the mortal plane, and he knew of seals and runes that would render her spirit captive.

Her husband would need to be factored into his scheme. She had been claimed, as such he could use him to ensure her cooperation if she were to display the same level of resistance he had encountered before. Yes, he would need both of them, but he would be ready. His flesh bristled beneath his armour, his mind flooded with the euphoria of so many pathways opening before him.

He focused his mind's eye upon the small tendril of energy, diverting a small amount of his focus towards feeding it. He would claim her energy centres one by one, slowly, to ensure his actions remained undetected. She would become his spy. She was positioned amid heroes, and her access to them would ensure he knew everything of their attempts to foil him. Or he would, once he had claimed the relevant chakra to allow him such observations. She would facilitate the birth of the future in more ways than she could imagine.

Everything was progressing as he required. Soon he would reclaim his bride to be, and with her gift he would remake the world, returning it to its true path. His niece's help would ensure any who would oppose him failed. The Skiá were merely the tools he required. They were his harvesters, the collectors of the materials he required to bring about the new world and, as with all tools, once they had exceeded their usefulness, they would be cast aside.

* * *

The Elemental Spirits, whilst connected to the mortal plane, each had their own domain. Their personal sanctuaries were only accessible by crossing through the appropriate portal in The Stepping Realm. To ensure their safety, each of the Great Spirits had designed a challenge, of sorts, to ensure those seeking their land were worthy of entering, and only those invited could pass through the portal to undertake the challenge.

The Water Elemental, unlike his brethren, had not always been a Spirit, nor had he been the original of his kind. He was once a god. Detesting the vanity and cruelty of those claiming to serve him he passed his domain into the care of another. As years passed, and time forgot him, he did not fade but became that which he was always intended to be, not a god, but instead a Spirit who ascended to become the Great Spirit of this element when poachers had killed the original.

He forged the passage to his domain, and gave the large body of water that would spring forth from near its entrance his blessings. In time a great castle, now known to travellers as Oureas' Rest, was built bordering his waters. Whilst the people paid homage to the ruling god of the ocean, the lake was freshwater, and there were those who still remembered to offer thanks to him for the bounty they received.

Seiken listened with interest as Alana relayed this tale, her tiny hands gripping her parents' tightly as she spoke with an excitement only possible for a child. There were many portals located within Darrienia, most serving to assist Oneirois in the transition from Darrienia's lands to their homelands which were found above the surface world, away from the influence of dreamers. As their race had a cardinal rule of non-interference, there were but a few methods to cross from Darrienia to the waking world, and one such place was where they guided Alana now. The threat to Gaea's Star was a grave one, and with Zoella speaking the will of their goddess the Oneirois could not deny them the intervention required.

Long had it been predicted that the five forgotten legacies would be revealed, and only then would the journey of the Chosen be concluded, and a new hero be born. The Chosen had discovered Darrienia, The Severaine, and through the revealing of both Sunrise and Remedy came to learn of two lost races, the Daimons and the Moirai, although, as predicted these events had not been a direct result of their own journey. Now, only one remained, one forgotten history. Seiken cast a regretful glance towards his daughter, the figure who would become the final legacy of the mortal world. A lost power would be reborn through her. Alana would become the Mitéra, the last of the legacies and the end of their journey. He wondered how much had been kept from him of the events that were to come.

Upon the vast lake numerous fishing boats could be seen as small angular shapes against a horizon of blue. If one had never gazed upon the ocean before this enormous body of water could easily be mistaken as such. Oureas' Rest had the largest trading port in the known world. The enormous lake eventually became several large rivers, cutting their own paths to the sea. Merchants seeking trade would sail these vast waterways to reach the castle's dock and unload their wares. Plain, forest, and mountains surrounded the outer recesses of the lake, and it was upon the shoreline of the most north-western range Alana's instincts had guided them to.

The sheer cliff faces towered above, and the waters lapped against their rocky path. Before them a large peninsula angled a steep descent, halting abruptly. Years of weathering had, to the untrained observer, worn the cliff's base into natural and twisting arches large enough for small vessels to sail through from one side to the other. Seiken, as would any who beheld magic, saw it in a different light. It was not a tribute to nature's power; it was in fact, a doorway to the very force that had created this beautiful entrance.

He tore his eyes from the scene before him to see Alana was already starting to wade into the waters. Her small teeth chattered, either against the sudden chill or as an expression of the pure terror he beheld in her eyes. He could not be certain which.

"Alana, you don't—"

"I made a choice, Daddy," she asserted, forcing a smile to her quivering lips, her eyes veiled with tears she refused to shed. "Besides," she continued her tone strangely adult for one so young, "fear is only a way to keep us safe. Without fear I would approach a lion with the same care as I would a kitten. But one would eat me."

"Yes, I hear those kittens can be tricky," Seiken jested, bringing a smile to her face. He scooped her up gently, "I wouldn't presume to change your mind, you have your mother's stubborn streak." Seiken cast a quick glance towards Zo and smiled. "I just thought it was time to show you a new trick." He placed her down, back upon the narrow walkway. "There are a few ways to do this, but let's start with the basics." He placed her small hand to the water's surface.

"Feel yourself drawing energy from it." He drew the energy, using his magic to manipulate hers.

"It's getting colder," she giggled feeling the strange sensation both at her fingertips and across her flesh.

"We're making it colder by removing energy to increase the surface tension, increase it enough and you can walk across the surface, too much and you'll create ice, which you could still walk upon." Seiken carefully directed her magic, keeping the working small, so not to affect anything but the area they planned to traverse. "Do you think you can manage now?" She gave an assertive nod, her eyebrows knitting together in a frown as her tongue extended from her lips in concentration. "That's it, not too much, stop just before it turns to—" a small frosting appeared upon the water's surface. Removing her hand against the sudden chill she turned towards her parents and grinned.

"A great first try." Zo smiled kissing Alana's forehead. "When you get really good, you'll be able to create the right tension not only through any part of your body, but also surrounding it."

"Why would I want to do that?" Alana questioned.

"Because you may want to stop yourself falling in if you slip, or maybe you'll need a longer path than your reach can extend. The drawing of magic is limited to a certain area, and doing just the area you need is more controlled which in turn allows you to keep more of the energy you absorb, rather than pushing it into maintaining the tension." Zo took her daughter's hand, channelling her own energy through her and walking her out onto the unfrozen surface. "Do you feel the difference?" Alana felt waves of heat rising through her legs, the water below her not even rippling with contact.

"Wow," she gasped. "But why do this when I can swim?"

"Because if you look at the gateway it's positioned above the water's surface. You need to be able to use this skill if we're to pass through." Seiken gestured towards the stone archways.

"Mummy, why does your magic feel different to Daddy's?"

"Every way to utilise magic in itself is unique. There are infinite ways to achieve the same results. Elementalists, like your Uncle Eiji, are a perfect example. No two skills are the same, and yet many can achieve a similar effect. Yours is different too, the way we each use and intertwine the energy within ourselves gives it its own unique signature." Alana, with a look of commitment snatched her hand from Zo's leaping forwards several paces. The water beneath her feet rippled while ice sprayed in her wake. Seiken stepped in, grabbing her hand and stabilising the energy flow.

"Focus on keeping the pressure even," he added as Zo caught up, taking Alana's other hand. She giggled again at the sensation of both her parents' energy flowing through her, seeing in her mind how each pattern was part of a whole and how they worked in perfect unison together. She looked between them, smiling before they stepped through the gateway together.

Chapter 20

A Plan

Rob sat at the table, poring over the ancient parchments with Fey and Acha, while Teanna decided she could be of more help preparing a meal, than looking upon the unfamiliar scrawls. Acha had only learnt some basic recipes, mainly the food that Eiji enjoyed since he was the only one she ever prepared anything for. She couldn't say she enjoyed the task, but to see his face always made the effort worthwhile. When Teanna had insisted she fed them, since she couldn't read their dialect, Acha had been somewhat relieved. Given the delicate fragrances wafting from the kitchen it appeared Teanna possessed some skill in the craft. It also allowed them some time to talk in private.

While they scanned the parchments—which were copies of copies, that originally had been transcribed from tomes and translated time and time again to make this broken Gaean script—Acha had explained the circumstances surrounding Teanna and, much to her relief, both Rob and Fey decided her safety should be their primary concern.

"I still cannot believe they have an archive," Rob mused turning the unusual paper over. It was not often things of importance escaped his perception. The writings were scribed on something known as stone paper. While they used mainly vegetation to make such things, it seemed records in need of preservation were scribed on stone parchment, which was not only waterproof but more durable. "This could have come in useful last year."

"There's nothing you would have benefited from," Acha volunteered. "Their records are limited to the many creation mythos, I hear the renowned scholars sit and debate the truth of life based on these." She gave a shrug, the Mythographer had assured her legends of the Skiá would be somewhere within this vast collection.

"Strange how something we've never heard of can have a written record," Fey muttered in contemplation.

"I've got it!" Rob exclaimed, jabbing his finger upon the dark sprawls. "It's... not what I was expecting."

"What does it say?" Acha asked enthusiastically.

"Skiá are of dark. When they touch their like a network between." Rob awkwardly spoke the broken sentence aloud.

"Their like?" Fey questioned, his face dawning in realisation as the words when spoken alone sounded as the meaning intended. "So... when they touch darkness they..."

"Can move between it," Rob muttered, pinching the bridge of his nose in thought, wondering if that was what the obscure message meant.

"How does that help us, does it say anything else?" Fey moved to stand behind him, reading the same lines over his shoulder as he rested his hand on the rickety chair's back.

"Nope, that's the lot."

"Why can't they ever write what they mean?" Fey despaired.

"They probably did, about a few hundred versions ago." Rob could not even imagine how many languages had come and gone, each not quite understanding the last as it was translated. The fact it made sense at all was a miracle. What they really needed was a means to contact Bray. In Misora he had access to knowledge grown from life itself which was then harvested and stored. Rob had witnessed Bray assemble a delicate weave of crystal lattice here, in this very room, and decipher the information within it. It had been a single leaf of a tree Rob could not even envision. If wisdom of the Skiá existed, Misora would have it in a form better understood than a text many times rewritten.

He gave a sigh, Misorians would be of no help. They lived sheltered and protected. Bray often said they will only watch, no matter the situation, always watching, never acting. Bray had been reluctant to return, wondering if he would once again be able to escape their vigil. The need to find Paion, or perhaps a desire for revenge at having been so masterfully manipulated, had seen him pursue this course. The fact his communications went unanswered did not bode well for the situation he had returned to. But this was Grayson Bray, by his own admission he believed he could even tempt Hestia into forsaking her oath. If that were true, escaping the Watchers should have been a simple task, so his lack of communication grew increasingly more concerning.

"So they can shadow-hop? There are few who can use such magic." Teanna emerged from the kitchen with a tray of delicacies. The scent alone caused their mouths to water as they realised how long it had been since they'd last had a chance to eat. "Come now, work off the table. Nothing is so important that we should not take time to savour a meal."

"What did you mean, shadow-hop?" Fey questioned, shuffling the papers and placing the documents back into the small leather pockets as Teanna served the food. She sat, tasting a mouthful before she spoke again.

"It's in one of our old fairy tales. Monstrous creatures could travel by possessing the shadows of those they had touched, allowing them to travel between shadows." She glanced around the table, smiling as she saw everyone was enjoying their meal. A silence descended, not one of them speaking until the plates were empty and they had thanked her for their food.

"I think our assumption of safety may have been a little premature," Rob said at last, stretching slightly in his chair as he rubbed his stomach contently. He had been thinking this over while they ate. If the Skiá could travel between shadows, then there was no where they couldn't reach. It was possible that someone within this city had already been compromised. The only real way to lose a shadow was in darkness, but it still existed and darkness was where they thrived. Looking around the table he could see he was not the only one to have such harrowing thoughts. Each gaze moved suspiciously from one shadow to the next, almost as if expecting one to move of its own accord.

"We're sealed here now anyway. Look, we know none of us were touched, right?" Fey glanced between them, seeing the doubt on each of their faces. The Skiá had almost surrounded them during their retreat to Collateral, fending them off with light and flashes had cast their own shadows far and wide as a result. It was entirely plausible their shadows had been touched. "Flosh, we've no way of knowing for sure, have we?"

"So the question is, what do we do now?" Rob poised.

"And how much light does it take to repel them? I mean, could they appear in someone's shadow, and go on a rampage or—Gods, this is infuriating. How can we know so little about a threat that's as old as time itself, what are we meant to do?" Acha glared at the crate of papers as if it had betrayed them.

"What can we do? Collateral is sealed." Fey shrugged.

"Perhaps their networks cannot travel beyond the land they are upon?" Teanna volunteered hopefully.

"When have we ever been that lucky?" Rob sighed, placing his head in his hands. It made no difference. They were trapped here now, for better or worse. With all the people who would have sought safe harbour here, fighting their way through the darkness to reach safety, it seemed impossible to believe at least one person had not created a passage for their enemy.

* * *

Daniel left Tony's with all the information he could have hoped for, and more. Whilst there was no immediate action he could take, there was a solution. He just needed to reach it. Chrissie, it seemed, had kept in frequent contact with him and his wife following their reunion. Just a few days ago he had received word she was planning to journey to Castlefort to see if they required any aid for those who had been taken ill. After all, it was no secret that they did not have the same resources at their disposal as Albeth Castle, and assistance for those suffering from unknown ails was always in short supply.

Emerging from the covering of the forge, he noticed the brilliant light now illuminating a majority of the city. The great beacon of the lighthouse was now solely focused upon the most populated areas. In the streets he could hear grumbling complaints, and realised they'd need to enlist a crier of some manner, to ensure a well-meaning individual didn't turn the light away believing it to be the result of some ill-conceived shenanigans.

With this thought in mind he hurried through the streets, seeking the Plexus. Short on time, he quickly explained the situation, and left the details in their capable hands. They sent a Herald to the bearer of Dynamism, requesting they begin to harvest more of the inexhaustible energy to ensure they could keep their lights aglow, hoping that this, along with the lighthouse's field, would keep them secure.

"Wita!" Turning to the strained tones of Alessia's voice, Daniel raised his hand, watching as the gathering crowd parted to allow her through. All eyes were fixed upon the lighthouse, while a murmur spreading through the crowd suggested the woman approaching had ransomed the lighthouse keeper at weapon-point unless he did as commanded. Taking advantage of the gathering, the Plexus relayed its first message as Alessia grasped Daniel's arm, guiding him from the busy streets to a more deserted area.

"Did you have any difficulties?" he asked when he could finally hear her above the rising noise of the crowds.

"Very few, and did you find what you were seeking?"

"I don't have a weapon, if that's what you mean, but I know where to start, the Depths of Acheron."

"You possess but half of a coin, how do you expect us to return?" Alessia questioned, knowing Adel could not currently channel the energies needed to create another tool of such power again for at least thirty-three months after creating two such relics within such short succession. Rites and rituals of the archaic arcane were taxing, it was one of the reasons this form of magic had been nearly driven into extinction. Adel paid the price of use, and could not complete any powerful workings until the moon turned red twice more. Daniel removed the small disc from his pouch, thinking how he was accumulating quite the collection of unusual artefacts. He fingered it tentatively, remembering how he had averted even Fate's gaze from the forging of the secondary relic.

"Alessia, you cannot accompany me. It is vital you reach Chrissie before anything befalls her," Daniel insisted as his focus snapped back to the present. There was no time for reminiscing. He needed to get underway.

"But, Wita, you—"

"As for returning, I intend to seek the aid of the only other person to have received one of these. I believe he still carries the other half." Daniel saw a small commotion begin where the crowd had gathered and led Alessia away, towards the port's borders.

"The treasure hunter?"

"Yes, between us we will possess what is needed to travel there and back." Daniel couldn't help but feel that Fate, whilst oblivious to his interference in events, was on his side, for the time being at least. He had not only learnt of the ore, but also possessed the means to retrieve it.

"I cannot allow this, Wita. The Depths are dangerous." Alessia's hands balled into fists as she attempted to suppress the outrage in her voice. The Eortháds had waited many centuries for a person with his potential, they had sworn to protect him, and yet he spoke of the need for them to distance themselves from this conflict, whilst he launched himself into danger.

"Then who better to have beside me than the only man who has faced its terrors countless times and returned alive?"

"Will you not accept an escort at least?"

"Alessia, I understand your concern, but the Eortháds are required to continue setting the beacons. The world is immense, the darkness containing the Skiá is spreading, thousands will die at their hands. We must do everything possible to save as many as we can until such a point we are able to repel them." Daniel had relayed very specific orders to the Eortháds. Large beacons were to be erected in places the cloud's shadow had not yet touched. He was uncertain if his feeling of foreboding had been related to the Eortháds or the wyrms involvement in this war, but he knew he could not risk either. They were to stay away from the shadows, and return to Kalia before the darkness touched any of them. They would do what they could, but he had reiterated, countless times, how essential it was for them to remain away from the Skiá.

"Repel them you say, but, Wita, do you have a plan as to how this can even be achieved?"

"Not yet. We must do everything possible," he stressed again. "Alana may eventually be able to stop Íkelos summoning more, if that's even his intention, but we still need something in place to destroy those who have already breached our realm. We need these weapons."

"We need a plan," Alessia countered firmly.

"And any plan must first start with a means to defend ourselves. In the meantime, each second we debate this only adds to the lives lost. We must get word to the towns. We must warn them of what is coming, advise them how to stay safe, and where to seek sanctuary until we can find a way to do what is expected of us." Alessia looked at him with such intensity he almost recoiled. Her calculating gaze was fixed upon him and he could see the thoughts racing through her mind. After what seemed like several minutes, she gave a consenting nod.

"We passed a Roost-house on the way in. Given the circumstances, I would suggest a bird will be the easiest method to convey a message." Alessia altered their course, leading Daniel towards the location she recalled having seen the large messenger aviary. She had paid this location particular attention for no other reason than the unusual looking bell tower. It had seemed out of place in the centre of the log cabin's roof, yet the age marked wood suggested it had been a part of it for as long as the structure had stood.

"The Plexus is also working on spreading the word, it's better they receive the message multiple times than not at all." Daniel entered the log cabin first, scribing the message with hurried hands, before passing it to the bored looking man standing behind the thick wooden counter. His droopy eyelids sprung open as he read the contents.

"Where is this going to?" he demanded in alarm. "Is this for real?" His hands trembled as he placed them upon the gnarled-wood counter. Behind him several birds, sensing the rising tension, screeched their alarm from their various perches found throughout the room.

"Everywhere, and very. How long before they're ready?" A ruffle of feathers glided past Daniel as one of the birds, previously roosting above, retreated to the calmer environment of the outside enclosure. The birds here came and went as they pleased, free to stretch their wings, and trained to always return at the sound of the tarnished silver bell suspended in the tiny belfry.

"I'll enlist aid, sir." Daniel was surprised at the ease of transaction, then again, since the events of the Severaine the Chosen had become well-known to many. He placed a pouch of coin upon the counter. The figure stepped back, giving the cord attached to the bell a quick pull until the sound of the bell peeling chimed through the air. Another flurry of movement filled the room as the birds resting relocated outside to their designated perches.

"You jest. I cannot accept coin from the hands of a hero. What use would it have if the message doesn't get received?" Taken aback slightly, Daniel replaced the pouch and gave an appreciative nod before turning to Alessia.

"This is where we part ways. Securing Chrissie has to be your top priority."

"It is not *my* priority, Wita. You understand my duty all too well," she protested sternly. "I shall be beside you, as is my place. Another can go in my stead."

"It has to be you. Please don't make me do it, you know I abhor such things," he pleaded, but the look in her eyes told him of the necessity. She would not willingly abandon him. Her refusal was certain, he could already see the creases caused by the narrowing of her eyes as she prepared to defy him, and it left him only one choice. A choice he was not happy with at all. "Alessia," Daniel's voice dropped, his face shadowed with regret. "As your Wita, I command you, secure Chrissie. Until we regroup, *she* is your priority, protect her as you would me." Alessia's face filled with astonishment, unable to believe he had actually just spoken those words.

"Wita, I—"

"You have your orders, Master and Commander." He felt the tightening in his chest, but knew nothing short of this would make her leave his side. She could not be beside him. Had he known of another he could entrust the role to he would have had her return home, but she was all he had, the only one he could trust. He just hoped she could avoid the Skiá. He was not eager to understand the void in his stomach that engulfed him whenever his plans thought of sending the Eorthåds to fight this war.

"But what of you?"

"We will regroup at the mercenary camp near the ruins of Weft. Have Chrissie protect them. You have your orders, *éaðmóde*!" Alessia bowed her head, before turning to depart. He at once regretting ordering her to obey, but would issue one final command. "Cépe." His voice was barely above a whisper.

"You take heed also, Wita," she acknowledged before departing. Daniel watched the door swing closed behind her and gave a sigh. He had never wanted such responsibility, but he also knew he was the only one who could see what must be done, unblinded by other loyalties. He hesitated for but a moment, listening to the scratching of the quill upon parchment before, with a deep breath, he departed once more for the Plexus. If he had any hope to succeed, he must first locate Rob or, as the Plexus knew him, Aeolos.

* * *

Alana glanced around in amazement at her surroundings. Water roared above and below, curling overhead like a wave, yet the tube remained in perpetual motion, creating a tunnel filled with mist, spray, and circular double rainbows. She had emerged upon the first of a series of stepping stones that marked a path through a tunnel which appeared to be the only way to continue.

Barely audible above the sound of the water, Alana could hear an unusual sound. In the distance, near the midway point of the tunnel, crouched a small figure, a child no older than herself, weeping. It was only as she turned to seek guidance from her parents she realised she was alone. With nothing else to do, no path to take but the one leading her onward, she jumped across the stones, growing ever closer to the sobbing figure.

"You're me," she announced, tilting her head with sudden realisation as the auburn-haired child lifted her gaze to look at her. The girl swiped the tears from her eyes and gave a nod. "How?"

"Water is a conduit of time. It means you can see things through it that were or could be. I only know this because I stood where you did, and that's what the other me said," the figure sniffed, once more wiping her eyes.

"So why are you crying?" Alana reached out, taking her mirror image in a soft embrace. "If you tell me why, I can stop it."

"But I said the same, when I stood there as you."

"And what were you told?" Alana questioned, the figure clenched her hands into tiny fists, wailing inconsolably.

"It was stupid, this whole thing is stupid," she bawled. "I wanna go home!"

"But we can't, we made a promise."

"Promise-smomish. I did it to make them proud, and now they're dead and it's my fault!" The figure wailed again, pushing Alana aside as she fled towards the portal's exit. The image of the retreating figure shimmered, vanishing from sight.

Alana swallowed, fear building within her as she looked at the path before her. It no longer seemed as beautiful as it had once been. With a little less spring in her step she continued to leap across the stones. At the end of the tunnel was a barrier of water so clear and still that it acted as a mirror.

"You saw what will be, why do you continue?" questioned a whispering voice.

"I made a promise," Alana's reflection answered as if it possessed a life of its own.

"Where are Mummy and Daddy?" she asked, the reflection acted as one with her once more, mirroring her movements perfectly.

"Safe, for now. Why did you agree to become the Mitéra?"

"To make them proud," answered her reflection. Alana realised that although she had spoken herself, her own words had not been heard, the voice of the reflection had drowned out her own answer, an answer she had thought this being would wish to hear.

"Alana, you cannot lie here, least of all to yourself. This is the first thing you must learn if I am to teach you. Lies breed danger for one who possesses power. You must always be honest, with yourself at least. Know the truth of why you do something, do not justify it with a partial truth. You saw the fate that awaits you, you spoke with your future self, learnt of the death of your parents brought on by your hand. Now, tell me, will you continue?"

"Yes," she whispered.

"Why?"

"Because turning back would be worse. You showed me the truth, so many mummies and daddies would die if I don't. I want to, but I can't be selfish. I love Mummy and Daddy, but other children love theirs too. It's not fair I should keep mine at the cost of all of theirs," Alana sniffed tearfully, her heart aching. The Spirits had shown her the death the Skiá would bring, the suffering, the loss, the pain. She wanted to think only of herself, she wanted to be wrapped in her parents' arms and hide away from everything that was scary. But if she did so, she knew she'd be denying other children the comfort she herself sought.

"You passed my test. I accept you," the voice acknowledged. "There is, however, a price you must pay should you wish to prove your worth. When you face me, I will take from you that which makes you immortal, and when we bind I will take something of what you are until you complete the rites expected of you. This is what will allow you to find me. Will you continue?" Alana looked upon her reflection.

"I'm scared," she whispered. Her legs seemed frozen in place, no matter how hard she tried to move them.

"Of what?"

"Failing." Alana extended her hand towards her likeness. She felt the cool touch of the reflection as it became water. At once she was looking back over the path she had walked, a reflection of herself departed in tears as another version of herself approached. Her brow crinkled in a frown as she tried to make sense of what she saw.

"Come, little one, turn and face me. We have much to do. My teachings take years to master."

"But..."

"Worry not. The time within our realms passes as slow or as fast as we deem fit. But it only ever moves forwards, never backwards."

"What of Mummy and Daddy?"

"They are safe, little one. They await your return in The Stepping Realm. No mortal before has entered my domain, and once you leave it is likely none shall see it again."

"Will it hurt?" she asked.

"Beyond what you can endure, and yet endure you shall," the Spirit answered in earnest. Severing the immortality from a being was the most agonising process imaginable. In ancient times it was used as a form of slow torture, prolonged as needed until all the necessary secrets were revealed. He had no desire to inflict such pain on the child, and whilst it would be over in seconds, this type of pain had a way of feeling almost eternal within those fleeting moments.

Alana, with her small trembling body, took several rapid breaths and, before she could convince herself otherwise, turned to face the Great Spirit of Water. As she looked upon him she felt the tendrils of magic penetrate her core, ripping and tearing her essence to claim that which had been promised. The agonised scream which left her, although short, would haunt all within his realm forever.

* * *

Daniel waited patiently for several minutes until the door to the rear area of the modest Plexus opened and the sprightly young woman, who had taken both his earlier request, and this one, returned. Her face contorted as she looked upon the parchment in her hands having third, and even fourth, thoughts about giving it to him. The Plexus had a closely guarded secret, and that this man would come in and request for such a thing to be done was unprecedented. She had sought the advice of her elder, who was just as perplexed that an outsider could have obtained this information.

"How did you know?" she whispered, relieved to see they were alone within the small wooden building.

"Your senior recognised me, that is why he agreed is it not?" Daniel nodded towards the door she had emerged from.

"Yes, but, what you asked for, it's kept between Plexus masters, and *you* don't even possess a sigil."

"You don't have to worry," he assured, "your secrets are still secure."

"How can they be?" she asked shaking her head doubtfully, still clutching the paper to her chest.

"I have no time for such fleard. The location, if you please." Daniel extended his hand towards the figure before him. As he raised his voice, he noticed the shadow beneath the crack of the door shifting, betraying the Plexus master's presence. The woman, also now aware of being observed, passed him the note. "Good day." Daniel turned and strolled away, leaving a coin on the counter for their trouble.

Stepping outside he took a deep breath before opening the parchment. Each Plexus member was given a sigil, a badge identifying them as members, which they only received after passing the trials. Its purposes were too many to count, but a nearly silent whisper had revealed to him one aspect of its nature which would prove of benefit to Daniel. As well as being able to connect with an impression to validate the possessor's identity, it also possessed an enchantment so that the Plexus could locate a badge bearer should an urgent need arise.

Studying the parchment he mentally mapped the location. A look of bewilderment briefly crossed his face as he realised not only where Rob could be found, but perhaps one of the reasons the woman behind the counter had been reluctant to present it. To anyone unfamiliar with the truth, it would seem nonsensical.

Daniel smiled slightly. He had spent much time documenting the area Rob could now be found, and knew him to be in the vicinity of Acha's home, in Collateral, or his sigil was at least. Pulling the gossip crystal's chain he clutched the star fragment tightly, wondering whether Eiji or Acha had retained possession of their piece, or if she was even there after the decision to avoid Collateral had been made. He was almost surprised when Rob greeted him with concern.

"You have their crystal?" Daniel questioned uncertainly.

"He stole it from Eiji," Acha called, taking a sip from her cup to disguise the smile. She raised her hand in a greeting. despite not being able to see him, she knew Daniel would be fully aware of Rob's surroundings.

"It wasn't like that," Rob protested. Already it seemed like so long ago sicne he had taken the crystal from Eiji's sleeping body in hope to find Acha and contact Daniel. The sudden thought saw him relaying his message. "I needed to warn you. Be on your guard, an Appraiser—"

"Our paths have crossed," Daniel interrupted. "But it just so happens I find myself in need of your aid."

"I'm not sure how much help I can be, but go ahead."

"I need to get to the Depths of Acheron." Rob removed a small coin from the folds of leather in his belt, and looked at it knowingly.

"How can I help?"

“Well, as you already realised, I need that, but I was hoping I could request an escort.” Rob glanced behind him briefly, towards a place outside the dome of vision the connection between the crystals afforded him.

“What do you seek from The Depths?”

“Ore discarded by the Gods. If we’ve a chance of fending off the Skiá, we need weapons that can hold fire and light. Can I count on you?” Daniel took a moment to survey his own surroundings and, seeing a small crowd gesturing in his direction, began to walk before he got drawn into a situation he didn’t have time for. There was a downside to being recognisable, people sought endless assistance.

“Always, but I’m afraid I’m not sure how much help I can be, Collateral is sealed.”

“How?” he whispered, the hairs on the back of his arm raised as he stepped into the shadows cast by an alley. He berated his carelessness, knowing he could literally not afford to be caught in the dark.

“I warned the council. They sealed the portals and changed the environment to one of perpetual light.” Acha revealed.

“Then you’re safe?” Daniel navigated the elongated shadow, searching for the closest stream of light. Spotting a stack of discarded crates he ascended, pulling himself onto the flat roof of an open top cafe. He heaved a sigh of relief, moving to sit in the centre and waited for the voices of the small crowd to gradually fade.

“We’re not exactly sure. We hadn’t planned on coming here, but it was the only choice given the circumstances. It’s lucky we did though, Collateral has a Mythographer, he allowed us to borrow their ancient texts. It appears the Skiá can travel between any shadows they have touched. Anyone here could be a portal, even us.”

“You’ve encountered them? What else did it say, is there anything that tells us how to repel them?”

“That’s how we crossed paths with Rob and Fey. We were heading to Lamperós. Of all places I foolishly assumed it would be safe, we were caught in their path. We escaped them unscathed, but we’ve no way of knowing if we’ve been touched.” Daniel fell silent for a moment lost in thought.

“As for your other question. Nothing, the only information we found was the passage about them travelling between shadows. If anything else was known, it was never documented,” Rob answered.

"It's no good." Daniel huffed casting his gaze to the ever darkening sky. The clouds moved at an alarming rate, even he did not dare guess how long until they converged to blanket the entire span of their world.

"What isn't?"

"As Wita I should be able to call on the voices of those who passed through the Gate of Shades. With the exception of one child, whose life was ended before the Skiá reached them, there's no one dead who's witnessed them." Daniel stood slowly to survey his surroundings. He'd been still for too long. There was no time to sit talking, he needed to keep moving. "Could it be possible we've jumped to the wrong conclusions?"

"If you heard and saw what we did at Eldnyng you'd not need to ask that." Fey shook his head as he approached the crystal, leaning in towards it to speak. "It was carnage, I'm telling you, nothing survived."

"What if... what if we're more than just something in their way? Maybe we're prey and everything we are is a means to sustain them," Rob pondered, pulling away from Fey, who stood too close for comfort.

"You mean they feed from both our flesh and essence?" Rob glanced to Fey. "You don't need to be so close, he can hear you just fine." Fey obviously wanted to ask something, but instead nodded, stepping back.

"I've been thinking on it for some time. Maybe they use the energy from devouring us to multiply. Given the rate the cloud is expanding I can't imagine there are enough of them to spread so quickly." Daniel paused again, screwing his face in contemplation. "Look, we need that ore, without it we've no hope to stand against them. This can't be how our time ends, not after everything we've been through. Listen, I can't do this alone, I'm going to need your help. You said the council sealed Collateral, but I don't believe that's true."

"It is, there are no portals." Fey once more leaned into the crystal to speak.

"Correct, but when Alessia insisted I stopped using them we erected a small Irfeláfa inside the pathway that connected to Kaila's portal. The tunnel itself doesn't exist but to those who know of it, and only those attuned can use it."

"I don't see how that helps us," Acha stated. "Unless you plan on coming here."

"Because you're one of us," Daniel advised. "You're family, and you've passed through with me already. It will recognise you, and any with you so long as your energy does not imply your actions are in duress you'll be able to use it at will."

"And what if it did? We're not exactly at ease," Rob advised skeptically.

"Then only she'd be transported. We protect our own. Acha, do you remember how to use it?"

"Are you sure that is wise?" Acha questioned glancing to her hand. "My blood is not exactly—besides, what if we're... what would we even call it, infected?"

"No one will be there when you arrive. I need you to leave immediately. Locate the symbol on the altar stone that looks like this." Daniel quickly sketched it on the parchment. "It'll take you south of Jones' camp. With any luck Alessia will have already arrived with Chrissie. If you are infected she'll be able to sever the link by cleansing your shadow. I need her to complete the rite with everyone in the camp and shield the area." Daniel's vision turned towards the lighthouse. "I don't know how long this will last, if they can travel within shadows I don't know how much security this precaution will provide. Listen, if you're going to use the Irfeláfa I need to recall the Eorthóds. For reasons I don't understand they can't be caught in this war. I can't risk them passing through after you and picking up something you may have left. Give me twenty minutes before you head out. I'll meet you at the camp. When Chrissie arrives it will be the safest place in the world."

"What is your plan exactly?" Rob poised.

"We need an army, one we can trust, and I need to arm them. We'll talk more later I've got to recall the Eorthóds and secure my blacksmith."

"Blacksmith?" Acha questioned in surprise.

"Obtaining the ore is one thing, but there are few who will be able to smelt it. If the worst happens I need him safe." As he spoke Daniel worked his way across the rooftops, sidestepping elongated shadows cast by the chimneys and the walls of adjacent buildings.

"You're bringing him to the camp?"

"No, they don't have the equipment to handle what he needs."

"But you've said it yourself, if someone infected enters..." Acha trailed off, she could see from the way he halted, tapping his forefinger on his forehead, he was seeking an answer. What they really needed, was another Chrissie.

"Leave it with me. We will convene shortly." With that Daniel terminated the link between crystals. He needed to find a way to isolate Tony and his wife, and any others who may prove useful. They needed to be safe, surrounded by light, and yet no one must be able to reach them and risk bringing an infected shadow to them.

Daniel's gaze fell upon the site used to gather Dynamism. In order to protect the delicate instruments used to harness the planet's rotational motion and convert it into energy, it had been constructed to be as secure as any prison. It was small, but if the lighthouse failed to keep the Skiá at bay, at least they would be safe there. The energy, even in its stored state, gave off light. If—when—the lighthouse failed, their domain inside the town would grow, but as long as the interior of the station remained secured, and no one entered or left, they would not only stay bathed in light, but the Skiá would have no means to infect a shadow to gain entry. He could address the problem of getting them out and to the forge later.

* * *

Zo and Seiken simultaneously felt their daughter's grasp being wrenched from their own. Their grip tightened, but it was to no avail, they had entered the portal with her, but they were not permitted access to the Spirit's domain. It was a test only she could face, but they thought they would have had more time.

Already they had told her how proud they were, how brave she was, how much they loved her. They had comforted her fears and tried to ease the burden. It was too heavy for the shoulders of a child, and they had been naive to hope she would not have to endure it alone. They stood trapped between two realms, both gateways were closed, they could neither enter the Spirit's domain nor return to the mortal world.

The Stepping Realm acted like steppingstones across the vastness of The Betwixt, a place which touched all realms that were and would be. The corridors between two adjoining places were as varied as the depths of infinity itself. Often the nature reflected a fraction of the domain which the gateway entered, and thus they stood between a corridor of flesh and Spirit. A simple place where an infinite illusion of water stretched on forever, and their bodies reflected the nature of both a physical and spiritual presence. They knew their daughter must have been granted passage to another gateway, one they could not enter.

"What do we do now?" Zo questioned, her vision focused on Seiken, marvelling in the brilliant radiance enveloping him. Pure and powerful energy surrounded him, gleaming as brightly as any she had seen. Twin essences fed and harmonised with each other like the twin nebula he had spent so much time showing her and Alana during their time in the observatory. His essence reflected the very core of his nature, and he was everything he should be, thus within this passage was an image of perfection in both flesh and soul. Her heart quickened as she beheld his splendour, and it was all she could do not to step forward to take him in her embrace. She traced her hand affectionately down the length of his arm, her gaze fixed upon him.

"We wait. The Spirit granted us entry here for a reason. The darkness is spreading, and it carries with it the Skiá. Alana needs us to make this journey, perhaps this is the Spirit's way of keeping us safe."

"Are you certain that's the reason?" Zo asked cautiously, her sight dropping to their interlocked hands.

"What other reason would there be?" Seeing the concern masked within her eyes he stepped in front of her, extending his hand to touch her face as she averted her gaze. "Thea, what aren't you telling me?"

"How do I look to you?" she asked, placing her hand upon his, once more locking their fingers together. She pulled away slightly, both of her hands now holding his as she kept him at arm's length.

"Beautiful, radiant." He smiled, attempting to close the distance between them as he leaned towards her for a kiss.

"Look again," she stressed, stepping back but still keeping their hands intertwined. She knew he could see it. She had known of it since first noticing the nature of this area, he just hadn't realised it. Be it denial or oversight, he saw only the beauty of his wife. He was blinded by her, so much so that he had been oblivious to the dark tendrils that snaked through her energy like veins. "The Appraiser, he must have missed some," Zo whispered. She released his hands looking upon the dark lines that slowly crept towards her torso from her left hip.

"We have time," Seiken stated assertively. He glanced around, as if desperately in search for an answer, a way to remove the poisonous energy that slowly tried to once more subdue his wife to the external influence. "We can—"

"We need a way to keep track of its progress, so we know how much he can learn from me. As yet it's not reached any of my chakras. We don't have cause to worry until here." She placed her hand upon her solar plexus. "Here he will have access to my energy, here"—she placed her hand upon her heart—"my emotions." She took a deep breath, "when he reaches my throat he can hear everything I can, and whilst he won't be able to force me to speak, he can stop me from expressing something. Through my third eye he will see all my left eye can, and when it reaches my crown I'll be his ears, his sight, and his voice once more. At least this time we know it's coming."

"You think the Spirit placed us here to warn us?"

"It's essential Íkelos does not learn what we are doing. We need a way to track the infection, something that by looking at me you will know how far his poison has spread and what precautions to take."

"Like an imprint," Seiken pondered, closing his eyes to mask the shadows of emotions he suppressed. "There is an old technique shamans used to track poisons," Seiken contemplated. There was a great power to this location, a convergence of flesh and spiritual energy. He was certain they could harness the energies needed to complete the rite.

"How did it work?"

"They'd enter the Spirit realm and place a vestige enchantment on the toxin. When they emerged from their trance they could still see the enchantment tracing the spread as if it overlapped the physical body. It's how they knew where to cut, or amputate, so that the person could be saved."

"Do it, we're as close to the Spirit realm as we can be here. We may not be shamans, but maybe here we could borrow their strength?"

"Actually, they used to do it between our world and theirs. They just thought of it as the Spirit world, but it was in fact the transition between being awake and dreaming. Powerful things can happen between realms if you know how to utilise the energies." He gave a reassuring smile, indicating that she should make herself comfortable upon the ground. The shimmering surface of the water rippled beneath her as she lowered herself down. Her vision once more ensnared as she looked upon her husband in adoration.

"Do what needs to be done, but when it reaches a point I'm more of a danger to you than an aid, you must promise you'll do what is necessary." Zo saw the look of concern in his face, his grip tightening on hers. "Promise me," she demanded.

"If the time comes, then I will ensure our daughter can do what must be done."

"That's not the same thing," she scolded, leaning up on her elbows to meet his gaze. He leaned towards her, kissing her lips with a feather light touch.

"Please understand, Thea, that's the best I can do."

* * *

Acha led Rob, Teanna, and Fey to the graveyard in Collateral. Gravel, lost beneath a layer of grass, crunched beneath their feet, betraying the presence of a path long overgrown and unattended. The sound of their footfalls echoed throughout the deserted landscape forcing their awareness to embrace the solitude of this place. The entrance had been difficult to find, a testament to the fact that, while it was present, it was a part of this land even the residents wished to avoid. Countless monoliths of varying ages filled the space, each visible surface was covered with names, some in lithographs familiar to them, others as obscure and unusual as the great city itself.

Once beyond the wall separating this domain from the living, the reach of these markers seemed to span beyond the horizon, trying to portray the sheer amount of lives Collateral had seen. It was impossible to discern how much of the landscape, filled by the endless tribute, was real and how much was an illusion marking the edge of the domain. There were no remains, as far as anyone knew. They burned those who died here upon a pyre, their only tribute was that their names became a part of the vast and endless sea of monoliths.

There was one monument, however, that served a different purpose, and it was crafted from a different stone. The obelisk was a deep black, flecked with white cristobalites. Pausing at its base, Acha removed a pan flute from her backpack and stared at it forebodingly. She recalled the beautiful yet haunting melody played by Eryx Venrent when last she stood here. He had charmed the passage open with the beauty of his song, and now it was her turn.

"It was all showmanship," she whispered reassuringly to herself moistening her lips. She traced her fingers across the off-white bones, before she hesitantly placed them to her lips and blew. When seeking guidance she had been told it was on par with blowing across the top of bottles to make them whistle, she'd not had much success with that either. Trying again she managed to create a strangled sound.

"What are you trying to do?" Fey questioned, as Acha made another attempt to tease sound from the instrument.

"I need to play each note with the last one being struck for the first time exactly two minutes after the first." Acha explained.

"Does it matter the order?" Fey grimaced as she tried again. He extended his hand, curling his fingers towards him in a suggestion to hand him the beautiful piece of craftsmanship and still the music that she was murdering. Once within his grasp he studied it with appreciation for a moment, examining the fine carvings upon the hollow tubing.

"No and you can repeat any you like, as long as each note has sounded and the highest pitch is only struck once," she stressed. "It's trickier than it looks."

"Could be its composition," Fey offered. "My father taught me to play as a boy, do you mind?" Acha gestured for him to proceed, he raised it to his lips, before pulling away slightly. "I'm a bit rusty, but it's just a matter of the notes right?" Acha nodded.

Fey raised the pan flute once more, starting with the longest, and he played a tune he had heard carried on the wind since he was a boy. He was not as unpractised as he suggested. Once a year he would visit the clearing, where his father had fallen to the eternal slumber, and play for him. Given its tones he had always thought it to be something similar to a lullaby and, except for the final note, which he simply added to the end, it fulfilled Acha's request. When he stopped, he looked up at Teanna who had been singing softly to his tune, her voice in perfect harmony with his melody. The words had resonated within her soul as the music had in his.

"Where did you learn that melody?" Teanna questioned in awe, as Acha approached the obelisk which now slid effortlessly aside to reveal a shaft descending into the ground.

"I couldn't tell you, until now I thought it was one of my own making, gifted by the winds, but you know it?"

"I've heard it every day since I was a girl."

"Where?"

"In Talaria. I was tasked with spending excessive amounts of time in the Rumination Room. It's a strange sensation being confined there, unbearable yet addictive. I would hear this song during the darkest torment, and it would keep me from losing myself. Now I know the purpose of that place, I also know what it was, it was the song of the Spirit Elemental calling to me." Teanna felt a flush of heat fill her cheeks. "But why you would hear it here, I cannot begin to fathom."

"Anchoring," Rob stated matter-of-factly. "If what you've told us so far is true, the Moirai fractured the Elemental Spirit and sealed fragments of him in the tethers Talaria uses to draw energy." Rob paused, thinking back to the time Paion had drawn a great tower from the skies. He had been both in awe of the monument, and in fear of Paion's power. To think Napier Village had been just one tether site, that other immense structures could descend and threaten their existence, was terrifying. He dislodged the thought, continuing. "If your presence kept the Spirit in check in Talaria, it would stand to reason there had to be a counterweight, a force here that would keep the balance, something or someone that would resonate with you."

"Are you clumsily implying we're soul-mates? Not possible, she's to be a Maiden," Fey intervened, returning the instrument to Acha.

"I'm not certain, but I've seen enough magic in my time to know your paths are somehow joined." Rob had learnt much during his time in The Courts of Twilight, and despite all he endured there, he would not trade that experience for anything, nor would he wish to have stayed. Lady Elaineor had mentored him in secret, it was she he had to thank for many of his skills, but seeing the web of magic enchantments was something he had always been gifted in, and although it was barely perceivable, there was something connecting Fey and Teanna. The longer they spent in each other's company, the more tangible it became.

Chapter 21

The Fallen Palace

As much as Alessia detested leaving Daniel's side there had been little choice. She had sworn an oath to uphold the wishes of this man. He was their Wita and whilst the Eorthåds were hers to command, his role saw him in a position of elevated authority when it came to certain areas. When he had suggested she left to locate and retrieve Chrissie she had been torn between her two duties, the one to him, and the one to the people of the world they had once vowed to protect. Daniel had stopped the Eorthåds from doing their sacred duty with a single command, and now had removed the choice from her. In some ways his order had been a relief and eased the burden of her dilemma, however, she feared for his safety.

The blacksmith had given Daniel the location of where he believed they would find Chrissie, and Alessia had made haste to the small village. She heard Nemean relay a telepathic command for all Eorthåds attending to the beacons to withdraw immediately and return to Kalia. She knew this request would have come from Daniel, and wondered what new insight he had gained which called for her peoples immediate evacuation. When Nemean relayed the discovery that the Skiá possessed the ability to traverse the shadows she had faltered, her gaze turning cautiously to all the darkness within the world, wondering if she was still as alone as she once thought.

She had questioned Daniel many times regarding why the Eorthåds were not to engage in the repelling of this threat, but he had never supplied a satisfactory answer. His resolve had been unwavering, his commands clear and beyond misinterpretation. Eventually she decided it would be wiser to ask no further questions, before he considered that she too should be excluded.

With this new revelation about the shadows she understood a little more about the threat he perceived. Whilst Kalia was part of the waking world, given its unique circumstances of existing between the mortal plane and Darrienia, it was constructed as much of a dreamscape as it was of reality. The sky above its coordinates would darken, but it was a change their land may not see. Nothing could gain access to Kalia without being granted passage, but she felt there was more to Daniel's insistence than keeping the island and its inhabitants secure, and it most likely had something to do with Kalia's link to Darrienia. Alessia studied each shadow as she ran, her muscles tensing and preparing for action with each sound she heard.

A soft glow in the distance confirmed the Elementalist's presence before anything else. The pale light illuminated the modest village in its embrace, allowing the area beyond its protection to also bask in its glow. The hue of the trees, instead of seeming welcoming, only appeared more sinister, their elongated shadows more pronounced in their retreat from the village. Each quickened step caused the surrounding debris, blown from shedding trees, to crunch beneath her feet, its frequent sound altering her to the increase in pace. Passing through the light Alessia rested her hand upon the recently repaired fencing, which served as a poor measure to keep the grazing chickens confined.

With a steeling breath, Alessia continued further into the town, noticing how the light from Chrissie's magic had shrouded the entire location, lightening every shadow as it infiltrated and spread through every crack and knothole ensuring every nook, cranny, and building was bathed in its gentle radiance.

Turning to survey the town Alessia startled as a wayward chicken scurried from a nearby barn, its rapid pace kicking up small plumes of the dry track as it hurried away. The wooden structures were mostly well-maintained, many with signs of recent repair work, as were the barns and stables found on the far borders. Hitching posts near the town's entrance next to its most prominent building, along with the scent of sweat and ale, suggested the large wooden cabin she entered near would be the tavern. A sign, crafted by a pyrographer, displayed the burnt letters that made up the name of the building. Alessia mentally sounded out the words and smiled. When first she had met Daniel, she understood the tongue well, after all, Gaeans spoke the language of the ancient beasts. Their writings also used a similar letter structure to her own, so it had been easy enough for her to understand, but sometimes she still had to resort to phonetic methods to hear the word formed by the letters.

Alessia approached the tavern, the heavy odours becoming increasingly more tangible as she reached the closed doors. Subdued tones of merriment exploded from within, causing her to startle, and realise for the first time the true extent of her own tension. Daniel had advised that Chrissie often accepted work while staying within an area, and more often than not it involved serving others. When she entered all eyes turned towards her, a quick glance across the curious faces revealed that, whilst the tavern was crowded, no doubt hosting a night of amusement for all residents, Chrissie was not among the unfamiliar faces. A nearby waitress hurried towards her, hooking Alessia's arm with her hand, enquiring what brought her here this night, while attempting to guide her towards a vacant seat. It was from this kindly woman Alessia discovered the person she sought would be found at the stables, giving aid to the Shoesmith. With little time to waste, Alessia gave hurried thanks and departed, relishing the cleaner scent of the air as the tavern's doors once more closed behind her.

"Chrissie, you must come with me, immediately." Alessia announced her presence firmly with her demand. Before her, scraping the hooves of one of the stabled horses, stood the familiar woman. Even without fully taking in her appearance Alessia had recognised the colours of earth and starlight of the woman's uniquely toned hair. Elementalists were known for their slightly unusual features, and it was Chrissie's hair which betrayed her as a wielder of such forces.

"I'm a little busy," Chrissie grunted curtly, before recognising the voice. "Alessia?" Continuing her work she glanced up to acknowledge her. Their paths had not crossed for many years, but Alessia had not changed in the slightest. Chrissie exhaled slowly, reflecting on how the years had added many a fine line to her own features, being a half-elf clearly had its advantages.

"We must go, the Wita requires your aid. He needs this—Alessia gestured outside towards the barrier she had erected—"but better." The harshness of her tone had clearly won her no favours as Chrissie turned her focus back towards the horse, examining its hoof closely before releasing it.

"And what of the people here?" Chrissie demanded, lifting a grooming brush from between two wooden pegs in the wall. Alessia suspected her brushing of the horse was merely a show of stubbornness. She knew little of these creatures, but given the smoothness and sheen reflected in the lantern light from overhead, its coat had clearly already been groomed.

"This is war. There will be casualties."

"War is it?" Chrissie kept her focus on the horse. "I thought it was an illness spread by shadows." Alessia's hardened glare softened.

"You are unfamiliar with the situation. Tell me, what is it you *think* we are facing, why use a barrier at all?"

"Information here is limited, you may not have noticed, but there's no Plexus based here. A traveller brought us news of a new disease and spreading shadows. The cunning woman here linked the two and so I raised a barrier, more to set the people at ease than..." Chrissie trailed off as she glanced in Alessia's direction. "Are you serious, about a war?"

"Wita Daniel is on a quest to obtain a weapon to be used against the Skiá. The threat is more than an illness and without your aid he *will* fail." Alessia entered further, eyeing the horse suspiciously as she felt the large brown eyes of the beast upon her. Wyrms she was comfortable with, but these creatures, horses, for some unknown reason, unnerved her slightly.

"And what would he have me do?"

"What you have done here, only better," she repeated impatiently.

"Better, better how?" Chrissie's fingers tightened on the brush, her anger bristling to the point the horse shifted uncomfortably. Blowing out a deep breath, Chrissie turned her glare to Alessia, setting down the brush on the stall's waist height divider.

"The defences here are weak. It is likely that there are infected amongst those living here."

"Impossible, my barrier spanned outward from a designated point." Chrissie stepped past her without courtesy, gesturing outside. The centre of this town had been marked by an old well. Its stone, mason walls had long fallen into disrepair, but being a monument, those living here had turned it into a planter for, what Alessia recognised to be, a young sugar-maple tree. Years from now, as it grew, she knew it would be a sight to behold, but for the moment it still lacked the height and thickness to be regarded as impressive.

"So you purged all shadows, even those unseen?"

"Well, obviously not those at point of contact with solid ob—"

"Then it is not safe. We have discovered they can create passages through shadows. There is a war to be fought, and Daniel needs your help in securing the mercenaries."

"He would have me turn my back on those here?" Chrissie gestured wildly, the set of her jaw hardening.

"This is war," Alessia stressed wondering how many times she would have to use this word before Chrissie understood the gravity of the situation, "and one where there are few with the capabilities and skills needed to fight it. As much as it pains me, there is only one person who can channel the light element. Without your aid the battle is all but lost."

"What would you have me do? I only possess one card capable of this. If I leave, I'm killing them."

"If you stay you are killing everyone. They are likely already infected." Chrissie's brow pulled in a tight frown at Alessia's words. "I understand it is not an easy decision. Perhaps I could help advise on some defensive measures." Alessia tried to soften her tone, but the longer Chrissie delayed the more lives she placed in jeopardy. If she could be certain the card was on her person, and not placed somewhere within the town's border unguarded—as it had been at Semiazá port when the Severaine raged—she would have incapacitated her and removed her choice long ago. This was no time for their shared stubbornness to be battling for dominance.

"Will they help?"

"Not really." Alessia shook her head as she inspected the town. It was set sparsely, the small buildings each a uninformed distance from their neighbours. Darkness would come to rest in every nook and cranny, every hollow and fissure, and this town had too many places where shadows could thrive. There was too much opportunity for infection, and few places that could be secured against such a force.

"You still don't know how to pull a punch do you?" Chrissie's shoulders slumped as she moved to perch herself upon the well. She closed her eyes, taking a slow deep breath which suggested to Alessia she had seen sense.

"You would rather I lie?"

"It's what you're asking *me* to do." Chrissie sighed. "Okay, fine. Help me set up defences, but Daniel sure as Hades better be right about this weapon."

"They have Dynamism here, correct?" Chrissie responded with a nod. "Then if you can purge their shadows, their chances of survival just increased. Here is what they need to do..."

A flurry of movement ensued, people worked together awkwardly, stepping on each other's toes to barricade the storage barn to the best of their ability. Chrissie's news brought with it woeful tidings, and she recognised anger on more than one face at the thought of her abandoning them, leaving them at the mercy of this enemy. They knew it was unwise to complain, she was a cleric, and when she was summoned it was her duty to answer. Makeshift shutters were nailed into place, draped with tanned hide in the hopes of preventing anything from coming inside. She had been vague about the threat, warning only of monsters who travelled in the shadows, after all, that was almost all she had been told.

While the skilled men and women patched and secured what would be their sanctuary, children scurried around gathering food and blankets, while the remaining people organised the lanterns inside in order to create the brightest, most encompassing glow. The only person not present was the Bearer of Dynamism, this young woman was busy harvesting the energy, storing as much as she could in the special cylinders. An act which would grant them safety for as long as the resources lasted.

Once the interior had been fully illuminated, Chrissie presented her card, slowly withdrawing the light barrier, her nervous gaze now studying the movement of every shadow. As Alessia made slight adjustments and checked for any weaknesses, Chrissie began to examine the townsfolk's shadows for any signs of infection, and purging those who had somehow, along their journey, been touched by the Skiá.

Alessia had been correct, the enemy had already been granted access to the people here, be it from a rogue traveller or an unfortunate hunting party, she was just grateful corruption was all they had returned with. It made sense creatures such as these would send scouts, doing so expanded their reach exponentially without raising panic.

When they left the brightly lit room Chrissie's face grew solemn as she heard them barricading themselves inside.

"I think I preferred the truth," she whispered looking back.

"What do you mean?"

"You said their chances improved because of Dynamism, you were lying. The moment they need to replenish its energy they'll be in the same danger as before." Chrissie let her vision wander from the storage barn to the small location several buildings away. If something was indeed lurking it would need only wait until someone made the journey across, or their light died. Either way the result would be the same.

"I was not lying. Dynamism is superior to flame."

"But you know it still won't save them."

"I know if you stayed here they would still die. At least with you helping us there remains a chance to cull the threat. Having you beside us could very well save their lives."

"Then why do I feel like I should be giving the rites of passage?"

"Because no matter your choice, people will die. It is never easy to know the faces of those you may condemn." Alessia allowed her own gaze to wander across the town. There was the unmistakable pang of regret, yet she embraced no sadness. Chrissie was vital to their success, and many more lives would be forfeit before this threat was vanquished.

"Oh, I'm condemning them now, am I?" Chrissie shrugged off the awkward hand of comfort Alessia had tried to offer.

"Come, the Irfeláfa is not too far from here." Alessia watched the light shield encompass them, protecting them from the darkness she herself had navigated in order to find Chrissie. "If I am contaminated, then this precaution will make little difference," Alessia observed.

"There was no depth to your shadow. You were right about one thing, there were people infected, their shadows went beyond." Chrissie had no other way to describe it but, when she looked at the cast image upon the floor, there was a clear and terrifying difference. She wondered if it was perceivable by anyone, or just those who could utilise her talents.

"You were successful in cleansing them?"

"I believe so, or I made them endure torture for no reason." Chrissie halted suddenly. "We need to detour." It was not a request. The firmness in her voice would normally have left no room for debate, but she knew Alessia was about to do just that. "Alessia, something's wrong, I can feel it. We need to head that way." Chrissie gestured to her right urgently.

"But that takes us away from the—"

"If you want me to come with you, do me this courtesy. Otherwise I'll leave you here." Chrissie altered her course, lengthening her strides, and was more than a little relieved to see Alessia had fallen into step beside her.

"Alright, just tell me what we are approaching." The area before them was bathed in shadows, if something survived it had either escaped the darkness' notice, or was part of its scheme, the need for caution was paramount. Something calling to the only person capable of wielding an opposing force could not be dismissed as a threat or trap.

"Something is seeking me." Chrissie's eyes narrowed but the melding of light and darkness made seeing any great distance impossible. She had not felt a pull like this for a long time and ignoring it was not an option. She placed a hand to her stomach as her gut knotted in discomfort. It was like an invisible tether tugged her towards the source.

"Something dangerous?" Alessia saw Chrissie wince. Surely that it was having a physical affect on her could not be a good omen. It ensured the possibility of her ignoring it was never an option.

"We'll find out soon enough."

* * *

The expanse of the Water Elemental's plane was beyond mortal comprehension. It was a clash of all this element was, springs, lagoons, oceans, rock pools, streams, rivers, and lakes all cast their varying hues upon an endless landscape. It was a paradise which had been the birthplace of many of Gaea's stars aquatic creatures, and as such was perfectly suited to their nature. Clouds of varying shades and types dotted a mottled sky where occasional great geysers sprung to life, erupting to shower the salt flats. In some places, fog could be seen rolling across marshlands and oceans. Everything that was born of water could be encountered here. This realm was its own world, as complete and perfect as any other. It was ruled by the Great Spirit, and any of his children were welcome within.

At first, Alana had watched with glistening tears as day turned to night, fearing for her parents, for the world she had left behind. It was only as the Great Spirit spoke with her, explaining how time within his realm moved at a different pace to the world beyond his domain, that he saw her smile. Tears, once formed from fear and concern, turned to those of relief as she pressed her forehead to his chest, bawling in the way only a child could. Until then, he had not seen the weight of worry the young prodigy had carried, and assured her that when she returned to her parents mere hours would have passed while she spent the years needed to understand all that she must.

As the suns rose, casting brilliant rainbows across the landscape, Alana had marvelled at the two brilliant orbs, how the larger red sun only traced the path of the horizon, while the smaller altered in shades, appearing more blue as it reached midday and shone down upon them from above. She marvelled at the red rainbows prevalent before the second sun rose. She had counted no less than twelve different types, some more vibrant than others.

She dove into the blue and green lagoons, trying to discover their inner most secrets while the Great Spirit watched her with nothing short of adoration. His children, unaccustomed to such creatures in their sanctuary, fawned over the young mortal, accompanying her in play, each eager to show her their homes and the wealth of knowledge to be discovered within. For the first half of a year, Alana hadn't realised she had been learning and absorbed everything around her with such ease that he had no doubt she was destined for the role they had bestowed upon her. Now that she swam almost as well as the nymphs, and knew his children's names and languages by heart, their real journey into the magic of his world could begin.

Through her time in play Alana had learnt much regarding the feel of the element she must master, how each manifestation reacted differently to her and stimuli, and began to understand osmosis, weathering, and more complexities than she had imagined could exist within such a simple solution.

Along with the manipulation of water, she was taught how to utilise the concentrations of minerals found within and separate the different chemicals, to create vapours that were either incapacitating or deadly. She had known water possessed great capacity for healing, but never imagined its devastating potential, not only when used as a natural force, but when applied in ways she had never considered, and this had been just the start of her journey. The other elements would bring with them new components, new ways to mix, meld, and combine their forces. A Mitéra was a force for unity, and as such she also had to be one of devastation.

He taught her nothing of gazing into the future, and she knew better than to question his reasoning. As she grew, she wondered about the method of his teaching. Never did he show her something and ask she duplicate the results, instead, by touch, he used her as a conduit, shaping the energy within her and asking she achieved the same. His was a sensory method of teaching, much like when her parents had first taught her to walk upon the water.

He had watched her grow as two years passed, and had seen the young child become something much more than she was upon her arrival. The playful nature of his children ensured the young girl still had some semblance of a childhood despite the weight of her lessons. Even in rest she was learning, be it through a lullaby sung by the sirens, or a bedtime tale told in the gravelly tones of the Graeae, who were the keepers of secrets and had much to tell of those uncovered by heroes past.

When at last there was no more she could currently learn, he knew her time within his realm must come to an end. Aware of what awaited her, the lessons and hardships she would face, he was reluctant to spur her journey onward. The young girl before him had become such a part of his realm that all within would feel her absence, and if she were to ever return it would not be with her child-like innocence. For two more days he allowed her laughter to carry across the shores, but he knew he could keep her no longer, and with a heavy heart rose from the crystal lagoon to stand before her as she sat upon its banks, watching as the rainbows faded and day became night once more.

"Is it time?" Alana questioned, her vision never straying from the horizon. He could see the most heartbreaking manifestation of his element as it shimmered within her eyes, spilling silently from her cheeks to catch the last remaining light.

"It is, Newt, we must seal our pact." His voice sounded almost regretful, but his features brightened as she smiled at his term of endearment. Just as a liquid could alter its form to its container, as the Elemental Spirit of water he could choose his at will, and unless taking form upon mortal soils he would never appear fully human. His visage remained transparent, and while sometimes treasures from his domain could be seen beneath his form, he knew this day Alana would see his unrest from the turbulences beneath his translucent skin. She had yet to see his truest manifestation, and he knew that once she departed she never would. "With our binding you will be able to call upon the powers of my element outside of my domain, but in order to grant you this boon our essences must be joined. I shall take something of yours, that you may keep my alignment until the rites of the Mitéra are completed."

"Are you sure this is the only way?" Alana questioned. She knew once these final steps were taken her path was inevitable, and the result would ultimately be the sealing of this powerful being. Her time here had allowed her to align to the element, but when she called upon the true brunt of his power, the force which she needed when she faced Íkelos, the consequences would be dire. As she was unable to complete the rites of the Mitéra she would lack the full attunement. By aiding her, the Great Spirits would become depleted and be imprisoned within their mortal shrine.

"Are you prepared?" the Spirit questioned.

"I am, Pigí," Alana nodded as he looked upon her with a smile. His own children, the water nymphs, addressed him as Megáli Pigí, Great Source, calling him father in their own way, and Alana had soon come to know him as such, and he too thought of her as kin. His true name, the name which would allow the Mitéra to channel his power, could only be discovered and bestowed upon her during the Mitéra trials.

"Then we shall begin. It is time for you to once more gaze at the source." Alana followed, a nervous skip to her steps until she stood above a small well spring, the place the Spirit had once said was the source of all water on Gaea's star. Her own eyes stared back, capturing her in a mesmerising thrall. No matter how she fought to glance away—to remove the strain of her body against the pressure encroaching up her limbs as the Elemental's aura began to merge with her own—she could not. The icy sensation pierced her flesh, bringing freezing heat coursing through her, droplets of sweat, unfelt through her burning agony, mingled with tears shed through unblinking eyes as she stood trapped within a frozen scream. Coolness began to wash over her as the stifling aura receded, the release of the pressure sending her tumbling breathlessly to her knees. Through her laboured breathing, as she attempted to dispel the tenderness of the air pressure upon her raw-feeling flesh, she heard his saddened voice as it whispered quietly, "It is done."

"Pigí, That wasn't as—" Alana gasped, falling forward onto her hands as the searing pain began anew. Its burning fury dancing across her flesh. This was a familiar pain, the same as she had endured to receive the markings upon her back. She clenched her teeth as she felt the icy burn of a new tikéta forming upon her left arm. She felt the tearing pain encircle her arm, leaving her breathless, wondering when she had fallen to her knees.

Sweat, formed by agony, trickled from her pale skin, casting ripples across the water's surface, adding parts of herself to the source ensuring that they would forever be as one. When clarity returned to her sight, she saw the beautiful ornament burnt upon her skin. In a similar fashion to the tikéta on her back, to the casual observer it would look as if she wore a piece of fine jewellery. Four feathers spun of water encircled her arm to create a mesmerising armlet. She touched the design with her fingertip, barely able to believe it was nothing but a brand. The feathers seemed to ripple with the movement of currents, and the whole design cast a shadow as if it were worn upon her flesh. Unknown to her, the design on her back had also altered, a new feather had appeared, shimmering like those upon her arm.

"Seek you now the phoenix, he must be the next to train you."

"Does the tikéta have any relevance?"

"It warns any who would look upon your flesh that you are ours. Each of us will mark you as our own, it ensures that even when we are bound to our shrines, you can harness a minuscule amount of our power, such is the only way to ensure that you will feel the call of the rites."

"Pigí, I'm going to miss you," whispered Alana, taking the solid vessel of the young boy in her arms. It was one of the forms she was most familiar with, a child appearing her own age who had grown alongside her.

"Our paths will cross again," he assured, releasing the seal on the gateway to The Stepping Realm, and diverting its path to reunite her with her parents.

* * *

The dark and twisting tunnels had been exactly as Acha recalled from her previous visit. If the floors had been coated with dust, she was certain their old tracks would have remained undisturbed. There was a daunting silence to the passage, as if nature had taken a baited breath to hide the life she felt dwelling in this vast underground network. She could feel its creatures, and the balance easily maintained in the absence of Man which kept this delicate ecosystem thriving. The sights were mesmerising, hypnotic in their alien diversity as strange and unusual plants and rock formations created the impressive expanse of the subterranean landscapes glimpsed in part through the natural breaks and fissures surrounding the tunnel. It was as she remembered, and yet somehow also more splendid.

As promised, near the location where the portal would have exited to Kalia, was the stone Irfeláfa. This marker had taken the form of a small stone plinth, but Acha recognised the runes etched upon its surface. She wondered who had been responsible for its appearance, the rock, rather than being placed, seemed to have been grown from the natural surroundings, making it a natural part of this world.

With but a measure of hesitation she spilt her blood, the ruby fluid channelled its way into the deep engravings found etched into the surface. The ivory-shaded marker paled in the presence of the crimson fluid as it trickled within each gully, never spilling a drop as it flowed to encompass the entire structure, giving life and magic to sleeping power within. Turning to the small group, she issued simple instructions before placing her hand upon the stone's surface.

Even Rob had been caught heaving after their second trip had concluded. Acha observed with sympathy, her own hand resting upon her unsettled stomach. Having experienced this method of relocation before she had been prepared for the consequences. Despite the disorientation, the awful sensations of being pulled and pushed, shredded and torn, she had handled this transition far more successfully than her first. She wondered how Daniel could tolerate its frequent use.

"Sorry, I should have warned you. It's not exactly a pleasant way to travel," Acha apologised, her stomach clenched as sweat formed on her brow. Raising a hand she took several necessary steps away from them. "We're safe, for now."

"What do you mean?" Fey questioned, his keen gaze surveying their surroundings.

"Truthfully? I live by absorbing life from things around me, hence—" she gestured to the space between them, before drawing their attention to the tree she stood beneath. A single branch of the evergreen giant had shed its leaves, whilst those around it remained rich and healthy. "I can control it now, but things like that consume a lot of energy. It has its benefits though, my presence, and apparently that of those I am near, is masked by the energy I take, making us indistinguishable from the surroundings, but if I concentrate while I absorb the energy, I can get some insight into the lay and dangers of the land and the things within it."

"And what did the land say?" Fey enquired.

"Shadows darken its borders and play in the darkness like the Anemoi through their branches, only unlike the spirits, they bring harm to those they touch. We should not delay, while our presence may be masked, eyes can still behold us. We must make haste to the camp." Acha thought back to Daniel's instructions and returned to the small stone marker where they had appeared. Without his directions she knew they would never find the mercenary camp, not with how well it was concealed. The protection they had implemented ensured it remained hidden to any magic, no matter its source.

* * *

Bray surveyed the area before them for what was easily the third time. Several small trees littered their surroundings, their purple flowers adding a spray of colour to the cold grey stones of the mountains. Small plateaus and jutting ledges provided a hospitable environment for plant life to thrive, while just beyond, the seeds fated to fall upon the cold rocks had buried themselves deeply and fought to spread their roots against the steep uneven surfaces.

Bray had guided them down towards the soft luscious valley, but in doing so it seemed he had lost sight of whatever it was he was using as a landmark. He crouched at the small spring that trickled from above, its thin sliver descending slowly to join the larger river below. After filling his leather skin, he drank deeply with cupped hands, casting the occasional glance towards Elly who, taking advantage of this brief moment, had sought shelter in the shade of one of the nearby trees.

"Are you certain you do not wish me to lead the way," Elly questioned, while nonchalantly plucking some of the tree's flowers from its branches. She held them to her nose briefly. Seeing his observation her posture straightened and she placed them in the small spring, watching as they turned and tumbled, snatched away by the rapid turbulent flow.

"Do you think you can?" Bray challenged as she shoved her hands into her coat pockets defiantly. "We are discussing something that has existed for a time older than either of us." He gestured onward, once more guiding their path.

"Your message said the golden peak, there are few here that would see such deceptive lighting, and fewer which would meet the rest of the description that was in your communication. When you consider the sun's position, vantage points, and such, there is only one mountain it could be and, I hate to be the bearer of bad news, but it is not within this range."

"And when you consider that the world's topography has shifted considerably since anyone even wrote in Othryian it is doubtful we are looking for a peak at all."

"You never mentioned the language," Elly muttered in silent contemplation. She felt the tightening of her stomach and quickly glanced around trying to find something that would give her some inclination as to their location. Her intuition suggested they were heading in the wrong direction. The more they walked this path, the more unnatural it felt; her instincts warned of hidden agendas. Horrific visions flooded her mind, making each step harder than the last. She didn't like it here for two reasons, despite her observations, she had no notion of where they were, and wherever they were set her every nerve aflame.

"As I recall, you never asked. Besides, you misunderstood the message. They weren't telling us to find a golden peak, they were telling me to find the battleground of the ten-year war. We have our own encryptions, not everyone can be trusted." Elly closed her eyes, bringing to the forefront of her mind the map of the world she had long ago known as home. Her eyes sprung open, her gaze once more panned the surroundings in alarm. It had been so long ago she had all but forgotten the lay of the land from that era. Seeing something of a hidden recognition Bray smiled. "And now you understand, we're not looking for a peak, but the scars left from its destruction."

"You knew," Elly whispered in realisation. "You knew where we were going before the note arrived."

"Not exactly. I knew where you fell into slumber, and given your deeds and Kronos' need for vengeance I imagined you were discarded not too far from his domain."

"You could have asked me." Elly felt her head spin. As she fought to control her panicked breathing, her anger towards Bray for deceiving her serving as a strong anchor with which to ground herself.

"There was little point. Whilst you slept in awareness you have no insight into where you were actually retrieved from, or what watched over you. You could not lead me where we needed to go, no one could."

"So if you do not know, how have you been guiding us?" she challenged, her cold glare fixing upon his amused smirk.

"Simple, every time you veered from the path I knew we were getting closer." He flashed her one of his annoying grins.

"Excuse me?"

"You don't recollect being here, or where here is, but your body does. You keep adjusting our bearings. Tell me, as the Lady of Knightsbridge, and having lived hidden within Phoenix Landing, how could it be you were unaware of Everburn? Given the location of both, you would most certainly have passed close to it before." The mountain range they found themselves traversing was situated between her two home locations, and many of the trade routes passed through the valley which cut a curved path through the impressive range to take advantage of the natural shelter from the seasonal storms and hurricanes that frequented the area.

"I travel through Collateral."

"Even when you don't, have you ever crossed these mountains, walked these hills?" Elly considered his question for a moment before shaking her head. "And why do you think that is? You're a woman who has traversed almost every inch of the world, discovered its secrets, explored ruins even gods of old have overlooked, and yet here is a range outside one of your homes you've never set foot upon. I knew we were close when you no longer recognised where we were. You've lived for years with it between your two main residences and yet, even now I've told you where you are you doubt me. You may as well confess that you, the seasoned and infallible explorer, are completely and hopelessly lost, and that's exactly how I know we are in the right place."

"What made you think it would be somewhere I did not know?" Elly suppressed the urge to release the frustration she felt building, knowing if he saw her exasperation it would only add to the arrogant, gloating, self-appreciative air already surrounding him.

"Because you were an adventurer, Mistress Lain. You have pilfered and plundered more than any holding that title. You do, however, show restraint, understanding not all treasures are for mortal hands, but still, you have gazed upon almost everything of real value this world has to offer. For you to not know of something means one of two things, it was either not worthy of knowing, or it was somewhere you feared to tread. Since I knew of its existence, but not its location I made the deduction it was the latter."

"I am *not* afraid."

"And yet as we've been talking you've once more altered our course." Bray placed his hand on the small of her back, leading her in a manner she now recognised. "I knew there was an inscription pertaining to the information I required, just as I knew you'd lead me to it by avoidance. Alisha was the one to suggest you may have the answers."

"The ink blob again?" Elly questioned dubiously, raising her eyebrow.

"The letter was a mere formality, as was the note I received by carrier bird." Bray gestured her onward through the narrowing of the track, their light footsteps disturbing the delicately balanced rocks and stones untouched by the passage of years.

"A deception so I would lead you here?"

"In a manner of speaking. But you're not really leading me anywhere, are you? Besides, we both seek the same thing, a means to protect those we care about from what's coming." For the first time Elly realised that the darkness cast by the clouds encroached, and more concerning was that the shade of what little sky remained suggested the sun would soon be setting. Hues of red streaked across the sky, bringing to mind old rhymes regarding shepherds, but she doubted these streaks could be anything more than a last and desperate warning before the sky became blanketed from all.

Elly, lost in her thoughts, wrenched backwards, trying to escape Bray's oppressive grasp as the yawning mouth of a distant fissure came into sight as they finished their descent through the Valley. Hidden by time, shadows, and foliage, she had been unaware of its presence until it was too late. The formation of cold sweat caused her skin to prickle, her stomach tightened as Bray's grasp increased to prevent her retreat. The very air surrounding her grew heavier, more stifling as they drew nearer to the unwelcoming passage.

"This is a trick!" she snapped. Bray turned to regard her critically before shrugging with a boyish smile that caused her blood to boil.

"If you feel that way it can mean only one thing, we're at the cusp of discovery. Now the question is, are you too afraid to discover what lies within?" She pulled her arm free from his touch, snatching his hand in hers as she rose to his bait.

"I have a bad feeling about this," she warned through barely suppressed anger at having being manipulated so completely. She knew he was toying with her, forcing her onward by challenging her bravery and curiosity. He knew she would not turn back.

"If you didn't I'd be concerned."

"What of the Skiá? What is to protect us once we are inside?" Elly gestured towards the darkening sky understanding that, even without the cloud cover, nighttime welcomed such sinister forces.

"What's to protect us out here?" He grinned, his expression suggesting he knew something of this place she didn't. Strangely, this mere implication was enough. Despite her instincts warning against proceeding, and every muscle protesting each step of their descent, there was no choice but to see it through. If for no other reason than to face her fears. Weakness was not something she could tolerate, especially in herself.

Creatures, once complacent in their sanctuary, skittered away from the noise of the intruders who invaded their home to clamber across the broken debris of landslides and jagged rocks towards a narrow opening in its furthest reaches. The once grand tunnels, long since collapsed and deteriorating, appeared more like large warrens snaking a path through the rock than the glorious structures they once would have been. The ground shifted with each carefully placed step, their weight measured tentatively to ensure their movements would not cause the precariously balanced rubble and delicately suspended boulders to come crashing down upon them from above.

After what felt like hours twisting and turning their bodies through nearly impossible openings, the confinement finally ended. The interlaced passages became larger until the tight tunnels opened into a spectacular corridor, allowing them to imagine how the path they had traversed could have once looked before falling to ruin.

Fractured carvings crumbled and peeled from the once smooth walls. Whatever message or tale they had once held had long been eroded by time's cruel hand as that which was once touched by divinity fell to the force of nature's power. Stone guardians lay broken, almost unidentifiable as their forms collapsed to once more become one with the element that had created them. Crouching, Bray scooped up a larger fragment, studying it intently for a moment before casting it aside. It had no value anymore.

"Welcome to the ruins of Mount Othrys." Bray's right arm swept before him in a grand gesture as he drew her eyes towards the area where the tunnels ceased and opened into an enormous cavern. Beyond it, in ruined glory, stood the palace which had once been the home of the Titans.

Through the darkness the details were indistinguishable, but the suggestion of its shape remained. Larger at the base it rose with gentle inclines to create spiked spires and towers. Large archways in the central area housed crumbled walkways, forever reaching to unseen paths. For the briefest moment Elly thought she had caught movement above, a darker shade of black moving like a shadow.

Elly knew the tale relating to the fall of the Titans well. Mount Othrys' ruin had been the final victory in Zeus' war against his father, and her own actions had presented Zeus the opening he had needed to deal a devastating blow. With his father dethroned, the Olympians mustered a final show of force, cementing their victory by destroying the Titans' landmark on Gaea's Star.

"These walls still stand because of you." Bray startled her from her reverie, his words seeing him the recipient of a questioning look. "Kronos vowed to exact his revenge upon you, as such he had to ensure your safety. Despite his intention being for your torture to be eternal, he wanted no injury at hands other than his own. Of course, other things have made this location their home now, and I am led to believe only the outer-shell remains fully intact. The protection only lasted until Night retrieved you from this prison."

"He never said this was where he found me." Elly held back a shiver as she examined each crumbled spire, each arch and brick, thinking how, if not for Night, she could be trapped here still. It was not surprising her mind had sought avoidance. This place had been a prison to her once before, it made her fear that returning in the mortal flesh would reactivate the curse she seemed to have shed.

"Or he did, and you can't recall. Where did you think he found you?"

"Sealed within a mountain."

"And so you were. It's only the details that escaped you. Shall we?" He gestured towards the enormous bridge that lay in ruin upon a moat of rubble.

"For something that was once home to the Titans it is smaller than I imagined."

"What god is not enlarged in the eyes of the devout?" Bray posed the question with a faint smile. "Besides, what you're looking on is only the uppermost spire, the only thing to have not been buried by time."

"You say that as if you know." There was almost a challenging tone to her voice. Bray had claimed to have no knowledge of this location, and her own fear served only to highlight his sudden familiarity with the structure they stood before. He had once served the Gods, and her unease insisted this could be nothing more than a ploy to see her returned to the place she should have remained. Crossing her arms, she turned to regard him with suspicion, looking at her he gave an exasperated sigh.

"Have I still to prove myself? Tell me, Mistress Lain, can you see the rest of the structure?" Bray gestured towards the crumbled stonework. As she beheld the fused and uneven debris, and how small jagged peaks extended from the ground as if part of a greater building, she had to admit evidence seemed to imply it was part of a larger construction, and so she decided not to argue further. "Now, do you plan on procrastinating and making excuses, or are you to accompany me? I always feel better with a lady on my arm."

"Or a snack within reach," Elly muttered under her breath before raising her tone to answer. "Fair enough. Let us proceed."

* * *

Each shuffle of movement, every rustle of the thickly foliaged leaves, put Rob on edge. Given the approach of the Festival of Hades it was not difficult to realise they were in the forest which bordered the Caves of the Wind. It was the only place he knew where Deciduous trees had evolved to no longer shed their leaves. While those elsewhere lay almost bare, many here still bore fruit, their harvest never yielding, even when the ground lay blanketed with snow. He could feel the icy, chill wind—the breath of Gaea—as it whispered through the heavily burdened boughs. He took a moment to absorb the atmosphere, to listen to the soft birdsong and the chorus of insects who, despite the darkness, offered comfort to those who would listen.

He knew better than to announce his deduction. From their conversation it was clear Daniel wanted to protect this camp's location for as long as possible, and so he played the fool, an act he was accustomed to by now. In some people's company maintaining this pretence was easier than others. Through his work with the Plexus he had discovered that adopting the mannerisms of the people he engaged with often turned situations to his advantage. He would mirror their dialect, mannerisms, even body language, but only ever subtly. Aside from his mentor, there were but two living people who knew of his former affiliation with The Courts of Twilight, Daniel and Bray. Being in the presence of either, often made this deception a little harder to maintain, especially since Daniel had already witnessed some of his skills.

"This camp, it's a mercenary one isn't it?" Fey questioned, pulling himself away from a hushed conversation with Teanna to fall in stride with Rob, who protected their flank as Acha led the way.

"Yes," he acknowledged, knowing Fey already knew this given his inclusion on the conversation.

"Why not visit the castles instead, and recruit those equipped for war? Why, with so much at stake, would your friend seek out a small bunch of cutthroats?"

"Precisely because there is so much at stake," Rob answered in Acha's stead, allowing her to continue counting steps. She pivoted, steering them to the left. "Their numbers will not be enough to make a defence, but with an army backing us..."

"Rob's correct," Teanna intervened. "I was under the impression he was looking for a small group he can arm, allies who will listen to him. Those who pledge allegiances do not take orders from others well. Besides, it would be foolish to assume the kingdoms haven't already deployed forces, and more so to think they would heed the Wita's advice."

"If nothing else he will have sent word to the kingdoms about the danger, and how best to protect the citizens," Rob interjected. "There are those who would see him only as a symbol of the Eortháds, a threat to their own power. His title and the appearance of the Eortháds has caused great unrest. It would be easy to plan an assassination amidst a war. He needs someone he can trust," Rob explained thoughtfully.

"So he's choosing hired blades?" Fey scoffed in disbelief. He had crossed paths with many mercenaries in his time, and trustworthy was not a word he would readily use to describe them. In some respect they were as bad as the bandits.

"He's choosing his brother's comrades," Acha interrupted sharply as she turned to address them. "What's more—" Rob raised his hand, interrupting her. The world fell into an oppressive silence. Even the sound of the wind seemed subdued. A sudden flurry of movement overhead seemed deafening as the birds, nestled in distant trees, took flight, retreating. His instincts were right, he had seen this behaviour before, when he and Fey watched the darkness being unleashed from the Mountains of Light. He glanced to Fey who tensed under the same realisation before their gaze turned to the silver-haired figure who stood between them.

"We need to move, now. Fey, take her somewhere. If our assumptions are correct, if they become aware of her, we'll be dealing with a swarm." Rob's tone was little above a whisper as he gripped the two figures, pulling them towards Acha in a small huddle so his words could be heard by only those they were intended for.

"She stays with us," Acha protested. "She's safest beside me." Acha turned, mentally retracing the steps before she continued to walk at a quickened pace.

"How can she be?" Fey protested, taking Teanna's hand in his to hurry to Acha's side.

"As I said before, my being here is suppressing the energy we naturally emit. As long as she's with me they won't be able to identify her. I would assume we would look just like everyone else in their eyes."

"That's why you were charged with her protection," Fey observed aloud. He remembered having similar thoughts before, when first she had mentioned it, but it had slipped his mind as his thoughts had turned to their survival in the darkened forest.

"That, and another reason."

"Such as?" Fey prompted, noticing that Acha's movements were becoming increasingly more nervous.

"It appears you'll see soon enough. We need to get to the camp, that's where they seem to be congregating." Acha's pace became a jog as fear assaulted her senses. She could feel the oppression along with the shift in nature before them. Something was happening, and if her calculations were correct, the faint hint of smoke she could now taste on the wind came from the direction of the mercenary camp. Her stomach knotted, they always took precautions to remain undetectable, there was no reason she should be able to find them without directions.

"You're going to walk us into a combat, into a battle we cannot hope to win," Fey challenged, his hand curling protectively around Teanna's arm as he also detected the smoke-flavoured wind. He lifted his vision to the canopies above, which masked any signs of the rising vapours.

"Yes, and you will have to trust me."

* * *

Once they had scrambled and climbed the broken debris that created the mound for this partially earth-devoured structure, Bray and Elly cautiously entered through the large gaping archway. Whether it had once served as a doorway to join two elevated structures, or it had simply been a window designed to permit observation across the lands below, could no longer be discerned. Time had destroyed the architect's grand design, that it stood at all was perhaps a miracle in itself.

Given the state of disrepair adorning the land-devoured structure, Elly had expected to find the area within reduced to rubble as the pressure from its destruction consumed all within its wake. Reflected by their dim light, small crystalline veins appeared to trace the outer extremities where the heat had once risen to such a level that stone became liquid, fusing the natural surroundings to this once magnificent structure. Crouching, she studied the intricate weave of fine and larger crystals. Their formations were unusual, but gave no insight into whatever befell the former home of the gods, nor why its downfall had ended so abruptly. She doubted it had anything to do with the slight pressure bearing down from above.

If what Bray had said was true, and Kronos *had* protected this location to ensure she remained unharmed, her body would have required a supply of air. If not for the large air pocket—that Bray kept insisting was a cavern—it would have been completely lost. Surveying the surroundings again she released a near bit her lip in contemplation, the scant light did little to reveal more of the true nature of that which surrounded them.

"It wasn't an air pocket," Bray announced, much to her surprise. "The ward erected where you slumbered caused the land to reform around it, rather than it be lost to the earth, but the existence of a passage granting access makes it a cavern."

"But the pathway was not always present," argued Elly. She knew he was right, but she didn't want to admit it. He had already achieved far too many victories for her liking.

"And wood is not fire, but when we set it alight that is precisely what we call it."

"Look at these markings," Elly stopped sharply, turning her full attention to the wall beside them.

"You're impossible," Bray shook his head, trying to mask his amusement. He approached the wall where, etched into the smooth surface of the stone, was a language he had not seen since he was a child. He traced his hand along the deep impressions and was overcome by a sense of nostalgia. "They're old."

"Can you read them?"

"Fragments." To the untrained eye many of the markings would appear to be territorial gashes left by animals. Humans were so certain of their own superiority that the consideration monsters possessed their own means of written communication was beyond their limited imagination. How wrong they were. He looked at Elly with a new appreciation. She had recognised this as a language, where most would have seen nothing. Unfortunately, it was a script Bray had only seen as a child, before he had been cast from the scare. He had witnessed it only briefly, when his sisters had read to him. Since then he had not encountered many examples, and in time the meanings of the markings had become a faded memory, one perhaps hastened by his own need to repress his nature.

"What does it say?"

"On the Hunters' Moon..." Bray frowned, willing himself to remember the etchings. "Something, something." He gave a sharp sigh, feeling almost ashamed. This script should have been his heritage, would have been, if he had not been born a male in a species where only females were allowed to live. "It's been too long." Elly's low-heeled boots echoed as she approached, placing her hand upon the etchings.

"On the Hunters' Moon the children of the árpyia and neráida were forced to seek shelter. Those who were once prey found a means to forge weapons from something which burned akin to the flames of Phlegethon, yet was forged from metal. Lives thought protected were lost to this magic ore, and numbers dwindled. Tribes, once enemies, united to claim the land of the fallen gods." Elly moved as if to approach the next segment, but found her path blocked by her bewildered looking comrade. Stepping around him, she marked her victory with a slight smile, approaching the next series of indentions. "The nest lay in ruins, and they burrowed, unearthing a stone they could not destroy. Upon it was the blessing of Aether and recognising its value they..." Elly paused looking for the final markings. Bray gently took her hand in his, drawing her fingertip along a nearly invisible line crossing the base of the final deep carving.

"Sanctuary," he advised softly, his voice no more than a whisper. He cleared his throat before speaking again. "It was easily overlooked. My kin communicate in many languages, but this word is something even those who cannot read recognise. It's short because it can mean the difference between life and death, and its etching is light because it is considered a weakness. To ask for sanctuary is a plea for mercy, or a request for safety." Elly traced her finger across the tiny etching again. "Here it represents them asking the named god to protect them. I must admit to being intrigued as to how you learnt this script."

"As you said, I have been an adventurer." Elly raised her eyebrow smugly at seeing Bray was not impressed with her answer. "I shall tell you the truth, if you tell me something I do not know about myself."

"Very well." Bray conceded, he had wondered how long he must wait before she sought to bargain. "It would appear that every cell in your body is still subjected to Kronos' suspended animation curse, and thus you will never appear older in the flesh than you do currently."

"Can they be destroyed, can I be injured, can I make new cells, can they heal, can I die?" she asked almost desperately. The twinkle in his eyes suggested this was precisely the response he had expected. His answer had only served to trigger more questions, many of which left her before she had a chance to still her thoughts.

"We said one thing. Your turn." Elly gave a huff, her need for answers was always prevalent, it was the reason she entertained his company. His response had been cruel, not even an answer but a catalyst to many more questions. She would appear no older, but was her time still measured? There had to be a way to tease some more from him. But first, she always kept a promise. She would answer his question, and next time be more precise in any bargain they struck.

"One cannot be touched by all godly wisdom and remain ignorant. Before doing so I had studied many languages, this one, however, I became aware of. It was subtle at first, I could see patterns in markings and understood their meanings. The more I looked the more I understood."

"So, you awoke the knowledge through subjecting yourself to stimuli, in this case, the markings," he mused.

"Was that a question, because if so I require another answer from you."

"It was not a question." Bray smiled seeing her disappointment. "I could provide another insight, if you are willing to pay the price."

"What price?"

"It has been some time since I lay with a woman of standing."

"No." The answer had left her before she had given it due consideration. To lie with him would no doubt be satisfactory, and she in turn would receive some further answers. She bit her lip, startling as Bray spoke.

"Satisfactory? My fair Lady of Knightsbridge, I am so amazing that I would ruin you for any who attempted to follow me."

"I will decline," she answered firmly, while another part of her longed to accept, if only to bruise his ego after the deed and remove some of his superiority.

"Very well, but know this, before our journey is concluded you will consent." A teasing, sinister smile played upon his lips.

"Fortunately for me I am well-rested."

"Seduction and temptation is a game we both play is it not? Whilst I have warned you what will be the result if you do not keep yourself adequately rested, that's not what I refer to." Elly felt her stomach tighten as Bray turned his back towards her to study the passage before them. "I am many things, but I do not force what can be given freely. I remain a gentleman, even *with* my nature." Elly watched him lift and wave the small lantern to examine their surroundings closer. The small tool cast a pitiful hue of pale light upon the darkness. The place they stood now had, from a distance, appeared to stretch on into the spire, but now they could see their passage was blocked by a dark stone, almost reminiscent of a shadow hidden within the shade.

"A dead-end," Elly observed approaching him with care, wondering if his warning had been intended to remind her of the need to rest. The adventurer in her told her to seek a path, but at the forefront was still the nagging fear, it was its voice which made observations about Bray's intentions, and caused her to doubt.

"No," Bray whispered, tracing his hand across a long triple score mark in the rock. "Or there would not be this warning to intruders. Besides, something is here." Closing his eyes, Bray inhaled deeply before releasing a frustrated breath.

"You mean the tribe still exists?"

"Possibly. This entire area has been enchanted. From the moment we first stepped upon this stone I've not been able to smell anything."

"Are you sure that simply does not just mean there is nothing here?"

"We are standing amidst earth and dust. This enchantment might fool almost anything, but for one detail," Bray paced slightly before approaching Elly, his eyes reflecting a look of such intensity that she failed to retreat from his advance. He lifted his hand, playing with the ends of her hair in his fingers.

"And that is?" Her voice wavered. He moved behind her, his hot breath sending small shivers across her neck.

"I'm famished, and yet I can't smell you." He licked his lips before stepping away. "Something is here, something that wants us to believe they've long departed."

"Then the question remains, how do we enter?"

Chapter 22

A Siege of Shadows

If there was one thing Íkelos enjoyed it was a challenge. A game of strategy and wits was the best way to spend the passage of time when there was nought to do but wait. He could feel the markers that had been placed upon his energy within his niece's body, so it appeared her condition had somehow been noticed. However, time had never been his adversary, and these small victories were nothing more than a distraction from the tedious task of having to direct his energy into keeping the tear—currently required to maintain the manifestation of the Skiá—open. The real game was still some time away.

Until his influence had penetrated the chakra relating to either sight or hearing he could only speculate as to where they were, and what plans they devised. He knew for certain they had been in the proximity of something powerful, something which reflected the true nature of body and soul. Such was the only way they could have noticed his spreading disease within her. Even Seiken, through the bond forged during the claiming, would not have sensed it unaided, after all, darkness moved unseen through the shadows, and his niece had beheld her share of darkness.

A slight chuckle echoed within the nightmarish helm. The final advantage, whatever their plan, would be his. There was no magic capable of being used within his presence, everything he was, his flesh, his armour, even his weapon had come from a forest that fed on and suppressed such powers. The sole exception was it had been made to ensure he could use that which already nestled within him, the unique magical signatures of the Maidens and the

Mystics. The other magics he had claimed were useless and had not even strengthen him as he had hoped they would.

It would make no difference what secrets they unlocked, what ancient magics they petitioned, when they confronted him all would be negated, leaving them weak, and so easily malleable. Even enchantments would fail in his presence, something he had recognised on first approaching this city. It seemed the wards protecting it were disabled in his presence, but its power returned as he placed an appropriated distance between himself and its markings. It was by this he gauged the ideal proximity needed to formulate his plan.

No matter what they unearthed, there was no power that could stop him. But their plight may inspire him in creative means to ensure their cooperation. He had been in the flesh for but a short time, and already the deep-seated need to raze and rebuild had turned from the spark of ambition to an all-consuming flame. Had his victory not been assured he may even have appealed to the Oneirois for aid, as beings of Darrienia they would see how the natural order, the way things should have been, must once more come to pass.

The Moirai had much to be accountable for and, soon, as Talaria came crashing down from the heavens in a ball of flame, their sins would be expiated by death. They had perverted the natural course of life, killed innocents, erased bloodlines, for the sole purpose of forging the future into one they deemed appropriate. One where their race had been mistaken as messengers from the Gods, worshipped, and given endless and unwavering love.

What elation the news of that prophecy had given him. He could not have divined a greater fall for the Moirai himself. To know the very forces they exploited doomed them, it was beautifully ironic. For so long they had manipulated such things to suit their agenda, and now it would be their end. He was almost certain Darrienia must agree with his ambitions, why else punish the ones who corrupted the course of Gaea's star?

There was only one thing missing, something essential to his plan, and that was the power Lavender possessed. Her divine gift had been one of life. Perhaps he should have realised that she would be the Spirit Elemental's counterpart, but her father had shielded their connection from all. The power she held, both as a divine creature and the Spirit Maiden was all he required. The Skiá no longer fully reflected those of the ancient enemies. He had adapted them, manipulated their forms. They were something unprecedented. Even now, as they were feasting upon the essences of people, tearing their energies asunder into the most basic seeds, and stripping away identity and life, they were granted but a fraction of the power these ancient forces had held. They were subservient to him, everything they took would be his to utilise, and with the magic that had once been Lavender's he would weave new life, restoring all to how it should have been. Then, perhaps even his mother, Nyx, would look upon him with favour.

Manipulating things into position without revealing his hand or presence would be a delicate process. What a gift his niece had been. She was the perfect medium or, at least, she would be. They may be monitoring the corruption's spread, but there were ways it could move beyond their detection. Such ancient lore was created to track the predictable flow of toxins, but predictability was not a fixed state for him. He could move in the shadows and given her Hectarian heritage his niece possessed something no other did, shadow chakra. Before this magic became extinct Hectarians were the only beings to possess a dual chakra system, it was essential for their balance, but few possessed the capabilities to realise this. Whilst Zoella's had been rendered inactive when Marise and she were separated, they were still present, and he could still utilise them to his own gains.

* * *

Chrissie's pace had been slow, but with each passing minute it became more brisk, more urgent, until she and Alessia almost travelled at a sprint. Before them, across the plains, they could see a small pinpoint of light, spirals of shadows formed around it, swirling in desperate attempts to penetrate the field.

"I thought you were the only one capable of such a feat." Alessia beheld a distant form encompassed within an orb of light similar to their own. The figure was clearly fatigued, the lurching of his body seemed to force his dragging feet onward, while protesting his every movement.

"I am, you're witnessing my great grandfather." Chrissie panted gesturing quickly towards the card in her hand, reminding Alessia they were carved from her ancestors' flesh. The figure stumbled towards them, the light revealing the form of a young boy grasping a card within his blood-stained hand.

Uttering a curse beneath her breath, Chrissie clutched the card maintaining her own barrier tighter, forcing more energy through her, extending their protection until it surrounded the boy, driving the shadows between them into a rapid retreat. Her light engulfed him, easing the young man's burden and releasing him from its grasp. He crumpled to the floor before them, the soft grass cushioning his heavy fall. Looking upon him Chrissie cupped her face in her hands, attempting to mask the look of horror.

Alessia was at the boy's side immediately, tracing her hands across him, studying each injury. His lips were dry, cracked and bleeding from a lack of hydration that was mirrored in his waxy, gaunt features. His clothes were dishevelled, torn and tattered and the scent of saltwater and sweat mingled with that of the urine, rot, and faeces which stained his clothes. The sole of his one remaining shoe was shredded, much like the mangled flesh of his bare foot. Evidence of a sock, long worn away by the journey was suggested by its tattered remains around the figure's ankle. The continued swelling of his limbs, and the strange angle of his wrist suggested he suffered at least several broken bones. How he had managed to walk was beyond her comprehension.

"Is he alright?" Chrissie crouched beside Alessia, a hand still cupping her mouth as she rocked backward and forward gently. The boy smelt of death, and she feared she already knew the answer to her question.

"He is exhausted. How he continued in this condition goes beyond simple preservation." She glanced to Chrissie, who released a somewhat strangled sigh of relief. "You knew he was seeking you, why?" Alessia asked firmly, as she applied drops of water from the leather skin to the boy's bleeding lips.

"How could I have been so foolish? I was young, it seemed like a good solution at the time. I enchanted the card so that whoever held it would become a herald."

"You used the herald's charm?" Chrissie nodded, surprised that Alessia knew of such things. "Necromancy was all but forgotten to this world, what have you done?"

"I was young. I only knew there was a great danger there. Hoping to protect them I left my cards in the care of a family. They were to keep it on them at all times, and if ever the seal restraining whatever force I sensed failed, it would activate and the possessor, or someone in the vicinity, would know to seek me or whoever held my cards." Chrissie paused, staring at the shallow rapid movements of the boy's chest. "Given the power I felt there, I didn't expect the possessor to still be living." Chrissie peeled a second card from the back of the first, one she had expertly grafted to the other in order to ensure this enchantment would activate should the danger be released.

"Well he is, barely." Chrissie quickly banished the energy from the second card and slipped both within the pouch to be reunited with the rest of her family.

The herald's charm was one of the many forgotten facets of Elemental magic. It used a special essence branding, and saw if the bearer died, or the preordained conditions were met, they would carry information to the one who marked them. The casting had originally been reserved for use on guards or soldiers in under-manned borders, or spies heading into enemy territories. The spirit would remain bound to the corpse and continue its journey until it reached the one who had placed the enchantment upon them. This had been the birth of necromancy. After great experimentation, it was realised that instead of relaying a message, the spirit could instead be manipulated to fulfil a duty. As the practise grew, it was discovered a fragment of energy from a recently departed soul could be diverted into a long decomposed body, creating creatures that could almost rival Cadmus' spartoi. As far as the Eorthåds were aware, the wyrms believed this form of enchantment had been extinguished when the Great Spirit Elemental's presence receded. Although Golemancers and adepts in other fields of the arcane had come disturbingly close with their own experiments.

"We have to take him with us. This is my fault." Chrissie acknowledged, knowing the only reason this figure had not spoken before collapsing was because she was already aware of the danger that had compelled him here.

"Agreed." Alessia looked over Chrissie cautiously, that she would even consider using such an enchantment made her feel uneasy. Whilst she knew Chrissie was not an Elementalist in the traditional sense, she had foolishly not seen the danger her unique method of channelling could pose. "We will take him with us, to ensure your hold on him has fully dissipated."

"It was only the contact with the card that resulted in this. I can't perform spirit branding, nor would I want to." Chrissie's reassurance eased some of Alessia's concerns, and yet, at the same time, the thought she could control a living host was in some ways more unnerving than the thought of necromancy being revived. She would have to keep a close vigil on her in the future.

"Given time he should recover, but he has travelled beyond what he should have been capable of. We can attend to him at the camp." Alessia lifted the young boy over her shoulder, not showing the slightest indication she was aware of the foul odours emitted from the figure. "Let us delay no longer."

Alessia briefly considered how many people would have journeyed through their Irfeláfa, and mentally promised to purge the magic, even if it meant each Eorthád would once more have to swear the blood oath. It was safer than having so many unknown elements being able to utilise a means that should be reserved only for themselves.

* * *

Elly joined Bray as he studied the barricade that barred their path. The wear of time and the gathering of airborne particles were a testament to its age, making it apparent this wall had always been part of the original construction. It appeared this archway—that they assumed had a practical use—was intended to be solely decorative.

Bray was convinced it was functional, and studied the surrounding area for hidden indentations or triggers, while Elly seemed more content to observe with a slight smile she thought was hidden by the shadows. He knew there would have been a means to open, elevate, or lower it, but whether by design or age it seemed the ancient mechanics were lost on him. The presence of the tribes and their markings suggested that, at some point, someone had found a means to enter, and this was the only location that remained fully intact, and free of debris, almost as if it had been maintained at one point.

"What did you say the tribe were, children of..." he prompted. Elly's slouched posture straightened as she pushed herself from her resting position against the wall, bringing his focus to the fact she was once more fatigued, but now was not the time to loiter. He had warned her of allowing herself to become depleted, but without any scent to fuel his hunger, for the moment at least, he felt no craving to satisfy his needs.

"Neráida and árpyia," Elly answered, casting her gaze in the direction of the etchings.

"So," he mused, his brows furrowed in concentration, all monsters had names other than those given to them by the humans, after all, they were not created by them. "We're looking at what you'd call harpies and fay." Bray tilted his head backwards, letting out a bemused snort as he saw the circular shaft extending above them. It was well camouflaged by the natural contours and shading of the surrounding stonework. A shadow hidden within the shade, he reflected on his initial perception of the area and berated himself for not thinking to study the space above them more closely.

"I do not suppose you can fly?" The corner of Elly's mouth twitched in a slight smile as she removed her dice from her sleeves. Hesitantly, she released them while focusing on the weapon they needed. There were conditions that needed to be met in order for her to create a weapon of her choosing outside of practice. It usually resulted in a weaker composition of the item forged, but it was worth the risk.

"You still carry your arsenal then?" Bray observed, hearing the clatter of dice against the stone corridor.

"I have expanded it since our paths last crossed."

"But what can you have that will get us up there? I don't believe a ladder is considered a weapon."

"Did you always possess such lack of imagination?" Elly questioned. "Besides, you would be amazed by what I could do with a ladder," she added as the dice vanished, duplicating particles from their surroundings until a weapon formed within her grasp. Bray, seeing the large frame within her hand, chuckled. He swept forward, all amusement fading as he reached out to steady her as her legs trembled beneath her.

"You've forgotten how much energy that trick expends. Have you even used it since waking?"

"So stop speaking and assist me," she gasped, surprised at how weak she felt. Bray was once again infuriatingly correct. This task had been a small feat when she was within the golem, but in the flesh it was considerably more difficult. She turned from him as he moved to lift the weapon from her grasp. "Do that and it vanishes," she warned. Positioning himself behind her Bray raised her arms, using his own strength to bear the brunt of the harpoon luncher's weight. Once the sights were approximately correct, he nudged her mind forcing her to fire. The bolt released with a surprising force, its metal tip burying deep within the shaft's wall to leave the attached tether linked to the remaining ammunition.

"What now?" he posed, as Elly moved slowly, placing the weapon to her back.

"There is a spilt in the lower belt, open it would you." Bray did as instructed, helping Elly to guide the launcher into place. He marvelled at all the subtleties woven into her coat and belt's design. To anyone observing it appeared finely stitched and decorated, but each section had been skillfully crafted in order to help secure any item from her arsenal. "As long as it remains in contact with me we should be fine." His fingers unhooked one of the half-belts that appeared to keep the garment fitted to her figure, and secured the weapon, ensuring it could still be removed with ease.

"Unless you collapse from exhaustion," he scolded.

"Then it would be best if we made haste." With a quick motion, Bray lifted her onto his back despite her surprised protest.

"Heed me well, Lady of Knightsbridge. I'm not falling to my death because you can't make the climb. Besides, if we're to scale the shaft I'm going to require your assistance." Elly stilled her protest, forcing her body to rest as Bray began to climb the rope. Its surface was strangely rough, it was only as he studied it he realised it had been made from finely woven stone, not fibre.

When they reached the bolt he was pleased to see it had penetrated the wall deeper than he had expected, allowing him to tentatively test its capability to support them.

"It is a mechanical broadhead. It should easily hold our weight," Elly whispered, seeing him clutching the uneven wall to give them some support should a sharp pull dislodge the bolt.

"A what?"

"Before your time. This one was designed to penetrate walls and open concealed blades to allow the users to infiltrate... for relevance's sake, let us say strongholds."

"Do you have another?"

"Just the one at the other end of the tether." Elly inclined her head as if to bring his attention to the second bolt, to which the end of the rope was secured.

"Can you aim it up there?" Bray pulled them up onto the bolt with tremendous effort, expending more energy than he would have liked.

"If you can brace us against the recoil."

"I'm stronger than I look," Bray boasted. "Even so, do it quickly." With cat-like grace he edged down the narrow, metal bolt until Elly could hear the rough surface of the wall as it scratched against the longer parts of her coat that billowed in the slight updraught. Understanding his intention, her legs tightened around him as she freed the launcher. Resting her arm on his shoulder for additional support, she squeezed the trigger. The force of the bolt's release thrust them backwards, pinning her painfully against the wall as the air was expelled from her lungs. Unable to compensate for the extra force, the weapon slipped from her grasp, the sound of its impact with the floor was absent as its presence merely vanished into the ether.

"It was expended, it would have dis—"

"Shh, you've still got work to do." Bray interrupted her attempt to justify why she had released it. "You need to remain conscious unless you want us to plummet to our deaths." He gave the tether—that ascended diagonally between the two bolts—a number of firm tugs until he was satisfied it would hold their weight. Briefly, a nagging concern surfaced about the bolts' longevity, wondering how long they would remain without the weapon or her touch to sustain them. He comforted himself with the thought that projectiles clearly possessed different rules to in hand weaponry.

"Assuming I can die," Elly pried, hoping, given their mutual fatigue, he may reveal something without thinking.

"Or that I can. Either way, the fall would be crippling and I'd devour you to survive."

"That thought is strangely sobering." Elly tightened her grasp as Bray surrendered his weight to the rope. She crossed her feet and arms across his torso, feeling vulnerable as the slight warm draught rising from below served as a reminder that there was nothing between themselves and the ground. She pressed herself closer, hoping her burning muscles could endure.

"Hopefully it's motivated you to stay awake."

"You could say that."

"Good, hold tight. We've still some distance to cover after we reach the bolt. You'll need all your energy if we're to make it."

"Or you could just take over my actions, again," she bit.

"I think you may be overestimating my current strength."

"And here was me thinking those of your kind were built for endurance."

"Trust me, I *am* enduring." The second bolt had struck only a few feet from the smaller opening above. Those last few feet would be the most taxing. He felt Elly's grip on him unintentionally slacken and increased his pace, pretending not to notice that the stone rope beneath his feet seemed to be thinning as it slowly shed dissipating grains.

* * *

Jones, swung his torch wildly as the rippling shadow circled back to continue its assault on the sentry it had surprised. Fire, was not something normally seen outside the masked protection of the buildings, but it was the only means he could think of to fight something made of darkness. His lieutenant lay bleeding, nursing a pulsating slash which, had Jones not witnessed the attack himself, he would have believed to have been inflicted by a large cat, rather than a thing with no substance. He didn't need his medics to tell him what he already knew, the wound was fatal. The claws, or whatever had shredded his flesh, had penetrated too deeply into his abdomen, and the rancid odour of perforated bowels and intestines permeated the air. He would have eased his suffering, if he could have spared even a single moment.

Signal fires crackled wildly, their light casting haunting images of sweat-soaked figures who worked in unison to create a sanctuary, but still the shadows crept through, riding the flickering darkness caught beyond the grasp of the fire's light. He was certain their attackers' numbers had diminished since their camp was becoming illuminated in the orange glow, but still the screams of his allies assailed his ears, carried on the billows of the smoke-laden wind, their cries becoming one with the roaring flame as silhouettes of life-long comrades and new recruits were torn apart before his horrified gaze.

"Form a circle around the beacon," he commanded. Sweat glistened upon his flesh, partially from the heat, and partially from looking upon a foe he knew they could not overcome.

"Jones!" he recognised the voice, despite the passage of time since he was last within her company. Through the fire's haze four forms emerged, sprinting towards where he and his men made—what Jones feared would be—their last stand.

"By Ares' Blade!" Jones, despite the severity of the situation, could not hide the smile, although given the situation it appeared more like a pained grimace.

"Rob, explain what we know," Acha requested, as she leapt the outer-ring of flames towards the central towering beacon. She scanned the faces of those present as they stood, red fleshed and panting against the stifling heat, between both heat sources. Dropping to her knees she extended her hands towards the aureole protecting them. "Please," she implored in a whisper of desperation, her eyes closed as if in prayer. For a moment she became still, the world around them silent but the the crackling of the flame. Her body slumped, crumpling upon the charred grass as the orange flames roared ferociously, rising to shield them from another assault. The fire shimmered with magnificent fury. In places its embers became nearly blinding as they danced the perimeter to defend the areas where darkness encroached.

"What in Hades, did she just become part of that?" Jones gestured towards the dancing flames. His paths had crossed with this woman on but a few occasions. He knew Daniel travelled with powerful companions, he had just never realised exactly how gifted they were.

"Her life-force is different," Rob summarised. He had witnessed her take control of something before. "It's just like with the blood," he reflected aloud on past events.

"What now?" Fey questioned.

"Never mind." Rob gestured dismissively before explaining to Jones all he knew of their situation and the enemy they faced. "She wasn't sure if this would work, or for how long. She is hoping to maintain the protection until Daniel can arrive."

"And Acha?" Jones jerked his head towards the slumped figure.

"Do not touch her!" Teanna shouted as one of the medics, seeing their commander gesture toward her, extended his hand to check for a pulse. The medic recoiled rapidly hearing the warning, wiping sweat from his brow as the flame's heat seemed to grow more intense and stifling.

"Teanna's right, you could interrupt the focus. Heck, I don't even know how this works." Rob glanced to Teanna. "She said her presence will suppress the entities' ability to detect the surrounding life. She's hoping they'll assume we're now dead and move on before—"

"Before we suffocate, or is there another reason?" Jones questioned, seeing the subtle exchange. He already felt the effect of the fire consuming the air beneath it, and although small areas opened, allowing fresh air to enter periodically, it was never for long, and the fire soon consumed it.

"How much do you know about her talents?" Rob shook his head. "Never mind, doesn't matter, she has a contingency plan."

"They're looking for me," Teanna stated, rising to her feet from her position beside Acha, satisfied no one else planned to approach. "Perhaps I have run far enough."

"Don't you dare!" Fey growled, grasping her arm a little too tightly as he pulled her protectively towards him in the same instant Jones had reached out to bar her escape. He knew Acha was tiring, to step through the barrier now would only result in minor burns, if any. The centre of the flame no longer burnt as fiercely.

"What's the contingency?" Jones questioned, mopping the sweat from his brow. He surveyed his men, he had lost some good warriors, and some newer recruits, but their numbers were still close to a hundred, and each of them felt the impending inevitability of death upon their shoulders.

"When she can't hold the flames any longer she will render Teanna unconscious, and fend the Skiá off until she can draw their focus. She plans to lead them away," Rob explained, his eyes fixed upon the flickering orange hues.

"It's a death sentence." Jones wiped his hand down his face, causing the blood splatter on his skin to streak his flesh.

"She's not certain about that. The Skiá don't want to kill Teanna, they need to capture her, so Íkelos can remove the power within her," Rob explained.

"Íkelos?" Jones questioned. He pivoted, hearing a loud thud as one of his men succumb to the thinning of the air.

"He's the one who summoned the Skiá," Teanna answered softly. "Please, I understand if you wish me to leave, it will lead them from your men."

"I'm not sure how men behave where you're from, young lady, but here we stand our ground until it falls from beneath us, and sometimes even after." His words were echoed with an exhausted chorus of aggressive agreement.

Jones sucked in a deep breath as the air around them once more became saturated with oxygen, it was only then he noticed how far the dome had receded. "Be ready," he warned, lighting a fresh torch, signalling for his men to do the same. Acha gasped for breath, her essence mostly returned to her body, while she ensured part of her still resided within the flames, attempting to hold the wall as long as she could.

"Te-Teanna," she gasped. Acha gave a sharp tug on her glove, allowing the touch-fasten seam to separate. Her arm shook as she raised her hand. Teanna could only gasp as their flesh met, before consciousness left her. Removing the talisman from around her neck, Acha placed it within Teanna's hand, knowing the part of her that was bound to the ancient artefact would be able to suppress her presence, it would protect her, even if Acha were to be embraced by death.

"Are you sure you know what you're doing?" Rob hissed, pulling Acha to her feet. "They eat souls too." Rob frowned wondering if he had come to this assumption himself or had heard it elsewhere.

"Keep her safe, and make sure she keeps my necklace with her at all times." The heat from the flames died as Acha withdrew the last of her presence from the fire leaving it a shadow of its once grand image. "Daniel will know what to do," she assured, casting a final look towards the group who watched in concern. With a deep breath and a nod of commitment she removed the final glove, leaving it beside Teanna, and leapt through the flames.

* * *

When finally Bray and Elly reached the pinnacle of the shaft, they were relieved to discover it emerged into a small cubbyhole. Eclipsed in shadows, and sheltered from sight, it seemed it had once been used to discard the waste casually thrown aside during banquets and gatherings. Beyond the caress of the shadows a glorious internal balcony stretched before them, circling the entire circumference of the tower. Marble banisters—that had once created majestic railings around the inner edge—allowed anyone to gaze down upon the lower levels. The banisters lay mostly crumbled in varying states of disrepair, but those which still stood strong were a testament to the artist. There were weavings so fine and complex within the marble it was amazing they survived being crafted, much less the test of time.

This mezzanine seemed to have been designed as a vista. At various places were large arched windows. Bray recognised the texture as being identical to the stone which had blocked their path, but looking out he saw not a solid barricade, but the world outside the tower. High above them was a solid ceiling made from opaque stones and below stood numerous internal balconies, cascading down, each occupying larger areas than the last until the final layer became the floor. Many of these tiers had areas leading from them, perhaps into internal rooms, and where such corridors and exits had crumbled, he was almost certain he could see evidence of old burrows.

After taking a moment to ensure their safety, he finally allowed himself to rest. Sweat poured from their fatigued bodies as they attempted to breathe past the exhaustion caused by the final moments of their climb.

"Get some rest, I'll keep watch." Bray looked upon his partner's dishevelled state and knew she could not continue for much longer. She beheld him hungrily, her ravenous gaze absorbing his every move. Even with their sense of smell inhibited by the enchantment the pheromones he emitted were still prevalent, and their strenuous climb had only served to strengthen them. The more tired and fatigued he felt, the more powerful his effect on any creature in his vicinity. The way she almost offered herself to him was testing his restraint.

"The Skiá will not wait for—"

"Better the world waits and receives a weapon, than we rush and it loses a saviour. *Sleep*." He put minimal influence behind the suggestion, but it was as much as his own fatigued body would allow. As her eyes fluttered closed he took a few moments to observe their surroundings closer and rein in the hunger that even now threatened to surface and send him into a frenzy. He could not lose control in her presence, he owed her more respect than that.

Lifting his vision towards the ceiling, his tired stare rekindled an old thought. Carefully he made his way to the balcony's edge, once more peering down. The floor below was not as clear as the one above, although now he focused on the details he realised why. The floor was covered with the discarded remnants of old bones. It appeared that if there were things still living within this tower, they no longer ventured to these altitudes.

Bray looked upon Elly as she slept, watching the heavy rise and fall of her chest as she sank into a deep slumber. He had waited long enough. Placing his index finger to his lips he suckled on it gently, coating it with saliva before positioning himself to lie beside her. She required sleep to recover, but he needed something far more substantial. He had warned her what would happen if she allowed herself to succumb to such an exhausted state. His hunger gnawed as he touched his finger to her exposed flesh. Feeling his skin fuse with her own he closed his eyes, savouring each moment as the energy of her life flowed into him. He needed her functioning, this was the thought he kept forefront within his mind as the seconds passed and he took what he dared.

* * *

Acha ran. Her heart pounded, unable to pump fast enough to compensate for the extensive needs. Her muscles burned with every movement as she forced one heavy limb in front of the other while her body cried out for relief, demanding she take what was needed from the world which, even now, drifted in and out of her exhausted gaze. She could replenish herself in an instant, gain renewal by stripping the life from the surrounding world, but to do so would be to release the mimic she held on Teanna. She forced back her body's warnings, its cries for sustenance with all the will she could muster.

The Skiá would not harm Teanna. Acha would be safe for only as long as she was able to deny herself what she needed. A long time ago she had no control over when she would consume the energy around her, but now she had a far deeper understanding of her curse. She knew better than to ignore the subtle warnings, but she had been given no choice. The quiet whisper of need now screamed at her, ringing like watchtower bells within her mind.

Acha's staggering steps slowed further, giving the Skiá the opening they had needed to surround her. Even so, she was certain they had been deliberately tiring her, after all, if they could shift between shadows, they could have ensnared her with ease. Her legs began to tremble, until finally they refused to allow her another step and crumpled beneath her. The darkness tentatively began to close the distance between them and, for a moment, Acha watched in terror as the surrounding land withered, and the shadows saw her for what she was, or rather, who she wasn't. She only hoped she had given her friends enough time.

A shrill screech pierced the air as the Skiá descended, and Acha became one with the darkness.

* * *

When Elly awoke upon the cold, stone floor she felt rested, but strangely disorientated. She sucked her dry tongue and was once again reminded how simple life had been within her golem. She sat slowly, her eyes fixed on Bray as she rubbed the back of her neck where aches and pains from the strange sleeping position seemed to have created knots of tension.

"Drink, you need to stay hydrated," he ordered as he turned to face her, thrusting a leather skin towards her. She uncorked it, drinking greedily, the cool water felt like heaven within her mouth until she tasted the subtle undertones of another flavour. She choked. When her coughing subsided he was watching her with an amused grin, and it only widened as she arched her eyebrow regarding him suspiciously. "Please, I have no use for such things. If I wanted you, you'd be mine." Her eyes narrowed slightly as she raised the liquid to her mouth before drinking more.

"It seems I am unaccustomed to such exertion, you were correct," she acknowledged, dusting the loose dust and stone chips from her attire after moving to stand. Their journey here was little more than a haze, already almost lost to her memory. She knew where they were, but wondered if when they left if the memory of this location would once more fade into obscurity.

"Eat, once we enter the lower levels there will be no time to rest." Bray gestured towards her discarded bag which lay a few feet from where she stood. "My assumptions were accurate. We are not alone within these walls." He once more turned his back to her, advancing towards the crumbled banisters.

"Have you seen something?" Elly asked after swallowing a mouthful of dried fruit. It wasn't much, but it would be enough to sustain her for the time being. Placing her hand within her pocket she clutched the berries and leaves harvested from one of the many trees they had passed on their journey here before placing them within her mouth.

"Not from here, but while you were sleeping I scouted below, there's definitely something here."

"What do you think we will find?" Elly approached to stand beside him, the knot in her shoulders growing tighter as she looked down. Her stomach tightened as her instincts warned the descent would bring with it danger or death. When Bray spoke, to her shame, she felt herself startle.

"Something new. If Fay and Harpies really have been cohabiting for generations, who knows what their alliance could create. Farpies, Harpay?" He turned to give a crooked smile, sensing her anxiety.

"Assuming the match is possible, they would likely slaughter you for such naming, and I must warn you, I would likely align with them."

"Fay can ensure conception. It's how they increased their numbers after they were almost hunted to extinction. How about Graysonious Brayicus?" Bray ventured, noticing the slight twitch in Elly's lips at his foolishness. She stepped away from the ledge, looking a little less apprehensive than just moments before.

"So we are considering a hybrid?" she continued, ignoring his tomfoolery.

"It would appear so."

"Any thoughts?"

"Given the abandonment of these levels I would assume they've lost the ability of flight. As I said, I scouted around a little while you were resting, even the bones are almost dust." Bray placed a delicate bone within her grasp, she studied it intently, examining the rows of jagged indentations upon the surface. She looked up at Bray, no words were needed.

Their slow descent remained cautious, their steps guarded while they took every opportunity to shelter within shadows and alcoves. As they reached the bone and dust coated floor, glimmers of the opaque crystal, that had been previously hidden, gleamed, reflecting the delicate light-stone's glow. It had surprised Elly to find such a treasure in Bray's possession. As its name suggested it generated a gentle light activated by the heat of a touch. It was not as powerful as a Hectarian spell or enchantment—or even a torch—but for now it served their purpose.

While Bray had explored, he had not taken the opportunity to examine the lowest level. He had thought his quick reconnaissance had excluded her more than enough, besides, she was like Rob, a natural born treasure hunter, and her skills of observation would serve him well, at least for as long as she continued to think her aid unnecessary. If she were to realise how desperately he required her assistance, she may just press her advantage. The dust and powder from the crumbling bones clung to their boots, rising and spreading with each carefully measured step as each movement cast the fine particles into the air. As they circled the room's circumference, the reason for this area's abandonment became clear, the descending pathway had been blocked by a cascade of crumbling rocks from above.

"You should rest some more," Bray advised pushing up his sleeves. "I'll get started on this." He knew it would not be as difficult as it appeared. Looking upwards, Bray had a new appreciation for the structure. Time had tumbled much of the deteriorating debris, but only that from the lower levels had come to rest on this bone graveyard. From the floor below, the weight would be impossible to shift, but with a clear view of what had fallen he could see it was only a matter of moving the larger rocks, unless, of course, the passage below was filled with debris. If that were to be the case then they may have to rethink their plan.

Chapter 23

Corruption

They could not sense the one they hunted for their master, but they knew she was close. The woman who had led them astray had fooled them, briefly, but she had also exposed their target's location. They were not fools, one could not mimic another without first having been in proximity to them. This woman, Acha, had another purpose now, she would take them to her. They had descended upon her, hoping to learn all she knew, but instead they discovered something spectacular, a means to retrace her steps. The essence they would normally devour possessed something they had not encountered before, a space. A place they could weave themselves inside in order to gain control, a means to infiltrate and seize the one they sought in their grasp, without having to concern themselves with the barrier their siblings reported now surrounded the encampment this woman had fled from.

There was something about this human, something different to those they had encountered until this point. She had injured one of them, but in doing so they had filled the void in her essence. This possession had not damaged her remaining sentience, instead she thought herself among their masses, aligned with their desire, and a part of their hierarchy. She, like themselves, bent to the will of their alpha and obeyed. Exactly how this had happened was unknown. The one of them who had touched her seemingly withered, but instead they felt his energy within her, heard his thoughts alongside hers. They would remain alert for others like this, their uses were beyond imagining.

They were both still present, but whether their sibling actually controlled this form, or if the woman had simply been brought into their ranks was unknown. It was something they could fully explore once their goal was achieved. This was now a vessel for their own exploitation, and there was a feeling of pride that their sibling had been the one to discover this boon.

The human body lurched, its movements erratic and unnatural as it staggered forward, leading them back towards the encampment it had once broken free from, but there was a danger there now, one they had been made aware of as they pursued this being. On understanding the figure this haunt of Skiá had followed was but a decoy, their siblings had resumed their attack. They were certain that the one they sought would be sheltered within the encampment, whether they could feel the unique strain of energy or not. Yet, their attempts had been foiled, their forces driven back, and all shadow-passages within had been severed. But they too had a new weapon now, one of them dwelt within the essence of one of their own kind, and they could pass through the warding, no matter how bright.

Stepping to the brink of the barrier the figure—once recognised by those inside as Acha—extended her hand towards the light. Her face twisted into a strange smile as the hum of energy chased through her flesh and her siblings excitement became palpable. She could hear their collective assessments, their joy that her touch seemed to mimic their power, allowing her flesh to absorb energy from whatever it touched in the same manner they did, only her pace seemed much slower, and was not limited to only living creatures. In the location where the possession had occurred the ground surrounding her had withered, but no death had been left within her footprints, leading them to assume her flesh alone would mirror their ability, after all, no human could do what they could. They were the devourers of life and the claimer of essences.

"You've returned!" The voice heard was deeper than the one forced to reply. Seeming to know their vessel the larger framed figure, a male, waved a greeting as he approached the barrier.

"Where is she?"

"As you left h—are you alright, you look..." The scream that curdled the air was heard by all within the safety of the ward as she stepped through, taking this figure by the throat until every ounce of resistance ceased, those still trapped outside the barrier rejoiced as they felt the energy within her swell, but the unique patterns of the essence was not joined with their own, it seemed in her possessed state, any power she mirrored was stopped at simple absorption of life. It mattered not, what she could do was incredible. She would be their mortal soldier, one who could walk where they could not. With her amidst their ranks there would be no sanctuary.

Acha's body stumbled forward, drawn towards the noise as more humans approached to investigate their ally's scream. Unlike her last victim they kept their distance, torches in hand despite the complete permeation of light. Snarls escaped her feral lips as she lunged towards them, sending them scurrying backwards with the roar of flames as they swung their torches as if they would defend them. Each step she advanced, the took in retreat.

A figure—a woman known to Acha as Alessia—blocked the path before her, protecting the dwelling she had no doubt her target would be sheltered within. The woman's black hair possessed a silver winged circlet which fought its way through the hair above her ears. As she stood in challenge, her fingers touched the blue teardrop amulet, allowing liquid metal to flow from within, coating her leather clothes to form a majestic armour known only to the Eorthāds. Acha studied the areas of weakness, the places where the shoulders, elbows, knees, and inner thighs were not kissed by the metal protection. Her eyes trailed back to the teardrop, now an ornament within the impressive looking armour.

Acha's charged forward, clutching Alessia's arm, waiting for the agonised cries which never came. With a sharp twist the woman struck her sending Acha stumbling backwards, her footing scrambling in the unbrushed foliage as her prey slipped easily from her grasp. Regaining her footing, Acha's lips turned into a ferocious snarl as she tried to understand why this figure had been unaffected by her gift. The only difference she could devise, with the help of her siblings, was with the first flesh had met with flesh. This time the Alessia's attire had shielded her from direct contact.

"Acha, hogae, understand, remember." Acha lunged again, her vision drawn toward the exposed flesh at the nape of her neck, but she got no closer. Alessia's sharp kick connected with her stomach, driving her backwards while her gaze scanned the faces of the crowd, looking for something. "Héo níedhæse ƿiþ þǣm eorðfæt hire ȝedǣlan." The urgent tones of her voice did little to force the understanding of her comrades. She glanced around in desperation, an action Acha interpreted as fear. "Talisman," Alessia demanded, her hand pushing Acha's charge aside as she sidestepped. Something soared past Acha, snatched from the air by her adversary whose hands traced rapid sigils, leaving a trail of magic as a brief afterglow. "Ic ræpe þu, I bind you."

Charging forwards, Alessia dodged another attack with the smallest of movements, turning again to barely miss the raking claws that had targeted her face. In a smooth motion, Alessia pivoted, her arm hooking around Acha's waist to pull her off balance to stumble over the extended leg. Alessia was upon her in an instant, not allowing her time to rise before pressing the talisman against Acha's exposed flesh as she flailed wildly. An icy sensation encompassed her protesting body, and all was lost to darkness.

* * *

Alessia sank to her knees beside Acha's body. The tension in the air was disconcerting, to the point Alessia felt the need to offer reassurance to the swelling group who had come to investigate what was happening.

"She is subdued."

"It would seem she must have touched a Skiá," Chrissie summarised. She had heard from Acha tales of something similar happening to her before. When their paths had first crossed Chrissie had been a prisoner. She had been found only thanks to Acha's contact with her captor, but she had taken too much of his energy, and had discovered it was nearly impossible to separate her own identity from his. "Quickly, help me purge her vessel."

"Can you divide the energy? The talisman is the greatest concern."

"What did you do?" Chrissie questioned, leaning in to hear Alessia's lowered tone.

"Acha's essence is stored within, are you familiar with the Djinn?" Chrissie nodded. "I used their recall enchantment to force her back into the talisman. The Skiá have contaminated her shadow, and her essence. Both must be purged." Alessia whispered, grateful when Jones began dispersing the gathering crowd.

"How is that possible, I thought they merely devoured us," Chrissie asked, keeping her tones low to match those of Alessia. She knew better than to openly discuss something which could be used to exploit one of her friends.

"She had to split her essence in order to protect Teanna, doing so left her vulnerable." Rob's voice intruded on their conversation as he made his presence known, drawing their attention towards him as he stood leaning casually against the vine woven structure where Teanna had been secured.

"You threw me the talisman, my thanks to you." Alessia nodded slightly. "You speak my language?" Alessia was aware of having fallen back into her native dialect during the confrontation.

"No, but I am familiar with a few of the words from... let's say a previous life, Þǣm eorðfæt, earthly vessel, níedhæse compelled and ȝedǣlan, if I remember, was to separate." Rob had much to be thankful for during the nightmare that was The Courts of Twilight, some of which was their drawing on ancient methodology to achieve the reproduction of creatures long extinct. Their master, Lord Blackwood, had wanted to create an army subservient to him alone, and much literature that should not exist within this time, had been referenced.

"I do not think I wish to know why those words are familiar to you, but I am thankful they are." Alessia spoke with care.

"You're right, you don't want to, but those days are long behind me. Whilst they made me who I am, they are not a reflection of the person I became." His words caused Alessia to relax slightly.

"The body is safe, have someone relocate it to a resting area," Chrissie announced, her attention now transfixed on the small talisman. "This is proving more challenging. The result was due to her essence and body absorbing one of them. If it had been her body alone then it would be easy, but cleansing a soul is far more complicated."

"Can it be accomplished?" Alessia questioned, seeing Chrissie focusing the secondary card's energy upon the small amulet.

"If not for Acha's essence needing to absorb energy from her surroundings she would be lost to us. There would be too much of their taint in anything she consumes at this time to fully restore her, she could very well consider herself one of them indefinitely. I'll need to channel this energy to sustain her, the light should replace the darkness as it begins to decay. But I can't leave the talisman unattended."

"What do you require?" Jones questioned, now that his mercenaries had returned to their duties, which at the moment consisted of preparing a pyre and raising a toast to their fallen comrades, his focus returned to Acha. Whispers amongst his ranks had already started to spread about the danger this woman posed. Had she not been recognised as a heroine she would have been judged instantly, but even they recognised she had not been in control of her actions, and the injustice of condemning her for an act beyond her control. Of course, understanding did not mean they could overlook the actions.

"Somewhere quiet where I will not be disturbed, preferably at a distance to her body so not to risk any overspill from the contamination."

"Before that, there's something else you need to do, if it is within your means." Rob spoke once more. Chrissie looked to him questioningly, gesturing for him to continue. "A light barrier alone is not enough. It needs to prevent passage from anyone not cleansed, otherwise anyone with a contaminated shadow could pass through undetected and your hard work would be for nought."

"What do you suggest?"

"A consciousness trap." Chrissie looked to him in confusion. "Your shadow purge causes people to lose consciousness, is there a way to weave this into the barrier somehow?" Chrissie's brow wrinkled in thought, after a few moments she nodded.

"I'll address that first, it should just take a few moments." She moved as if to hand the card she was focusing the energy through to him, but after a moment of hesitation passed it to Alessia, along with her simple instructions.

* * *

"Acha?" The voice echoed within her ears, causing each syllable to reverberate. "Step back, she's coming around." Her body felt heavy. Fear flooded through her as a cold sweat trickled an icy path down her flesh. Through unresponsive eyes all she could see was darkness. Darkness such as that which had threatened to devour her. She tried to fight the paralysis, finding it as unrelenting as that which had bound her for centuries after her essence had been traded to Hades.

"Release the binding, she's safe." Another voice echoed. Acha thought she should recognise it, but the distortion was still too intense to allow her to place its owner, but trusting the words she allowed herself to relax, convincing herself to stop fighting against the pressure bearing down upon her.

"Are you certain it's purified, she won't attack again?"

"Certain." At once the invisible pressure holding her in place released. Acha's eyes sprung open, taking a few moments to adjust and focus on Chrissie and Alessia who stood over her. Their heavy gaze scrutinised her every movement. Her hand rose instinctively for her talisman. "It's safe. We had to take some precautions." Chrissie banished the light seal around the amulet and placed it within her hand.

Alessia had been aiding her in enabling the link between Acha's body and the talisman to reconnect to a point where she would regain consciousness. It had been a difficult process. Chrissie had been replacing the dark energies with that from the light card, while Alessia had used her own magic to bind Acha's body, permitting but a minimal connection between the two to remain. A connection that was carefully regulated to ensure the vessel survived without Acha's essence occupying it. They had not realised the danger of the initial separation until the body itself had begun to change and deteriorate. It was only then they realised Acha's essence had been the only thing which kept it functioning. Whilst they both knew much of the woman, they had never been certain how her talents had worked.

"Teanna?" Acha questioned, her energy returning. She glanced around, noticing for the first time she was in one of the biotecture structures of the Mercenary camp. Trees and vines had been encouraged to grow around shelters until they had created a perfect replica of the internal structure, allowing the internal frame to be removed. Even now Acha was impressed at how they had encouraged nature to build their homes. Even the bed beneath her was formed from interlocking roots, somehow, this realisation made it a little less comfortable than it had been just moments ago.

"Safe, although she's a little shaken. The Skiá know she's here, but they can't breach the barrier," Chrissie comforted.

"Shadows!" Acha sat rapidly, causing the two mercenaries who had been keeping watch outside to startle, their hands seized their weapons as they turned sharply ready to enter, pausing only as they saw Alessia's signal.

"We know, Rob filled us in on the details. The area is secure."

"How did you find me? It was me you found, wasn't it?" Acha's voice trembled slightly, recalling the touch of the Skiá upon her flesh and the power of their energy flooding through her. She raised her hand, seeing the familiar slender fingers, complete with the occasional freckle, not that such a thing meant anything to one such as her. She could have easily been forced into another vessel if her existing one had not survived the confrontation.

"It was." Chrissie spoke over whatever Alessia had been saying, drowning out her words entirely.

"How?"

"You weren't hard to miss. Let's just say if you weren't tethered here we may have had a problem." Chrissie attempted to comfort her.

"Not true, it would be more accurate to say that her split tethering caused the incident," Alessia revealed, the scowl on her features showing her clear displeasure at having being so disrespectfully silenced.

"What do you mean?" Acha questioned, throwing back the coarse blanket as she swung her legs over the edge of the low bed, offering them her full attention. Her movements once again caused the figures just outside the door to tense.

"Alessia forced you back into the talisman." Chrissie moved across the compacted-earth floor, stretching her arms as she walked the small area until she stood at the door. After a nearly silent exchange of whispers she pulled it closed, dimming what little illumination had entered. For a brief moment Acha found herself wondering why the encampment was bathed in light, until she recalled that Chrissie would have erected a barrier on her arrival. The light energy took a moment to find the imperfections in the wooden structure and weave its way through to illuminate the room. It came in small rays at first before expanding to fill the void completely.

"How?"

"I know something of soul and Djinn magic."

"I am not a Djinn." For a moment Acha questioned her adamant statement. She had never been certain exactly what she had become during the fifteen centuries she had spent bound in the talisman. She had slept, with the fates sending her dreams of how the world had changed. But she would be a fool to believe herself unaltered, after all, she had awoken unique, and with traits she had not heard of another possessing, except for the god who had once been her mortal father.

"True, but your essence is bound to a container none-the-less. I had no other choice but to hope it would achieve the required result. We needed to stop you." Chrissie let out a groan from her braced position against the door, her head lowering. "It is the truth, would you rather I—"

"Stop me? What did I—why are their guards stationed outside?" Rising to her feet Acha glanced between the two figures in the small enclosed space. It was only then she noticed another amongst them. Rob sat on the other side of the room, his fingers idly playing with what appeared to be a small dart. Fear knotted her stomach as she realised he was there to subdue her should the need arise. "What did I do?" she questioned again when it seemed as if no one would answer. Her vision bore into Alessia, knowing she had never been one for placation.

"You fled into the Skiá with a trace of Teanna's magic. When they realised you were not her... how do I explain this?" Alessia questioned, somehow finding herself unable to force the words into a language that was almost second nature for her.

"Easy." Came Rob's voice from across the room. "You went out with half a soul, you left a space, it came back occupied."

"The Skiá possessed me, is that even possible?" Acha could scarcely believe the shrill tone she had heard belonged to her.

"Not unless you're you. At least we learnt something," Rob announced. "It's too dangerous for you to do anything like that again."

"What did I do?"

"Absorbed their memories and filled the void in your essence by consuming theirs. You lost your identity, you were all but one of them and brought them here, into the camp, seeking Teanna. If Chrissie hadn't already arrived, it is likely we would have fallen to you." Acha felt her knees weaken in realisation, she backed away until she felt the bed behind her, and slowly lowered herself to sit.

"She's safe?"

"The part of you still bound in the talisman shielded her from detection. I don't know if they would think her moved, but it seems darker out there. You were one with them, what can you tell us?" Rob pushed.

"Daniel was right. They absorb us to multiply, they create bridges through shadows by which to travel, but the shadows must be of something living..."

"Trees, plants?" Alessia interrupted.

"No, nothing rooted. Human or animal, but not plant, rock, monster, or mineral." Acha applied a gentle pressure to her temples as she filtered through the rapidly fading insight. It was always the same, whenever she absorbed the life from someone she briefly retained their memories, but they rapidly faded. She focused more on what remained and gasped as the image of a family charging towards her with smiles and open arms invaded her thoughts.

"Monster?" Rob pressed, seeing her pale.

"Those born with part of the Skiá's composition. The Skiá were part of their creation, and so they cannot be used. That said, they are kin and may fight together if the Skiá could locate them." Rob released an audible breath. Another image assaulted her as she tried to probe deeper, Jones stood next to her, weapon in hand as they repelled bandits from a village who had refused to pay the demon hunters' fare.

"At least I don't have to worry about him then," Rob muttered to himself, relieved to discover Bray should be safe. "What else?" Rob pressed. Knowing what her touch would do, and given the alarm that was taking root, he feared she had realised what she'd done. "Don't think on that, concentrate on the Skiá."

"It's all a bit of a haze, not like when I normally touch someone. I don't really remember anything just impressions."

"You should rest. If you think of anything, let us know." Chrissie exited the small area, the encounter had left both herself and Alessia exhausted. Whilst Alessia had not used her Elven magic, she had called on something much deeper, a gift inherited from her father, who had been a wyrm in human form.

It was only now, as the sky was eclipsed by darkness, she realised how much of her own energy had come from the sun, and this realisation brought with it a deeper understanding of some of the reasons Daniel may have forbidden the use of wyrms. Not only would their essence be a feast for the Skiá, but the shroud blanketing the world would have weakened their power considerably, and the corruption of either a wyrm or a rider could mark the beginning of a dangerous transition, one once thought impossible but in itself carrying a great threat. His insistence made much more sense. If they were to intervene and be tainted, they could unleash a terrible curse upon the world they were sworn to protect.

Times had changed, as had the rules, and they needed to be more careful.

* * *

Daniel hurried. His every step measured in shades of grey as he wove avoiding the amassing of shadows, their dark tendrils casting a frightful landscape, one which could spell his end with a single mis-step. He sprung between scant areas of lighter foliage, praying he survived the run, praying his allies had succeeded in their own missions. His heart pounded louder than his hurried steps, than the sound of twigs grinding and splintering beneath his feet. He focused on his objective, reaching the camp. After this he could turn his mind towards the journey to the well, to another trek through shadows and terror in order to reach The Depths of Acheron.

Whoever had thought to construct the well had been attuned to the world. It was situated upon a large convergence of ley lines. When this energy combined with the raw desires, hopes, and dreams that were transferred into a coin by its possessor, there was every possibility a wish would be answered. But if a person skilled in the almost forgotten archaic arcane had crafted that coin, then nothing was left to chance, except for the impossible.

Creating the coin had been an exhausting and powerful process, more so because a second one had been fashioned in secret. Events which yield objects of such power were always observed by the Gods and fate, but Daniel had found a way to shield knowledge of the second coin's existence, by having Acha present to conceal the massive amounts of energy generated and dispelled in its creation. It was for this reason alone they could now enter the Depths of Acheron, and only because each party in possession of a coin had used but half.

The coin was forged from two sides joined together by a simple twist. Half was needed to gain entry, the other half possessed the same power and would have allowed them to leave, but Acha nor Rob had used both fragments.

Casting a furtive glance towards the dark blanket of swirling clouds, Daniel lengthened his stride, his fast-paced walk becoming a jog as movement seemed to flit between the shadows. Long ago, Jones had told him this forest had once been referred to as fay forest, and had been home to small magical creatures, but Daniel did not believe such creatures caused the flashes of movement currently caught in his peripheral vision.

The encampment had altered from Daniel's last recollection. Following their journey to find a means to seal the Severaine, he had visited this vicinity several times, marvelling at the biotecture structures, grown and moulded to become homes. Their location was a closely guarded secret and, as such, all possible measures were taken to ensure that even the most skilled Elementalist or tracker could not detect life in this vicinity. The large barrier of trees and single stemmed shrubs were a welcome sight, but it was the presence of a light barrier that caused his quickened heartbeat to slow. Chrissie was here, and Alessia was safe. He released a breath which caught again as he tried to devise a means to dismiss her. Her presence was now more of a danger than an aid, and he knew he should have had her return to Kalia long ago.

Daniel's run became a full-out sprint. Whilst there was a barrier of light, there was also a circle of darkness, elongated shadows stretched in every direction, and he was certain he could see within some the pulse of movement. He fought his way through the barricade, feeling the sting of thorns and broken branches pull at his hide clothes. He knew there was a natural passage through this tangled wall, but he dared not spend the time to find it.

A wave of instant relief washed over him as he broke free of the entanglement to stand before the barrier. Even then he knew better than to breach the light, everyone inside would have been cleansed, for him to enter so brazenly would be to risk contamination. He called out, looking upon the hidden buildings with a new appreciation.

He had been here in both hours of light and darkness, and was still amazed at how seamlessly nature had been manipulated around the frames of buildings. Distinguishing dwellings from the natural domain was impossible but to the trained eye. The only true sign of human life were the small tables and seats, made by manipulating plant growth. Any not knowing this was in fact a mercenary base, would assume it to be the work of magical beings, after all, such mythology was how Daniel had first conceived the idea.

Daniel's older brother, Adam, had joined the mercenaries at a young age and risen through their ranks with Jones—Daniel's contact here—always at his side. This location had become his brother's centre of operations and Daniel had seen the foundations of the project when he had visited at seventeen. That had been the last time he had seen his brother alive before he was slain by Marise Shi, the notorious assassin.

When next he visited many years had passed, and Jones had seen him at his lowest. To this day he still felt a tug of embarrassment whenever he visited. After the release of the Severaine he had fallen into a downward spiral of despair, taking relief however he could find it, almost at the cost of his life. He had made much progress, but still looked back on those days with shame and regret. Over the years he and Jones had formed an alliance, swearing to be at each other's beck and call should ever the need arise. Most, in Daniel's position, would have sought to petition the aid of the defence forces, from both Albeth and Therascia, however, he knew first hand they would not lend him aid.

When the Eorthráds had first made their presence known in the aftermath of the Severaine, both kingdoms had refused an alliance. Before coming to this decision they had conversed with The Order. It was told they deemed any who worshipped alternative gods and spirits, or were in service to magical beings, as heathens and had no place upon these lands. It was a certainty that if they knew the Eorthåds moved to stop the spread of darkness, The Order would view it as an ally rather than the enemy it was. It was better they knew nothing of their movements and sought to drive it back on their own, unwitting allies were better than those who would outwardly and openly sabotage the efforts of salvations.

The towns the Eorthåds had aided, and most of the cities, did not harbour these ill feelings. From what Daniel had divined, the Order lived in fear of a force being unleashed that would threaten their own position of power. Anything which took prayers from the Gods stood in opposition of them, and they would stop at nothing, even the extinction of all life, to ensure their most feared prophecy would not come to pass. The first part had been realised when the first wyrm was seen within the sky.

The Order believed the Gods would save the devout. If they envisioned this threat being confronted by the Eorthåds, then they would do all they could to aid the darkness' spread. The enemy of their enemy would be thought an ally, after all, they had the protection of the divine on their side. This was but one of the many reasons the Eorthåds could not stand beside him in this conflict; their presence would create more problems than it would solve.

"Daniel!" The familiar sound of Chrissie's tone served as a welcome reprieve, pulling him from the thoughts he had withdrawn within as if to create a barrier to protect himself during his time of vulnerability.

"Wita, praise be, you are unharmed." Alessia stepped forward, casting a scornful look towards Chrissie as she raised her arm.

"He's been infected," she announced, noticing his shadow appeared unnatural, as if it held depth as well as darkness.

"Purge him," Alessia commanded, worry framing her brow.

"Wait!" Daniel raised his hands. "It won't hurt the host in the hope to spread, correct?"

"We don't know, but you can't enter The Depths with something so dangerous in tow. Imagine what its exposure to the things there could breed, you'd never purge every shadow." Rob joined them at the boundary, nodding his head in a gesture of greeting.

"You're right, of course," Daniel conceded.

"Perhaps it clouds the minds of those they tether, in hope to better spread?" Alessia suggested, seeing Daniel mentally wrestling with his thoughts.

"No, I was just wondering if there was a way to turn it to our advantage. If I'm correct, then it may be just what we need."

"Ásæge!" Alessia demanded harshly, but as Daniel began to explain her demand was apparent to all present.

"How long passed since I called out, and if the Skiá were nearby why didn't they attack? The answer is simple, they need to spread to protected places, maybe they even know my destination, I couldn't say. The thing is, next time I may not be so lucky—"

"Lucky?" Chrissie questioned in outrage, Daniel raised his hand placatingly.

"If what I believe is true, and they won't hurt the infected, then I've just answered my main concern."

"Which is?" Rob prompted when Daniel fell silent.

"How to reach the wishing well unharmed." Dawning realisation reflected in each of their eyes. "While infected I can walk untouched… the problem will be purging the connection before entering The Depths."

"*I* was going to escort you," Chrissie stressed firmly.

"You only possess one card of light, and it's needed here."

"Correction, I only *had* one card of light. Dainan returned the one I'd left in the care of Lamperós. I'm not hindered by only being permitted one per element."

"Don't tell me that's why the Mountains of Light, had light."

"No, but it was, maybe still is, the sealing ground for a powerful darkness. I left the card there after visiting as a young cleric. It worried me whatever it was would break free and spread before word could reach the outside world. I ensured it would activate light protection and a herald enchantment on any who held it if the danger arose."

"You knew something dark was there?"

"Why else would so much light be needed, if not to restrain something? I wasn't certain and, truth be told, I've travelled to so many places I can't remember which story it was that made me think there was a danger. It was more of a feeling, as if I could sense something deep within the mountains. Better to safeguard than to regret." Chrissie gave a slight smile. "Of course, if you're insistent of keeping this bane then I won't permit you entry here. I've not only created a light dome, but a ward, you can't pass without being cleansed." This was true, but what she failed to mention was that anyone wishing to enter could not be conscious. Wards were difficult for her. The combination of various elements to produce a goal was something few masters could do, but since she channelled her power differently it was possible. A ward to prevent entry, however, had to have conditions upon it, and the only one she had learnt thus far was a means to prevent any passing unless taken by slumber or unconsciousness. In this instance it served her well, any who entered had to first be cleansed, and the purging of a shadow was anything but bearable. She only knew of this method because she had happened upon the details pertaining to its execution in an ancient scripture once belonging to a member of The Order.

"You truly have a second card?" Daniel glanced to Chrissie who nodded, producing one of the soft leather cards, he grimaced slightly as his focus was drawn to the hard textured leather remembering how these cards were carved from the flesh of her ancestors.

Chrissie was not like normal Elementalists, she could not channel the power. Her body possessed the necessary attunement but, as with all her bloodline, she could only draw upon the power through the cards. Each one possessed a different elemental affinity, and this alone ensured Chrissie could use elements that other Elementalists had no alignment to. They didn't rely on the spirits' presence or blessing. The other difference was that, unlike others, she could leave an enchantment or spell in place by leaving the card in position. He had never fully understood the concept of it not needing her present to work, but he intended to find out.

"It's your choice, Daniel, place you trust in either the light or the darkness," she smiled playfully.

"Purge it. Darkness is fickle, and deceptive. It was only a consideration because I saw no other means."

"Good to hear, this may hurt a bit."

"Hurt, why?"

"Because I'm going to sever your shadow so a new one can be born untouched."

"But that's impos—" His words froze as every muscle in his body became rigid, the world around him succumbing into an unparallelled brightness as all darkness was burned away before his frozen gaze. A searing pain began to spread through him, his every pore aflame. He could hear distant cries of anguish that he knew, on some deeper level, belonged to him. He felt as though he suffered for an eternity, as if his flesh was being stripped from his bones one painful layer at a time. His blood turned to vitriol, and his mind fought for some reality beyond the agony, finding it only when he succumbed to unconsciousness' sweet embrace.

* * *

Bray wiped the dust-stained sweat from his forehead as he bent to lift the final slab. His muscles ached and protested against the laborious task. He was actually relieved when Elly came to assist him in sliding the final piece from their path. The spiral staircase below was deteriorated, fragmented, and collapsing, but possible to navigate with care.

Bray crept towards the crumbled banister of the newly accessible balcony. Looking down, he could discern a blue stone embedded within what would be the base of this tower's floor. The faintly illuminated tablet petitioned his attention only briefly before his focus was drawn to a more immediate concern. Circling below were dark shadows, gifted in flight, as they played and chased with each other in what he assumed to be their mating ritual. Streaks of energy and magic trailed behind some of the darker forms, attempting to draw the attention of their potential mates that perched on the balconies below, watching the display.

He watched the mating dance with interest. The full moon was almost upon them, and with it came the single most powerful time of year for a monster to conceive. He still remembered the tales told by his sisters of how a monster conceived on the full moon of this month would be granted a power beyond that of their peers. He would have dismissed their claims, but their tales had been embedded deep within his core, after all, he was the sole male of their species to survive, and his sisters swore that his conception had aligned with the moon in this manner.

"Do you think that is the stone?" Elly whispered, moving to stand beside him. She cast a wary gaze down the multiple tiers, her vision moving from the hexagonal stone towards the orange vines which coiled and wrapped themselves around crumbling relics as their thick, earthy tendrils twisted and coiled upwards. She had seen many places where nature had reclaimed areas constructed by man. Given time she knew Gaea could reduce even the greatest cities to rubble, and yet here, despite her first impressions of the vines being overgrown, there seemed to be an order to them, as if they were being deliberately guided to support areas of failing structural integrity. The more she examined them, the more areas she saw that seemed to be supported by the tendrils.

"We're going to have to proceed slowly, and quietly. Things will unlikely be in our favour should we be discovered, even if most pair off before we reach the tablet." Bray swallowed realising how close she was, and how much his base urges still burned.

"Pair off?" Elly questioned, watching as one of the figures took flight, spiralling around another as if in an invitation to dance before they departed into one of the many dark burrows lining the walls.

"Think of this time of year as mating season for our kind. I know I'm desirable, but not all the tension you're feeling is from being so close to me." His voice was but a whisper as he turned towards her. Stepping closer, he tucked her hair behind her ears, his fingers playing with it softly as he ran them through its remaining length. She watched his tongue as it moistened his lips and heard herself gasp as his ravenous vision raked along the contours of her figure until his eyes met with hers. Succumbing to the moment he leaned forwards as if to place his lips to hers, his eyes closing as he prepared to savour her taste. But his advance met only with air as she turned away to place a few small paces between them.

"Then by all means go and join them." Elly stepped back further, readjusting her hair to how it was just a moment before his unwelcome touch. Bray inhaled deeply, turning his vision towards the ceiling for a long moment. Being so close to all this energy, even without his sense of smell, bordered on torture. He was famished, barely able to keep himself from surrendering to the frenzy building within him. While he couldn't smell her he could still taste her, just as he could taste her longing. Clearing his throat softly, he took a long draught from his leather skin, hoping the fluid within would return him to his senses. Toying with her was all well and good, but in his current state he could no longer discern where the line between play and prey was situated.

Bray once more took the lead, stalking carefully between the shadows. Ever vigilant, his hand grasped Elly's as they wove between the crumbled areas of cover, seeking to shelter themselves from any creature above whose attention may stray. Their numbers were thinning, the glow from above becoming less vibrant with each pair that departed, but still they were too many, but the lower they descended the more foliage seemed to shield their path. Rustles of distant movement set their senses on edge as they wove between the enormous orange vines that spewed from the large opening which may have once led to an internal garden. The steps gave way to brier slopes that caught their clothes, rustling a near silent alarm as they moved deeper into the overgrown terrain. Vegetation thrived around them, large trees towered near the far reaches of the room, their leaves a faded white, indicative of being fed by magic rather than sunlight. The unusual shades of this internal world seemed oddly natural against the ivory backdrop of the tower's walls, and the manipulation of vines and tree growth to support the more damaged structures above spoke of some manner of external influence. It was easy to envision the entire lower level now thrived with such life, and the calls of distant wildlife did little to persuade them otherwise.

He placed his hand softly upon Elly's arm, bringing them to a stop before their final descent. Just below, the terrified squeals of an animal pierced the silence, the scuffing of its hooves against the ground as it tried to careen its way to freedom echoed in time with its cries. Flashes of movement drew their attention to the two young creatures playfully pursuing their prey, intercepting the boar at its every turn. When they had tired of the game, they descended upon their meal, and Elly and Bray received their first real glimpse of the beings that called these ruins their home.

The creatures seemed part human in facial features, but their mouths extended beyond what was expected. Their small pouting lips, with the seductive Cupid's bow, curled naturally into an enticing smile. But such delicate features were deceptive, as noted when their lips parted. Something sensual became horrific as the seam, stretching from ear to ear, became visible against their china-doll complexion, their jaws splitting, opening in a serpentine fashion to reveal the predatory teeth spanning to their loosely hinged jaw.

Large black eyes tracked their prey with a predatory gaze, while their noses, which may have once been partially a beak, had shrunken until nothing but a slight peak remained. The creatures' bodies seemed more bones than flesh, and the lithe frames allowed their elongated leaf and feather wings to lift them from the ground in flight. Their arms, back and tails were the only place where the smoothness of their skin was disrupted. As their taloned feet touched the floor an aura of magic surrounded them. Bray had to blink to ensure his eyes did not deceive him, it was no illusion. Whilst within the air they were a form of harpy—altered through centuries of breeding with the fay—when their flesh made contact with the ground their form shifted again, becoming more fay than beast.

The feathers receded, leaving slender arms with long fingers tipped with sharp talons. The plumes collected at their heads, cascading down from their scalps to create soft and beautiful hair while the leaves gathered around the shapely contours of their body, covering the places any modest human would avert their gaze from. Their eyes remained larger, but took on a hue of brown and greens, becoming more human, but when they smiled, the slightest hint of the extended seams of their mouth could still be seen. The young male on the left sunk his nails deep into the dying boar's chest cavity, as the young female watched, awaiting the gift he would deliver in courtship.

The adolescent male extended his hand, offering the female the bloody heart, her lips parted revealing the monstrous jaw as she took the first bite, allowing the fluid to pool in her mouth, spilling from her lips before she pressed her mouth to his so they could share first blood. With this ritual complete the two creatures descended on the dead animal, tearing and shredding its carcass, altering their limbs and forms as they desired.

Lost in the glory of their shared feast, they remained unaware of Elly and Bray's slow approach. Perspiration traced their skin as they crept forwards, utilising their surroundings as a barrier, hoping the sounds of their masked footfalls would go unheard amidst the tearing of flesh and shredding of entrails. On tenterhooks they navigated past, pausing each time a head cocked or movement stilled. Several long and taxing minutes of burning muscles and shallowed breathing passed until finally they were far enough away to consider themselves safe. Even so, their steps remained guarded, light and careful, as they navigated the foliage, unaware if others lingered, as they made their way towards the central part of the room, the place the blue stone had been seen from above.

There were no more shelters, no more cover between themselves and the knowledge they sought. Above, the mating rituals continued. Dark shadows swept across the floor, cast from the soft afterglow left by the males. With great care they approached the tablet, dropping quietly to their hands and knees, their fingers tracing across the places the blue and white stone fused with the floor. Upon the surface were vaguely familiar characters, but there was no time to struggle over the possible translation. Bray looked to Elly, glancing above at the predatory creatures.

'*Can you read it?*' Elly looked to him, shaking her head. The question had been nothing more than an idea placed within her mind. Screams echoed from above, shrill cries as the movements became frantic and creatures once seated watching the displays took flight, circling.

"They're telepathic," Bray groaned. His act of discretion had achieved the opposite effect, instead of concealing their presence, he had, in fact, announced it.

"Hold them off," Elly demanded quickly removing her coat as the creatures began to dive. Her hand disappeared within the lining, finding the tiny hooks and eyes within. She released each one in turn before pulling a piece of cloth from inside and placing it upon the tablet. Swinging the coat around her shoulders once more, she slipped a small rectangular block of beeswax from one of the two belts on her coat and began to rub, causing the inscriptions to appear upon the cloth's surface.

Bray laughed despite himself. It was no wonder her reputation had always preceded her. He lifted his gaze towards the descending creatures. He was hungry, beings such as these would prove nothing more than an annoyance. A great shriek echoed through the chamber as ruby fluid tore from its confused owner to answer the call of the Empusa.

He had told Elly that monsters generally did not devour one another. There were of course exceptions, and he held a position of predominance within the hierarchy, but one with a major advantage. Empusae were known to be an all female race. His survival had been a mistake, one which would challenge what people believed they knew about these monsters. The Empusae needed flesh to survive, but this was only partially true, they required something more, they required blood. The inability to create new blood vessels was something not apparent in the females until they reached an age capable of conception. This race were known for their ability to seduce men, and it was through their casual dalliances the females extracted the blood required to live. Males, however, were born with this trait already present, and as they could not feed they were left to die. There was another difference between the males and females, daughters mirrored their maternal species, but males, whilst Empusae by nature, appeared to look like their fathers.

Bray's sisters had decided to take his life into their own hands. His conception had aligned with the Festival of Hades, and they had known if he could live he would become something remarkable. After their mother had discarded him they sheltered him in secret, feeding him the fluids he desperately needed to live. By the time his existence was discovered he was a young boy, but he was still immediately cast from the scare. Being male, Bray did not possess the organs required to feed, and his expulsion had been a death sentence. Or so they had thought.

Hunger has a way of changing a creature's nature, and Bray was no exception. He could not take the blood in the same manner as his sisters, but he could still call it to him, as he had discovered one fateful day.

Veins and arteries tore from the creatures above, the blood answering his call to rain down upon him. He scarcely used this method to feed, puberty had changed his saliva to allow the merging of his flesh to another's, facilitating his need to feed. Whilst natural, calling blood to him without a touch was not the solution to the problem he had once believed it to be, but the cause of one instead. It was too primal, too undisciplined, and to use it was to embrace that part of himself he kept controlled. Bray's eyes developed a red hue within the span of a single blink, tinting as the frenzy took hold.

He felt his own awareness begin to recede as the predatory instincts surfaced, shifting the spectrum of his sight until every creature began to appear the same. Gone were their identities and distinguishing features, in their place, the collection of pooling fluids and blood vessels outlined the forms they held as the blood of his prey called to him. Unlike the females he had no need for flesh, human sustenance was adequate, but when he was hungered it was so much harder to control his impulses, especially when the blood contained the taste of magic, sex, or fear.

He focused upon the flailing forms above, savouring the touch of their life essences as they rained down in torrents, but there was another creature in the room. One who needed to be savoured. Like his sisters, his presence induced feelings of lust and longing, after all, the taste of fear, whilst enjoyable, was nothing compared to the euphoric pallet presented when his prey had reached the heights of pleasure. Once he had gorged himself, he would take his time to savour this one, but for now those things meant it harm, and it was his to be enjoyed, and his alone.

Chapter 24

Eidolon

Elly saw the alteration in Bray as he tore the blood from the creatures above. His eyes matched the red hue of the fluids raining down upon him. His lip curled into a feral snarl reminiscent of a smile as his skin turned crimson. Watching him, she no longer knew which predator she should be more wary of. He culled the attacking swarm with ease, and yet she could sense part of his bloodthirsty attention remained fixated on her. Once more she found herself questioning exactly what he was. She knew he was of the Aphrodisia Clan, but could discern little more.

He moved more like a beast than a man, launching himself at those who dared swoop down. His body wrapped around them dragging them to the stone floor where he tore them apart from the inside out, before moving onto the next. He was fast, calculating, and executed everything with a deadly precision. No longer feeding upon them, he simply plucked them from the air, killing for sport, until their attackers decided survival was preferential to this onslaught and retreated. Part of her hoped he would pursue.

Elly, despite being lost in her thoughts, dabbed away the sprays of blood from the newly waxed cloth before she carefully stored it back inside her coat lining where it would be buffered and protected against the elements, ensuring nothing of importance could be lost. She had done this so many times it was second nature to her. As the elongated shadow fell upon her, she found her breath hitched. Standing quickly, attempting to increase the distance between them, she opened her mouth to speak, but found the words trapped with her throat.

A firm hand grasped her shoulder while his arm snaked around her waist, pulling her close with such force the impact of their bodies was almost as hard as that of his lips as they crushed against hers with such raw, unfiltered desire she almost felt herself swoon. Betrayed by her own body, her pulse quickened as she responded instinctively to his dominating advance. Melting into the kiss, her own desire matched his hunger and passion until he recoiled, firmly pushing her away. His hands flew to his face in repulsion before he turned aside, expelling the green pulp from his mouth. A smile teased her lips as she attempted to regain her composure as he glared at her in disgust, his eyes once more returning to their normal shade of mesmerising green.

"Chasteberry," she divulged, her tone etched with amusement as he continued to scrub at his mouth. "A woman has to protect herself from predators after all." She grinned, watching in amusement as he swilled his mouth with water from the flask before expelling it with disgust on the ground. She had harvested the leaves and berries from one of the many Chaste Trees they had passed during their journey. She had known she couldn't trust his nature, especially since having woken to feel the unmistakable tingle of his touch upon her flesh.

"You tried to poison me!" Bray spat again, although a glimmer of amusement was evident within his eyes.

"You tried to eat me," Elly countered flatly. "Besides. You have been consuming it yourself, did you not think I would identify the berries' flavour in the water you gave me? If I didn't know better, Grayson Bray, I would say you had tried to protect me." She raised her hand to her neck where she knew he had fed from her.

"I warned you what would happen if you let your guard down around me," he admitted, seeing her gesture. "But given these circumstances I was attempting to be a gentleman." Elly stepped forwards, briefly touching her lips to his in a gentle but seductive kiss.

"Try that again, and I *will* kill you," she warned, patting his cheek gently with her hand.

"Kiss me like that again, and I may just take the risk," he retorted with an impish grin. "But how did you know it would dispel the frenzy?"

"It does not, or you would carry it with you to retain control." Bray chuckled, realising this woman certainly lived up to her reputation. The taste of Chasteberry *was* appalling to him, but little more. Her observations had once more been astute. He basked in her presence for a moment, appreciating everything she was before forcing himself back to his senses. He was too old for such tomfoolery, but there was no denying she was indeed a temptation. Something was special about her beyond the blood which coursed through her veins, she was astounding. He saw her watching him with a smile, and quickly diverted his gaze towards the exit.

"Shall we, my lady? It is better we do not dally, the atmosphere here is too complimentary for my nature."

Bray began to lead the way, cautiously glancing over his shoulder. Somehow, he had clawed himself back from embracing his nature, once more imprisoning the monster within him, but her kiss, that kiss had almost overpowered his senses, turning the desires he projected into others back onto himself. He would have to be very careful when keeping her company, but he'd known that from the moment he'd first taken her blood. She was different, lethal. Despite what he asserted, he was no longer at the top of the hierarchy when he stood beside her. She was dangerous, and when she came to learn the complete truth of what she was, he was curious to see what she would become.

"Do you think we will be granted passage?" questioned Elly softly. Bray closed his eyes, seeing the carnage he had unleashed, and the lives needlessly wasted.

"Sometimes it is safer to let the monster pass," he muttered. "You saw the inscriptions, can you decipher it?" Bray questioned, changing the topic.

"Partially, I think it will take us some time."

"Then I suggest we head to Collateral. We can seek safe harbour there and gather the supplies we need."

"Collateral will be sealed. News of the Skiá will have reached them by now." Elly started the ascent in silent contemplation, once they were almost to the debris they had cleared she spoke again. "If we are where you say we are, then there's a town north of here, Eidolon,"

"The ghost town?" Bray questioned, he had heard rumours of this town, it was sometimes called Felglow, a town said to shine with an eerie light for the fourteen days before and following the festival of Hades. This cursed location had been struck from the maps, with warnings scrawled upon each parchment about the dangers therein. Never had a single place instilled such fear, as such, it was avoided at all costs. He looked to Elly. "It's Dekatreís." This insight held far more than a declaration of the month, this he already knew, and Elly, understanding his realisation, was surprised he had not reached this conclusion sooner.

"Of course, when better to pierce the barrier to the Skiá than the time when the border between all realms are paper thin?"

"The Festival of Hades, is in four days."

"And we have less than that to decipher this. We must be prepared, because that is when the war will really begin."

* * *

When Daniel's eyes flickered open he felt sore. His flesh and body appeared unscathed, and yet the rawness of his skin suggested it should bear the wounds of a thousand battles. There wasn't a part of his body that didn't hurt, or muscle that didn't ache as he slowly attempted to move. His vision quickly panned the modest dwelling to see Alessia watching him intently.

"Wita, are you unharmed?" Her voice pounded through his throbbing skull, but already the effects of the purge were waning.

"Like with yourself, it will pass shortly." Chrissie's soft tones were a welcome reprieve to Alessia's more abrasive dialect. Moving his blurred vision towards her he could see the sympathetic expression she held also mirrored by those around him. The room began to stretch and warp as he pushed himself up, only to find himself being steadied by Alessia's firm grasp as she assisted him back into a seated position.

He forced himself to focus on one specific feature, a small stalk growing inward through the solid lattice. Its budding green leaves seemed so intense against the bark of the trees. Inside these buildings had been left as natural as possible, the curves of the trunks and shoots giving each place its own unique features. Staring at the small stem, he wondered how many residences still possessed the internal wall frames, and how many had become nothing more than a natural, but manipulated, shelter. He blinked again, forcing back the rising tide of nausea, aware of the heavy silence as they waited for him to speak.

"By all the Gods and Spirits, I thought it would be something painless, like flooding the shadow with light." He swallowed a lump in his throat, gratefully accepting a wooden cup from Alessia and drinking deeply.

"No matter how bright some darkness will always remain, be it in the fold of a cloth or beneath the sole of a shoe. It's like that old saying says, darkness reigns at the foot of a lighthouse. My only option was to tear the shadows from you, so the ones that returned would be new and untouched."

"Again, that's impossible." Daniel moved his arm, watching his shadow mirror his movements with interest.

"And yet I did it. Although, to be honest, if not for one of my relatives being an inquisitor for Mirage Lake then I doubt it would have been documented." Chrissie averted her gaze from his as she spoke.

"They know of this torture?" His voice came out a strangled cry as voices from the ancestors confirmed the many atrocities that his mind pictured at the thought of that location. Their voices were relentless, their bombardment of such horrific information caused his temples to throb so much Chrissie's response was almost drowned out by their voices.

"Thankfully not. I used my position to retrieve it before it could be uncovered."

"And now, what became of it?" A small sigh escaped him as the voices fell into silence. Elementalists had no place beyond the Gate of Shades; as such, thoughts centred around such knowledge always stilled the voices.

"We burned it," she replied, her hand dropping to the pouch secured on her belt. "There are no copies, no way they could recover the technique. It is, for all intents and purposes, lost. I confess I felt compelled to read it, perhaps I knew I would need its aid, but there are things written there that still haunt me in the night."

"How did you even know to look for it?"

"Luck and happenstance. I'm the last of the Kigenso nobles, a name and title I had long discarded. When a certain somebody tracked me down and saved me, the Keeper of Records witnessed my return to Albeth and passed on a message originally intended for my father."

"And you trust it did not pass into anyone else's hands?"

"I do, it could only be unsealed by his flesh." Chrissie gestured meaningfully towards her card pouch. "It's our way, but the line ends with me."

"You're young yet." Came Jones' voice as he entered. "I know plenty of young men who would fall over themselves for a night of—for an evening with a lovely creature such as yourself." Jones gripped Daniel's arm firmly in greeting, but Daniel could see it was a means to assess his current condition. "Why is it that all your friends are so stubborn? Is working with me really such a chore? I've offered good pay, even tempted her with our chef's cooking. Honestly, Daniel, if you're insistent on flaunting them can't you at least make powerful allies who are a little more open to temptation?" Daniel chuckled, when first Jones had met Eiji he had attempted to recruit him, and he had no doubt he had tried the same with most of those who had escorted him here in the past. Daniel's laughter died as he thought of his friend, a sombre expression creasing his brow. "That serious? I wondered where he'd got to, seemed to me at a time like this he'd be at your side. To business then, what brings you here?" Despite the small residence now being hot and overcrowded, Jones, sensing Daniel had still not fully recovered from the purge, made no attempt to move their conversation elsewhere.

"Would you believe I need an army?"

"We're at your disposal. We assumed it was something like that." Jones gestured outside, as if to indicate the protection that surrounded them. "You sent all your strongest allies to our door. It's lucky for us you hold us in such high regard."

"I swore you an oath. Even without your assistance we—"

"Enough said. What can we do?" Jones interrupted before Daniel could finish. It was not wise to have him dwell on this thought longer than necessary. He believed what he was saying, but Jones knew if their aid had not been needed he would not have come to them so readily. Sometimes even allies had to be sacrificed for the greater good.

Daniel was new to this kind of leadership. He was asking people to place their trust in him and their lives in his hands. Jones could already see the burden of its weight upon his shoulders. He had seen Daniel at his worst, and whilst he had overcome his hardships, there was always a chance that he could once more succumb to his past frailties. Such was the burden of leadership.

"Do you have a means to contact other camps?" Jones nodded in response. "I'm taking Rob to The Depths of Acheron. I need you to gather as many mercenaries to this location as you can. This is our stronghold, nothing gets in without us wishing it."

"The Depths of Acheron?" Jones questioned with the same disbelief as Blacksmith Tony had.

"Not the underworld. It's a realm beyond our own, there's no time for explanations. In essence we need to gather its ore to craft weapons."

"Weapons?" Jones questioned despondently, as images of their near defeat resurfaced. He had lost many good men and women to those creatures, and nothing they tried had so much as touched them. "It's no use. I can tell you first hand, steel or metal won't harm these things. If Alessia and Chrissie hadn't arrived when they did..." Jones shook his head.

"I'm not about to risk your lives on a whim. This ore is the only answer I can find. Light hurts the Skiá, and forged correctly these blades will burn." Jones looked doubtfully to Alessia. He had witnessed many the failed attempts of weapons which used oil and metal. "I will not ask you to fight beside me, nor will I ask you to do anything I would not be willing to do myself."

"Do you have blueprints?" Jones questioned, his hand extended.

"With my blacksmith."

"He's not here?"

"No, your forge is not sufficient. As fine as your smithy is, he's not... he's not Tony. He's the only one who can smelt and temper the ore. I've safeguarded him as best I could."

"Don't misunderstand, I trust you, Daniel. If you give us weapons, we will fight with them, if you sent us out there with twigs we'd still give you one hell of a battle. Our lives will be yours, and we have already pledged them willingly. I cannot fathom what we are against, give me man or beast any day and I will find and exploit its weaknesses, but give me legend and monsters and I'll drown in what I don't know.

"I am a commander for things of this world, but you are the hero who has overcome god, myth, and magic. You're the one who will lead us, of this there is no doubt, and I give you my mantle willingly. Be warned though, it weighs heavily, are you certain this is a path you wish to tread? Would it not be better to advise one already familiar with the weight of such leadership?" Jones let his vision stray to Alessia, who gave him an appreciative nod. He had just moments ago swore not to broach this subject, but he thought too much of Daniel not to. He could not let him think this burden was his alone, standing beside him he had two competent commanders, and either would shoulder the weight of lives in his stead.

"Whether I am ready or not, this is the duty of the Wita. I will not shrug off the burden of leadership because of fear that I cannot make the right choices. No one but myself should be asked to hold responsibility for what will pass. I am weak and inexperienced, this I know all too well. I hate to lose those I care for, I never wanted this responsibility, but it is mine to bear, and I have a plan. Don't assume I will ask you to follow me blindly and put your lives in something unproven." Alessia straightened as if to protest, knowing what he was about to say. "I will trust my life to these weapons before I would dare ask any of you to do the same." Jones sighed, placing a hand to shield his eyes. Standing before him was no longer the young brother of his former commander and closest friend, but a man who rivalled Adam's memory itself.

"You've too much of your brother in you. Don't you realise we'd take you at your word? You need not prove anything."

"Yes, I do," Daniel stressed. "I am Daniel Eliot, Wita to the Eorthāds and defender of the realms. I will ask no one to do what I myself would not, and I will fight beside you, look the same danger in the eye, knowing I gave you the best chance when before there was none. Yes, lives will be lost, but they will not be stolen on account of my own cowardice. I will test the weapons. If they fail, then better they fail me than you. This is war, between mortals and monsters. No quarter will be given, least of all by me." Daniel glanced around the small room, seeing a mixture of reactions to his words. Alessia leaned closer, her hand resting lightly upon his shoulder.

"Defender of the Realms?" she questioned with a smile. He gave a shrug, it had felt right at the time, but now he simply felt embarrassed.

"Too much of your brother," Jones repeated, slapping Daniel firmly on the back, but his eyes held a great deal of respect for the young man before him. "Just don't end up like him, there's no reason for you to die alone."

"Well then, I guess that's our cue to be going, I mean, what else can be said to top that?" Rob interjected lightheartedly.

"Well, before you dash out into the shadows, it would be wise to be protected. Besides, how do you plan on getting to the well? Collateral is sealed," Chrissie questioned. The current affairs of the world had been discussed in depth as Alessia had escorted Chrissie to the camp. It was important everyone knew the dangers and limitations brought upon them by what had occurred.

"We'll use the irfeláfa, we have keystones concealed near many places of power."

* * *

Eidolon was magnificent to behold. The daunting peaks of the western mountains sheltered the small town, while a small stream cut a jagged path through the landscape providing fresh water before coming to rest at a fresh water lake found deep within the forest. While home to many species of trees a barrier of pine flanking the northern region acted as the sole warning needed to deter people from venturing within.

An old wives' tale suggested any approaching a forest of pine should turn back. Fables told they had once acted as a barrier to prevent evil from crossing. Back then it had been believed that malevolent forces could only spawn in certain places, and had to shroud themselves in protection from the light of the world in order to traverse it. The shed pine needles pierced the wards they erected thus preventing them from passing into the world beyond the pines.

When Eidolon had first been founded they had played on this mythos, planting young saplings. It had been built as a sanctuary to any Méros-Génos seeking to escape the persecution, or even to offer shelter to those who had fled their master's cruel and ill-tempered hands.

As time passed the town grew and slavers, seeking to swell their profits, became more daring in their ventures. Méros-Génos lacked the rights of humans and were often preferred for dangerous labours, thus when they discovered this defenceless refuge it became a harvesting ground. No matter how they reacted, or what defences they erected, the slavers would find their way through, targeting the young and defenceless. When it became apparent this brutality would never cease, the Méros-Génos began plans to relocate, gathering what few belongings and possessions they had. The night they planned to leave was when their very own miracle occurred. The forest, and everything within, came aglow.

Since then, during the twenty-eight days surrounding the Festival of Hades, those daring to approach would bear witness to a terrifying sight. Ghostly figures and spectral animals roamed the eerie glow of the forest within the pine boundary, and rumours of this town being touched by the darker forces of Hades spread as quickly as the glow.

Little did the superstitious people realise that this illumination had been caused by the introduction of a rare species of flower. Once a year they released their pollen sending luminescent dust into the air. Wildlife would spread the pollen, causing their forms to resemble terrifying ethereal figures. The spores coated everything, people and plant alike, and the result was the haunted and harrowing reputation of the town, and the subsequent abandonment of any and all hunting there. It was believed to enter the forest was to invite curses and misfortune.

"It's a town of Méros-Génos," Bray observed noting the very distinctive style of buildings. He gave up trying to remove the clinging dust from his person. The more he tried to brush it away the more it spread and the brighter it appeared to glow.

"It is enhanced by heat. That is why it is brightest around the town and the woods just glow modestly." Elly motioned towards a small circular building closer to the mountains than any other.

"Could we use this as a weapon?"

"The illumination is not sufficient to injure the Skiá. For the immediate future they will understand it clings to anything of substance and keep a cautious distance. The moment one of them consumes something that has been in contact with the pollen Eidolon will no longer be safe."

"Lady Elaineor," a warm voice welcomed, as a figure rushed out to greet them as they approached the building. "Look at you glowing, you're positively radiant." The figure stepped back to observe her fully. "This must be a first, it seems the spores have taking a strong liking to you on this occasion." Elly smiled. Whilst her golem had been affected by the pollen she had always remained dull, not like those who had the warmth of life running through their veins. "Come inside, it is a nuisance, come, come. Can I interest you in some shimmering stew, how about some embers mead, or glowing grapes?" The figure chuckled in good humour. During this time of year everything was aglow, be it food or drink the pollen permeated everything. "There's something different about you," she observed.

"News has reached you of the Skiá, Briana?" Elly asked, plucking one of the glowing orbs from the offered bowl, she grimaced as she bit into it.

"Ah, I guess they were the gooseberries, you never can tell." The figure chuckled offering the bowl to Bray, he raised a hand in polite decline.

"The Skiá?" Elly prompted.

"It seems to be the newest neology, everything is Skiá this, or Skiá that, even our birds bring messages of Skiá." The figure flapped her arms in frustration, sending clouds of brighter pollen into her immediate surroundings.

"Have you thought of seeking refuge?" Bray questioned.

"Looking like this?" asked the humanoid form flatly with a smack of her lips. "If we ventured anywhere looking like spirits of the damned the only thing we'd find is a spear in the gut. Besides, even when the dust settles there's no guarantee we'd be welcome. You said it yourself, we're Méros-Génos." Bray hadn't realised his observation had been overheard.

"It does not mean what it used to," Elly offered.

"You're a sweet thing, worrying about us, but best you be on your way before it really gets into your pores, then there's no dusting it off. You're always welcome here, you know that, but we'd rather you didn't bring his like. The Strigoi have a taste for some of our kind." Elly looked to the woman in confusion, whilst she was unable to read auras like the woman before her, she knew for certain Bray was not Strigoi.

"He's—"

"Apologies, we will be on our way," Bray interrupted, grabbing her arm. "Besides, Lady of Knightsbridge, if you open the inscription here we'll lose any hope of reading it."

"You've brought a rubbing?" Briana questioned with intrigue.

"Do you mind?" Elly questioned shrugging out of her coat.

"Will you vouch for him?"

"On this occasion." The figure gave a nod and Elly presented the cloth. Briana wafted it through the air, covering it in as much of the airborne pollen as she could before disappearing through the back with it. "I know you are not Strigoi," Elly whispered. "Why let them think otherwise, why can't she identify you?"

"I would rather they remain unaware of their mis-classification. Such a thing has saved my life frequently, surely you of all people can appreciate the boon of being underestimated."

"What *are* you?" she whispered in frustration. Still after all this time she could not pinpoint his origin.

"Such an intimate question. I'm an enigma, perhaps you would like to solve me?" Bray waggled his eyebrows suggestively. "She said we could use the closet."

"She did no such thing, and neither will I." Elly snapped. She turned her back to him as she heard Briana's approach, the cloth in her hand now bore the same luminescence as everything else, except for the inscription which seemed almost as if it burned with light.

"That should preserve it nicely." The figure cast an awkward glance towards Bray. "If you plan on remaining, please keep him from sight. The elder would rampage if he knew."

"We will depart soon enough, but could we trouble you for some supplies, we are going to need to make something."

"You can use the closet, it's not much but it's empty." Bray turned to Elly with the impish grin she had learnt to hate. "Keep him out of sight, and as soon as you know what you need let me know."

* * *

When Alana emerged her gaze was drawn instantly to her parents, they sat in silence. Her father's arm was wrapped around her mother's shoulder as she rested her head upon his shoulder. Sensing the sudden movement they both turned their gaze in her direction, and it was impossible for her to miss their bewilderment. For her, time's passage had felt natural, but given what Pigí had told her, for them mere hours had passed. She rushed forward to their awaiting arms, burying herself within the security of their embrace and absorbing the warmth and comfort of another. It was only as she pulled away, and gazed upon them through older eyes, that she realised there had been concern passed between them in the brief look they had exchanged.

"It was my immortality," Alana answered the unvoiced question, her mannerism already mirroring that of an adult despite appearing only eight years old. "I agreed without delay. If death is not a fear, then all I must face would hold no meaning." She saw her mother's vision flick briefly to her father once more. Alana, however, ignored this fleeting observation. "Pigí said we should visit the Phoenix next." She skipped ahead, not looking back to see if they would follow.

She had been prepared for this difficult transition, and tried to portray the nature of the child they were losing. It was as her water-father had said, when she accepted the role she had also agreed to orphan herself. It was a regretful transition, but necessary given the urgency of her plight. "Come on, I hear his feathers shed embers that burn for days." In her peripheral vision she noticed her parents begin to follow, their posture indicative of understanding what they had already lost.

Alana leapt through the portal, her light steps leaving ripples across the water's surface. The warmth of the air upon her flesh filled her with energy, and the call of nature was a long forgotten melody. For the past two years she had known only the company of creatures of water. The sirens sang with beauty that had often helped ease her into slumber, while the Naiades, Nereides, and Oceanides had taught her games and mischief, and the Graeae told her fantastical stories of history. She had known an entirely new world, a place where those sworn to Pigí sought rest and salvation from the rising threat. The many species had accepted her, for she was their father's protege, but she had also been warned that if she called upon their aid outside his domain, there would be a price for their assistance.

The water realm had been busy, creatures some would call monsters sought sanctuary, speaking of an ancient evil rising and darkening the sky. Looking up, Alana saw for the first time there was no sun. The sky above was blanketed in dark clouds.

With a firm nod of her head, she spun upon the water. Her graceful movements produced a dance of beauty as her precise steps sent sprays of mist into the air to fall like gentle rain. She concentrated, yet also lost herself to the joy of the movements, her hand reaching down in a final motion to touch the surface and send small droplets into the air. They shimmered, but the absence of the sun meant her dance had not produced the rainbow she had hoped.

With a sigh she stopped her dance upon the water, her gaze turning skyward once more to the darkness. She knew then that this would not do.

"That was beautiful," Zo applauded as her daughter's head hung slightly.

"It was ditchwater. But the proclamation has been received," she pouted.

"Proclamation?"

"To those creatures still dwelling here. The dance is a ritual announcing my birth as one of Pigí's children. I had to perform it in his realm and this to cement the elemental pact."

"We will make haste to your next destination, but if you can, would you share with us your story? We've missed you."

"I missed you too." Alana jumped from the water to the rocky shores, her balance faltering as she found herself on the firm earth. Tumbling forwards she somehow missed her parents' outreaching arms, her head striking the cliff's wall. She raised her hand, wiping away the fluid which trickled from her brow.

"Sit still. I'll have you patched up in just a second," her mother fussed, pulling a salve tin from her satchel. "It must hurt, you're being really brave."

"Hurt?" Alana questioned, raising her hand to feel the enormous swelling just before her hairline. Even touching it triggered no sensation. "No, is it bad?" She waited, expecting to feel the sting of her mother's healing as the salve was applied. It was a sensation she remembered so well from all her falls and broken bones from her over adventurous exploring. Alana had never understood why she needed mending, after all, she was meant to have been a creature of pure energy, but it seemed there were other laws at play in Darrienia as well. Her mother had explained it to her, but it had been beyond her understanding, and it was too long ago now to recall. What was remembered though, was that her mother imbued her salves with energies from Darrienia, to ensure she could utilise her healing magic whatever plane they were in.

"All done. You've been so brave." She once again saw her mother glance in her father's direction.

"Was it just your immortality he took?" her father asked, pulling her to her feet with a playful twist so she faced the direction they would be walking.

"The fusion needed something from me. Since my essence is complete but not yet mature something had to be taken before a part of him could be added, otherwise his energy would have spilt out and simply been lost. Why?"

"Because your injury should have hurt. Just be careful, being unable to feel pain is a blessing and a curse, especially since you've lost your immortality."

"Oh, Daddy, I didn't lose it. I *gave* it to Pigí as payment for my tutelage. See." Alana, for the first time, revealed her newest tikéta, and for but a moment allowed her parents to gaze upon it, before pulling her sleeve back down. She studied her clothes with a critical eye. "Why do they still fit, I have grown, haven't I?"

"Of course you have, but your clothing is from our home. It's adaptive," Seiken explained.

"Yes, of course it is. Sorry, Daddy, it slipped my mind for a moment. Now shall we go, how are we going to travel, can we ride a wyrm?"

"It's too dangerous. We have been granted permission to use the Irfeláfa."

"Oh," she sighed in disappointment.

* * *

The well was precisely as Rob recalled. The irfeláfa was situated just a few minutes walk from the ancient structure. To reach it, they had fought their way through the luscious undergrowth, lined with concealed brier and bramble, until they reached the overgrown path. As it had when last he stood in this very spot, the well stood proudly in the serene clearing. Its rafters were still covered with vines, their flowers still prevalent despite the approach of the Festival of Hades. In fact, as he gazed upon it, he realised every detail was exactly the same, preserved in perfect detail down to the last petal. The same patterns of mist seemed to rise from within and, as they drew nearer, the small glowing orbs he had seen before blinked into existence, only to vanish should he try to focus upon one.

"Déjà vu," Rob muttered, scratching the back of his head in contemplation.

"The location allows for the preservation of form. In the depths of winter it would appear no different than in the heights of summer," Daniel explained. He plucked a petal from one of the vines by way of demonstration. Instantly it dissipated into a fine dust, drawn back to its position on the plant before reforming.

"Why is a wishing well the gateway to anywhere?" The last time he stood upon these grounds he had been filled with thoughts of his daughter and fairy tales, and still a part of him lived in the past within his memories of her. There wasn't a day that went by he didn't miss his wife and child. His hand slipped into his jerkin where his fingers rested upon the hair clip his daughter had once made to ensure his safety. He looked to Daniel, remembering he owed this man a great and personal debt; ensuring he survived The Depths would not come close to settling the balance.

"What holds more magic than the power of wishes, dreams, and hopes?" Daniel poised, pulling Rob from his thoughts.

"Does every wish made here come true?"

"No, although the probability is greatly increased given its location on the ley line convergence. There's a greater chance luck will touch the wisher, but also a greater chance that ill-fortune is returned. It really is a coin flip."

"That's why no one visits?" Rob stared deep into the darkness of the well. His stomach lurched as he recalled the last time he had stood here. Roots had erupted from within, dragging him and Bray down into The Depths, the transition had not been a pleasant one. It was strange how such a picturesque masonry well could stir such dark memories.

"People visit, but only those desperate enough to risk a curse in place of a blessing. Most can only find this location once in their lifetime. That you stand before it again is, in itself, a gift."

"Does that mean the likelihood of a curse is doubled?" Rob took a long draught from his leather skin before blowing out a deep breath. He saw Daniel glance to him, no doubt detecting the strong odour of alcohol. He offered it to Daniel, who took a guarded sip before choking.

"Under normal circumstances," Daniel wheezed, clearing his throat and eyeing the leather skin cautiously as he handed it back. "But the coin we possess is part of an ancient pact. The well retains its powers so long as it answers the plea of any who toss such an item within."

"Any plea?"

"Only those achievable in the mortal realm, by mortal means, if luck and good fortune are in abundance."

"So it couldn't bring back the dead?"

"No," Daniel placed his hand on Rob's shoulder briefly before withdrawing. "But it could bring someone on the verge of death back to health, after all, nothing is absolute until that last breath is taken. By this same power, we can open a passage to The Depths of Acheron, to the exact place we need to be."

"And where is that exactly?" Rob queried, deciding it was time to learn as much as he could about what they would face. The Depths of Acheron were extensive and diverse, and he had travelled the twisted domain more than most. He hoped he could do what he had mentally vowed and keep Daniel safe.

"The Lorn of Hephaestus." Daniel seemed to look to him for recognition, perhaps hoping he had ventured there before.

"The Gods have gardens in The Depths?"

"Lorn, not lawn," Daniel chuckled, releasing some of the tension that had been building. "The place Hephaestus cast out that which he felt unworthy of being tempered. Thanks for that," Daniel grinned, knowing the motive behind the comment. "Are you ready?" Removing the coin from his pouch, he took a moment to appreciate the sheer complexity of what he held within his grasp. The two small interlocking discs were etched with ancient symbols and imbued with such power he imagined just holding it would cause a feeling of the potential stored within to echo upon his flesh, and yet, it was cool to the touch, weighing no more than the average coin. Sliding his fingers around the edge he twisted the two parts, separating them into their individual pieces as he approached the well. The whispers of invocation leaving his lips seemed to be both echoed on the wind and rise from the well as he released the first coin, focusing on their intention while grasping Rob's arm tightly with his other hand.

* * *

Despite the forest lining the borders of Phoenix Landing being shielded against detection magic, upon their arrival Alana took a moment to gather her bearings before leading the way.

This area had once been home to Zo—or more precisely the assassin Marise Shi who she had once shared both body and soul with—for nearly a decade. Beyond the complex, steep and jagged peaks of the mountains and dormant volcanoes, concealed within a natural barrier, stood the Courts of Twilight, a town, and Blackwood's mansion, a place Zo had once lived.

Marise had possessed a temperament as fiery as her red hair. She was the darkness born of Hectarian magic when Zoella's own alignment favoured light. All things with Hectarian magic had a balance, and Marise was created by the external manipulation of her internal balance Zoella had fought so hard to maintain. Even now, Zo recalled little of her time with Blackwood. One thing she did remember, however, was Marise's love to drive the settlers of Burntbush away when they attempted to slowly relocate to the richer soils near the mountains' base. Fires would ignite the sky, and to all who observed it seemed as if the volcanoes erupted, burning the town to cinders and ruin. Eventually they decided that with the combined danger of the volcanoes, and the bandit clans who sought to take advantage of the forest's natural properties, keeping their own town on the forest's outskirts was their safest option.

Within the forest that caressed the mountain's base was an ancient and rare tree. Zoella, thanks to Eiji, knew the tree's name to be Fenikkusu. Through the insight gained she had come to learn that each of these trees had their own gift, and the suppression of locational magic attributed to this area was but part of its purpose. Its objective was to protect and restore the phoenix, sacrificing its own branches to the eternal flame to rekindle this magnificent being should the need arise, thus allowing it to be reborn within the temple deep below the earth.

Zo herself remembered little of the challenges she had faced in Hephaestus' temple, and yet the one thing she recalled with some measure of clarity was the discovery that the magnificent fire-bird had been bound to the Grimoire of Fire. She remembered almost nothing of their exchange, except for the burning need to ensure this magnificent creature did not fall under Marise's control. She searched her memories, hoping to impart some wisdom upon her daughter, but her recollection of that time was vague, mere impressions upon a flowing stream moving forever further from her reach.

The great Fenikkusu stood as a giant, overshadowing the trees in the forest, towering above them like a king, and yet unless someone stood before it, its existence was shielded. It eclipsed all in both height and width and upon its bark small saplings, native to the surroundings, sprouted giving the impression they had been drawn into it to facilitate its growth. High within the impressive canopy the multitude of leaves were apparent, yet not one seemed to be specific to this tree. Instinctively, Zo knew this was another means used to camouflage itself. To possess its own distinctive leaf would be to allow others to locate it if its leaves were shed.

"Sproutling Mitéra, I was informed to expect you." The tree's leaves whispered in an absent wind as the voice penetrated each of their minds.

"Greetings, great tree. I seek entrance to Phoenix's realm." Alana stepped forward, crossing one leg over the other as she extended her arm forwards in a sweeping bow.

"Such is your right. It is, however, a path you must walk alone."

"What of the Skiá?"

"Whilst you are within the realm of the Great Spirit, your Tikéta will channel its energy through myself and shelter any beneath my canopy. I will attend to your parents, such is the Spirit's desire. It would seem he owes his freedom to your mother, and will ensure the debt is repaid in full. So, Sproutling Mitéra, are you prepared?"

"Can you tell me anything of the trial I must face through The Stepping Realm?"

"How wise you are, to realise your first challenge was within such a place. But I can speak nothing of it. It is a test, and how you answer reveals more than you would realise."

"Then it's a riddle?" Alana pushed playfully.

"All life is a riddle, and you are forever being challenged, Sproutling Mitéra. Come, I shall reveal the path."

A deep rumbling shook the ground around them as earth and stone raised under the force of the tree's massive roots. These appendages were the Akegata species' most noted feature and were visible to all in a complex woven lattice around the base before they submerged into the soil. It was theorised that these tendrils held the weight of earth and stone to create hidden tunnels and passages for the magical creatures of the forest. The tree's roots alone stood higher and thicker than any of them, yet were knitted so tightly no access could be granted.

Compacted soil cracked and rose as the roots creaked and groaned, slithering and uncoiling at an alarming pace for something so immense. The heavy scent of decaying earth and fertile soil filled the air as the roots retracted, opening a passage barely large enough for Alana to step through. She hesitated briefly, glancing backwards towards her parents, knowing that when she returned she would once more have aged, and before long the fond recollections she had of her childhood would be a distant memory, yet such memories would still be fresh in the minds' of her parents.

The weight behind the look she gave caused her mother to give a saddened smile, no doubt realising the same thing as her daughter had just moments before. Turning back towards them, her arms extended so they might embrace a final time before the start of her journey. She heard their whispers of encouragement, and felt their sadness and pride. With that small comfort she pulled away, not daring to look back a second time in fear she would hesitate further. Time was of the essence.

Chapter 25

The Lorn of Hephaestus

Rob beheld the shattered landscape. Never before had he seen such desolation, and he had traversed this realm more than any other human. The flat barren stone shone with a reddish tint, and what looked to be intermittent jets of scalding water and steam hissed from gaping chasms and gorges. Mist hovered high above their heads, like gossamer clouds, never descending from the height reached by the tallest geyser. It was from this canopy a sickly glow of opaque light seemed to radiate.

Broken islands cast dark silhouettes against the glowing moats as if the life essence of this land was being forced, in all its burning radiance, through any fissure it could find. At the far reaches of this great expanse, beyond the scarred lands and crumbing plains stood a place of curious intrigue. The manner in which the eerie light sparkled upon its surface made its nature indiscernible, although Rob had seen a similar occurrence before, when sunlight was reflected upon the surface of metal.

"If I was Hephaestus, I would be having words with my gardener," Rob mused, noticing Daniel was mentally exploring the lands before them just as he had moments ago. "If I know anything from my journeys to this place, it's that there is no chance that is water, scalding or not." Daniel crouched at one of the smaller fissures, peering inside.

"It's not," he confirmed, watching the movement of the strange substance below. "If I were to guess, I'd say it's some form of highly pressurised energy."

The heat in the air was oppressive as they walked, their flesh burning with each movement. Sweat had drenched them in the moments since their arrival, causing their clothes to stick to them uncomfortably. Scalding or not, this energy generated heat, massive amounts of it. Daniel tugged on his collar, but the action seemed to only succeed in allowing more of the unbearable heat to assail him.

"Visible energy?" Rob panted, wiping sweat from his brow, only for it to be replaced seconds later with a fresh layer.

"You witness it everyday with Dynamism. Think of this as this realm's natural equivalent."

"Dangerous?"

"The closest comparison I can draw, if you think of it as magma you probably won't be too far off."

"Deadly then."

"That would be my assumption."

"I'll take point from here," Rob announced suddenly, as the hairs on the back of his neck began to prickle. Such a sensation was never welcome, especially here. "By the way, what's the plan for moving the ore? For the amount you're going to need, you're going to want something more than just that satchel." Hearing this Daniel clutched his bag closer to himself instinctively.

"Don't worry about that. Let's locate the ore first. We can discuss the details later."

"Yeah, it's probably a bit too late for me to be asking now anyway." Rob surveyed their surroundings once more, something was watching them. He had spent too long fighting and surviving in The Depths not to recognise his body's reaction to danger, but as his vision panned across the open landscape he could see no hint of threat; then again, the things that thrived here had done so for countless cycles. They knew how to conceal themselves and, more disconcertingly, how to hunt.

"What is it?" Daniel questioned, his hand resting upon his collapsed staff as he watched Rob's posture stiffen further.

"I'm not sure, but we're not alone." Rob realised his own hand was resting upon the thin needles he kept tucked within his belt. These, and his crossbow, were his weapons of choice, they were the only ones he had ever truly trained with. He carried others, he would be a fool not to given that a glimpse of a blade was often enough of a deterrent. In a reflexive motion he ensured his crossbow was correctly loaded and within easy reach. The weapon had been custom designed to suit his needs, and was smaller and lighter than most. Its weight in his single-handed grasp offered comfort. It had saved his life more times than he could count.

"What are you thinking?" Daniel queried, increasing his pace to draw level with the treasure hunter.

"I think we may find some clues ahead." Rob gestured forward, where his vision had caught the slightest hint of movement in the distance. It was a few moments later he saw Daniel's look of recognition as the flicker of movement became the billowing of decaying rags, flapping wildly in the updraught from a nearby fissure. Cautiously they made their advance, their pace steady, their senses alert, as they picked their way closer.

One thing Rob had learnt from his countless ventures into The Depths of Acheron, was that it was rare to be the first person to leave a footprint upon the vast and varied landscape he would emerge into. The difference was, however, unlike other poor souls, he had been the only one to return. Even to this day, his ability to navigate and survive this frightful domain had turned him into somewhat of a legend amongst his peers. Squatting next to the twisted figure, Rob allowed his vision to roam over the remains of the lone adventurer. The unusual composition of the bones seemed to suggest they had been melted and fused in places. He looked on, absorbing its every detail while his instinct warned him something was amiss, but his mind couldn't quite discern what.

"There's no sign of gnawing," Daniel observed. "No indication of blunt trauma." Using his staff he adjusted some of the decomposing clothes and inhaled deeply. "No flesh, marrow, or soft tissues, that explains the lack of any odour. But the fusing is interesting, it's not something you'd expect to see on someone this young. It's not a natural fusion either." Daniel produced two coins from one of his pockets, placing them within the hollow eye sockets. Given the state of the body it was no longer possible to place a fare within the mouth.

Rob watched him, his own heart aching. Just a year ago he had discovered this man, and his friends, had paid the passage for his own wife and daughter to the underworld. For six long years he had lived in fear of them being stranded. Their bodies had never been found, that he knew of, but it seemed during their travels Daniel, Eiji, and Acha had happened upon the ruins of Weft, and ensured each person lost to the rage of the Severaine had receive their fare. Seeing Daniel perform this action as second nature suggested he had seen far more death than any one man should.

"Wait." Rob froze suddenly, noticing the cause of his momentary disquiet. It was something they had both overlooked, something which came with a distressing realisation. "This body's fresh, a year at most." Daniel glanced to him in request of an explanation. "The hallmark." Rob gestured towards a partially eroded dagger fused to the fingers of the deceased, before pulling a very slender needle from the inside seam of his jerkin. There, engraved towards the base of the needle, was the same identifier as on the weapon's pummel. "This smithy only set up shop just under a year ago."

"So even if this was from opening stock..." Daniel tapped his lips in contemplation. "The lack of damage would suggest he must have been poisoned, or perhaps, immobilised, sealed inside something maybe?" Daniel posed thinking how the clothing seemed to appear more burnt than decomposing.

"Like an amoeba?" Rob questioned rising to his feet.

"It'd have to be—"

"Large?" Rob questioned, his foot connecting with Daniel's boot in a bid to get his attention. Daniel turned slowly, a cold sweat already forming on his flesh as he recognised the fear within Rob's voice.

Daniel looked upon the creature with awe. Visible through its thick membrane, swirling currents of energy broiled within it like tropical storms traversing the undercurrents of its composition. Whilst it was not, an amoeba this amoeboid creature possessed many common traits. The thick cell membrane, whilst rigid enough to hold its looming three dimensional shape also possessed enough fluidity to allow it to ooze upward from the crevice in its own version of movement bending and twisting in a manner only possible for a thing of this nature. Distorted, yet just about visible within the liquid-energy endoplasm were food vacuoles, many still possessing the half-devoured remains of small mammals. All the while, throughout its ascent, its many pseudopodiums stretched out hungrily, extending in their direction. Deep within its core a large eyeball rotated, seeking its prey. Through the churning fluids, the numerous optical nerves from the enormous orb, extended outward, connecting to unseen parts within its core, yet it's complete rotation while it studied its surroundings showed its connections in no manner restricted its fluid movement. Daring to move, they discovered its focus snapped directly to any motion they made, and the extending tendrils responded.

Rob nudged Daniel softly, the viscosity of its form, and the deadly nature of the energy it stored within meant none of the weapons they carried would be of any use.

"We could do with some magic about now, you don't happen to know any?" To Rob's dismay Daniel shook his head. "But I thought you were the Wita, don't the Eorthãds have magic?"

"Some, but being the Wita means I'm a sage who can commune with the dead, and seek their wisdom."

"So... you can't call them here to your aid or anything? A spirit army diversion would have been great about now."

"It's not spirits as such, it's hard to explain, but no, I can't make anything take ethereal form."

"Pity." Rob shrugged, removing a handful of what appeared to be soft marbles from one of the many pouches on his belt. "Here, but use them sparingly."

"What are they?"

"Magic." Rob gave a mysterious smile. He tapped the surface of one, causing strange lights within to pulse. The light's flashing brightness seemed almost like lightning, piercing against the duller shades from above. He tossed it towards the creature, its single eye tracking the movement. "Run," he whispered, grasping Daniel's arm as the small marble came within reaching distance of one of its pseudopodiums. As Rob knew it would, it reached out, drawing it into its body.

Daniel did as he was told, his stomach tensing as he prepared himself for an explosion. Leaping the crevice onto the next island they continued to run.

"It doesn't explode?" Daniel asked, glancing over his shoulder to see the creature's eye swing around internally as it attempted to track them, all signs of the flashing marble had now vanished, consumed by the energy within.

"I don't even want to know what kind of toys you played with as a child," Rob retorted after clearing the next jump onto yet another crumbling island. He flicked another to activate it before once more throwing it towards the creature.

"Surely it'll know to ignore them by now."

"Doesn't matter, it has no eyelid."

"You're blinding it?" Daniel paused, briefly glancing backwards in astonishment as the creature devoured another marble. Rob grabbed him, encouraging him onward.

"It automatically tracks movement, it can't help but look. They're not much but..."

"Residual imaging. You're positioning us in the areas that will be shielded by the after image once it looks away, genius." Rob's feet skidded as he altered their course, tossing another marble.

"Feel free to help out," he encouraged. Daniel remembered the marbles in his hand, and tossed another. "Flosh," Rob panted, seeing the ripple of movement ahead. They were just a few leaps from the reflective surface that had first drawn their attention, but the break between them and it was filled with movement.

"You've got a crossbow, right?" Daniel questioned, his heart hammering as he saw the creatures rising as if to form a barricade.

"I've thought of that already, even my best bolt wouldn't make it through, I sacrificed power for size." He gestured towards the small weapon.

"I don't think it would make a difference anyway," Daniel resigned. "It'd burn up before it could do any damage. I have an idea how to pass, but you're not going to like it."

"I like the thought of meeting my end inside one of those even less. What are you thinking?" In response, Daniel removed the leather card Chrissie had loaned them from the safety of his inside pocket, his gaze holding Rob's firmly.

"We use it now, you said it yourself, they've got no eyelids. If we attack with something bright enough it should stun them. They'll fall back allowing us to pass."

"She channelled it for a second use right?" Rob questioned knowing the first had expired when they entered the well. Daniel nodded. "Do it, without it we've no chance."

"If I do we have no chance against the Skiá either."

"Did no one tell you I've the luck of Tyche?" Rob jested.

"Someone told me that once too," Daniel chuckled, thinking back to Amelia. "The luck of Tyche and the brains of a turkey."

"Sounds about right. Then together we're a force to be reckoned with. Why are you still talking? Do it."

Daniel nodded in firm commitment, drawing a deep breath he focused on the power within the card. When Chrissie had presented it to him, she had done so with a firm set of instructions. Elemental magic was brought into form by visualisation. In order to protect them he needed to feel the power she had channelled into the card, and shape it with his mind. Only when he had a firm image, could he release the vision, causing the energy to manifest. On their journey here he had needed to envision a barrier surrounding himself and Rob, creating a protectional bubble around them through which no darkness could penetrate. Channelling the energy now he envisioned something entirely different.

Light burnt across the air, its blaze as dazzling as the sun. Fine forks of burning energy chased towards the unsuspecting prey, its silent impact staggering, halting the slithering advance. Near silent choruses, like songs beneath the ocean waves, cried in anguish as several creatures, dazed and blinded, lost purchase on the ledge tumbling into the burning currents below. Rob reached out, grasping Daniel, who stood dazed. His firm movements guiding him, wondering what had encouraged the Wita to observe the blinding flashes. He whispered commands, instructions to keep them moving despite the impairment.

By the time they had reached the crevice, Daniel's vision had virtually recovered, allowing him to see the mass of forms they had woven carefully between. They stood paralysed, but the rippling of their membranes, and the subtle twitching of their pseudopodiums suggested their recovery was imminent. With a final leap, the two men cleared the distance over the crevice, their pace quickening as they hoped to place as much distance between themselves and the creatures as possible.

* * *

The tunnels that stretched before Alana were dark, beyond any darkness she had experienced before. Even in a lightless realm small creatures or nature's magic often found a way to create some illumination, no matter how dim. But this had been complete and all-encompassing from the instant the tree's roots had sealed the path behind her. Alana recalled her fear of the dark, the thoughts that monsters played in shadows. But whereas human parents would offer comfort to their child in misguided lies, her own parents had known better. They knew there was a reason to fear the darkness, but they also taught her simple spells she could use to protect herself.

"Night-light," Alana whispered remembering how she had been taught to say her desire aloud to see it manifest. She had questioned why everyone else could do it at will, but she had to invoke it, her mother had said the words were just a means to channel her intention and, eventually, with practice she could do it without invocations as well. Alana held her open hand out before her, but where normally a dim orb of magic would throw light into the darkness, the only response was an increase in the cold pressure that had crept across her flesh. "Dispel," she whispered, her breath catching. The pressure eased a little, but the darkness remained as stifling and oppressive as ever.

Even realising the futility she squinted into the darkness, trying to force her mind to distinguish shapes from the endless expanse of nothingness. Hair-like tendrils clung to her face causing small whimpers to escape as images of the creatures who made this place their home crawling upon her skin assailed her. Extending her arms before her she probed blindly until the sensation of movement beneath her fingers upon a damp wall caused her to squeal. She froze involuntarily, aware of the scuttling sounds made by the surrounding life. A tear escaped through her heavy lashes as she clamped her hand across her nose and mouth, which only served to amplify the sound of her gasping breaths to such an extent that all other noise was lost. The rapid tattoo of her heart chorused each panicked breath, and for a moment she feared she had lost control over her body as her legs refused to obey her desire to turn and run.

"I can do this." The fear in her voice did little to offer the reassurances she had intended. Yet, on some level, as the reverberation returned her muffled words, she found in them a measure of comfort and the noises beyond that of her own fear serenaded her once more, this time with more clarity than before. Sounds, which had once been a source of unseen fear, began to sing their own song, speaking of the nature and location of the choir surrounding her.

Slowly, Alana began to place one foot before the other, freezing with each new sound, using its pitch to estimate its size and nature. Small rapid scuttling, she hoped, translated to little creatures. Long slithering belonged to snakes or other legless animals, and the pitch of wings in flight allowed her to estimate their size, the higher the pitch, the smaller the creature. She found herself questioning how these beings could navigate in such conditions, wondering if they possessed some manner of echolocation or if they used their other senses to guide them, just as she did now.

Pausing, she became aware of an opening beside her, the feeling of space was staggering. Sounds assailed her from every direction, almost overwhelming her already strained hearing. It seemed she stood at a crossroad. The choice seemed impossible. The noises were so many and so widely varied.

Tentatively she took a step forward, her throat closing as she gagged. The stench of death and rot emanating from that direction was almost unbearable. Taking two rapid steps backwards a trembling sigh escaped her lips as the stench weakened. She had been aware of the strange odours for some time, but had been so focused on the noise of her surroundings she had paid her other senses no heed.

Turning to her right she began to walk, but the lack of sound in the tunnel unnerved her. It was as though everything around her had grown still. It was then she felt the base rumbling beneath her feet, movement. It was something large, predatory if the silence surrounding her was any indication. With each passing second the vibrations grew stronger. The echoing of a timbre growl reverberated throughout her chest, speeding her heart, causing her to turn and run down the only passage that remained. She tripped and stumbled as her hurried steps caused her balance to falter and her feet to snag upon the uneven ground.

She was unsure how long she had run for, how far she had travelled staggering through the darkness until realising the vibrations had stopped. She could feel the warmth of fluid seeping from her hands and knees from her many falls, but without any pain to hinder her pace she crept on. The world once more expanding beyond the tunnel her fear had created.

Her skin began to tingle, at first she thought it was nothing more than the heat that enveloped this tunnel growing in intensity. That was until she drew back and the feeling faded without transition. Extending her arm she moved her hand before her, mentally drawing an image of the places where the strange feeling was strongest. Stepping closer she allowed its energy to wash over her, realising that the sensation was something beyond heat, it was magical, a portal. With a steady breath she stepped forward, immersing herself within and passing through.

A blazing light momentarily blinded her, forcing her eyes to close, reopening in a squint only when they had chance to adjust to this new environment. Light flicked before her from sunken fire pits that edged the room while large stone scones stood at staggered intervals across the stone floor. Seeing what lay before her she realised she had only now entered The Stepping Realm, that all which came before her emergence here had been but a prelude to the challenge.

Her nose twitched, alerting her of a vaguely unpleasant odour just seconds before she felt herself being thrust forward, deeper into the room. Spinning on her heel she turned, confusion knitting her brow to find herself alone. She scrutinised every shadow, seeking evidence of something concealed themselves within, but nothing could be found. The faint scent returned, drawing her gaze towards the blazing fires causing her to wonder if its source came from within, but she knew there was no time to indulge such curiosity. Straightening her clothes, she set her focus towards the other side of the room, the only place where the surrounding fires didn't burn and took another step forward. The sound of her footfall upon the floor had barely registered when the force struck her again. The strength of the blow surpassing the last, sending her tumbling to the ground, where her motion stilled abruptly as her head collided with the wide base belonging to one of the fire braziers.

Warm fluid spilt from the wound, her fingers briefly testing the severity of the painless injury as she attempted to blink away the disorientation. Reaching up, she grasped the brazier pulling herself to her knees. The scent of burning flesh stung her nose, forcing her gaze to her raw blistering hand. She moved uncertainly, her pace quickening to a run before something struck her with such force she felt her body spin and heard the socket of her shoulder dislocate as she impacted with the floor. Despite the lack of pain, her vision swam as dizziness overwhelmed her, intensifying as the overpowering smell grew stronger.

* * *

Bray looked doubtfully at the over-sized copper coils as they twisted and wrapped their way around a cylindrical tube to spray out at strange angles from either end after being bent and wrapped to support several, roughly-cut gemstones. The translation of the tablet had been difficult, even with Elly's vast knowledge of ancient dialects, cuneiforms, and scripts.

He had watched her labour away, her tunnel vision unaware of anything else that occurred around her. She muttered and mumbled, mused and ranted until, with a growl of frustration, she clenched her fists, resisting the urge to destroy the bane of her life as she complained how much easier such things had been in her golem. Seizing the opportunity, Bray had stood behind her, sliding his hands onto her shoulders to gently ease the tension knotting them. He knew the information was within her, but despite her focus she had been unable to decipher the text. On seeing her tire he used his influence encouraging her to read to him, and to her own amazement the words had flowed from her with ease. But it had been exhausting, for both of them.

What he held now was the result of their labour. Looking upon its cobbled-together design he wondered if, perhaps, he had been premature in his actions, especially since it had found its way into his grasp for testing.

"Proceed," Elly encouraged, leading him further from the town's borders. If anything went awry it was essential they were as far away as possible. Over the years she had become fond of the people there, and although she would never admit it, had been responsible for not only the initial rumours to ward people away, but also for the introduction of the flower that kept them safe.

Elly had never really had any great fondness of flowers, yet in Collateral she possessed her own garden, a collection of vibrant beauty and deadly deceptions that had once been her way of measuring time. Each decade she allowed herself a personal errand, to seek out the rarest flower and see it grow within her garden, a place it would forever be preserved. Such was how, a chiliad ago, she had happened upon this breed. The natural hybrid was fading, its longevity was short lived, its cultivation failing. It had been doomed to extinction, yet in her garden she had found a way to revive it. When years later she had happened upon this town she knew it would be the answer to their problems, but it had taken her a full lunar year to create enough cuttings. It had been a difficult task, especially ensuring it would not grow beyond the boundaries of the forest, but the people of this town had seen too much hardship and persecution, and Elly was a firm believer that a sanctuary should be just that.

"I don't see why I'm the one who has to put his life on the line," Bray complained, pulling her focus from one of the flowers which occasionally closed before expelling a cloud of spores into the air.

"If you can guarantee it would not kill me, I will gladly take it." Elly reached forward to grasp it as Bray stepped back, wafting his hand to divert a flurry of falling leaves from his path. "Should I interpret such reluctance as a sign?"

"It would not be very chivalrous of me to allow a maiden as fair as yourself to put herself at risk." Bray rubbed his free hand down his trousers in a vain attempt to clean it before placing it above the other on the metal casing. Instantly he felt the pressure of his feet upon the carpet of fallen leaves increase as an invisible weight bore down upon him from above. A distinctive crackling erupted from the metal as sparks of lightning danced upon its surface, spanning out across the wires and beyond their touch at numerous angles. The pollen's glow upon him faded as the light crepitated around them. "It's a shield?"

"No, it is a weapon. It is brilliant, but by the Gods is it deadly," Elly whispered in awe.

"What do you mean?"

"Multi-pronged, light-emitting energy from infinite angles. You are wielding magic in its rawest form."

"I have no aptitude for such things."

"And that is precisely why it is deadly, look at your feet." Bray looked down, noticing the decaying foliage had lost all its glow and continued to shrivel and decompose at an accelerated rate. "It strips the magic of life to allow you to wield it." Elly's thoughts instantly turned to Acha, the only other being she knew with the ability to draw life from her surroundings. Their paths had not crossed for some time, but she couldn't help but wonder what effect her touch would have upon the Skiá.

"We can't just hand this thing out to the masses, think of the—"

"Exactly. A weapon like this, with such devastating potential, serves a purpose other than just wielding magic."

"What do you mean?"

"If we can craft enough, we can bring something even more powerful to the war, and with it lies our only hope of destroying the Skiá." Elly's face shone with elation as she processed this new idea. It stirred something within her she had not felt long before returning to her human flesh, fervour.

"You can't be implying what I think you are!"

"We would need to duplicate this on a grand scale," Elly continued as if she hadn't heard him, her voice quickening as her adrenaline spiked. "If we can arm a small platoon, and have them stationed at a single location that should be sufficient. The only thing we do not possess is a means to draw the Skiá. We need something, the target of their master's objective—"

"Are you insane? Do you even realise what you're suggesting. It would be mass-suicide." Bray forced the outrage he felt into expressing his words, but her excitement was contagious. He could feel the power behind her emotions, her raw drive and passion and felt now what he had when first their paths had crossed centuries ago. A growl vibrated within his throat as the intensity of her spirit called to the beast within. It was no wonder she had been a hero. She was often calculating, efficient, methodical, and kept her emotions closely guarded, but what he now witnessed, this part of herself she kept buried, was spectacular.

"No, it would not be suicide, not if the aim was for a greater good, Mass sacrifice, perhaps, would be more fitting," she debated energetically. The wind shifted, but did little to dispel the energy surrounding her.

"Do you not see any problem with what you're suggesting?" Bray growled, trying to force himself to remain rational and objective.

"Well, if you have a better plan then by all means tell me, but until you decide to save us this is what we have. War is never ideal, and it does not come without sacrifice."

"And will the soldiers you recruit know the cost of their actions?"

"Does a farmer tell the pig they are being led to slaughter?" Her voice softened, and the emotions that had ran so rampant just moments ago were forced back behind the indifferent facade. She once more suppressed her passionate soul, as if she had realised for the first time the cost to those who would follow her.

* * *

With every blink the residual imaging from the explosion of light began to fade from Daniel's vision only for him to find it captivated by another sight. When they had first entered the Lorn, where they now stood had been nothing more than a reflection of light in the distance. Standing here now, the reason became apparent.

The deep crevices in the cracked and fissured landscape hissed with the pressure of the energy building below. The ground vibrated underfoot, groaning with its burden as it forced another glob of molten metal from below to begin the formation of a new structure to join the other highly polished silver spears that littered their surroundings. Hundreds of shimmering trunks towered above them, creating a mesmerising jagged forest of gleaming metal, their leafless branches as sharp and dangerous as any trap as they were expelled and cooled into formations that were both deadly and beautiful.

"By all the Gods and Spirits," Daniel gasped, absorbing every detail of the sight Rob had already become accustomed to.

"I don't think we have cause to worry about any of those things following us here." Rob observed, ducking under several jagged prongs. "Us getting out, however, is a different matter entirely."

"Don't worry about that, it's in hand. This will be easier than I anticipated." Daniel paced the circumference of one of the trees muttering to himself. Reaching into his satchel he removed a blue jewel before placing it upon the surface of a tree, where it remained fixed. He selected ten more of the trees, and repeated the same process, each time attaching a nearly identical gemstone. "Now for the difficult part," he muttered glancing to Rob. "I hope this works."

Daniel placed his hand beneath his coat, his fingers activating the gemstone he kept concealed beneath. He drew in a sharp gasp as he felt the liquid metal begin to pour from within to craft the armour bestowed upon him by Nemean. All Eortháds had their own protective equipment, forged to enhance and align with their role and affinities. Daniel remembered the awe he had felt when he had first witnessed Alessia's retract into the gemstone she wore as a pendent. Feeling the pressure spread across his torso he touched it again, stilling the process and causing it to reverse, as it did the stones upon the tree thrummed in resonance, and in turn, caused that which they touched to be drawn into them.

Rob stood, his mouth agape, as he watched in disbelief. He had seen this man retract his armour on one other occasion, but for some reason it had slipped his mind, until now. Daniel fell to one knee breathlessly, his hand still beneath his coat, feeding the energy required for this process through his own gemstone. It was not something he was well-versed with. The Thegnalar, even Nemean, had oriented his training on his connection to the ancients and building his endurance and skill, rather than on the focus and direction of energy. Since Daniel possessed no magic, the skill had been lower on their list of priorities, despite the one thing he could use it for.

As Wita, his own armour could be attuned to Alessia's and the Thegnalar, ensuring should he behold any danger, the activation of his own defences would in turn trigger their own, along with any other who was in his vicinity. With great effort he could also reverse the process. It was a responsibility he had refused in fear it would one day be exploited Before his departure, Nemean had granted him eleven of their armament crystals attuned to his own for the task he was now undertaking.

Daniel leaned forward, supporting his weight with his free hand, waiting for the completion. The detriment of this attunement was that it exhausted his energy, physically and mentally. He felt his vision start to fade as the crystals completed their task, his strength waned as he forced himself to endure through the dark motes swimming before his distorted gaze.

"Hey, are you all right there?" Daniel could barely manage a nod as he felt Rob's hand grasp him. But what he needed more than the support, was for Rob to gather the crystals now his task had been completed. As if he knew what was expected from him, he eased Daniel to the floor, looking over him one final time before leaving his side collecting the crystals with haste, while his vision remained trained upon him. On his return he helped Daniel into a seated position, touching his leather skin to Daniel's parched lips and noticed his confusion as he realised the sweet mead he had just consumed was not what had been in the last skin he had drank from. "I came prepared," Rob shrugged. "It's honey mead, you looked like you needed some sugar." Daniel accepted more, this time drinking deeply. He could feel the sugars from the alcohol both rejuvenating and sedating his body.

"Water," Daniel gasped. He could already see Rob's bemused and somewhat quizzical expression. He seemed to think for a moment before shrugging apologetically.

"Mead contains water," Rob answered. Hearing this, Daniel chuckled softly, grasping his satchel and pulling his own leather skin from within. The coconut water quickly countered the building effects of the mead, but still he was exhausted.

"You really need to lend me one of these," Rob teased studying the crystals, his voice holding enough longing to reflect the truth of his words.

"Help me up," Daniel requested as he returned the gemstones to a small pouch which he placed back inside his satchel. "It's better not to linger." With great strain Rob pulled Daniel to his feet.

"I don't fancy our chances if we come across any of those oozes again, are you sure you won't rest?"

"The crystals weren't designed for this purpose, they'll only contain this substance for a short period of time. We need to get moving."

"Okay, but how do you propose..." He watched as Daniel fished the remainder of the coin from his pocket. He turned it over in his fingers before placing a hand upon Rob's shoulder and dropping it to the floor with a wish. "I thought you needed a—" His words froze as an overbearing pressure seemed permeate the air surrounding them. The ground at their feet began to quake, the stone dissolving into mists of light until they felt themselves plummeting downward, twisting and turning at an alarming speed until they were propelled upwards from the well. The Depths of Acheron were always unpredictable, but one thing Rob had never grown accustomed to was the fact that directions and orientations within held no relevance to the place they emerged.

There had been no hesitation, no delay in using every means at their disposal to escape the gelatinous creatures. The final protection of the light card had saved their lives, but as they stood now, in a world blanketed by darkness, it was impossible not to be consumed by the foreboding dread of their situation. They were alone, in the dark, without any means of defence. The scenery rustled around them, movement stirred from the undergrowth as shadows leapt and played in a motion that may have only been the shifting of the wind throughout the trees. But something lurking. A darkness that could almost be seen weaving towards them, its pace quickening, its presence drawing closer. Daniel glanced to his satchel knowing if he fell here Alessia would know, and she would ensure his journey had not been in vain.

* * *

The pressure pinning Alana down eased, allowing her to drag herself back to her feet. Her left arm hung limply by her side, unresponsive to any attempts to move it. Despite the lack of pain she felt the warmth of tears streaming down her face, stirred by the sight of her injured body and the blood coating her hands from the wound on her forehead. Regardless of what future awaited she was still a child, and she was afraid.

She sniffed, calming herself in the only way she knew how, by breathing as Pigí had directed her. Long, deep, slow breaths.

The glimmer of sweat upon her skin sung of her fear, one she tried to repress. If there was something lurking, determined to prevent her from reaching the portal, then its nature wasn't too dissimilar to the insects in the tunnels. They had been present but unobserved. The only difference came in the nature of concealment. A small tremor passed through her tiny body, her vision once more surveying the lay of the land. The portal wasn't far, but if with every strike its strength increased she wouldn't survive to make the journey. A tear rolled down her cheeks, creating the slightest noise as it impacted upon the ground causing her to tense, her foot slid backwards in partial retreat from the noise which, while almost silent, seemed too loud against the roaring flames.

The obnoxious odour assailed her senses, a yelp escaping her trembling lips as she stumbled backwards. The tearing force of pressure sailed past. The force of its momentum caused her clothes to billow, creating yet more movement and noise, another source for it to follow. The prevailing scent warned her of its approach, the pressure of its direction. Spinning on her heel she pivoted, evading the blow, her movements becoming continuous, the flow of a dance much like the one she had learnt within Pigi's realm, but she was but the follower, the leader, the scent drove her steps, its presence propelling her onward as she circled the braziers. Her pace quickened, confidence mounting as she began to predict where the scent would next emerge based on how she placed her feet or moved her arms.

Then everything changed. Her foot froze mid-stride as the expected odour did not return. The pressure surrounding her welled, before realising her mistake her leg was propelled from beneath her. She struck the floor heavily, screaming out in frustration.

The stalactites blurred in and out of focus through the dampness of her eyes. But her tears were not of grief but indignation. She knew the lesson, knew to utilise all her senses, yet when one had stopped it had disrupted her focus, she had ignored her instincts. Wiping her eyes, she felt the pressure build again spurred by her movement. It was not being as forgiving, it would not let her lie in self-pity. With a roll she pushed herself to her feet.

Closing her eyes she once more embraced her senses, feeling for the pressure, listening for the movement of her clothes. She thought back to how her mother used to scold her for throwing the cleaver burrs at Rowmeow. After one of their games of sticky buds, her mother had spent hours grooming the small pods from his fur, only for him to depart and return later, both himself and Alana covered in the same pods. He said he was teaching her to dodge and aim magic through the use of harmless projectiles and, whilst his explanations seemed to have merit, Alana often thought he only insisted on this game because he liked the attention he received afterwards. The pressure here was like that of those pods, it was small, concise. Yet unlike her childhood game being struck had dangerous consequences. Stealing her focus she moved again. Embracing the dance while being hindered by the jarring motion of her leg.

The fires before her seemed to cool, opening her eyes she confirmed the portal was barely a few paces away. Excitement renewed, revitalising her, until she saw the large pit spanning the distance between herself and the portal. She knew making such a leap would be impossible, even before being injured. Moving again, a plan formed within her mind. This energy, this attacker, had led her in an extravagant dance, but she had learnt the way it moved, and now would utilise it. As her steps froze at the edge of the fire pit, her eyebrows furrowed, waiting for the expected blow. When it struck it did so with a jarring force, her small frame barrelled forward, the buzz of energy as she struck the wall cam as a welcome relief for barely a second before she struck the ground landing in a heap before the most fantastical being she had ever laid eyes upon. Try as she did she could not draw her gaze from his burning feathers. They were everything the myths had promised and more.

"That your first teacher removed your pain was fortunate." The phoenix's voice invaded her mind as he observed her damaged limbs and blood streaked appearance. "My lessons are brutal, and the cost of being within my presence is often paid in pain."

"Great Spirit of Fire, I, Alana, seek your training. What cost would you extract from me?" She blew her damp hair from her eyes in a small attempt to make herself appear more presentable.

"To teach you all I must, I will accept a tribute of your inherited magics."

"What will become of that I learnt from Pigí?" Alana questioned, a frown creasing her flustered brow.

"It was not a gift you were born with, as such it will remain unhindered. I speak of the gifts passed to you by your family only," he clarified.

"I accept your fee and offer it willingly." Alana gave a sweeping bow, invoking a strange screeching sound from the phoenix as it extended its burning wings.

"Please, do not do that within my presence again." There was amusement in his communication that made Alana believe the noise she had just heard was in fact a laugh. "Ladies do not bow, least of all the Mitéra. You will learn to show your respects appropriately, and your poise and balance is in clear need of attention." The creature screeched again in good humour. "But know this, little spark, once you have completed the rites, you will bow to no one, remember this well. By bowing you show subservience and place the person before you in an elevated status."

"Except yourselves?"

"Not even us, unless you think it necessary for a child to bow before their parents."

"What of respect?"

"That is why you are granted a voice. Show your respect and intentions through how you speak and act. Once our rite is completed I shall heal your wounds. I would warn you of the suffering you must endure, but with it you are already familiar. Know that whilst your former master relieved such a burden from your physical body there is no buffer to quell the embers of pain to the essence. I will retrieve your inherited magics, and in its place add your alignment to myself. As before, when you are competent, I will complete the fusing and by doing so borrow something from you. Are you ready to proceed?"

"Yes, Great Spirit," Alana consented, preparing herself for the agony she knew would follow.

* * *

The comforting embrace of the tree's canopy reached out across the blackened heavens. Birds sang, and animals grazed, despite the unnatural darkness that had descended upon their world. Squirrels foraged, collecting nuts from nearby trees before retreating back into the safety of their dreys, away from watchful eyes. Zoella, who was normally captivated by such sights, did little but pace beneath the tree's umbrella, turning on her heels, only to walk back once more, repeating this pattern in a constant loop.

There were many things she contemplated, as she heard the rhythmic crunching of autumn foliage beneath her boots. By her own estimation Íkelos could manipulate her energy. She could feel his corruption surrounding her solar plexus chakra, and his touch on all those below so he could exploit her for his own purpose. His infection had already succeeded in the first steps of once more forcing her to speak his will and using the gift Darrienia had bestowed upon her to his advantage.

She had been pacing for some time before noticing Seiken was still standing at the base of the tree where their daughter had last been seen. His gaze followed her every move, and it was only as her vision met with his she realised he had been studying her. He looked away briefly, trying to conceal the depth of his concern as their eyes had met.

She felt the tightness in her chest, warning of the dark tendrils' proximity to the next chakra, and confirming that all which lay below had been claimed. Seiken, seeing her unease, moved to take her hands in his. His expression more open about his examination. He examined her slowly, assessing the spread, before tearing his eyes from hers to avert his gaze as he faltered.

"Will you excuse me a moment?" he questioned formally, causing her pulse to quicken. She looked down at herself, trying to see whatever he had. It was a pointless endeavour since she knew the vestige enchantment was only visible to him. "No, it's not what you're thinking," he assured, placing a hand tenderly upon her arm. "I just realised I need to relay an urgent message to Alessia. It has just occurred to me, I must ensure she knows the dangers of letting the wyrms, or even the Eortháds, leave Kalia. I am certain Daniel has realised, but—"

"You can't plan to leave the protection?" Zo glanced meaningfully towards the tree's outstretched branches. She placed her hand to her chest where the gossip crystal normally hung around her neck, feeling its absence. All things considered, they had decided it was safer in his hands than hers.

"It extends to the forest's edge. When Fenikkusu said canopy, he was referring to his veil of protection. Our crystal will not work within this forest as it seeks to locate and connect to another, but perhaps it will where the barrier is weaker." Seiken glanced past her as he spoke, as if navigating the distance he must travel.

"Then I should come with you," Zo asserted, turning. Reaching out, Seiken grasped her arm, pulling her back into his firm embrace and held her tightly, easing her burdens in the way only a loved one could. His fingers teased gently through her hair before he pulled away to place a gentle kiss on her forehead.

"As much as I would enjoy walking with you, one of us needs to be here in case Alana returns. In some ways this may be her greatest challenge."

"Why, what do you know?"

"What do you remember from when you gazed upon the phoenix?" Seiken questioned, knowing she had limited memories of that time. They had spent many a night, snuggled together beneath a blanket, overlooking the vast and varied landscapes of Darrienia, discussing just this. Zo had never forgiven herself for the actions Marise had taken, despite being unable to control them.

There had been nights of long and emotional conversations as parts of her jaded past resurfaced, reigniting a loathing in herself it seemed impossible to shed. He would listen with understanding as she spoke in depths of the many horrific things she recalled, not knowing these were but the tip of an iceberg in a very tumultuous sea. There were things he knew she had done that should ever they come to surface, she would never be able to forgive. Actions which affected people she loved dearly.

"I only saw him within my mind, but he was beautiful," Zo whispered, in a far-away tone. Her mind revisited the image of the magnificent fire bird. "I remember thinking that looking upon him was akin to gazing at the sun." Zo raised her hands to her mouth in realisation of what Seiken implied. "Years will pass for her."

"She will need one of us to be here." Zo nodded her understanding. Seiken once more pulled her close, placing one final tender kiss upon her dusk-pink lips. She felt the sensation of his touch lingering long after he had left and become concealed by the dense foliage.

Chapter 26

Promises

Alana wiped the sweat from her brow, panting heavily. She knew this challenge by heart, which was just as well given the price of her training. At first, after the forging of the pact, everything appeared the same. From her first day the phoenix had made his expectations known and never did their routine vary. For three years she would crawl to her resting place at the day's end, her limbs burning and magic expended. Phoenix would embrace her within his healing aura and his children would tell her tales of their plights. In Pigi's realm she had been a child, playing and learning, here the rest came only when her tasks were completed, and even then she recognised the tales and games for what they were, lessons. She learnt their languages with ease and their identity through how the heat of their aura danced.

The first time her gaze had rested upon the magnificent lava caves she had grown silent, feelings of trepidation and awe bubbling within her as she beheld the realm of fire. Their first day had been nothing more than a tour of the prominent places, locations her studies would take place. She remembered saliva growing thick within her throat as she looked out across a river of lava, small pillars of varying heights stood within, leading to barely visible natural footholds, that skirted around deadly waterfalls and majestic views. Pyrophytic plants created precarious walkways and stunning landscapes their thick insulated leaves would serve as a source of food and hydration for beings like herself, who required such things.

When phoenix had explained the landscape before her was intended for her training, to hone her skills, balance, endurance, and strength a heat prickled across her skin that had nothing to do with her surroundings. She never imagined being able to reach the end of the complex terrain, let alone being able to return to her starting location.

Each day they would train her body to exhaustion, only then, when her limbs were shaking and unresponsive, would they move to the place he had chosen to have her study the essence of fire, learn its ways and how it could be utilised alongside its opposing element, water.

Over time, the reason for the routine became apparent. Each day she would walk the same paths, run the same courses, and practice channelling the Fire Elemental's energy in the same places. As the months passed the once vibrant shades began to dull. At first she paid such changes little heed, believing she was simply becoming accustomed to this environment, yet with each day her sight grew dimmer, bringing new fears to surface. Seeing her distraction the phoenix had explained the unavoidable cost of being in his presence for extended periods of time. Whilst her pact with the Water Elemental had delayed the effects slightly, it could not stop the natural affliction. No one could gaze upon such burning intensity for such an expanse of time without sacrifice, not even the future Mitéra.

On hearing this Alana had understood why, when they first met, he was pleased that Pigí had taken her pain. He had said 'the cost of being within my presence is often paid in pain.' Alana was certain if not for the price of fusing with the Water Spirit she would have experienced agony as her sight was slowly burnt away and her world descended into eternal darkness.

Many things made sense to her now. She had found her way to The Stepping Realm without the aid of sight, learning to trust her other senses. Within the transitional area she had faced an unseen foe, one that encouraged her to apply what she had discovered in the vast entangled networks of darkness she had encountered beneath the tree, proving she could endure the price of his training. She was certain had she failed, the Great Spirit would not have offered her his insight.

Alana sank to her knees, exhausted, and turned towards the familiar sensation of his aura she felt to her right. It had taken but half a year for her sight to fade completely and, during that time, in the hope of prolonging this fading sense, the phoenix had attempted to take on many forms, but whilst the vibrant fires appeared dulled, the effect of beholding him was very much the same. The warmth traced contours within the air, suggesting his shape to have taken on one of its more humanoid apparitions. Heat that would cause any normal mortal to blister and burn encompassed her hand as he helped her to rise in one of the many gentlemanly gestures she attributed to this fiery lord.

"The challenges before you are great, little spark. You have proven yourself capable of wielding my energies. Sylph will help restore some awareness to the world you have lost. The time has come for you to rejoin your parents. For you, three years have passed in my care, you are nearing adolescence and this will be the last time they see you as their little girl. Grant them this luxury."

"I remember them bringing me here, their faces, but I fear I may not know their voices. I understand this will be difficult for them, but most of my childhood memories are of my time with you, Pigí, and your children."

"Yes, you are rather unique in the sense the Great Spirits will raise you. You are the first Mitéra we have taken in this fashion. There is much about you that will change how we proceed, and whilst we are on the subject of progression, are you prepared for the fusion?"

"Having experienced it once, I can say I will never be prepared, but I am ready. What will you remove?" Alana felt the warmth of his aura embrace her, and remained still and silent.

"Since you came to us so young, the price for what I must extract may seem severe. Are you sure you wish to know?" Alana nodded. "Due to your limited experience before coming into our realms, I must temporarily extract both your passion, and your ability to feel happiness."

"I will be miserable?"

"No, the absence of one does not always mean an abundance of the other." Alana dipped her head in understanding, slightly relieved. "Then the time has come to seal our pact. Step forwards." Alana did as instructed, mentally preparing herself for the pain that would follow the appearance of her newest tikéta. Even having prepared herself, after so long without feeling any physical pain, the agony that coursed through her seemed more intense than the last time she had endured.

* * *

Elly plucked her hat from the coat stand, gracefully positioning it in its familiar place before tracing her fingers across the seam disguising the concealed blade. Unshuttered and plunged into darkness, the forge stood abandoned, even absent the glow of embers, while the same cold oppression caused her skin to prickle. The streets had been understandably empty, yet someone had possessed the foresight to turn the lighthouse's beam upon the city. Dark clouds loomed overhead, but at least it appeared they were aware of the imminent danger, which meant she would probably find Tony somewhere safe.

"Are you certain a blacksmith could fashion this?" Bray questioned. There was more to this design than coils and twisted metal. There were intricacies a calloused hand, hardened and numbed by endless labour, could surely not duplicate.

"We need him to smelt and cast the metal. The inventor will have a solder and the means to attend to the more delicate needs, while the port-based apothecary healer carries the crystals we will require. We did well with what we had to hand, but a more ergonomic design will grant more confidence for those wielding it," Elly explained approaching the large open doors to survey the port. The salty sea-air carried the cloying odours of seaweed and decaying fish from the lower tiers where countless hauls had been hastily discarded.

"Sure, there's nothing like confidence when being led to death." Elly glared at him, pulling her coat down before raising her collar against the chilled wind.

"So," she mused, studying the lay of the land once more, "if I knew enough to turn the lighthouse onto the city, where would I hide the weapon-smith?" Elly drummed her nails on the empty display counter near the exit, briefly considering how unusual it was for such a thing to be void of wares.

Bray tracked the path of the lanterns which lined the streets. The glass containers still thrummed with the power of Dynamism. Just a few places of business had been left fully aglow, as if to suggest that careful consideration had gone into these actions. Homes he could understand being awash with light, but businesses were less likely to be a refuge to people seeking shelter or a place to cower and huddle in fear against an unknown attacker. There was something else which struck him as unusual, the lighting patterns of the lanterns seemed to join from each location to create a single walkway.

"Dynamism," Bray muttered to himself before stepping outside.

"Pardon?"

"If I wanted to ensure the survival of a select group of people, people whose services I thought I may need, Tailor, Tinkerer, Blacksmith, Glassewryght"—Bray gestured towards the buildings still bathed in light—"then I would probably possess enough foresight to also know there is only one place in this city that will never want for light, no matter how dire the circumstances." Bray motioned towards the place where all the lit paths converged, the building housing the Dynamism collection conduit.

"Someone has gone to great lengths to ensure their security," Elly observed leaving the forge to march the lit path towards the small building on the outskirts of the port.

"Yes, and we should be careful not to endanger them needlessly."

"Stop talking and use that already." Elly gestured meaningfully towards the metal casing currently held extinguished in Bray's grasp. No sooner has she spoken, when its once vibrant sparks charged the air around him. Tendrils of plasma crackled, burning in electric shades as they caressed the spaces between the metal spokes before flickering outward like the tongue of a viper tasting the darkness around it, seeking its prey. Her vision watched its dance, the way its energy seemed to track the movement she herself had been watching with interest. Without pause for thought she placed her hand to Bray's back. Forcing him from the safety of the path and beyond the barrier of light encasing the town. The tendrils grew angry, clinging to the metal until it was akin to Medusa's hair, hissing and writhing to become a force of power so intense it left the contraption with a deafening crack, streaking through the air towards its foe. It was with no small measure of relief she watched as the creature recoiled retreating back into the shadows.

"What the—"

"They will not hurt *you,* remember?" she shrugged nonchalantly.

"I said they won't *devour* me. It was betwixt and between if they harmed me," Bray fumed, his cold glare held her while the slight crinkling around the corner of his eyes suggested he was not nearly as annoyed as his tone portrayed. He had known she wanted to test the weapon, and their journey here had been uneventful to the point they both had wondered if this device could protect anyone. He shuffled back onto the lit path, huffing out a sigh.

"Oh, it appears you were fortunate then."

"I will consent to you exploring *any* of your whims at my expense, but desist this attitude immediately," Bray growled seriously. "Do not think your nonchalance has me fooled, but it may deceive those to whom your outlook matters most. Mark me well, Mistress Lain Exerevnitis, the allies you seek *will* know they are samded before the weapon even touches their hand. Most will not expect to return, most will gladly stand in the face of conflict if they think it's a battle of worth. You will *not* treat them with the disregard you just showed me in order to shield your own remorse. Their lives have been shorter than yours. They have friends, family, loved ones. They are not tools, they will offer the most valuable thing they possess because you will ask it of them. You will show them the respect they are due."

"Do you think I am unaware of this? I have seen countless mortals perish during my lifetime," Elly stated flatly, adjusting her hat.

"And that is precisely why you conceal yourself behind this callous shield now. I saw that spark of passion you deny yourself, the reality hidden beneath the shield forged from too many years of loss and remorse. The soldiers who will take up arms will not do so because it is their duty." Bray stepped before her, reaching forward to smarten her hair slightly. "They will do it because the Lady of Knightsbridge, daughter of Lord Blackwood, asks it of them, and she must be the person she has always been to them, their protector, not their callous executioner. You oversaw Blackwood's domain in his stead and ensured they had food in times of famine, and water in times of drought. You faced a hydra for this very city to ensure the safety of those who lived here. It was you who protected them, and they will not hesitate to fight should you ask it of them."

"Then they are fools." Elly felt the words almost stick in her swollen throat. She turned away from Bray, hating how easily he read her. He had seen both her excitement and turmoil. Almost no one had ever seen beyond the character she portrayed. She remained cold and calculated because lifetimes of grief had taught her to distance herself, and still despite the act it was a lesson she had never truly learnt. That Bray had recognised this in her was infuriating.

"No, they are the bravest and most loyal people you know, and that's why it hurts."

"I have watched many of them grow from children, just as I watched the port grow from nothing at the hands of their distant relatives. Even before the facade with Blackwood, before providences and monarchs, this port has been my home. It was here I met my first husband, and his distant relatives still live here to this day," Elly whispered, lowering her head slightly cursing the rising emotions she had once so easily pushed aside and sealed away. Over the centuries she had taken many husbands and wives, but he had been her first. A man she had married for no other reason than love, and now she would ask for aid from what little of his bloodline remained, and in doing so perhaps even end his line forever.

If there was one regret she harboured from her first love, it had been the fact as a golem she could never birth a child. His family continued on through brothers and sisters, and a promise passed on dying lips was sworn that she would watch over them. As decades past, she aided from afar in discrete ways, from negotiating with the hydra to send great hauls their way, to ensuring when the Severaine struck the one person capable of aiding them found their way to this port. It was by no coincidence Chrissie had heard this location had been devastated. While rarely present this town was hers, its people one remaining fragment of her love. She flinched as Bray placed his hand upon her chin, raising her gaze to meet his own, pulling her from her thoughts.

"Is it not better they die for hope, rather than without it? Tell me, would you rather face overwhelming odds for those you love, or wait hopelessly for a threat to consume both you and them? I understand, why do you think I sought your aid in the first place? Creatures such as myself rarely have the luxury of kinship, but I would die beside Rob, against impossible odds, before I drove a wedge of distance between us to spare myself the grief."

"You are correct. I cannot be distant. Why should I hide and protect myself while they risk everything at my request? No, I must be the person they need me to be, the leader they would be proud to serve under. Thank you, Bray, for clarifying things. I will not only fight and bleed beside them, I will lead their charge."

"Wait, what?" Bray questioned abruptly.

"You are right. Blackwood's people have always looked to me to guide them. This time should be no different, I will be their point man."

"What you're suggesting would be suicide, you can't be—"

"Sacrifice," she corrected sternly, "and why should I ask something of them that I am unwilling to give myself." Elly hesitated briefly outside the modest dwelling. Light escaping from the small cracks beneath the door cast an eerie glow upon the ocean mist clinging to the damp cobblestone paving. "Once we have successfully produced our first duplicate, take the one you have to your comrade. Stand by yours as I will stand by mine."

"As you wish, but remember our agreement. You will only get your answers once my friend has his weapon, so you will need to survive."

"I think if I survive I may already have an answer, do you not agree?" Elly chuckled.

"Answers are often allusive, and truth can change. I will see you on the battlefield, Cerelia." Elly's lips parted as she heard him speak this name. She felt a warmth flood through her as the shadows of another voice whispered that name. When she was a young girl her mother had died, passing her into the care of her employer, a man who felt responsible for her mother's death, and yet had orchestrated it for his own gains.

When asked her name as a child she had called herself Lain. As was so often the case in her era, nicknames were formed by adding ikin to the end of a name, and shortening it. Those named Cerelia became Laikin further shortened to Lain. As the years past the name given to her by her mother became lost and forgotten in a shaded history and from Lain her other aliases, Elaineor, Elly, and Lee were born. Bray's words had not only given her something she thought had been lost through time, but something so much more, certainty. She knew now, without a doubt, he could give her the answers she sought. If he knew enough to address her as such then he surely knew all there was to know.

"Why did you call me that?" Elly questioned softly.

"Because I want you to have no doubt as to who you are, and who you have been. The name Cerelia means both mistress and lady, so let your actions from hereon reflect that."

"We have delayed enough, let us begin." Elly balled her hand into a fist and knocked upon the door. There was work to be done. She glanced back towards Bray. "And, Grayson, *never* call me that again."

* * *

The groans and sighs of the ancient roots once more parting, disturbing the forest around them with its slow movement was all the prompt required for Zo and Seiken to rise from the small mound of dried leaves where they had sat waiting. For a moment, as the figure stepped from the darkness below they remained motionless, watching as she inhaled deeply. As her bare feet touched the autumn leaves her attire evolved and adapted, absorbing the colours around her to create supple garments in preparation for their journey.

"Alana." Zo, unable to hold herself back any longer, rushed forward to place her hand on her daughter's forehead and assess the damage. Her striking blue eyes, which had once been the mirror image of her own, had altered, but they were not quite what she had expected to see. She cupped her hands on either side of Alana's face to study her more intently, an act which caused Zo to realise exactly how much their child had grown.

Her electric blue irises had dulled, clouded over and yet, the manner in which they had done so was spectacular. Looking into her daughter's eyes was like staring at some of the most breathtaking astronomical sights she had ever bore witness to. The clouding in her eyes looked like the gas and dust of spiralling galaxies while different colour saturations shone from within, appearing as pinpricks of blue and purple stars. The whites of her eyes had once turned bloodshot causing fire to outline the iris in golds and reds before fading into the white background.

"Phoenix protected me as best he could, but even his power was limited in regard to this," Alana explained as her mother's touch remained. "From your silence it must be worse than I imagined," she assessed with a shrug. Once more her voice betrayed an age unexpected for a person of her current appearance.

"Alana, you're beautiful." Seiken encouraged his wife to withdraw her touch.

"So much so that I rendered you speechless?"

"Remember a few months ago, when the observatory showed you the Helix Nebula," Seiken began, he saw his daughter frown no doubt trying to recall something that, for her, happened so long ago.

"Indeed," her tone was unimpressed, bordering on pouting which brought a smile to his face. "They said it was a giant eye, watching, ready to tell on me if I caused any more trouble." Despite the years that had passed for her, Alana remembered the sight well. As a child her stomach had tightened and she had been filled with fear, truly believing there was something out there, an eye in the sky, that watched her every move and reported on her actions. It had made sense at the time, after all, her family had always known when she was up to mischief, even with whole rooms separating them. She had sworn to behave, and not try to sneak in and use their toys again. Despite being terrified, now she recalled the image she remembered its beauty.

"Well, let's just say it's a sight that pales to you." He reached out, stroking his daughter's face. Alana raised her lips in an empty smile.

"Is it far to The Caves of the Wind? We should not keep Sylph waiting."

"What was the cost?" Zo questioned, a little harsher than intended. Her daughter's smile had brought a flood of unwelcome memories. She had seen such an empty smile before. She herself had worn it often.

"Inherited magic, that which I received from your heritages." Alana touched the bracelet that was still secured upon her wrist. Time had been kind to the leather charm. She remembered it as a gift from her grandfather and, over the last three years, had developed a habit of fidgeting with it. She liked the feel of its varying textures against her fingers. While being coarse leather it also felt soft, like a cooling breeze where it touched her flesh. She remembered thinking how it had felt different when she had been with Pigí. "Grandfather's too, I guess," she whispered through chattering teeth, realising for the first time how cold it was now she was no longer in a domain dominated by flame and heat. Seiken touched her shoulder, and she felt the comforting weight of a warm hide coat form from the magic imbued within her clothes.

"That was a powerful gift," Seiken observed thoughtfully. No less than three types of magic flowed through his wife's blood alone. Zoella had been born of a union between a god and a mortal of an ancient Elven ancestry, not only that, in life she had been the last wielder of Hectarian magic and, for a brief moment, become a Primitive, a servant to magic itself, as she had battled against Marise Shi. As for himself, he was a timeless and powerful being, not only the Prince of Dreams, but something so much more, something his own people could not see. He possessed two souls, and both were his own, one was his from when he was born an Oneiroi, but his true power lay within the second soul, the primal soul of the wyrm god that he sheltered and protected as its reincarnation. That gift of magic had been no small price, nor had the immortality she had offered to the Water Spirit. He almost feared what the remaining two would ask of her.

"Is saving the souls of the innocent something that can be gratified with a price?" Alana questioned, tilting her head to one side slightly.

"No, you misunderstood. When one magic is removed it leaves a void that in the presence of other magical beings will, overtime, be filled. What you received was powerful."

"I don't understand, explain."

"Very well." As he turned his open hand over particles from his clothing drew towards it, reforming, spiralling and condensing upon his outstretched hand until within his grasp he held a small saucer filled with water, upon which stood a candle covered by a glass beaker. "Inside the beaker is air, in this scenario it will represent the gift you gave. The water will be the attunement you require to be able to use the phoenix' element. In their current state there is no possibility of change, but by lighting the candle"—the wick sprung to life at his request, burning with a dull yet fierce flame—"that's to say removing your magic, a void is created allowing the vessel to draw whatever is needed from their environment." Seiken gestured towards his display as the candle extinguished to leave the beaker half filled with water. "As you can see, the water doesn't occupy all of the glass, there is still a void, a place neither claimed by your old magic or new. Your body will naturally compensate for this vacuum which will allow you to use the two elements you possess in unison. Fire, and water, such hybrid magic needs its own reserves which are created from this process meaning you won't just be able to use fire or water, you can use both in combination.

"Sylph will build on this also, making this hybrid foundation larger. I would pose that your dream magic would be another toll, it's not something inherited, but something natural to those of Darrienia, and would have worked to transfer hereditary skills into ones that can be used in our world, as for what the last thing could be, I don't know of anything left which would create such power," Seiken mused.

"Speaking of Sylph," Alana interjected, "we should be on our way. Thank you for the explanation."

Seiken exchanged a quick glace with Zo, their daughter had always enjoyed watching his simple 'non-magic, magic tricks,' as she called them, but now it didn't even raise a smile. He closed his eyes, groaning slightly as he realised what he had done. The fact she had not thought to mention her lack of vision rendering his demonstration ineffective, reminded him she was growing up quicker than he and Zo had ever expected. When her next trial was completed, they would be more like travelling companions, than parent and child.

* * *

Whilst he knew there was no need to hurry for his own safety, Bray found himself atop a 'borrowed' mount, pushing it to move faster. He himself had little cause to fear the Skiá, and if they opted to turn on one sharing their own blood, thanks to Elly, he had the means to defend himself. Rob, on the other hand, would not be so fortunate. It was only thanks to the blacksmith he had some notion as to where his friend would be found, eventually.

His and Elly's parting had been nothing more than a promise to meet on the battlefield. Once Rob had the weapon Elly was owed some answers, and he would fulfil his obligations. The blacksmith, Tony, had started smelting the necessary items to fashion a better version of the weapon he now possessed. With the supplies he had gathered while Elly talked Tony through the process, he had little doubt they could outfit a small platoon. His only concern was, with the amount that could be fashioned, there would still not be enough.

The gnawing in his stomach warned him of the ever increasing number of Skiá. Instinctively he knew when they gathered enough energy from devouring essences, they could birth a new creature by asexual reproduction. The more they devoured, the more their numbers increased, and their reach had spread far.

Long grasses whipped across the mount's legs sending spiralling seeds rising into the darkness above, their pale pappus consumed by the blanket of darkness. Even the vibrant shades of wild flowers were muted as they bowed their head to the artificial night as if in prayer. But no prayer of this blackened land would be answered, even should the Gods wish to intervene the stifling operation of the ebony clouds would cushion their ears to even the most desperate of pleas.

The horse he rode had been encouraged into submission, this alone was the reason it was not overwhelmed with the panic any living thing should feel in the presence of such monsters. He knew the moment the mount was free of his influence it would bolt. As such he drew it right to the thick brier that protected the entrance to the forest where he and Rob had ventured once before.

Elly, having heard Tony relay the tale of Daniel's visit, knew Daniel well enough to understand some of his thought processes. If he were to attempt to retrieve this ore, then he would have recruited someone with detailed knowledge of The Depths, and Elly's former protege, Rob, would be the logical choice. Neither had made the connection between Bray's friend and her young ward from the Courts of Twilight until Bray had spoken of Rob's countless journeys to The Depths during small talk as they had walked from Eidolon. But having heard how this man braved The Depths, she had been certain his friend and her old student were one and the same.

To see his friend standing beside the worn rafters of the ancient well would have been too much to ask for. There were tracks, signs of movement but the heavy brush had been so disturbed it was impossible to discern if the newest tracks were even created by human footfall. For a brief moment, as he watched the hypnotic dance of the scarcely visible motes of light from his shelter, he wondered if his plan had been too hasty.

There was no way of knowing if they had already departed. Teasing rustles of the wind through scantly foliaged trees seemed to hold more than just the whispers of autumn's song. Crouching, he listened, his hand upon the cold earth as he isolated each sound and movement. He was not alone and knew even the shadows walked in whispers. His grip tightened upon the crudely fashioned tool in his grasp, it was better to avoid using such methods for as long as his hearing would warn him of danger's approach. Elly had been correct, this tool was dangerous. He shuddered envisioning what any great number combined could do. His knuckles turned white, his fingers cramping the sweet scent of the flowers surrounding the well grew fainter as he turned silently. He had just been about to search for further tracks when he heard the familiar voice of his friend coming now from beside the well.

Bray spun, his need for stealth discarded as the darkness stirred and whispered as it glided towards its unsuspecting prey. Brambles clung, snagging his clothes adding precious seconds of delay as he realised how far from the monument he had strayed. In his hand, the weapon sprang to life at his will, the tendrils cracklings excitedly, reaching out in the direction of the threat, ready to strike. He pushed his legs harder, begging the energy to unleash, he needed to be closer, faster. The shadow's touch was almost upon them. The energy from his weapon writhed as his feet skidded in the loose debris as he thrust himself before them causing the lightning to discharge in a display that even Zeus himself would have appreciated. The shadow recoiled, but the tendrils were still wild and angry, unsettled on which direction they should face as unearthly sounds echoed around them. He didn't dare question how it knew what to attack, assuring himself this magic would rise to challenge anything he or it deemed a threat.

"How'd you find us?" Rob questioned in awe, watching as his friend wielded an unknown power against their would be attackers.

"You didn't take heed of my advice," Bray observed, grimacing at the levels of poison still within his friend's blood. One reason travelling with Rob had been so easy was because, even if Bray slipped into a frenzy, the blood coursing through Rob's veins was unappealing due to the high toxicity produced by the generous amounts of alcohol he consumed.

"Good job, if you sniffed me out like some kind of hound," Rob teased with a lopsided grin.

"That is *not* what happened," Bray assured.

"Yet here you are."

"I could just as easily leave, and take my weapon with me." As Bray raised the metal shaft another bolt of magic struck out, causing the encroaching shadows to once more recede.

"What is that?" Daniel questioned, stepping forward to look upon the prongs of energy expanding from the surface. He stepped back suddenly, noticing the cost for its use.

"Indeed, you're wise to be cautious, Wita." Bray flashed him a smile, surprised to see it caused Daniel to blush. A realisation that suggested he was hungrier than he believed. He had intended to eat at the port, but his path had only crossed with Tony and, strangely, his palate had not responded at all to the hulking figure's presence.

"It's stripping the energy of nature to generate magic, it's deadly." Daniel crouched, examining the ground close to Bray's feet.

"That's where you and Elly are in agreement," Bray advised, "but the scales have to be balanced, we can't leave the Skiá unaddressed and this is all we—"

"It's genius!"

"Wait, what?" Rob intervened hearing the unmistakable excitement within the Wita's voice.

"How many of these are at your disposal?"

"This was the prototype," Bray responded, wondering how both Elly and Daniel could be so instantly excited about something so blatantly dangerous.

"And you, are there any adverse effects?"

He circled Bray a little too closely, his fingers tracing across his shoulders as he sought for any indication of a toll on his body. "Not that I know to... well, I feel heavier. The pressure of the energy makes me less reactive, slower," Bray assessed.

"Who are you arming with these?"

"Elly is gathering those who will follow her to battle. But I hear you had other plans?"

"Yes, we'll need that too. But this is just what we were missing!" Daniel's eyes seemed to sparkle. "If we execute things just right, we could even win!"

"You've lost me," Rob began.

"The power of these is just what we need. Our weapons, once forged, will injure the Skiá, maybe to the same extent as the magic from this does." He gestured wildly towards Bray.

"Wait, hold on," Rob interjected, pushing his hand through his hair. "So you have two weapons that you believe can only injure the creatures."

"He's talking about using it's other effect." Bray, seeing Rob's confusion, motioned towards the spreading death at his feet. Elly had suggested the exact same thing, she was only lacking in one aspect of her plan. In order to utilise this force scattered troops were of no use. She needed a means to draw the Skiá to a single location so the combined effect of the damage they were causing would be enough to draw the only thing capable of stopping the Skiá.

"Can we do that much damage?" Rob asked in disbelief, now clear on their unspoken intentions.

"We have to. There's no way we alone can stop them. We need something greater than ourselves, something so powerful that it has sparked fear in every generation of god since the dawn of time. We need the Severaine."

Chapter 27

Preperation

Long ago Sylph had made his home within the Caves of the Wind. At this time, there had been many who mirrored his nature. The sylph were beings of beauty once thought to have been human. Many of his kin had been female, for more often they were found to be more vain than the male. It was said vanity was impure and in great excess corrupted the essence to a point that even the Underworld could not claim the soul. So in a way, those corrupted became echoes, shades walking the land, but their inability to pass through the Gate of Shades made them different in nature, and this difference was how the sylph were born. This was but one of the tales Alana had heard, another was that they had always been Spirits of Air, and it was they who controlled the clouds and mists with the beating of their wings. There were more tales of origin than she could count, but she had appreciated her parents recounting them whilst they walked through the forest. It made the uneasiness that hung between them just a little more bearable.

There were more theories than could be remembered but, over time, like the power which sustained the creatures, the myths faded. With the Severaine sealed, and the Star of Arshad removed from the Mountain of the Spirits, the magical balance faltered, driving creatures of myth and legend to seek refuge in places of magical significance. The final calamity had come with the sealing of Hectarian magic. Even the power of the ley lines faltered and the sylph, along with other lesser mythical creatures, began to fade until only he, their king who ruled from the Caves of the Wind, could exist outside his domain.

The caves had a power of their own, bestowed upon them by a consciousness far beyond the understanding of the gods. This deiform blessing had protected both himself and the gateway to his realm; just as being sealed in the temple of Hephaestus and bound to the eternal flame had sustained the phoenix during these dire times.

Each of the four had their own story about how they survived the fading magic and retained a presence on the land, keeping it in order and balance. There were, however, seven Spirits, and these beings through their existence created balance. For one to cease its existence would be for calamity to befall the land and for balance forever be turned askew. They had been made to protect the world, maintain the balance, and retain order while the primordial gods defended their realms against the enemies who attempted to infiltrate the small part of the great unknown they had claimed for their own.

When Gaea had first gifted mankind with her own vein of magic, it had been from the source of these Great Spirits that Elemental magics had been born. That four still remained unbound was the sole reason this magic still endured. Whatever had occurred to bind Light, Darkness, and Spirit had placed a seal at the very core of that tree of magic and as time continued to pass the results were becoming more apparent.

With equal absence also came a balance. As seasons changed darkness would rise and fall, ebb and flow in natural tides, keeping rhythm with the world and nature. But that balance had now shifted. Darkness filled the land and with no Spirit of Light to correct the flow and restore harmony there was only one hope to staunch the rising tide that consumed them. That hope was the Mitéra, the only person capable of standing in the presence of the one who had discarded the natural order.

In banishing Íkelos lay the only solution. Without him to sustain the breach the creatures would be forced into retreat allowing the fabric between the worlds to repair and a precarious equilibrium to emerge. Yet the cost of this one action had far spanning repercussions, some of which could only be spoken about hypothetically. With all the guardian Spirits sealed the world would begin a gradual decline for without these Spirits air would become stale, water stagnant, fires die and soil become barren, without these Spirits the very life of Gaea would slowly fade. There would be enough energy of them within the Mitéra's essence that she could conjure small boons, and she would need all the blessings she could muster when the time came for her to begin her journey to the shrines to free those who would be bound.

"We're here," Alana announced. She was aware her father had been talking before this, but her attention had strayed to this warning tale, something both Pigí and Phoenix had spoken of with her before she left.

The Caves of the Wind were a place which gave birth to many fables, tales of their magnificence were heard far and wide. This awe-inspiring mountain range towered high across the large southeastern peninsular of Albeth, lining the coast and descending into the waters below. The forests which covered the remainder of this land had adapted to the icy breeze forced from the caves. Some said, beneath this land Gaea slumbered and the wind drawn in and released by this landmark was her gentle breath. The new breath being expelled was cold, waiting to be warmed by stories of the world before returning to her.

There were secrets hidden and lost within these caves. Kronos himself had used the intricate caverns and waterways below to store an item he thought would one day help him reclaim his throne. This relic of the Titans was long gone now—retrieved by Marise Shi during her quest for the Grimoire—but even with its absence the caves' power did not falter, and thus, Sylph had remained sheltered when magic had all but been lost. The release of the Severaine had seen a new order arise. The potency of magic was returning, and this devastating force punished any who sought to harm Gaea, while creatures who relied upon magic to exist, returned from slumber.

The icy wind chased across the land, dipping long grasses as they bowed to its powerful presence. The cushioned sound of life beneath their feet dulled, replaced by the hollow echo of their boots upon the rocky terrain. Whilst the entrances were many, the choices for a beginning were few. Each cave would somehow connect to the others, and it would be Alana's place to uncover the secrets within. Her parents could go no further.

"Alana." Zo took her daughter's hand within her own, her vision shifting from the cave's darkened maw to their intertwined fingers for a brief moment before raising her gaze.

"I understand. For you but a few hours will pass, be safe." Alana slipped her hand from Zo's to approach the opening before her. Seiken wrapped his arm around his wife, drawing her near as Alana walked with an unsteady gait, the toes of her boots scuffing the ground while her outstretched arms sought guidance. They watched as their child reached the opening, her hands tracing the porous rock before her journey continued and her small frame became consumed by the darkness within.

"We're the parents, shouldn't we be the ones protecting her?" Zo asked softly.

"By blood alone, Thea. Alana may be our daughter, but we are not the ones raising her. She is destined for something far greater than you or I could have offered. An immortal forced to mortal planes to be raised and trained by the Spirits. She is what was intended for the Mitéra from the beginning."

"I don't understand,"

"When the Great Spirits first took a Mitéra, it was a means to prevent the elements from war. Each one bound itself to a single essence so they could keep their opposing forces in balance. When this divine essence was lost the Great Spirits attempted to claim a mortal to fulfil the role of keeping peace between gods, spirits, monsters, and mortals."

"But our time has never known a Mitéra."

"Few have. Part of this reason will be due to the imprisonment of the Spirit Elemental, and the unexplained loss of those of light and darkness."

"But that alone isn't the whole reason, or Alana could not become the Mitéra now."

"In the past, the mortals chosen for this role by the Spirits have all failed. The force of the elements within them, combined with their own life experiences saw them corruptible. Ultimately, their paths would turn from salvation to destruction. But a Mitéra should walk neither path. Like a Hectarian they should strive to keep a balance, but those raised by humans often see favour in their own kind. A true Mitéra should not differentiate between species, merely assess intention.

"Alana will keep order, and broker treaties between magical beings and humans. She will be the one to hold all things accountable, and because of this she will become the single most feared force this world has seen. Empires will be built around her, some seeking to please her, others wishing her demise. She will herald the return of the old order, and there are many who will be displeased to see such a change on the horizon."

"Is it wise for one person to hold such power?"

"What I speak of is a long time in the future, and some tasks awaiting her will seem impossible, but if she succeeds, she will herald a new dawn."

"Why are you telling me this now?"

"I see you are struggling." Seiken pulled her into a firm embrace, kissing the top of her head gently with a tenderness that caused her skin to heat. "Knowing this, the future which could await her, may lessen your burden." His voice held a hopeful lilt as he looked upon her.

"We forced this choice upon her," Zo whispered, wrapping her arms around Seiken tightly, her eyes prickled with tears as her focus rested on the monumentous range before her. It was a network of subterranean tunnels, a maze whose very purpose was to disorientate and repel, and now her child, her blind child, had entered alone with nothing to guide her on her path other than her own destiny.

"No, she chose it."

"How can it be a choice when to do nothing was to end all life?"

"Doing nothing was still a choice."

* * *

Elly stalked the streets of Semiazá Port, a lantern held high despite the lighthouse's illumination. The rings of light amplified by the ocean mist were a beacon for those who trailed behind her. While apprehension stilled their voices, their footsteps echoed down the damp and winding streets as she led them through the maze-like entryways towards her goal. With weapons in hand, it mattered not if they strayed into the shadows and so the shortest route was travelled swiftly. She glanced over her shoulder, a half smile on her lips.

She had spoken of threats, of heroes and honour, and they had followed her without question. Taking up arms willing to fight and die beside her in the name of this cause, in her name. Whilst there had been no shortage of volunteers, she had chosen but a few, those who suited her needs. Yet she needed more allies and there was but one place where she still held favour. Knightsbridge. But therein lay a problem. Even on the fastest transport, armed as they were, the journey would take days. It was time she did not have to spare, time she would not have to think about had Collateral not been sealed. So when she had seen that first marker, the first white pebble that shone a pale blue as if touched by enchanted moonlight, it was as though her prayers had been answered.

The blue stones converged before a doorway, their illumination still visible despite the light flooding out past the partially drawn drapes. Its light was blinding and created by a fire few could stoke. The house, by normal standards for those in this profession, was not just modest, it was diminutive.

"Wizard!" Elly struck the door thrice in summons noting the warmth from the wooden panelled door increase with each impact. He had stoked the fire, but it seemed the spell was less than stable if her knock could cause its heat to shudder. She knew when Hectarian magic had been extinguished the fleeting number of wizards had taken to the shadows under the pretence their magic too had failed. They had faded into the background, using their skills to turn profit and embrace a usually luxurious life-style.

From somewhere just inside she heard an almost silent curse uttered, followed by the creaking of footsteps on ancient floorboards. "I am Elaineor, Lady of Knightsbridge, you did not ward, your steps are audible, and I seek your aid." Something resembling a large sigh sounded from the other side of the wooden barricade.

"Well, best you come in then, you *and* your army." The voice was younger than she had expected, but sound meant nothing to those who could manipulate the very waves of energy and magic. She placed her hand upon the metal handle. The tarnished surface was cool against her grasp while the wooden door itself still roiled with heat. It turned smoothly, offering neither protest nor resistance as it opened inward to reveal a black-haired young man. He squirmed slightly under her scrutiny, straightening his over sized moth eaten robe. He was not at all what she expected. "Yes I get that a lot." He seemed to shrink a little before her gaze. "As for what you seek, yes, I can, but it will need to be two groups." Passing him a weapon from her stash she raised an eyebrow at him quizzically. "Of course I know to dispose of it once the threat is gone." He gave a pained sigh, turning his grey eyes towards the ceiling for the briefest moment before taking a few steps backwards as Elly gestured for her army—as he had referred to them—to step inside. The uneven floorboards creaked and groaned in protest as the small group filtered inside. Each one of them casting a brief but fearful gaze towards the lanterns burning with wizard's fire suspended from the wooden ceiling rafters.

"Do not touch anything," she warned, seeing one of her group extend a hand towards a shelf filled with amber bottles. A small smile lifted the man's features making him appear momentarily younger.

"I've been expecting you since you started recruiting, knew you'd find me." He sighed a third time, slapping his hands at his side as the small crowd shuffled in. "Your kind always do."

"Since words are clearly not required—" Elly waited. The last wizard her path had crossed with had no gift for reading thought waves.

"No I'll not come. Someone's gotta look after the young ones. Wouldn't be much of a guardian if I left them would I? Knightsbridge is it?" Elly gave a nod, narrowing her eyes. By now she would normally have seen the tell of a glamour, be it a shimmer of light or the smallest fracture in image. But his guise of a young twenty-year-old held firm. "Shall we?" Kicking a large dusty rug aside from the furthest part of the room he smiled, his eyes brightening with the gesture as he encouraged her towards the runic circle. "No offence, but I don't want you here longer than needed. You'll bring trouble to my threshold. Split your troops and swear you'll leave me be. I'm not causing trouble for anyone."

"You would do better to shed the robes if its obscurity you seek. I know of no wizard who still wears them." She smiled slightly as he pushed the long sleeve up to his elbows. Elly nodded as she motioned for half the men and women to join her.

"I don't usually wear them," he defended a little too quickly as Elly began to divide the small group of people. With the first group decided, she turned her focus back towards the young man, he had shuffled in worn slippers towards one of the many book-lined shelves, his fingers tracing the spines of the tomes casting a spray of fine dust into the air with his hurried movements. After a few moments his finger paused, tapping a book before sliding the ancient tome from its resting place.

Approaching the runic circle she watched him cast a cursory glance over the awaiting group before the crinkling sound of ancient parchment brought an even heavier silence to the air. Opening the thick, weighty pages he blew three times across the scattered letters upon the page, forcing them into their correct formations to reveal the spell. His hand held the slightest tremor as it was placed upon the time-worn upon the page, his face contorting in concentration.

"Wait, you are a novice?" she asked in alarm, seeing the words of power animate upon the page as they began to ascend his tanned fingers, his aura swelled with the power of the words as the black ink danced just beneath his skin, the letters and symbols marking each visible part of flesh in perpetual motion. He lifted his gaze to hers with a sheepish smile.

"Good luck." He raised his arms in a magnificent, somewhat flamboyant, gesture. She opened her mouth to protest, but before a word had even formed she was struck by the release of power, words scarred the air with mystical energy, activating the symbols beneath the group's feet. Her world became nothing more than characters and blinding flashes of light until the ink dancing before her flashed in the final throes of a raging storm and everything became dark. Wind chased through unseen streets as Elly hurried her disorientated allies aside, her own vision still not recovered. It was only mere seconds before the remainder of her modest group appeared exactly where they had stood just moments ago.

"Blasted wizards," Elly snorted, as several of her group vomited from the less than comfortable transition. All things considered it could have been much worse. She had never known a novice to control so much wizard's fire unaided before, but a promise was a promise, even once this journey was over she would leave the young man in peace. "The residents will be seeking shelter in the town hall," Elly assessed, watching as the sparking weapons flared to life, firing bolts of energy in rapid succession. "I should thank the Research Plexus. Let us see who has survived and make plans for our attack."

* * *

With the use of the irfeláfa, the return to Semiazá Port had been far easier than Bray had anticipated. He was more than a little relieved not to have to make the long trek, especially without any form of transport. The Festival of Hades was drawing near, with just a final sinking of the sun between them and what would be the final stand between Man and shadow. Darkness had smothered the light and yet still distant glimmers, like stars across a blackened sky, gave rise to hope as towns and cities heeded the warnings carried to them on the wings of messenger birds.

Despite how quickly their journey had been completed, Elly was no where to be found.

* * *

When Elly had departed she had left Tony, and those under his protection, with two of the crafted weapons at their disposal to ensure their safety now that the sanctuary had been breached. There had been brief talks of further replicating the devices, and whilst Tony watched with a knowing smirk, he saw the frustrations rise as the remaining artisans were unable to duplicate what their collective group had accomplished. He knew Elly well enough to know that the final part of the forging had been completed by her own hand to ensure these devastating devices remained few in number. To have such a thing reproduced at whim would be as dangerous as the Skiá themselves.

In lowered tones, with muted words, Elly had sworn to him that once the threat had passed, so too would the weapons become useless. As the hulking figure had cast his sight over the prototype he had come to the conclusion this vow had something to do with the enchantment and carvings which she had scored upon the surface of all but the original.

Seeing Daniel standing besides Bray his first reaction had been one of disappointment. His stomach sank, until he saw not a trace of defeat in the young man's eyes. Reflected within them was something he had seen before, hope, and whilst the figure before him appeared empty-handed, as his vision searched him, he felt his skin prickle in anticipation. Tony gestured Daniel towards the forge, following him after exchanging quiet words with Bray regarding Elly's intentions.

Tony had given the young man barely moments alone, and yet when he entered the secured area he was astounded to behold the vast quantities of metal now filling his workshop. Large and jagged trees shimmered throwing dazzling reflections from his forge's embers. These magnificent specimens had been carefully arranged, ensuring a clear path to the stone hearth and firepot.

Approaching with care, Tony closed his eyes, his calloused hands caressing the metal trees as the ore sung to him its secrets. He touched it softly, with every bit the care and tenderness he had once used when caressing his wife, and his expert touch revealed its every mystery. What once had been discarded from Olympus for its impurities, had been beautifully reformed into an ore of the likes one such as he had only dreamt of.

"Daniel can you secure the castings?" Tony broke the silence. He gestured towards the hip height container which stretched from one side of the room to the other, reluctant to relinquish his touch upon the seductive metal. A small smile tickled his lips as he saw Daniel's expression, no doubt wondering if such a structure had been present when last he had visited here.

The skin around Tony's aged eyes crinkled in eager anticipation of what was to come. Every blacksmith dreamed of forging their crowning glory, an item which reflected their very soul. For Tony it had always been his unfinished business. Never had he encountered a metal that needed his touch, nor an individual worthy of unlocking his true potential. Until now.

* * *

As Daniel approached the area Tony had indicated, he noticed the large container was filled with sand. The tops of small partitions were just visible peaking from the sand. In the centre of each was a corked clay mould. Hoping to be of aid, Daniel walked the length slowly, checking the positioning and stability of each. With his task finished he returned his focus to Tony, astonished to find a number of the metal trees had already succumbed to Tony's skilled hand.

Wiping the soft glistening sweat from his brow, Daniel turned towards the forge to regard it suspiciously. Being close to it he could feel the heat pouring from the embers, and yet along with the heat came a frigid air. Instead of negating the heat, the two intense temperatures seemed to work in unison to both scald and freeze. He would have liked to examine this peculiar phenomenon more, but his need to focus on the instructions from Tony made dwelling on such things impossible, and his concentration saw the whispers which may have offered answers silenced.

"Give me a hand with this," Tony requested.

Daniel followed his lead, pulling on the thick elbow length gloves as Tony demonstrated how to remove the small white hot vat from the glowing fire with a pair of tongues. He guided Daniel through the process, removing the cork from the mould before lifting the lid from the molten fluid. As Daniel followed Tony's direction, he noticed the liquid was not the orange to yellow shades he had come to expect from molten metals, it seemed to glow pure white.

When the many smelting pots had been emptied into the casings Tony approached the next tree.

Removing his gloves, Tony clapped his hands, rubbing them together vigorously before drawing a blade from his apron across his palm. He saw Daniel wince slightly, no doubt noticing the numerous slashes upon his hands from when he attended to the other trees. Rubbing his hands together again they became tainted with his ichor, once satisfied he approached the next tree, laying his hands upon it. At his touch the metal seemed to melt, becoming as mailable as putty.

Manipulating the size and shapes of the segments he removed, he placed them in the smelting pots, while offering a mischievous wink in Daniel's direction as he stood awestruck. "Did you really not see the fire in my soul?" The blacksmith laughed heartily. "This is what I was born to do, what all those of my line were born for. We are metal workers, blacksmiths, and the ore is ours to command."

"I assumed it was a metaphor," Daniel gaped, blinking as the forge somehow appeared larger than just moments before.

"Speak of this to no one, you are the first outsider to see our blood magic. Now, the latest molds will be fired, go set them in the other pit. The casting will save us time, but there's still much to do."

* * *

Alana hesitated. Hanging back within the shadows she listened to her parents discuss the future she would bring. Their confidence in her caused her chest to tighten. They spoke as if she had already vanquished the looming threat and freed the Spirits from the imprisonment that helping her would force upon them. She wished she shared their certainty.

A gentle whisper of icy wind tickled her face, encouraging her to realise it was time to move on. Phoenix had said the Spirit would guide her to the portal, but whilst the wind gently teased across her flesh, it did little to guide her uncertain steps. She stumbled forward as her foot twisted upon another dip, and this time she barely caught herself before tumbling to the ground. The path before her was littered with stones and debris, each one slowing her pace and making her blind journey more difficult.

It had become so easy to believe herself adapted to her blindness. In phoenix's realm she had navigated with ease, and even her journey here had been an easy walk. It was only now she was alone, struggling, falling, that she realised her error. She had known the fire realm's every nook due to her training and how it had been conducted, and here, absent her parents' subtle guiding touch she was having difficulties with even the simplest of obstacles.

She shivered against the growing cold, raising the collar she wrapped her coat around her tighter, bowing into her fingers in the hope of restoring some measure of warmth. Since leaving the fire realm she had been filled with an unnatural chill, one which intensified as the world around her became colder. She heard the slow transition from compacted earth to the crunching of ice beneath her feet, its smooth texture creating icy walkways across the once uneven surfaces. The bitter sting of the biting wind caressed her face once more, urging her to the right before a mighty gale erupted from her left with such force the sound of her clothes being beaten by the winds echoed as it chased its howling path.

The unmistakable pressure of the world above baring down upon her made her falter. The air was crisp and silent, and for a moment even the ever present howling of the winds seemed to die. Her fingers burned from the cold creating contradictory sensations across her flesh. She was so cold, and yet places of her felt aflame. Her brow furrowed, for a moment as she remembered that while burns would be left unfelt temperature was still able to create such strong sensations. Phoenix had told her it was due to the difference in the way the body responded. Pain caused one reaction, while thermodynamics created another. Even through the tingling of her fingers she was certain she felt something more, a tickle of familiar energy. She placed one hand to the cave wall while her other extended before her. With each step the sensation grew stronger until the hum of the portal's aura was all she could feel. With only a breath's worth of hesitation she passed through.

Alana paused once through the portal, straining her eyes, willing them to see. Each time she had traversed The Stepping Realm there had been a challenge for her to overcome. This room seemed silent and still. As she took a tentative step forward, the sound of gravel crunching beneath her feet made her stop once more. Bending, she scooped a handful of the small, loose stones, and tossed a few forwards. Silence was her only response, it seemed as if the area before her was nothing more than a gaping chasm. Bending down she removed her footwear, filling her socks with the small pebbles as an idea formed. Carefully she crawled forward, feeling for a walkway with her outstretched hands. To the left side was a thin beam, taking a few of the stones she scattered them forwards, listening until the noise upon the narrow surface stilled.

Her fingers curled around the sides of the narrow walkway as she progressed slowly, carefully feeling for each turn as she created a mental map of her route. Small beads of sweat trickled down her forehead, her stomach lurching as the path seemed to halt abruptly. Biting her lower lip she mentally retraced her steps, but thus far her path had not deviated. Removing a small handful of stones she began to scatter a few across the air before her, listening intently. The skittering of pebbles to her left brought relief, but as she extended her hand she found no ledge. Listening again as she released another handful she tried to gauge the distance before rising unsteadily to her feet. It was further than she was comfortable with, but there seemed little option. She threw a few more stones frowning as the small projectiles impacted upon her clothes. Reaching forward her hand located another ledge just above the height of her hips. With great care she pulled herself upward, not daring to question how it was supported in fear that such things would cause whatever magic conjured this room to collapse.

Over, under, down, and through, her journey reminded her of the time she learnt to tie her laces, and her own mental map had become as tangled and nonsensical in her mind as when her fingers had first tried to create a bow. No longer crawling, she walked tall, trusting her feet to alert her of any sudden alterations. Her pulse quickened as she realised how hopelessly lost she was, her mind filled with images of walking in endless circles and never finding reprieve.

When her toes curled beneath the firm texture of gravel, she feared she had walked a complete circle back to the start. The tickle of energy from the portal, however, offered her silent reassurances, its position opposite to the place she had first emerged. Rolling her shoulders she tried to shake free the tension before, with no small measure of relief, she entered sylph's realm.

Winds from the four cardinal directions chased over her flesh, bringing the touch and scent of all the four seasons to greet her. Blooming flowers contrasted against autumn decay, icy snow against summer's heat. The winds howled, calling out a greeting as they chased through the land. She could feel the warmth reflecting from the shelter she was within, and her mind's eyes brought to her an image of an impressive tree. This tree made even the ancient Fenikkusu seem like a sapling. The base was hollow, and where she stood, within its centre, was the place all four winds would meet.

"Mitéra cub, I thought I would have to retrieve you. My puzzle is not intended for one lacking in sight." The sylph were beautiful creatures, and none more so than their king. Whilst in the mortal realm he could assume the visage of a man, his natural form in this realm was that of a white tiger possessing wings feathered by mist. He used these magnificent appendages to form and shape the clouds, as well as direct and summon storms, just as myths had once suggested. But there was nothing even he could do to stir the dark blanket concealing the heavens from the land.

"The walkways were invisible." Alana realised, muttering her thought aloud. "The gravel was to help find the path."

"Correct. I used air pressure to create invisible platforms. You did well. Are you prepared to make a pact with me? If so I ask for something fleeting yet powerful, something that would provide inspiration and terror, hope and escape to mortals."

"You want my dreams?" Alana questioned.

"You show wisdom, but no. I don't seek your dreams, rather the magic you could use to give rise to them and influence their power."

"Dream magic? Phoenix already took my magic," Alana advised apologetically, heat flushing her skin as her stomach tightened in fear.

"He took that which you were gifted by your kin, not that given to you by the land in which you were born. Your natural birth magic is what I seek."

"I accept your terms, and offer my dream magic willingly." Alana closed her eyes, a meaningless gesture but one that helped to prepare her for what she knew was to come.

"When first we begin, I will teach you windsight. It will take some time to understand, but it will ease the burden of Phoenix's lessons."

"Windsight?"

"All will become clear, or clearer at least. Let us begin."

Chapter 28

Blades' Awakening

The clear chiming ring of the age-old hammer and anvil serenaded the workshop in a harmonious and rhythmic chorus. For a moment Daniel allowed his eyes to close, listening to the composition of all who had come to assist in this monumentous task while Bray stood guard, his weapon at the ready. The initial whispers of awe, as the brilliant shade of the crafted metal from Tony's cast, were soon replaced by strenuous murmurs punctuated with blood and sweat as people worked until their arms failed to lift the weight of a hammer, and another crafter took their place.

Glistening in the light of embers and magic just over one hundred blades lay ready. The metal had stretched further than any had imagined possible. At set intervals, Daniel would emerge, collecting scraps, filings, and shards returning them to the sealed forge where Tony would craft them into arrowheads. But the smelting and clay casting of ore was not all he had accomplished.

"Here." Tony approached Daniel as he entered with a pouch of newly collected fragments. The smell of flame and rancid sweat filled the forge area and, for the briefest moment, as he waited for Daniel to close the shutter between his forge and workshop, Tony looked upon those who had come with pride. Their work was crude, but without it the weapons would be useless. He had trained many apprentices in the art of polishing a blade, smoothing out the coarse edges, and sharpening it, and now he looked on with satisfaction as his own workers schooled those willing to assist. These blades were not intended to be used against one another; but having them tempered and treated as if they were, would only improve their function. Once they were polished, there was one final thing required, they key ingredient to the process, and it was something only he could do. Something his blood upon the metal had started.

"What's this?" Daniel questioned taking the small piece of wrapped leather from the giant man's hand.

"That's what eyes are for, take a look. I took measurements while you were busy, but I thought it might come in handy." Daniel removed two cylindrical objects from the pouch and looked at them with confusion. "I've not made anything like it before, so it's a first. Most of the swords back there will break once the fire leaves them, few will survive as only splints, and only those I take from birth to presentation will endure. You don't wield a sword, so I made you an enhancement." Tony gestured towards Daniel's staff.

Daniel unhooked his weapon from his belt, snapping it into one solid structure before presenting it to Tony. "As I suspected, there's some strong magic in there. This'll give you the protection of the blades, but it won't damage your wood." He slotted the two cylinders onto each end of the staff. Rubbing his fingers across the metal he stretched it slightly, fixing it in place before twisting a molten coil from one end to the other. As if knowing what was needed from him Daniel touched the staff, collapsing it into its fragments, and returned it to the blacksmith who smoothed, the metal's edges along the five separate segments. "Now it's what it should be." He passed the weapon back to Daniel as he surveyed his work. "That's one fine weapon you've got there."

"Thank you." Daniel grasped Tony's calloused hand in a show of appreciation. "I'll find some way to re—"

"Don't you be getting any notions about being indebted. I've told you before, I owe you a debt that can never be repaid."

"If you're certain." Tony nodded. "Then thank you, but from this day you should forget any notions about being indebted." Tony chuckled at hearing his own words turned back upon him.

"Come, I've six special weapons crafted by my hand from birth and they are awaiting presentation. Who you give them to is for you to decide, but know they can never be turned against you, nor will they be damaged in battle, except by one of its likeness or greater, and anything greater would belong to the Gods, and even you should take heed about meddling in their affairs."

"And you say I owe you no debt." Daniel shook his head in disbelief.

"Come now, I've just awakened a hundred blades, and the festival of Hades is nearly upon us. My time is short." Tony turned his back to Daniel, hoping his slight slip had been overlooked, when the young man spoke Tony's broad shoulders relaxed.

"The Festival of Hades what has that—" Daniel abruptly fell silent, his hand leaving an imprint in the dust-ladened wall that now offered him support. He hadn't factored in the time of year. Íkelos was drawing the Skiá through a tear between realms, but their numbers must be being limited by the strength of the veil. If he were to discover a means to create a permanent rift it could only be achieved during the time when the veil was at its thinest. In that one horrifying moment his blood turned to ice causing a cold sweat to prickle upon his skin. If Íkelos achieved this, their defeat would just be a matter of time. He wondered if anyone else had come to this same realisation.

* * *

The icy gale blustered through the trees, joining with the howling of the caves to create a melody found only in this one location. Shifting slightly, Seiken tried to find comfort as they sat upon the cold rocky terrain. The heat from Zo's body as she rested against him with her eyes closed was the only warmth he could find. He pulled her closer as her muscles twitched slightly, suggesting she was dreaming. Her ability to dream was a skill they would need to explore. It could this was nothing more than the manifestation of omnipresence, a skill to send an astral form to another location. Recently he knew her dreams had been prophetic, and with the spread of Íkelos' influence throughout her, it was likely their connection was becoming stronger. He felt her startle, her vision quickly surveying their surroundings.

"Íkelos is widening the tear," she whispered.

"You saw him?" Seiken kissed the top of her head delicately.

"He was somewhere below ground. It's taking all his strength to keep the fracture in place. It seems it is required to keep the Skiá active."

"There was something else?" Seiken questioned, sensing her hesitation.

"There was a shrine. He's channelling strength from whatever is sealed there, but how he does it, it's almost as if he wants to ensure the seals remain intact."

"That would make sense." The new voice startled them, adjusting their gaze they looked up to see Alana stood before them. "It is doubtful that if it were to be unleashed it would allow him to syphon such large amounts of energy."

She was no longer a child on the verge of adulthood, but a young lady, and her clothes were too small for her forming curves.

"Dream magic?" Seiken questioned placing a hand on his daughter's shoulder. The clothes adjusted, growing and altering until they were a comfortable fit. Her hair had been cut, shortened to her shoulders and curled to look windswept by a clearly skilled hand.

"Thank you. Yes. There is only one Spirit who awaits us. We should make haste, this journey is nearing its end."

"What was the other price?"

"What does it matter?" Zo closed her eyes, placing her hand upon her daughter.

"Compassion," she advised. "How was it you knew where to find us?"

"Sylph taught me windsight, a way to see by feeling air currents."

"Alana."

"I understand this is difficult for you. But there is no time to delay. We must reach the Earth Spirit. It nears the Festival of Hades, if the tear is still open it is likely never to close. The boundaries between the worlds are weakened, and this damage could become permanent. After I have finished, I will be counting on you to get me to him, *that* is your duty. No matter what happens, it is the one thing you cannot forget. Do not hesitate."

"What do you mean?"

"Let's go, those of Kerõs are aware that we will be arriving."

"Kerõs, that's where Daniel went to visit Xantara," Zo mused. "Then once again we move full circle."

"We conclude my lessons where the threat first began. How far will we need to travel?"

"Not far, the irfeláfa is on the boarders of their forest. Alana, I wanted to—"

"Save any concerns until after." Her snipped reply interrupted Seiken. "Let me partake in this final lesson, and after I will answer any questions or concerns you have." Alana placed her hand upon the small stone. "I have changed, it is doubtful you or it will know me." Her words were not intended to hurt, but she could see they had.

"Your essence has altered but your blood has not. As my kin the gateways will always be yours to command," Seiken comforted, offering his daughter his hand as she stepped over the moss-coated stone circle barely large enough for them to stand within. His foot swept across the debris in the centre to reveal a small marker that came aglow the moment his blood made contact with it. The familiar distortion took them in its stifling embrace and within two blinks of their eyes the forest had changed. No longer within a land of eternal evergreen, autumn's hand had painted the landscape in vibrant shades turning deciduous trees into a plethora of colours. Plump rich berries lined flourishing holly bushes which sang a testament to the rich and fertile soils. To gaze before them was to behold the true majesty of nature in all her glory.

The people in Kerõs had been awaiting her arrival. She was greeted by Leona, the acting Maiden and the woman Alessia had woken from Darrienia when Xantara had been taken by Ádlíc. Their words were soft spoken, and their arrival had caused an unnatural hush to fall across the small town. People averted their gaze, while others openly stared at the young woman who would become Mistress of the Elements. Tales of the Mitéra were a legend that none ever truly believed. The Great Spirits rarely chose their own Maiden, but allowed others to don the mantle minus the greatest boons. These Maidens would not be blessed as those born for this title were. It was a rare occurrence, and yet each Spirit had taken a Maiden of their own and now, before them stood the embodiment of all their power. The one they would swear featly to.

"Welcome, Mitéra." Leona bowed, a gesture Seiken and Zo returned, whilst Alana stood proudly before her. "We were told of your arrival. I am to escort you to our sacred place. I am told you will know what to do."

"Why are their no Skiá here?" Zo questioned, noticing that, although the town was plunged into the same darkness as the rest of the world, there was no movement within the shadows.

"Has there been any at the gateways to the other Spirits' realms?" Leona asked softly. Zo thought for a moment and shook her head. "Each Spirit protects their transitional domain from the incursion of other elements. The Skiá are born of darkness, and so, you would find them only where that element dwells, which in its current state is vast indeed. Their protection is why you have been able to travel their gateways unhindered. Their domains are small, but they will be sheltered."

"We should let Daniel know. If he is still evacuating, we could have him usher people to those areas." Zo moved to grasp the gossip crystal before once more recalling it was no longer in her possession.

"There will be time for that later." Alana stepped forwards turning to face her parents. She studied them for a moment, recalling all the fragments of her childhood she could. Advancing, she wrapped her arms around them. "Whist you didn't raise me, you will always be my parents, I will never forget that." Zo and Seiken hugged her tightly before she pulled away to follow Leona, the town's leader, through the village and into the woods.

"There is so much I want to ask you," Leona began.

"There is no time. Promise me, you will watch over them until I return. They don't know this yet, but they are about to lose their daughter."

"What do you mean?"

"Each Spirit has requested something of me. If I pass his test, the Earth Spirit will ask that I surrender my time line."

"What does that mean?"

"All who once knew me, all I have done before my paths crossed with the Spirits, will be forgotten. They will not recall having a child, they will not remember I have aged as my journey progressed. All that I was, and all that I would have been should I not have accepted this duty, will be his. I was once immortal, my time would have been endless, and the infinite power of endless possibilities is powerful indeed. Even you will not remember this conversation, you will know only that you await my return."

"Then why tell me?"

"Why not? I alone will remember all that has been, and this final sacrifice will set to right the passage of time for any involved by simply removing my existence from those who knew me."

"You have sacrificed a lot in order to protect us from this threat. We shall not forget what you have done for this world." Alana looked back from her position by an old hollow tree that housed the portal to The Stepping Realm. She offered a smile which didn't quite reach her eyes and uttered just three words before stepping through and vanishing from sight.

"But you will."

* * *

Daniel stood in awe of Tony's skill. Within the forge, placed upon the rear table ready for inspection, were the promised weapons. A sword, a halberd, a short sword, a bow—clearly designed to be adaptable for close quarter combat—a dagger, and a cestus. Tony moved to stand beside Daniel as he admired his work.

"I don't know who you travel with, but this somehow seemed right. They're all for you to present as you see fit, except for the bow." Tony stood with his hands on his hips, looking over what were, without a doubt, his finest works.

"Thank you," Daniel whispered, his voice lost to emotion as he looked upon the impressive weaponry before him.

"You're not going to ask about the bow?"

"Who is it for?" Daniel rasped, still almost speechless from all this great man had done for him.

"This is for the Mitéra. I charge you, Daniel Eliot, with its deliverance into the hands of the woman who will restore order. It will not serve her yet, but I have been asked to relay to you two things in exchange for the use of my gifts. First, you will covertly ensure she has training in both bow and staff combat, this weapon will suffice for both, agreed?" Daniel nodded, a perplexed look crossing his features. "And second, this cannot be presented if the Skiá still possess a foothold. From what the flames revealed the path is, as yet, inconclusive."

"I accept. Tell me, do all blacksmiths possess Pyromancy?"

"No, the only futuresight we hold comes from the work we complete at an anvil. We know its quality, and if its suited to the hand of its owner. Nothing more. I rarely craft with things that have touched the hands of the Gods. One would almost think this ore had been discarded with purpose." Tony gave a shrug, it was better not to dwell on such things. Before him lay his greatest work, the finest weapons he had ever forged. The sheer sense of pride and fulfilment was like no other. A look of sadness crossed his face briefly, but not unseen by Daniel.

"What is it?"

"Never mind. On to business." Tony waved his hand in a sweeping gesture across the table. "These are yours, may they serve you well, Daniel Eliot, Wita of the Eorthåds and Defender of the Realms."

"Thank you, I accept graciously." Tony faltered slightly, his body overcome by weakness from the hours spent at the forge and anvil. He had achieved in one day what should take months, thanks only to some notable intervention of forces beyond his understanding, and perhaps some aid from the realm which had become Tony's keeper many moons before. These weapons had needed to be forged, and subtle manipulations by a god who knew well the boundary to circumvent promises had ensured that this had come to pass. So crucial was the act he had just performed, that each year since his wife's death he had returned to this forge, awaiting the time his skills were in demand. In all those years, Elly and Daniel had been the only ones to seek him, and thus they alone had found him.

This panoply of armaments held great significance, but the rest, those which passed into the care of other hands to be finished, would eventually fail for they had been forged in haste. The weapons for Daniel, however, would become something greater than the Wita's life span would witness, but with him it would start, and their legacy would continue through those he passed them on to.

Seeing the trembles now wracking the blacksmith's weary body, with a hand upon his arm Daniel guided him towards the small rear table. Wiping a dusty bamboo cup on his shirt, he poured some lukewarm water from his leather skin, his hand fastening around Tony's to bring the cup to his parched lips.

"Will Elly be returning?" Daniel asked as Tony drank deeply.

"You know the Lady of Knightsbridge? No, she is already seeking to rally those who will follow her. Why do you ask?" Tony questioned, seeing Daniel's eyes flit across the table.

"We have been both ally and enemy, and one of these, despite my better judgement, seems intended for her."

"Then you best find her in battle." Tony smiled slapping Daniel on the shoulder. An act which would normally be so jarring, seemed weak.

"May I leave the bow in your keeping?"

"Did your dreamer friend never show you how to store your staff?" Tony hiked his eyebrow curiously to see Daniel looking at him in confusion. "The young lady who sent you to my door all those years ago, she was the one who crafted your weapon, was she not?"

"Yes," Daniel stammered wondering how he could know this.

"Do you remember anything unusual about when she gave it to you?"

"Not really. She pulled it from her satchel. Although, I wondered how it had fit in there, even in its folded state."

"She made you that too?" Daniel nodded, his grip instinctively tightened on his own satchel. "I'm just a blacksmith, but I'd suggest you have a talk with that friend of yours. Now, I must lie down, I've never felt so depleted." Without even moving Tony placed his head upon the table and was soon snoring. For a brief moment Daniel considered throwing one of the coats from the coat stand over him, noticing once more how chilled the air was considering the roaring flames of a forge were so close. The sweat on Tony's brow persuaded him otherwise. Returning his focus to the weapons on the table he carefully wrapped them in the leather bindings, knotting them together to make them easier to carry.

These weapons were everything he had needed them to be, metal that would come aglow with divine light. His heart quickened at the thought of seeing them in action, of testing them to prove their value, but he knew better than to delay. Time was no longer a luxury and arming his allies had to become his primary focus.

* * *

Impressions danced within Alana's mind. Her fingers brushed the tips of long grasses as she walked releasing more of their delicate aroma into the air. She watched in her mind as the long stalks swayed within the almost absent wind that brushed against her flesh with a gentle touch. Within the luscious surroundings there were but two places which drew her focus. The first was a grove of tightly knit trees creating a circular barricade no mortal could pass. The branches and roots interlocked together, with barely a space between them for her windsight to exploit and the second, an area of nothingness, a small location without vision or texture which she recognised to be either a portal or a reflective surface, but the low hum of energy suggested it to be her exit.

The long grasses ended to become a landscape of earth and bark as if this soft ground had been carefully manicured to surround the small grove. Her brow furrowed as she continued towards the portal, the hum of energy remained consistent, not increasing in strength. She knew even before she extended her hand towards its surface the portal was too weak to complete its required task.

Something more was needed of her, like all her transitions through The Stepping Realm, here too there was a challenge to uncover. Clearing her mind she allowed her focus to become submerged in her surroundings. Her skin prickled as the lukewarm breeze continued its journey, carrying upon it a sweet aroma which caused saliva to pool within her mouth. She inhaled again, slowly, tracing the succulent scent back to the small grove she had passed. Her fingers brushed against the rough bark as she detected the slightest vibration from within, a power which mirrored the nature of the portal.

Cautiously, she used the small divisions where the trees had intertwined together to form an impression of what lay inside. Her mind returned images of a pedestal upon which rested a spherical object. It was from this orb she felt the energy being emitted. Slowly she walked the perimeter, searching, without fortune, for a means to gain entry.

Samaras grew heavily on the branches above, their rustling melody joining in harmony with the sonorous choir of bees that only now seemed audible. Closing her eyes Alana allowed her mind to wander back, a smile upon her lips as she thought of all the lessons she had learnt and the tales she had been told by the spirits and their brethren. She knew at once what she needed to do. In a place such as this there was only one nature spirit who would answer her call.

"Oh, Meliae, hear my plea. I call upon the compassion of the honey nymphs, of those who once nursed Zeus, and dwell within the ash trees. I, future Mitéra, ask for your aid to pass into the Earthen Realm."

"And in return?" several voices questioned in unison, as the impression of movement stirred from within. Alana thought over her lessons with the Spirits, of things they would consider of worth and value. While man craved gold and riches, nature spirits held other things in high regard.

"A favour," Alana announced clearly. "I will owe you the debt of a favour to be called upon as you need it." A hushed whisper tickled the branches of the trees.

"Words have power here, do you know the price of what you speak?"

"I understand that this is the highest valued gift I could offer, and that when you call upon me I must answer."

"You must not only answer, but do as you are bid. We will bind you to your word," warned the voices.

"Will you help me?"

"We will. Once our pact has been bound we will give you the means to pass through to our protector's domain." The ground at her feet began to soften, causing her to retreat a single step as through the oozing mud a vessel began to form, heating and baking itself in its creation until a clay vase filled with a foul and viscous fluid lay at her feet. "Swear your vow upon it and make your pact."

"In exchange for assisting me in my passage through this place, both now and in the future, I swear upon the water of..." Alana grew warm, realising she had no idea what she swore a vow upon.

"Styx," the voices offered softly.

"I swear upon Styx that I will owe a favour of their choosing to the Meliae, to be called upon once, in their time of need." The vase before her tipped, shattering back into the raw form of mud and earth releasing the stench of decay as the water oozed from the vessel spilling the foul substance upon the once fertile land, and causing all which its droplets touched to wither as Alana jumped backward, beyond its influence. A few moments of silence passed as the offensive fluid soaked into the ground. She knew from lore that Styx was the river of hatred, the water was polluted by this emotion, the foulness caused it to congeal and decay like the essence of those harbouring such emotions. She also knew it was where divine vows were promised, and any forsaking such a swearing would be condemned to Styx's judgement.

"It is done." From above, several of the Samara separated from their tree, spiralling down in a majestic dance seen only by this type of seed pod. As they landed at Alana's feet the seeds merged, creating, what looked to be, a pewter ewer, no taller or wider than her own thumb, excluding the handle. Attached to the handle was a silver chain, which Alana placed around her neck. "The value of what you have offered exceeds this one deed thus, in balance, this ewer will last until Ares returns to the place in the celestial heavens he now occupies, that's approximately two years on the mortal plane. You need only consume it once to forever be granted permission to pass through the barrier. This gift is precious, and once you have passed through the barrier it will replenish you when you feel weak or sickened. But be warned, use it sparingly, and only in times of great need."

Alana nodded her understanding before lifting the small jug to her lips, as she did so she saw the insides fill with honey. She savoured the taste of the rich ambrosia. As she lowered it, she felt a strange sensation across her wrist. Tracing her fingers over the small weal she felt a long vertical line, with five smaller horizontal lines emerging on the right side. Below it was the shape of the ash tree's leaf. "It is the script belonging to the trees. This one identifies you as a friend to those of the ash tree. The small leaf shape below shows you are in our debt. The swelling will lessen, but your skin will remain embellished by our mark, may this be the first of your many alliances." Alana was about to thank them, but realised such words would only serve to increase her debt.

"I will abide by my pact and await the day I honour my obligations. Fare thee well, Meliae." Alana, still tracing her fingers over the new markings, returned to the portal and without delay stepped through, an act she was proud of considering she was preparing to surrender her time-line. A sudden thought crossed her mind, she would have to ask that her debt be remembered.

"That is noble of you child, but also the reason they marked you. They know what you will give to train with me." The rich voice resonated.

"Then, they will not recall our encounter?"

"The details will remain visible to their kind through the tikéta, as would the pact and alliance be stored in any future agreements you make. Tell me, why did you offer them such a blessing, when a simple please would incur a smaller and instantly satisfiable debt?"

"If I simply said please they would have me clean their grove, or find some menial task that has no real value, but what I gain in return would be significant. By giving me passage to your domain they have offered me the final stage of my training, that which I need to become the Mitéra and vanquish Íkelos. If I offered any less the exchange would be unjust."

"But with your time-line erased they would not know."

"But I would," Alana answered sharply.

"You did well. You saw the value of their aid and unlike those who failed, you did not attempt to cheat those aiding you. In return you have earned a great gift." Alana's hand rose as if to touch the ewer and stopped, her fingers moving to her wrist. "And you recognise it, I see you have been raised well. The Meliae rarely offer their script, normally they present only the marker of debt. Now more than ever I believe we made the correct choice."

"I have one request, regarding my time-line. If it is possible, I need for those involved to remember they were with me on this journey, not who I was, or how I've aged, but something was shared between them during my absence that is best not forgotten, plus, I need their aid to reach my destination."

"As I said, you recognise the importance and value in things. It shall be done."

Chapter 29

Íkelos' Spy

Alana strode through the village, her head held high, her shoulders back as she passed the modest dwellings. Their homes were simple, no more or less than what was required. The faint earthy scent of the hide tanner's oils mingled with ripened fruits from the nearby orchard. She walked with confidence as those inside their homes looked out in awe, gathering in doorways and exchanging almost silent whispers. Her auburn hair was secured in a low ponytail, the shorter strands clinging to her neck giving the impression of a fringe that had long grown out.

The training with the Earth Spirit had taken her the longest yet and had presented the most difficult challenges. There had been a time when doubt had crept in, when she wondered if she could truly do the things expected of her. Now, however, she was confident, certain she could fulfil her role. While barely a few hours had ticked away, five years had passed in his realm, five long, frustrating, and trying years, but it was time she had needed to learn the workings of the final magic, and how each of the other elements could interact together. The Spirit had seen it appropriate to present her some new clothes, nothing complex or decorative, but they would offer some protection. He had his spirits weave clothes of hide, cotton, and leather. Nothing befitting her title, such apparel would be earned from her visits to the shrines, but this would offer her some protection against the elements. A hide coat, with a large cowled hood covered a cotton shirt and soft leather trousers.

"Mitéra, how went the blessings of the Spirit?" Leona questioned, hastening to fall in step beside her as she walked through the town. Until this moment, Alana had wondered how everyone would recall her purpose for being here. Her earth father had said they would know of her presence, and of her mission, but he had not explained the details.

"Everything is complete. Where are my guides?"

"They await you by the town's borders." Alana nodded, dismissing the woman with a wave of her hand before strolling to her parents.

"Thea, Seiken, I am prepared," Alana announced, studying the fatigued figures before her. Although she was the one who had aged, her parents looked older now than she had ever seen them appear as the weight of worry and exhaustion reflected in eyes which no longer held their once welcoming smile. When they crossed into this realm they were relying on the energy emitted from those sleeping to sustain them, but few could sleep in times such as these and with such drought so too came the weakness she now witnessed as her mind's eye absorbed their every detail.

They no longer knew they had lost their daughter, but the rewriting of their time-line had taken a greater toll on their energies than any other beings, especially given the adaptations that had been needed to ensure they continued to guide her and recalled everything of importance.

"The Spirit has offered his blessing?" Zo's voice held relief as she rose to greet her, dipping her head slightly in a show of respect.

"I have completed all the blessings. I am primed to confront Íkelos and seal the rift. Is everything in order?"

"We are prepared to regroup with those facing the Skiá, Mistress Alana," Seiken confirmed. For a moment she wondered why he did not lower his gaze as most should given her title. It was then she realised the identity of the man who had once been her father. Neither he, nor her mother, would have cause to show her any submission, and yet her mother had.

"We should not delay. It would be better to simply proceed to our destination."

"Mistress Alana, of those fighting the Skiá many will lose their lives. To see you, to understand we have a chance, will bring comfort even in the face of certain death. Our destination is Lamperós, with our method of travel it would take but a few moments in detour. Their role will be pivotal to our success, our presence, however brief, is essential," Seiken asserted, taking his wife's hand in his own.

"As you wish, Seiken. However, the Festival of Hades approaches, each delay reduces our chances of victory." She could feel Seiken's cold stare upon her as her mother touched his arm. She delayed their departure just long enough for him to kiss her mother's forehead in a sweet gesture of their love, before she resumed her march from the village back to the irfeláfa.

* * *

Daniel wiped the sweat from his brow, glancing towards Rob with a smile. Their somewhat unskilled display of swordsmanship had proven their point, even if it had forced Alessia from the sanctuary to take up arms beside them and ensure their safety. Clearly, neither of these two men were well-versed in wielding such weapons, not that it mattered for Daniel. He had only ever shown proficiency in combat with the staff that had been forged specifically for his hand to overcome his disastrous incompetence in melee. Alessia had no choice but to cover them as they charged towards the camp, brandishing their new weapons with all the skill of a child mimicking their favourite hero of legend. Their ungraceful dash did, however, demonstrate that the light-infused swords could indeed be trusted.

Her stern expression let Daniel know she thought his actions were reckless, even if he were being true to his word. She could not condone him placing himself in danger to ensure those who fought for him knew the weapons could be trusted. That said, when her fury at his stupidity waned she had to admit that to reach them from the Irfeláfa without encountering any hostility would have been nothing short of a miracle. It was more the lingering outside, to ensure everyone saw their dangerous display of unskilled bravado, that had given her cause to drag him towards the barrier, like a mother scolding a child. Thanks to his actions, she also had to endure another shadow purge, but when they awoke it would be time to discuss tactics.

The moment Daniel's eyes opened he dragged himself from the floor to his feet, somewhat unsteadily, before making his way to Jones' home. It was a place he was familiar with since he had stayed there when it had belonged to his brother, and again when they had journeyed to seal the Severaine. Even now he couldn't remember if Jones had told him it had become his own dwelling since he had assumed his brother's position.

"Does mother hen know you're out of bed?" Jones teased glancing up from his hunched position at the folding, oak table with an amused smirk. Daniel felt his face flush, knowing facing Alessia was something he had yet to do. He was *not* looking forward to that conversation. "We need a plan to draw the Skiá to one location, and I think I know just the place." Jones' calloused fingers tapped lightly on the map drawing Daniel's focus towards the plains just east of Seine Weir. "I just don't know the how."

"Leave that to me." As if encouraged by his words, Daniel noticed Jones straighten, an invisible weight seeming to slip from his shoulders. The low crackle of the fire was the only sound within the modest dwelling for a few short moments until Daniel spoke again. "I have an idea, but you have to do as I say." Dropping his voice to an almost inaudible whisper, he leaned down, his hand upon the rough grain of the table as he placed his lips by Jones' ear and began to relay the plan. With the approach of footsteps, Daniel stood, glancing towards the closed door before returning his voice to normal volume. "One last thing, perhaps the most important part of this is that Teanna stays safe. We must keep her with us, at the core of the army."

"Actually, Wita, Teanna will accompany me." An unfamiliar voice intruded on their hushed conversation. "I require the one who would be the Spirit Maiden as my escort. Such is my right." Both men rose to their feet by instinct, turning their attention to the figure at the door.

"By Ares' Blade, Daniel, where've you been hiding this one?" Jones had an eye for talent. He had attempted to recruit many of Daniel's allies through all manner of friendly bribery, but he would fall to his knees to serve the vision before him. She was beyond his control, together they could take the world, she could be the magic to his steel.

"Not the time, Jones," Daniel whispered. As the figure stepped inside he had needed to blink, for the space of a breath he had thought it had been Zoella who stood before them, but as reality and logic prevailed more questions surfaced than he could ever find answers to. She strode towards them, her head held high displaying an air of confidence her mother had never mastered.

"You have what I seek?" As she extended her hand sharply, Daniel's gaze fell to the tattered leather bracelet upon her wrist, before looking to the figure once more, almost as if to confirm his initial assessment.

"Alana, you're a woman, but how?" Hearing this the figure dropped her arm, something close to surprise knitting her features and drawing attention to her unusual eyes.

"I should have realised one claiming the title of Wita would not be influenced by my time-line sacrifice." There was a hidden meaning to her words, and Daniel realised that he alone now knew of this woman's origins. "Of course I am a woman, influence such as mine cannot be harnessed by anything less."

"What is your plan?"

"Íkelos dwells deep within The Mountains of Light. I plan to offer him an audience with Teanna in exchange for safe passage and diplomatic negotiations. Perhaps an arrangement can be met where your war can be avoided." She narrowed her eyes poignantly towards the two men, before her features grew stern as if to challenge them to contradict her.

"You can't just take her—" Daniel raised his hand, silencing Jones, his eyes never leaving Alana.

"Did Zo come with you, what does she think of this plan?" Daniel queried.

"Zo?" Alana questioned, her lips turning in a slight smile. She knew exactly who he meant.

"Forgive me, I mean your guide Thea," Daniel corrected. Alana nodded, inclining her head towards the door.

"Such questions bear no relevance here. Grant me Teanna and I will deliver you victory. If it brings you comfort perhaps you can plan for *if* I fail."

"If that is your wish. Shall I send her to you?"

"Yes, I will await where we first awoke. This area is... disorientating. Nothing is as it appears, but I can retrace my steps with ease. Oh, and send her protector too, the one who keeps Teanna's presence shielded," Alana ordered.

"How did you—never mind I don't need to know." Alana gave a sharp nod before turning on her heel, exiting as sharply as she entered.

"Gods, Daniel, who was that? I've never felt an Elementalist with such raw power."

"She's not an Elementalist," Daniel revealed, his vision transfixed upon the closed door.

"A demi-goddess, a goddess?" Jones posed with increasing excitement. "Do you think she's aligned? You know, we could use someone like her." Jones smacked Daniel's arm playfully, trying to ease the tension, but he continued to stare towards the door with an expression of awe.

"She's most certainly aligned." Daniel approached the window, watching Alana depart before returning to Jones and speaking in a tone barely above a whisper. "The woman you just saw is the future Mitéra."

"Mitéra?"

"You know how the people out there answer to you? Well, one day the Elementals, their Maidens, the Spirits, magical beings, us, and anything in between will answer to her. She could walk as an equal with the Gods."

"How did you know she'd come?"

"Because I was there when she was called. We needed something to stop the threat, to match the power of an old god, and it was she who answered. Jones, if she needs Teanna there's a reason, let's accommodate her wishes, but before you go," Daniel placed a roll of cloth on the table, "I'm not one for ceremony but it is a necessity here. I, Daniel Eliot, Wita to Eorthháds, willingly bestow this sword unto you, my ally. May it serve you well." Daniel looked at Jones' face as he lifted the weapon from the table, his face awash with astonishment.

"Ares' Blade," he muttered, his delicate grasp cradling the weapon as if it were a newborn child.

"Not quite, but it is likely made from the same ore."

"You're serious, aren't you?" Jones asked, unable to tear his gaze from the expertly crafted weapon. Never in all his years had he seen or held a blade so fine. "I don't know what to say."

"Just swear you'll stay safe. Before our newest guests depart there is still much we must discuss."

"Then I should make haste in seeing to the request." Jones turned the sword over studying its every detail. It was relativity plain, and yet magnificent. It was a tool crafted for purpose, not aesthetics, and it was beyond perfection. He placed a firm hand on Daniel's shoulder.

"Please do. In the meantime, I need to speak with an old friend."

* * *

Zo startled as Alana strode purposefully from the building. For a moment she wondered what exactly had drawn her here, and how long she had been standing outside this complex structure. Once Alana had left, Zo wiped her hands down her face, wondering if Seiken had also awoken in a daze. She scanned the area, seeing him engaged in quiet conversation with Acha, as his gaze fell upon her he smiled, gesturing for her to join them.

She raised her fingers to her temples, massaging them slightly as a feeling of foreboding expanded from her stomach. She didn't remember waking here after Chrissie had purged their shadows. It was a realisation that brought too many unpleasant memories to surface, memories of bloodshed and violence. She took a deep cathartic breath, she had been feeling unsettled since learning of the corruption's return, but surely Seiken would have warned her had anything altered, should she now be a danger to what they were trying to achieve.

"Hey, Zo." Daniel emerged from the building, pulling Zo back from her wandering thoughts and stilling her advance towards Seiken. "She's really something isn't she? You've travelled with her, what do you think of her idea to take Teanna with you? It seems a little risky."

"She wants to do what?" Zo was dumbfounded. Surely that was the worst thing they could do, presenting Íkelos his desire on a plater would not differ from him retrieving her by force.

"Her plan, it's not what I was expecting," Daniel admitted, raising a hand as he spotted Seiken. Jones was with them now, his hand slipping into the crook of Acha's arm as he escorted her away.

"What's her plan?"

"She wants to take Teanna to him and see if they can come to some manner of agreement and settle things... diplomatically." Zo's expression looked horrified.

"You can't be serious? What was your plan, surely something better than offering the poor girl on a sacrificial altar?" Zo glanced in Seiken's direction, his beautiful brown eyes were transfixed upon her, his piercing gaze caused her heart to skip as he closed the distance between them until his arm encircled her waist, pulling her close.

"I wanted to keep her with us. We need a means to draw the Skiá to one location."

"So either way she's bait." Zo crossed her arms, resisting the urge to shake her head.

"But at least my way there's an army between them," Daniel pointed out.

"Thea, can I talk to you a moment?" Seiken's hand cupped her elbow as he pulled away, leaving a gentle kiss on her temple. He exchanged a brief look with Daniel who, with a nod, excused himself to the place Alana was to meet with Acha and Teanna.

* * *

Íkelos allowed himself to relax. Drawing his hand from the obelisk he stretched his fingers. The time was approaching. He no longer needed to draw the energy through the tear to maintain the Skiá. With a swipe of his armoured hand the fracture between his realm and this knitted closed. How easy this would be. He had possessed concerns when the woman wielding light had enveloped his spy, but his energy was not made of darkness, and it remained untouched. How freely they all spoke before his niece, not realising she was already his ears. Her husband was a fool, so fixated on watching the amassing energy around the heart chakra he had failed to notice the contamination of her throat. He had snaked along her dark meridians, disguising his progress by the sheer collection of energy surrounding her heart.

He listened through her as the woman they had escorted from Kerõs spoke words as sweet to his ears as ambrosia. She must have been a diplomat of some description. He could not recall having heard her name before, but that she would think to bring Teanna to him was most fortuitous. His Skiá, nor the corrupted who would have once been able to grant them access, could now enter the mercenaries' camp. For a brief time he had feared he needed to wait to corrupt his niece's energy fully to use her gift once more. Yet now, this woman would deliver to him all he desired.

People never failed to surprise him. He would never have considered such diplomacy in the face of war, and that the men and commanders stood cowed in her presence showed her to be a person worthy of great respect. They dared not argue with her, meaning, he had preparations to make and seals to erect. His former bride would come to him, and with her the power he needed to fulfil his ambitions.

The time for diplomacy had ended when The Order had sought to suppress the birth of the Maidens, killing infants so that their own gods and power remained unchallenged. They had failed this time because he had intervened. Those taken by the sickness known as Ádlíc would be the only living Gaeans to survive his devastation.

* * *

Acha looked at the figure before her in astonishment. Despite having witnessed miracles and mysteries, what she had just been told defied even her belief.

"I'm not sure about this," Acha admitted, glancing towards where Teanna sat waiting. Acha curled one of her long locks around her finger, shifting her weight slightly as she considered the implications. She had heard tales of monsters and magic users with such abilities, but to think it was something she too could achieve seemed impossible, especially since she had spent many years embracing rather than fearing her curse.

"It is a simple progression. The ability is already present. Do you not alter when you take possession of a new body?" Alana's sightless eyes seemed to penetrate into Acha's very soul as she scrutinised her. "In order to do this you already have some control over your appearance. What I am suggesting is an alteration based on the energy you absorb. Surely you have heard tales of old shamans drawing on aspects of the lesser spirits?"

"I'm not a shaman," Acha asserted.

"In some respects you are correct, however, that amulet you wear was crafted by a powerful, if not corrupt, one. Spirits once loaned shamans their power by entering an item in their possession and energy sharing. They would do this willingly and leave as they desired. Yours, however, was designed to be a trap. Permanently binding the spirit within. To achieve this, a part of the crafter's magical essence would have been melded with the amulet in order to ensure the possessor could manipulate the forces they snared. By doing so, as the talisman's keeper as well as occupier, part of their skill is transferred to you. That is why you knew to leave it with Teanna to keep her veiled." Alana released the talisman letting it fall back around Acha's neck, causing her to wonder when the woman before her had taken it in her hand. She was normally protective of this relic, yet Alana had known exactly where she had concealed it.

"How can you know this?" In times past during old adventures Acha knew Daniel had spent much time looking into the origin of her talisman, hoping to someway unearth its secrets. But aside from a few of the symbols appearing in ancient shaman rituals he had uncovered nothing more. She scuffed her feet across the wooden flooring, thinking how she perhaps should have asked him again since his ascension into the role of Wita. The fact no tomes existed on making a duplicate suggested it was of a knowledge that could only be earned, not cheated. There was no shortcut to power in most magic.

"I am to be Mitéra, I know much of the forgotten realm of spirits. The embellishes on the surface show it as an attractive trap. It would lure a free essence inside and bind it, allowing the wearer to manipulate the power possessed by whatever they had drawn to them. Since it was discarded, it activated the failsafe and your own essence was allowed to enter the flesh of one no longer amongst the living in order to free yourself or, as you found out, inhabit it as if it were your own. Believe it or not, in times of old, many shamans sought to snare nymphs and other beings to use them to sate their physical needs, but the main use was to allow them access to the creature's innate powers. Few could design a trap this comprehensive though. It's ancient, but I feel no decay in its power."

"What does that mean?"

"It means your essence is safe within, until such a time you choose to release it to reincarnation. I have answered your question, now, if you would accommodate my request." Acha glanced towards the wooden screen, ensuring all the windows were covered as Alana raised her hand. Acha mirrored her posture, their flesh not quite meeting.

Alana saw the concentration cross Acha's brow, as her breathing became focused and rhythmic. She stood for three long minutes before Acha let out a frustrated sigh. "Have confidence, do not doubt me." Alana scolded. "Let me show you." Placing her hand on Acha's chest, above where the talisman lay fastened, Alana forced the change. Acha stood before her panting, aching, but unaware of any external difference. "You have surely felt the alteration of bones when you take a new vessel. It draws the imprint from the energy of your essence. If you focused on a different imprint it would allow you to take another image for as long as you can retain it. Unlike when you partially possess a form, you will not be privileged to the information they hold, but nor will you leave space for other things to enter the void left." Alana paused as if confirming something. "Another thing to be cautious of is that their ailments will not hinder you. The impression energy reflects a person in their truest form, the one they would take in the underworld, as such it does not reflect injuries."

"You said this was a trap, how was the Skiá expelled?" Acha raised a hand to her throat, realising her voice had altered. "Wait, I'm you?" She placed her finger to her hair, noticing the rich alteration in colour as the silky texture passed through her slender fingers.

"The talisman is not intended for dual occupation. When your own essence returned in full the charm sensed the unbalance and worked with your light caster to expel the alien force, besides, you were never actually possessed as such, you just were admitted into their ranks by consuming too much of their power. Only you are bound to this. When you are whole nothing else can gain entry. And, yes, I shared a fragment of my energy so you could see the truth of my words. Except, you may appear to be me, but you don't have my power, or my blindness. Your facsimile is skin deep only and, as you always do, you mimic the energy aura of the power you've absorbed. At a glance it would be impossible to discern which of us was real." Acha lifted her hand as the energy began to diminish, watching the rippling of flesh and bones as they returned to her normal appearance. Their frames were similar, and the discomfort minimal.

"That was...unusual," Acha mused as she studied her hands once more.

"If you cannot bring the change about yourself, I can force it upon you if need be." Alana stopped, her direction of conversation altering drastically. "Teanna, you are to accompany me. If Íkelos is not open to negotiations, I will take your power myself. The question remains as to how I can approach him to request our meeting and passage. I am hoping a mere announcement would suffice. If not, then I will need to think more on it. Be ready within the hour. Now, I have to speak with the Wita. He may control the army, but he needs to understand his place." Alana pivoted, leaving the two women to watch after her in confusion.

* * *

The enormous banquet table, within the town hall, was ladened with all the supplies and resources the panicked townsfolk had managed to gather as they were sent fleeing from their homes by the monstrous din created by the warning bells. When the Severaine had run rampant these alarms had been set in place, and the people trained to the point that, on hearing the toll, their instinct was to gather what they could and retreat to the town hall. Few even questioned what the danger could have been.

Inside, people huddled afraid, but with no understanding of the threat. All they knew was that when the dark storm clouds began to loom on the southern horizon, they were called into hiding. The town hall had been secured completely, windows were barricaded, and doors were bolted. Elly alone, with the exception of the Research Plexus Founders, knew of another means to gain entry once this building was sealed, but the cost of passing through was steep, too steep to risk thinning the number of soldiers within her ranks.

Elly merely announced herself at the door, and those within had, without concern for their own safety, unbolted and unbarred the thick iron barrier and granted her entry. Words of relief and pleasure at seeing her alive washed over her as she glanced across each face of those seeking shelter. She recognised all of them, except one. The single voice who had not called out a greeting, who had seemed to protest against the opening of their sanctuary. She regarded him with a cautious smile, seeing his obvious discomfort at her presence.

"Your lord requested you leave the door barricaded. Why did you not comply?" she posed softly, her vision sweeping across the attentive crowd.

"Because he is an outsider, and you will always be our lady whether you hold the title deeds or not." The voice belonged to a stocky middle aged man, one Elly recognised as captain of the guards.

"Has he been unjust, treated you unkindly?" she questioned, her vision focused upon the captain. He ruffled his hand through his hair, unconsciously stepping behind one of the smaller tables to create a barrier between himself and her.

"No, my lady, he has stabilised trade in your absence."

"Then, perhaps he is treating you unfairly, overtaxing, being unreasonable with his demands?" The sound of Elly's footsteps on the tile floor echoed as she advanced to run her finger across the table that separated her from the secondary figure of authority within.

"No, my lady," he responded with a tug of his collar. His gaze flickered between Elly and the people uncomfortably.

"Is he sending you on dangerous missions, putting your lives in jeopardy?" she continued.

"No, my lady."

"Does he ignore you when you beseech his aid?"

"No, he listens to our grievances with a fair and impartial ear."

"Then why did you deem it necessary to ignore his concerns?"

"Because, my lady, we know you would not bring danger to our doors. He doesn't have that insight, we meant no disrespect." Elly gave a nod, turning herself to look upon the figure who sat elevated above all on the second tier of the room.

"I trust this display has satisfied you. Lord of Knightsbridge, I am not here to reclaim my title, nor do I bring danger on my heels. The people here find you satisfactory, and you are now aware that they only acted against your wishes because of their knowledge regarding my own commitment to them. Now, let us put this behind us." As the new lord met her gaze she smiled slightly, seeing a visible reduction in the hostility he had regarded her with just moments ago. He leaned back, relaxing into the large wooden chair—a chair she had once sat in to resolve disagreements amongst her people—raising a hand as if to bid her to continue.

"Welcome home, Lady Elaineor." The Lord rose to his feet, impressed at her subtle diplomacy. "What brings you to our doors?"

"The world is changing. You have faced threat before, stood against the terror of The Severaine, but never has the danger been so real, so permanent that I cannot see a means of victory, at least, not without your help. I have been on a long and exhausting journey to uncover ancient secrets that will help us combat the threat that is the Skiá. Using the words of the Gods themselves as a template, we have crafted a weapon capable of injuring the creatures lurking in the darkness, creatures who seek to tear our very souls from our flesh as they devour both."

"A weapon?" Elly raised her hand, silencing the captain's enthusiastic interruption as he moved to take his once familiar position at her right side.

"I have come from Semiazá Port, with these brave men and women. They can vouch that the power of these devices has kept them from harm, driving back the Skiá. They are brave, and have sworn to fight for my cause. However, our numbers are not adequate for the task we must complete. To any who will stand beside me I will, here and now, present gratuity to the Plexus to be delivered to their next of kin, a person of their choosing, or to be collected by themselves should they return." Her eyes flitted to the Plexus Master who nodded, understanding he would be keeper of their agreement. "I may not have my land and titles, but I have wealth beyond what you could imagine. I will ensure that the reward is substantial enough to support those left behind comfortably. This truth will be confirmed by those who already stand beside me."

"And where will you be, my lady, while you deplete this land of its warriors?" The lord's face twisted with a snide smile. While Elly had shown him diplomacy, he sought to expose her as a coward. She met his accusation with a pointed stare holding such a weight of threat she saw him flinch.

"I will take point. I ask no one to do what I will not, nor give what I am unwilling to. As any great leader would, I will lead the charge." The lord seemed to falter at her words, no doubt having expected her to remain in safety while others fought to their death in her name. He saw the approval swell through the city's residence and knew his land and title were still his by her grace alone. He seemed to swallow, regretting his attempt to shame her. Elly raised the corners of her mouth in a subtle smile at his response.

"Lady Elaineor, you know we would seek no compensation," the captain began.

"But you will accept it. If we fall, if we fail, there is no tomorrow. The barrier is thinning, the Festival of Hades is nearly upon us, and if we cannot drive back the threat then we will be consumed by it. I have twenty weapons remaining. They need no skill to wield, and those who join me are unlikely to return.

"I do not ask for your strongest warriors, only for those who are willing to stand, fight, and maybe even die beside me." Elly could see the hands twitching, ready to raise when she asked for volunteers, but instead she asked something else from them. "I require a map, my allies require sustenance. When we are prepared, I will ask for twenty people to accompany me. I will let you decide for yourselves, but be ready when we depart."

Elly strode across the room to stand before the Plexus Master she had indicated earlier, a man not belonging to the Research Plexus, but to the Hunters' Plexus. It had been a deliberate choice on her part. There, she issued a large quantity of paper currency, a form rarely seen given their indicated value. One note was worth more coin than could be comfortably carried. "When the decision is made, report here, and the Plexus Master will attend to the contract. Some of you may think to turn down the coin. Do not. Take it to ensure the future of your kin, refusing it does not prove you any more loyal, and would only cause me to question your ability to follow orders on the battlefield."

With those words Elly worked her way through the crowd, towards where she knew the map she wanted was located. She would march her troops out into danger, but as yet, she still had no means to draw the Skiá to her. Her plan was infuriatingly incomplete, but there was no time to delay. Action was needed now, and the plan could be created on the move.

Chapter 30

A Path Through the Shadows

The glow of the lantern was lost amidst the illumination of Chrissie's light enchantment, and yet something about its presence still added a comforting touch to Jones' home as it stood perched on the edge of the table the small group had gathered around. The wooden table creaked and groaned in slight protest as Daniel leaned across towards Alessia, divulging the details of his plan to her and Bray in lowered tones. Beside him, keeping silent vigil on their surroundings stood Alana, an appreciate smile tugged at her lips as she listened, while surveying the camp or the danger she knew lurked within.

"You're taking a significant risk," Bray acknowledged, sitting up and leaning back in his chair to stretch out his stiffening muscles.

"But do you think you can do it?"

"Rest assured, I can find her. But to do what you're requesting I will need sustenance, and it will be enough to render whom ever I take it from unable to participate."

"To track?" Daniel questioned in disbelief.

"If it were merely tracking you were requesting, then no, but you're asking for much more." He rolled his shoulders, trying to recall the last time he had eaten enough to sate him. What Daniel asked would be difficult. Yes, ultimately it was a search and recover mission, but the energy he would require to succeed, even if he didn't meet with resistance, would be draining.

"Who do you have in mind?" Bray's vision lifted to Alessia.

"She would suffice." Bray had scented her unique bloodline from the moment their paths had crossed. Her blood would give him endurance and strength beyond that he could obtain from even a dozen men, and in a concentration they both could manage.

"Alessia?" Daniel turned to her, seeking consent. She shifted as the focus of the group moved to her, and he could clearly see the conflicting emotions.

"Wita, I am to protect you."

"It is your decision, I will not order you on this. However, Alessia, please remember I have my weapon and an army at my back. I have already requested your abstinence from this conflict. If you wish to protect me then this would be the best way. I cannot have an Eorthád, not even yourself, upon the field of this battle. Kalia alone is safe from the Skiá's reach. Know that if you did this it would bring me comfort to know you are safe and you are aiding me the only way that ensures our security." He placed his hand on top of hers, begging her to understand. They had engaged in this conversation countless times and even knowing some of the danger she still wanted to stand beside him.

"To not be beside you is unthinkable, but if I do not agree to this you are saying I put you in worse danger." She rose to her feet, extending a hand towards Bray not looking to Daniel as she spoke. "Let us conclude our business but, Wita, hámsíðe." Her voice was stern, but her features softened as she looked over her shoulder. "Come home," she whispered softly.

"We can proceed here." Bray took her hand in his as he rose to his feet, guiding her around the chair until she sat. He saw Alessia's cheeks flush with colour as she looked upon those who would witness such private acts. "My lady, forgive me, I forget you know my true nature. For this act I don't require that level of intimacy."

"But I thought..."

"My sisters always require such dalliances but I remain a gentleman, when the mood takes me," he added with an impish grin. Alessia's stiffened posture relaxed slightly.

"It is time I checked on Teanna. Escort me, Wita." Alana gestured in the direction of the door as he looked hesitantly between Alana and Alessia, who sat rigidly in the chair with her eyes closed. As if she could feel his gaze upon her she gave a sharp nod.

"Of course."

* * *

The ward of light encompassing the mercenary encampment stilled on an imaginary border that lay some distance from the natural barricade which had once been manipulated to shield this location from accidental detection. Despite all within the enchantment being awash with light, there was a burning intensity to the barrier's edge that cast brilliant and pure light into the world beyond. But the brighter the light, the darker the shadows of things not within the enchantment's snare. Vines and grasses cast long and jagged tendrils across a dark and haunted landscape where even the sunflowers, once used to tell the time, bowed the heads in nyctinasty appeared dead rather in slumber, a prophecy that could soon come to pass without the sun's awakening kiss to break the curse upon the land.

Zo wrapped her arms around herself as she absorbed the details of the landscape with sadness. Her Hectarian heritage had once seen her attuned to nature, and she could still feel the life energy slowly dissipating from the world around them. Seiken's arm slid around her, pulling her close, but even his warmth brought little comfort as they waited for the rest of their small group to arrive. She didn't want to challenge the Mitéra, but Zo had a foreboding feeling about her plan.

"She has all the guidance she needs. You must trust in her," Seiken comforted, seeing the apprehension marring his wife's features. He was being careful not to speak Alana's title aloud where darkness as shadows could hear, as had been agreed by all some time ago.

The fact Íkelos would not know of her identity was the only advantage they would possess. Seiken frowned momentarily, wondering what made him certain Íkelos would not know of this great power when she had been sent to them in their time of need. He shook his head, assuring himself it was something to do with the fact she had been too young to be awakened, after all, that was why they had escorted this woman to meet with the Spirits.

Alana was finalising the details with Daniel, and would be joining them with Teanna shortly, which allowed them a few moments of privacy. Seiken glanced around at the shadows which seemed to writhe and pulse as if they knew something important was about to occur. He watched the semi-solid forms began to materialise before dissipating back into nothingness. The vision stirred dark thoughts about how these things were kin to Epiales, and of the loss he had suffered at the hands of these creatures. As his vision once more settled on his wife he re-swore a silent vow to protect her not just for today, but forever.

"Has it spread?" Zo questioned fearfully, seeing the intense manner with which Seiken beheld her. As if snapping from a trace he turned her gently to fully face him and brought his attention to her heart chakra.

"It's not penetrated yet." He could see the dense amassing of energies engulfing the area surrounding the energy centre, its vibrant green aura dulled by its presence. It was not yet claimed but he doubted, given the hairline blemish through it, that it would remain so for long. For the briefest moment he indulged himself in the delusion that this influence could not claim what already belonged to another. He focused on the wisps of his own essence, the part of him that had fused to her when the rite of claiming had been completed. It defended her fiercely. Even at the chakras already corrupted he could see the turmoil and battle within as his energy fought to liberate her with every bit the perseverance he would. Rowmeow had implied that his claiming her was the sole reason she retained her own will after speaking Íkelos' true name, but until now he had thought this to be misguided optimism.

"Are you sure it is safe for me to join you?" Seiken's jaw clenched as he bit back his fresh welling fury. He recognised that look and had hoped never to see it again. It had no place within her eyes, no claim upon her soul. She was worried about them, about what her presence could mean. Anger churned within his stomach, his glare enough to cause all life to wither. Íkelos would pay for this. He would pay for every fear and doubt, every second of uncertainty and moment of heartbreak, every tear. Once silent birds taking shelter in the world beyond took to flight as an aura of rage consumed him. A deep breath was not enough, nor two or three. Nothing could dispel this burning rage, and yet he needed to be collected. Leaning forward he cupped Zo's face gently, claiming her mouth in a passionate kiss, crushing her lips with desperation before resting his forehead to hers, closing his eyes he spoke a soft yet powerful vow, his timbre voice adding strength to such quite words.

"I trust no one else more than you. I would die if you commanded it of me, just as I would if ever we were parted. You are my missing half, my very life, and I swear to you he will be made to regret this. It may not be today, it may not be tomorrow, but it will be soon. This I promise," he whispered before pulling back. He kissed the tears from her cheeks. "Today we face Íkelos together, the one who put this corruption within you. If you weren't beside me there's the possibility he'd bring you to him. Better you stand amongst us than be used as a hostage."

"Are you sure it's safe, bringing Teanna with us?" Zo forced the words through a throat swollen from hearing his whispered emotions.

"Everything you are seeing is for her." Seiken saw the concentration of shadows had increased as they spoke. "Perhaps Alana is correct, her presence with Íkelos will calm the Skiá."

"Are you ready?" Zo turned to see Fey, the young man who seemed always to be at Teanna's side, walking alongside the nervous looking silver-haired figure.

"Are you?" Zo questioned, searching the woman's eyes. Without speaking she simply nodded, biting her bottom lip. Fey placed his hand upon hers, causing her to flinch.

"Skiá." Alana's voice rang clear and true as she approached the barrier. "Go to your master, tell him we seek to treat with him. I have the being formally known as Lavender with me, and request for safe passage for myself and my comrades." The almost inconceivable whisper of shadows quietened before the darkness seemed to peel away from the area before them. "Know this, should I sense deception I will not hesitate to kill her, and claim the power as my own." Teanna's hand tightened on Fey's arm at hearing these words. Leaning closer, Fey whispered something, soothing her nerves slightly. Alana did not turn to look back at the small group, such an action would have been meaningless anyway, she simply stepped through the ward. "We have safe passage. Let us use the irfeláfa, and hope his benevolence remains until we are granted an audience."

"If not?" Teanna questioned hesitantly.

"If not I'll kill you myself," Alana asserted without remorse.

* * *

Íkelos drew on his link to the Great Spirit of Darkness, utilising the shrine as a medium to syphon the raw powers and energies he required to become the wielder of shadows and master of darkness. All answered to his whim, to his control of the Spirit that had been sealed for cycles untold by his own hand. The Skiá were his eyes, their whispers his ears. Weaving his awareness through the network of shadows they created he listened as a woman, the diplomat he assumed, addressed the darkness, seeking safe passage. It appeared while they were willing to attempt diplomatic negotiations, trust was a commodity they would not indulge.

The shadows writhed at his touch, quivering in his presence as if they were sentient beings. They bowed to his will, his mind capturing their very essence and drawing them back. Each blade of grass, each flower, shed its darkness, and light from the barrier surrounding the encampment extended outward, drawn into the void to create a balance. He wove its path creating safe harbour from the place they stood to the portal stones.

He observed as the illumination filled the locality where shadows had reigned. A symbol of his commitment, his agreement to granting them safe passage. He would do everything within his power to honour their request for negotiations, that was, until his machination reached fruition.

Teanna would be his, his niece would be incapacitated and her magic bound leaving her powerless to fight the final spread of corruption. She would aid him, or watch the one who had claimed her suffer. As for the diplomat and the ranger, he would allow them to witness his victory. There was nothing powerful about their auras, they would prove little challenge. When they stood before him, with the Oneirois neutralised, there would be no defence, no protection.

He knew the pathetic army still intended to draw the Skiá, and he knew exactly how they planned to do it. His niece had overheard Seiken speaking with Acha. His Skiá would not fall for the same trick twice, however, to have so many essences grouped together in one location was too great a lure. They had demonstrated their weapons could injure them, but what did they truly hope to achieve? There was no force they could muster that could stop the Skiá, only he could drain them of their energy, only he could repel their attack. If things went awry he would have hostages at his disposal; mortal, vulnerable hostages, some of whom his niece loved dearly, as she had proven countless times over the years by jeopardising, even sacrificing, herself for their sake.

He had watched this small group with curiosity. They were symbols of hope, people of power. It was time they were quashed. Few would be afforded the luxury of bearing witness to the dawn of the new world, the return of order.

* * *

Daniel stood sheltered, eclipsed from view as he witnessed the events unfold. He felt his fingers sting from the power with which he clutched the tree's bark as he watched the shadows draw back and light from their own barrier cut a path through the forest. He knew where that path would lead, and that Íkelos was aware of their method of travel caused an uneasy knot to twist its way through his stomach. His eyes tracked Alana's movement, a darkness in his eyes making it evident he was none too pleased with her tactics. There had been but a few things they had agreed on, their presence with him would cause the distraction needed to pull the Skiá to them. Light washed over the small group as they departed, the shadows beyond the light writhed in excitement, but never attempted to draw back.

"Acha, are you certain you are all right with this?" Chrissie questioned as a silver-haired figure stepped cautiously from her concealment inside one of the small abodes. She had stayed hidden for a reason, the plan's success relied on a certain level of deception.

"It is as Alana said, the duplicity will cause confusion in the Skiá. They will flock to me, seeking to fulfil their duty unrestrained while Íkelos is otherwise engaged and distracted by having the real Teanna before him. It is the only opportunity we have to manipulate them beyond the sight of their master." Hearing the soft-spoken voice Daniel turned to look upon the image of Teanna, she was dressed identically to the figure who had moments ago departed, thanks to the quick work of the tailors she was a flawless duplicate.

"Is everybody ready, do we all know our parts?" Daniel questioned, the departing of the group through the thicket had been the signal for his forces to gather.

"When Seiken alerts us to their arrival, we should be in position," Jones confirmed. They had a narrow window in which to execute their plan.

"Chrissie, I know you don't want to hear this, but you need to stay here, keep this sanctuary safe. Watch over Alessia, she cannot be permitted to join this conflict."

"I would be better watching over your army," Chrissie countered.

"We'll have one card, a small sanctuary to fall back into, but we need her safe. *I* need her safe." Chrissie nodded reluctantly. Seeing this Daniel turned his focus to the mercenaries.

"The Skiá will come in force. We will set flash traps, signal fires, and try to keep our position as bright as possible. We will divide into two teams. The first team will engage the enemy, when you start to feel fatigued, head to the sanctuary, swap your positions with someone there, and take over the loading of slingshots, wrapping torches, binding flash bombs, firing arrows, or whatever needs doing. Keep the Skiá alert, and most importantly, away from Acha.

"Acha will be situated here"—Daniel drew a cross in the dirt on his sketched layout—"and the Skiá will be trying anything possible to reach her. Keep her surrounded and protected at all costs. We hold until Bray brings Lady Elaineor to us. Her numbers will ease some of the burden, as will her weapons, and I need not tell you, they are pivotal to our success."

"And then?" Chrissie questioned, her arms folded in an expression of displeasure at being left behind.

"Then, we pray to the Gods, Spirits, or whatever you believe in, that this works." He allowed for the troops to study the layout before dragging his foot over his crude plans, smoothing the dirt at his feet. "Let's move out."

* * *

Alana followed Fey as he led the way through the parted shadows, his stalking movements indicative of the danger he perceived. Despite requesting him as her guide, she could tell he was uncertain as to why she had chosen him for this task. He did not realise his own importance. His presence was essential because of his ties to Teanna. Despite only knowing her a matter of days they had developed a deep connection, as it should have been. He was her Fanger, although his latent abilities had not yet awoken his presence still complimented hers.

The Fangers were guardians of the Maidens, but when the Spirit Elemental had been sealed away their skills became latent, leaving the Maidens with no mortal protector. Although, protector was a loose term. Fangers had been created to compliment their Maiden's abilities, to support or protect depending on their capabilities. They calmed the fires of anger, or stoked the embers of fury. Alana had recognised him for what, and who, he was the moment her windsight had touched him, thus she knew Íkelos would recognise his underlying potential, but the precautions she had taken ensured he would not sense the bond between Fey and Teanna.

Alana's footsteps stilled, the crunching of autumn leaves beneath their boots growing silent as Fey raised his hand, requesting the party to stop. They were not yet at the irfeláfa, but Alana could feel a familiar pull of transitional energy before her. It was a softer pulse than the portals she had used to pass between realms, but the manner in which the energy oscillated revealed its nature.

"What do you see?" Alana questioned. Windsight was a powerful boon, but it could not see beyond the visible. She sensed the portal opened somewhere within this world, hence the softer pulse, but without her sight she couldn't ascertain where. For her, looking upon a portal was no different to looking upon a mirror, she could see the surface that would hold the reflection, but not the image within.

"It's the Mountains of Light," Zo answered recognising the shape of the most prominent peaks. "Although, Mountains of Darkness might be a more apt name for what we're seeing."

"Since that is where he can be found it seems we can trust him with our passage." As she responded the small party witnessed the distant image within the portal shift, as if it had been waiting for their agreement. The dark hue of the mountains became more vivid as they watched the landscape draw nearer, peaks sailed past pulling their focus to a distant city high within the sheltered peaks. Waterfalls cascaded in majestic views only to vanish into the blackness beyond. Closer and closer to the city the reflection grew until they looked upon it from the grand bridge which granted any seeking entry to Lamperós access. The thick, heavy, arched bridge acted as the sole entrance and exit to the town. It crossed the first of the swollen rivers and stood just several feet from the place it cascaded down into the second tier of the magnificent waterfall that once drew crowds. This bridge was forged from stone, and had perhaps even been weathered into existence by the magnificent falls. Its once smooth contours bore the signs of time well.

"It appears he wishes to take us directly to him," Seiken observed, critically studying the surroundings. His eyes were drawn to the figure who stood upon the centre of the bridge. The armour he wore painted a visage he was all too familiar with. Íkelos had been called Melas-Oneiros for a reason; his presence had brought nightmares to the world of Darrienia. Before his confinement in the forest of the Epiales, a place which existed in the Betwixt, Darrienia had known only peace.

"Is he alone?" Alana queried as the silence drew on. She could not behold the breathtaking sights of the snow-tipped mountains rising in the distance, or the haunting mists which swelled from the banks of the bordering forest. She knew nothing of this city, of how water cascaded down from above to create crashing waterfalls and fast flowing rapids straight through the town to turn ancient waterwheels while the glow of the mountains chased through the streets, normally illuminating the tightly packed houses whose jagged and uneven rooftops almost mirrored the razor points of the mountains themselves. But in her mind she could see him, Íkelos, his visage a vision gifted to her from the Spirits when first they had spoken to her of this future. She could see him clearly in her mind's eye donned in armour that looked as though he had been flayed while creatures and people trapped beneath his muscle and sinew attempted to push free. The demon mask was twisted in a perpetual sneer that had haunted her dreams for well over a decade.

"It appears so," Zo answered with a nod. Behind him Lamperós appeared to be deserted, not a single movement stirring to indicate any life was present. The sight sent a flood of icy fear down her spine. She had never visited this location, not that she recalled, but she had images of an overpopulated, bustling city. The city itself, alien to the darkness of his surroundings, was bathed in a dull light, as if to suggest they had no cause for fear. "He has illuminated the area, but it is a double-edged sword, it makes the shadows darker, easier to conceal something within," she observed critically.

"Light? I thought his intention was to draw the Skiá here, why would he illuminate the place of his casting with something they are averse to, could we be mistaken about his intentions?" Seiken mused.

"Either way, we should treat the shadows as a threat," Fey muttered, narrowing his eyes as he too scanned the portal. He placed his hand upon Teanna's shoulder in, what he hoped to be, a comforting gesture. She rewarded his effort with the faintest smile.

"The Skiá are still prevalent, there is no question he is seeking to exploit them. If not to overrun us, then why?" Teanna questioned.

"I doubt they were merely a hunting party. If he's keeping their numbers finite, then... what is their purpose?"

"Another question for our growing list. Keep your focus on the shadows, let me know if you see even the slightest hint of something suspicious. Now, relay the message to your comrades, and let us see what awaits us," Alana instructed.

"I will, although, I feel very uneasy about this," Seiken answered, his fingers brushing against the gossip crystal. He took a few paces away from the small group before relaying the agreed message to Daniel.

* * *

Concern and unease must be contagious emotions, because their tells were worn upon the faces of all. Keeping their voices low and their steps light Daniel's party followed in Alana's steps. Despite their attempts of silence such a large mobilising group was anything but discrete. Drums, crates, and barrels were affixed to many of the mercenaries' backs, adding extra weight to their footfall and time to their slow progression. While the path of light still tracked through the forest, Daniel clutched Chrissie's light card tightly, keeping the channelling active. The illumination surrounding the group spilt into the shadows, driving back the threat but as they advanced the land behind them once spared the oppressive touch once more became consumed.

As they walked, Daniel recalled his final orders to Alessia. Once she was strong enough Chrissie was to escort her home to Kalia in order to complete a task of grave importance, the purging of the altar stone thus ensuring any who had used the irfeláfa to travel would no longer be able to do so until oaths and pacts were sworn anew. While he was unsure if the Skiá could travel via this means he needed to be certain any potential threat was quashed.

Bray had left Alessia exhausted, but she had insisted he took as much as he could need. Daniel's entire plan hinged on him finding Lady Elaineor, and Alessia had given more than she should have, of this Daniel was certain. She had teetered on the verge of unconsciousness, and still had begged him not to leave. There was an unspoken acknowledgement between them, and understanding of why he made this request to secure Kalia. Even before leaving he had doubted he would return. Lives would be lost, and his would most likely be amongst them. He wanted the Eorthåds to be protected. They would bring hope should his plan succeed, and if not, perhaps one day they could find a means to expel the Skiá. Their land existed between dream and reality, on the border and as a gateway between both. As such, it could not be entered by conventional means, except for those accepted by the island, or those permitted to use the irfeláfa.

"Are you okay?" Jones' hand fell heavily upon his shoulder as he gathered the group around the small stone. He knew the look that haunted Daniel's eyes all too well. He had seen it on Adam, Daniel's brother, when he had led his men into danger. Each single life bore down upon his shoulders. "Can I tell you something your brother once told me?" Daniel swallowed with difficulty, barely bringing himself to nod. "Out there things will happen quickly, fear will flood you, people will die. When you reach your limit, when things around you happen too fast, stop. Take a deep breath, shut out everything else, and focus on what you need to do. You'll find you have more time than you think if you take control, rather than be controlled. Fear distorts time, take it back, breathe and focus."

"My brother said that?"

"His version was more inspiring, but that was the gist of it." Jones' friendly eyes twinkled. "If we make it through this, can you remember me telling it better?" Jones joked, his smile fading as he saw Daniel's expression darken. "Daniel Eliot, we have chosen to stand beside you, to fight for hope. Our lives are not on your shoulders, we alone carry them, and if need be we will lay them down, but not at your feet, do you understand?"

"And yet, I see the same concerns weighing on your brow," Daniel observed quietly.

"Do as I say, not as I do."

"Everyone is ready." Teanna's soft voice interrupted the intense look shared between Jones and Daniel. He saw Jones mouth a word to him, in response he took a deep breath and released it slowly.

"Okay. I've never tried to move this many people before, but I've been told it's possible. Ready?" Daniel felt several hands upon his shoulder as the group adopted the agreed positioning, each person holding onto two others, one in front, and one to the side. Those closest to him paced their hands upon him. "On three..."

* * *

Íkelos watched the shimmering surface of the portal begin to distort. The effect was similar to watching a figure emerge through a perfectly calm lake, the image rippled, parting to allow those from the other side to step through. As their small group gathered on the opposite side to the bridge he drew in a long deep breath, savouring the clean taste of the mists and nature. They hadn't seen the second portal yet, the one he had conjured just to the side of the bridge suspended in midair. Its surface reflected another image, one of their counter-force. While light surrounded the group as they prepared to make a stand of their own, the Skiá circled them at a distance, creating a storm of darkness around the group who worked on creating beacons of light. His threat was clear, they were already at his mercy. They had brought Teanna to negotiate with, and in turn he was demonstrating his own power. Their allies were ransom.

"Greetings, I thought while we discussed terms of surrender it would be prudent for you to witness what is at stake should you fail to satisfy my demands." Zo rushed forwards onto the bridge, closing the distance between herself and the minute images, hoping to discern more of the threats her friends faced, hoping to somehow warn Daniel. It wasn't until Seiken's arm grasped at her waist, pulling her back she realised Íkelos had retreated several small steps and the etchings upon the bridge's surface came aglow with the same darkened power as the mountains.

"A trap," Seiken whispered seeing the shimmer of a ward before them. It took barely a moment for him to understand why this force had not blocked their path previously, and with this realisation came a new found dread. He tightened his grasp on Zo. Íkelos' home, the Forest of the Epiales, had one very specific and dangerous trait, it suppressed and fed on magic, and so too did Íkelos' presence enforce this aura of this suppression.

"Not of my own making. I'm sure you realise there is a purpose to this city being built within running water. Spirits and those whose life is tethered to other realms are not welcome here."

"Alana—" Seiken attempted to voice his concerns, but instead she interrupted.

"Go, see if you can help the Wita. You are no longer of use to me," Alana commanded indifferently, as she stepped through the barrier onto the bridge. Íkelos' trap had solely prevented her parents from advancing. "Teanna, Fey, stay behind me." Alana didn't need to glance backward to see her parents were not only denied entry, but had been prevented from leaving by a single new addition to the carvings. To reveal her awareness of this, however, would be to lose an advantage.

"Well, yes, that I do acknowledge." He gestured towards the newer symbols roughly carved upon the bridge as Seiken discovered their retreat was also barred. Trapped within the small boundary, the two Oneirois could neither advance nor depart.

"Íkelos, we came here to negotiate." Alana's words were clipped, implying her frustration.

"Yet you come with a Fanger, and Oneirois." His image distorted slightly as he strode towards them, but his steps were carefully measured to ensure his distance kept the entrapment active. "If anyone should be concerned about deception, would it not be myself, the one cornered and outnumbered? Although I suppose the odds are more in my favour than you would believe, after all, I have the Willsayer on side. Or I will, as soon as I claim the final chakra. You were tracking the spread, and still you failed to see she was already my spy. I guess it is true, the heart really is your weakness, you never thought to look above it." Zo's face filled with alarm as she glanced from Alana to Seiken. "I know your every plan, I heard your every scheme, because I had her listening for me. You were wise to bring Teanna to me, but even now I cannot spare you."

"What is it you hope to achieve?" Alana questioned, standing her ground.

"Restoration, of course. Paion almost had it perfected, but his method was too inept. He would have destroyed the very souls I need to bring about the rebirth. How power has corrupted the minds and turned natural order askew. But you can die in the knowledge that your essences will become a thread to weave something new, something greater. Except, my dear niece, for yours.

"You will stand beside me, a trophy, a means to enforce my wishes on any who would threaten the new order, and with your husband as a hostage, even the Gods would dare not move against my plans." Zo gasped, falling to her knees as an invisible force constricted around her throat. "For years you believed you escaped my forest untouched. Long have I planned for this day. I helped to bring you and the Prince of Dreams together, and you will aid me willingly, or he will be the one to suffer. I've seen those claimed driven to madness by the torture of their possessor. How long do you think you can resist and endure when the one who claimed you cannot know death?"

"You want to rule?" Zo gasped as Seiken crouched beside her. She attempted to calm her erratic breathing, ignore the sensation of the tendrils crawling beneath her skin knowing this was a ploy to frighten her. The others he had claimed had been unnoticed, this one should be no different. She hadn't felt him claim her heart, and for him to say final suggested this was the only one left. She resisted the urge to claw at her throat as her breathing became laboured.

"Why do you people always think it is about control? Did your own father not teach you anything? He and I are not so different. We both want restoration, we both want to salvage what we can of this corrupted world. His way failed, even with the Severaine unleashed those of power remain unchallenged. My way is pure. You don't rebuild on crumbling foundations, you tear them down and start anew."

"Where does Teanna fit into this?" Fey questioned, shielding her protectively as Alana turned, attempting to discern a means to free her parents.

"She's the missing piece. The Maiden of Spirit, a former goddess. She alone possesses the power I need to rebuild the essences the Skiá are devouring. I will change and shape people into what they should be, and I will give them the ruler they were destined to follow."

"I'll not help you," Teanna called from behind Fey.

"Have you still not realised? I don't need your help, only your power," Íkelos snarled. Patience had been his forte for time immemorial, but now he no longer wanted to wait. As the three remaining obstacles advanced, he moved with swift grace and speed, flinging Fey aside with a backhand that possessed enough force he was thrown from the bridge crashing down into the swelling currents below. His armoured hand closed around Teanna's throat as the diplomat stood paralysed by his display of power. "After all this time..." The composition of his armour began to writhe. The vines within—once indistinguishable from muscle fibres—pulsated with excitement, making visible the aura of magic the woman struggling within his grasp held.

Her energy was a vibrant white, almost dazzling, but as its tendrils began to peel away to be consumed by his touch, he saw the darkness beneath. "What trickery is this?" he growled seeing the dirty blemish and the truth disguised beneath the surface. "You dare play me for a fool?" The vision before him warped, bones adjusting beneath his crushing grasp until her true visage emerged. Acha's long hair whipped around her as she clawed at his grasp around her throat, her bare hands having no effect on a power that had already once before left her helpless.

"Acha!" Zoella screamed her name in fear as she saw who he held, no doubt remembering the time both she and her half sister had fallen to his forest's lore many years ago.

"You seek to be devoured?" he mocked. "So be it." He released her sharply, striking her across the face with his heavy gauntlet. The impact caused her to stagger, her knees weakly struggled to hold her weight after having so much energy torn from within her. She had no time to react as the next blow came. Tendrils of shadows expanded from within the suspended portal, ensnaring her as the roots of his forest once had, dragging her flailing form from his sight until her screaming image appeared within, plummeting towards the sea of darkness below. He heard the sobbing of his niece, her mournful cries. "Teanna will soon be mine. Witness now the fate of those who dare deceive me." His gaze snapped towards Alana, "And you—"

"I invoke Champion Warfare," Alana announced, standing from the etchings which bound her parents, to sever his words sharply. Before they had departed, everyone had sought to offer her some small wisdom, and Rob had warned her these words held great power. He had used them himself. It was a creed honoured by even the most unscrupulous characters. Ultimately their confrontation would result in combat. There was no negotiation, not unless there was a scenario where losing the Spirit Maiden and her divine gift was acceptable. There wasn't.

"You and I, the victor claims the powers of the other." Íkelos laid down his terms. "You with all at your disposal, against me as I stand." Íkelos plucked a stone from the ground, gesturing for Alana to approach. He placed her hand upon his.

"We as we stand until a victor emerges," Alana confirmed. She felt the magical vibrations emanate from the stone. Íkelos opened his hand, the stone became dust which he released to the air, bringing his arm around quickly he stuck Alana, causing her to stagger backwards, the smear of blood already upon her lips.

"I should warn you, I possess the power of the Mystics, and of the four Elemental Maidens." Alana did not rise to his bait. It was better he was unaware of her own alignments. "I should have mentioned, I was using the shrine to relay commands to the Skiá, but I will give you the respect of my undivided focus. Words have power, and your challenge prevents me directing them. They will show no restraint to bring me my runaway bride." Alana did not glance toward the portal, there was no reason to, she could not see beyond it, but she knew what would be occurring. The Skiá would congregate in mass to the place Teanna stood. "There is one more thing I forgot to mention, my flesh was born of the Forest of Silence, magic is powerless in my presence."

"Are you going to stand there talking, or shall we end this?"

Chapter 31

Ancient Powers Collide

Their plan had been simplistic, yet brilliant. Thanks to Seiken's awareness of the true spread of corruption, and their real plans being schemed in whispers, Íkelos thought Teanna was within his grasp, and the Skiá thought she was amongst this group. The conflicting realisations kept them wary. It gave Daniel's warriors something they had desperately needed, time. Time to hastily construct the signal fires, time to prepare their assault, and time to organise the sanctuary. Having been briefed beforehand, the mercenaries moved like the tendrils of a single entity, each performing their designated task both independently and cooperatively.

There was no telling how long this respite would last. New beads of sweat accompanied each second of hurried motion and silent labour as apprehensive eyes searched the restless shadows.

Teanna stood in the centre of the sanctuary, clutching Chrissie's light card to her chest with a trembling grasp. She tried to clear her mind, to distance herself from knowing that the people before her had one sole purpose, to keep the darkness from reaching her. Through the bustle her gaze met with Daniel's. As if drawn by her unease he wove a hurried path between the thrum of activity until he stood beside her.

"How you holding up?" he questioned softly, wiping his forehead with the back of his hand. The heat from the flames surrounding them was stifling.

"In earnest, I'm terrified," she admitted in hushed tones as tears misted her eyes. "What happens when he disco—"

"Give that no thought. Acha knows what she's doing, you've felt the effects of her touch yourself."

"But..." She turned her gaze towards the floor, unable to bring herself to look at the people who would defend her.

"You're a pawn, bait," Daniel asserted firmly. "You're here because I needed you here to draw them to a single location. Don't misunderstand your role. You're important but, these men and women, their lives are on me, their actions by my command." Daniel had attempted his sternest voice, and was aware it was not as severe as he hoped. "While you're safe the Skiá will flock to us. It's our only chance to be rid of them."

"With weapons that can but hurt them?" she challenged.

"We are relying on something far more powerful than what we, mere mortals, hold."

"Something the lady will bring?"

"Something our collective power will summon." Teanna heard the unvoiced end to that sentence, the unspoken words, 'I hope,' rang in her ears louder than anything surrounding them.

"And if we fail, if an infected shadow breaches the sanctuary, or if your lady does not arrive, where then, pray-tell does that leave us?"

"In no worse situation than had we stood by idly." Daniel placed a hand upon her shoulder, trying his best to keep the tremble of fear undetected.

"And your weapon, the staff I've witnessed you carry, where is it? It is magical in nature, surely it is essential."

Daniel looked, with not quite shielded concern, to the halberd Tony had forged, his grasp upon its cool metal surface tightening. For years now he had trained with the same weapon. A weapon crafted for him by Zo to transfer insight and perception into action. The user needed no expertise in combat, only knowledge, and for that reason it had been the perfect—the only—weapon suitable for him. The halberd now in his possession was not without its charm. Its axe blade and hook—with a little imagination—looked to be a wyrm in flight, and the long thin spikes at either tip made it incredibly deadly. It was aesthetically pleasing and functionally perfect, for someone who knew how to wield it, someone like Alessia.

"It's not *too* different from my staff." Daniel seemed to be reassuring himself more than her, an act further emphasised as he twirled the halberd, treating it as if it were the tool he was so familiar with. "I just need to remember it has blades, doesn't detach, reflect magic or—look, it'll be fine. Let me worry about the melee. Your focus should be on maintaining the sanctuary." He offered a good-natured smile but she could still see the weight of his concern.

"But what if I—"

"Teanna, all you need to do is stand, and think about the barrier surrounding us. It won't extend beyond its reach, it won't weaken, but given that we needed to travel with it, Chrissie had to make it so it required focus to be maintained, otherwise it wouldn't have made the transition between places." He saw the doubt clouding her eyes. "Hey, if I can pretend this weapon is magical, you can think about a haven, agreed?"

"Agreed."

"We have beacons, flash bombs, flaming arrows—"

"Don't forget the slingshots!" added Rob as he moved to stand with them. Meeting Daniel's eyes he inclined his head towards Jones, relaying a silent message. "That fused ammo I've made is some of my finest." Daniel shot him an appreciative look as he took over comforting Teanna so he could address other matters. "Besides, Bray's a knight and a gentleman and, surely you know, gentlemen are never late, especially when there's a damsel in distress. You just think about protecting these folks, and let us worry about everything else."

"It's just..." Teanna's voice trailed into silence as she let her sight roam across the scene before her. Inside the dome of light small scattered piles of slingshot ammunition and arrows lay at designated intervals. The arrows stood in large oil filled quivers, ready to be ignited, and many small fires littered the area to make such a task an easy one. Bundles of wood and metal, cloth and powders, surrounded the area closest to her, to allow people to craft more, thus keeping the supply constantly restocked until their resources were depleted.

Small groups still unloaded supplies from their bags—most of which seemed to be crates and barrels with straps affixed—while others set and prepared caches near the barrier's edge. Her gaze found Daniel through the crowd once more, he was speaking with Jones, their animated gestures a sign of scarcely suppressed nerves as they spoke quietly, confirming and rechecking everything was progressing according to their plans. Outside the barrier was awash with deep and vibrant shades of lavender and wildflowers that spanned endlessly until the distant forest's borders. The trees looked dark and foreboding, barely visible through the encroaching mass of darkness that twisted their natural visage into more haunting images.

The mercenaries had divided into teams, wading their way through ankle deep grasses as they assembled to take their predetermined positions. The smell of sweat and fear carried on the wind with sulphurs and phosphates, oil and wood. No more than four mercenaries stood together, they would fight back to back, protecting each other's flanks, protecting her. Their experience in teamwork showed, and whilst the air was filled with the unmistakable tension of the coming battle—a battle which would decide the very fate of life—they stood united, as comrades.

Teanna allowed her gaze to venture further still, to the darkness that surrounded them. It broiled and writhed. In that one moment, as she watched, she knew not only the Skiá stood within the shadowed mass. The very source of nightmares walked amongst them. The Skiá were using the natural veil conjured by their uniformed presence to conceal something larger, their own mystikó óplo, a force that those gathered had not even thought to prepare for. Creatures that were the source of nightmares, creatures that could, if needed, walk in the light if only briefly.

"Epiales," Teanna whispered, recognising them from her studies in Talaria. Her warning came out strangled as her throat constricted. Íkelos was no fool. The Skiá could not touch her without inflicting the fatal injuries she had witnessed when they had laid siege to the mercenary camp. He needed something physical to retrieve her. She was certain they couldn't pass through the complex barrier that had surrounded their former base, but it was clear they had been drawn to the mortal world as physical manifestations. A field of light alone would be no match for them. "Epiales." Her voice failed her again as she tried to scream the word for all to hear, to warn them of the danger they could not yet perceive.

Excitement seemed to brew within the shadows, as a single shimmer from above, almost unseen but for its distortion, fractured the air. It was gone within a blink, and yet something of it remained behind, a figure whose last breath had cried out in terror. Acha. The form plummeting from above was dressed like herself, it could only mean one thing, Íkelos had already uncovered the truth. She watched in horror as Acha's body was swallowed by the darkness, lost forever in the tides of the blackened forest.

"Fortify!" Daniel's loud cry rang through the air, causing postures to stiffen further just moments before the battle began.

* * *

Alana allowed the impression of her surroundings to wash over her. Windsight gave her an amazing view, bridges, movement, air currents, and hiding places. Anything the wind could touch, with focus, her mind could see. She could see her father, offering comfort to her mother, but this was how things were meant to be. She alone could stand against Íkelos. The Fanger was lost and Acha had been thrown to feed the beasts. Both she and Acha had known he would see through their ruse, but she had not expected it to be so soon. She had hoped to learn more of his plans, of the purpose of the Skiá, and a way to stop them.

Alana knew she still held an advantage. He spoke of his body being forged of things which devoured magic, yet she felt the disturbance in the currents around her as he commanded the elements to obey his will, proving not all magic was suppressed. Plumes of water erupted from the surface of the river, hurtling towards her. Waters rained down as the bulk of the shoots were driven with such force it caused the bridge to rumble beneath her feet. Raising her hand she captured the flow, focusing her strength into forcing it back towards their manipulator as she wrestled the control from him. She rolled as a second volley showered down from above.

"A water Elementalist," Íkelos observed seeing the way the water coiled above her, its flow winding like a mighty serpent being unleashed. Mist flooded the bridge, mingling with the fog which rolled in around them as Alana severed the unity of the flowing water, dissolving it into a fine, harmless spray that soaked her clothing in mere seconds while she drew excess moisture from the earth. She wiped the hair plastered against her skin with her hand, concealing her steps within the natural billowing movement of the moisture. The confusion in his voice had barely been disguised, he had spoken of his presence suppressing magic, and yet here she stood, his equal, using that which should be silenced. He closed a little more of the distance between them, perhaps assuming he was too far away to stifle her abilities.

She knew what needed to be done. She had trained for this moment, but he had more power than expected. Her only advantage was his arrogance. He thought he alone could wield magic, but it was clear the forest of the Epiales, a place her parents had told cautionary tales of when she was an infant, had made some allowances so he could still use certain energy signatures. Little did he know she held the same gifts as those he had stolen. After all, he would not entertain the notion of something impossible.

A barrage of waves crashed over head, stealing her breath as the force fractured the weathered stone parapets sending remnants of ancient and broken fragments tumbling and grinding across the bridge's surface, sweeping it through the large decorative openings. Her footing slipped as the powerful current knocked her feet from beneath her, her fingers clawed for purchase as earth and rocks gathered, its solid formation splitting and redirecting the raging tide, while her mind unleashed earth-splitting tremors at the location she had last seen his dark silhouette. The river broke free of his control, calming once more as her attack staggered him. Taking advantage of his slight disorientation she charged through the settling mist, lunging forwards, fracturing earth from his feet to pelt him, driving him backwards until they were both on even footing.

Earth became mud, falling harmlessly around him giving rise to dust as he baked it with fire, flooding the surroundings with a dust cloud. Alana froze, whilst she could see through barricades of water, her windsight was unable to penetrate barriers of earth. She listened intently, trying to hear above the roaring of the water. She felt the chill encompass her too late, ice ruptured from the water soaking her clothes, sinking deep into the ground to bind her in place in long sharp spears.

"Earth and water, what a master you must have had." Íkelos approached. "I'll enjoy this feast, young one, look at you, you could have been spectacular. So much power. But now it is useless." His armour began to glow, forcing her own energy to answer in kind. "Don't struggle. You displayed skill, but I possess the strength of the Mystics, and just as I used their power to draw the energy from the water, so too will they let me draw the power from you in this realm." Íkelos extended his hand, the pulsating of energy within his armour growing more rapid as tendrils of vine and ether uncoiled to reach towards her. With each advance she could feel the syphoning pressure of his aura pulling her energy towards him while she fought to resist.

Small plumes of condensation escaped her lips as she embraced phoenix's element to raise her body temperature. Focused on her task, on manipulating the energy within, she attempted to ignore his slow and draining approach as her stamina waned. She squirmed within the ice's grasp, pulling deeper on the heat. Echoing within his footsteps she could hear the drip of ice becoming water and pushed harder, expelling the scalding power. Ice dissipated into steam as Íkelos lunged forwards, his extending hand glanced her shoulder as she leapt aside, her movements as fluid and graceful as water itself as she feinted her retreat, using the rising steam to conceal herself as she slid behind him.

With swiftness and accuracy she struck, her open palm thrusting squarely between his shoulder blades. The power behind the blow was weak, unable to even unbalance his wide stance, but damage had never been her intention. As contact was made she unleashed a power from within, channelling it through herself into his body and releasing everything the Great Water Spirit had bestowed upon her, forcing it into Íkelos to seek and reclaim the Water Maiden's essence. Her released attunement bound his with perfect precision and harmony, tearing it from his possession. Mist rose from his armoured body as the last of this stolen element's power disappeared with her own into the ether.

* * *

Teanna wanted to close her eyes, to look away and plug her ears. Screams tore through the swarms of darkness, mimicking those of the battlefield's first dead to create a chorus of eerie echoes that spread throughout the darkness as the whirlwind of chaos and violence bore its fangs like a rabid beast. Flaming arrows, crackling with flash powder, created blinding arcs across the sky, their targets carefully selected as fire rained down death in places where markers and planning had warned allies not to tread. Seemingly random signals pierced the air, a warning to the mercenaries of which area was about to be ignited with blinding fury. Even despite these precautions Teanna knew not all arrows would fly true, not all eyes would be undazed, and not every warrior would hold their position.

The Skiá had goaded the mercenaries, drawing them closer before peeling back and unleashing the monsters which roamed within. Their dark figures locked to a single charge. Their battle cry echoed with the haunting sound of fear and nightmares. Screams of child and adult, animal and beast, amalgamated with primal sounds that even now resonated with the ancient parts of mortals' brains. Darkness had been feared for a reason, and two of those reasons surrounded them.

The sound of the god-forged metal impacting the not-quite organic flesh of towering monstrosities did little more than create openings for faster, more agile creatures to exploit. Teanna could see it all, feel it all, as if part of her was somehow connected to each person before her. The most terrifying thing, the thing that unsettled her more than the darkness, more than the fear, was that those who fell were being left alive. Left to suffer before becoming a feast for beings more powerful than anything they had faced before.

Those closest to her wrapped and crafted ammunition in a rapid flurry of well-practised movements. Their stony gazes fixed solely on their work, drowning out the cries of a battle they soon would become a part of when others fell back. She wished she had their resolve. She wished she had their focus. But all she could do was stand in the centre of the massacre, hearing the screams, aware of the suffering, and waiting for the darkness to carve a path to her.

* * *

Íkelos felt the power of the Maiden leave him. The water still under his control slipped from his grasp, quieting the swell, returning the river to its natural state as its remaining torrents cascaded magnificently from the bridge, spilling over the sides before joining with the rest of the flow in the lakes below.

"What are you?" Íkelos growled, turning to face her. His words were met only by the sound of a second strike, unexpected, unanticipated. His adversary lost no time in regaining her focus, or catching her breath. Her first blow had been followed immediately, catching him unprepared as his mind reeled and he tried to discern what had occurred.

He staggered backwards, feeling the threads of energy once again invade his essence. His grasp of the Earth Maiden faltered, his confusion almost paralysing before survival took root causing him to leap back in time to evade the third attack. He had felt her own energy binding his. Her power was somehow equal to that he had taken from those blessed by the Spirits.

While he evaded her advance, he wondered how such a force could have been overlooked when he had used one of the Daimons to scry for powerful magic. The simple answer was, it couldn't. He had detected every potent esoteric power, that was why he had been able to locate the Maidens, those who he himself had shielded at birth, as well as pinpoint the Mystics. Nothing could have escaped his gaze, and yet here stood a woman who had matched two of his abilities in power.

He needed a moment to think, to assess her latent abilities and discover what lay beneath her guarded aura. Something was shielding her true capabilities from him, and for some reason, even close proximity had no effect on the power she wielded. He dodged another rapid succession of strikes, his balance faltering as the ground grew uneven underfoot. He rolled aside, he had seen enough to know he had an advantage, he had been close enough to witness her sightless eyes.

The roar of flames surrounded them as the howling winds rose. She may have possessed the skill to nullify his earth and water alignments, but there wasn't an Elementalist alive who had mastered such skill in more than one, that she held two was impressive. Three would be unheard of. By using her power to seal his she had left herself powerless, except for, perhaps, a few novice abilities that her former master or masters may have possessed.

The figure before him froze, overwhelmed by the bombardment on her other senses, the noise, the heat, the air currents. Wasting no time Íkelos struck out, fanning the fire with the air, sending streams of molten flames towards her. She had moved, but not quickly enough. He watched in satisfaction as her body skimmed across the ground, her rapid movements stopped only by the impact of her body upon the sturdy brick structure that marked the entrance to the city.

The rickety groan and creak of the waterwheels masked the sound of his almost-silent advance. He looked down upon her in disdain as she attempted to pull herself upwards, her limbs trembling as she reached up to the stonework, using its solid support to aid her. His hand extended, grasping her firmly, dragging her to her feet with such force he felt the tear of fabric beneath his solid grip.

He looked upon her, his gaze slowly dismantling her own protection as he attempted to strip away her mental defences. He had to know where this power came from. Drawing his vision to her face, all too late he saw the crooked smile upon her lips. He had fallen for her ploy, she was not as injured as he had thought. Her leg kicked out, connecting with his torso.

Íkelos felt his grasp release as the pressure of energy propelled him backwards. It raced through him, seizing the Fire Maiden's magic and tearing it from him. He felt the force of the strike continue, forcing him backwards, pinning him to the wall. It was only as she stood before him, panting for breath, he noticed the tikéta. The torn fabric displayed an unmistakable marking, one he had longed to see. This young lady could use all four elements with power and mastery beyond that of the Maidens, an impossible feat but for a single person.

He flinched as she placed her hand upon his chest. The powerful wind magic pinning him in place ceased as the final Maiden's energy was released from his capture. Íkelos moved quickly, striking out with such force Alana tumbled head over heels. He was livid. Crouched before him, covered in dirt and blood, had been the Mitéra. She was young, too young by at least thirteen moons to have earned the title attached to the magic she had brandished.

"You fool, what did you do?" He struck her again. There was but one means for her to have obtained the power she wielded, she had to have taken parts of the Spirits into herself. Without completing the rites to open the correct meridians she had doomed the beings that aided her to imprisonment. He could see her essence now, a perfect mortal copy of the once magnificent being. Remaking her would be simple, but with the Spirits bound to their shrines there was no being capable of recognising and naming his recreation. His entire plan unravelled before his gaze. Without the Spirits, no new Mitéra could rise.

Íkelos glanced towards his niece, she and her husband fought desperately to find a way to break the runes binding them, as he watched their struggle a smile spread across his face. Zoella had already provided the answer, a means to locate another Spirit, the only one no longer bound. He glanced skyward recalling her words, Talaria will fall.

In a single breath his plan changed. He would need Teanna alive to manipulate the Spirit, as for the woman before him, the patchwork Mitéra made from clipped and fused essences, she was useless, the Skiá could feast upon her so he may recreate her true brilliance.

* * *

Something had shifted. Zo could feel Íkelos' energy still snaking through her, she could feel its advance as it attempted to gain control. The pressure of his will, his desires, bore down on her as nearly audible whispers. There was a frustration within them, an anger that made her fear for their lives.

"Seiken, can't you do something?" Zo begged. She had witnessed his power, his ability to find and exploit fractures in spells and logic.

"Thea," he sighed softly, he knew what she was thinking. When she had been lost in the Forest of the Epiales he had come to her, warned her, but the price of doing so had been high. "The forest's silence is less effective on me, but in this realm there's nothing I could do. Why do you think he trapped us rather than just barricaded our entry?"

"Then, we're useless. What is even the point of being here if we are powerless to be of aid?" She sank to her knees, her vision burning into the symbols which had bound them in place. She recognised them. They were the same as those used by the Moirai. She covered her eyes realising he only knew how to detain them thanks to her. "I am sorry, this is all my fault. He knew you were coming, he knew your plans, he even saw through me how to accomplish this." She gestured towards the markings, bile burning her throat.

"Thea." Zo turned, feeling Seiken's hand rest gently upon her shoulder. "I've known since Phoenix Landing how far his manipulation reached. When I left with the crystal it was to warn Daniel, but it was you I cautioned him against. We decided to turn his spy against him. Since then, everything you've heard has been carefully scripted. Did you not question why no one addressed Alana by her title? We feared there may be a fusion with the forest's magic, but this also told us that it would have to have made allowances for certain magics to be utilised. With the Maidens' power inside him, only the Mitéra could mirror the magic needed. We had to keep her identity safe. He could hear through you, but he doesn't know your thoughts."

"What do you mean?" Seiken shifted, moving to sit beside her.

"Íkelos was bound to behold us as a threat, as I say, the forest's effects are less on us. Daniel devised a plan to destroy the Skiá, but in order for it to work we needed to buy time. While Íkelos was focusing on Acha, thinking she was Teanna, he was unaware of Daniel's pieces being manoeuvred into place. While we still don't know the true reason for his bringing the Skiá here we know they are vital to his plan. If we were to remove them then his plan becomes hindered."

"What aren't you telling me?"

"We are here in the capacity of The Chosen, but our presence is not intended to resolve this conflict, and yet it is essential to ending it."

"How?"

"You're going to be the courier to the one thing missing, the only thing that can stop Íkelos, The Hand of Deliverance." Zo's brow furrowed at his words as she pieced everything she knew together. She and Seiken carried no weapons, they were trapped, there was no way to retrieve anything.

"How is that even possible, you don't mean?" Zo glanced to her battered satchel. She never travelled without it. It possessed medicine, remedies, potions, and alchemical tools, but there was something else about it too. The embroideries and enchantments she had placed upon it many years ago had given it a very special property, one she had included when she crafted a satchel for Daniel when she thought they would never cross paths again in this life or any other. "But I never showed Daniel how to use it."

"No, but I did."

* * *

Daniel's grip on his weapon tightened as he watched a charging shadow fix its stare beyond him, beyond the start of the sanctuary, to Teanna.

From its shape alone he could tell it was not one of the many large creature resembling hippopotami. These horrific beasts, with their giant gaping mouths stretched to impossible lengths, would bare their bone-breaking long teeth before releasing swarms of smaller creatures or tendrils from their gullet. Despite the appearance of the Epiales—the waking visions of nightmares made flesh—the mercenaries, to their credit, held, seemingly unperturbed by the ghastly forms before them.

Perhaps it was as his brother had one said long ago, killing a monster is easier than killing a man, and sometimes a man must become a monster, if only in your own perception. Daniel understood his brother's logic. There was a distance of comfort between taking the life of something different and something from your own species, at least to most.

He had prepared those who stood with him as best as he was able. Unsure of what the Skiá could be he had spoken of the Epiales, of how they manifested in the forms of nightmares, and he spoke of darkness and terror and its many forms, but even he had not been prepared to cross paths with the beast that now charged. He had never seen so much as a sketch, or even a footnote, of such a creature; but as his vision fixed upon the three horned beast, the voices of the ancestors became deafening. The thing charging, with its head lowered thrusting back and forth in goring movements to clear its path, was known as an Odontotyrannos.

Its three horns protruded like fine tempered blades from its forehead. Its skin, while looking similar to hide, shimmered like scales as the light from flash bombs and cascading arrows streaked the sky above. It tore through enemy and ally without mercy, propelling anything in its way into the air as it thrust them from its path under the direction of the shadowed figure upon its back who steered it towards its sole target, Teanna.

Daniel's eyes roved across the shadows, across the blood soaked grass. His own mind drowning out the cries of the dying, while mentally tracking a rapid path to intercept the creature. He moved without thought, trusting his instincts, trusting his body would not betray him.

Using the halberd he sprinted forwards, lowering the butt spike and using it to vault into the air towards the enormous creature. Twisting and tucking the weapon beneath his arm he braced himself for the jarring impact. Landing with a precision he had Alessia to thank for, he drove the tip deep into the creature's flesh. It howled, yet its pace never slowed. Jostled from side to side, Daniel's fingers missed the hilt on Tony's short sword once, twice, his fingers finally grasping it as his grip on the halberd began to falter from the brutal momentum.

The creature's enormous rump twitched as it let out a nightmarish shriek, yet it continued to advance, unhindered by his effort. Daniel's plan had been simple, mount the creature, throw off the rider, and divert its charge. But as the shadowed mass he thought had been a separate entity, shuddered and lurched Daniel saw the hide of the creature ripple, sliding the rider towards him. Two seemingly independent beings were fused in one nightmarish visage. He struggled to hold on, all too aware of the rider's advance.

Everything was happening too quickly. The world around him sped by, screams of allies and howls of Epiales overwhelmed his hearing while the acrid stench of battle flooded his mouth with each laboured breath. It was all he could do to retain his grip, to stay rooted in place as he clutched his embedded weapons with cramping hands. Burning arrows exploded before him as archers, seeing the danger, focused their aim on the charging beast. Projectiles targeting the moving rider whizzed by, too close for comfort splitting the air with fire and whistles, and still, all he could do was flail, jolted by each of the creature's thundering steps, as the rider slid ever closer. He needed to pull himself upwards, to gain purchase, but his muscles were burning, his strength waning.

The last hours of his life flashed before his eyes, the gathering, Alessia, his talk with Jones. As a flash bomb exploded to his left the words they had exchanged rang clear, like a divine bell overshadowing the noise and chaos, and heeding the words passed down from his brother, Daniel took a deep breath. It was nothing, remembering to breathe, focusing on that one thing. Yet in that instant everything became clearer. He pushed aside the world beyond himself, the overwhelming bombardment of his senses, and focused on solely what he needed to do. As the creature's rump twitched again, he used the momentum to pull himself up onto its back, ripping the short sword from the beast, he whispered the word bestowed upon them by Blacksmith Tony. As the sword continued its arc his weapons came aglow with the divine light that slept within the ore. Using the force of freeing the blade to gain power the sword's rapid momentum sliced the rider in twain. For a moment nothing happened, then, as if shaken free by the beast's rapid charge, the two halves peeled away with a sickening organic squelching sound to sag beneath the creature.

The Odontotyrannos let out a blood curdling roar. The sagging masses hung like loose skin at its underbelly, tangling underfoot, reducing the speed of creature's thundering charge as it began to draw the severed flesh back into itself. Pulsating bulges beneath its scales began to grow, pushing upwards slowly near its massive, muscular shoulder blades. Seeing his opportunity was limited, Daniel released the halberd, his fingers coiling around the gaps in the scales as he dragged himself towards where the rider first sat. With the sword grasped tightly, he focused on his target, the one area of weakness he knew to exploit, the creature's horns. Blow after blow he chipped away, until, with a howl, it veered from course, bucking and twisting in an attempt to throw him off. But Daniel had one experience it could never have imagined, he had ridden wyrms.

His thighs clenched, and his muscles burned as he held himself in place, continuing to hack at the creature until the horns, all sharing a single bone core, were severed. He brought down the blade once more to bury it deep within this core severing the artery and thrusting the through to its brain. The creature tumbled, a mass of shadows poured from the wound, erupting like blood but reforming the moment it became airborne. These powerful arterial-like sprays took on a new manifestation, separating and coagulating until the newly formed winged creatures flooded the air, but he only saw them briefly as the hulking mammoth beneath him collapsed.

Daniel pressed himself tightly against the creature as it fell, instantly regretting the instinctive decision as the impact of the ground slammed against him with a pressure that ripped the sword from his grasp and, by some miracle, left him alive but pinned beneath the screaming beast's deflating and shrivelling form.

Straining against the oppressive weight, he tried to pull himself free. His attempts doing little more than creating deep grooves in the ground and shredding the grass beneath him as he twisted and writhed. Above, he watched as the creatures formed from the Odontotyrannos' blood—Meganeura, a silent voice informed him—swooped down on unsuspecting targets. These creatures, however, weren't those from ancient legends. Twisted by nightmares they became something more, something horrendous that attached itself to its prey with leech-like jaws that traced their legs like the suckers on a kraken, while their venomous teeth devoured their meal.

Their large wings made them easy marks for the archers and catapults, many fell screeching to the ground, neutralised before being able to secure themselves to an unsuspecting being. Daniel extended his arm, his vision fixed upon the short sword that had been thrown from his grasp during the impact. His fingers grazed the blade as he attempted to draw it closer. Flexing several times, he rolled his shoulders, straining, all in an attempt to grasp it. He was vulnerable, exposed; unarmed and pinned beneath the remaining bulk of the Odontotyrannos. His heart pounded, sweat causing his skin to become slick. He tore at the grass, hoping to somehow bring the sword even a fraction closer.

The rustling of wings surrounding him grew louder as creatures, drawn by the scent of his blood from his nicked fingers skimming the blade's tip, sought to find its source. Only as a volley of arrows rained down, forcing Daniel to hug himself closer to the beast, did he see the crimson stains spreading beneath him. His pulse echoed through his ears as the creature's fatty tissue ignited where arrows pierced, releasing noxious odours into the air as the flames charred and melted its flesh. He stretched again, his shoulders protesting the over extension as he feebly gained precious few inches from the slickness of the ground beneath him. It was almost nothing, but it had been just enough to grasp the sword's tip.

His blade penetrated the flesh, spilling foul fluids upon him as what seemed to be rotting entrails and muscle streamed from the wound in a seemingly endless supply. He attempted to hold his breath, turning his head one way then the other, his hand pushing against the wound in an attempt to still its disgusting discharge until he had no choice but to suck in the putrid air. His stomach contracted with each heave and gag as the taste the rotting fluids assailed his nose and mouth. His arms flailed as he shoved the building entrails from him. Despite their volume, the pressure pinning him did not relent.

Chapter 32

Destiny's Path

Fey clawed at the riverbank, coughing and spluttering water. He gasped and heaved as he attempted to heft himself up the steep bank, his hands slipping in the thick sucking mud. Reaching out he grasped a root, his slick hand threatening to slip as he kicked and slid in the earth. The water's forceful manipulation had saturated the normally dry banks, and the frosted ground had drank the frigid fluids hungrily.

A downward glance reminded him the currents had not yet calmed, and his grip tightened, fearing he would lack the energy to fight the currents and undertow again. For a moment he stopped struggling, his limbs burning from his fight to reach safety. Those few seconds felt too long for his tired muscles, but they were enough to allow him to begin the struggle anew. He thrust his hand upward, his feet slipping and scraping, trying to find the traction needed. His fingers coiled around a higher root but he was drained, exhausted, and it was several moments before he found the strength needed to drag himself up. He lay, panting for breath, his muscles trembling and for just a few seconds, allowed himself to savour the feeling of warmth being reflected back to him from the mud.

He knew time was of the essence. Whilst Alana's quick but subtle reactions had saved him from death by ensuring the water became a barrier protecting him rather than a crushing tidal wave, he was far further from them than he would have liked. He could see the bridge, streaks of fire caressed the air, leaving burning afterglows and sprays of rainbows as water and fire magic merged.

Staggering to his feet he pulled himself unsteadily to the tree line, leaning on the rough trunks for support, trying desperately to regain his composure. He did not understand why Alana had chosen him for this task; it seemed like something expected from someone who was more than a simple guide. Alana had informed him he was something called a Fanger, and was bound to Teanna. Apparently, lifetimes ago, he had been the guardian to deliver the blow that separated Íkelos' body from spirit allowing the Mystics to seal his essence within the Forest of the Epiales. He had been born for this task, to protect the Maiden of Spirit and was to use that bond to allow them to once more seal the threat. To do that, however, he needed to be there. Mopping his brow, his fingers left trenches in the thick mud that now adorned him.

There would be but a small window of opportunity once the essence of magic from the four Elemental Maidens had been removed. It would come at the time when Alana would be forced to draw on the power of the Goddess' Tear, but while Íkelos still possessed the body forged from the forest he could syphon power from that domain, tipping the balance of power and condemning Alana to the prison in his place.

Fey hurried. His legs and lungs burning from the exertion as drying mud cracked and broke free from his stiffened clothes. He saw the flash of movement in the shadows, the glowing of predatory eyes, and cursed silently as he made an effort to steady his fatigued breathing. Whilst he knew the Skiá had now been drawn to Daniel and his mercenaries, there were still other predators to be wary of. Fey froze. Before him the guttural growl of the wolf looked down upon him from the rocky verge. The shadows behind him began to encroach, echoing the snarls of their alpha. He stood still, listening intently, and he could hear the quiet whines of pups. Raising his hands Fey took a step backwards. He lifted his gaze to meet that of the alpha.

His father had always maintained that this would be a sign of hostility yet, for Fey, he had discovered that when he looked into the eyes of another animal it was almost as if they sensed his soul. Perhaps, he thought, it was something related to the fact he had been bound to the Spirit Maiden. Creatures of the forest rarely attacked him, and it always seemed to be humans he needed to be cautious of, those who hid their souls and intentions through lies and masks. Animals, however, had no need for pretence. As their tether extended the snarls of those surrounding him silenced, and he and the alpha shared a silent understanding.

The alpha's growl ceased, but his teeth remained bared. His beautiful silvery head turned towards the forest, in an indication he would let him pass, but not this way, not near their pups. Fey nodded slowly, and carefully sidestepped. The wolves parted, allowing him entrance into the trees. He was aware of their stalking silhouettes continuing to pursue him, keeping their distance, observing him intently until they were satisfied he was far enough away. Only when they left did he begin to run. The detour had added minutes to his journey, and each delay put everyone in further danger.

* * *

Rob surveyed the battle, his nimble fingers making quick work of constructing more flash bombs. Overwhelming odds like these reminded him of the years he had spent exploring The Depths of Acheron. He had journeyed alone through the terrifying domain, facing beings and creatures he thought had been born from nightmares. But he could see now that the monsters in The Depths were just animals, albeit evolved and terrifying animals. The things the mercenaries struggled to hold back, they were the true face of nightmares.

His fingers worked autonomously while his legs grew restless. This was not the place for him, and he knew it all too well. He felt the call, the pull of something from within the shadows, and he knew it was a cry he must answer.

Bright flashes illuminated the battlefield like lightning, their rapid succession bringing highlights to the more serious scenes of battle. For but a second he glimpsed a dark silhouette felling a massive beast before the scene faded, only for flaming arrows to glint from shimmering wings as hundreds of creatures erupted from the fallen monstrosity.

Seeing the winged creatures descending he pulled his small crossbow from its tether on his belt. His aim tearing through the creatures' wings with ease, until he had only a few, very specialised, bolts remaining. He looked for a bow but, knowing they were in the hands of people who could use them with the skill and precision, he relayed orders as the swarm descended in mass upon the fighting mercenaries. Arrows streaked the air severing wings and splitting the large segmented bodies.

Rob's eyes once more scanned the battlefield. He could feel the distant pull growing, the call was becoming louder. Somewhere amongst the Skiá was a portal. He glanced towards the sky, wondering if the full moon was upon them. He instantly cursed his foolishness as his vision met only with the thick smothering embrace of the black clouds. Night or day, it all looked the same.

Rob glanced towards Teanna, their eyes briefly meeting through a sea of sweating muscles and exhausted warriors as he advanced. Being unexperienced in melee, watching this woman and instructing those within the sanctuary on wrapping flares and flash powder alchemy, had been his designated role. However, if his theory was correct, if he truly felt the tingle of energy, then he was certain he could prevent the Skiá's reinforcements arriving. Somewhere, in the mass of bloodshed and shadow, was a gateway, he could feel the pull of the magical web binding it as it prepared to open.

He studied the features of the terrified figure before him as she wiped the strings of vomit from her face with a quick swipe of her arm. He knew she had never seen a war. Given her past it was unlikely she had even seen bloodshed. She stood frozen in place, whispering words in a dialect he was unfamiliar with. He took it to be a prayer, a way to focus on the sanctuary she believed her thoughts maintained. Her vision always seemed to snap to the most horrific scene, scenes of man or woman being torn apart, the churning howls of agony. It was almost as if on some level she was connected with the battle, connected to each mercenary within. Another bout of vomiting reflected every fatal injury. Tears streaked her face, her eyes unblinking as she took in every moment of the carnage with vivid clarity.

"Teanna." His firm voice drew her attention from the place dust and earth rose from the creature Daniel had slain. She had thought for certain it would reach the sanctuary, that it would claim her. Part of her had hoped for its success, then this senseless slaughter would be over.

"I understand, go." He saw her mouth the words, but her voice failed to accompany it. He nodded, glad he had thought to suggest to Daniel that they kept her mind occupied with the thoughts of the sanctuary. They had both come to the same conclusion, but he had voiced it. Her distraction was essential and her crucial role would keep her focused on something other than the death surrounding her. While she thought she was the hope of those fighting, that she kept them safe, she would not contemplate foolish or rash actions. Chrissie had even managed to add a minor enchantment to the card, so Teanna focusing on the barrier would divert negligible amounts of energy, enough to give the ward the feel of Teanna's energy and thus drawing any stray Skiá into the fray.

Rob sprinted, pausing only at the sanctuary's edge to cast a final look back towards Teanna. Embraced by the light she looked like a goddess standing upon a field of Lavender, watching the wars of man with tear-streaked cheeks flushed with horror. He turned his vision away, the darkness looming seeming all the more foreboding after glimpsing her almost awe-inspiring visage. With a breath and a ill-considered notion of a plan, Rob charged into the fray. Instinct guided his steps as he jumped and wove, ducked and careened around creatures, sliding beneath the clashing of claws against weapons his focus never faltering. Their allies were too few, the enemy too vast. But he would turn the odds in their favour, he had to. He was probably the only person amongst them who could *see* a magical web, not to mention possess the skill and knowledge of how to sever one.

With burning muscles Rob wove and dodged in ways that defied belief, ways that had saved his life both in the past, and present. As he pushed his way into the Skiá, a haunting thought plagued his mind. The Epiales had given this shadowy force an advantage, so why weren't they attacking, what was stopping these shadows from joining the fray and clearing the path to Teanna? The Skiá would be unable to penetrate the light, but if they reached the start of the barrier then most of the mercenaries would have already fallen, along with the weapons capable of harming them, leaving the Epiales free to claim their prize. A cold shiver coursed through him. With such a clear tactical and numerical advantage, why had they yet to exploit it?

* * *

Taya sat proudly, scarcely disguising her frustration at not being able to accompany her brave warriors. While few in number, when news had reached them of how Rob was to enter the fray, it had been as if a silent call to arms had rang throughout their great city. Not all Daimons were fighters, some would slip unnoticed amongst the ranks of healers, but those who could, would mount an aerial assault. She had felt no small measure of pride when her most trusted warriors came to her bearing arms, laying them at her feet in a silent request. No words had been needed as they knelt before her, ready for battle. Her permission had been nothing more than a decisive nod. Had they not approached, she would have beckoned them herself.

From their time trapped within the Betwixt they had developed a method of travel none so far on this world had duplicated. Leather, bone, and sinew had been skillfully woven and crafted into a frame capable of supporting the weight of one or two of their people. With their wings extended, even with no wind to carry them, the release of their magic would grant lift allowing them to take to the sky. Unless their magic was in demand, Daimons' wings remained part of their internal skeleton, breaking free from the flesh to create membrane webbings of magic as they released their restraint on the great power they held within.

Geburah was the last to approach, his unearthly wings forged from Lampads' magic cast an eerie glow upon his armour while the two score of Daimons averted their gaze, hurrying past his enormous frame to prepare themselves. Taya smiled to see he had donned his battle helm. It rested upon his head as if it were part of his own skull, its composition identical to his own flesh in order to portray a terrifying image. The intention had been for the large horns to invoke further fear into the hearts of those he faced by fully embracing the visage of a demon from their legends. She only hoped he would be recognised as an ally and not mistaken for one of the nightmares made flesh. He stepped aside, allowing Yuri to approach and kiss her tenderly. Her heart fluttered as she beheld him adorned in the magnificent armour of a king. Lightweight, but imbued with magic, nature, and even its own healing reserves. There was no question he could command a room with but a glance, just as he had commanded her heart from the moment their gaze had first met.

"Fear not, we shall return, and I will not have you wait for me as long as I did for you." Yuri smiled, lifting her hand to place another delicate kiss upon his wife's cool skin.

"I only wish I could be in attendance, damn this infernal contraption. What right have I to rule when I cannot fight beside my people?" Her gaze lingered upon Yuri's sculpted armour appreciatively, just moments before her grasp tightened on the the metal of her chair's arm, her frustration evident as she berated her own weakness. She should be amidst her people, *she* should be securing the future. The Sfaíra was intended to be the keeper of the realm, a protector and leader. Confined in this manner she was of little use to anyone.

"There will be other battles," Yuri comforted, "other means for you to place us in awe of your formidable talents."

"Yes, do behold my formidable skill of sitting, and waiting," she accosted, biting her lower lip to prevent further slips.

"Patience is an undervalued virtue." He kissed her forehead softly. "Time grows short, the Kyklos report Rob is already aware of the portal, it will only be a matter of time before he finds himself in need."

"We must ensure he can reach it. There is little point us having endured what we did to raise our land to the light if we now lose the world to darkness. I once vowed to give you the sun, now you must return my gift," Taya instructed.

"I will, Sfaíra."

"May the Spirits and ancestors watch over you."

* * *

Acha groaned, blood spilling from her mouth as she moved ever so slightly, enough to feel the swelling against each and every broken bone. The fluid from her mouth spilt onto the saturated ground, mingling with the spreading death that coated the barren landscape that had been stripped of life to sustain her fatally wounded vessel. Her chest burned and rattled as she struggled to pull in a laboured breath while her head throbbed painfully in time with her rapid, shallow pulse. Each movement was agony, each second torture, as she mentally sought new sustenance, enough to allow her to roll to her side, expelling dark red clots in the place of bile.

Darkness surrounded her like a stifling blanket. The only light came from distant signal fires, beacons that seemed too far to even dream of reaching. She was unsure how long had passed since Íkelos had cast her through the portal, but she had vomited several more times, each vile expulsion easing the pressure in her chest as her body stripped the life from anything and everything it could seek out and touch, grass, flowers, even the Skiá.

The events from the past minutes were nothing more than vague impressions. Sweat poured from her as she slipped in and out of consciousness, but each time she awoke, the pain had lessened. Acha heard a whispering presence in her mind, a vague suggestion of confusion. Something nearby wanted to attack, to lash out and swarm with the Epiales as had been their intention, but they were waiting on the command, the voice of their alpha.

Acha's head began to throb. Flashes of an attack led against her, of her body instinctively drawing the energy from those who attempted to devour her. It was with a shivering realisation she recalled the claws digging deep into her broken body. The most powerful Skiá amongst them claimed feasting rites just moments before she tore the essence from it devouring it and its followers.

Embers of panic were doused by the recollection of Alana's words. As long as she didn't attempt to place herself in any other thing, the Skiá could not possess her, not like they had before. Her body would not be theirs to control, but that was not the only danger. Digging deep she allowed her mind to embrace the part of the Skiá she had absorbed and whispered but a single command. A command that took all her strength.

"Hold."

She felt the eagerness of those surrounding her, their numbers fewer than the darkness they travelled within would have any believe. With that command she felt the strain of each Skiá tethered to her. The bond of the alpha ensured its word was law, and its will was enforced upon all others. She had considered this a hive-mind, but while subservient to a single being there was a constant challenge being issued to the role of leader, only the strongest mind could control the hive, and at this moment they thought it to be her.

The pressure of their desire to charge was, in a way, a challenge for supremacy. Should she fail to restrain them, the will that broke her desire would become the new alpha and lead the charge on her friends. She didn't know how long she could suppress them for, not in her current condition.

Digging her fingers into the dry earth she dragged herself along, begging to feel the tingle of life beneath her grasp. The tethers from the Skiá sustained her, allowed her to dominate their will. But she could not afford to absorb much more of their energy, and her body was failing, and with it, her consciousness. It was with a deep-rooted horror she realised why they still considered her to be the alpha. They only waited to charge because, as she had devoured the essence of those surrounding her, she had given the order to unleash the Epiales. Her will, her power from consuming the Skiá, had been so absolute in that one exchange she not only consumed but became the alpha, and as they peeled back to unleash the nightmares, she had ordered them to wait for her command to charge.

She was weaker now, but the energy she had consumed had strengthened her will while the desire to protect her friends had continued to restrain them as her body had healed. That did not change the fact they were growing impatient. They felt their leader's judgement to be poor. It was everything she could do to quell the rising rebellions that assailed her mind, attempting to overpower her command. If she lost consciousness again the battle would be lost. Luscious greenery wilted at her fingers, her broken body leaving a trail of death in the wake of her movement. For each bit she consumed, she felt the resistance in her renew only for it to diminish at their ceaseless attempts to wrest the mantle of leadership from her.

The Skiá's will was not the only desire she had to contend with. For a long time she had ensured she had enough energy in order to maintain the fragile balance she required to live. Her time with Eiji had fuelled her beyond needing external sources, replenishing her while making his prolonged existence around other people possible. Both had an aura of power, where as Eiji's excessive energy would act like a poison to those in his presence for too long, Acha could inadvertently strip years from a person's life just for them being close to her at the wrong time. His absence was telling, and coupled with her injuries her body was starving, on the verge of death, and at times like this she lost her precarious rein on its control. Her need called out to her, demanding she surrendered, but to do so would be to strip the life, all life, from everything. Man, woman, ally, enemy, her curse could not differentiate, and human energy was the easiest to absorb, it needed less work to be adapted into what she needed.

Between the mental battle with the Skiá, and the need to repress her own nature she was perhaps the most deadly agent of this battle. Even the slightest waver in her resolve, the most inconsequential slip and she would not only unleash the Skiá, but would potentially cause the demise of her allies herself. She gritted her teeth, weaving her fingers in the long strands of grass as they crumbled into dust. She needed more, more to fend off the Skiá, more to satisfy her body.

The bones in her neck ground against one another sickeningly as her attention snapped towards the alluring pull of easily harvestable energy. It had entered the shadows, and she wanted it for her own. Tendrils of energy reached out, chasing across the ground like roots beneath the soil until they rose, coiling around her target. Images of a child, a wife, and a loving home flooded through her mind and the pressure in her chest eased a fraction. This figure, this man, could offer her just some of the resistance she knew she needed. He had strayed into the Skiá's territory, surely he had sought death.

"Mine," Acha growled possessively, feeling the movements of the Skiá as they honed in upon the feast. She was assaulted by their protests, but with her vigour renewing dismissed them with ease. They relinquished this prey, focusing instead on their will to attack.

* * *

Rob clutched his chest, his legs buckling as an unknown force assailed him causing his head to spin and his strength to wane. The shadows churned around him, yet kept their distance. He could see the shimmer of energy from his target before him, the vision took his mind back to a simpler time. One where he and his daughter had walked the woods on frosty mornings, seeking the winter food and berries. The frost and dew upon the spiders' webs had fascinated Tabatha. His hand trembled, digging into his jerkin pocket as he sought the touch of comfort.

The warmth from the hair clip washed over him, his aching muscles relaxed. He had ventured here unprepared. It may have been unintentional but it seemed he would be joining them soon. How he had longed for this day, longed to surrender to the warm embrace of death and return to his wife.

"Don't you dare," a voice scolded. With great effort he lifted his drooped head, his vision blurring to leave residual impressions of the grass as he sought to focus on its newest target. Where the web once stood were the silhouettes of two figures. Figures he longed with all his heart to be reunited with. His head drooped against his will to watch the wilting and decay of the grass beneath his bent knees. "I said, don't you dare!" His wife had always possessed a no nonsense tone.

"If you're here then it's already too late," Rob whispered with a chuckle, his voice lacking any power.

"You have responsibilities. If you think for one second you'll find peace taking the easy route just remember my scorn, now multiply it by eternity." Rob heard himself cough another weak chuckle.

"I'm sorry, my love," he whispered. He wanted to tell her he would take an eternity of her scorn over another moment without her, but his words found no voice.

"Daddy, Mummy's making her angry face." The young voice warned, flooding his slowing heart with warmth. Despite feeling so weak he managed to curl the corners of his lips into a smile, closing his eyes as he listened to the sweet serenade of a voice never quite forgotten.

"Mummy's only pretending to be mad, she knows I've no say in this. It's my time or else you wouldn't be before me now."

"Idiot," his wife scolded, her tone soft. In the space of that single word she had moved to stand beside him. Her hand, while possessing no form, rested upon his face, sending a tingle of energy through him as she crouched down to look upon him. "I'm here because it's the Festival of Hades, and you're about to do something idiotic."

"Why break the habit of a lifetime?"

"Because you have a job to do. Haven't you realised that yet? Everything that has happened has brought you to this point. You alone can stop the Epiales' reinforcements that, even now, are amassing at the boundary of this forming portal. You alone can see the web, you alone can destroy it."

"I can't... whatever this force is, it's stronger than me."

"Nuh-uh, Daddy's a hero, like Herakles, only better! And I should know," Tabatha bragged, he could see her in his mind's eye, chest puffed out, hands on her hips with a dangerous fire in her eyes she had inherited from him.

"Just resist a little longer. Do that for me, love." The soft voice soothed his fatigue. As much as he wanted to obey and please her he could feel his energy leaving him. Once it was gone, like the grass beneath him, his life would be next. As his mind clouded his wife's touch grew more substantial. "Just a little longer," she whispered. "Please, for us."

* * *

Sweat trickled down her back as Elly ushered her small army behind her, while Bray protected their flank. With each rapid flicker of movement, each solid step of the predators upon the ground, she cursed her own shortsightedness. Many of her army had only ever wielded hoes and fishing nets, and those who had once experienced battle were past their prime and had long seen the muscle and instincts forged in battle turn soft with age. She had believed their only foe would be the Skiá, yet, to her dismay, there were things of solid form patrolling. Elly knew them to be Epiales. Bray had caught the unusual scent long before their approach. From what he could tell, they were few in number, but given their strength and composition, even a few could fell her warriors.

Her hand grasped the scythe fate had dealt her, while Bray, skirting around, placed his hands upon her waist, his fingers skimming her hips as he claimed one of her daggers. She did not like these odds. Proficient in nightmares and invoking fear, the Epiales played to their own strengths releasing a piercing shriek that echoed in chorus through the air, almost masking the pattering of a rapid charge. Light on her feet, Elly leapt left, while Bray dashed in the opposite direction, both in time to cause the charge to veer and the creatures to once more vanish into the shadows. These beings were clever, they were testing them, seeking to expose their weakest defence.

"Hold formation," Elly hissed a warning, knowing Bray had noticed the same thing as she. The attack had been an attempt to scatter the weaker members, making them easy prey. "I promised you a battle, and you will see it," she asserted. "Leave this to us, focus on keeping your weapons active."

She moved again, surprised how she and Bray worked as if they were a single unit. He lunged sideways as an assailant altered its path, his weight wrapped around the darkened creature, driving the dagger to its hilt into the hide of the indescribable being. Elly swung her scythe, the weapon's range allowing her time to sever the lower jaw of the snarling mass before spinning on her heel to deliver a staggering blow to the head of another. The sounds receded, but she knew all too well nightmares were silent and had no footfall. She glanced to Bray, relieved to see he too had returned to position. "Can you not just," Elly extended her hand in a gesture he understood. He shook his head.

"They're more figment than flesh, it isn't blood that flows through them." He raised the dagger as if to prove his point, she could see the dark fluid become mist upon its surface. "We need to stay closely knit. I can confirm the presence of five." She heard the warning in his tone. They had barely held against three, with such odds their chances were slim, and it would only take one person falling to an attack, one opening too slow to be defended, and the group would panic. Panicked people were unpredictable.

Tensing, Elly readied her weapon, sweat glistened upon her brow and she knew without a doubt the nightmares would taste her fear, although it wasn't them she was afraid of, it was failing the people who were relying on her. Once more the patter approached before the surroundings fell into silence. The Epiales were taunting them. In a rapid flurry of movement she saw Bray dart to the side, his arm extended as shadows merged creating a beast hurtling through the air in a silent pounce. The creature's teeth clamped around his limb as he twisted, using his strength, he pummelled the Epiale hanging from his arm against another that tore from the shadows.

Elly's movements became strained, techniques which had once flowed from her so effortlessly were harder to execute under the pressure of fatigue. She controlled her breathing, listening, predicting. The crackling light of the small squadron glinted off the whirling metal of her scythe as she defended them with everything she had and more. Her movements became a dance, while Bray's movements, in contrast, became more savage, more aligned to the more primal part of himself. They circled and protected the small group, but the attacks became a barrage, affording them no rest, no opportunity to breathe. Casting her glance towards the sky, Elly felt herself weaken as she witnessed the creatures above making a rapid descent. Bray appeared to have seen them too, his lips curling in a growl as he tore the limb from one of the creatures with a loud cry. It didn't seem to matter the injury, this species of Epiales seemed to recover, altering their form, adapting.

With a whispered curse, Elly continued her defence, knowing there was no chance they would survive this battle. The creatures surrounding them were smaller than they had been on their first attack, presumably as damaged parts dissipated and flesh had been reformed, but the reinforcements sealed their fate. They were too tired, and her army, too inexperienced. She had thought they may scrape a victory if their stamina held, but now had to admit such a thought had been wistful at best. She would do as promised, she would defend them until her final breath, however long that would be.

* * *

Fey wiped the sweat from his brow, his pace slowed as he crept from shadow to shadow. He had only the element of surprise on his side, and he intended to exploit it. He cautiously approached the place where the two Oneirois were being held captive. The one named Seiken acknowledged him with a nod, while his wife, Thea or Zo—he wasn't certain as everyone seemed to have their own preference—watched the exchange between Alana and Íkelos in horror.

Seiken reached out, slipping the satchel from her grasp, presenting it to Fey. With a silent nod of understanding he placed his hand inside, feeling around within until his fingers touched upon the same energy he had felt from within Daniel's own bag. His fingers pierced the enchantment to touch against the cool metal within. With precise and firm movements, he removed the staff, noticing the name, engraved upon its surface, had altered to his, at least temporarily.

"You know what you need to do?" whispered Seiken, placing his hand upon Fey's shoulder, positioning himself to ensure his frame blocked any indication of Fey's presence.

"One clean strike," he acknowledged. He allowed his eyes to study the weapon in hand, a weapon Daniel was entrusting to him. Since accepting the role he had known this moment would come, but had been unprepared for the almost disorienting touch of the magic within as it extended to greet him.

"Just one, you can do this," Seiken encouraged. Fey flipped the staff together in the same manner Daniel had shown him back at the encampment before they had departed. He took a deep breath, remembering everything Daniel had told him in private. His muscles grew taut, his exhausted body rejuvenating from the adrenaline and fear now coursing through him. Suddenly he saw it, an opening. His muscles tightened as he exhaled. Propelling his body into action he tore across the bridge, the silhouette of Alana and Íkelos burned into his vision. His mind looped with a single monologue of what he would do. One strike, one strike and the nightmare would be over.

Chapter 33

Irony and Destruction

Alana lay writhing on the ground, her posture clearly one of fear and defeat, but he had expected no less. She had no time to learn from the Spirits; she was just a patchwork Mitéra with parts of their essence fused to her own to allow the power needed to vanquish him. A power she had wasted in freeing the Maidens' energy from him. He approached with long strides causing dust to rise in his wake. A smile, hidden by his helm, crossed his lips as she pushed herself backwards as he approached. He was clearly the victor and it was time to claim the spoils.

Her defeat was obvious, portrayed in her very posture. All that remained was for him to claim his prize, should she still possess anything of worth. She had depleted herself in their brief skirmish, using loaned powered from the Elemental Spirits, but in doing so she had lost her only advantage, now the Goddess' Tear was useless in her possession. He had sensed its presence, but her reluctance to wield it meant she knew the truth, should it be brandished against him it would be she who became the captive, especially now, he still possessed the power of the Mystics, and she had nothing, no way to tip the balance of power to her favour.

Rage still coursed through his veins as he looked upon the bloody and battered figure before him. No man should inflict such suffering upon a woman, least of all the Mitéra. But physical assault had been his only option. Her sightless eyes had made his manipulation of nightmares irrelevant. Had she known of them at all her senses would have told her of their falsehood making their grip on her impossible. Now she was subdued and he had banished the oath, he could draw more power from his realm and feed the emptiness within him created by the absence of the Elemental Maidens.

He would need her alive for the Skiá to prey upon, but to leave her conscious was foolhardy. There was no telling what she would do. If she were to end her own life before the Skiá descended he would not be able to obtain what he required. No two essences, living or dead, possessed the same pattern as this one, and the world would not survive until she was reborn and of age, not now that the Great Spirits had been bound by her foolish actions.

Íkelos focused his energy, towering above her like a king before a peasant. He needed just enough power from his domain to fracture body and spirit. Then he could draw her consciousness away, render her body sleeping until he had time to reconcile the situation. For the moment the Skiá were wild, consumed by their desire to please him, and bring his target to him. Íkelos let out a bitter chuckle, seeing the irony of his own manufactured desires and those he had forced upon the Skiá.

"You could have been magnificent," Íkelos lamented. "Such a waste." He reached down, pulling her to her feet, supporting her weight as she hung limply, unable to even fend off his grasp. Her head lolled with each movement he made. "No matter." His free hand enclosed around her forehead, his body startling as she opened her eyes.

His armour began to coil and writhe as the roots emerged from within to dig deep into the ground. In alarm he attempted to finish his task, to unleash the energy he had built. "How are you doing this?" he growled as the tendrils from his torso lashed out to coil around his arm, dragging it back and away from her.

"Quickly," she gasped. Her words made no sense, not until a figure came into sight in his peripheral vision, locked into place he could do little more than observe as the charging figure advanced at speed, a staff lowered as if he were a jouster, aiming to deliver his final and devastating blow. He did not have to turn his head to know what was wielded like a lance in the Fanger's unskilled hand, he knew that weapon well. He knew its every engraving, and could feel the resonation from its core of magic. It had been his bane, his demise, and by his will it had been scrubbed it from existence. Or so he had believed.

"The Hand of Deliverance," he wavered. "Impossible. It was destroyed."

"Surely you of all people understand that anything destroyed can be recreated. And a Mitéra is more than just the sum of her parts." Íkelos looked upon her seeing the well of power previously shielded. His skin prickled, he had thought her to be nothing more than a pastiche. He had never imagined she had been trained, that she had access to the true power of the Mitéra, allowing her to use all as one. His own terms had condemned him, *'You with all at your disposal, against me as I stand.'* A Mitéra had more at her disposal than magic, she had her maidens, any beings she had made a pact with, and more troubling, the Fangers, all were at her disposal and he had granted her consent to use them. The woman he held within his paralysed grip was destruction and creation itself, or at least she would have been.

He locked the vision of his niece in his mind, knowing there was only one hope to evade the fate which it appeared awaited him. With one final push, he forced the words to her lips.

* * *

Elly's heart hammered in her chest as her rapid breathing almost froze. Within moments the dark shapes would be upon them. The threat was evident, they aimed towards the centre of the group, It would be nearly impossible to defend them all. She felt the sweat pouring from her as she repelled another attack, the creature tumbled backwards into its advancing ally. Tensing, she prepared herself to intercept one of the aerial attackers, with carefully measured steps she backed away, before using the moment to leap. A solid force struck her, pulling her from the air and thrusting her to the ground heavily. Her scythe's snath dug into her flesh as it became pinned between her and the attacker. It was a few moments before she realised it was Bray upon her. Strings of saliva poured from his mouth as his rabid gaze fixed upon her. She squeezed her eyes closed, her strength failing as she attempted to thrust the scythe upwards to free herself.

When he had found her, she'd had been concerned about his accompanying them to the fray. This battle had been too much for him, he could no longer rein in the beast he had unleashed in order to protect her troupe. She winced as she felt him move, waiting to hear the agonised death cries of those she had chosen from the volunteers, waiting to feel his touch upon her skin as he did what his nature demanded and fed. When neither assailed her, she opened her eyes, witnessing the sparks of magic trace through the air as four warriors protected them.

With renewed vigour, Elly pushed on her scythe once more. This time she met no resistance as Bray willingly moved, allowing Elly to retake her position with no small measure of relief.

The sound of leather billowing upon the wind could still be heard from above. She cast a grateful glance skyward as the formation broke away, no doubt ensuring that the reinforcements offered were sufficient before heading towards the pinnacle of battle.

She had known the path would be treacherous, but had not realised exactly how desperate things would become. Elly quickly glanced amongst the new faces within the crowd, committing them to memory. Their timing had been impeccable. When they had descended from the skies she had feared the aerial assault would be their demise. She had prepared herself for anything, except for the beings landing to take up arms beside her. Fortunately, it seemed Bray had recognised their scent.

Magic streaked the air, adding light and temporary enchantments to weaponry. With their greater numbers the five Epiales were soon the ones in danger, magic burnt their flesh, as targeted strikes relentlessly assaulted them, dissolving them little by little until all that remained was the dark evaporating mist which Elly had once witnessed upon Bray's dagger.

She nodded appreciatively, before taking point once more, and leading them onward into the darkness.

It had been impossible not to notice the sudden tensing of the figure next to her. Bay's steps halted so suddenly, that the person behind had collided with him. Bray looked to her, a rare expression of weight and seriousness upon his face before he glanced deeper into the veil surrounding them. When his gaze returned to her, she lifted her chin, granting him the permission he seemed to seek.

"Go," she commanded. With a forced smile, he gave a slight bow before disappearing deeper into the shadows as they continued their path towards the fray.

* * *

Bray looked upon the pitiful, slumped figure of his friend as he knelt amidst the mass of shadows. The weapon he had given Rob was still clutched tightly in his friend's grasp, yet it gave no flicker of life. Despite this, the Skiá maintained their distance. For the briefest moment, as he looked upon the pale and dewy flesh of his friend, he feared him dead. The silence was absolute, but as his own senses calmed through the vacuum of sound came the slightest comfort, the slow beating of a heart, a rhythm so subdued it was almost like an animal in hibernation.

"If you're going to do something, now would be good," Rob's voice growled as his heart rate began to quicken. "For the life of me, I can't find the source of this trap."

"That's because it's not a trap, as such," Bray conceded as he mentally examined the ground around his friend. He looked to his hand, he had felt something similar to this touch before. Yet never had it been delivered in this manner. Bray searched his thoughts, he had expected to come face to face with a breathing vessel, one he could manipulate, but this was wild magic, unleashed for a purpose. "I just know I'm going to regret this," Bray chuntered, stooping beside Rob. "Just get that forming portal closed quickly." Bray, being a monster, could see the amassing energy but he had no skill capable of dispelling it.

Bray crouched to where the energy tendrils had snared Rob, he could see the decay of this attack casting deathly webs across the surroundings. He hesitated, unsure if this would produce the desired effect, but he would take the risk, it had to work, or he could be caught in the same net. With a sharp intake of breath he placed his hands upon the ground. At once he could hear the sentience of the energy, the order it was given. With great effort he forced a single word into it, 'Complete.' He felt his energy levels depleting with the effort of convincing the intelligence within the magic that Rob lay dead. But the effort was not without reward, Rob fell forward without grace as it released him from its grasp. Panting, he pulled himself upright and staggered on exhausted legs towards the webbing.

The tendrils receded quickly from their prey's location, its rapid retreat leaving seared marks upon Bray's otherwise unblemished skin. Slumping to sit, he watched as Rob forced his shaking hands to steady as he unleashed one of this long thin needles to strike a mundane patch of soil. Despite Bray seeing nothing, but for the tiny piece of metal piercing the debris-lined ground, he felt the pressure across the land ease. By this alone he knew Rob's weapon had struck true, as it had done each time Bray had seen him use it to dispel a web created by magic.

The area surrounding them grew just a little lighter, breathing a little easier, but the Skiá were watching. Quickly Bray retrieved and activated Rob's weapon, at once unleashing the serpentine snakes of plasma. Bolts of energy streaked the air, leaving scars of afterglow as they chased away the circling shadows, buying him the time he needed to retrieve his friend, who had once more collapsed to his knees in a fit of exhaustion.

"What were you thinking coming into this?" Bray scolded, hooking his arm beneath the exhausted man's shoulders. He pulled him forward, his own energy more depleted than he would have liked. There was no denying the need to feed was becoming more necessity than whim, but a battlefield presented ample opportunity to do just that. However, his first priority would be to guide his friend towards the powerful prayer he could hear resonating within his mind. There, he knew there would be some measure of sanctuary.

Once Rob was safe he would feast, paying the passage for those who sated him before searching for Elly. Something about the look in her eyes as their paths had once again parted, felt unusually permanent.

* * *

Zo dropped to her knees, her fingers woven tightly within her hair as she bit back a cry, her teeth drew blood as they sunk into her lip. She focused on the sensation of pain, of the coppery taste flooding her mouth, anything to push away the clawing presence that assailed her mind. The image of Fey charging before her burned into her vision, becoming overlapped with a ghostly visage, an image of his will as she witnessed this mirage stumble, faltering upon uneven ground causing the strike to glance off Íkelos harmlessly and strike Alana, freeing him from her touch and magic. This was his will, his path to victory. She squeezed her eyes closed, trying to ignore the compulsion, the command for her to speak.

The warmth of blood streaked her face, she could feel Seiken's comforting embrace. His arms draped around her shoulders as he knelt behind her. She focused on the feeling of his breath on her ear. A breath which she knew held words of comfort unheard through the pain which caused her body to tremble. She felt the words building in her throat and tried to swallow them. Her tongue moistened her lips as her voice rang out through the virtual silence to pierce it with a deadly precision.

* * *

Íkelos felt relief wash over him as the sound of his niece's voice penetrated through the air. It was only as he felt the jolting impact of the strike he realised the words she had spoken had not been those he had forced upon her. He felt the displacement instantly. It was as though his essence was fixed upon the tip of the staff and thrust from its home. The armour and flesh forged from the forest begin to dissipate. Vines, leaves, berries, and metals fell to the earth under the force of gravity, slowly dissolving as the energy from the realm channelled through him diminished.

He was but an echo, yet he was far from powerless. He turned sharply to Alana, who held the Goddess' Tear firmly in her grasp extended towards him.

"This city is no place for shades," she announced as the light of the four Spirits surrounded her. Her aura appeared aflame, creating a rainbow of energy that danced upon the penumbra of shadows. Light rose from within her, piercing the crystal, shattering and splintering the brilliant colours within its multi-faceted surface, only for it to be expelled as something new, something that wove and reknit itself into a complex webbing which ensnared him completely, like a spider wrapping its unsuspecting prey in silken threads, as it drew him in, pulling everything he was into the prison that awaited.

Even in defeat Íkelos smiled. The figure before him had truly been the Mitéra. She was everything he would have hoped, and given time she could be again. His niece's prophecy had betrayed him, but at the same time it had returned the order he had sought. He felt the power of the crystal envelop him, and once more heard Zoella's words.

"Gaea's star will be restored, its lands and dangers returned." She had spoken the voice of Darrienia, the only force which could have pushed aside his own will.

A victory within a defeat. That was something he could accept. Besides, if Geburah found a means to escape from this prison so too would he. He would watch with interest as the world became how it should have been before man, gods, and Moirai perverted the natural path in a quest for power. He had fallen this day, but he had done so in victory.

* * *

Battle raged below. Masses of dark forms cluttered an overpopulated landscape while explosions of light, and fire tipped arrows, streaked the sky. Had they not been highlighting a scene of such devastation and carnage it would have been a sight to behold. Little remained of the natural purple hue of the grassland outside the illuminated sanctuary. Dark fluids and bodies of the fallen covered the once lavender flowers, turning the serene blessings into a macabre landscape. Even from their vantage, the haunting cries of the Epiales and the sounds of battle pierced their ears, rising above the noise of the wind battering upon the gliders' sails.

The Daimons rained their magic down, grassy coils enveloped the fields, momentarily restraining and delaying their enemies, while offensive attacks caused devastating blows that created a path through the carnage so that their healers could breach the sanctuary, and spread word that the remaining air-borne units were allies. Arrows whistled unnervingly close as those on ground assumed anything within the sky were their adversaries. But their aid was duly noted by their enemies. Forms below twisted, giving birth to wings as they propelled themselves into the air bringing the battle skyward to those who rained destruction from above. Large forms circled. Gliders twisted and turned, rotating to evade deadly claws.

Shards of splintered bone rained from the sky as a spiralling form wrapped its winged serpentine form around Geburah's glider, crushing it. Wasting no time, he severed the harness, pulling his mace and hammer free. In a display defying belief he secured himself against one of its elongated legs, hefting his Herculean form upon the writhing monster. Its cries pieced the air, calling smaller creatures to its aid as Geburah used the spikes of his weapons to gain traction and vantage. Pressing himself closer to the creature he kicked his legs, his armoured boots dazing the small swooping forms unfortunate enough to come within striking distance.

Opening its giant mouth the creature exhaled, its foul breath bringing screaming wraiths hurtling into existence, causing the leather of the remaining gliders to coat and crackle with ice. Geburah, seizing this moment, drove the spike of the hammer into the creature's eye. Pain exploded as its ear-piercing cry staggered him, his footing slipping as his balance failed. Swinging the mace he pummelled the creature, trails of matted fluid and yellow-tinged gore streaked the air. Fumes burnt his nostrils, acidic and potent, identifying the sulphuric odour, Geburah expelled the magic from within his multi-coloured plumes, bringing the maddening fires to life. Blue fire chased the fluid through the air, erupting as it touched the gushing wound. The scent of burning flesh and noxious fumes surrounded him as the creature caught alight, its massive body plummeting towards the floor in a ball of flame.

The ground erupted in a cloud of dust, fire, and gore, as Geburah called on his remaining magic to protect himself from the damage of impact. Staggering from the blast, his ears ringing, he cast his blurring vision skyward, watching as his allies held back the wraiths with their own magic. Frost met with fire and lightning, causing torrents of rain to fall upon the already gore-slick ground. Light caught the rain, casting brief explosions of circular rainbows. Behind him, in the shadowy veil, he could see the crackle of weapons belonging to the small group they had assisted on their journey here.

Weapons in hand, his corded muscles glistened with sweat and blood where parts of his armour had shattered. Burning embers of blue, purple, and green feathers shed as he moved, his spiked, bludgeoning weapons clearing a path to ease the advance of the warriors he knew would follow. The battle zone looked and sounded like the depths of Tartarus, and he, with his impressive stride and powerful form would become its blood-soaked master.

* * *

Daniel could feel the low reverberation of each pained grunt as he struggled against the bulk of the great beast pinning him to the ground. Even slick with its entrails he gained no reprieve from the oppressive weight. Around him, battle waged on, the sounds of combat, explosions, and screams—both of allies and mimicked by nightmares—carried on the barest trace of a wind that did little to alleviate the stench of decay and death. There was no denying the Epiales' numbers were faltering, but so too did their own. Neither force was gaining ground and their own force would deplete faster than those of the nightmares. It was a losing battle, even now, and Daniel was painfully aware that the Skiá had not yet advanced.

His focus was drawn to the dark veil that surrounded them. The swirling, writhing shadows were in perpetual motion, but within he saw hope. Flashes of lightning illuminated the more dense areas, lightning accompanied by the thunder of marching feet. Daniel released a pent up breath. The approaching illuminations meant only one thing, Bray had done it, and their arrival had brought with it a slight reprieve. He allowed his head to fall back onto the grass, witnessing for the first time the allies above who had joined the fray.

Their gliders defended against horrific wraiths in a battle of magic that none within his army could have withstood.

"Need a hand?" Jones towered above him, his skin soaked with the blood of ally and enemy alike. As Daniel nodded, Jones thrust his shoulder against the place the beast's corpse pinned Daniel, but still its bulk would not budge. "You sure you can feel your legs?" Jones queried, he had seen too many crushing injuries to not recognise the dangers. Having witnessed Daniel's heroics there was no question as to exactly how long he had been trapped, but the battle had been too fierce, too unrelenting, to even consider lending him a hand until now.

"Don't ask me how, but I seem to be trapped between folds. Aside from minor damage—"

"Protection of the Ancients." Daniel turned his head sharply to see the figure who had spoken as she continued to impart her wisdom in the authoritarian tone he knew all too well. "An ethereal barrier said to occasionally protect those worthy from fatal blows. I must confess, when Bray said you required assistance I did not think he was being so literal." Elly examined the beast, pacing its length before crouching to examine the area surrounding Daniel, her nose wrinkled slightly. Moving her hand across the corpse, she made quick calculations before plunging her sword deep into its flesh in a similar manner to that Daniel had previously, and drew the blade across, parting the beast's flesh with ease. As she cut Daniel felt the pressure lessen. Elly thrust her blade in once more. Jones' hands seized Daniel's arms tugging and pulling, gaining inches.

"Just like birthing a calf," Jones grunted with a humorous smile as he fought the resistance until Daniel finally slid free from the folds of the beast releasing a fresh torrent of gore, adding a macabre truth to Jones' jest.

"Can I assume this is your plan for drawing the Skiá?" She gestured towards the shield of light having already assessed who could be found at its centre.

Daniel pulled himself to his feet, spitting and heaving before lifting the blood-soaked short sword from the ground. He wiped it as best he could before turning towards her, with a serious expression.

"I, Daniel Eliot, Wita of the Eorthåds, present this weapon to you, Lady Elaineor of Knightsbridge. May it serve you well," he announced formally as he extending the weapon's hilt towards her, knowing he had to seize the opportunity immediately. Elly snorted a chuckle, to think *he* would offer her a weapon in the midst of battle. She grasped it, instantly freezing as she recognised the touch of the metal and the skill of the crafter.

"I accept," she whispered, tracing her finger down the perfect blade. Producing a handkerchief she wiped the remaining fluids from it to behold its splendour. She had never seen work of this mastery, at least not in the hands of man. She looked upon it in awe, taking in its every detail in a manner of seconds before she spoke again. "So, Daniel Eliot, enlighten me. How exactly do you plan to draw the Severaine here?" His eyes looked down to the other weapon clutched within her hand. "I remember a time the thought of killing would see you retreat. You do understand what you are suggesting?" She quirked an eyebrow as she studied the gore coated figure before her as he attempted to wipe some of the congealing mass from his face with disgust.

"None of us will survive, but—"

"There is one thing you're overlooking," Elly interrupted. "You need more than what we have at our disposal here. You are going to need her." Elly inclined her head meaningfully towards the shadows.

"Who?" He winced, pressing his hand to his side to staunch the slow trickle of blood from an earlier injury.

"Gods and dragons' teeth. Do not tell me you did not realise she was alive in there. Acha you fool. You need to amplify the damage to bring the Severaine here. You need it sprinting, so to speak, not just ambling along. If my weapons alone were enough it would be on our heels already."

"She's alive in there?" Daniel swallowed in disbelief, his attention fixed upon the writhing veil of darkness. "I thought for certain Íkelos had killed her, if not him then the Skiá."

"Seriously? You know her nature better than most. This is a field of death, even had her body perished—oh, you thought his presence would render her talisman ineffective given her experience in the Forest all those years ago." Elly smiled a cold and calculated smile. "You believed you had sent her to her death. Tell me, why do you think the Skiá have yet to attack, who do you think is restraining them?" Elly thought back to how Bray had reacted on entering the shroud of shadows. There was only one thing which would have caused him to leave her side at that time, his friend had been close, and she had recognised the concern and fear within his eyes as easily as she had felt the stifling presence of Acha's gift. Her holding back the creatures was not without cost. "I do not believe she can restrain them much longer. We need to conclude this. I will lend you my force. They are not battle ready but they can use my weapons against the Skiá should their ranks move. The Epiales, however, fall to yours. Wait for a signal, then have everyone draw as much energy into their weapons as they can. Your plan has merits, but in order for it to work it requires a catalyst." Daniel hobbled forward, his eyes set firmly on the shadows.

"Then—"

"Where do you think you are going?" Elly challenged sharply. "*You* have an army to command. Leave Acha to me. I know what must be done, and despite your commitment I do not believe you can do what is necessary." Elly gave a nod towards one of her soldiers, indicating he was now to follow Daniel's command.

"What do you mean?" Daniel queried.

"Give the order to fall back to the first marker, and hold your ranks there until you see the alteration, it will be impossible to overlook." She began to leave, her vision fixed firmly ahead for a brief moment. "When you see it, make haste to the sanctuary," she called back over her shoulder. Daniel saw Jones nod, drawing his fingers to his lips he gave the sharp blow on the shrill whistle worn by all commanders as he issued the unmistakable signal to fall back to the first marker which stood several feet from the sanctuary.

"Wait, what do you mean?" Daniel questioned again. Elly gave no answer, she simply strode across the battlefield, ignoring all within her path until she became nothing more than the hint of light from her weapon in a sea of darkness.

* * *

Elly walked amidst the shadows, marvelling how well their camouflage disguised their lack of numbers. The shroud generated by the Skiá was impressive, creating an impression of strength while playing on the primal fear of the dark. The effect was no more than that of a bird fluffing its wings to appear larger. The weapon in her left hand crackled, occasionally lashing out with its brilliant burning tendrils to drive back any force which dared approach. While the shadows had made their force seem larger, it was still impossible to determine just how many creatures glided through its concealment, it could be as few as ten or as many as thousands. All she knew for certain was very few crossed her path.

With purposeful strides she followed the vines of death which snaked across the ground, turning all within its web to death and decay. She knew the feel of this magic. She had recognised its oppressive weight when her army had traversed this domain. Forcing the required intention towards the weapon in her right hand she took a brief pause to marvel at the radiance of the light which began to glow from within. The darkness seemed to retreat from her proximity dispelled by both the divine glow and the tendrils of magic. As she walked she pondered what this weapon would become should she live long enough to see its evolution.

The light from the blade cast a sickly glow upon another creature within the woods. Acha's ringlets, now solid from the setting of mud and fluids, moved stiffly in the stifled wind, casting Elly's mind back to the time she once had gazed upon Medusa. This historical gorgon had possessed the same feral look within her eyes she saw reflected in Acha's. Neither gorgon, nor the power of this girl, possessed the ability to petrify her and so, Elly's pace never faltered.

Acha knelt upon the deadened earth, seeming somehow smaller than Elly last recalled. Her lips turned upwards in a vicious snarl. Fresh tendrils erupted from her body seeking out new life to sustain its master, yet strangely they steered away from contact with Elly, making her wonder if there was still hope for this young woman after all.

"Desist this foolishness," Elly commanded. The exhausted figure raised her bloodstained, mud-encrusted face slowly as if in challenge. Elly reached forward, grasping the material of Acha's dress to drag her upward, onto her feet. "I can see it is already too late for reason," Elly acknowledged as Acha's head jerked spasmodically as she tried to comprehend the situation unfolding around her. "You are too dangerous to remain unchecked. The Epiales have all but fallen. That means you alone could still deliver Teanna into his arms. I had hoped there may be another way, a way to save you."

"What can you do?" hissed Acha's barely human voice. Elly thrust forward, her blade buried deep into Acha's kidney in what would be a fatal blow to any mortal. But Acha was not mortal. The tendrils grew thicker, their pulsing energy delivering more sustenance and rapidly closing the wound as Acha laughed manically, drawing more of the energy of the Skiá tethered to her by her status as alpha.

"Something long overdue, Acha Night." Elly struck out again, dealing several precise, fatal blows in quick succession, penetrating each critical area with ease.

* * *

Bray and Rob rushed towards the barrier with limping exhausted strides. Both were barely strong enough to stand as they fought their way across the field of death. The few remaining Epiales pursued those who retreated and the brave heroes who had returned to the fray in an attempt to drag the wounded to safety. The range weapons were striking true, offering cover for the small groups still hunting through the entanglements of body parts for the trapped or wounded.

Their attention was elevated, looking for the movement of either ally or enemy, but their path lay empty. Reaching the barrier the two men collapsed in exhaustion. Bray patted Rob on the shoulder before pulling himself up.

"What are you doing?" Rob panted, waving away the approaching medic. There were others who needed aid more than he did. The groans and pleas of the suffering were a deadly chorus carried by the wind. A chorus that rang in the ears of all now the sounds of battle had all but faded.

"If there's anyone alive out there I'm probably their best chance at surviving," Bray responded, moistening his lips as his attention was drawn to the place the wounded were being laid in order of condition, from critical to minor injuries. Those with fatal wounds were being attended to by one of the temple's priests who had followed the mismatched forces accompanying Elly. Bray could hear the beating of a heart and the rush of blood within his ears as hunger gnawed at him from within. It took a moment to realise Rob was addressing him.

"I don't mean to be rude but have you looked in a mirror lately? You're barely amongst the living yourself."

"Another reason I can't stay here," Bray whispered, swallowing the pooling saliva. "At least not until—you know." He tore his gaze from the wounded, casting it across the battlefield where blood-soaked grass and corpses marred a once picturesque landscape.

"Listen up." Jones' voice pierced the air. "I need everyone who can to take up the weapons. Form a perimeter."

"That's my cue," Bray whispered with resolve. He tossed Rob his weapon. "It's been my pleasure."

"Grayson Bray, I hope you're not skipping out on our arrangement," Rob scolded, fumbling the catch.

"I am nothing if not a man of my word. I have a lead on our other matter, or will assuming she does nothing foolhardy. Until my return, just grasp that hair clip of yours firmly and hope for a miracle."

"You know, don't you?" Rob questioned solemnly. Bray hesitated, turning back to help his friend from the ground. He gave him a firm hug, patting his back with all the energy he could muster. The inevitability of the situation hung as heavily as the dense clouds above.

"Of course." Bray's eyes briefly glanced to Teanna before he pulled away, slapping Rob firmly on the shoulder. "I'll be back. I will stand beside you until the end, but if I don't go now I've got a feeling she's about to do something very foolish."

"Does it really matter, given the circumstances?"

"Have you learnt nothing," Bray teased. "When facing death who better to have at your side than one who can—"

"Charm the lock off a chastity belt?" Rob chuckled, hiking an eyebrow as he saw Bray's gaze fixed on Teanna. For a moment she returned his stare before glancing away.

"That's not all I am accomplished in. On that note, I bid you good day." Bray raised his hand in a mock salute before taking off across the former battleground.

* * *

Acha's body slumped towards the ground, her mind slowing, fading, as her identity became clouded, and her thoughts no longer solely her own. She had taken too much of their energy, too many of their memories and everything she was slowly became relinquished to a single desire. She had fought this loss of self, as she had years ago when she had taken too much of Fenris' energy. But this time it was different, despite her efforts her body continued to seize the energy needed to heal, and with each second the memories of the Skiá who had fallen to her became stronger than her own until their thoughts were all she knew.

Whispers and demands filled her every fibre. She raised her heavy arms with a twisted smile upon her lips. She was the alpha, the commander of these forces and the time for delay had passed. The figure standing before her had said in this form she could take Teanna to their master, and that was precisely what she intended to do.

Acha's head lifted to stare at the figure before her. She needed more power, more energy to control this form and retain dominance as the alpha. The warmth of life flowed from the wounds of this flesh too quickly. The minds of those who would take control challenged her will, demanded she relinquished her position to one stronger. She would not. Their imaginary tethers shone through the strange sight of these human eyes. She grasped them, drawing on their energy as they tried to fight her for control.

She felt the waves of life rushing towards her, the cries of her allies as she began to devour their life to repair herself. She would complete this mission, even if she had no choice but to stand alone. Her brethren could not touch the mortal flesh, but her hands could. Their sacrifice made sense, besides, their master would surely recreate them, but right now he needed someone capable, someone who could fulfil his demands.

The cry which left her lips as she feasted was one of both agony and elation. It was a sound of neither man nor beast, yet was made from everything found within the recesses of nightmares.

The figure of the mortal still stood before her, her weapon poised, striking once more before she could fully heal, causing more of the furious energy to flood into her vessel. An unnerving sensation consumed her as she realised how ravenous she was. The energy being drawn was powerful, all-consuming, addictive. She wanted more, needed more and her body knew how to take everything she desired.

The creature before her slowly backed away, unheard words suggested by the movement of her lips. But Acha could no longer hear them. She could only hear the cries for fulfilment, only feel the hunger this vessel had once known how to suppress.

Chapter 34

Fractured Release

The tension released from Alana's body as she dropped to her knees, the crystal still held firmly within her exhausted grasp. The final deed had taken almost everything the Spirits had given her. In turn they had been sealed, torn from their own domains to await the day she was called to their shrines. If that day ever came. Already she could feel their power, their influence on the land, soils, water, air, and on nature itself, wane.

Their powers had not deserted her completely. She still had aspects of them fused to her essence, and now she understood why they had done this. This small fraction—that had come at the price of a part of herself—allowed her to harness what little of their powers remained in the world around them. Her windsight was present, but unlike before when she could focus and see all around them, she could now only behold her immediate surroundings.

She was the Mitéra, but the powers she now harnessed were but a shadow of what they had once been, and they would remain this way until she completed her pact. She felt her body tremble with exhaustion as Fey crouched before her.

"Alana, you did it," he whispered in awe.

"I was foolish," she snapped, her fists grasping at the dust that lay before her. "The Skiá he unleashed are sealed within this realm. There's no stopping them. There is nothing more I can do. I thought with his defeat they too would be vanquished."

"Mitéra." Seiken addressed her with respect as he stood still sealed within the barrier. "Not everything will fall to you to bear. You are no island, you are not alone. Have faith in your allies, in those you know and have yet to meet."

Fey reached down, assisting Alana to her feet. Her weary steps dragged across the sediments of dirt and soil left upon the bridge. She asked Fey to guide her hand to the newest of carvings upon the stone structure, those which had created the prison for her parents, rather than offering the town a sanctuary. As her hand touched them she sent a weak pulse of earth through the rock, targeting only the newest symbols in such a way as to rewrite their purpose. The invisible pressure she saw surrounding her parents dissipated, but the protection against shades remained.

"Tell me," she whispered, shuffling forward to sit beside them, knowing this would be the final time she would be in their presence. "Tell me what you witness." She inclined her head towards where the portal's shimmer had started to diminish. She could see its energy waning, and wondered how the warriors had fared.

* * *

Elly felt a hand grasp her arm, pulling her firmly away from where Acha stood shrouded in an aura of shadows. Earth crumbled into dust at the young woman's feet as Bray pulled Elly along beside him.

"You're a fool if you believe you will see the Gate of Shades as you are," Bray hissed as he dragged her dazed figure behind him.

"And how am I?" Elly snapped, regaining some of her composure. She had expected something to occur, but the sheer power that pulsed through Acha was immense and destructive. It had bore down on her, stealing her breath. She had intended to back away, but then another thought had captured her. There was an adventure she longed to have and she could not do it here. She had vowed to lead the charge of those who followed her; it made sense she should be the first to greet them in the afterlife. After all, there was no escape from what was coming, what she had just unleashed, not for them at least.

"As I believe I informed you when our paths first crossed, you are divine. Did you think you could become the vessel for all divine wisdom and not undergo some metamorphosis yourself in order to contain it? Yes, you were cursed by Kronos, and like everyone else you believed it was so he could return to exact his revenge. A logical assumption, considering." Bray pulled her harder, his peripheral vision warning of the cloud of dust and death rising behind them. "But those who have gazed upon you, those who would presume to make assumptions, have not seen what I have."

"And what have you seen exactly?" Elly challenged, the glow from the sword that hung limply in her hand intensified as if warning them of the encroach of the ever-present danger.

"Ask me later," he whispered, glancing over his shoulder, his hand gliding to the small of her back to encourage her onward.

"Why did you intervene?"

"I told you, you will not see the Gate of Shades, but with my help, with planning, you would not be the first being of flesh to enter Hades' domain."

"And in return?" Bray glanced backwards again, her hesitation was delaying their retreat. He stopped, heaving her over his shoulder in an undignified manner. She was weary, so the gentle suggestion not to resist penetrated her mental defences with ease.

"I seek a Moirai by the name of Paion. If I aid you with your quest, I ask for payment in kind." He ran with death on his heels, his speed increasing until he saw the thinning of the darkness. He twisted, removing Elly from his shoulder, and noting her look of gratitude. Breaking through the shadows he looked before them. People still scoured the corpses of the battlefield for survivors. The field knew solely their movements. The final Epiales had either been slain or had retreated back into the cover of darkness.

"Fall back!" Elly's voice carried across the plain with an undeniable authority. Her voice sharp and crystal clear. Movement on the field stopped as the command echoed. It was barely a second before they obeyed, and those hunting for survivors abandoned their task to retreat to the sanctuary. Not one had frozen in fear at the shadows and death that pursued. "Activate weapons." Elly charged through the weak defensive line, readying her own weapons. Bray lifted the device from her grasp to leave her with the sword as he saw Daniel's rapid and furious approach, a fresh dressing already stained with blood seemed so bright against his dark hide clothes, and for a moment Bray wondered why he had not used the armour he knew was at his disposal, before realising it was likely for the same reason no Eorthåds could be found here.

"Go," he whispered.

"Draw on the energy, forget targets, give them a display of power they will not soon forget," Elly commanded. Weapons fired to life as those loyal to her did as they were bid. Others looked to their own commanders, who relayed the command to shield Elly's warriors. Daniel grasped her arm, pulling her away from the front line.

"What did you do?" he growled, seeing the power of the encroaching death.

"Your entire scheme rested on these few weapons posing enough threat that they would draw the Severaine. Surely you had already realised if that were to be the case then—"

"What did you do to Acha?"

"In terms you will understand? I made it necessary for her to absorb enough energy from the Skiá that she no longer saw the divide between herself and them, and thus forgot the power she spent every breath restraining. It is a similar state of mind to when she touched Fenris, her identity has been lost to the memories of those she absorbed, causing her to be consumed by the Skiá's energy and will."

"I will make you pay for this," Daniel growled. The sparking of lightning from those around them cast haunting shadows on his stern face.

"You will not need to. There is no method to stop this rampage, not until she can absorb no more, and the damage to her body was already extensive. This shield of light will not protect us, not from what is coming." Elly paused, knowing that Daniel knew this already.

"Then why, on no less than two occasions, have you ordered us to fall back to it?" Jones questioned approaching from Daniel's right, his eyes fixed on the death and decay that rushed before them.

"Hope," Daniel whispered in understanding. She had wanted to give them hope of surviving. His body tensed as he felt a familiar power begin to saturate the air. This was it, the force they had enraged was upon them. The end was here.

The guttural roar of the wind shook the very foundations of the earth. Particles of light separated, breaking free from the barrier to drift like ocean spray across the battlefield, soaking into and illuminating each blade of grass, each corpse, until the land itself was saturated in the glistening hue. The land devoured the light drawing it within itself and amplifying the magic already within its core. Areas of concentrated energy rippled like veins and arteries, with finer capillaries narrowing and reaching out to connect everything.

The pressure was so intense those who drew breath found themselves paralysed. Every muscle, every fibre, was frozen beneath the strength and power of what was approaching. This force had razed great cities and toppled kingdoms. This power made the world anew and sought to reap vengeance on those who dared harm its mother. A crime, for which each of those present stood guilty.

The Severaine had no reason, no logic, just the primal desire to defend its mother. For years it had slumbered, rarely needing to remind Mankind of their place, not since last time. Now was different, now it had awoken filled with wrath and vengeance as it heard the cries of Gaea. Their attack had been precise, local to one of the ley lines, a place of power, and one to which damage could not be ignored.

Magic chased across the sky, erupting across the velvet blanket in blinding, furious explosions in a display the Gods would know to fear. The temperature plummeted in seconds causing plumes of condensation to rise from flesh and land, misting the surroundings as heat rose from the bodies of the soon to be dead to mingle with the remaining warmth of autumn soil. The sky rumbled and growled it fury as enormous hailstones began to rain down furiously from above. The Severaine was coming, and it had marked all for death.

* * *

Teanna felt the world around her fracture as her vision was drawn once more to the man she had briefly met, the one named Bray. She felt his thrall, his command to reach out to the one power who could still be of aid, the Spirit Elemental. His demand had stirred something within her she hadn't known existed, a link between herself and the Spirit. In that instant she saw through eyes that were not just her own. She simultaneously stood upon the field of battle and lay within the Rumination Room. A feeling of comfort and belonging washed over her, along with the barrage of conflicting emotions she knew this place for, and now she understood the reasonings behind such fractured emotions.

'*I can aid you,*' whispered the Spirit's voice within her mind. '*But we are not yet as one. I have yet to claim you. I am not whole, and such assistance will come at a cost, to both of us I fear.*'

"Please, help me help them," she begged aloud. Her mortal eyes bearing witness to the approach of the power she knew would destroy every life here. Those who had fought so valiantly to protect her, to keep her from Íkelos' grasp.

'*I will use what little power I have in this severed form. I will be forced to seek mortal hosts to contain me until such a time my fragments can reunite. Until that day you will slumber, awaiting the time when my touch will awaken you. What I am to do will be dangerous to both of us, do you consent?'*

"I care not for myself. Please, help them," Teanna begged.

'*As you wish, my Maiden.*'

Teanna felt the energy surging through her. Light from above pierced the clouds just moments before an enormous landmass broke through the thick blanket above. Crackling tendrils of energy streaked the sky from the structure. The energy seemed to be drawn towards the barrier. Each jagged bolt reinforced its strength as the survivors became stationary, whether bearing arms or dragging and carrying the injured deeper into the sanctuary, all movement stilled, paralysed by the Severaine's approach.

Across the expanse Teanna saw Acha, her form rigid enveloped in the consuming energy that spread a blanket of death around them. The darkness to her light, they stood in contrast to one another. Amidst the energy, the roaring of winds, the mental, anguished cries of the injured, and wails of the Skiá, Teanna could hear Acha's tormented scream as the energy of the Severaine's power wrapped around her and began to nullify the most potent threat. She wailed in agony in a voice both Skiá and human, in a sound so haunting even above the roar of everything else it could be heard.

* * *

The ground near the central disturbance began to fracture. Wrapping and encasing Acha's rabid form, attempting to smother her power beneath the land and quash her vessel. Yet the more damage the Severaine inflicted, the more powerful her destruction grew. Threads of magic linked between her and the lives of her shadowed allies that fed her, allowing her to thrive even within the Severaine's embrace.

Fire spewed from the fissures, pushing lava vents to the surface to heave forth its molten rage, yet still, nothing touched these creatures of darkness. Wind, fire, and ice, all drew together, striking with a violence known only to nature. The force of the elements combined sending currents of multi-toned light cascading across the land, each connecting with the Skiá, burning their shadowy form in a true purge of darkness, while the Severaine's power shred their shroud and utilised the unseen light from above to draw down light's fury and consume the blackened clouds until the sun's rays could once more kiss the land and but a single entity remained within a circle of death. Acha's cries became more human, more terrified as her skin peeled back to reveal sinew and bones as the Severaine's energy tore through her unprotected mortal flesh as if it possessed no substance.

Witnessing all, as if she were a part of it, Teanna cried out; her arms extended, her head craned towards the heavens as a shadow from above, the origin of the light which strengthened her barrier, became fully visible through the blue sky. Talaria was falling. The Spirit Element had finally shattered the remaining bonds of its prison in a feat necessary to aid her.

Its fractured form passed through her, enhancing the barrier before being deflected. A faint glow was all that kept Talaria's unnerving bulk in its steady descent. In that one moment, as her eyes began to cloud she realised why there had been a prophecy, why Talaria would have fallen. Had they not began their descent her need for the Spirit Elemental's aid would have been so great it would have torn them from the sky, pulling them from their orbit.

Teanna felt her knees buckle beneath her as another fragment of the Great Spirit struck her. In her mind she saw Talaria. The Virtues guided the land's descent towards the coldest climate the oceans of this land had to offer. She saw the Severaine, shredding Acha's body until nothing remained. She witnessed the gliders, carried upon the winds being whisked from danger. Everything she witnessed was through the eyes of the Severaine, and it in turn saw her.

For the briefest moment it felt the energy the Spirit Elemental poured back into the world through her, the energy it took to shield those who had summoned it beneath a barrier of life. It saw an ally, and as quickly as it had appeared, the pressure of this terrifying force receded, and the faint glow of all things living which had heralded its arrival began to return to their darkened shades.

As the final fragment of the Elemental pierced Teanna she saw with the sight of each of the severed fragments as they hurtled across the lands to find vessels in which they could survive until it could become one once more. The card creating the sanctuary slipped from her fingers as her body fell to the ground, and during the moment of disbelieving silence, as people realised they had survived, she slipped into the promised slumber.

* * *

Daniel dropped to his knees as the tension released him. His once frozen breath was drawn deep into his lungs in rapid succession, causing his head to spin and the world to darken before his exhausted gaze.

"Was that, an island?" Jones gasped, his heavy arm slapping Daniel's shoulder weakly. Several afterglows of light still burnt across the sky. The land beneath them remained aglow with the fading radiance the Severaine's presence had drawn.

"Talaria," Daniel panted, too tired to wipe away the sweat that streamed down his face.

"The Skiá, are they... I mean... what in Hades was that?"

"That was the Severaine. The only force I know of that could shred the very essence of something as powerful as a god." The dust across the land slowly thinned, blown away on gentle winds which tickled the faded energy of the ley lines until their glow was no more, and they could see the true horror of the battlefield. The corpses of the Epiales steamed and withered under the powerful light of the midday sun, sending their vile odour into the acrid air. Crushed lavender flowers were soaked with blood, and within the place they sat, the area they had known as their sanctuary, a new species bloomed to mirror the reddening of their once purple brethren.

Beyond where the light had shielded them, beyond the graveyard where carrion birds tentatively flew and scavenged, stood an area of perfect and complete death, where stagnant water, dust, and barren earth marred the land. Daniel staggered to his feet, the words and sound of the survivors lost as he pushed his way past them. His lurching steps carried him ungracefully through the field of death towards the toxic lands. He tripped and staggered, stumbled and faltered, over the freshly broken ground and severed limbs. Fire and embers spat from the newly formed fissures, releasing vents of heat and steam he barely saw and avoided as he pushed his way onward into the petrified forest. His vision locked in place, and everything surrounding his focal point was lost to his exhausted mind.

"It has to be here," Daniel whispered, falling to his knees at the very centre of the decay. His hands fervently searched the dust and rubble of the crater marking the place his friend Acha had last stood. Jones, as tattered and battle-worn as he was, had followed him, falling in to offer aid, dragging his own hands through the layers of dust to mirror Daniel's actions.

"What are we looking for?" he questioned, his hands tracing through the dry and barren sand. A hiss of steam erupted from below, swelling and breaking the surface seconds before an odorous combination of sewage and viscous fluids spewed into the basin. The grotesque liquid began to rise, more small fissures appearing to feed it with this foul fluid. Grabbing Daniel's arms, Jones pulled him away, his hands covering his mouth as the liquid took on a putrid glow, that was both green and red depending on how the light reflected upon its tar-like surface.

"It doesn't matter," Daniel whispered, watching the slow rising of the bubbles. The sickening pop as they broke their surface to release the noxious odours sounded like the cracking of bones and caused his stomach to churn.

Daniel turned towards the place the sanctuary had once stood, his vision seeking a solitary figure amongst the celebrating mass. When he failed to see her he realised something else. It had taken more than just light to protect them from the Severaine.

"Where's Teanna?" Daniel asked, once more checking each face within the distant crowd.

* * *

Rob watched in silence as Bray skulked away to follow his former mentor, Lady Elaineor. He had vowed to make contact when he had news on Paion, but he had another promise to keep first. Rob worked his way to the inner circle, where medics were tending to the most critically injured. Amputating limbs, cauterising wounds, whatever it took to keep the person before them breathing, until help could arrive.

He noticed, with a smile, a small number of Daimons, working along the humans, his vision scanned the battlefield for Geburah. More than once he had seen the brilliance of his plumes illuminating the darkness and causing the horrors of battle to become more intense to any who gazed in his direction for too long. Whilst the healers still remained, it seemed those who had taken up arms had departed amidst the chaos. His brow creased, recalling the muted movements of the Daimon healers while all others remained frozen in place by the Severaine's power. It seemed this great force, for reasons he could only imagine, did not have the same effect on them as on those who could not channel the magic of nature itself.

The aftermath of war was horrific. The dead outnumbered the living, and he knew of those who had survived, many would wish they had fallen in battle, and more still would fight this war for the rest of their days. Mercenary or not, there were things that happened here, powers and forces witnessed, that could never be unseen. There were things no mortal eyes should ever behold, and they had gazed upon them for too long.

After today there was no denying monsters were real and darkness was a place of terror. It was a shame that few would realise the true lesson of this day, that with enough faith a victory can still be clawed from impossible odds.

Rob crouched beside Teanna. The medics had made her comfortable, but with no visible injuries she was the least of their priorities. In his mind he replayed the images of the powerful lights penetrating her, enhancing the barrier to shield them. It was only as he considered this he realised the final burst had not come from above her, but from within.

With a quick cursory glance around he scooped the limp figure into his arms. Albeth was a long walk from here, but as far as he could tell no messenger had been deployed to request aid for the injured. He would act as herald and also place Teanna in their care. If he was correct, if Alana had been successful, the Mystics would slowly be awakening. He had a feeling, however, the same would not be true for those belonging to the Great Spirits. Something told him that the Maidens would not awaken until the Spirits were once more able to walk upon mortal soils.

Rob walked slowly, Oureas' Rest central in his mind's sights. The end of battle was a strange thing. People celebrated, attended to the wounded, but ultimately were lost. For those upon the field everything had changed, and yet the world remained the same. The flurry of movement would abate, the celebrations would fade, and slowly, like he himself had, those involved would dissipate, thinning the crowds.

Rob glanced behind him one final time. He had witnessed the birth of the Mitéra and the falling of darkness. There was no question that this would not be the last field stained with blood. His sister had worked for The Order, and if there was one thing he knew it was that they feared losing their status. The birth of the Mitéra was a threat to their power, and if they realised she walked amongst them there was no telling what they would do to end her quest before it could begin.

* * *

Bray fell into step beside Elly. Her brisk pace continued east, towards Karabi Port, or perhaps her destination was the college which stood in close proximity to it, he couldn't be certain.

"Do you ever listen to that body of yours?" Bray scolded. "You need to rest."

"I would be, had you not intervened. You said I would not see the Gate of Shades, so tell me, Grayson Bray, what have you seen, and why do you think I would not be permitted death?"

"My lady, there is a huge leap between not seeing the Gate of Shades, and not being able to die."

"What did you divine?" Bray reached into his pouch, pulling out a small mirror. He stepped before her, thrusting it unceremoniously before her frustrated gaze.

"A goddess walking amongst man, perhaps?" He quirked an eyebrow, allowing his impish smile to tease his lips. "I know it is not what any woman wishes to hear, but you're no goddess. You are, however, sufficiently different not to know the afterlife, only rebirth. You've yet to realise the power within your blood. It is more than just fluid, your every cell is charged with wisdom itself. You are both divine and mortal, simultaneously."

"Íkelos once referred to me as a divine, mortal dreamer," Elly mused, attempting to remove some of the stains from her face, but only succeeded in smudging them further.

"I doubt he would do so for the same reason as I would. You forget, only someone such as I could reveal your true nature." Elly lifted her gaze from the mirror to meet his.

"Can I age?" she asked abruptly.

"No. Every cell in your body remains bound by Kronos' curse. Your body will never alter in age, and the cells made to repair and replace damaged ones will be exact replicas of those they replaced."

"Can I die?" Elly whispered, pushing the mirror back towards him.

"Even an immortal can die, if the right conditions are met," he answered softly, knowing she saw the mischievous reflected in his eyes.

"You know what I am asking."

"As I mentioned, you are simultaneously divine and mortal. It's betwixt and between. Flip a coin, your answer depends on which side of you is dominant at the time." He saw something alter in Elly's posture, she seemed to shrink before him ever so slightly. "What is it?"

"It was not what I expected," she whispered.

"You should be pleased. Surely there are things you wish to do, things you have previously denied yourself?" He felt her shudder beneath his touch before she pulled away.

"I have but one adventure. I seek to release an essence from eternal torture."

"Infiltration of the underworld? Compared to some of your journeys it will seem dull."

"And yet, it is the only thing I desire." Elly twisted a broken leather cord within her fingers as she considered her options.

"What's that?"

"A debt to be repaid, but first I need to stop at the college to use their tools. What of you?"

"I'm famished. It would be ungentlemanly to have you wander alone on a day such as this. I will escort you, besides we have a partnership to solidify, and I have more to tell you."

Chapter 35

A New Path Awaits

Beside Eiji's bed, Daniel, Zo, and Seiken sat, awaiting his awakening. One by one the Mystics had regained consciousness none-the-wiser as to the events which had occurred during their slumber. The Elemental Maidens, however, remained unresponsive, as Alana had predicted before parting ways with those who had aided her.

"This is the last time." Seiken's voice grated within Eiji's confused mind as his awareness slowly returned. "You heard the prophecy. Besides, this world has the Mystics, Spirits, The Severaine, and now even the Mitéra. It is time for you to let go. This world must learn to look after itself."

"But—"

"But nothing. They have all manner of forces to watch over them. It is time we watched over our own world. With no master to command them the Epiales will pose more danger than ever before."

"Hey, I think he's waking up." Daniel's voice shushed them from the other side of the bed as Eiji felt his heavy limbs finally begin to respond. His eyelids fluttered and his vision burned against the brightness of the room. He heard the rustle of movement as Daniel drew the heavy drapes across the window.

As Eiji's eyes adjusted his tired gaze searched the faces of his friends as he tried to recall what had happened, and why he was lying in what appeared to be a healing room. He studied them, seeking for answers, but instead saw their haunted expressions. Sitting in alarm he shoved the thin blankets from his torso. He had seen this expression before and remembered it well. It caused his stomach to tighten as he looked amongst his friends, counting them, studying them, and already knowing that there was one person who was not amongst them.

"Where's Acha?" he questioned hoarsely. His gaze focused on the door, hoping to see her silhouette against the brightness that flooded in from the hallway.

"How much do you know about what has happened?" Daniel posed gently, resting his hand upon Eiji's arm.

"Where's Acha?" he demanded again, his gravelly voice feeling like sandpaper against his throat.

"She... that's to say—"

"You really are idiots." A dark shadow obstructed the light from the hallway, causing each head to turn towards their visitor. Daniel rose to his feet sharply, the scorn in his eyes evident. Elly raised a hand in a placating gesture before tossing a small pendent onto the bed where Eiji lay. He had moved his arms as if to catch it, but his limbs had grown more sluggish and unresponsive than normal.

"What am I meant t'do with this?" he questioned. His fingers tangled in the highly-polished, heavy silver chain of the pendent as he lifted it from the covers.

"You are in a hospital, people die here all the time. Must I spell everything out for you?" She suppressed a smile as her words reminded her of their first journey together. She glanced towards Daniel as if she wanted to say something more, but instead she simply bit back whatever remark had been brewing.

"How did y—" Daniel snatched the pendant from Eiji's grasp before he could finish, raising it to the light he tipped it first one way, and then another, examining each and every marking on the amulet's surface.

"Relax, it is unaltered and what is within was spared from the taint. I did what you should have had the foresight to do." She looked meaningfully between Daniel and Eiji, both of whom should have recalled Acha could retain possession of a vessel for a limited time without contact with the amulet. She had proven this on at least one occasion she knew of, when Marise had killed her. "If we keep exchanging debts like this, one may just have to consider us allies," Elly mused as Eiji plucked the charm from Daniel's grip, relief flooding through him as he realised what it was. The chain was different, but the talisman remained the same.

"Or friends?" Eiji offered. Elly chuckled, raising her hand as she turned her back on them to leave.

"I believe this once again balances the scales, we are even. Thank you for the weapon, Daniel Eliot." Eiji reached out his hand, stopping Daniel from pursuing her.

"Even," Eiji reiterated firmly, rooting him in place.

"No, it's not that. It's just..."

"Y' didn't think t'take it y'self?" Eiji proposed. Daniel shook his head. So much had happened since he first learnt of Acha's nature he had failed to consider it. All that had been on his mind had been how the Skiá had possessed her when she left the talisman with Teanna. He had been so fixated on this he had failed to consider the time she possessed other bodies, or even existed without its contact. He felt foolish. The reason Acha had seen the need to split her essence at that time was because she was simultaneously protecting the mercenaries and leading the Skiá away. She had needed to be in two places at once, and this was the sole manner by which it could be achieved. He looked towards the door, grateful that at least someone had considered it. "I think I'd like t'hear what happened," Eiji motioned towards the empty seat at his bedside.

"Are you not going to..." Zo gestured towards the charm in his grasp.

"No need. She'll find me when she's ready." Eiji smiled slightly. Acha had been reborn from death at least twice that he knew of, and only for the first time had she needed to be in contact with the amulet. The second time she had sought them out, reclaiming it from her corpse to bind herself to the new vessel. He had no doubt, that when the time was right, she would find him once more.

* * *

Just months ago a fight for survival had played on the fears of all, ushering a new awareness to the human mind. Yet now, life had returned to normality, for most people at least, and Alana found herself surprised at how quickly people adapted and forgot the events that could have spelled the end of their very existence.

She had excused herself, slipping away from her parents once the tidings of the battle had been revealed. She and Fey had journeyed to Semiazá Port, where they would eventually part ways. Alana had used Fey's knowledge to learn about the lay of the land, the workings of this unfamiliar world, and with his duty done, he had decided he would take up residence in Albeth castle, to await the awakening of Teanna. The one he was bound to as Fanger.

As a temporary farewell, since he knew their paths would cross again in the future, he had taken her to the small tavern that overlooked the port. The atmosphere was subdued, several small tables had a few patrons who dined quietly on local delicacies creating a scent of freshly cooked fish and vegetables that mingled with ale and mead along with the subtle fragrances being emitted from the large fire hearth where those fending off winter's frost now gathered. Fishermen spoke of coming snow and bragged about their latest hauls, while taking draughts on spirits to warm themselves from the inside out in preparation of their next voyage.

A small lantern flicked on a table between Alana and Fey. Her fingers rested tentatively upon the rough-hewn surface that in some places still possessed hints of its long stripped varnish finish.

"Are you certain you will be okay?" Fey questioned, as the fair-haired waitress placed a bowl of stew before them both before, on seeing Alana, she described where everything she needed could be found.

"I am to meet with the Wita. It seems he has news on a location I can rest until my journey begins." Her fingers hesitated over the spoon for a moment before taking it within her grasp. Her world was not as clear now as it was before she had faced Íkelos, but such was to be expected.

"You remember what I told you, about the Plexuses, and how to get in touch with me?"

"I do. Your schooling has been invaluable. It will still be many moons before I come of age to make the journey, and whilst I am impatient I still must await the summoning. Once my objectives are completed, the Spirits will gain their freedom once more, and their Maidens will awaken. Until then, I must keep their remaining power within me."

"What of Teanna?" Fey questioned, lifting his empty bowl from the table to hand it to the passing waitress.

"I do not know. What she did, she did as unclaimed. Her Elemental partner is fractured, I imagine only when he is reunited can he repair the damage that was inflicted." Fey consumed the last piece of his bread before rising to his feet.

"It appears your guest has arrived, and so, I bid you farewell, Mitéra." He dipped his head politely before taking his leave, nodding politely to Daniel.

"Until our paths cross again, Fanger." Alana acknowledged. "Wita, will you be sitting?" she questioned, gesturing towards the place Fey had just vacated.

"I thought we could walk. There is a friend of mine I wish to introduce you to. His services have been invaluable to me, and I hope he can perhaps be of aid to you in the future." Daniel stood patiently, waiting while Alana finished her meal. When she rose he placed something within her hands. "I had Alessia weave you a hat."

Alana traced her fingers across the wide brim, and with a smile placed it on top of her head. It was an unusual weave, designed to shade her eyes from any who would look upon her, while the ends of the back and sides had been left long, loose and twisted to run down the length of her own hair.

"It is ideal," she acknowledged, thinking how frustrating it was when people realised she was without normal sight. The design would keep her eyes shielded, and the wild ends would draw attention from her face. "Who is your friend?"

"A blacksmith. I have another gift for you, one crafted by his hand. I thought he may like to see who was receiving it." He offered his arm, smiling as Alana accepted.

"Blacksmith?" a voice called from the tavern bar. "We've not had one of those around these parts for a few years now, not since Tony passed." Daniel turned sharply towards the bar. Where the patron removed his hat in a show of respect for the deceased.

"What do you mean?"

"Followed just a few days after he lost his wife. Though you should know, I've heard it said around the approach of the Festival of Hades there's been some strange sounds in that workshop, some folk even claim to have spoken with him." The man replaced his hat, his expression remaining solemn.

"You jest?" Daniel's voice came out nothing more than a whisper.

"I do not. He was a good man. I think that's why no one has taken over the forge, see for yourself if you don't believe me. They've never so much as moved his tools."

"Then how do you explain... I mean..." Daniel trailed off, leading Alana at a brisk pace towards the abandoned forge. The flash of sadness that played on Tony's face as he presented his finest work replayed in Daniel's mind. He recognised it now, Tony had known he would never forge anything greater than that which he had done, and as such, he would finally rest. "The Festival of Hades," Daniel muttered.

"Something troubles you, Wita?" Alana questioned.

"No, nothing. It seems we had help beyond that we expected. I guess that makes this gift even more special, since it was made for you, Mitéra." Daniel placed his hand inside the satchel, unlocking the mysteries as he had been taught, before pulling the finely crafted bow from within. To an onlooker it would be nothing short of an act of magic. He placed the large weapon in Alana's grasp, he could already see it would be a perfect fit whether used for melee or range, as had been its maker's intention. Her long slender arms meant the bow was only a few inches shorter than herself. Studying the weapon as she traced her hands along it he noticed something he had failed to see before, and smiled. Just as his staff was linked with magic, the same power would conjure the string of a bow. "May it serve you well. On that note, I should take you to the village we spoke of. There's a small dwelling near its borders that once belonged to the wise woman, and it seems you are her sole surviving relative, thus lands and titles have been passed to you." Alana nodded, understanding his intention.

"Lead the way. While we walk, tell me once more of my parents. I feel this will be the final times our paths are destined to cross in this manner."

"It is safer that way," Daniel acknowledged, knowing he alone knew this young woman's true identity, and how quickly she had grown to become the figure this world had needed, and would need again one day. "What would you like to know?"

Dear reader,

We hope you enjoyed reading *The Dream Walker*. Please take a moment to leave a review, even if it's a short one. Your opinion is important to us.

Discover more books by K.J. Simmill at https://www.nextchapter.pub/authors/kj-simmill

Want to know when one of our books is free or discounted? Join the newsletter at http://eepurl.com/bqqB3H

Best regards,

K.J. Simmill and the Next Chapter Team

Printed in Great Britain
by Amazon

54491820R00310